ALICE OSEMAN

HEARTSTOPPER

VOLUME 1

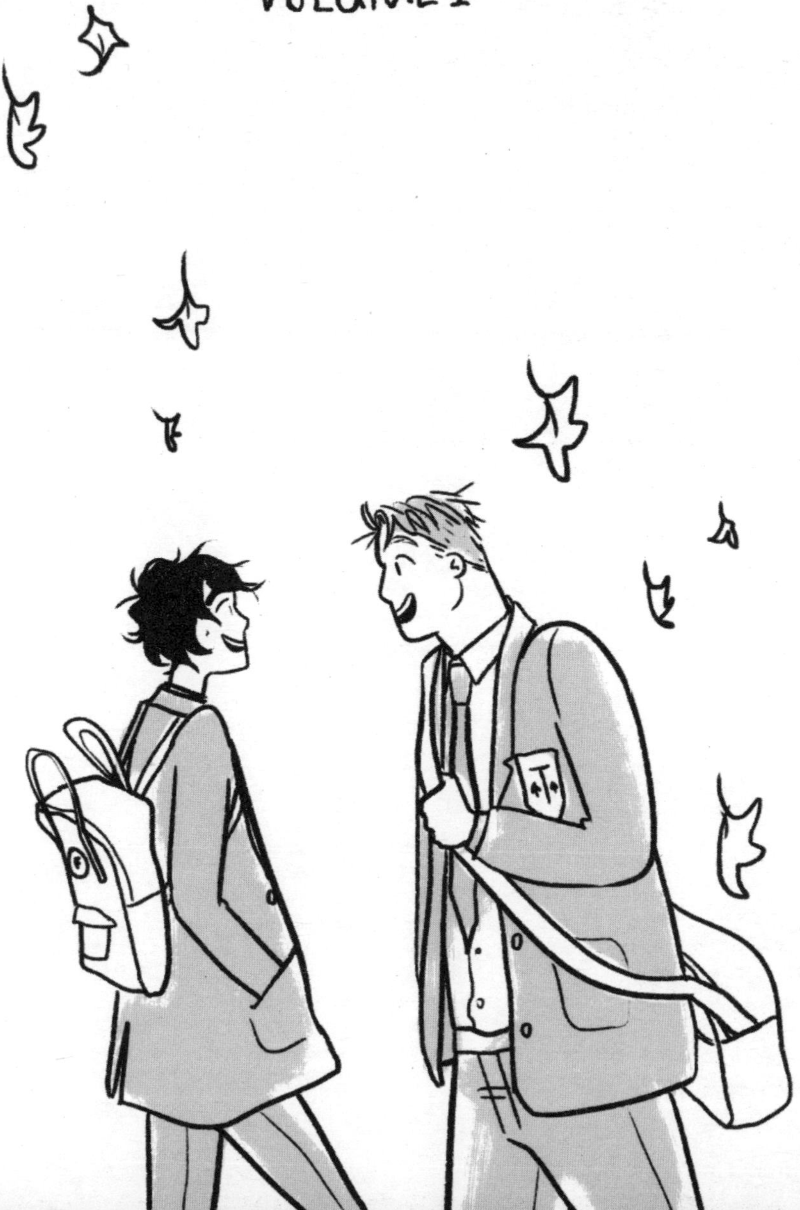

HODDER CHILDREN'S BOOKS

First published by the author as a Kickstarter edition in 2018
Paperback edition published in 2019 by Hodder & Stoughton
This paperback edition published in 2022 by Hodder & Stoughton

5 7 9 10 8 6 4

Please be aware that this book contains depictions of physical assault and verbal homophobia.

This comic is drawn digitally using a Wacom Intuos Pro small tablet directly into Photoshop CC.

A CIP catalogue record for this book
is available from the British Library.

ISBN 978 1 444 96892 7

Printed and bound in Great Britain by
Clays Ltd, Elcograf S.p.A.

The paper and board used in this book
are made from wood from responsible sources.

MIX
Paper from
responsible sources
FSC® C104740

Hodder Children's Books
An imprint of
Hachette Children's Group
Part of Hodder & Stoughton Limited
Carmelite House
50 Victoria Embankment
London EC4Y 0DZ

An Hachette UK Company
www.hachette.co.uk

www.hachettechildrens.co.uk

www.aliceoseman.com

CONTENTS

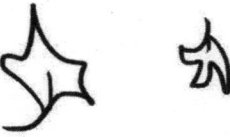

1. MEET

January

Messages
08:01
Ben
Library?
Mon 14 Dec
K
Music Room 2?
Wed 16 Dec
Ok
Library?
Thur 17 Dec
Yep

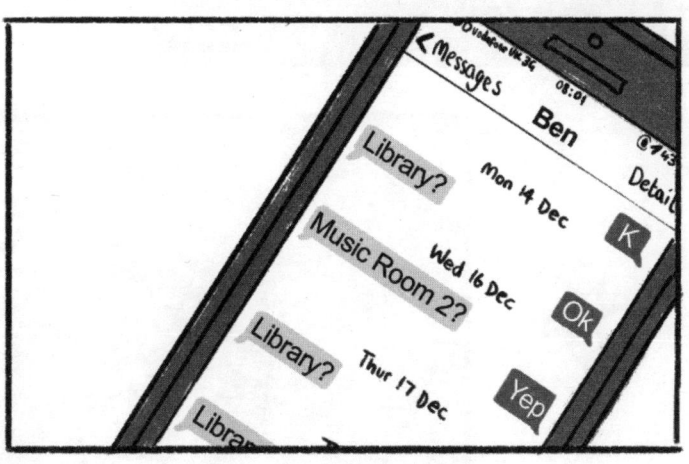

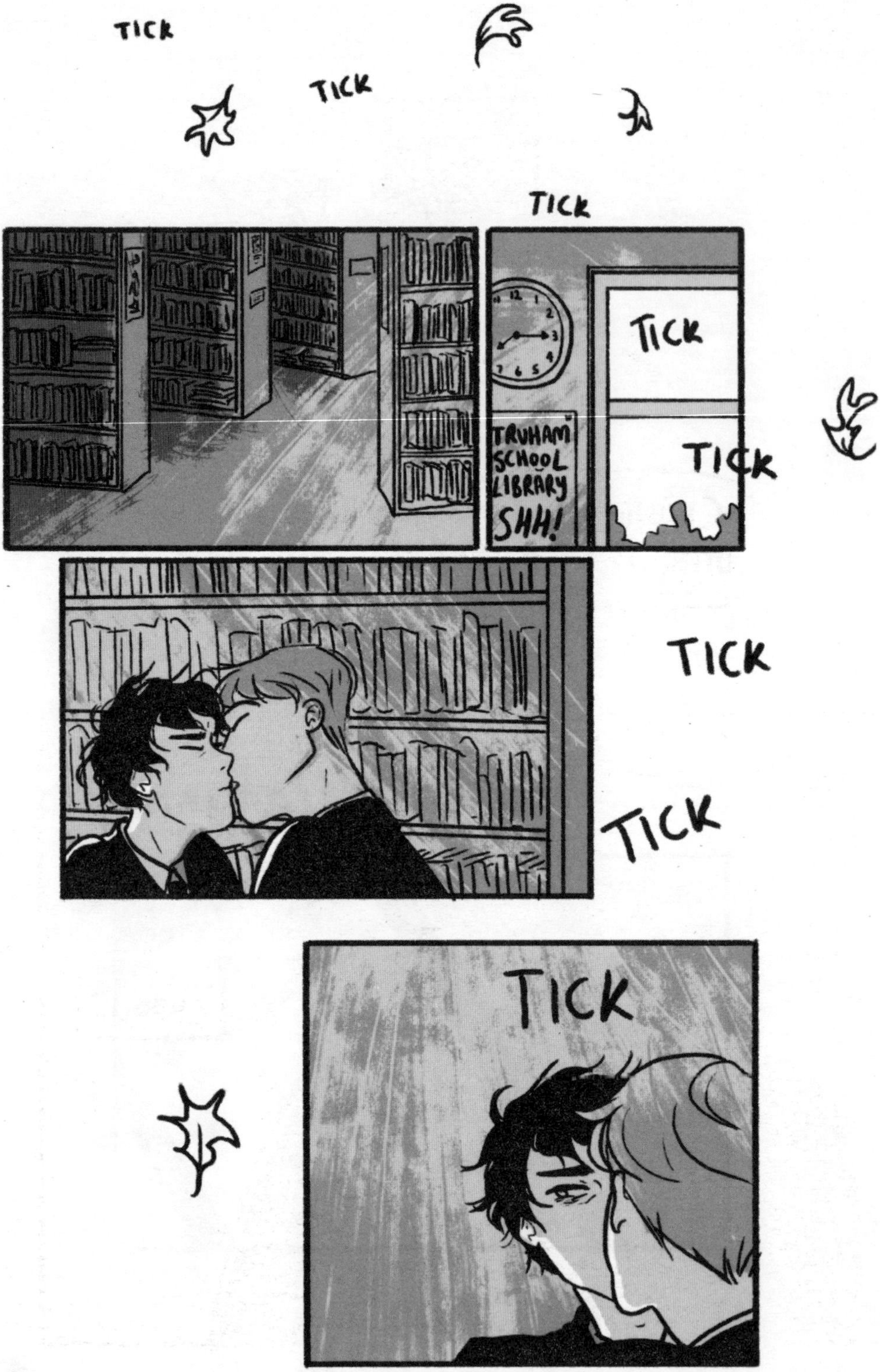

TICK
TICK
TICK
TICK
TRUHAM SCHOOL LIBRARY
SHH!
TICK
TICK
TICK
TICK

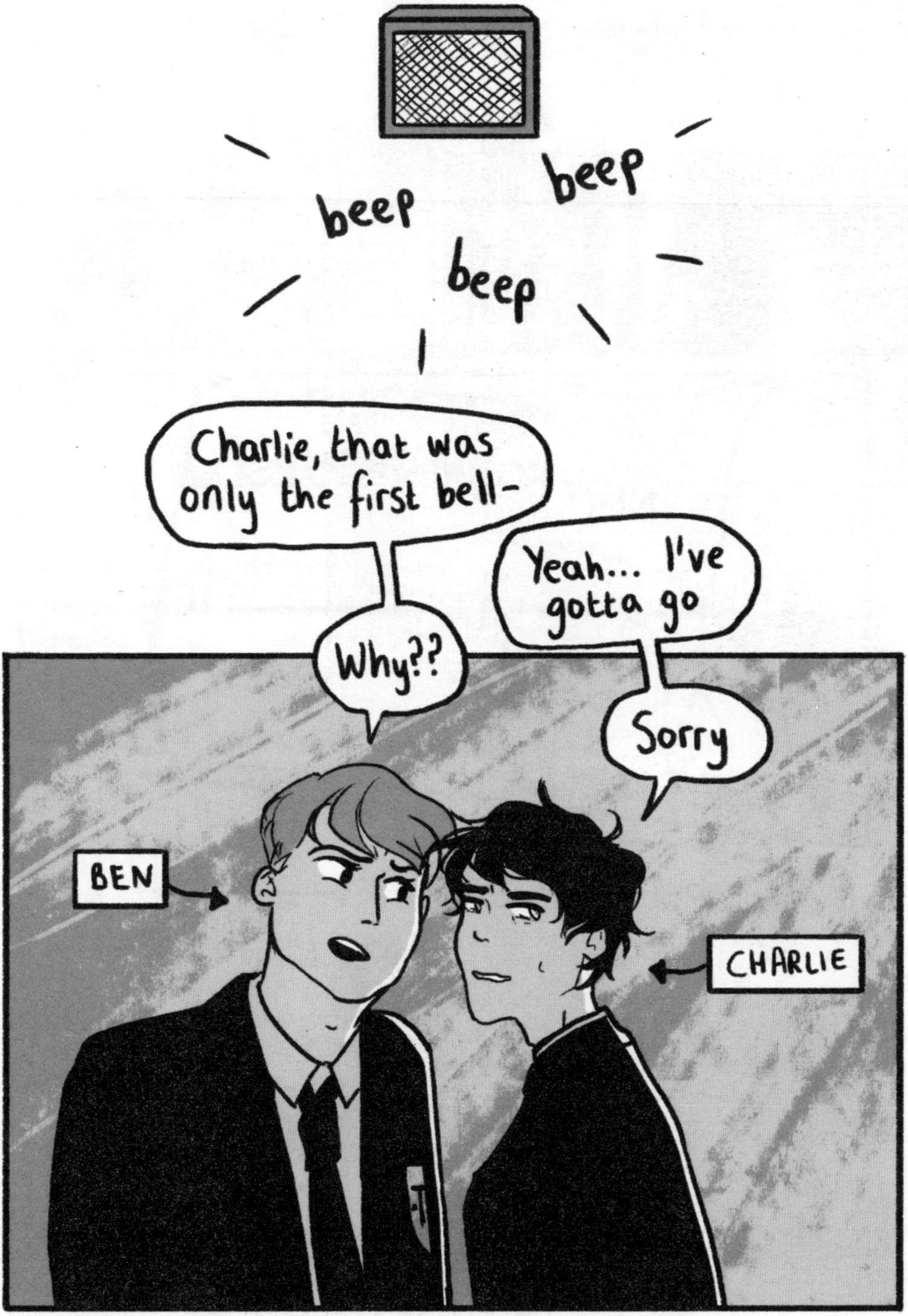
beep
beep
beep
Charlie, that was only the first bell-
Why??
Yeah... I've gotta go
Sorry
BEN
CHARLIE

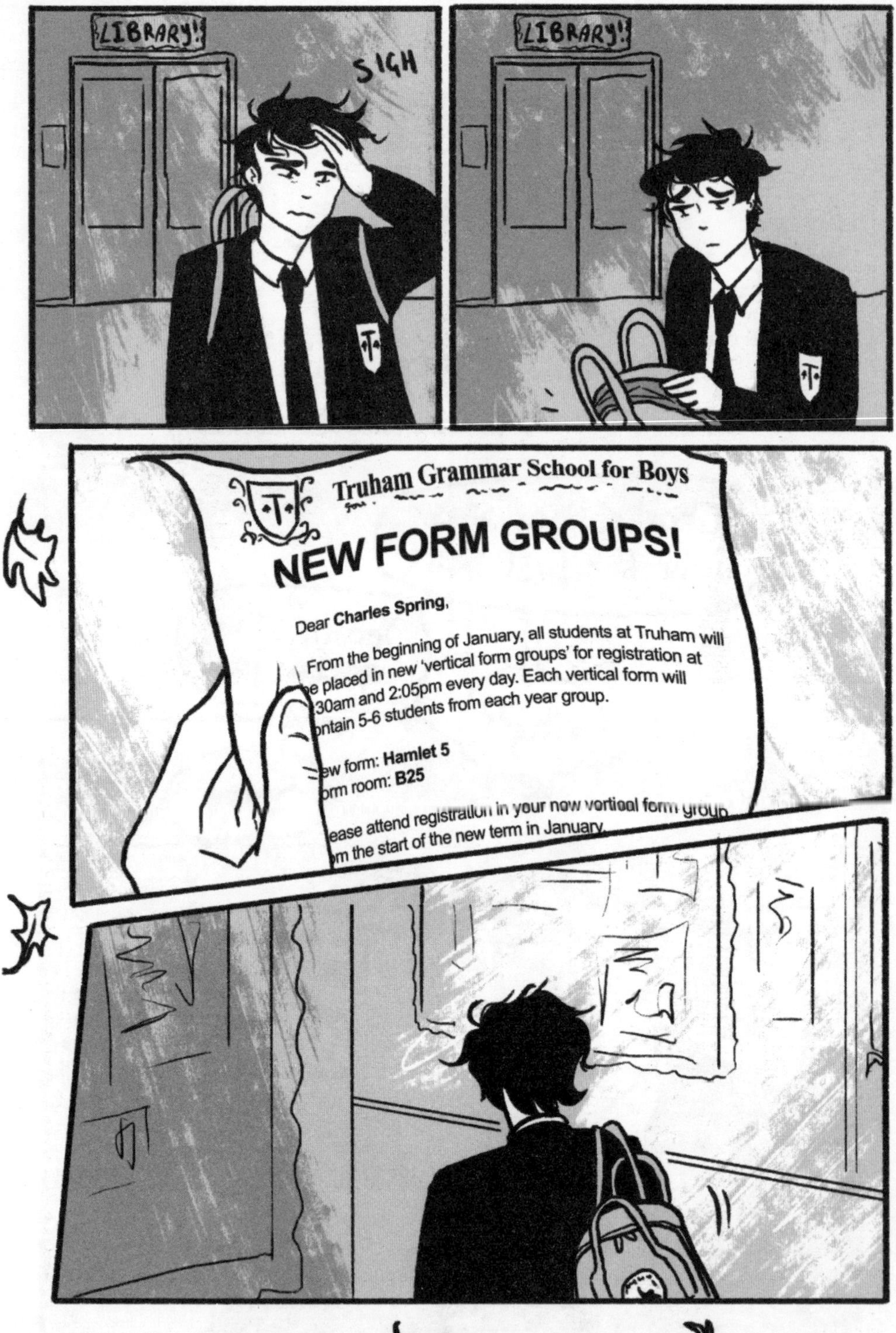
LIBRARY!
SIGH
LIBRARY!
Truham Grammar School for Boys
NEW FORM GROUPS!
Dear Charles Spring,
From the beginning of January, all students at Truham will
e placed in new 'vertical form groups' for registration at
30am and 2:05pm every day. Each vertical form will
ontain 5-6 students from each year group.
ew form: Hamlet 5
orm room: B25
lease attend registration in your new vertical form group
m the start of the new term in January.

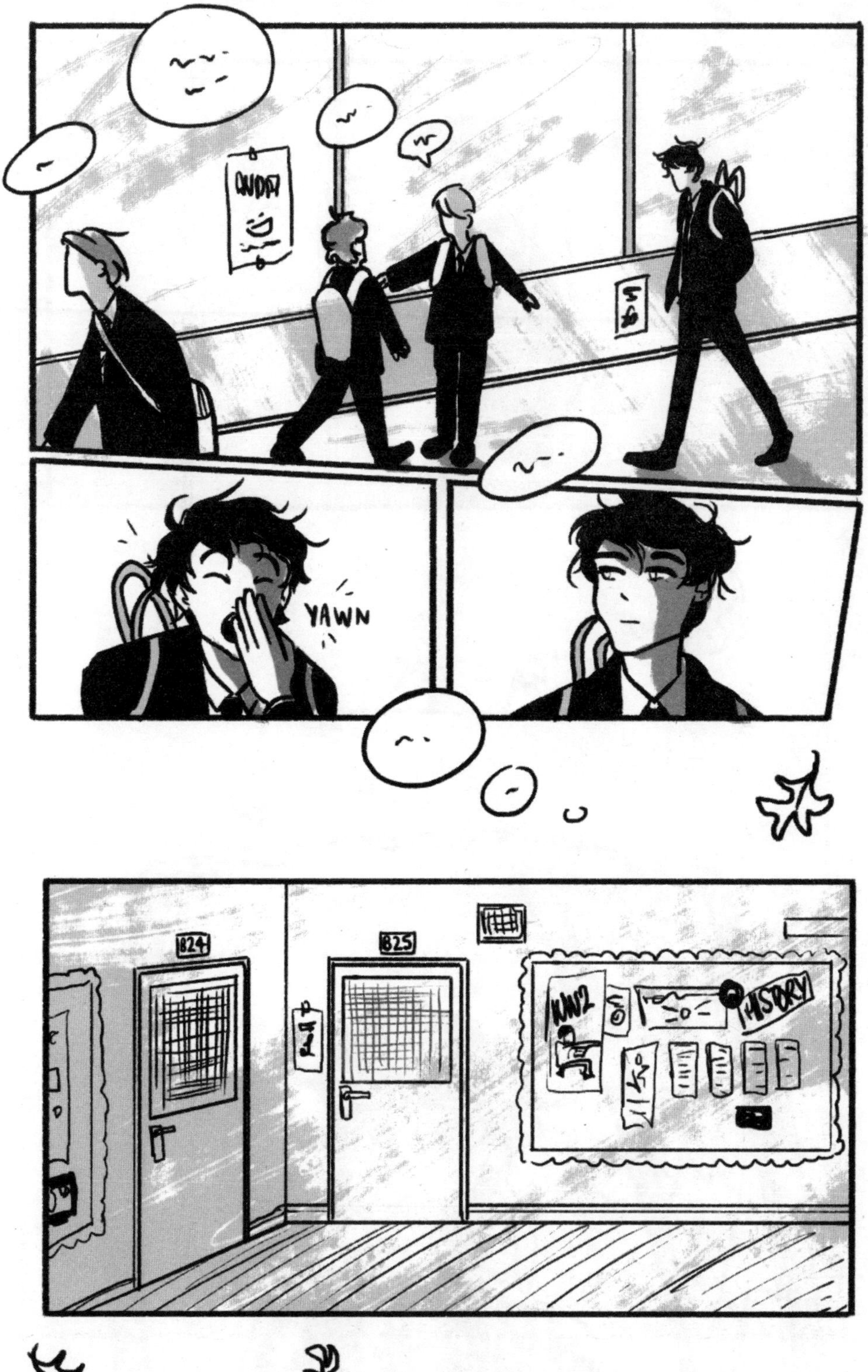
YAWN
824
825
WW2
HISTORY

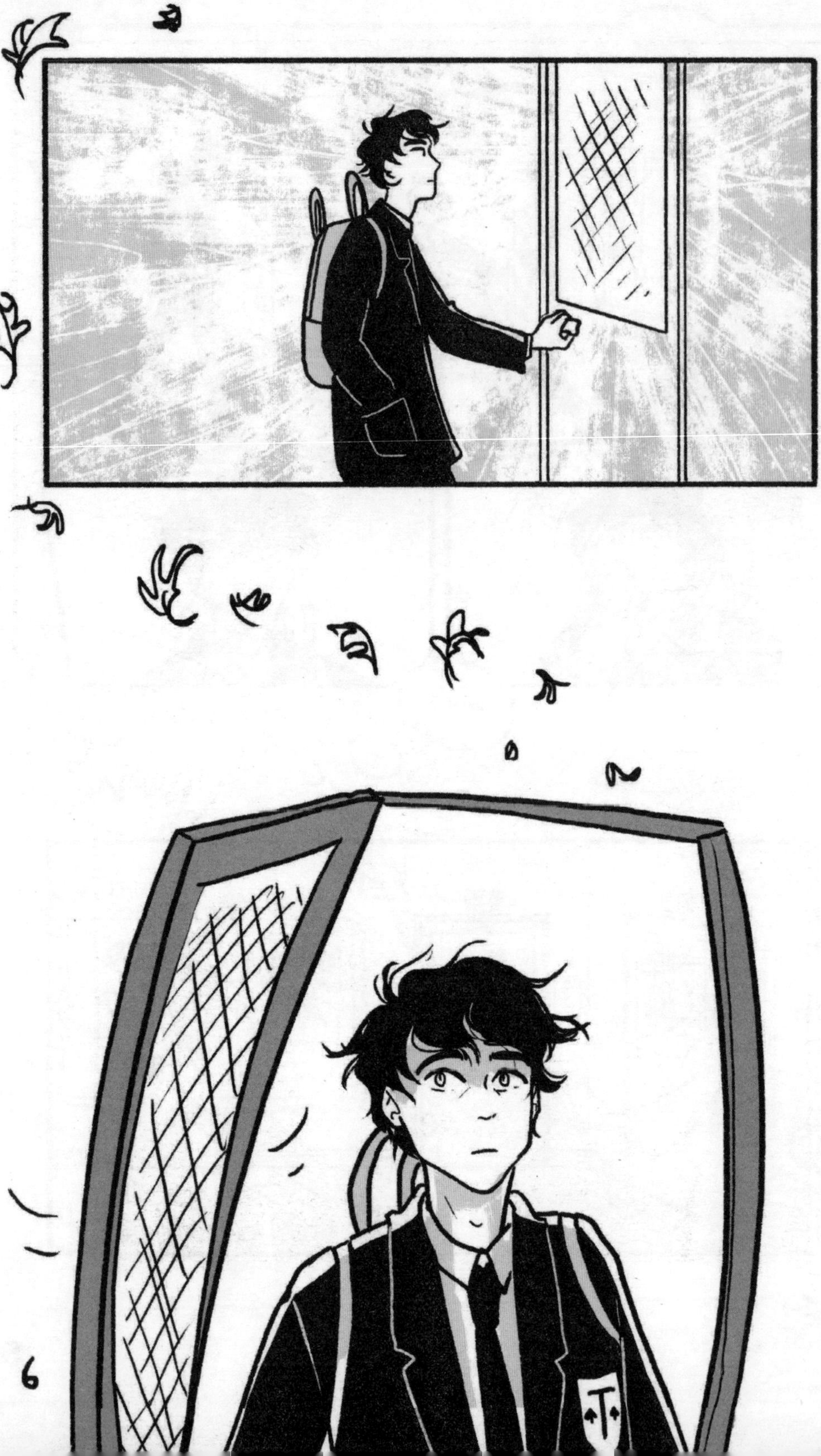

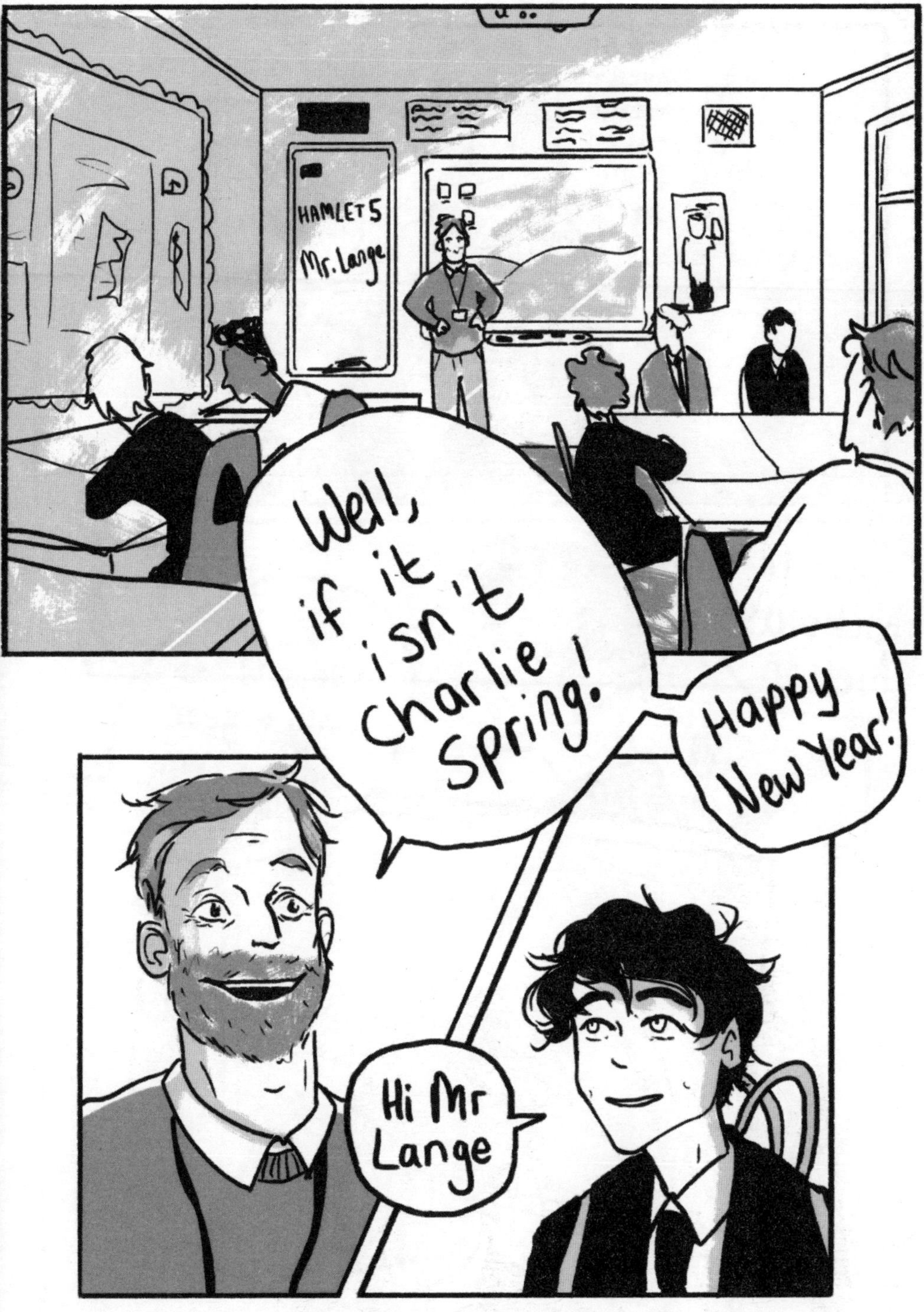
HAMLET 5
Mr. Lange
Well, if it isn't Charlie Spring!
Happy New Year!
Hi Mr Lange

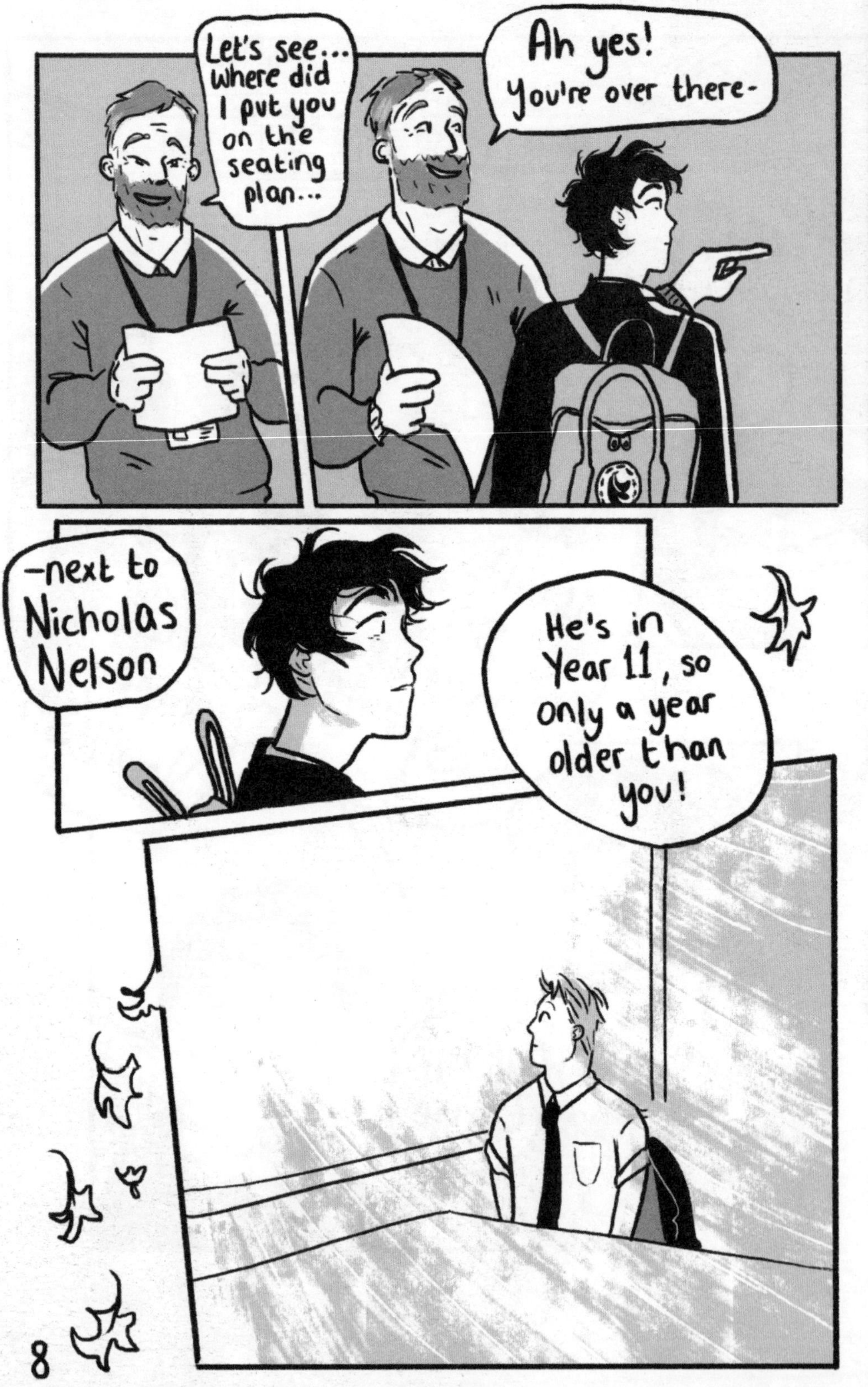
Let's see... where did I put you on the seating plan...
Ah yes! You're over there-
-next to Nicholas Nelson
He's in Year 11, so only a year older than you!

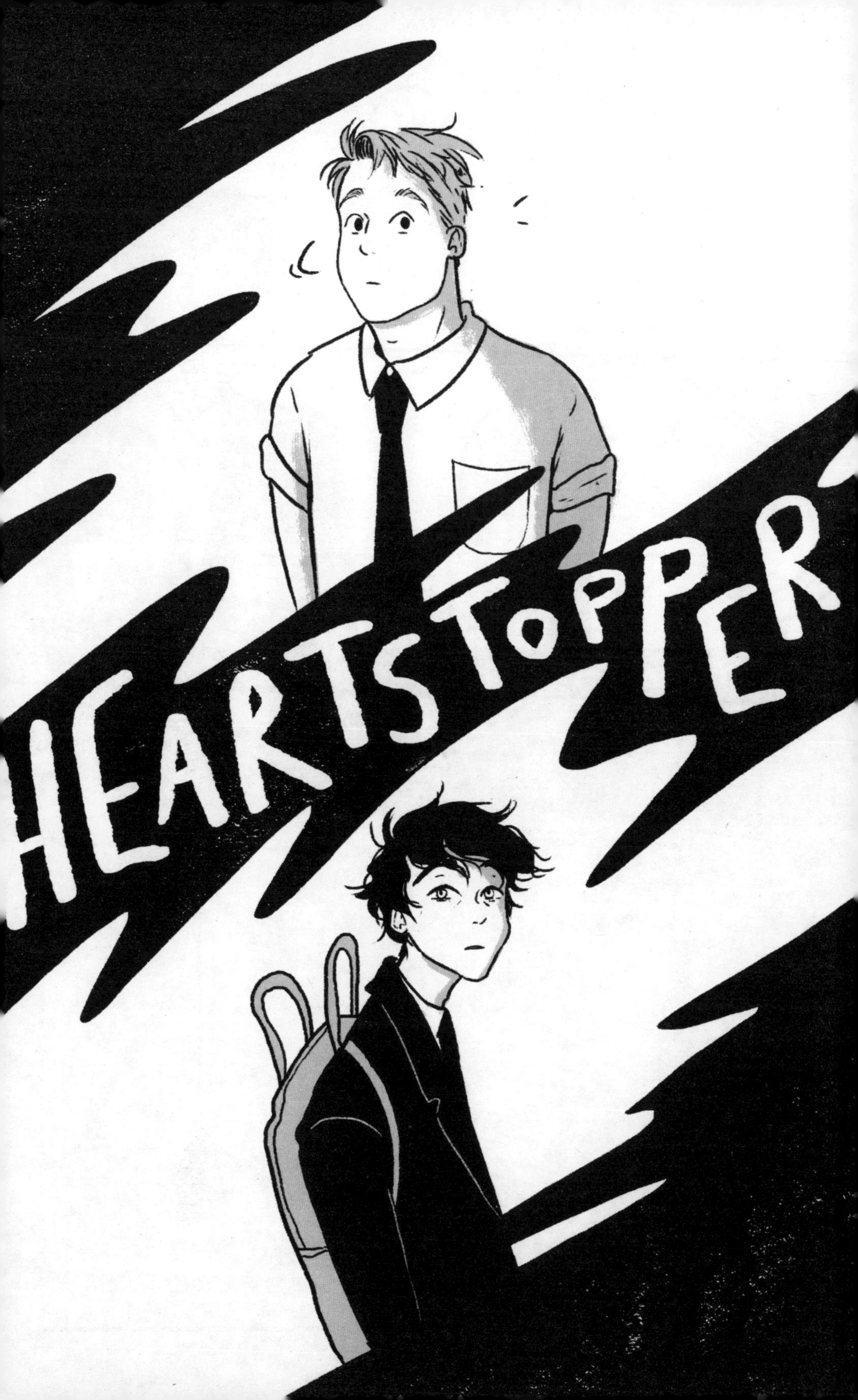
HEARTSTOPPER

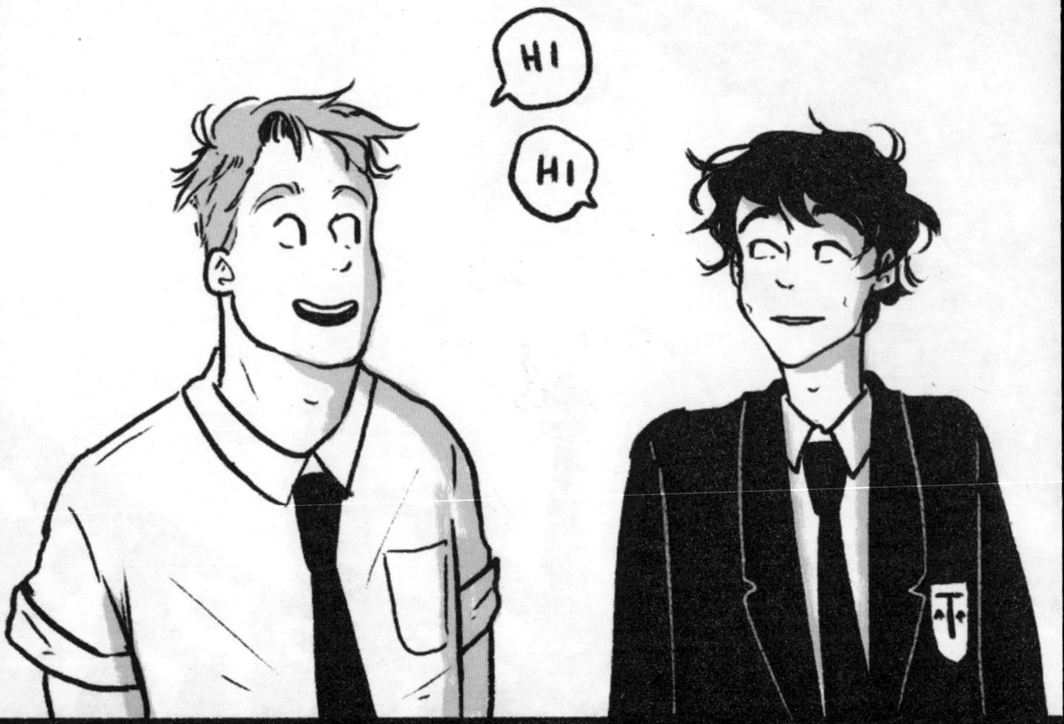
HI
HI

A COMIC BY

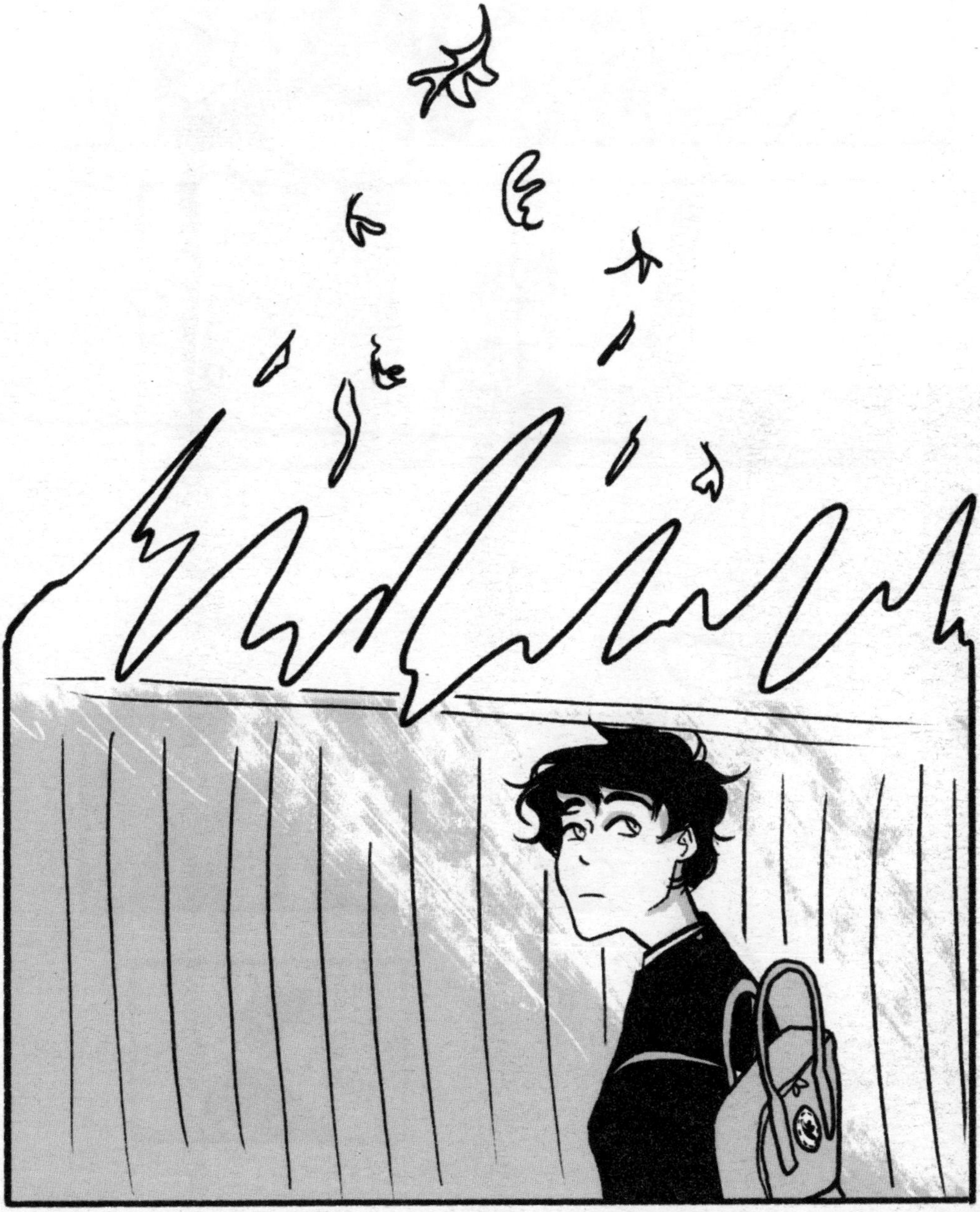

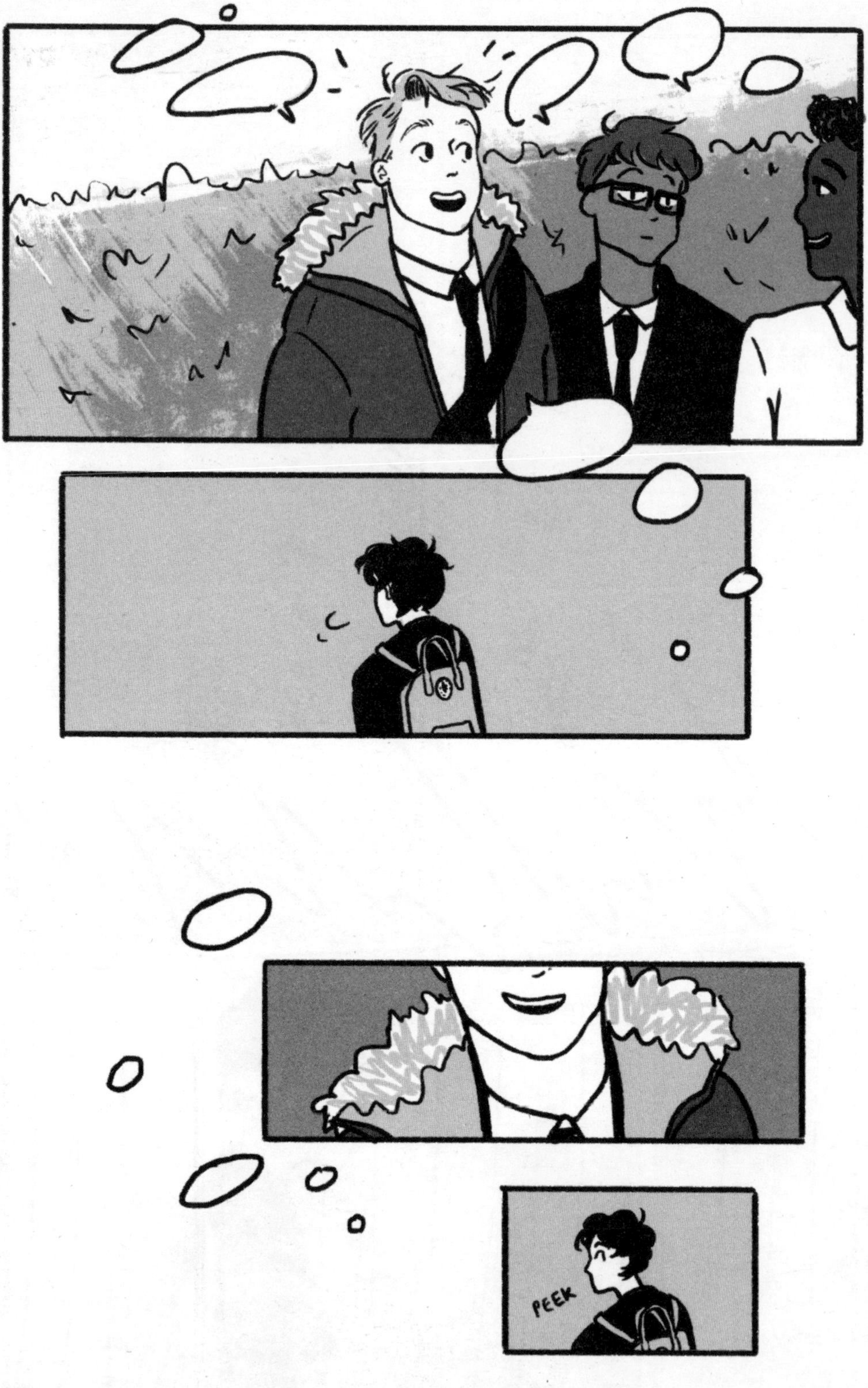
PEEK

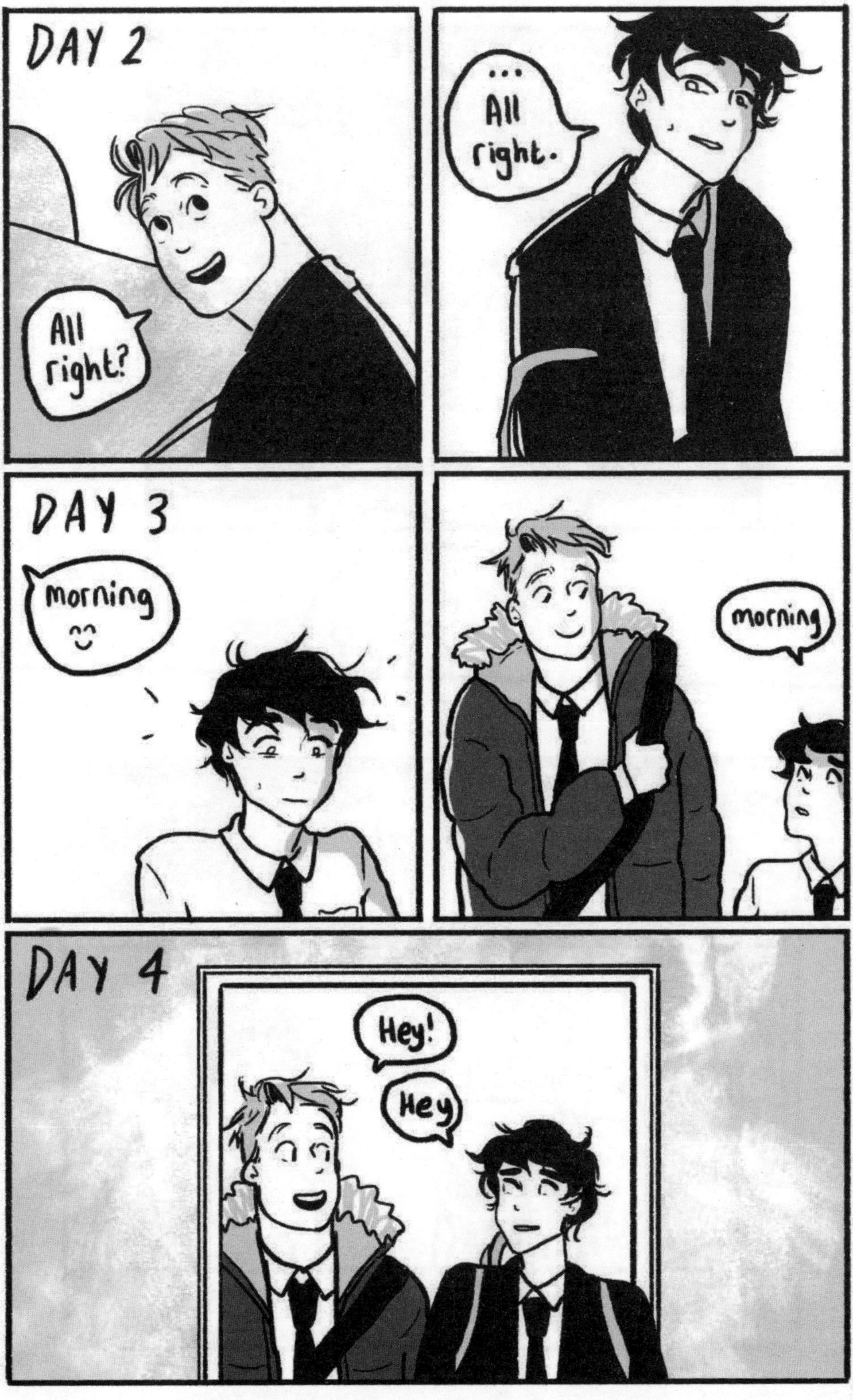
DAY 2
All right?
...
All right.
DAY 3
morning
^^
morning
DAY 4
Hey!
Hey

Why does he always say hello to me every single morning? Is it a joke? Is it like the guys who used to bully me last year all over again? He's probably just making fun of me. Why else would he talk to me? He's not even in my year group. He probably thinks I'm gonna hit on him or something-
Er... Charlie?
you don't have any tissues, do you? My pen.. er.. exploded

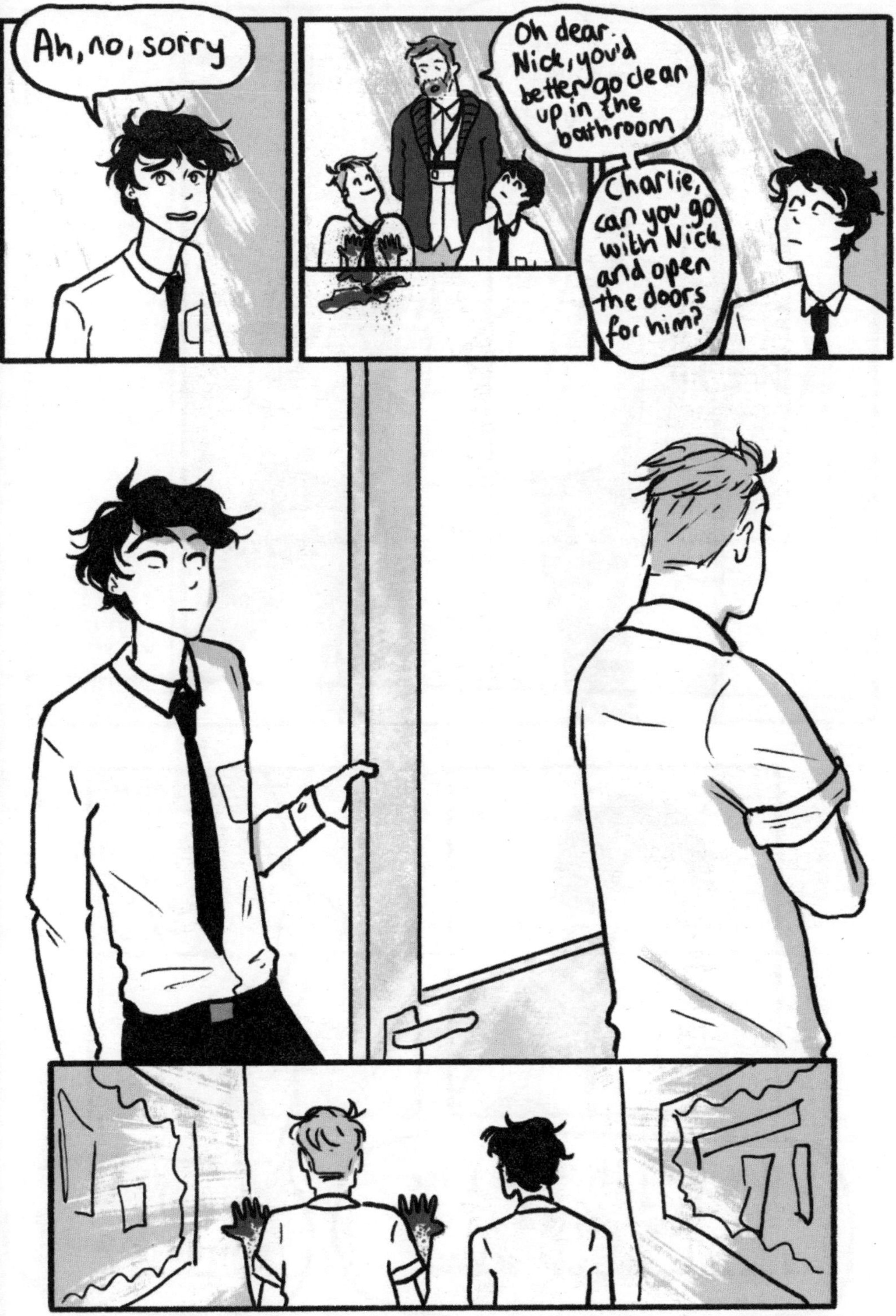
Ah, no, sorry
Oh dear. Nick, you'd better go clean up in the bathroom
Charlie, can you go with Nick and open the doors for him?

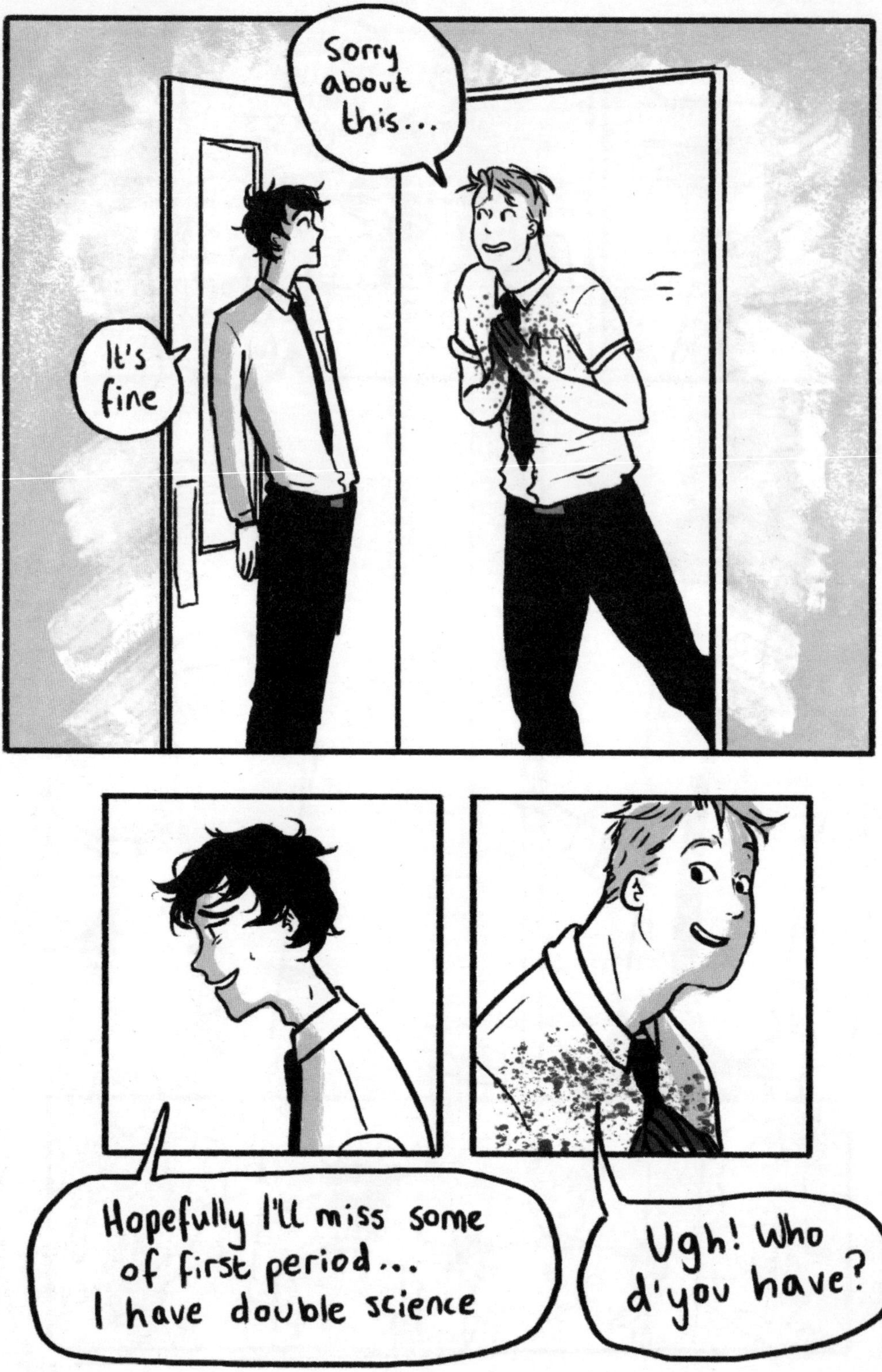
Sorry about this...
It's fine
Hopefully I'll miss some of first period... I have double science
Ugh! Who d'you have?

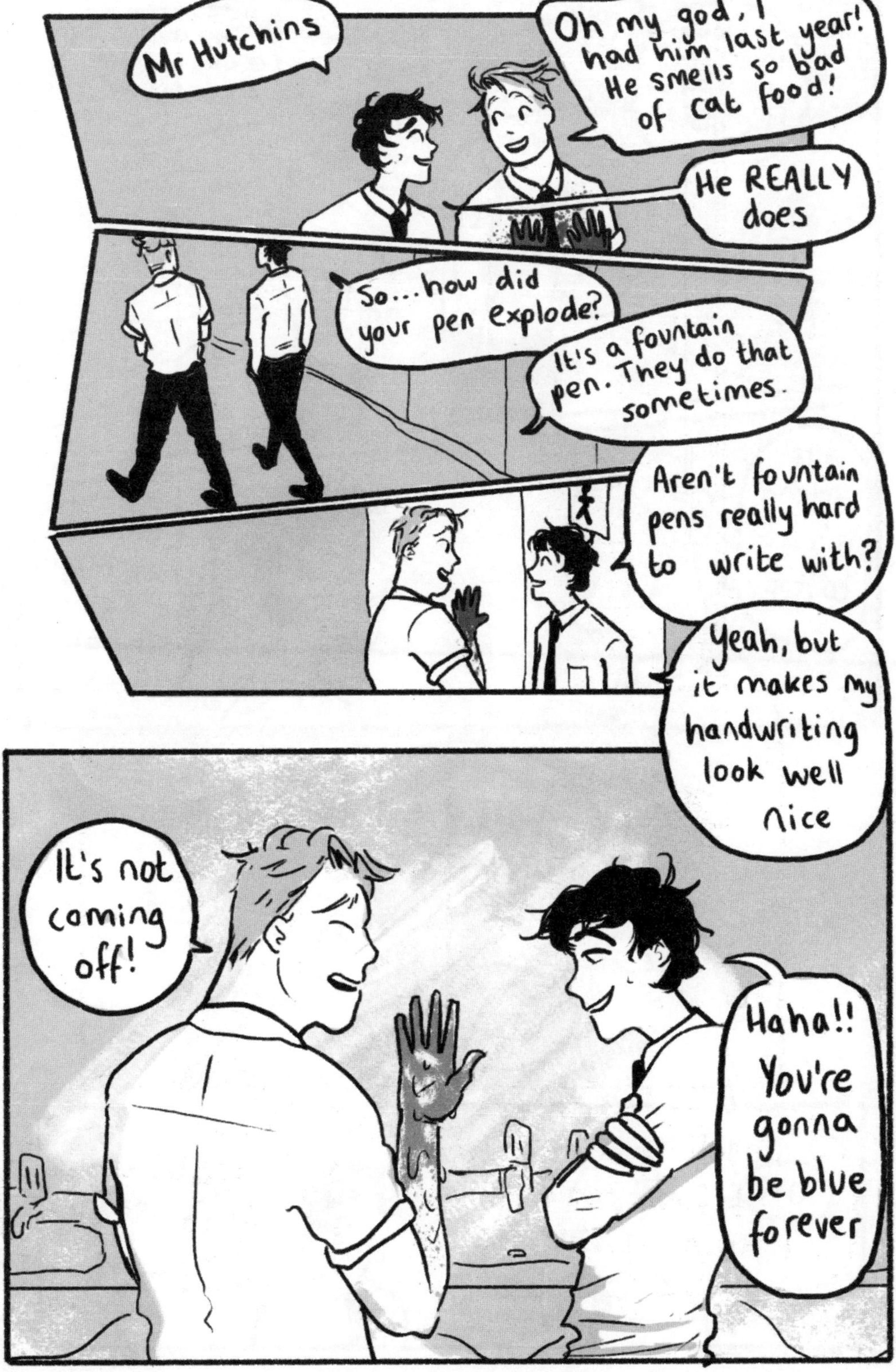
Mr Hutchins
Oh my god, I had him last year! He smells so bad of cat food!
He REALLY does
So... how did your pen explode?
It's a fountain pen. They do that sometimes.
Aren't fountain pens really hard to write with?
Yeah, but it makes my handwriting look well nice
It's not coming off!
Haha!! You're gonna be blue forever

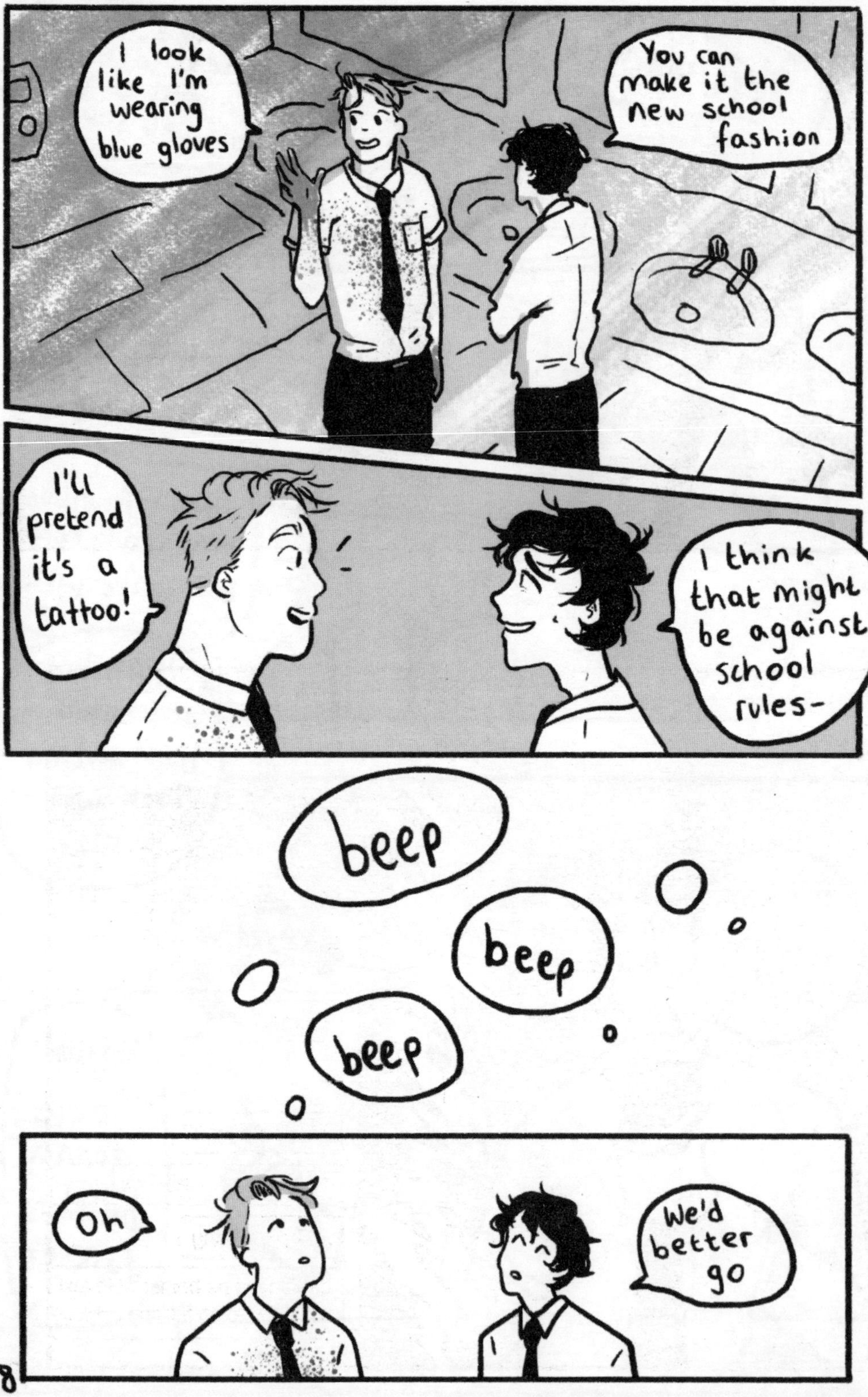
I look like I'm wearing blue gloves
You can make it the new school fashion
I'll pretend it's a tattoo!
I think that might be against school rules-
beep
beep
beep
Oh
We'd better go

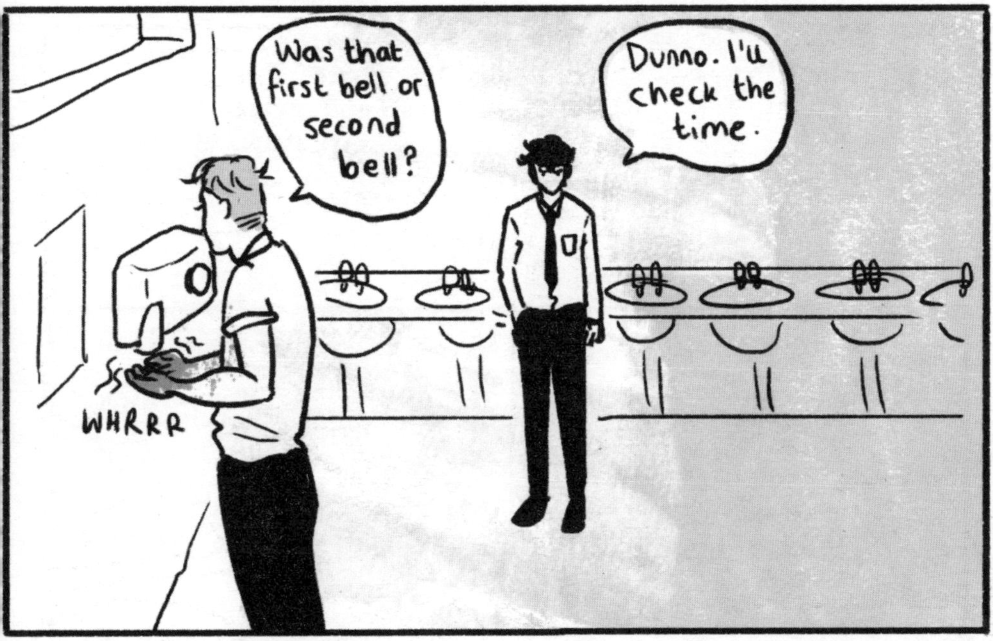
Was that first bell or second bell?
Dunno. I'll check the time.
WHRRR

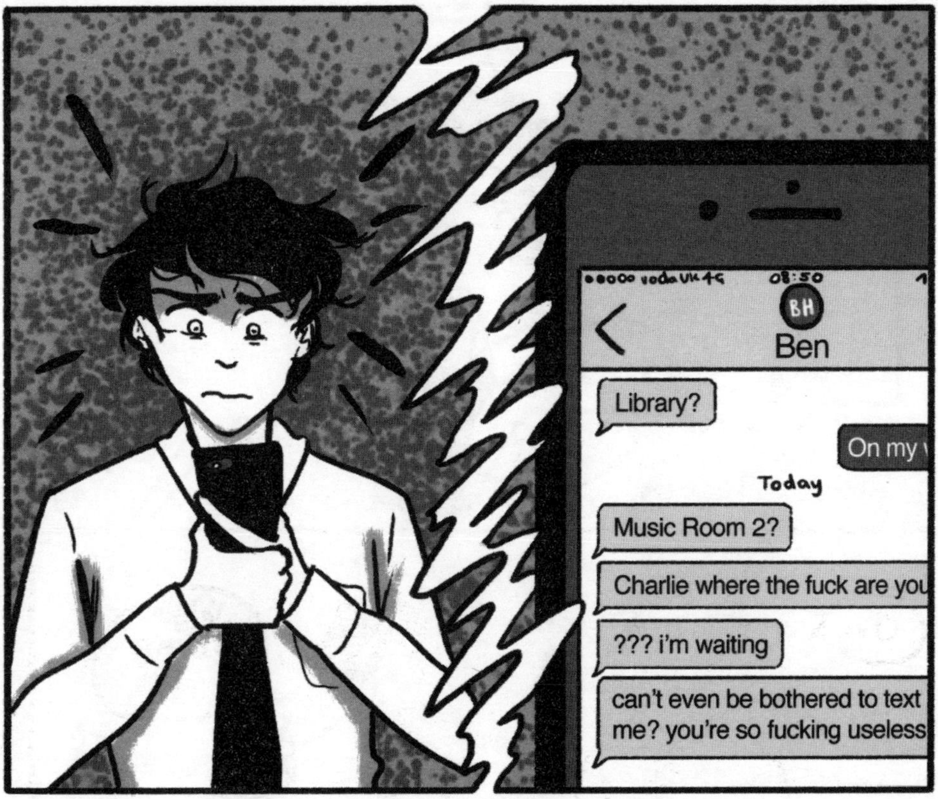
Ben
Library?
Today
Music Room 2?
Charlie where the fuck are you
??? i'm waiting
can't even be bothered to text me? you're so fucking useless

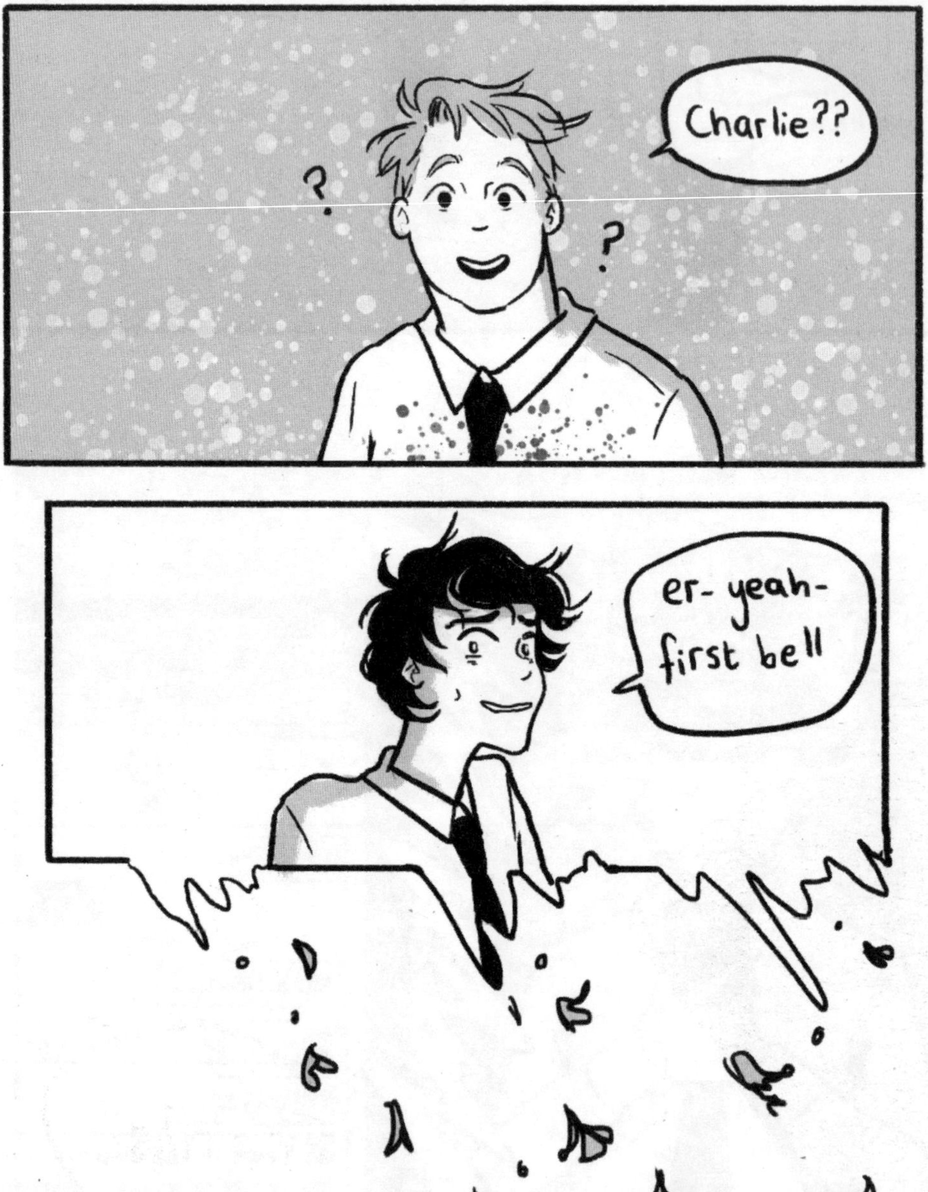
Charlie??
?
?
er- yeah-
first bell

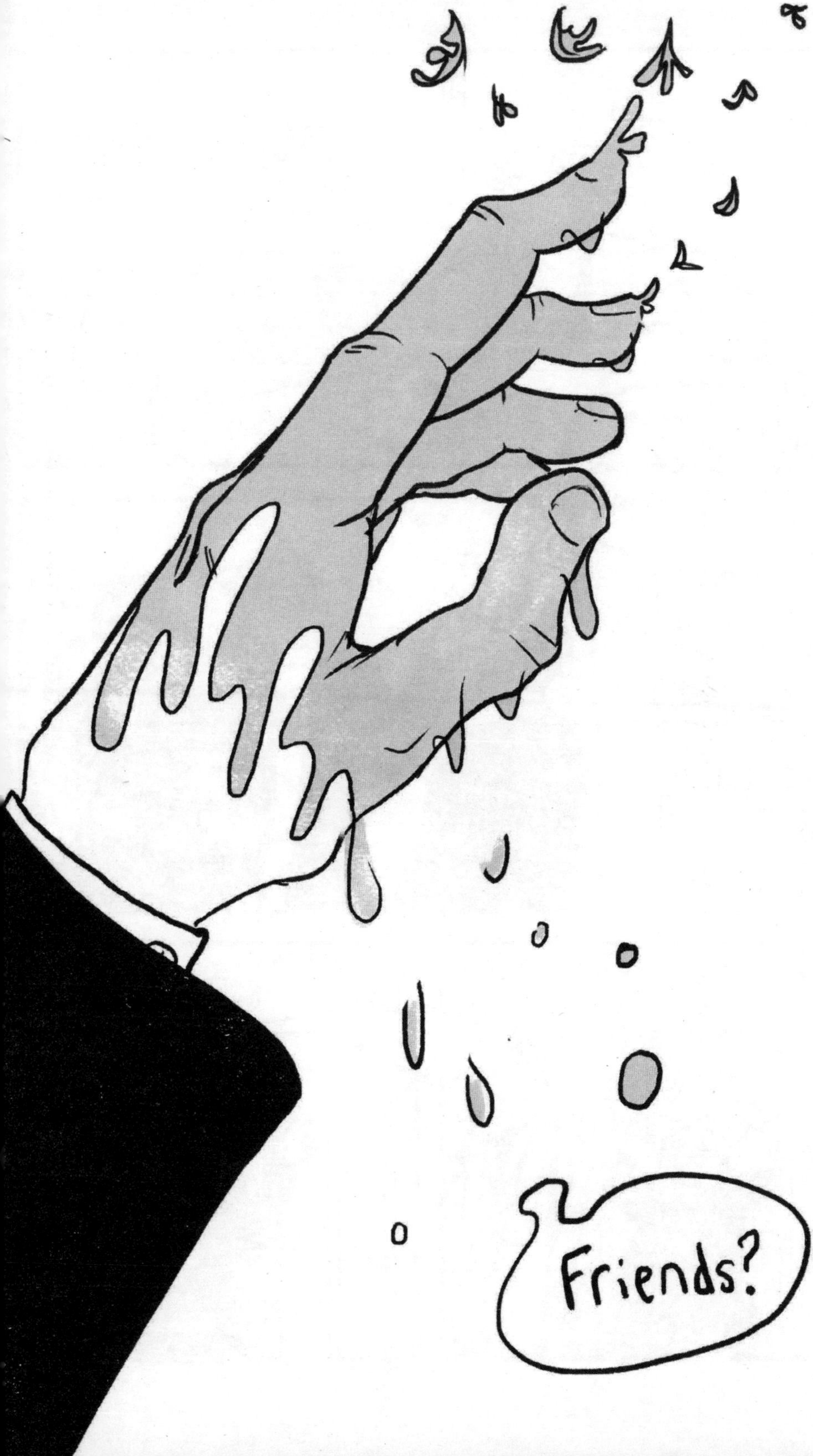
Friends?

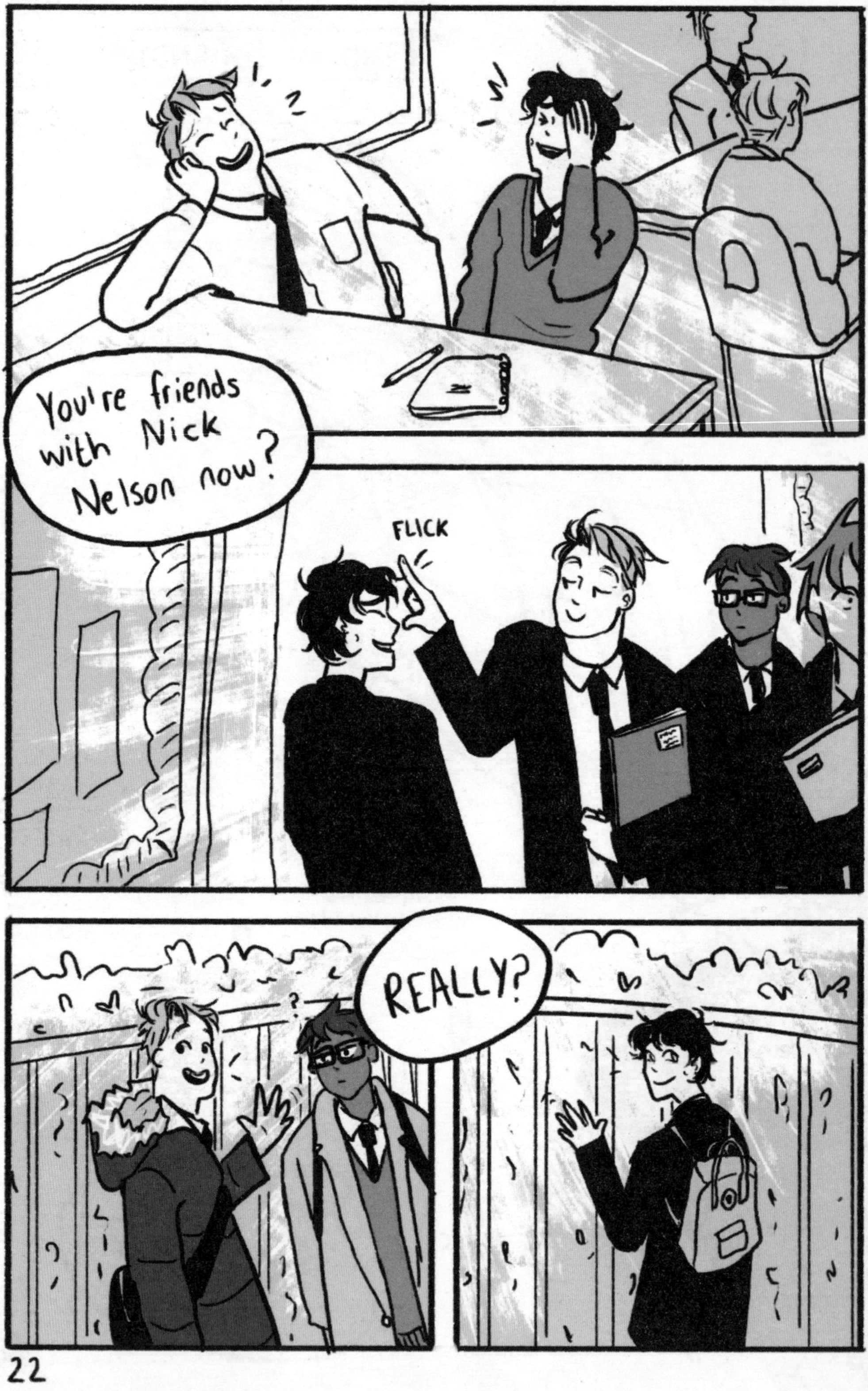
You're friends with Nick Nelson now?
FLICK
REALLY?

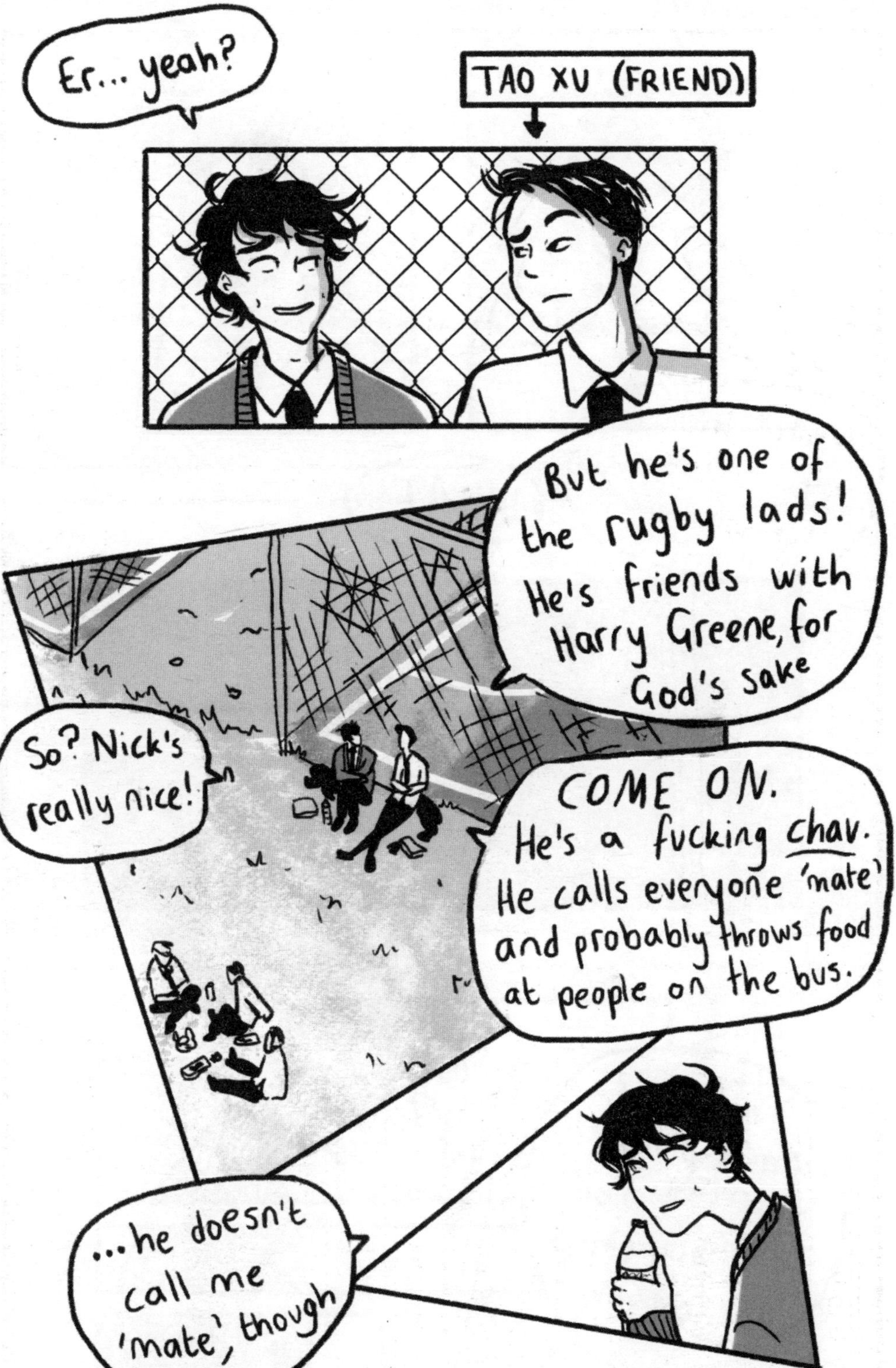
Er... yeah?
TAO XU (FRIEND)
But he's one of the rugby lads! He's friends with Harry Greene, for God's sake
So? Nick's really nice!
COME ON. He's a fucking chav. He calls everyone 'mate' and probably throws food at people on the bus.
...he doesn't call me 'mate', though

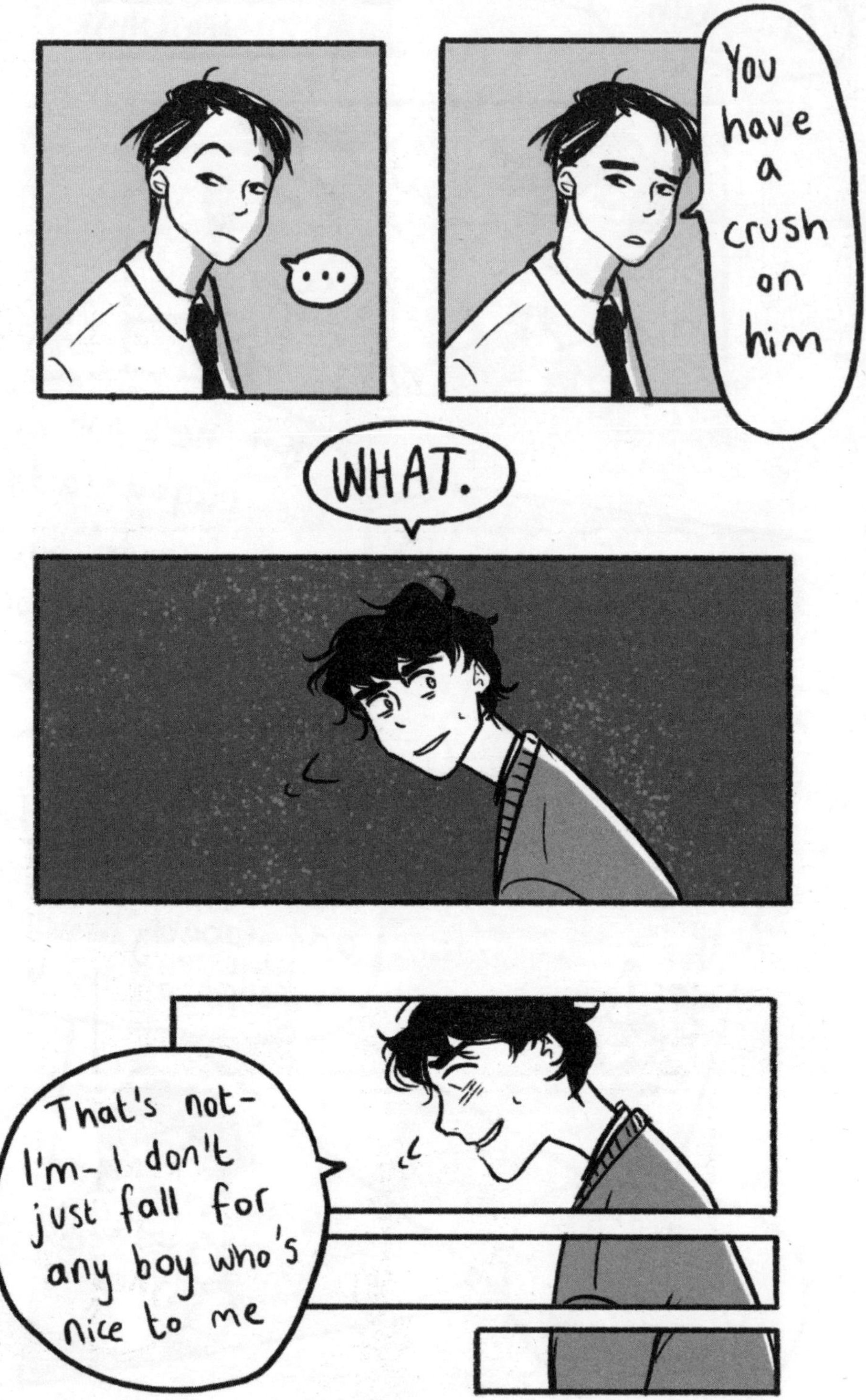
...
You have a crush on him
WHAT.
That's not- I'm- I don't just fall for any boy who's nice to me

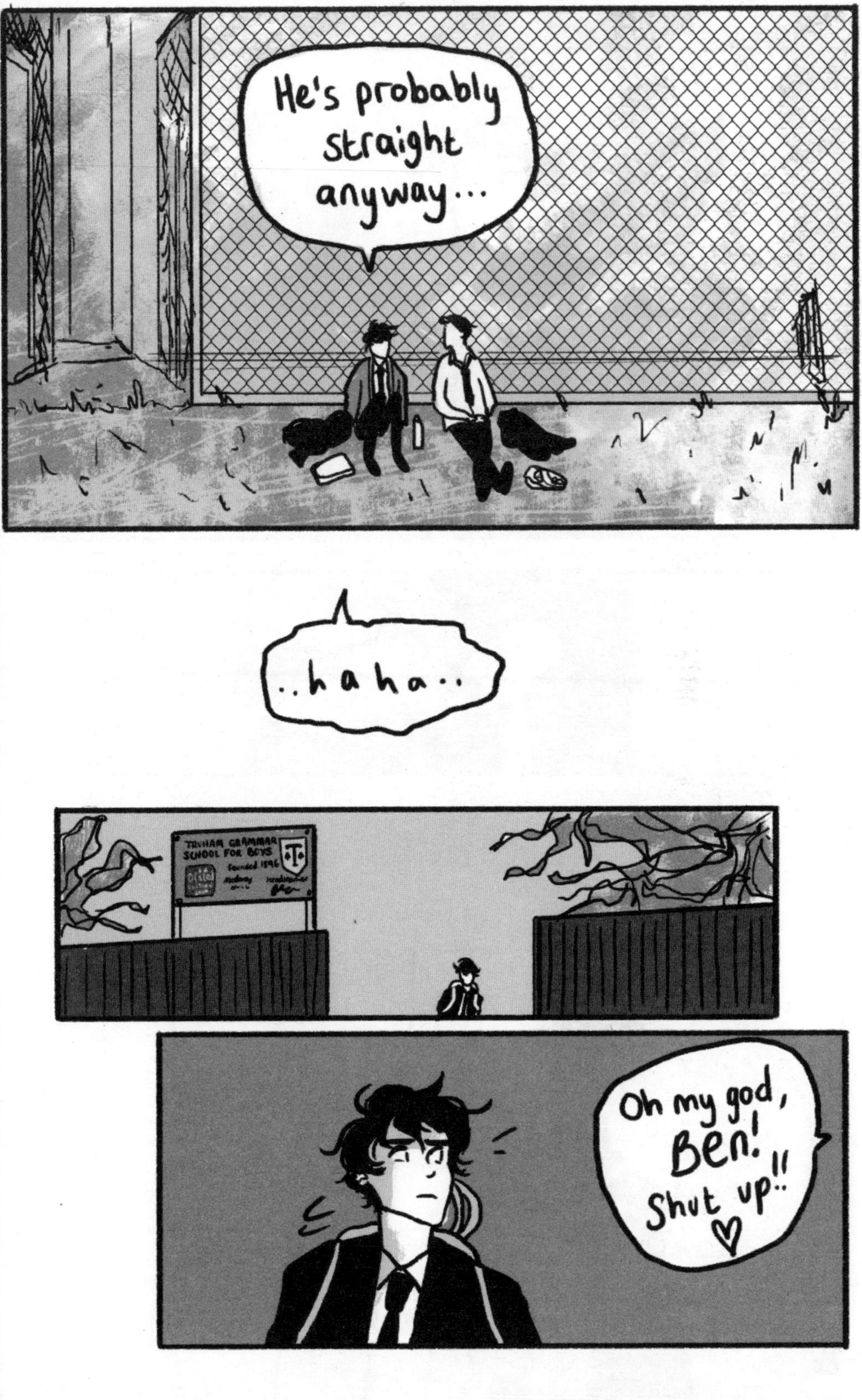
He's probably straight anyway...
..haha..
TRUHAM GRAMMAR SCHOOL FOR BOYS
Founded 1896
Oh my god, Ben! Shut up!! ♥

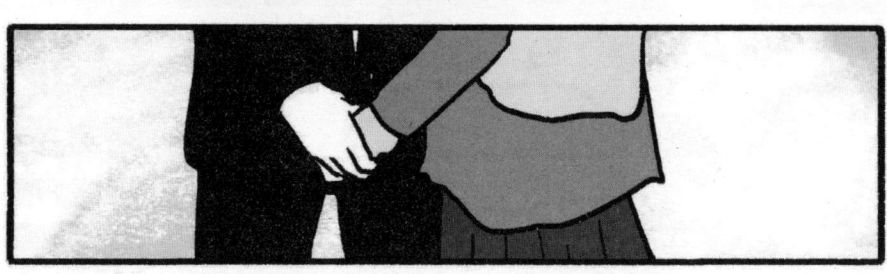

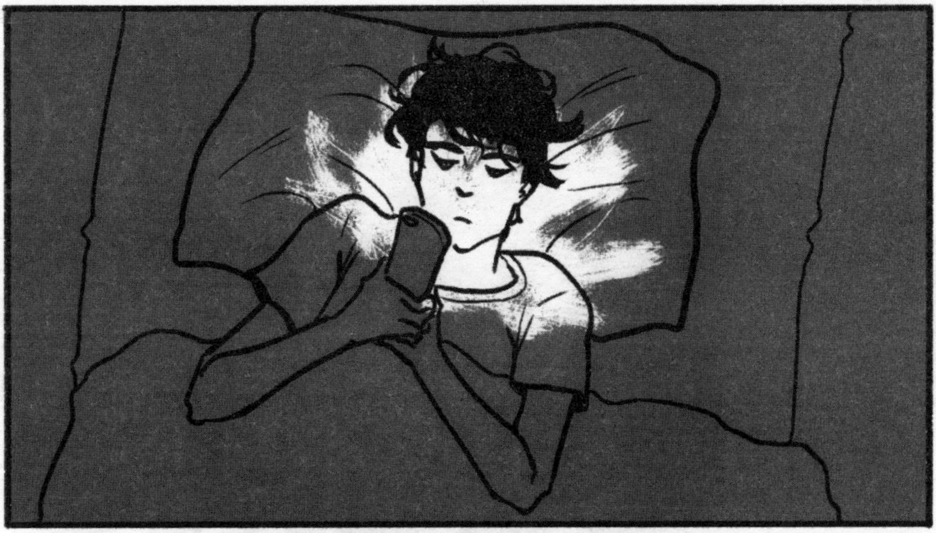

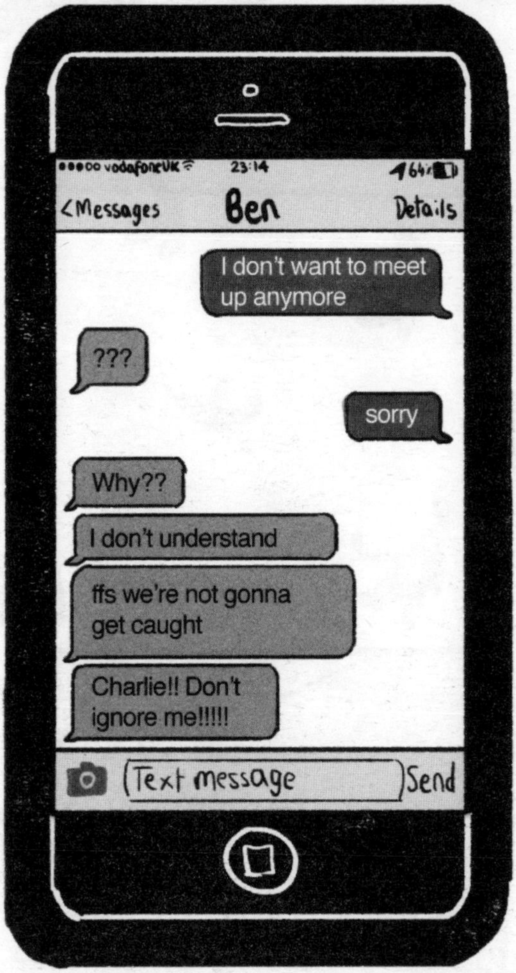
●●●○○ vodafoneUK
23:14
64%
<Messages
Ben
Details
I don't want to meet up anymore
???
sorry
Why??
I don't understand
ffs we're not gonna get caught
Charlie!! Don't ignore me!!!!!
Text message
Send

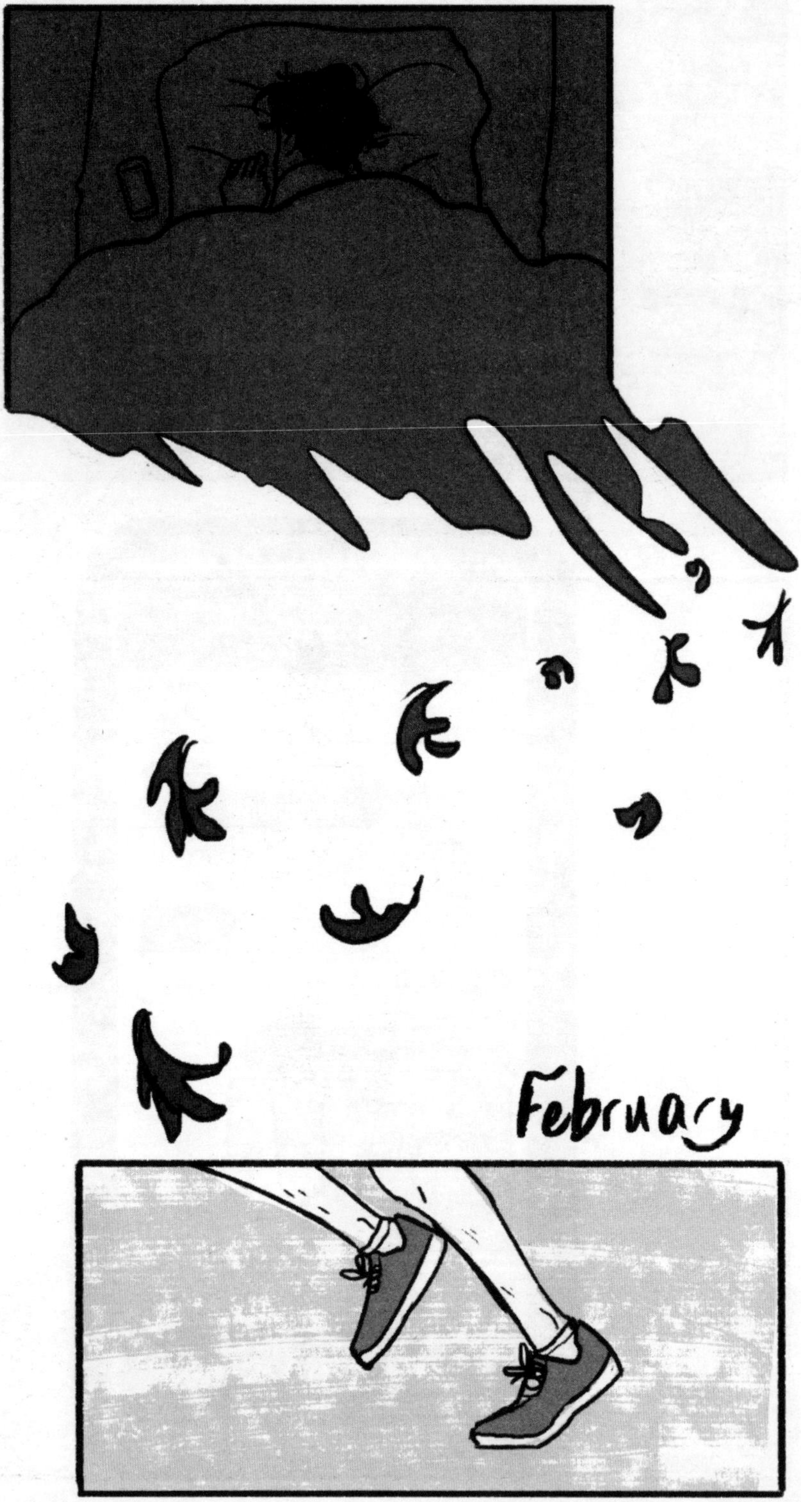
February

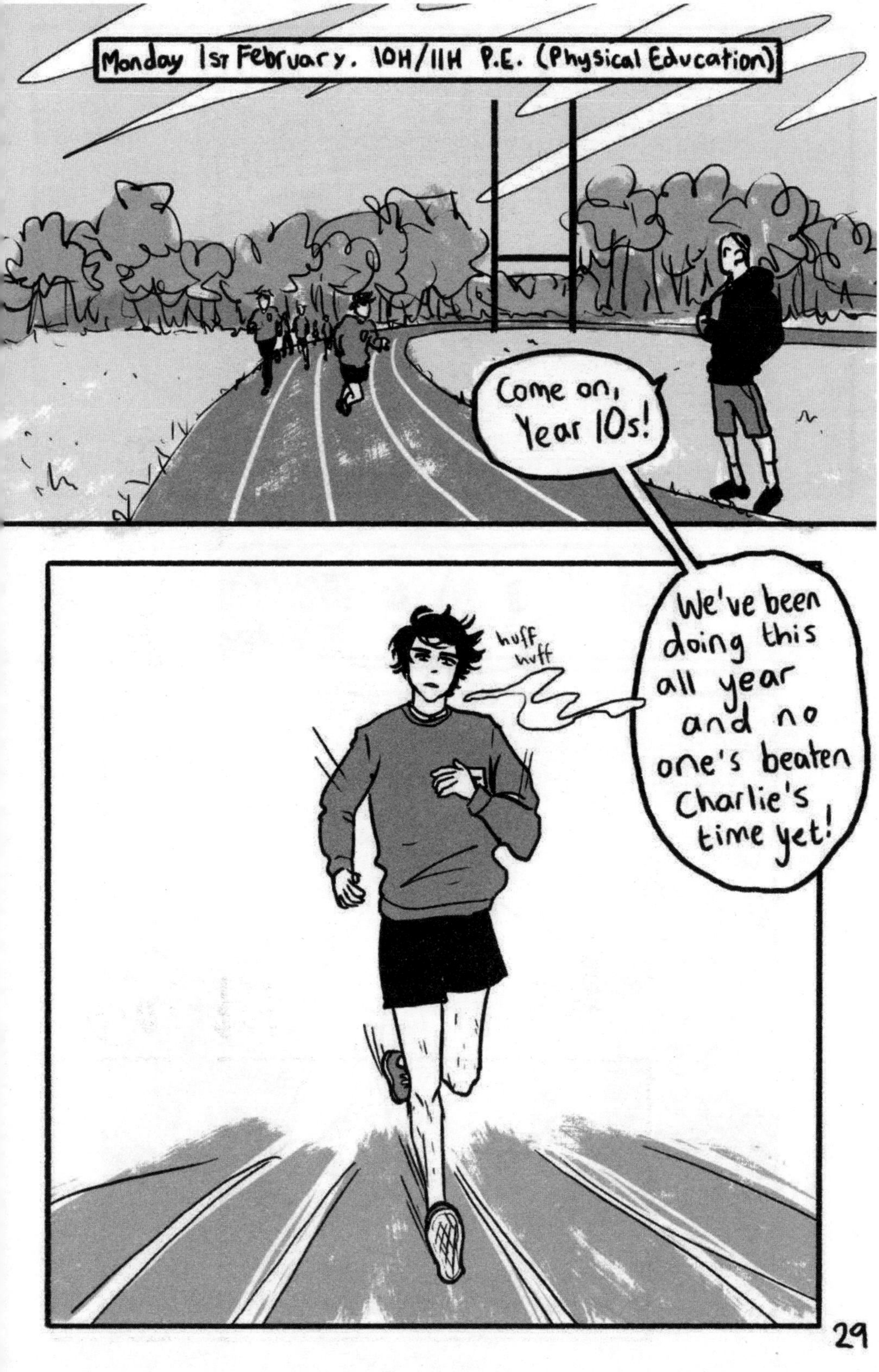
Monday 1st February. 10H/11H P.E. (Physical Education)
Come on, Year 10s!
We've been doing this all year and no one's beaten Charlie's time yet!
huff huff

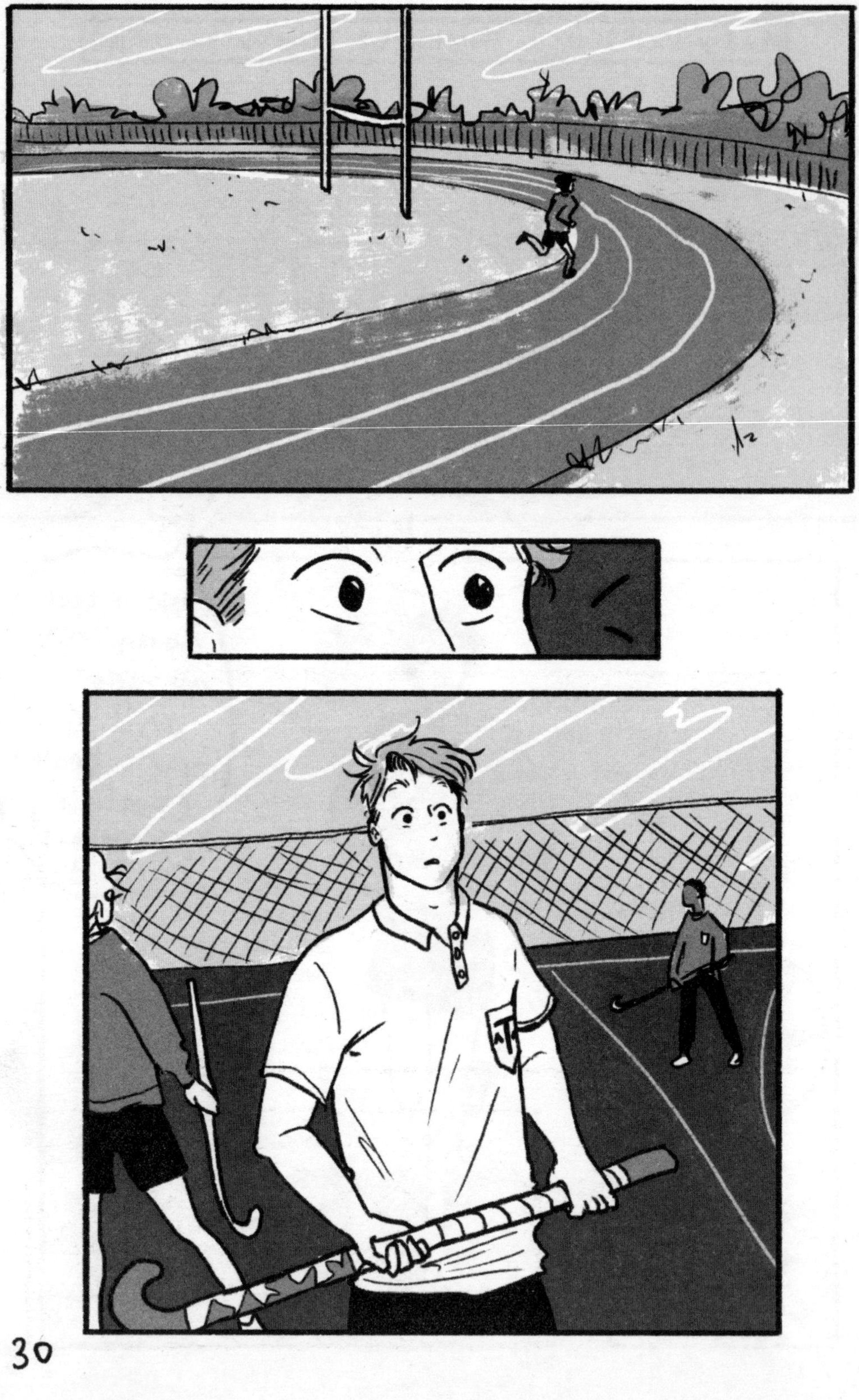

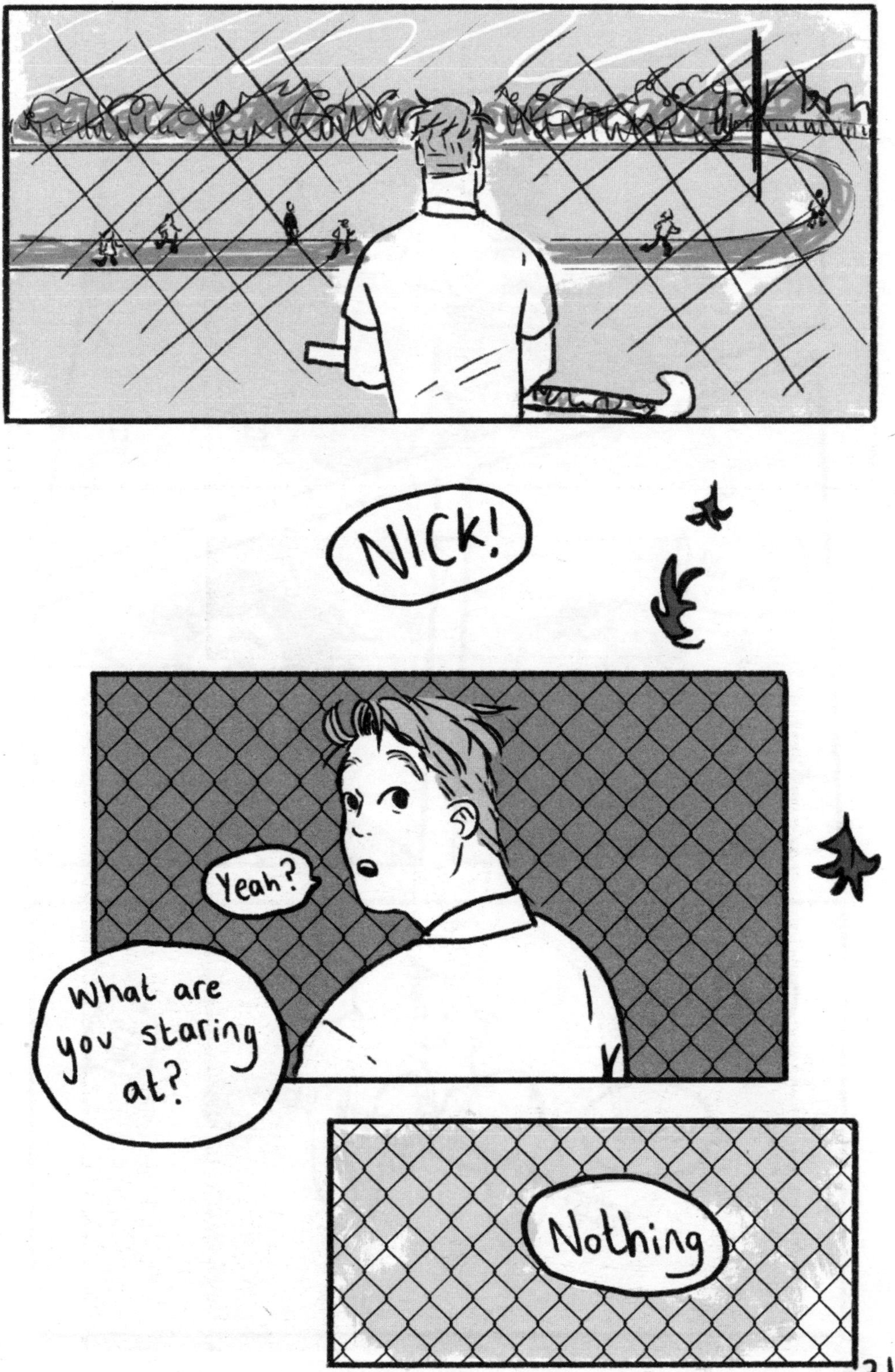
NICK!
Yeah?
What are you staring at?
Nothing

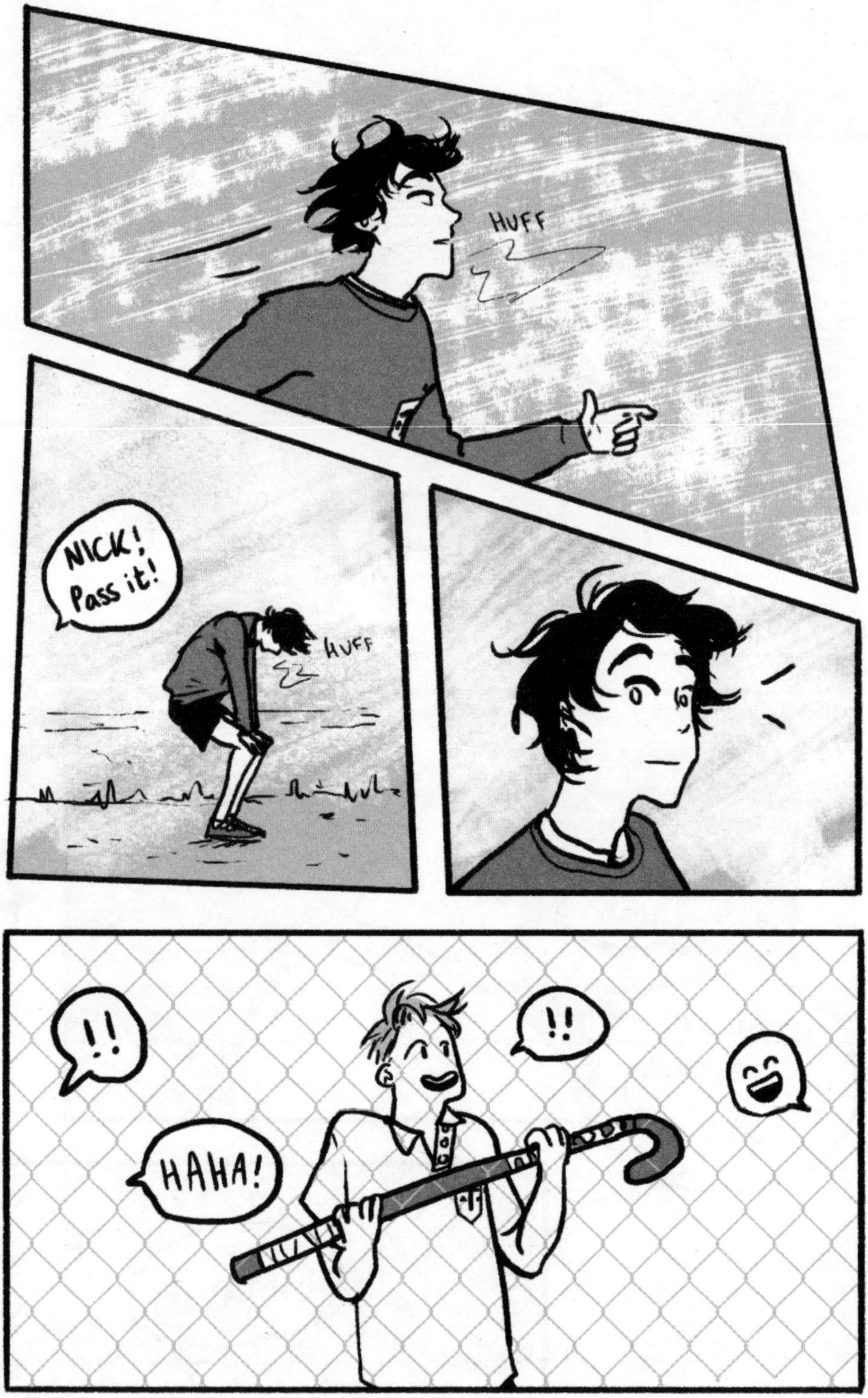
HUFF
NICK! Pass it!
HUFF
!!
!!
HAHA!

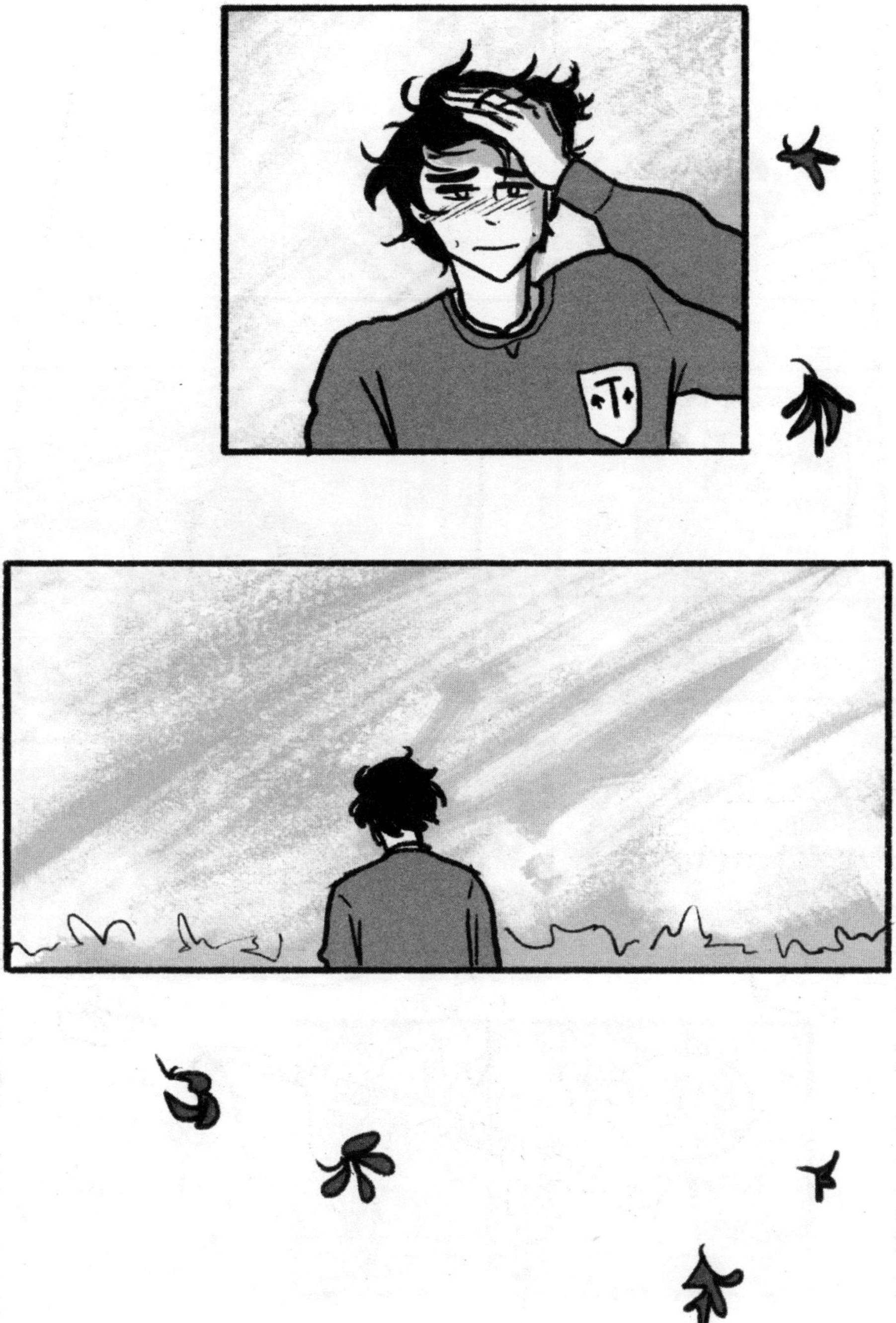

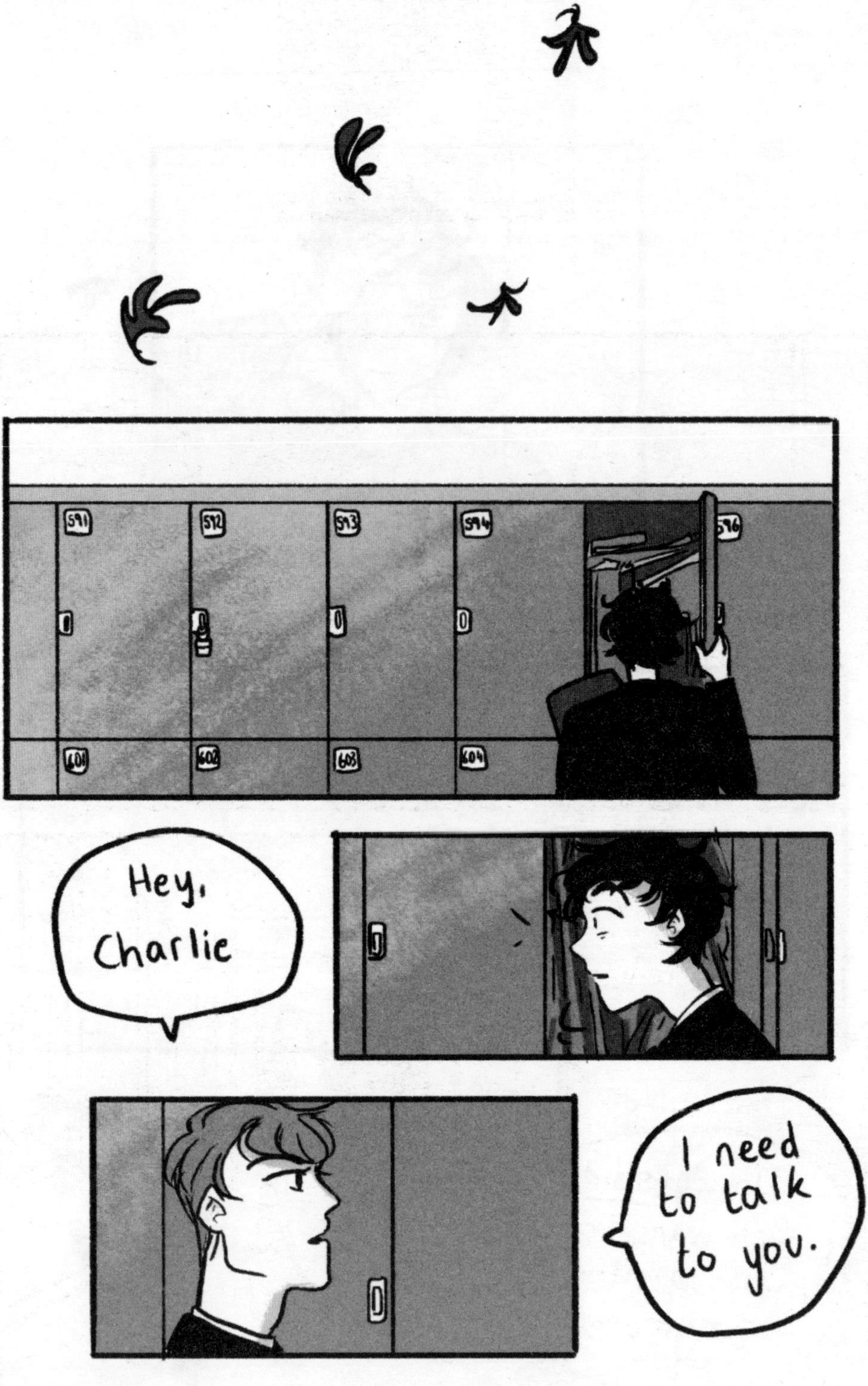
Hey, Charlie
I need to talk to you.

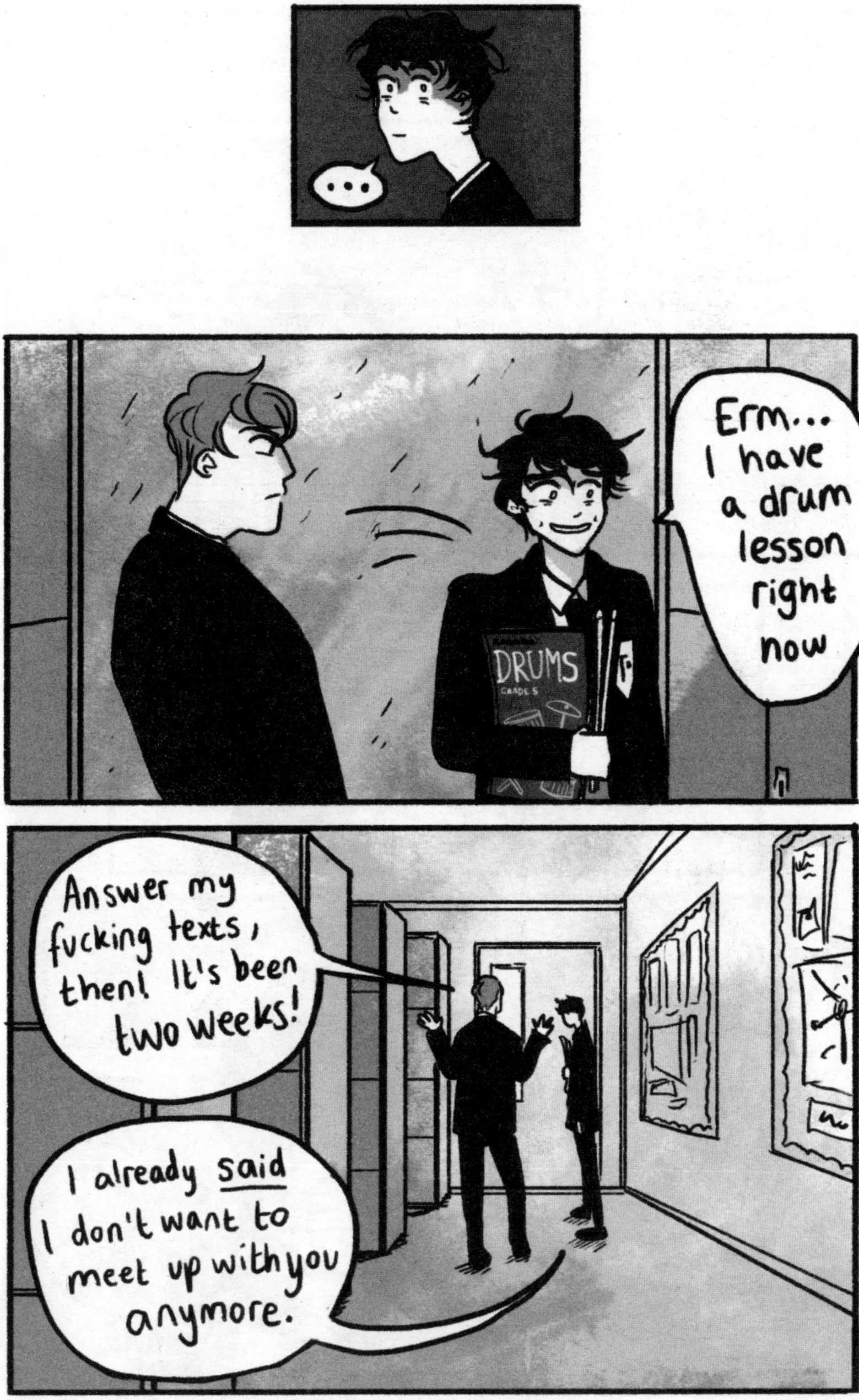
...
Erm... I have a drum lesson right now
DRUMS
GRADE 5
Answer my fucking texts, then! It's been two weeks!
I already said I don't want to meet up with you anymore.

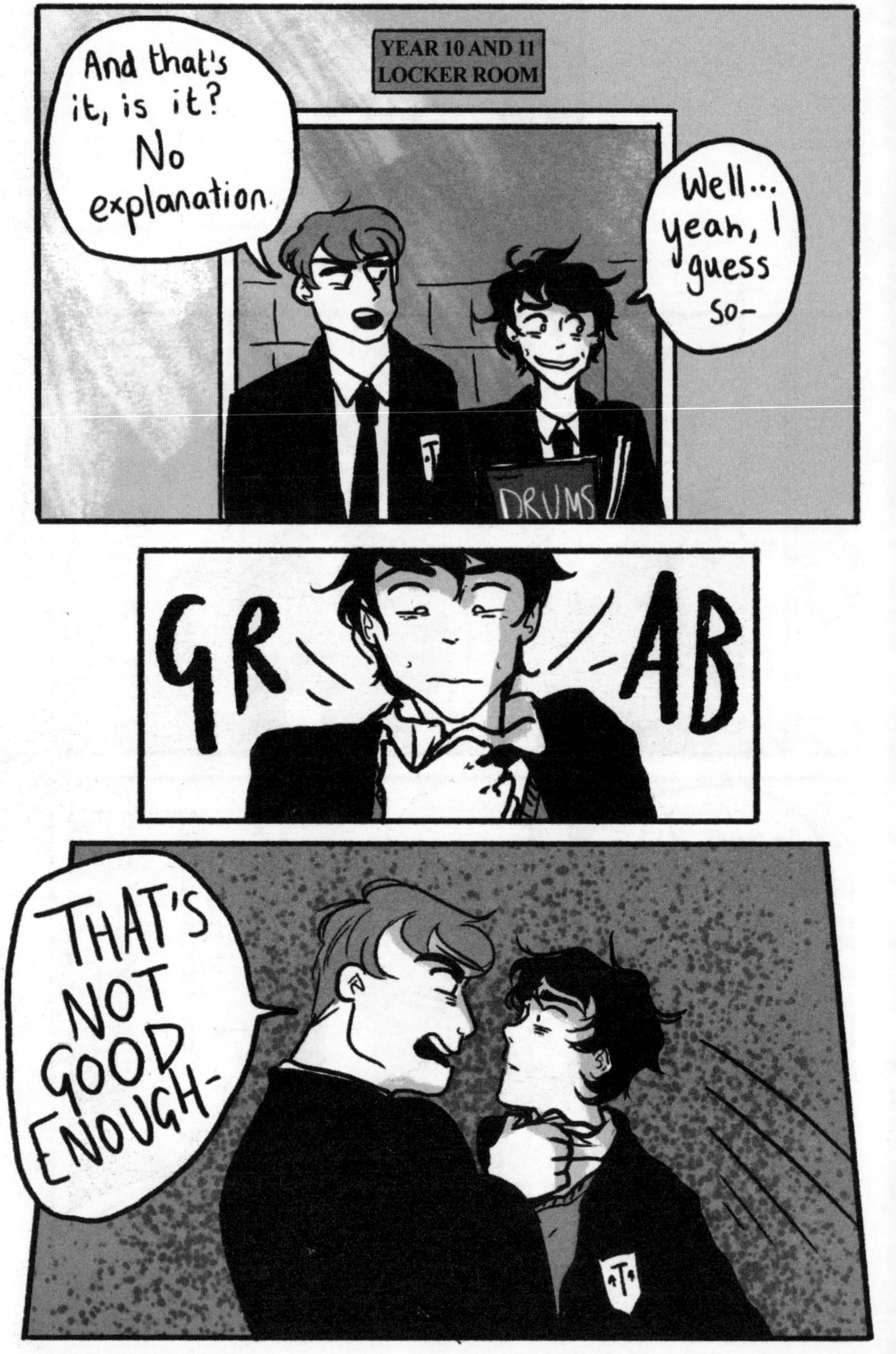
YEAR 10 AND 11
LOCKER ROOM
And that's it, is it? No explanation.
Well... yeah, I guess so-
DRUMS
GRAB
THAT'S NOT GOOD ENOUGH-

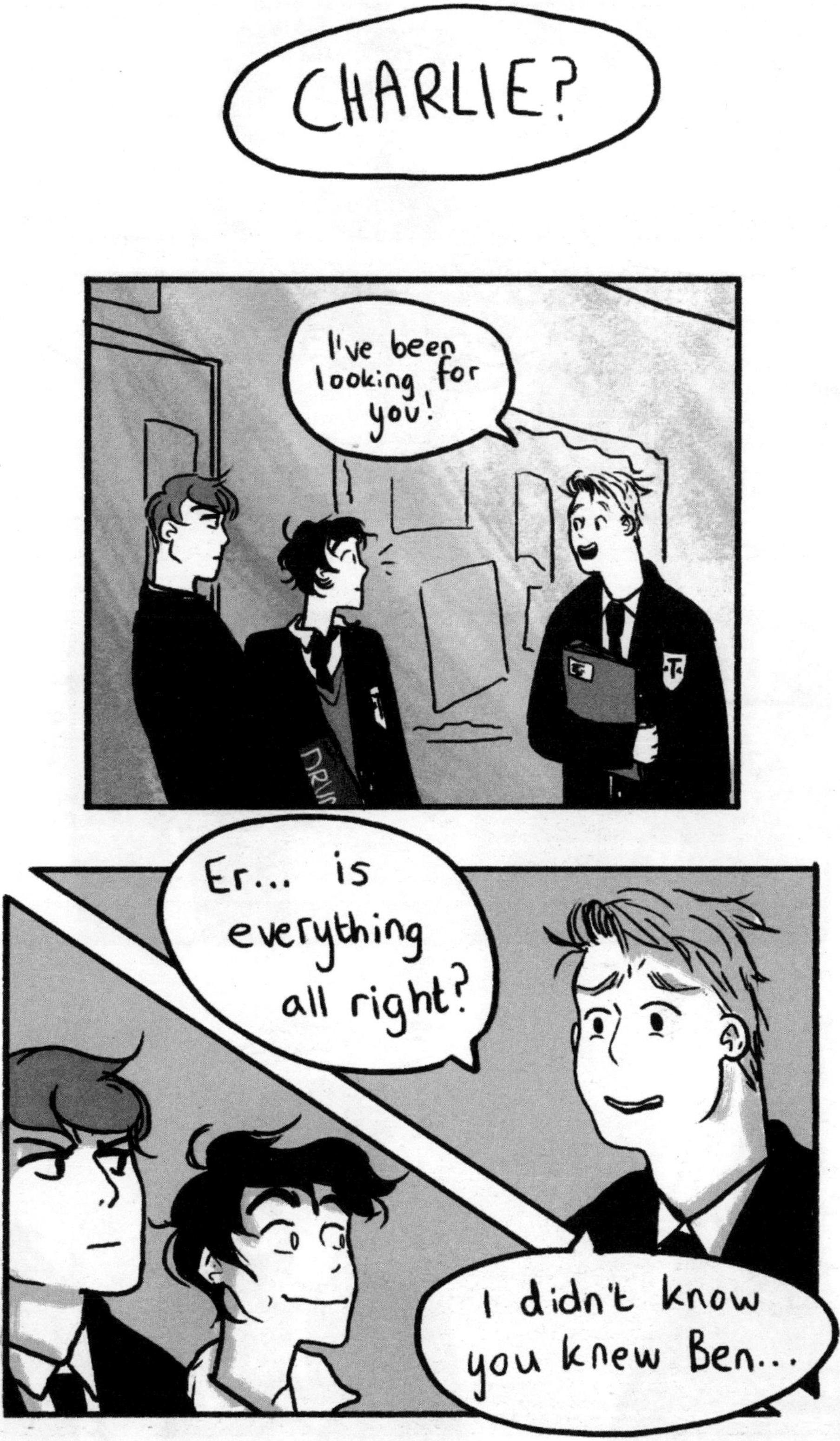
CHARLIE?
I've been looking for you!
Er... is everything all right?
I didn't know you knew Ben...

Erm... yes?

we'll talk later, Charlie

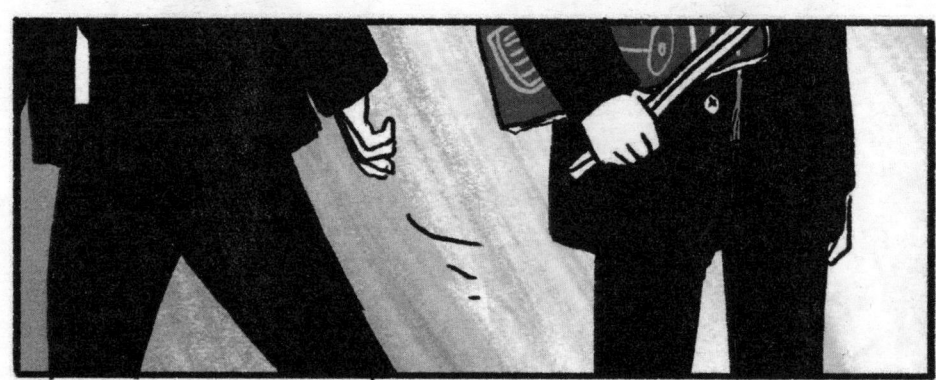

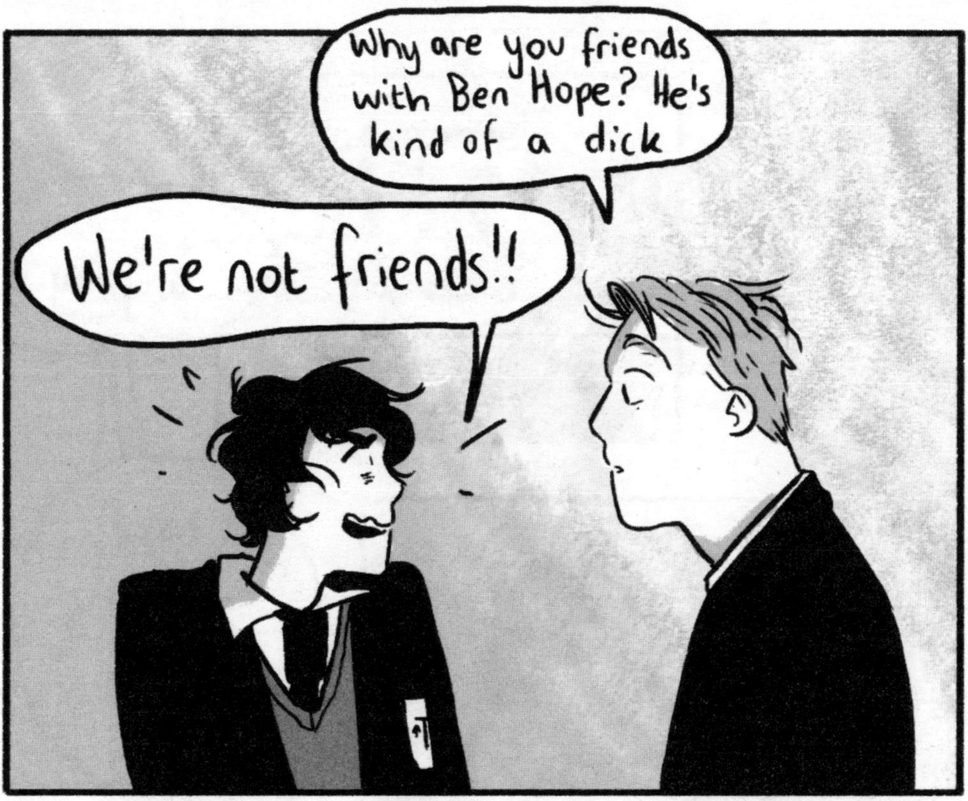
Why are you friends with Ben Hope? He's kind of a dick
We're not friends!!

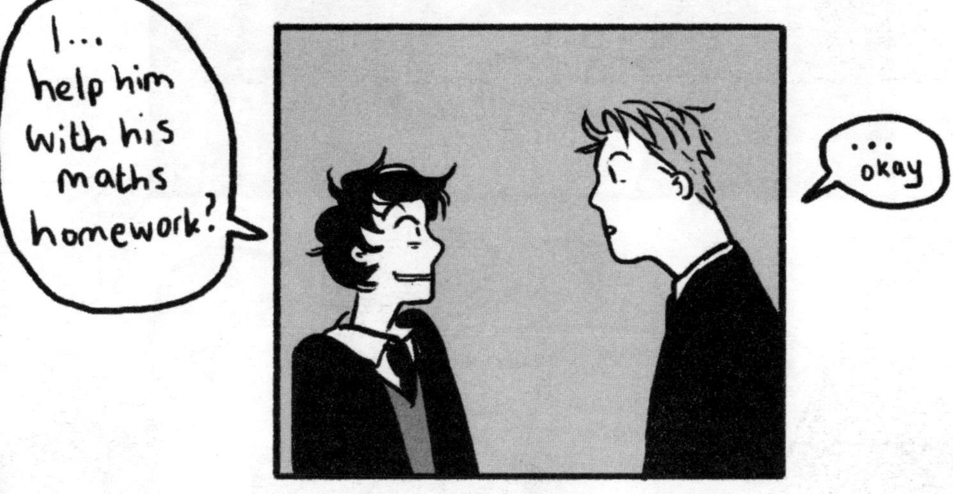
I... help him with his maths homework?
... okay

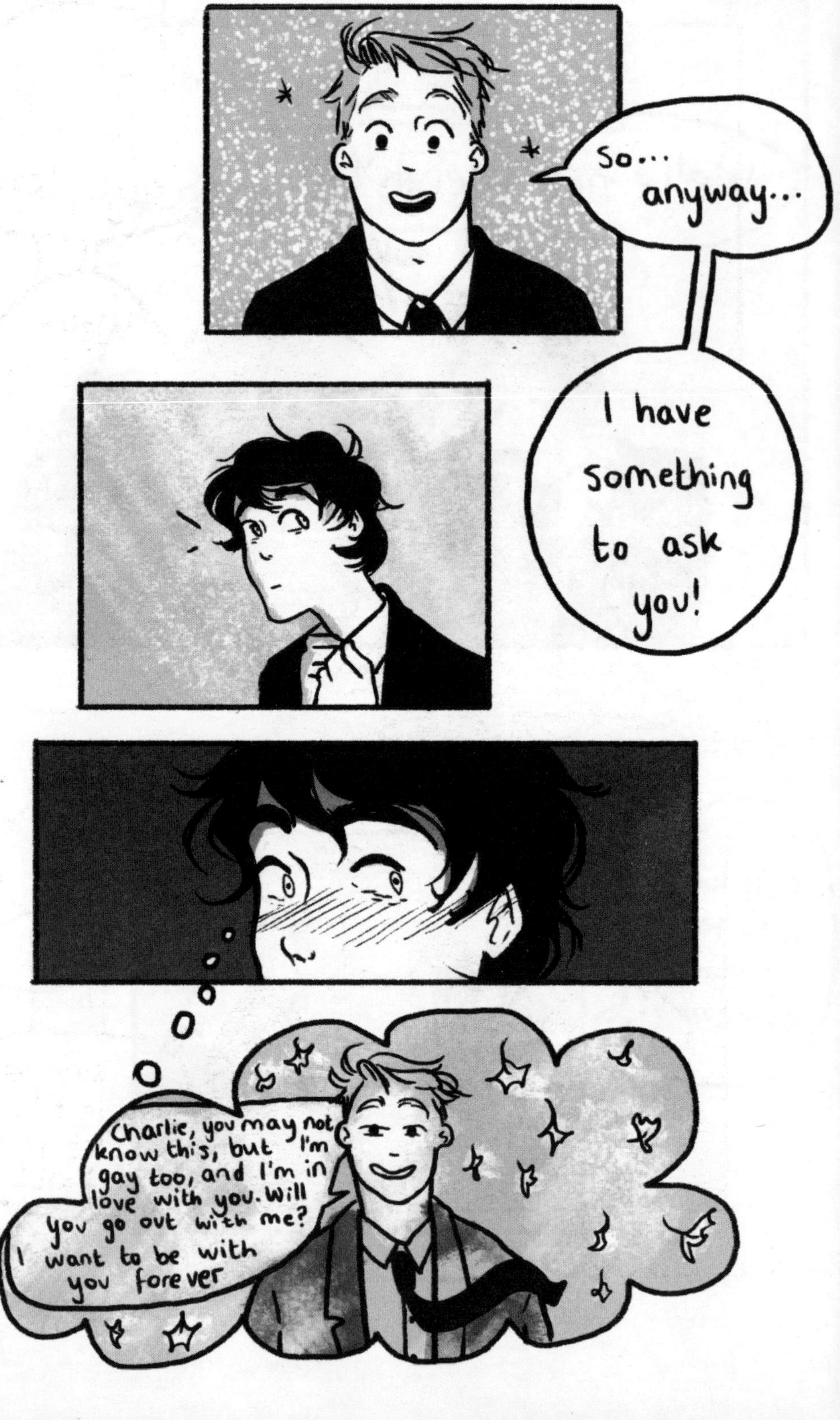
So... anyway...
I have something to ask you!
Charlie, you may not know this, but I'm gay too, and I'm in love with you. Will you go out with me? I want to be with you forever

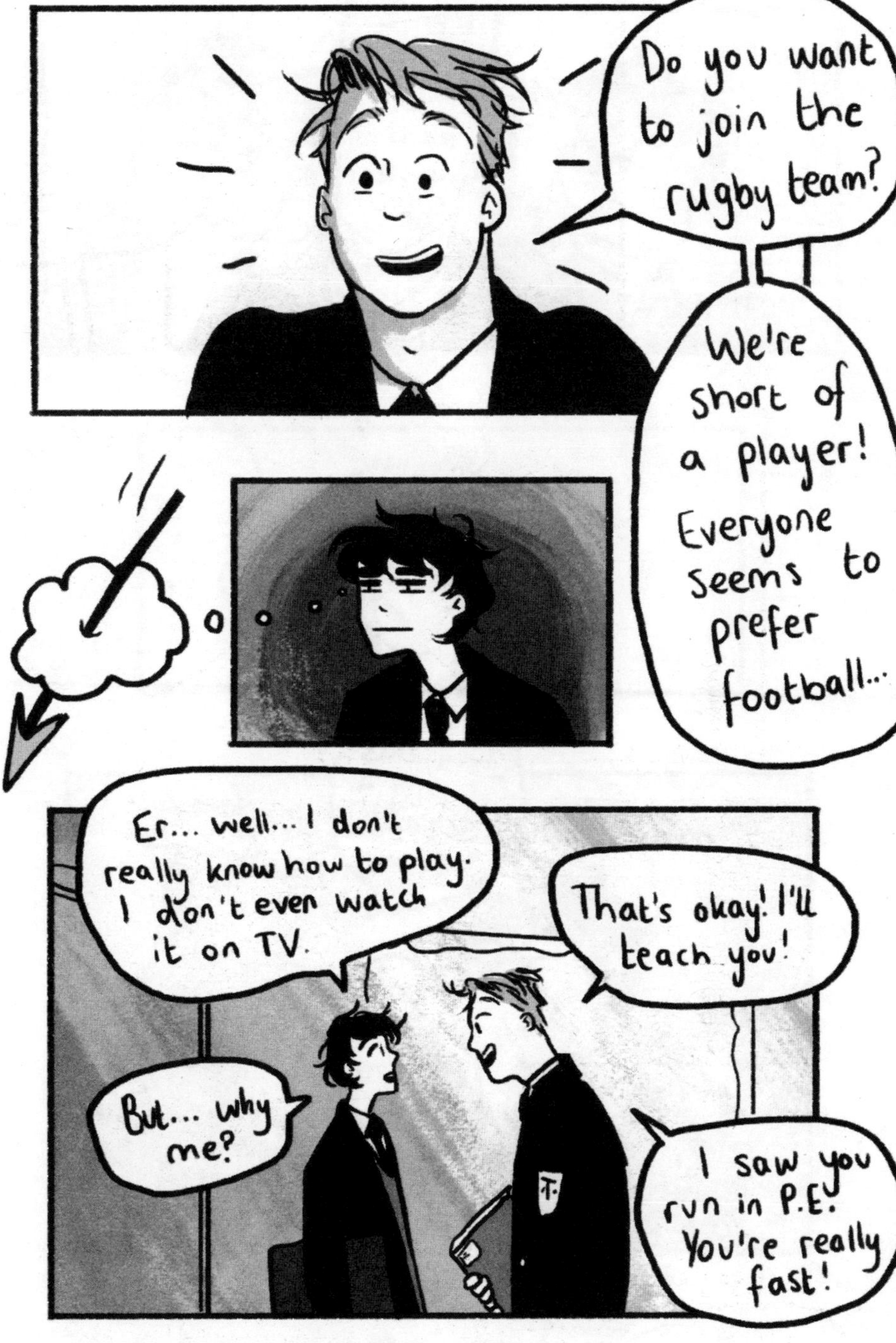
Do you want to join the rugby team?
We're short of a player! Everyone seems to prefer football...
Er... well... I don't really know how to play. I don't even watch it on TV.
That's okay! I'll teach you!
But... why me?
I saw you run in P.E! You're really fast!

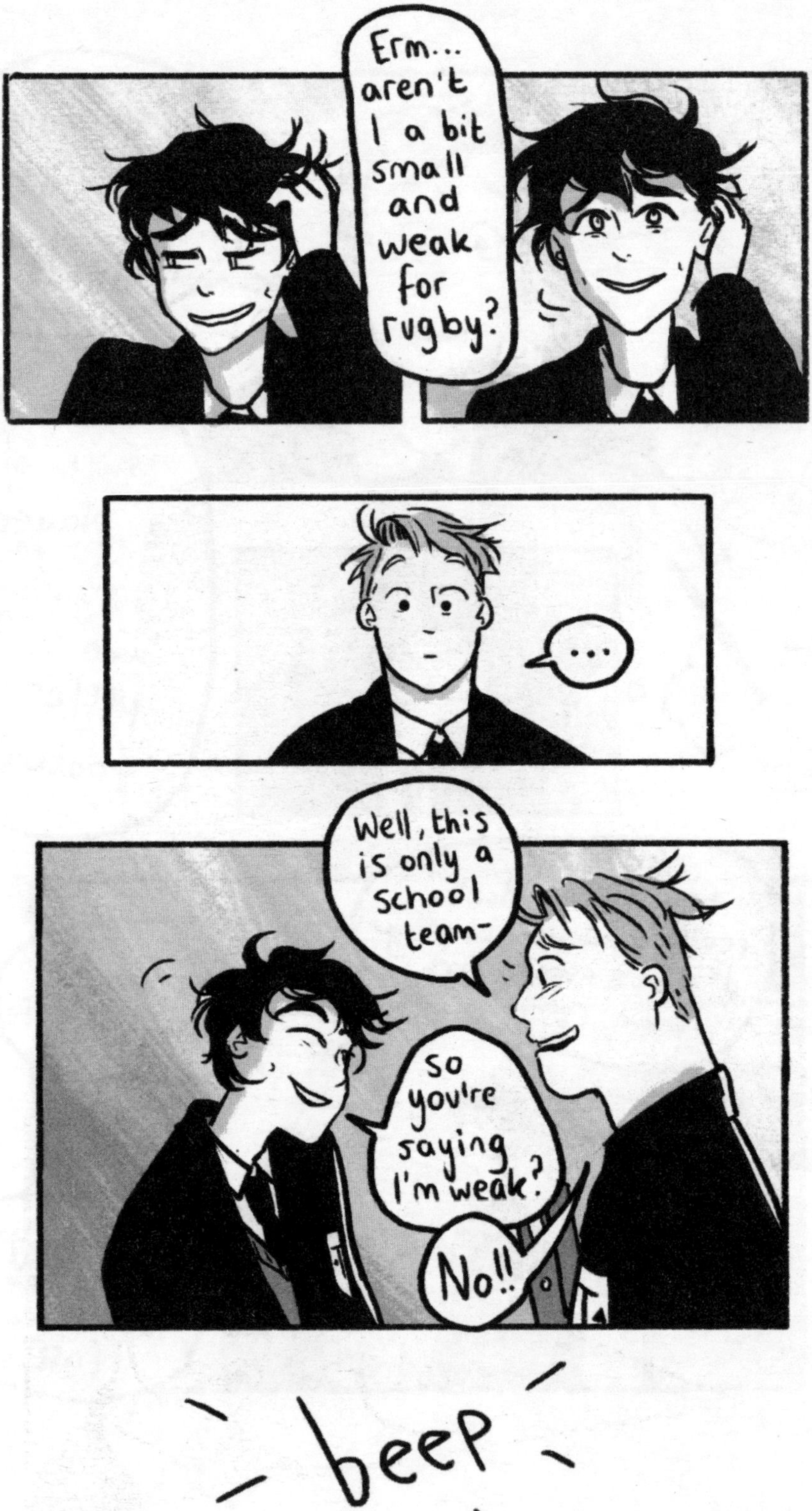
Erm... aren't I a bit small and weak for rugby?
...
Well, this is only a school team-
So you're saying I'm weak?
No!!
beep

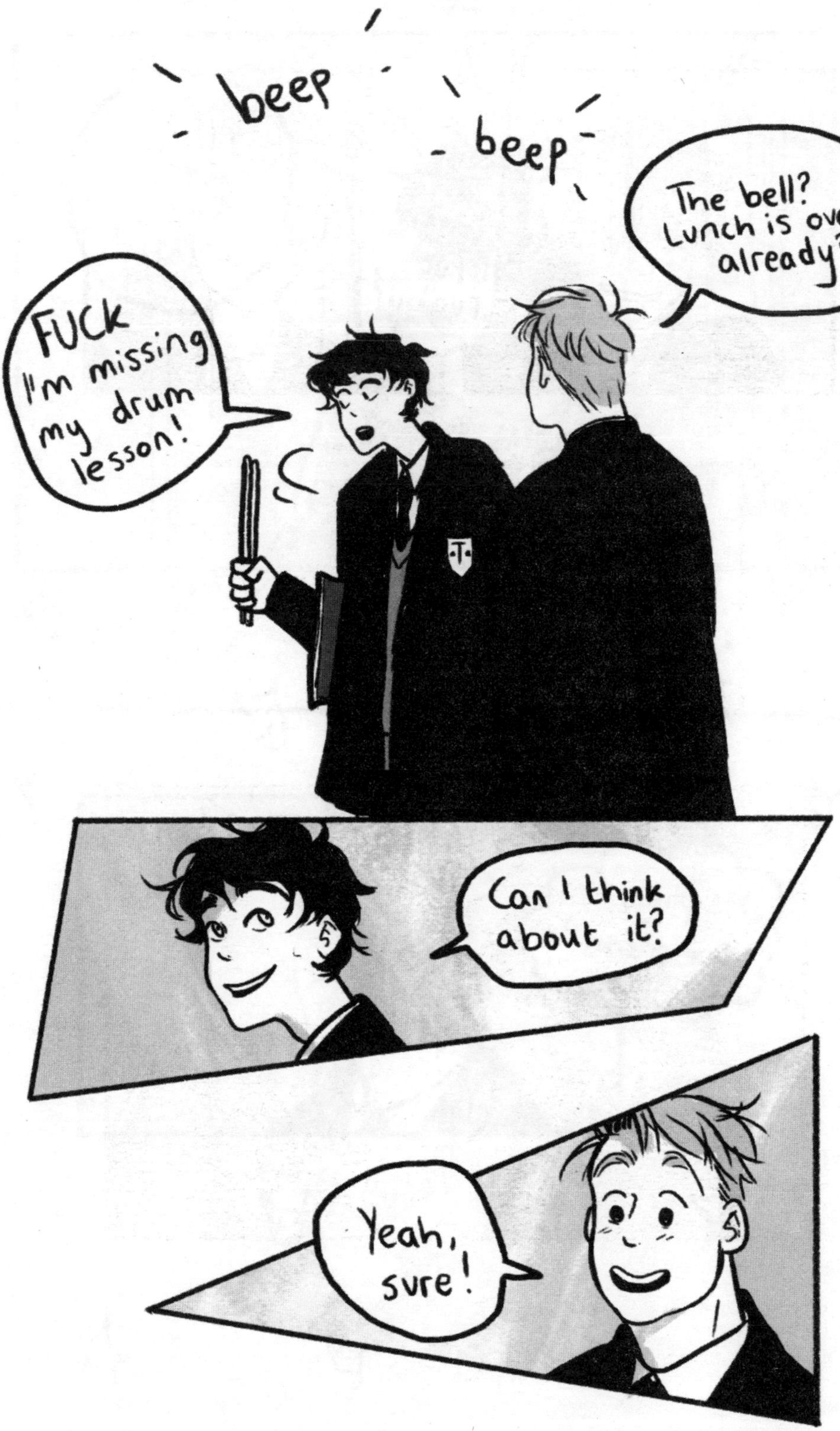
beep
beep
The bell? Lunch is over already?
FUCK I'm missing my drum lesson!
Can I think about it?
Yeah, sure!

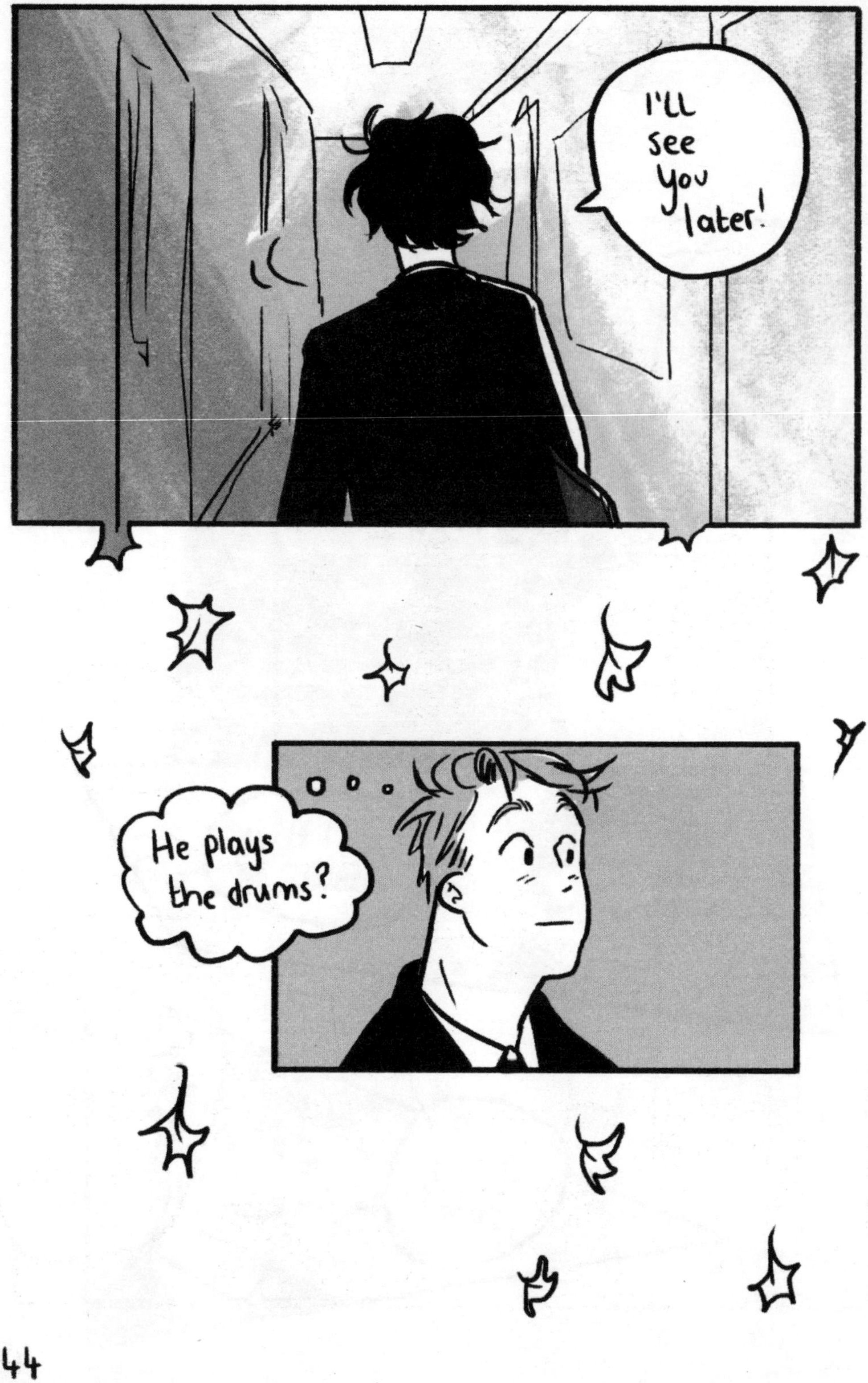
I'll see you later!
He plays the drums?

ONE WEEK LATER...

Charlie Spring, though?

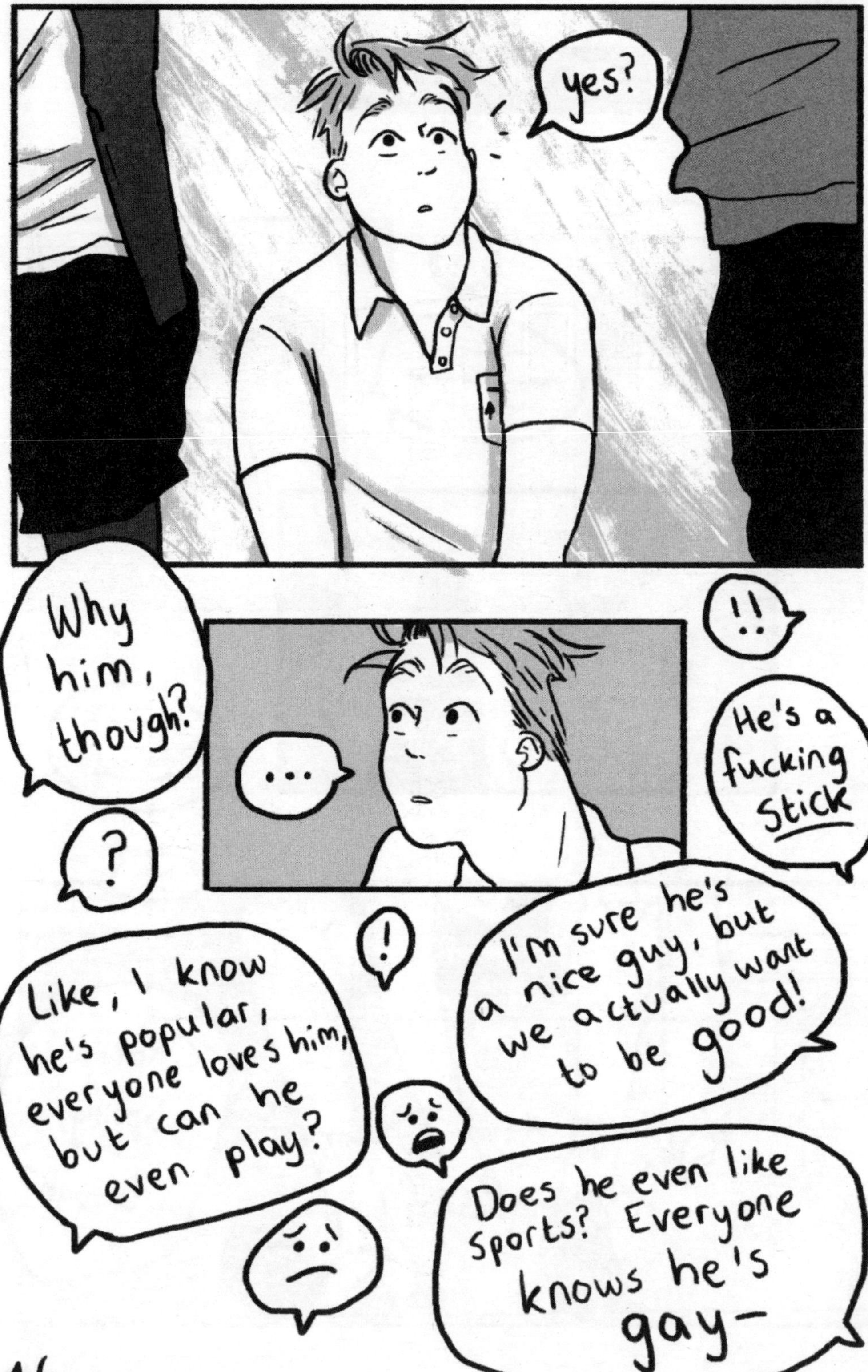
yes?
Why him, though?
...
!!
He's a fucking stick
?
!
Like, I know he's popular, everyone loves him, but can he even play?
I'm sure he's a nice guy, but we actually want to be good!
Does he even like sports? Everyone knows he's gay-

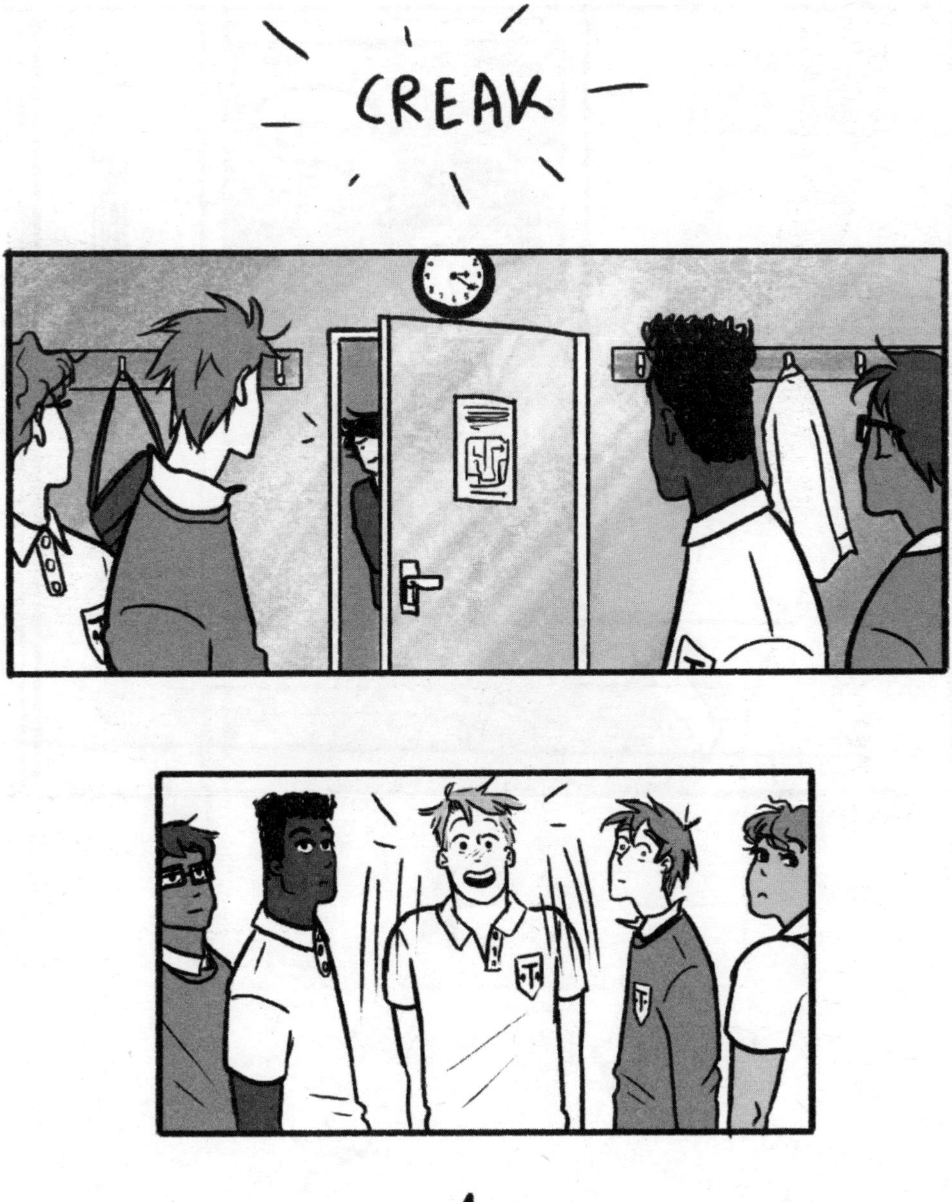
CREAK
Hey!

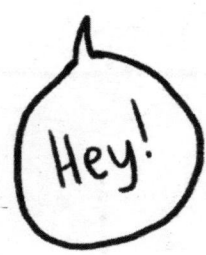

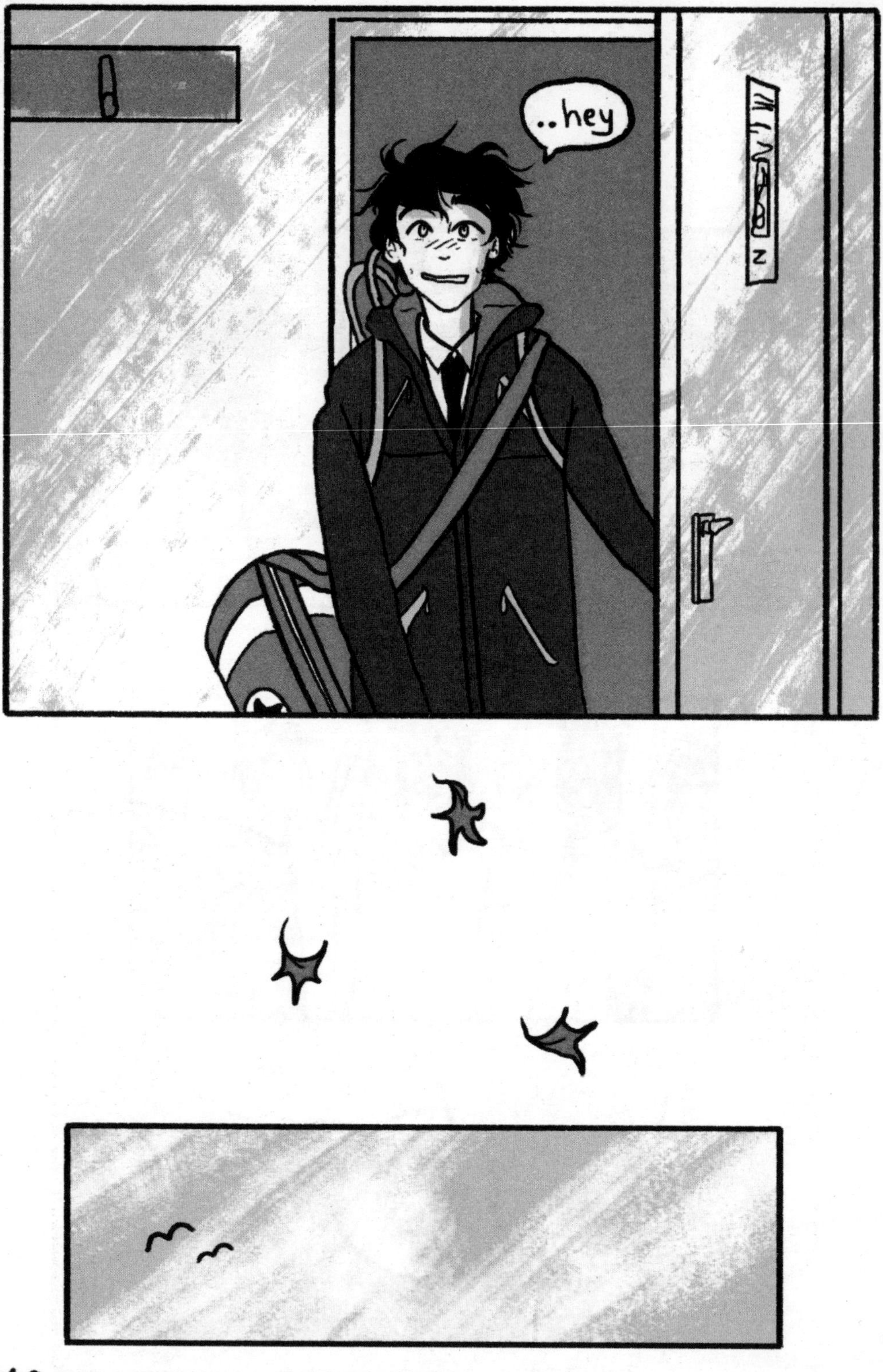
..hey

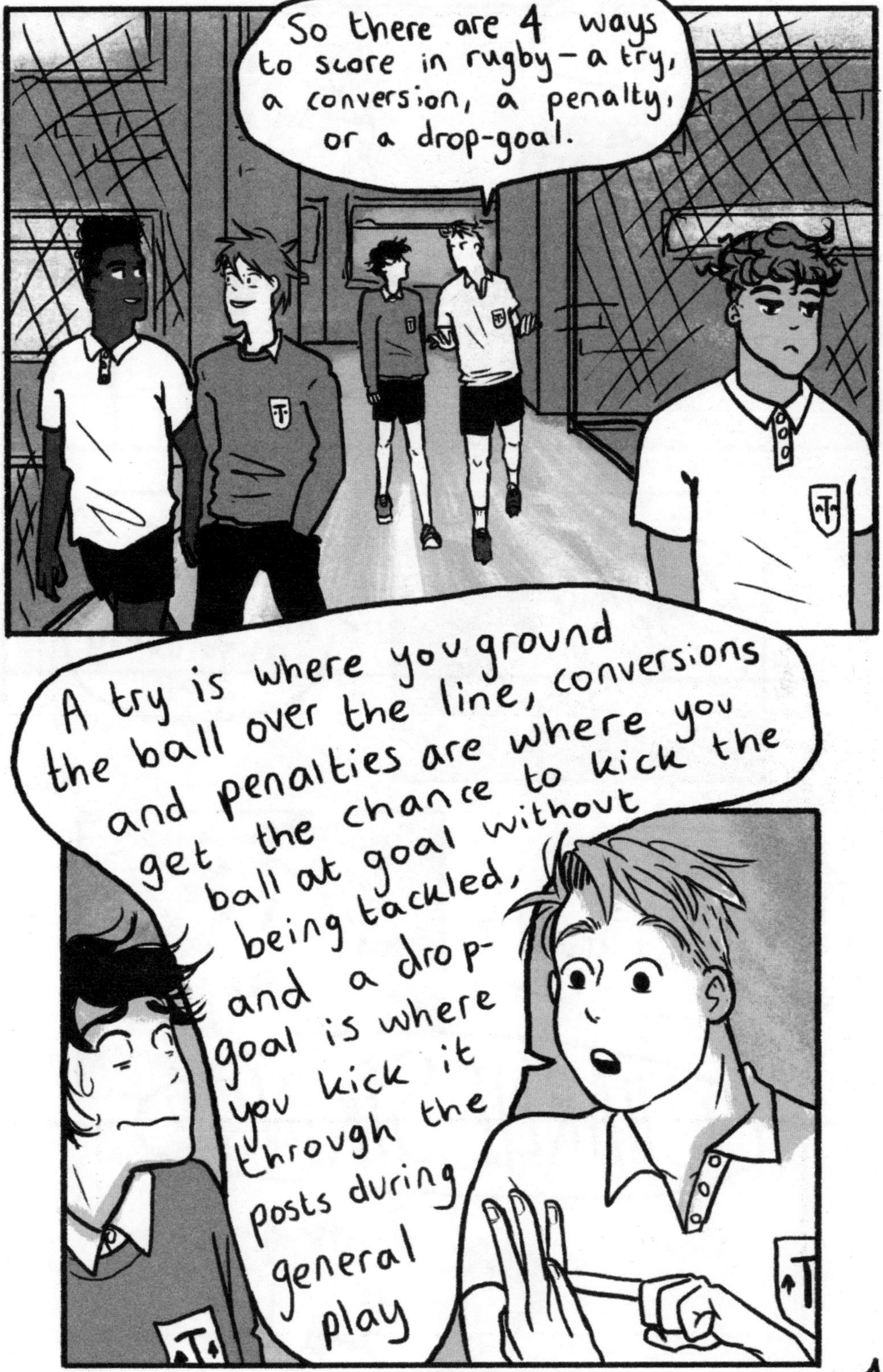
So there are 4 ways to score in rugby – a try, a conversion, a penalty, or a drop-goal.
A try is where you ground the ball over the line, conversions and penalties are where you get the chance to kick the ball at goal without being tackled, and a drop-goal is where you kick it through the posts during general play

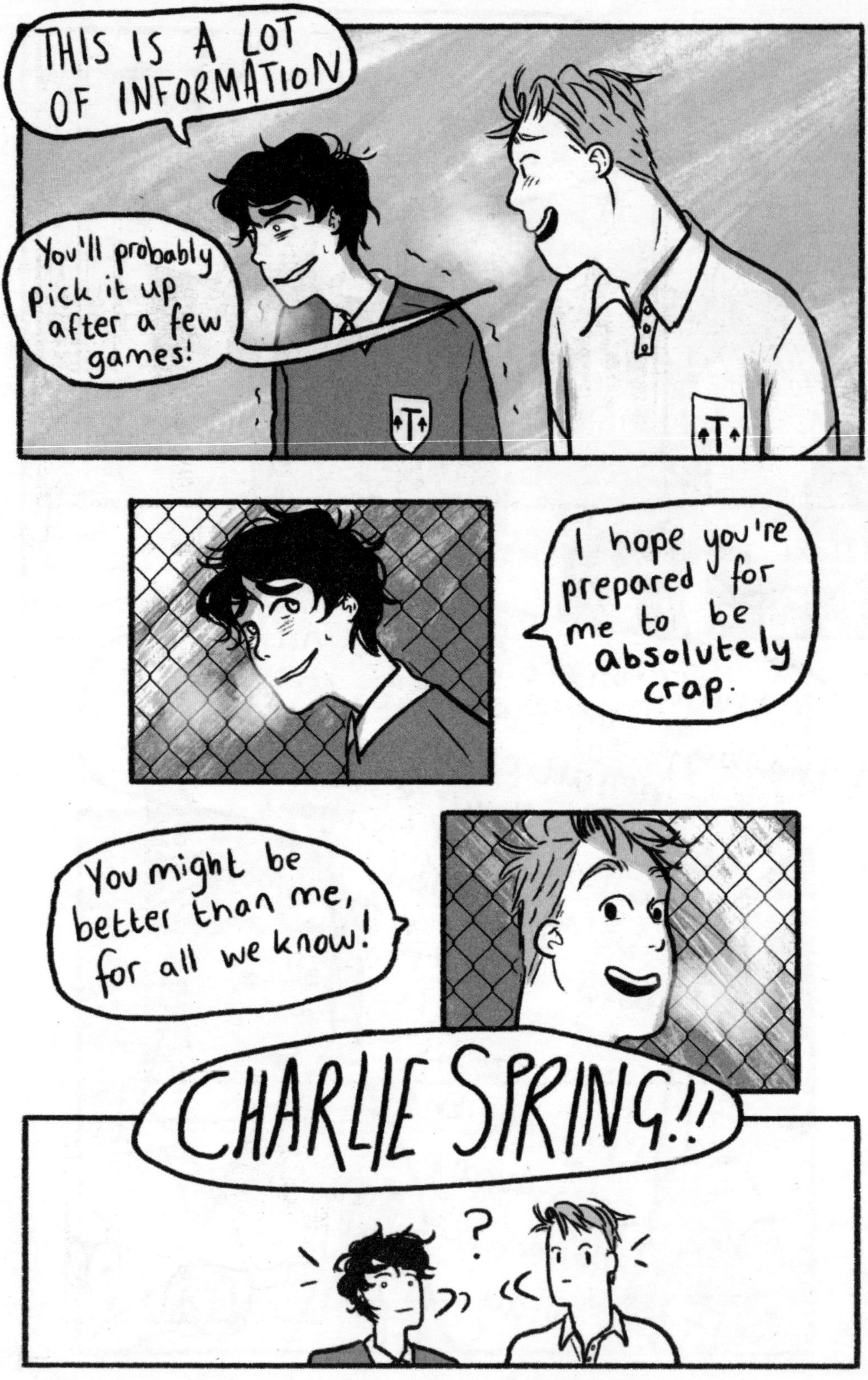
THIS IS A LOT OF INFORMATION
You'll probably pick it up after a few games!
I hope you're prepared for me to be absolutely crap.
You might be better than me, for all we know!
CHARLIE SPRING!!
?

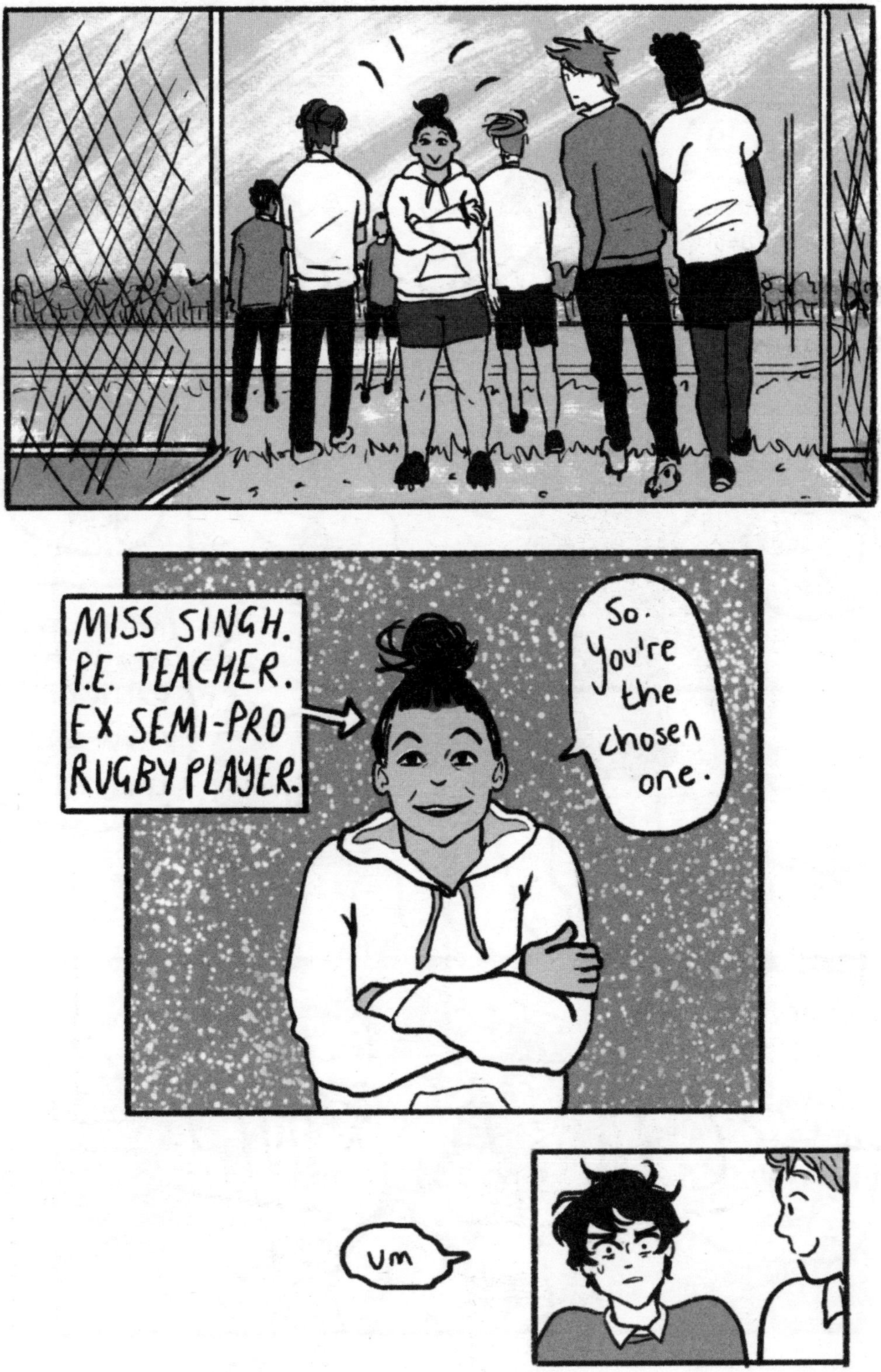
MISS SINGH. P.E. TEACHER. EX SEMI-PRO RUGBY PLAYER.
So. You're the chosen one.
um

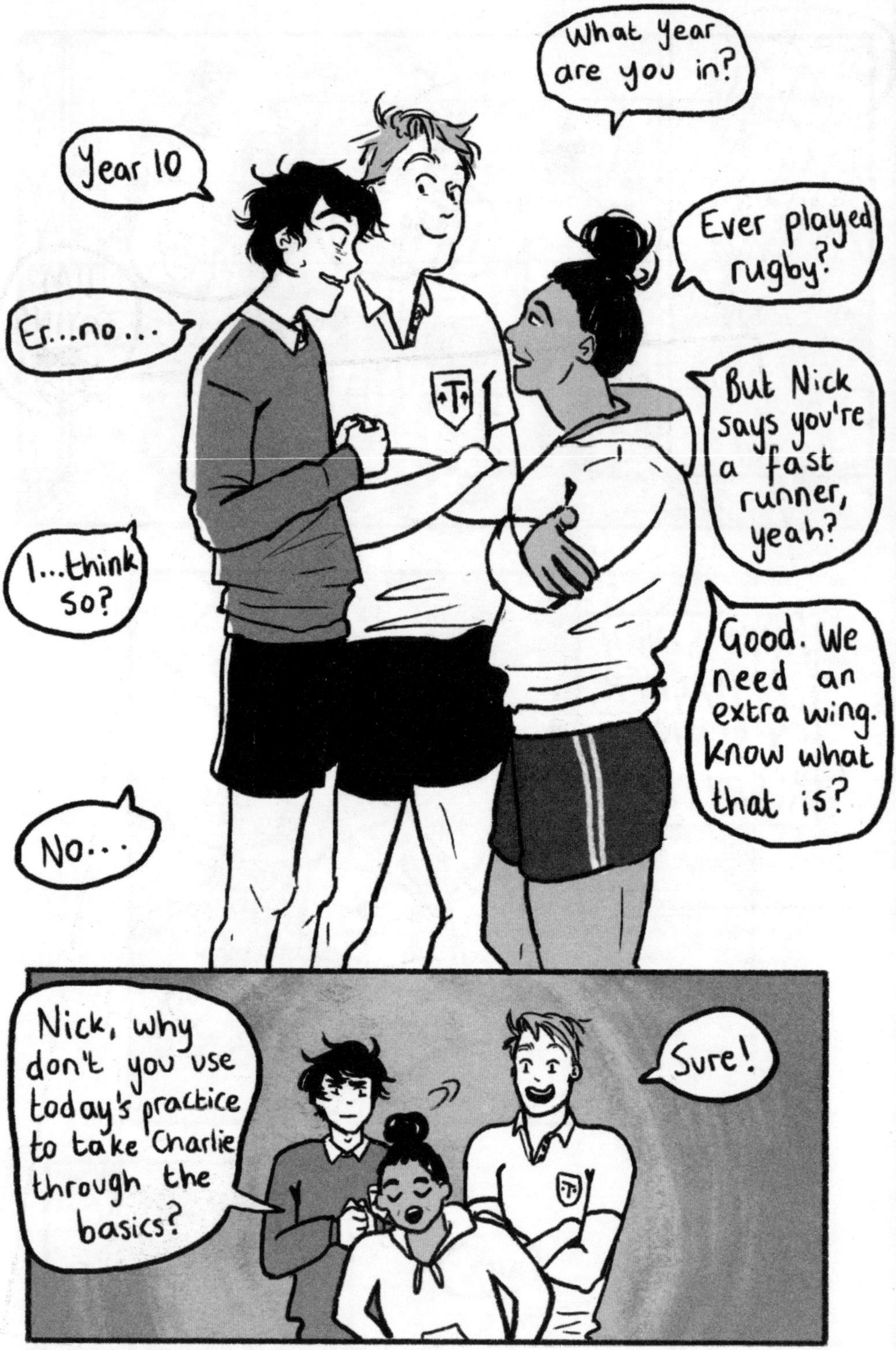
What year are you in?
Year 10
Ever played rugby?
Er...no...
But Nick says you're a fast runner, yeah?
I...think so?
Good. We need an extra wing. Know what that is?
No...
Nick, why don't you use today's practice to take Charlie through the basics?
Sure!

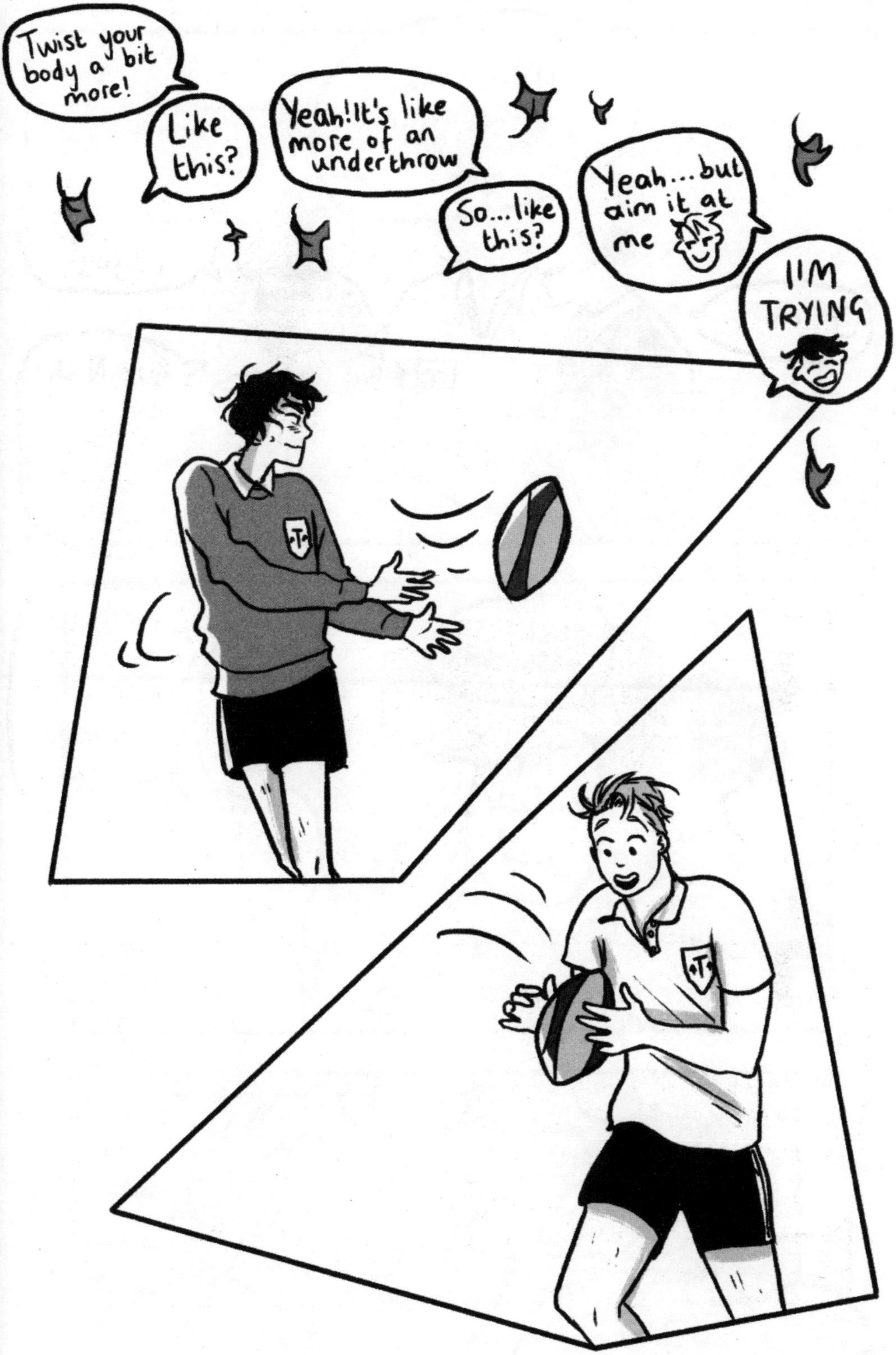
Twist your body a bit more!
Like this?
Yeah! It's like more of an underthrow
So... like this?
Yeah... but aim it at me
I'M TRYING

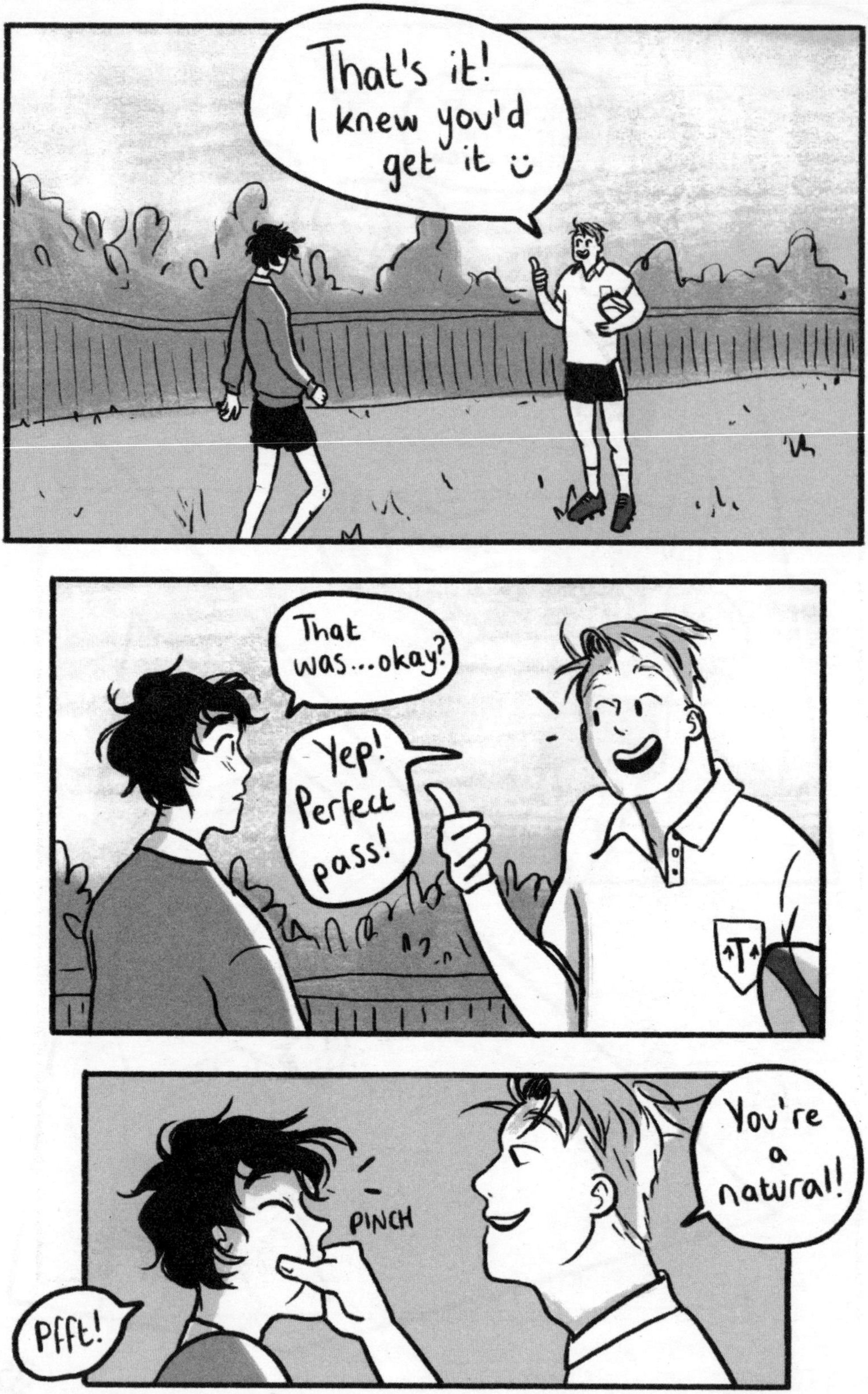
That's it! I knew you'd get it ☺
That was...okay?
Yep! Perfect pass!
PINCH
You're a natural!
Pffft!

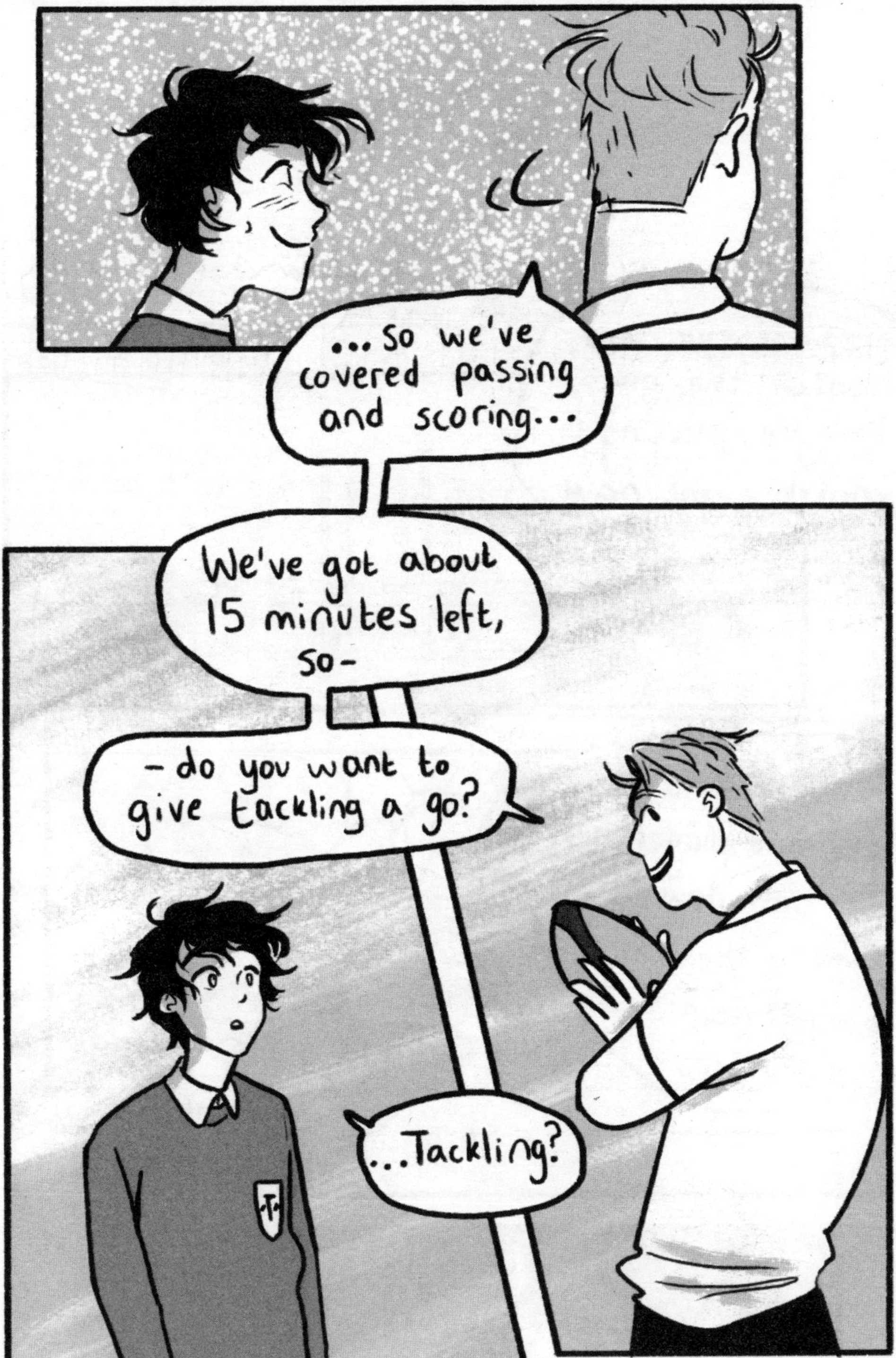
...So we've covered passing and scoring...
We've got about 15 minutes left, so-
-do you want to give tackling a go?
...Tackling?

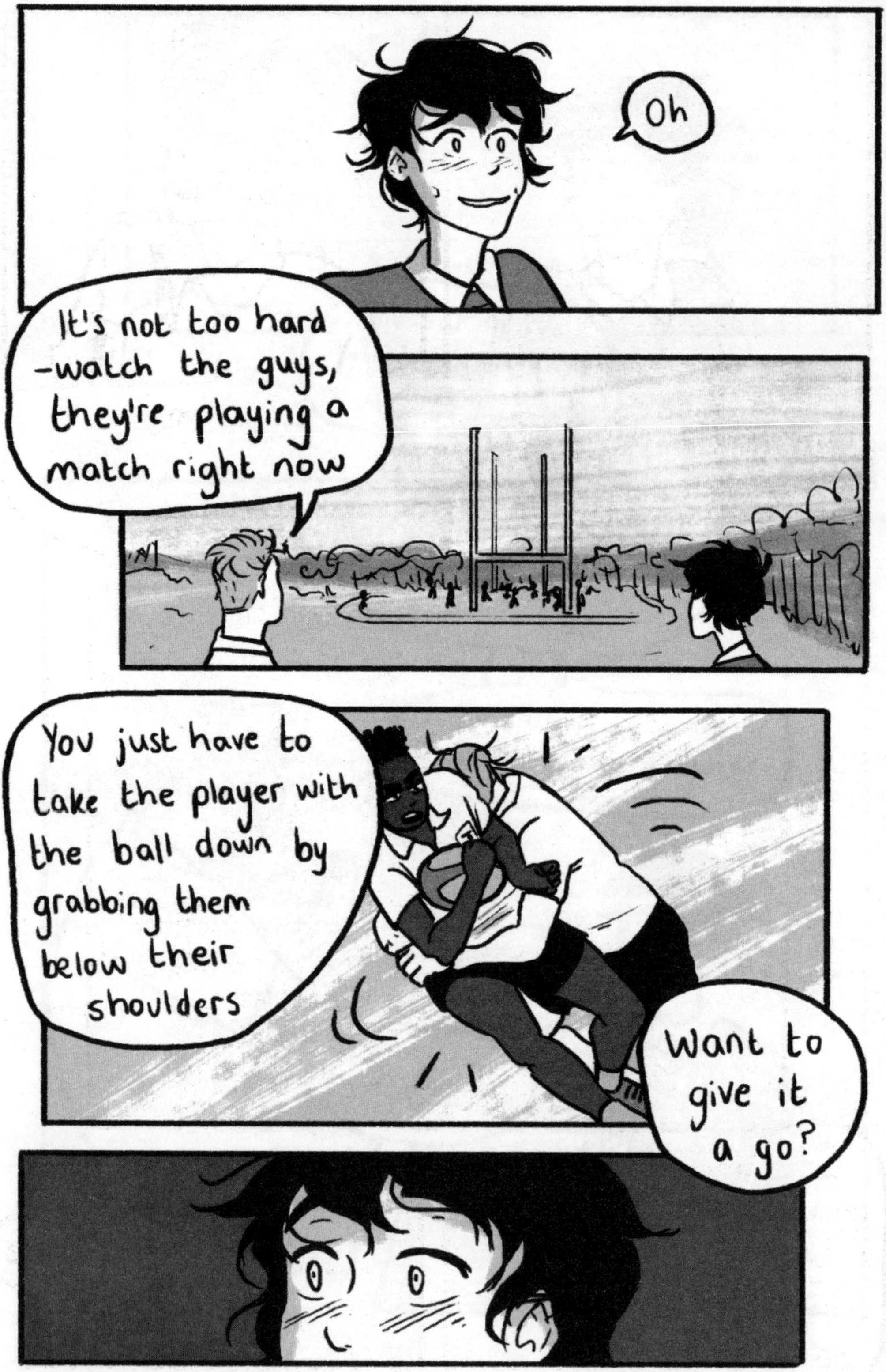
Oh
It's not too hard -watch the guys, they're playing a match right now
You just have to take the player with the ball down by grabbing them below their shoulders
Want to give it a go?

I am definitely way too weak to do that

Excuse me — where is your 'can do' attitude?

Give it a go. Just run at me. I won't dodge!

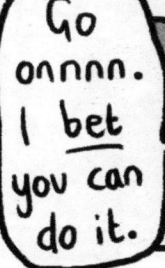

Go onnnn. I bet you can do it.

...Fine

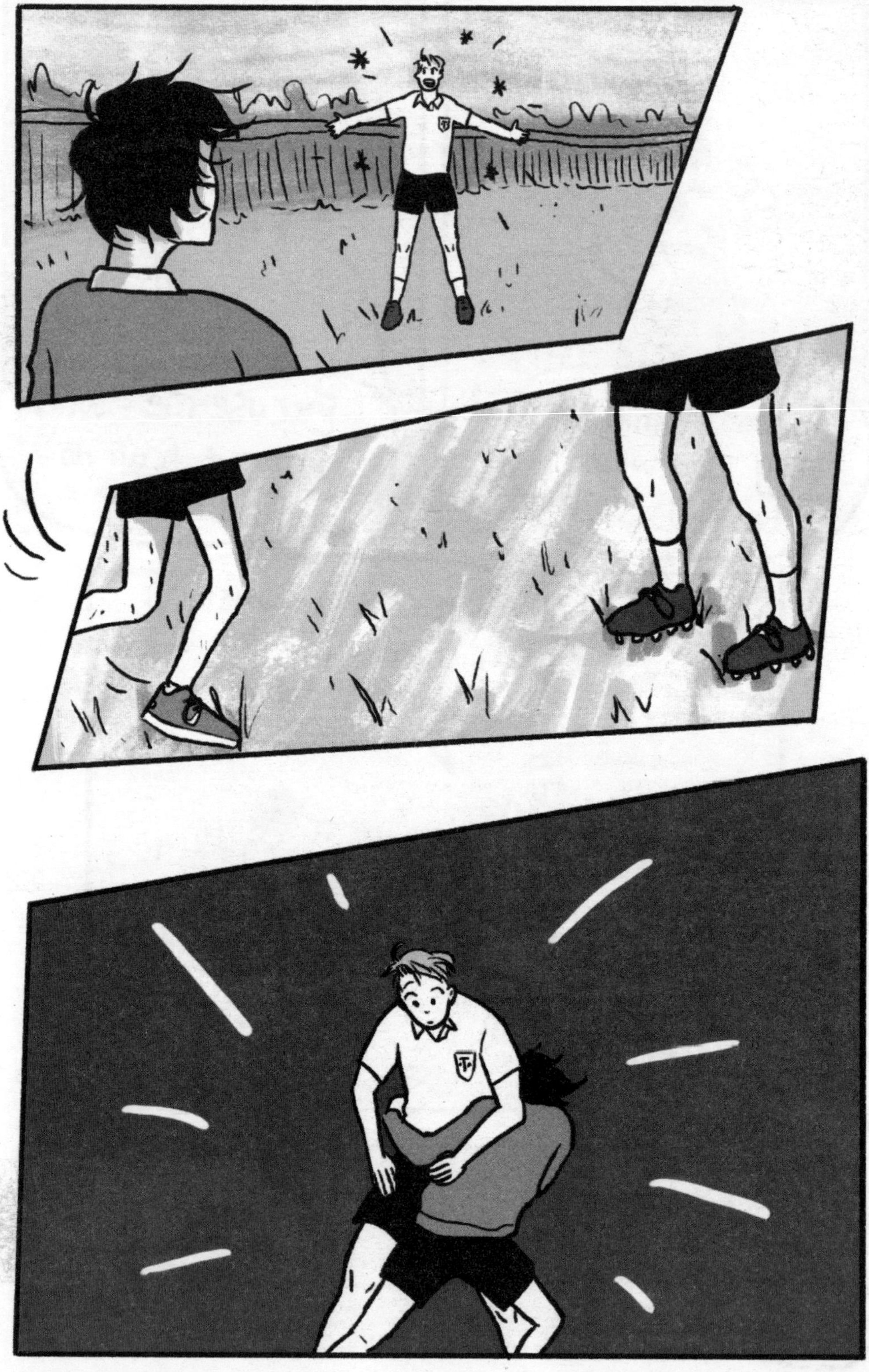

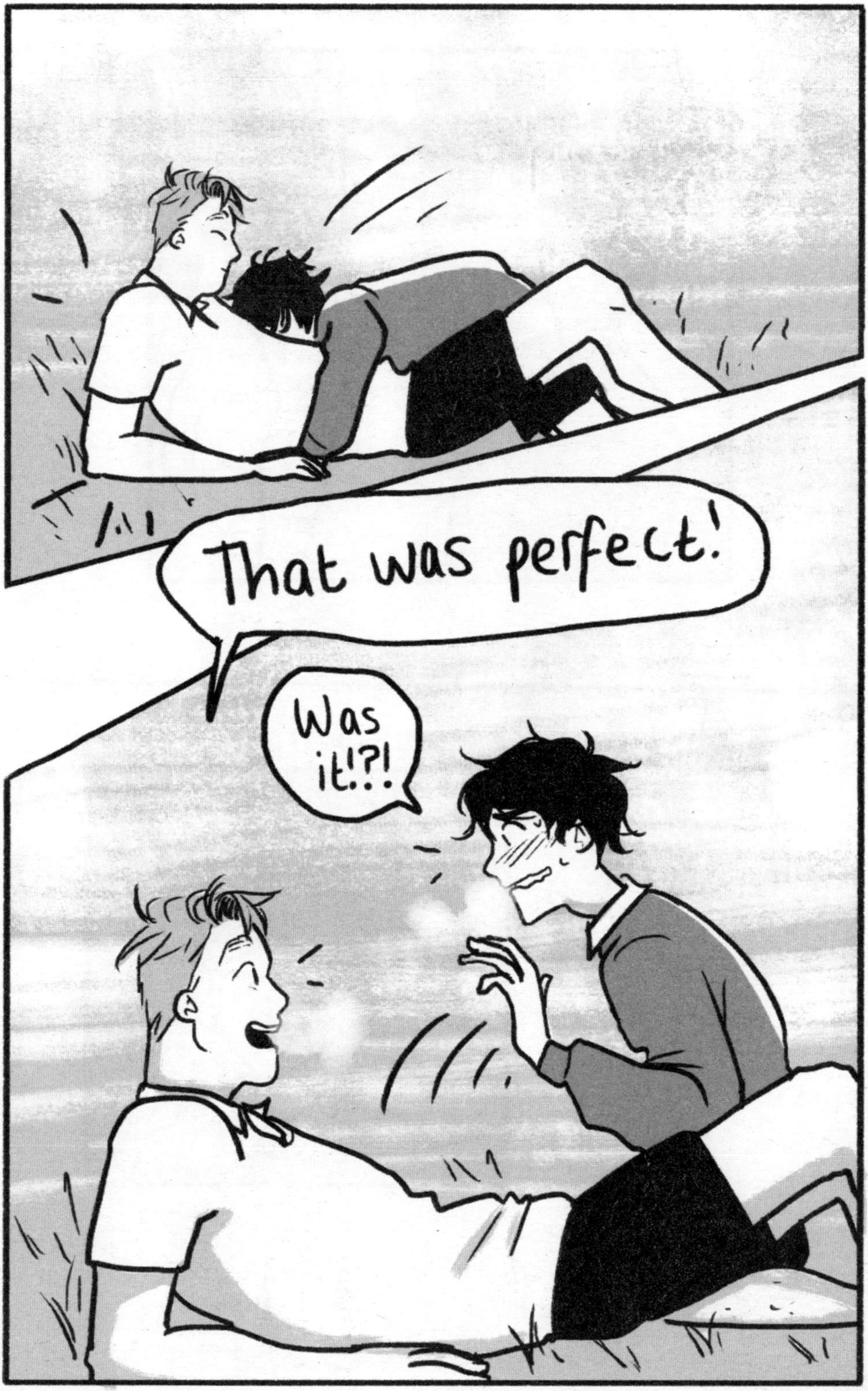
That was perfect!
Was it!?!

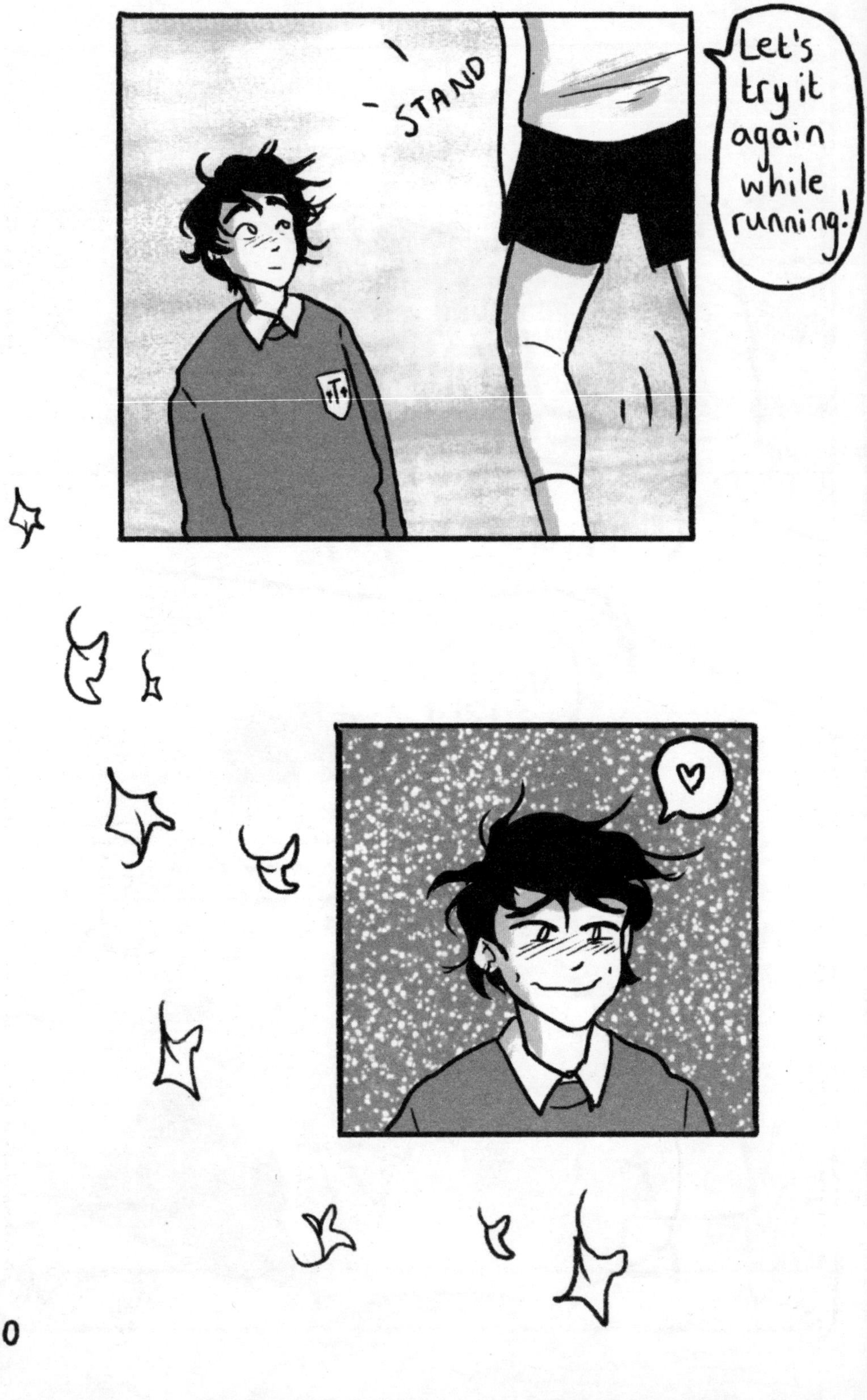
STAND
Let's try it again while running!

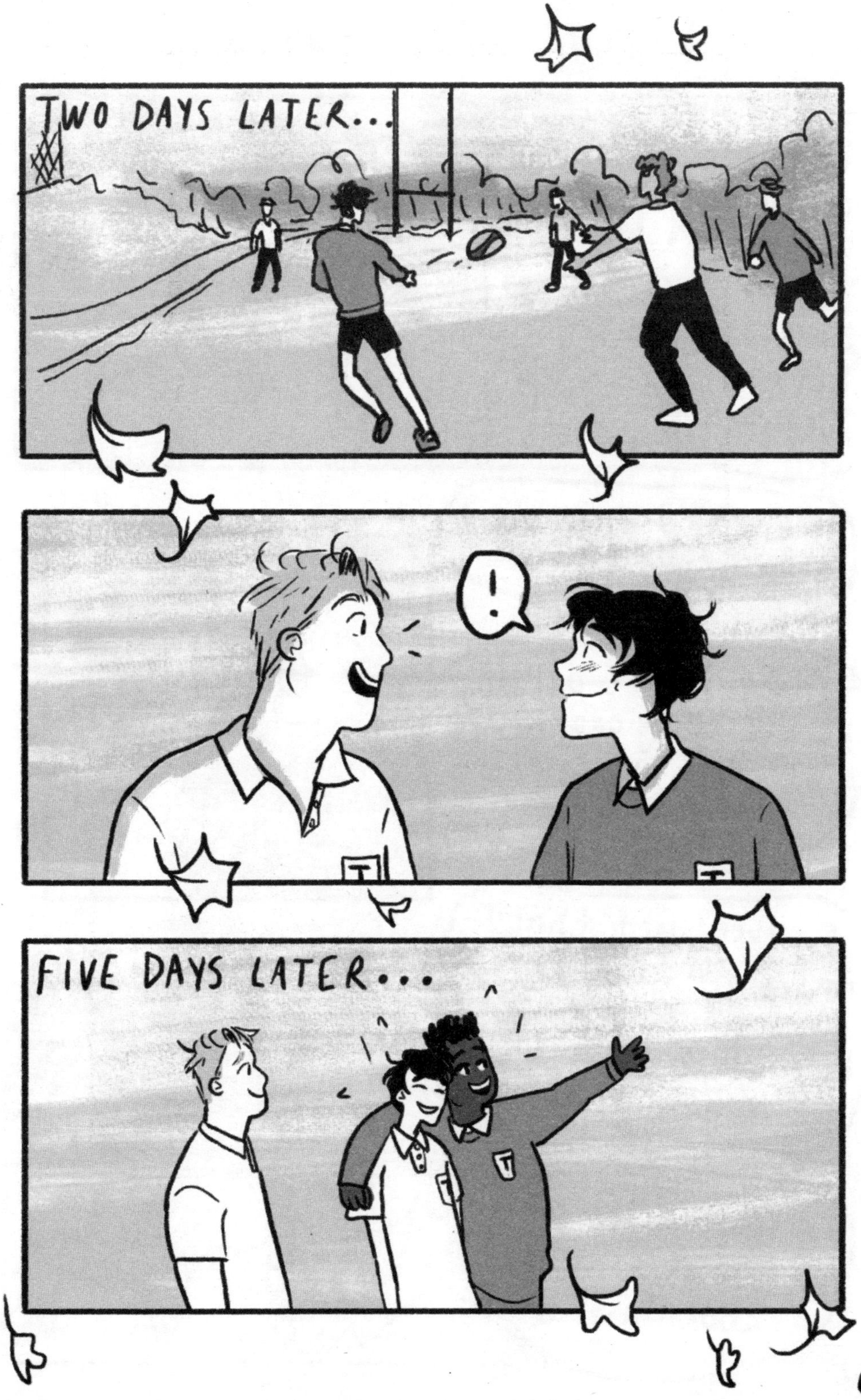
TWO DAYS LATER...
!
FIVE DAYS LATER...

ONE WEEK LATER

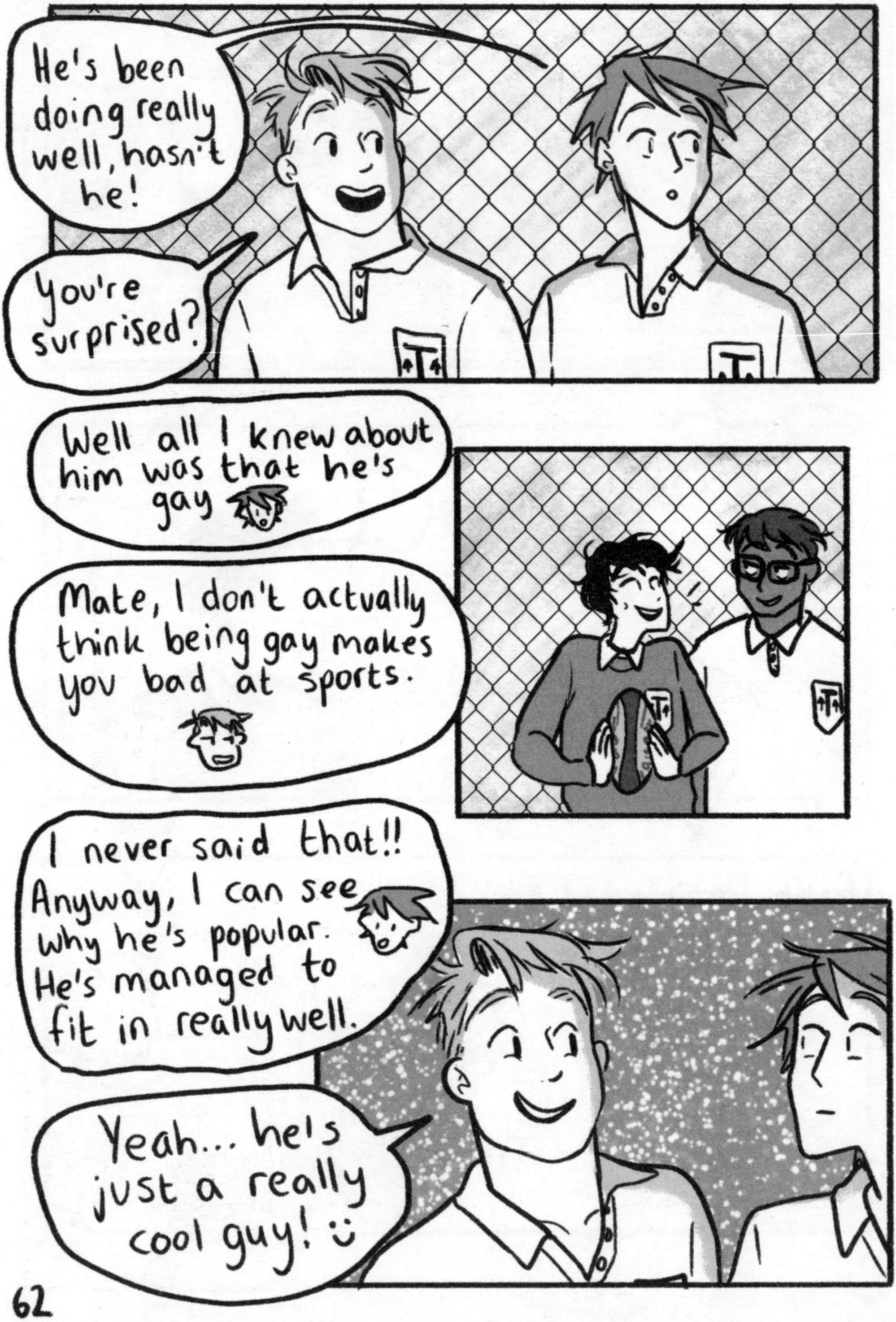
He's been doing really well, hasn't he!
You're surprised?
Well all I knew about him was that he's gay
Mate, I don't actually think being gay makes you bad at sports.
I never said that!! Anyway, I can see why he's popular. He's managed to fit in really well.
Yeah... he's just a really cool guy! ☺

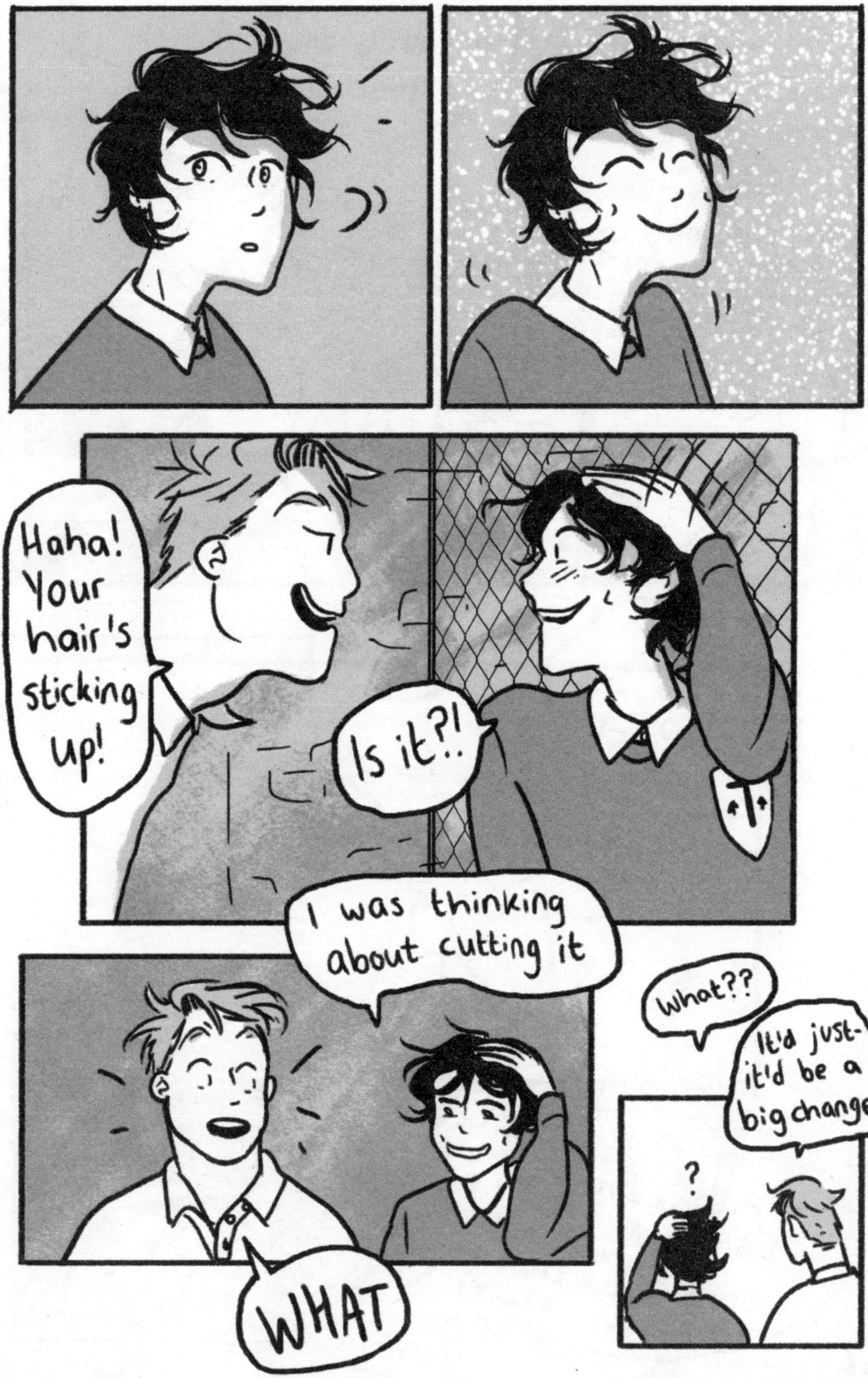
Haha! Your hair's sticking up!
Is it?!..
I was thinking about cutting it
WHAT
What??
It'd just- it'd be a big change
?

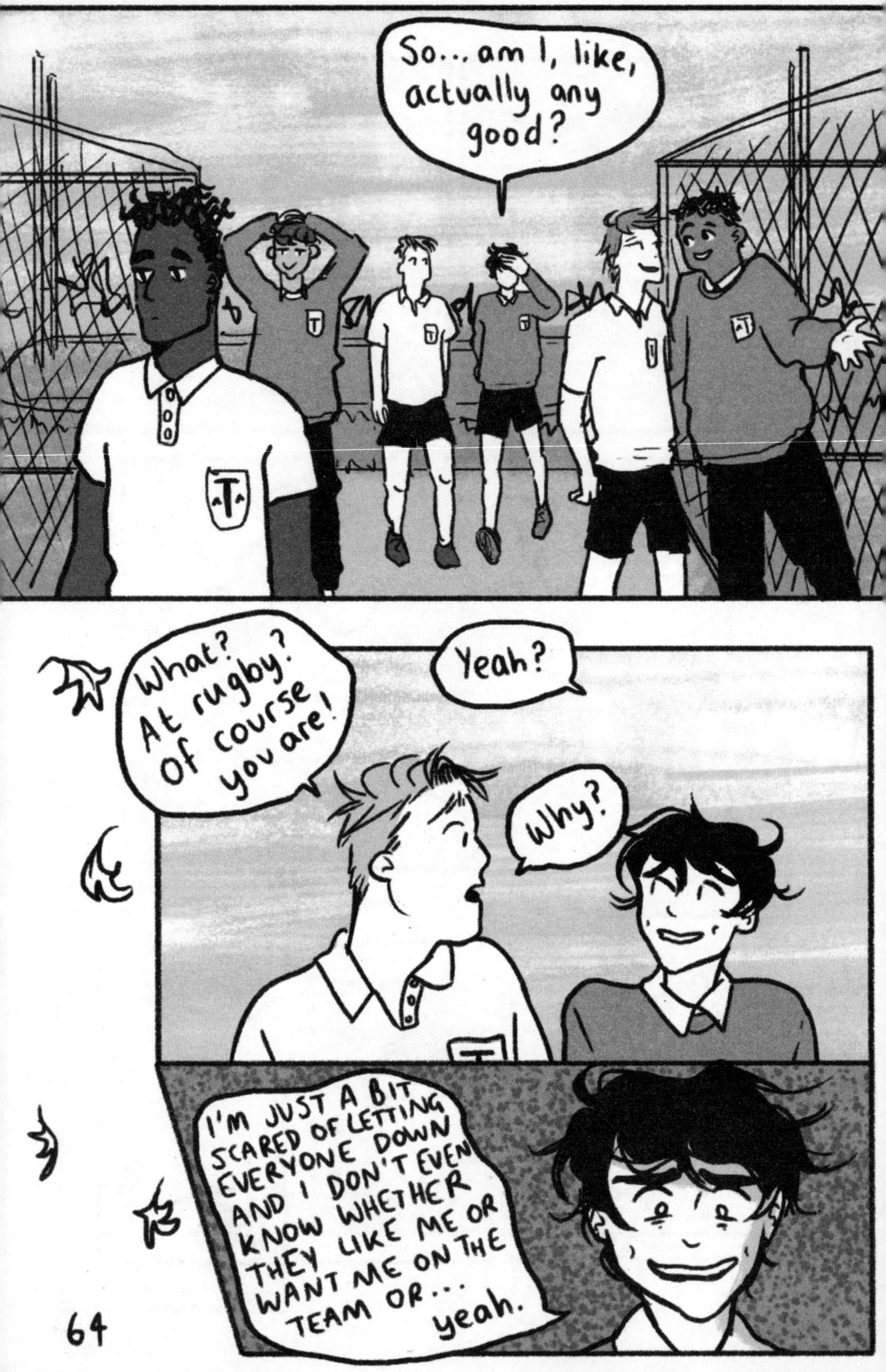
So... am I, like, actually any good?
What? At rugby? Of course you are!
Yeah?
Why?
I'M JUST A BIT SCARED OF LETTING EVERYONE DOWN AND I DON'T EVEN KNOW WHETHER THEY LIKE ME OR WANT ME ON THE TEAM OR... yeah.

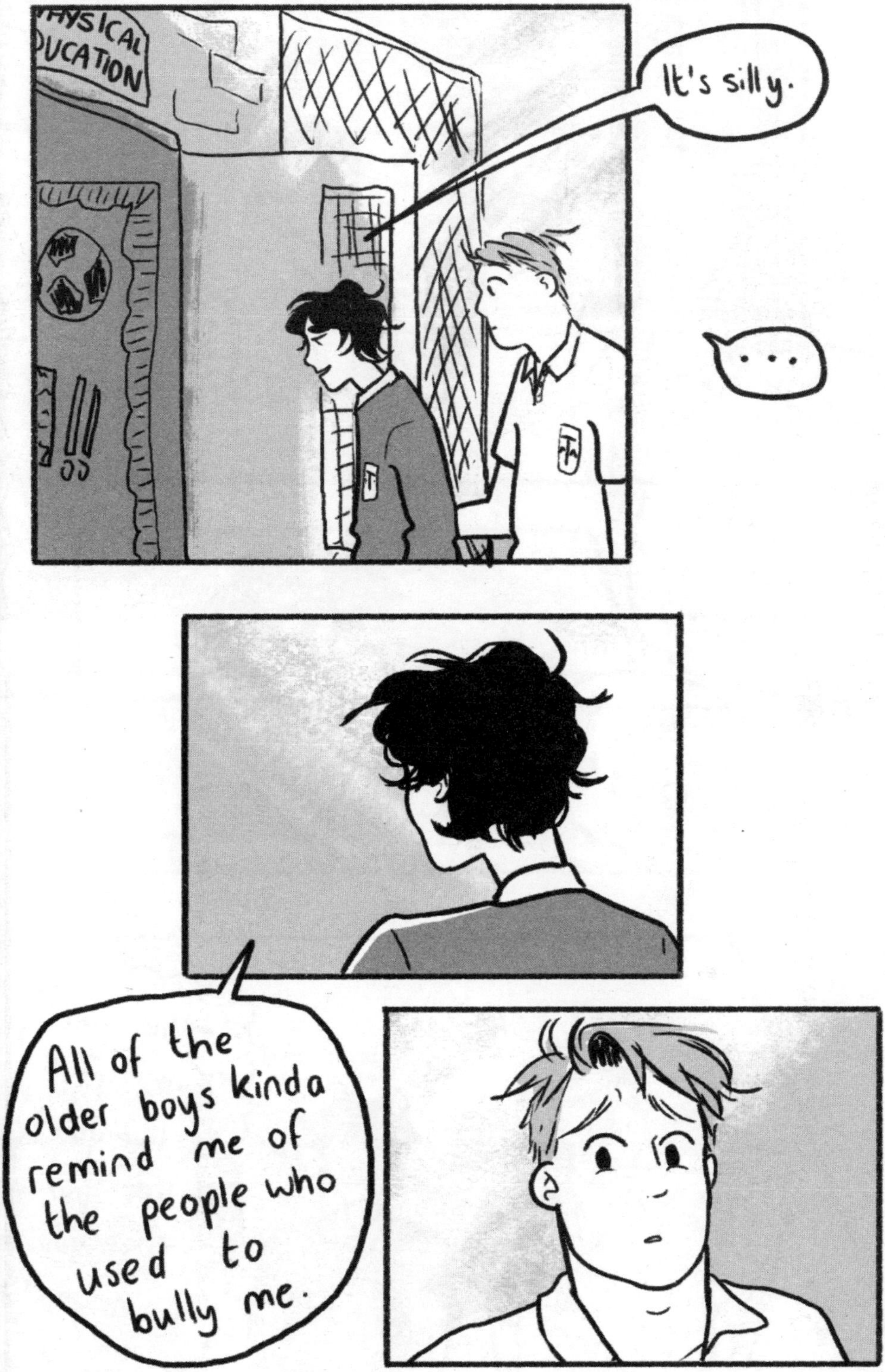
PHYSICAL EDUCATION
It's silly.
...
All of the older boys kinda remind me of the people who used to bully me.

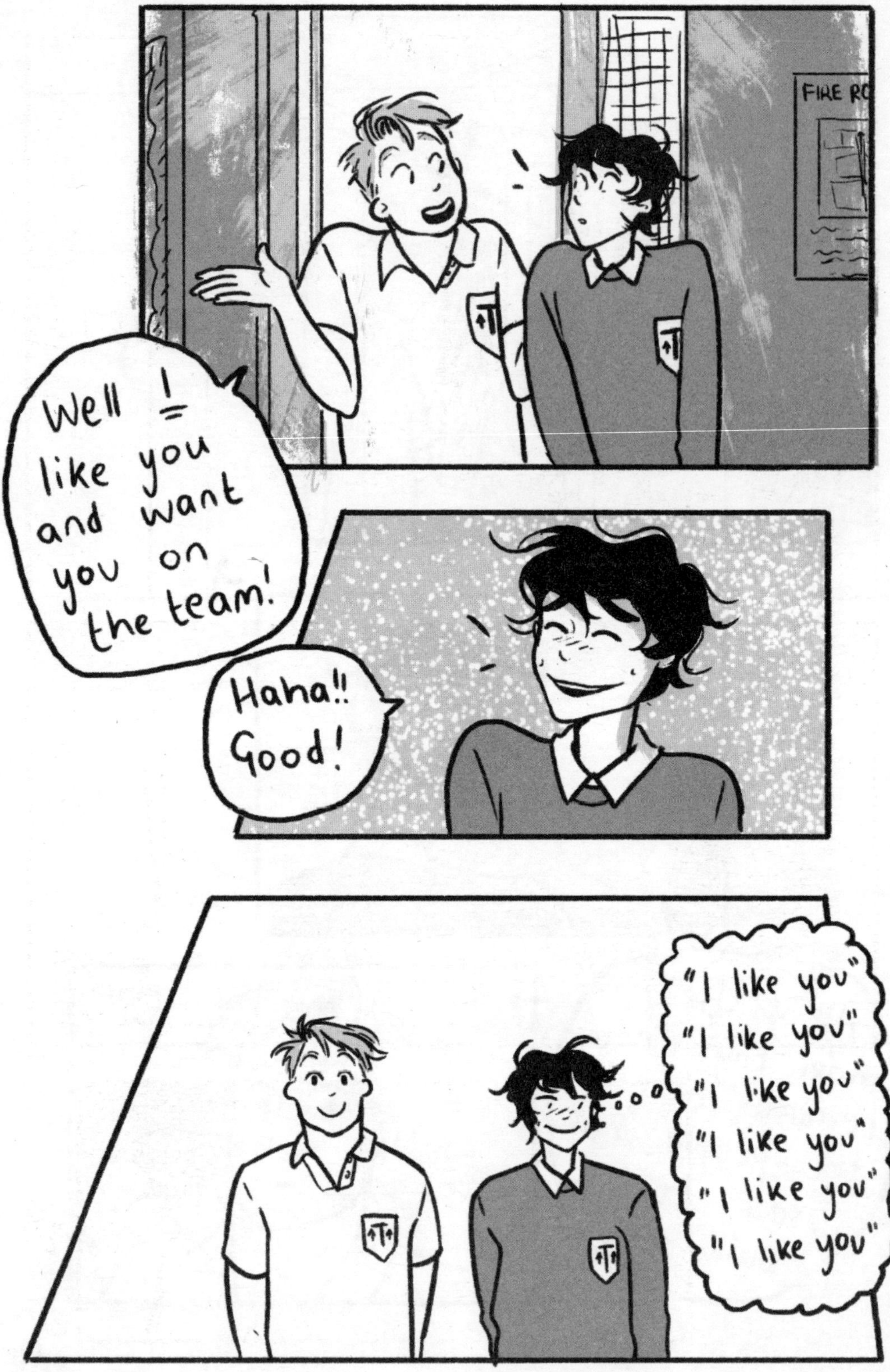
FIRE RO
Well I like you and want you on the team!
Haha!! Good!
"I like you"
"I like you"
"I like you"
"I like you"
"I like you"
"I like you"

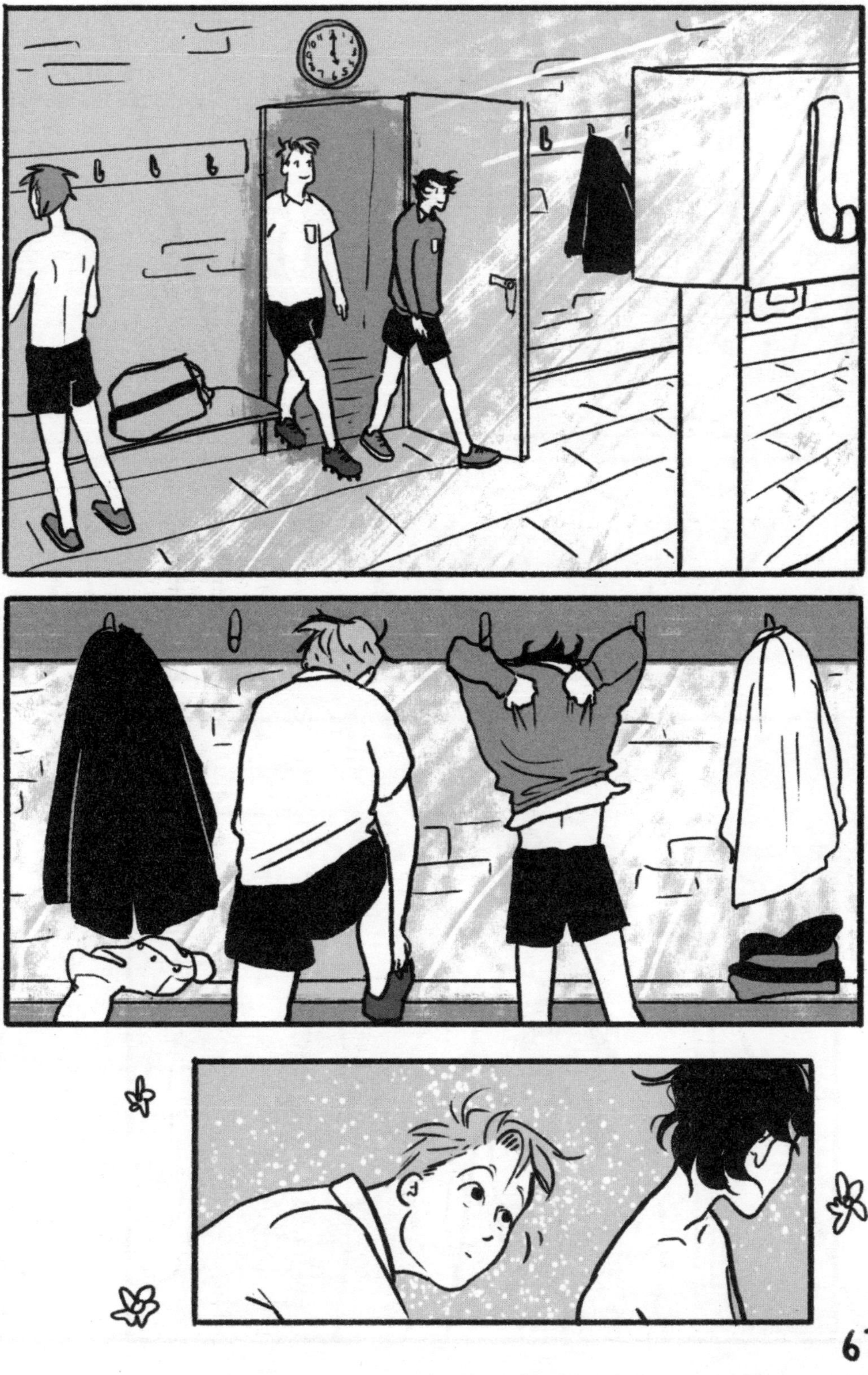

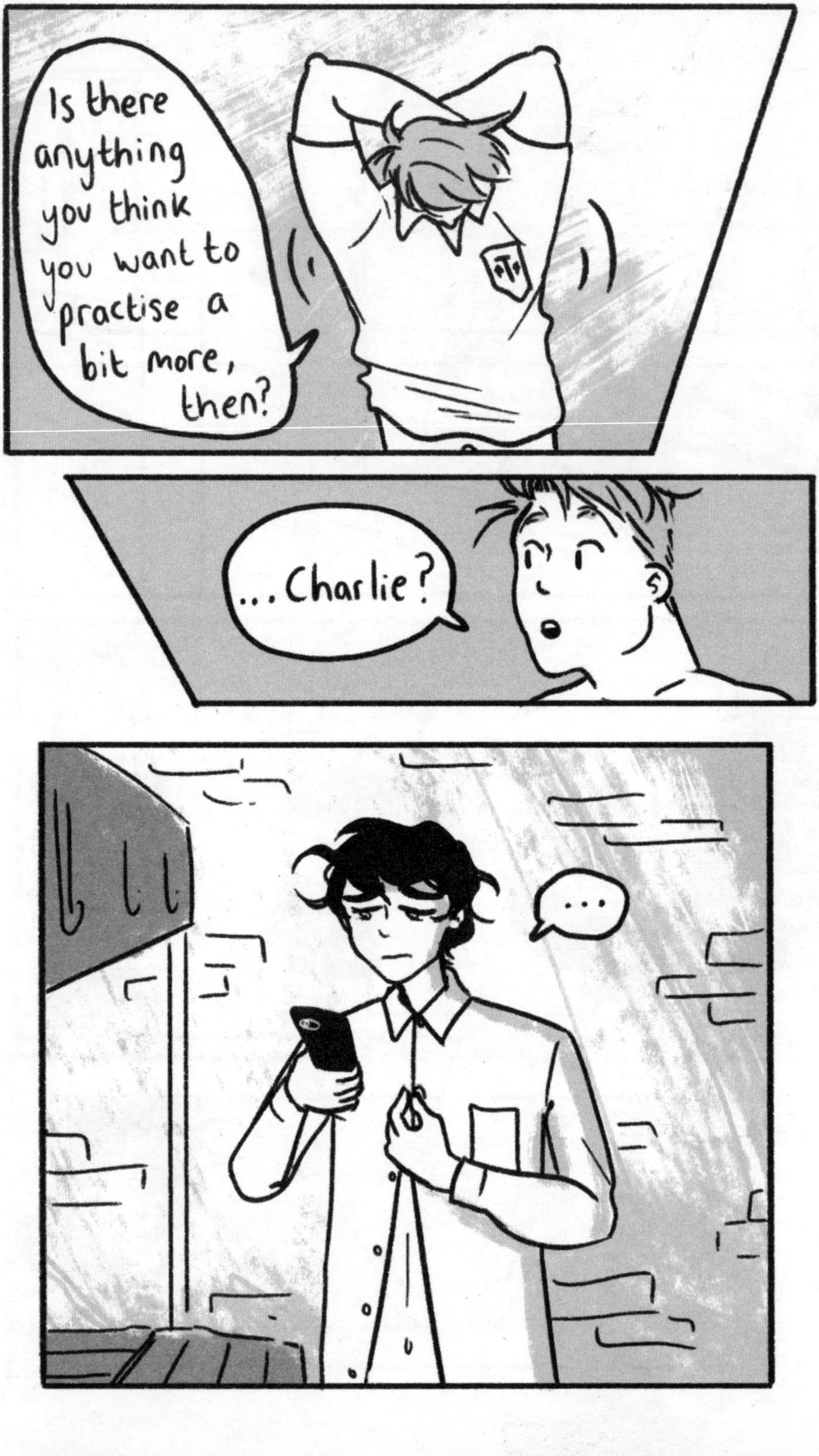
Is there anything you think you want to practise a bit more, then?
...Charlie?
...

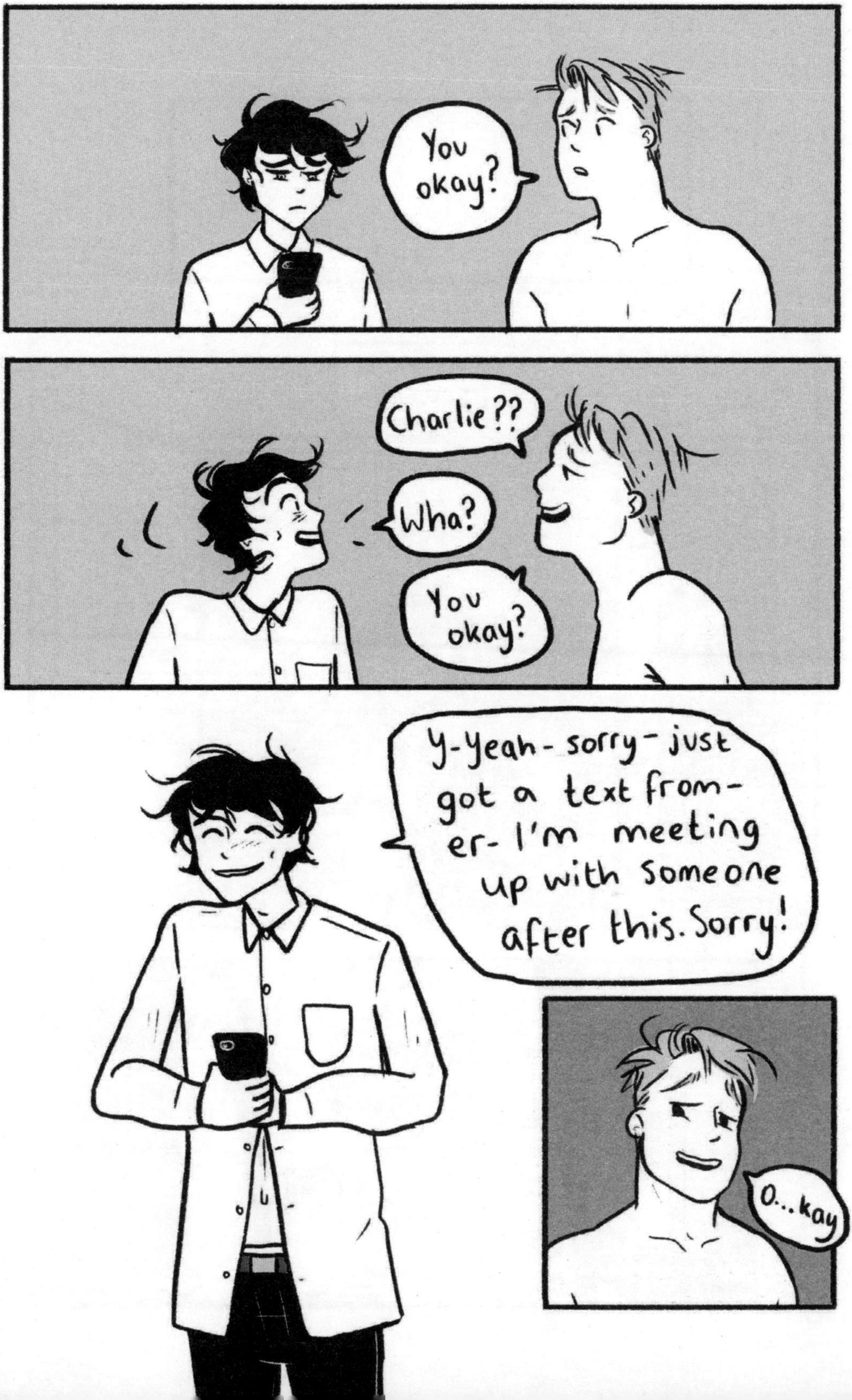
You okay?
Charlie??
Wha?
You okay?
Y-Yeah - sorry - just got a text from - er - I'm meeting up with someone after this. Sorry!
O...kay

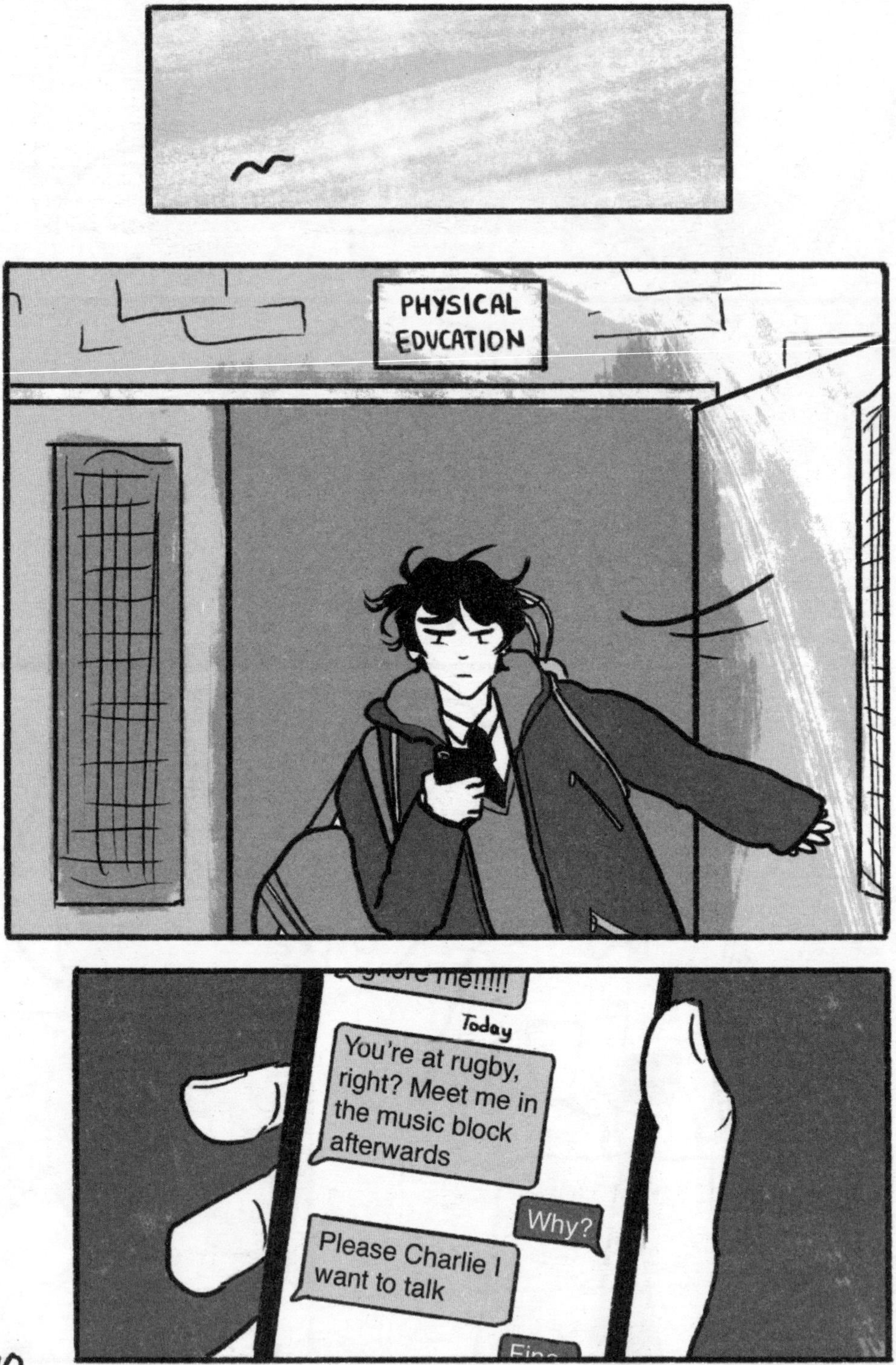
PHYSICAL
EDUCATION
Today
You're at rugby, right? Meet me in the music block afterwards
Why?
Please Charlie I want to talk

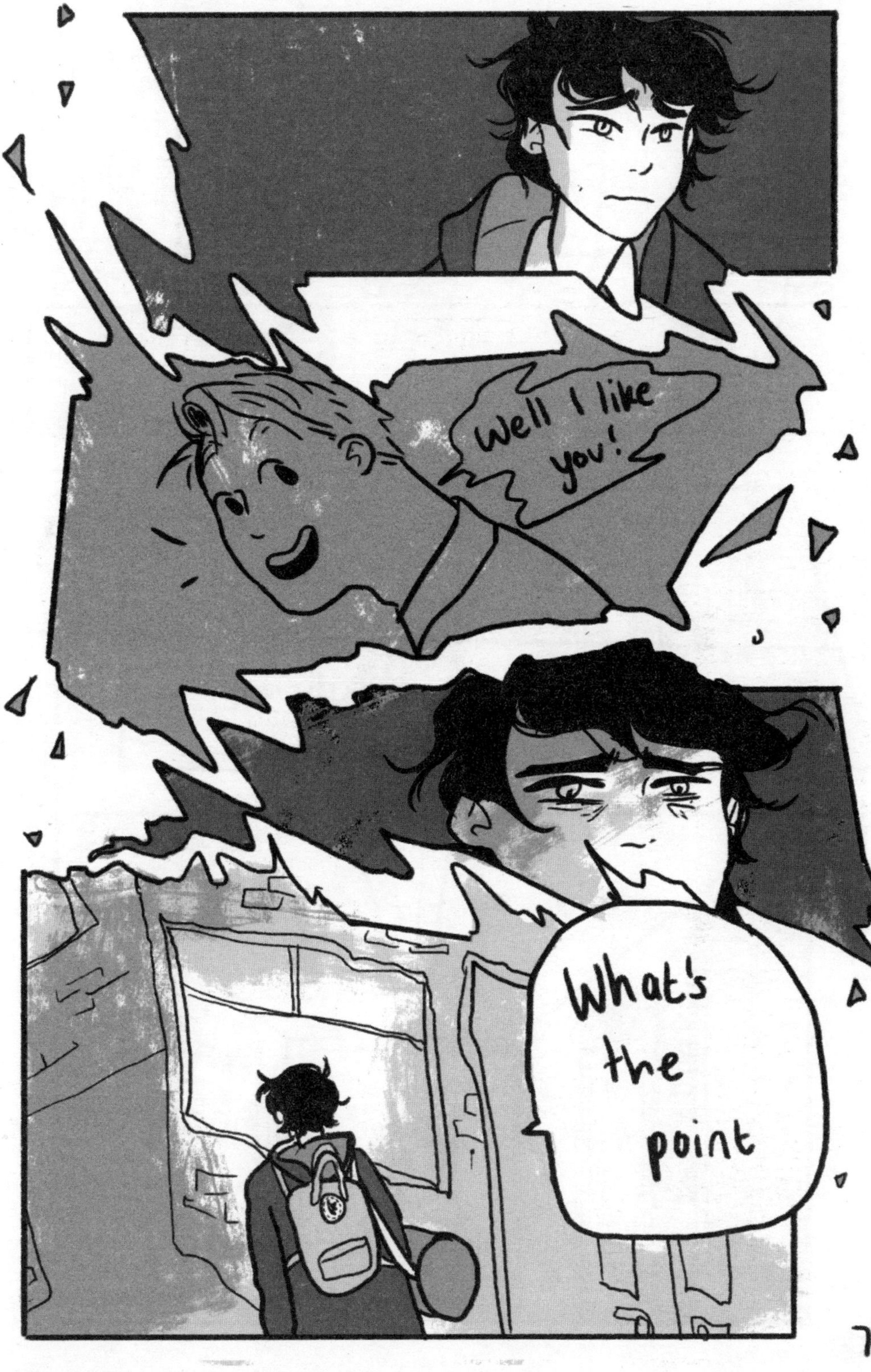
Well I like you!
What's the point

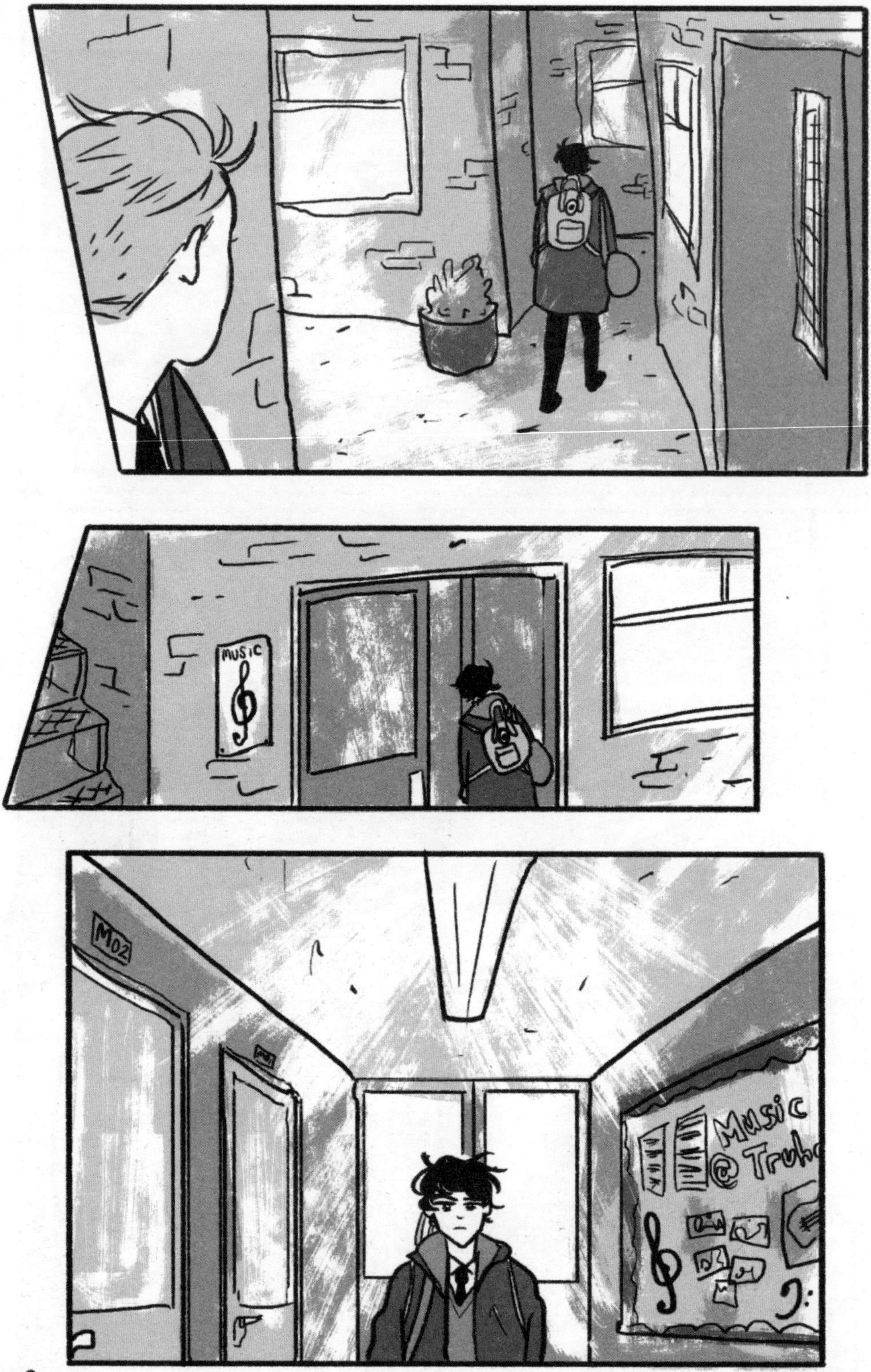
MUSIC
M02
Music
@ Truh

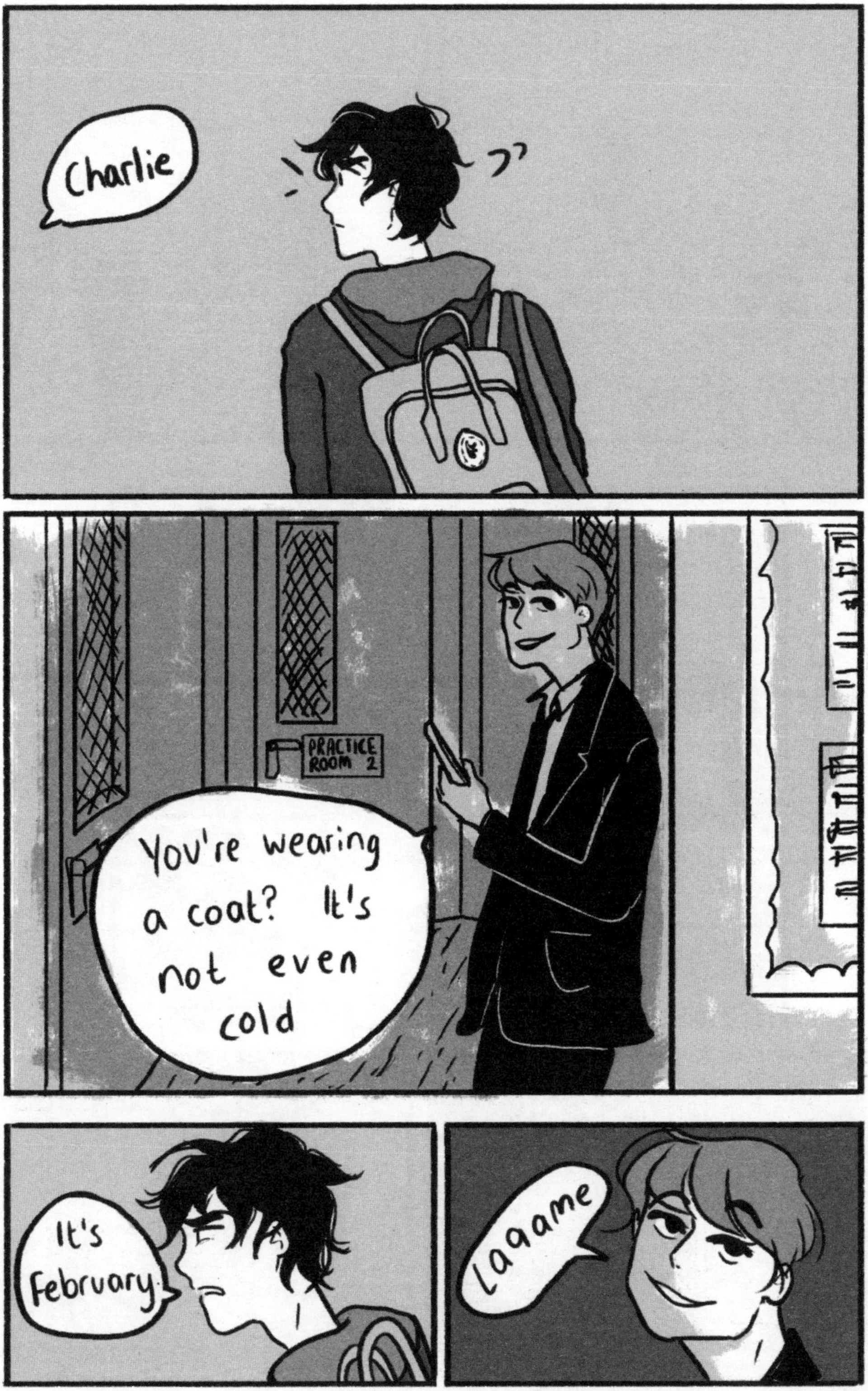
Charlie
PRACTICE ROOM 2
You're wearing a coat? It's not even cold
It's February.
Laaame

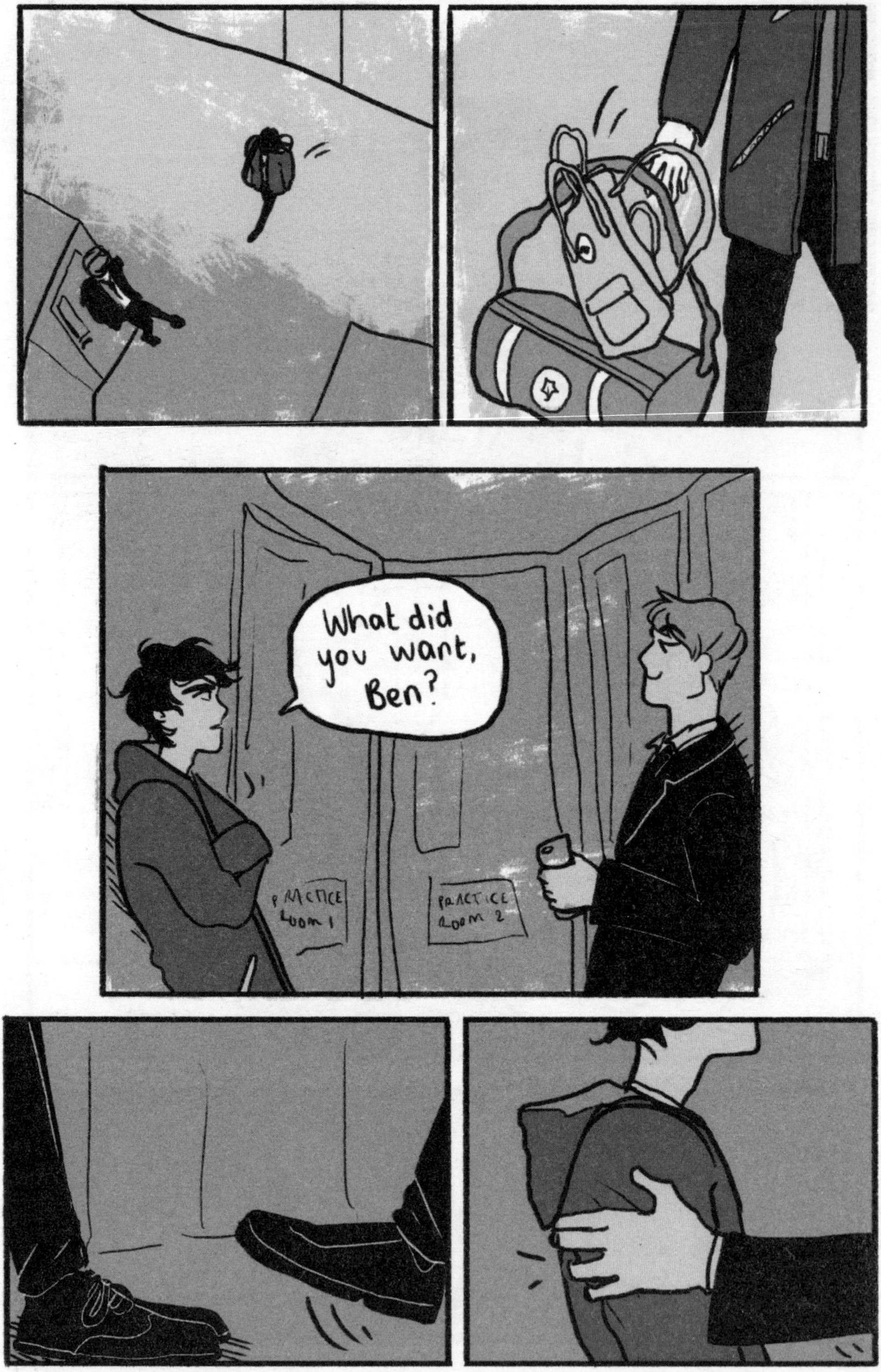
What did you want, Ben?
PRACTICE ROOM 1
PRACTICE ROOM 2

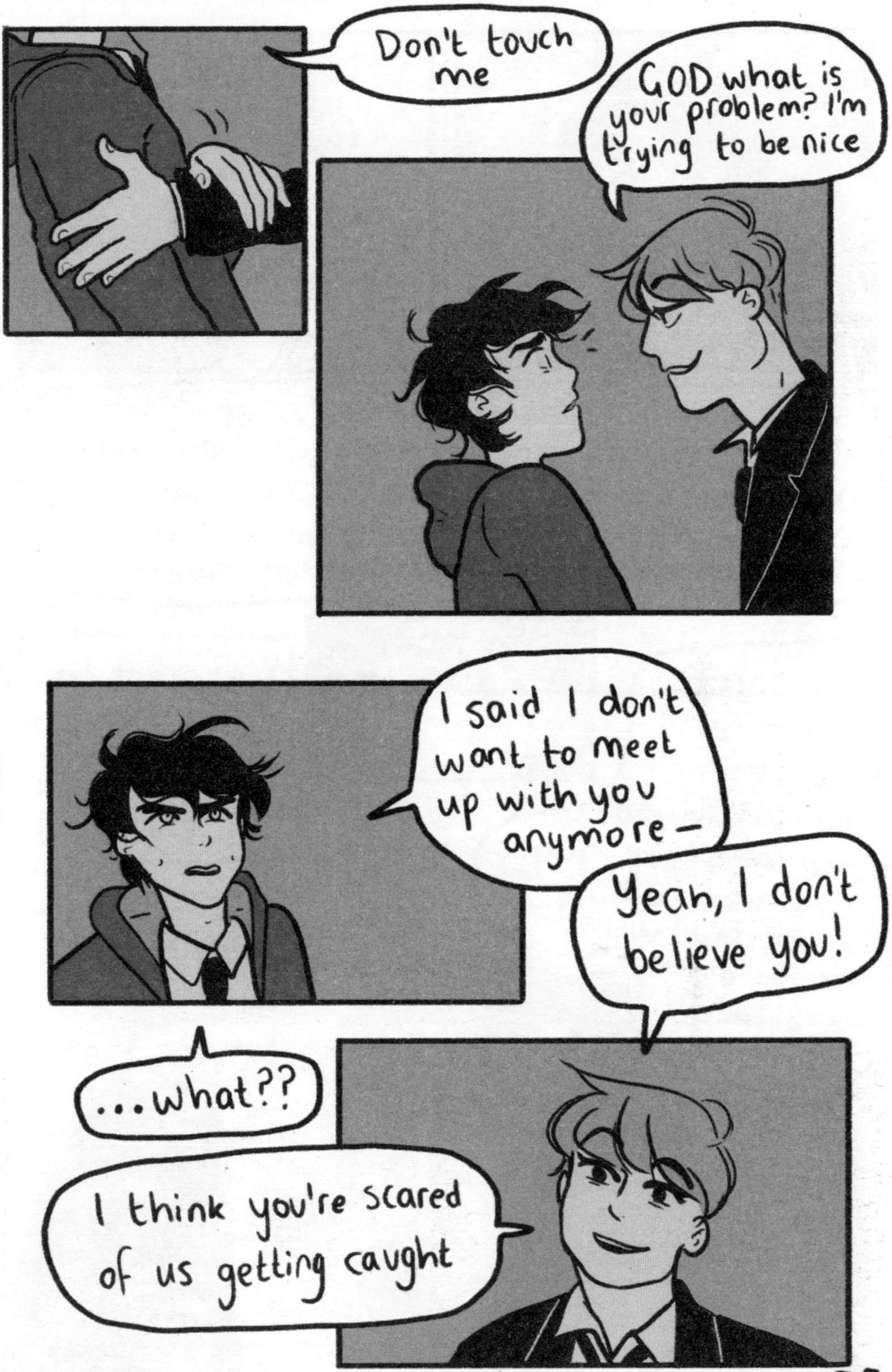
Don't touch me
GOD what is your problem? I'm trying to be nice
I said I don't want to meet up with you anymore–
Yeah, I don't believe you!
...what??
I think you're scared of us getting caught

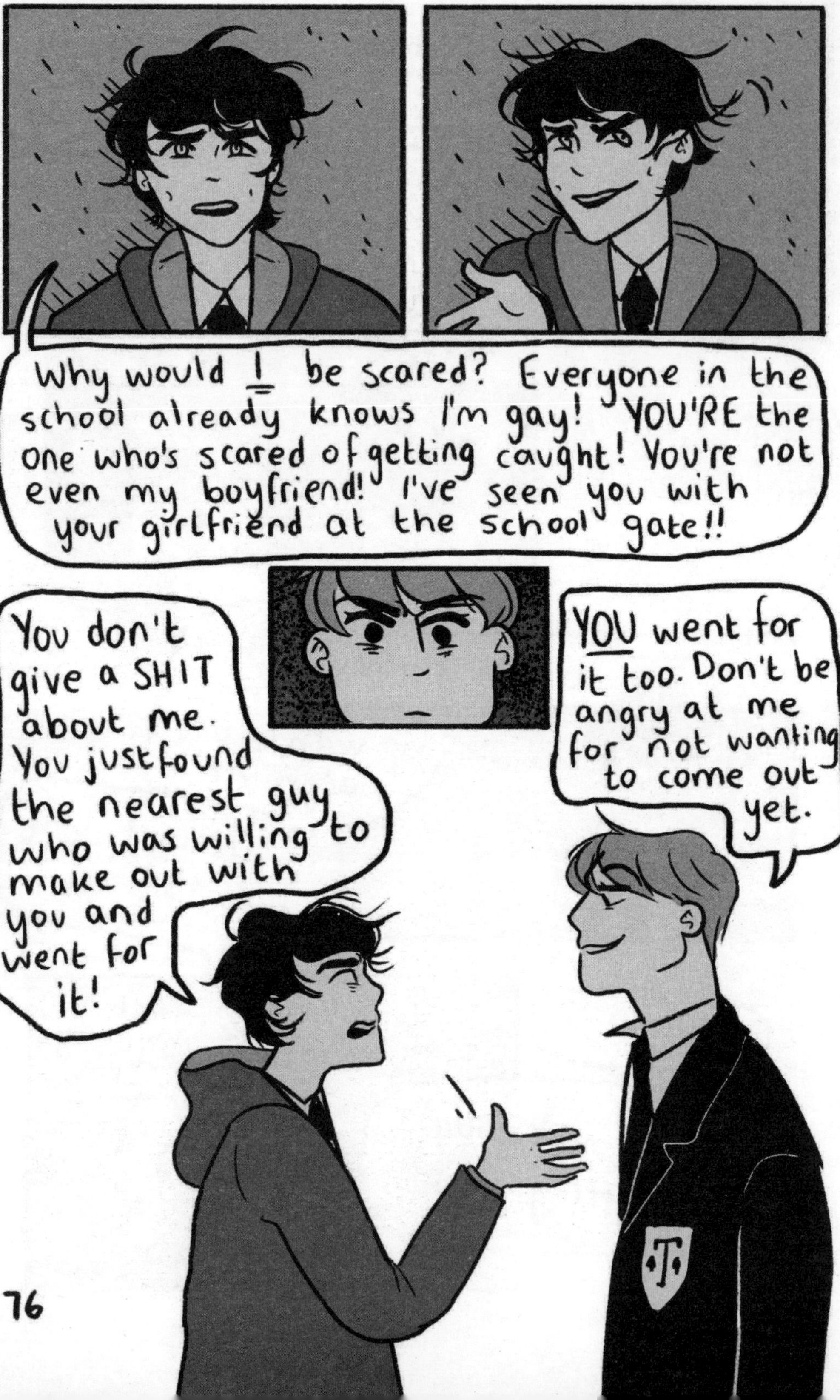
Why would I be scared? Everyone in the school already knows I'm gay! YOU'RE the one who's scared of getting caught! You're not even my boyfriend! I've seen you with your girlfriend at the school gate!!
You don't give a SHIT about me. You just found the nearest guy who was willing to make out with you and went for it!
YOU went for it too. Don't be angry at me for not wanting to come out yet.

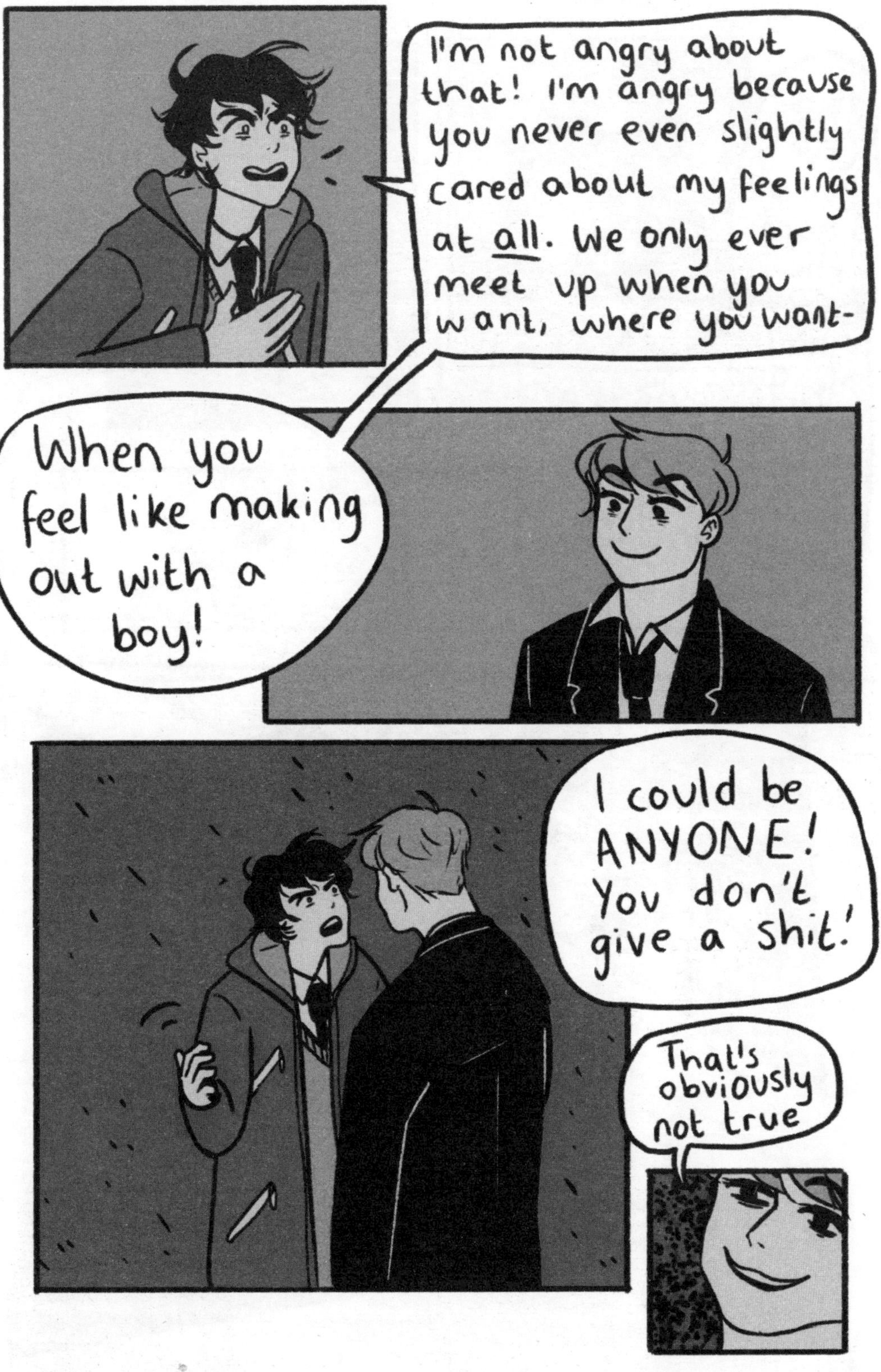
I'm not angry about that! I'm angry because you never even slightly cared about my feelings at all. We only ever meet up when you want, where you want-
When you feel like making out with a boy!
I could be ANYONE! You don't give a shit!
That's obviously not true

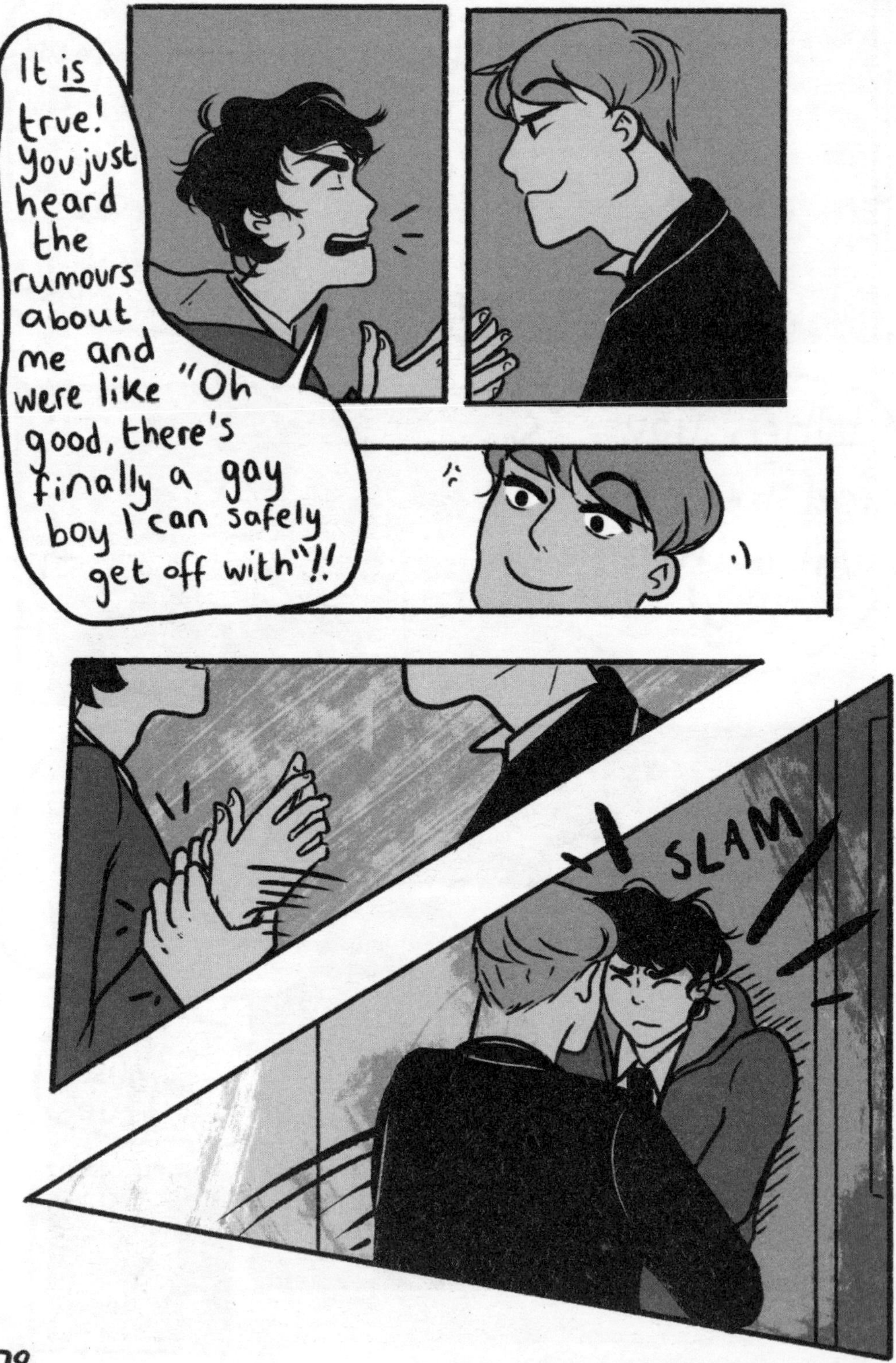
It is true! You just heard the rumours about me and were like "Oh good, there's finally a gay boy I can safely get off with"!!
SLAM

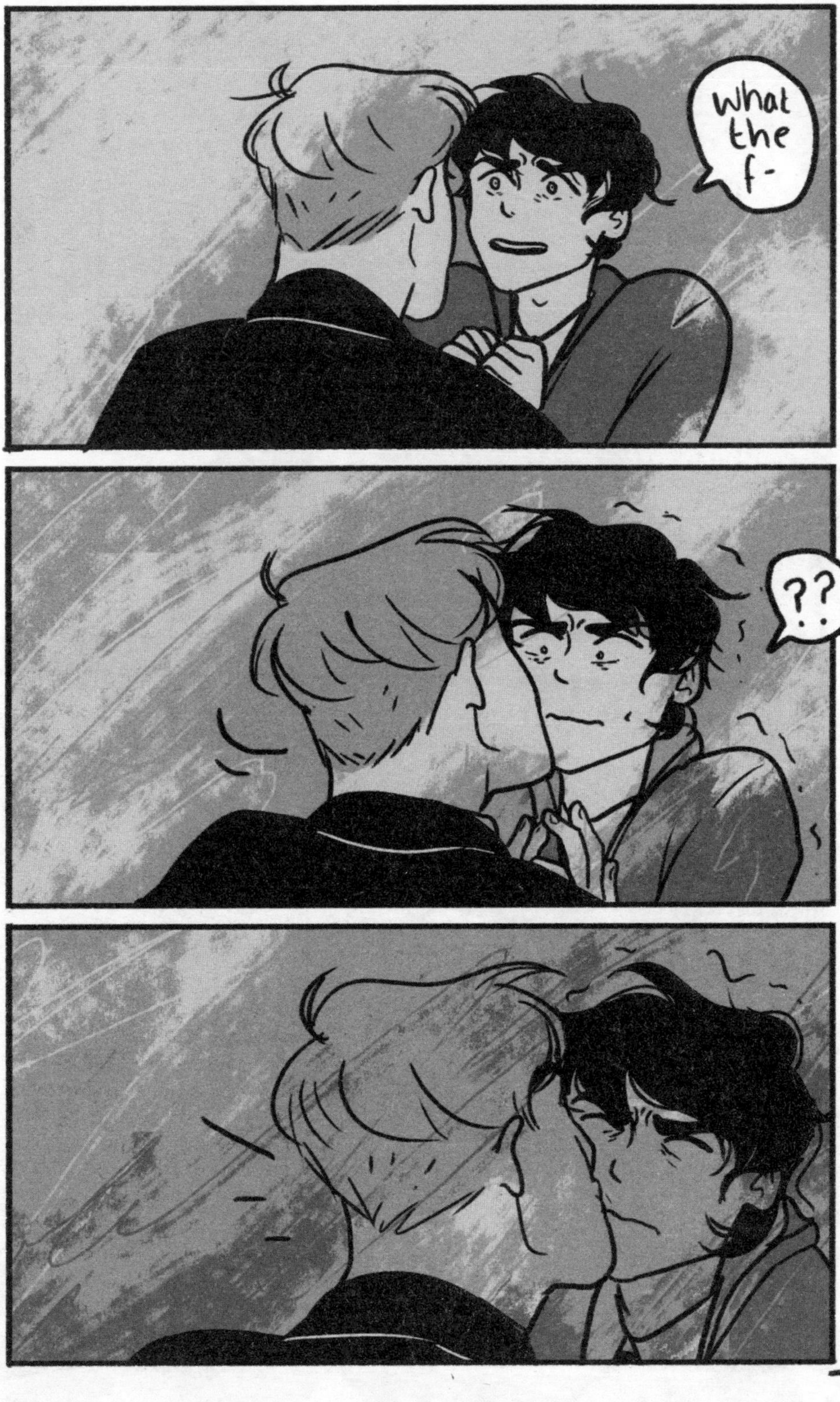
what the f-
??

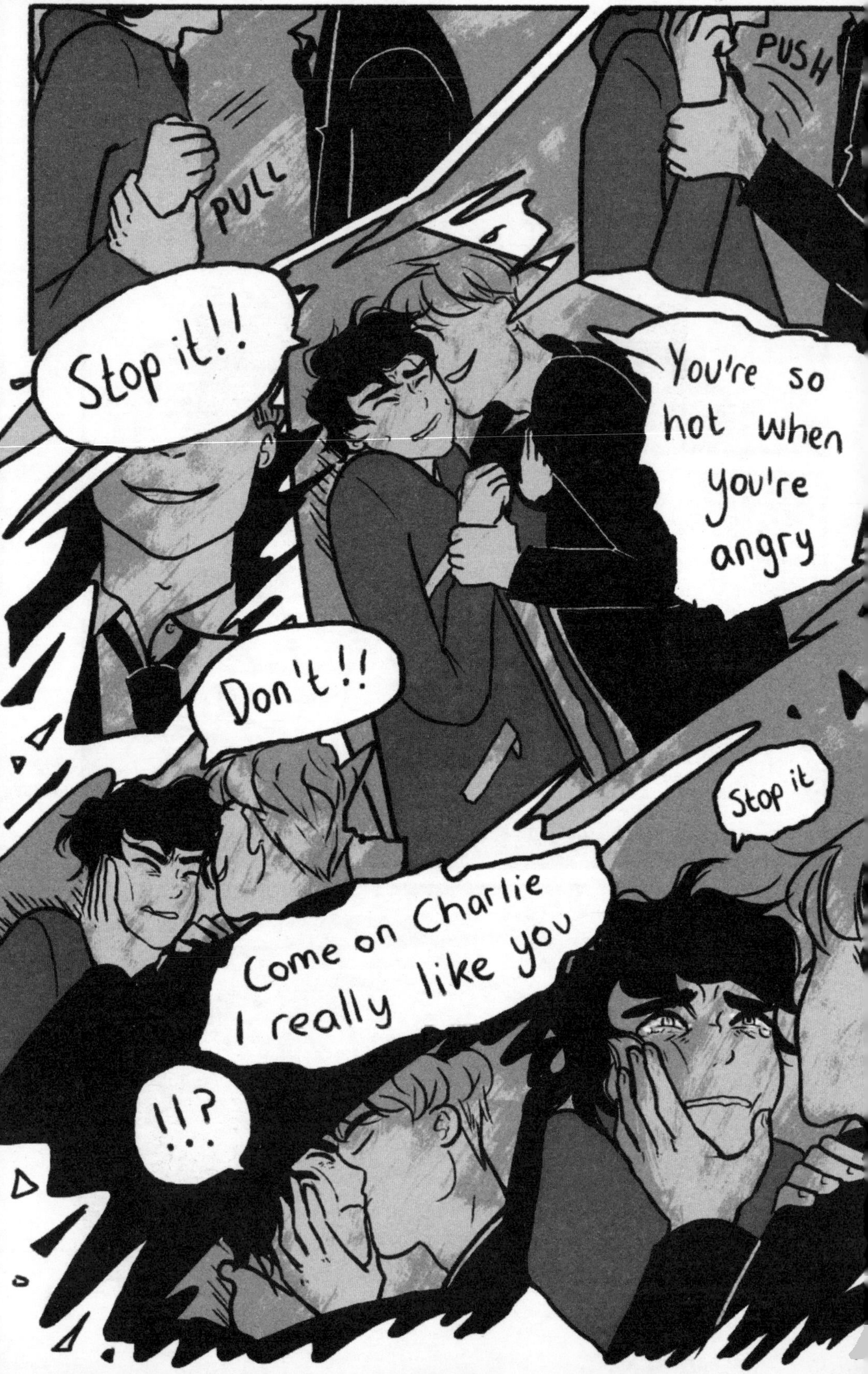
PULL
PUSH
Stop it!!
You're so hot when you're angry
Don't!!
Stop it
Come on Charlie I really like you
!!?
...

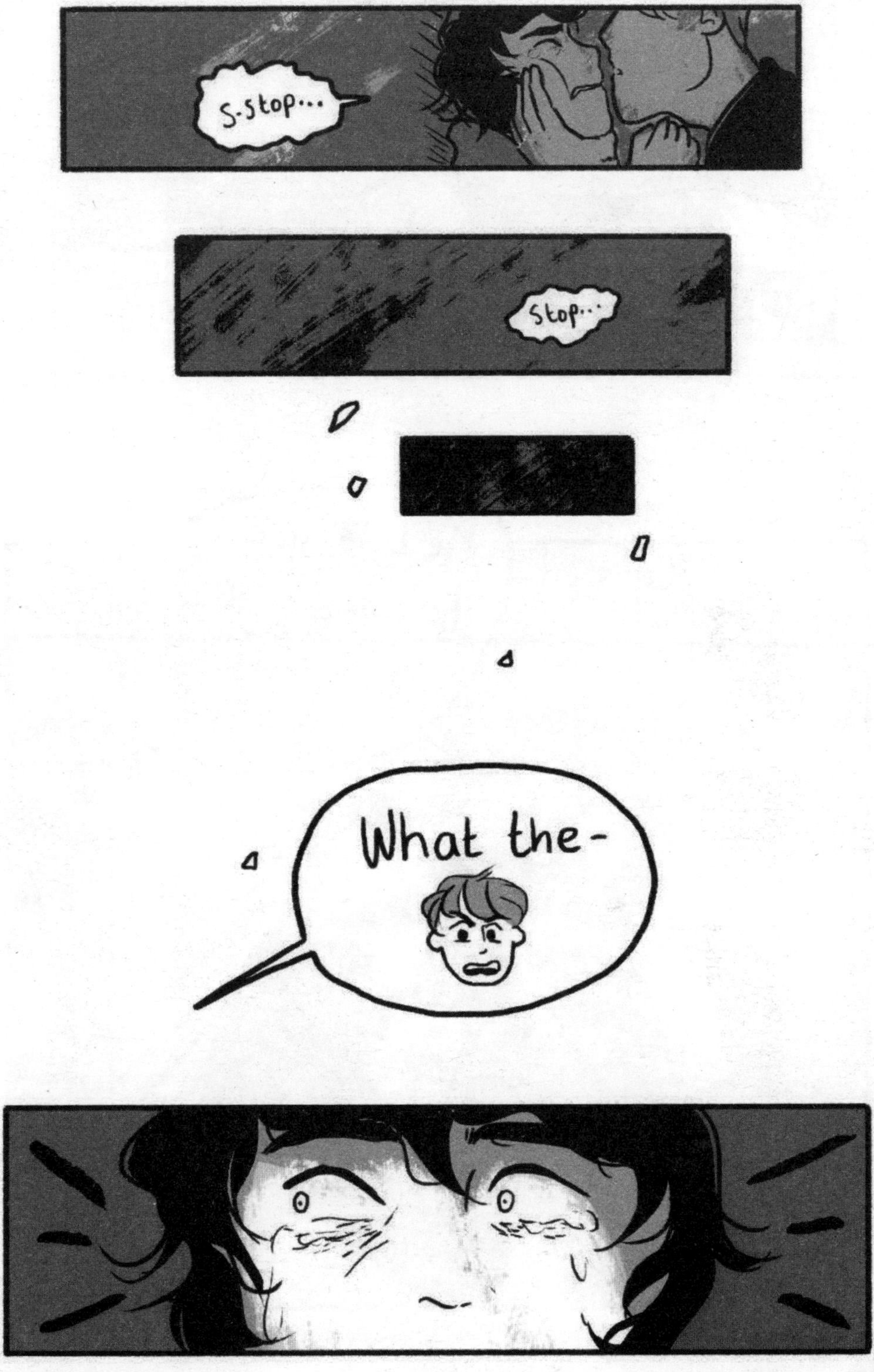
S-stop...
Stop...
What the-

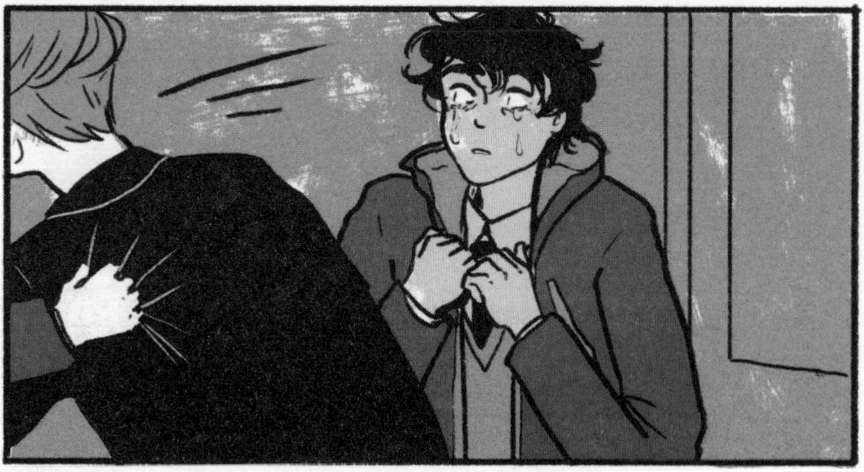

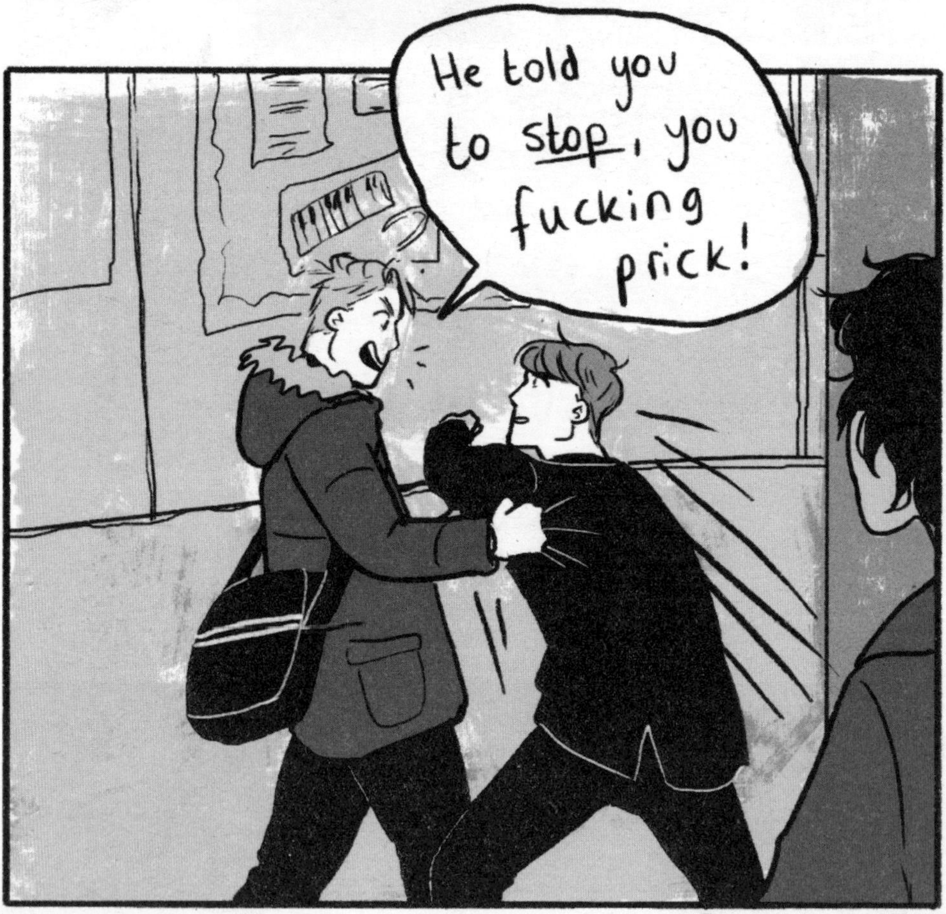
He told you to stop, you fucking prick!

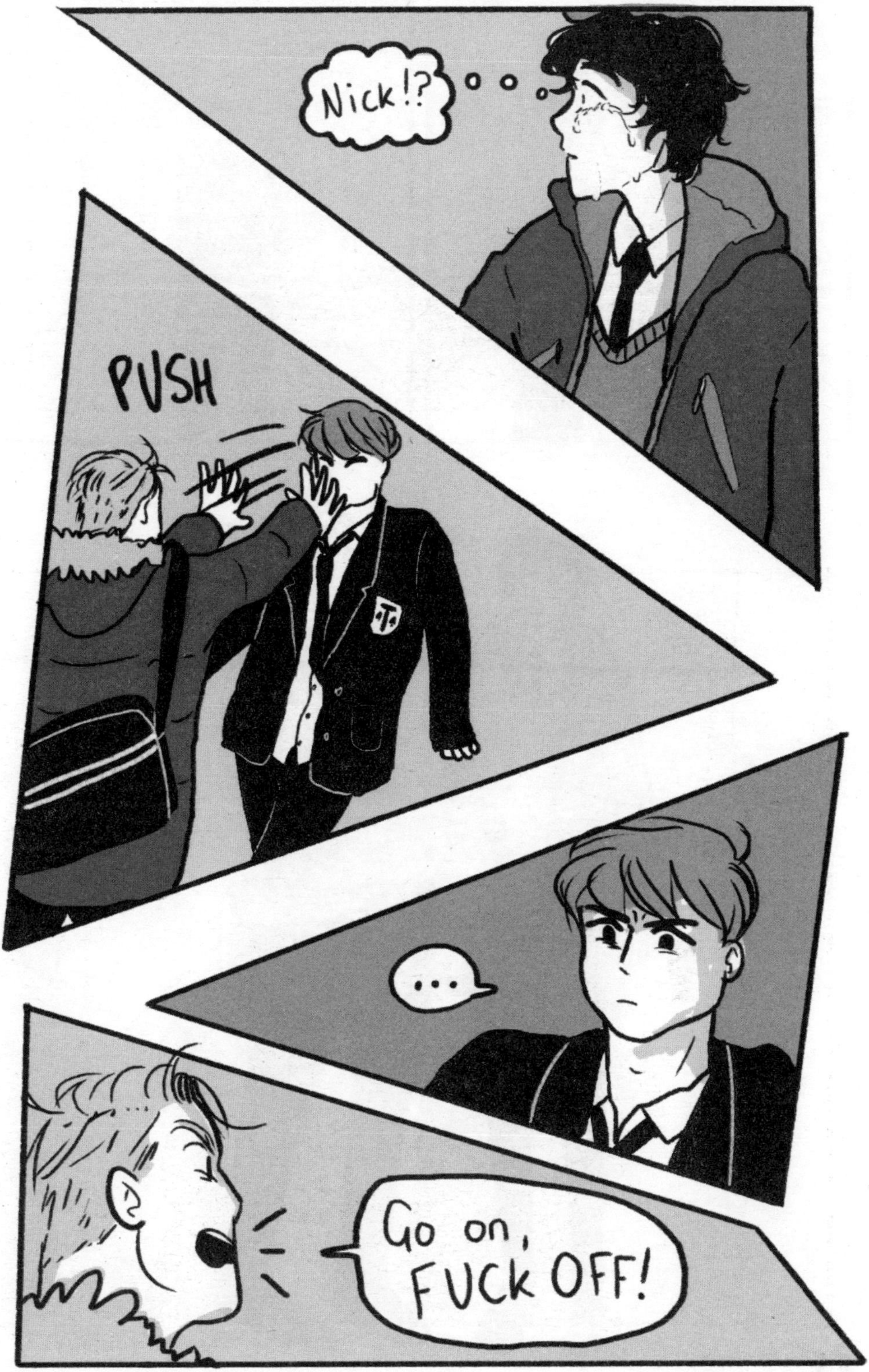
Nick!?
PUSH
...
Go on, FUCK OFF!

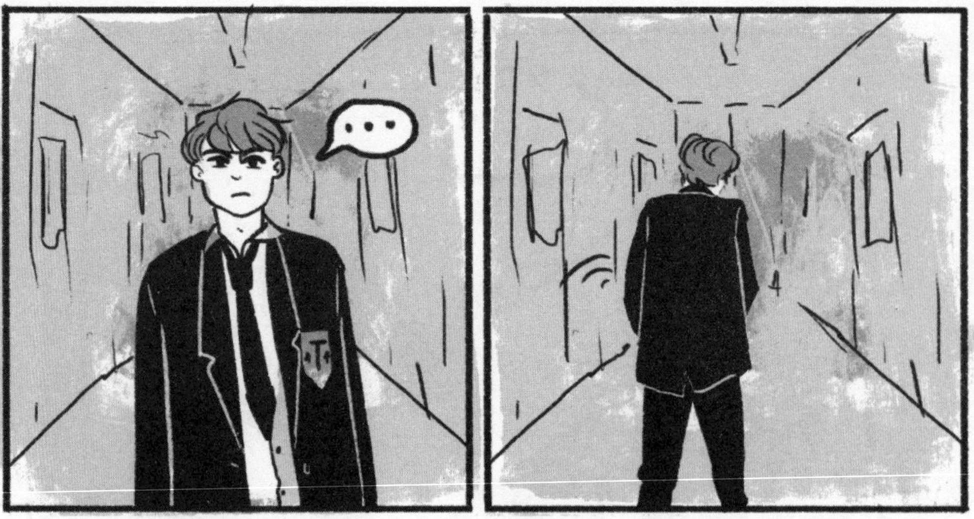
...

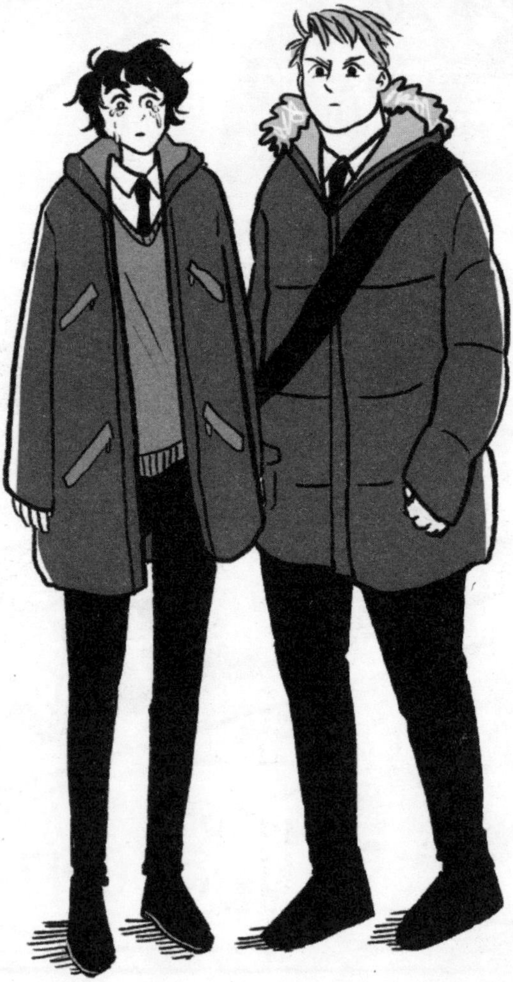

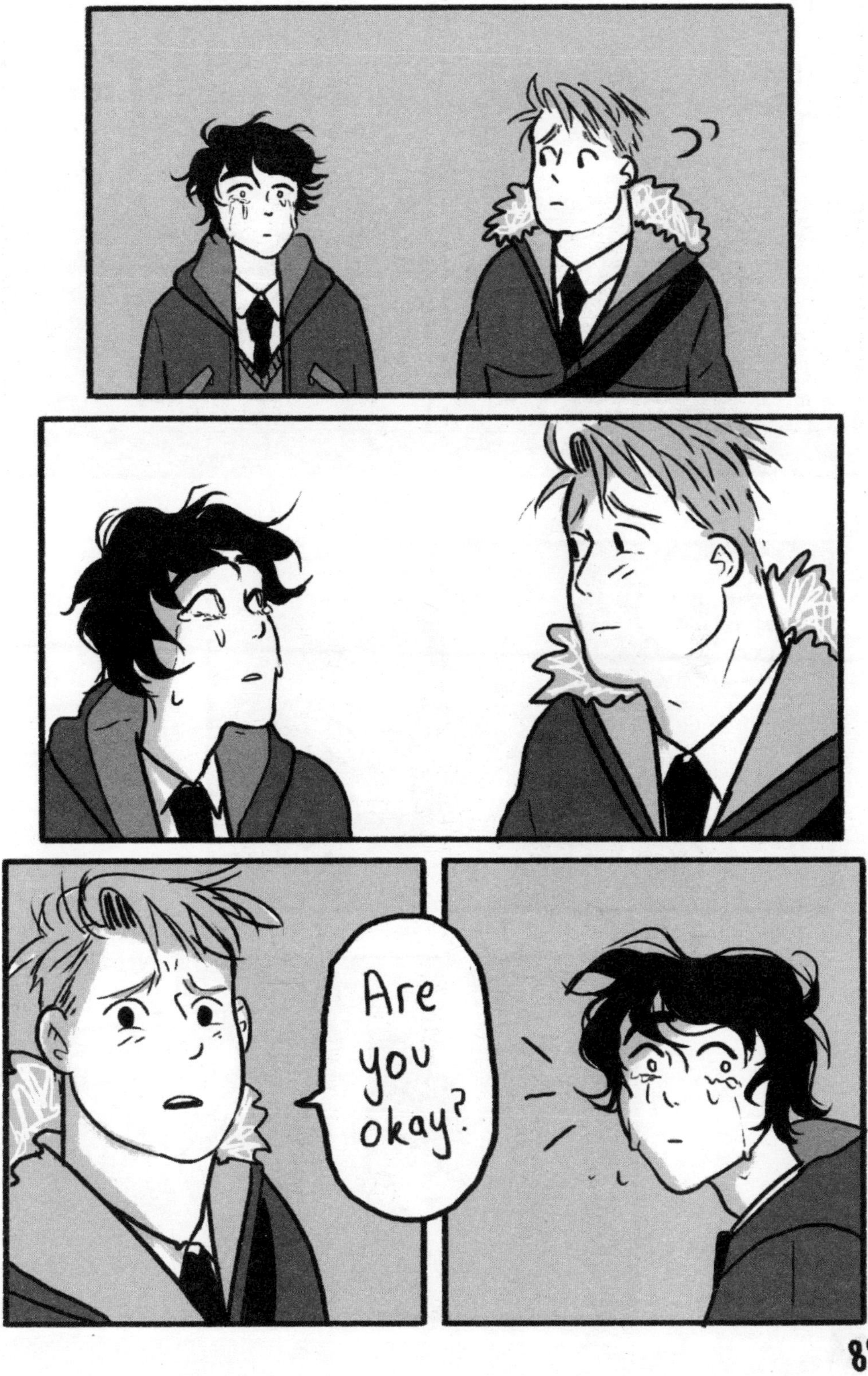
Are you okay?

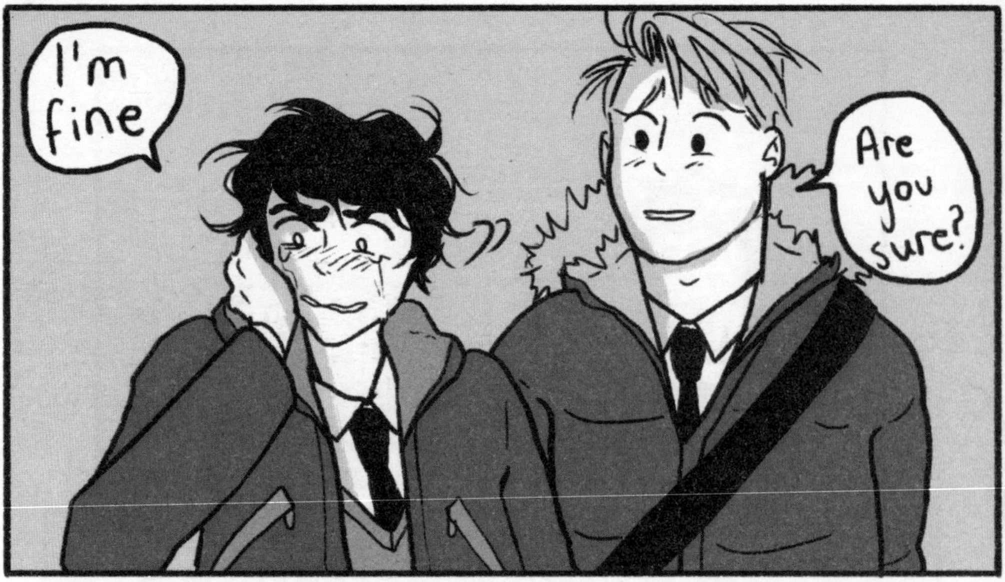
I'm fine
Are you sure?

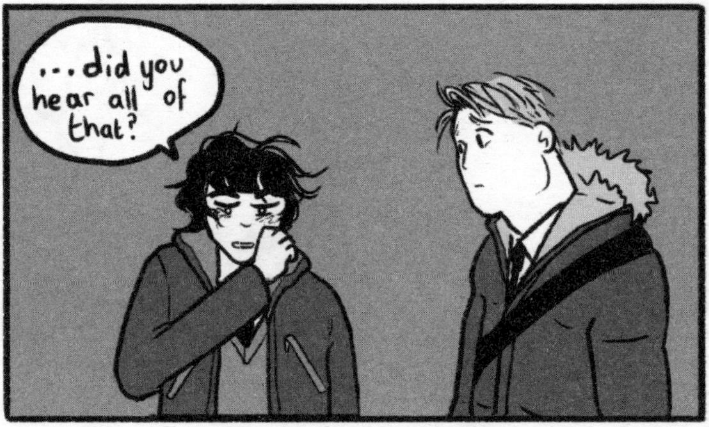
...did you hear all of that?

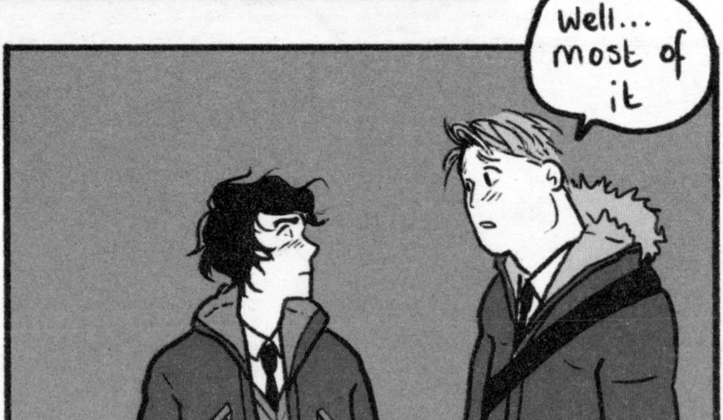
Well... most of it

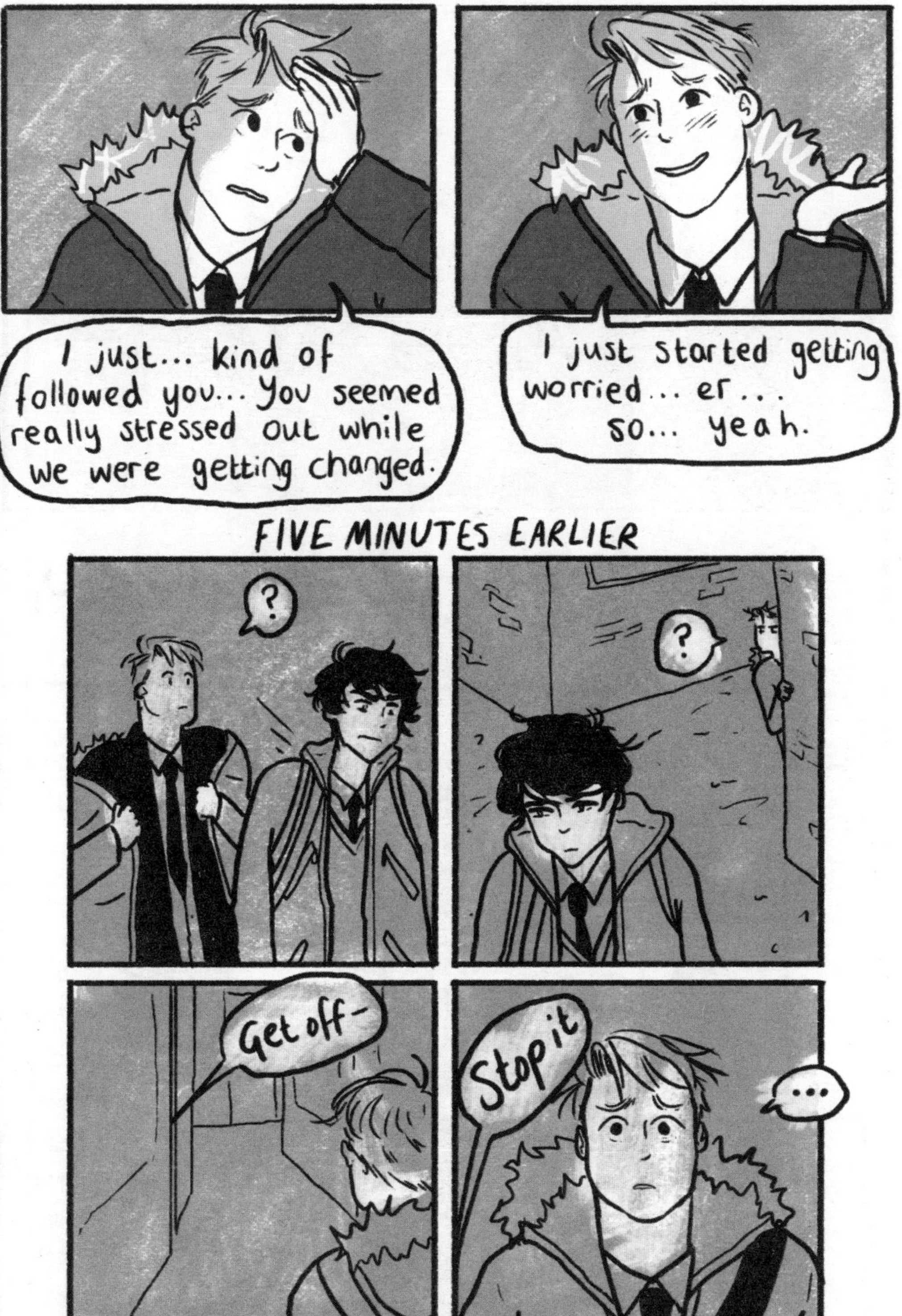
I just... kind of followed you... You seemed really stressed out while we were getting changed.
I just started getting worried... er... so... yeah.
FIVE MINUTES EARLIER
?
?
Get off-
Stop it
...

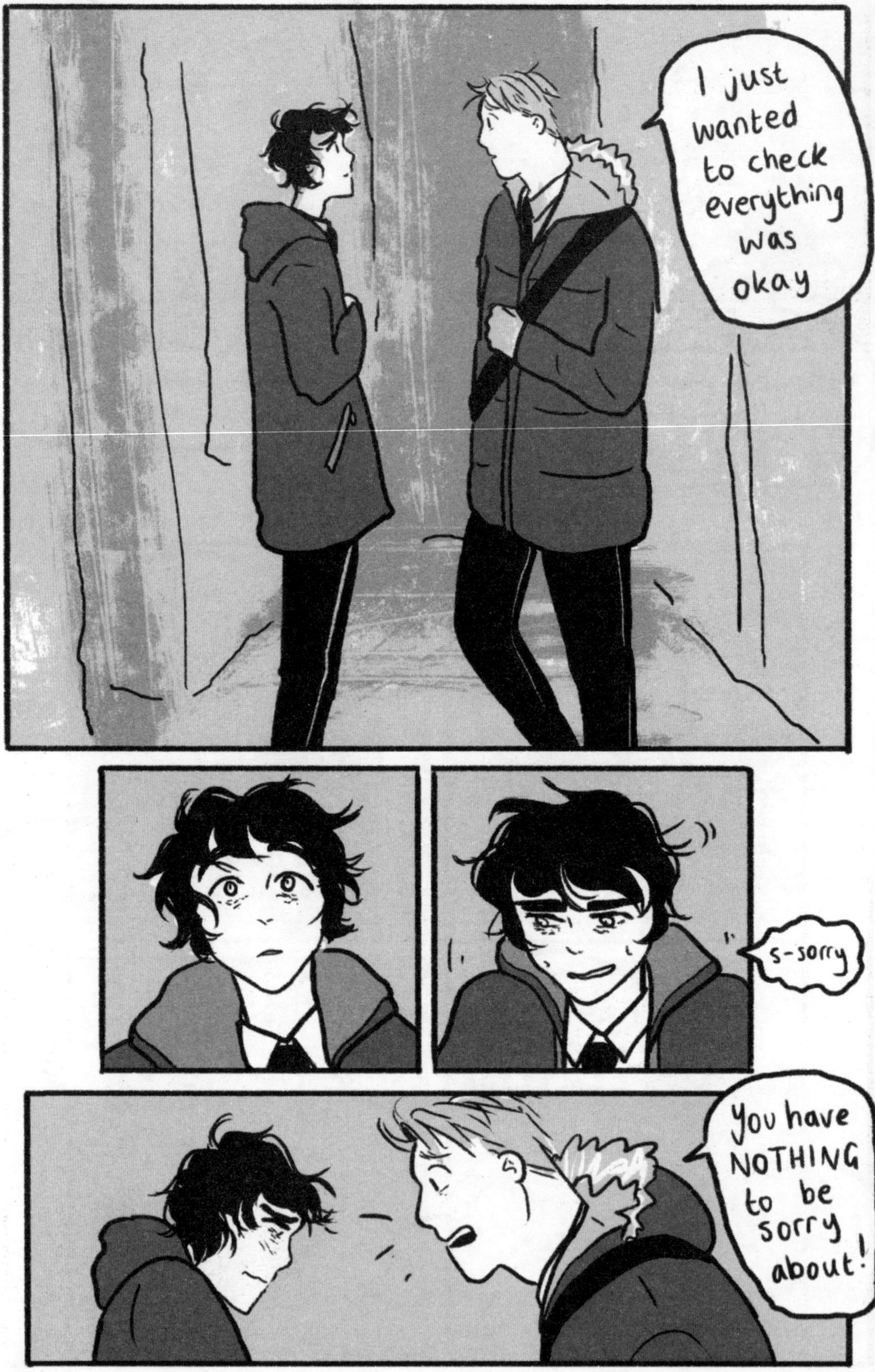
I just wanted to check everything was okay
s-sorry
You have NOTHING to be sorry about!

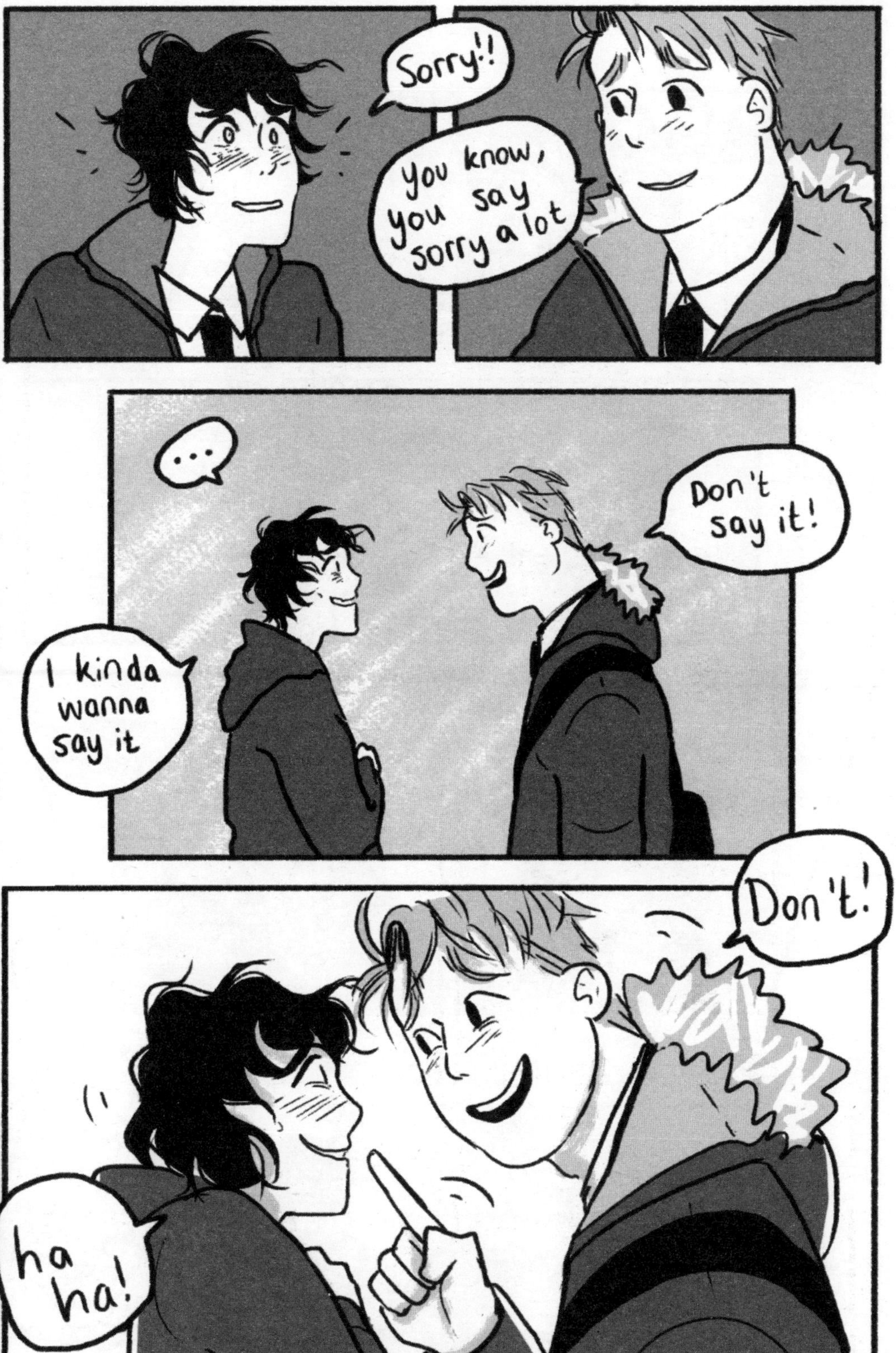
Sorry!!
You know, you say sorry a lot
...
Don't say it!
I kinda wanna say it
Don't!
ha ha!

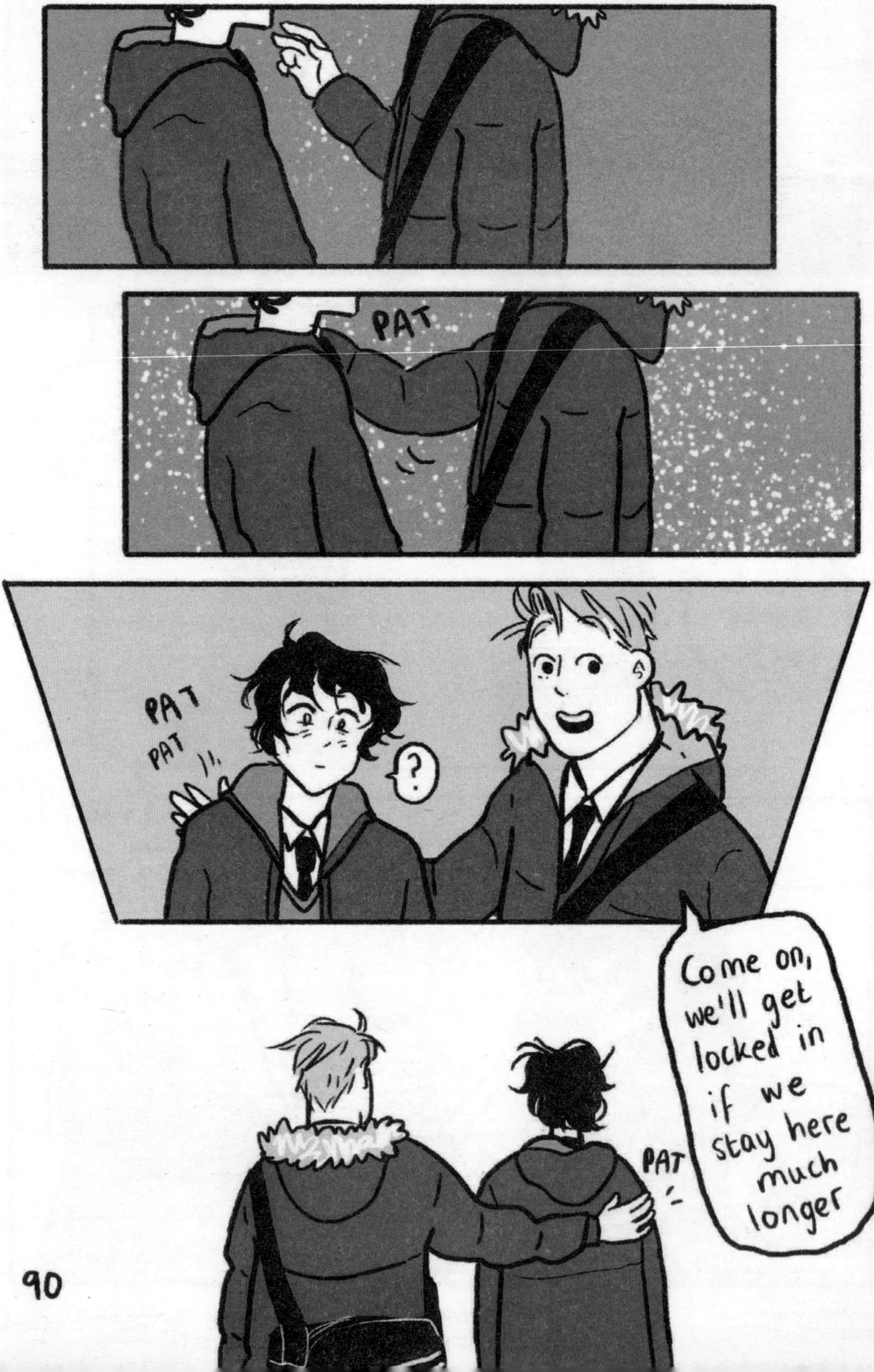
PAT
PAT
PAT
?
Come on, we'll get locked in if we stay here much longer
PAT

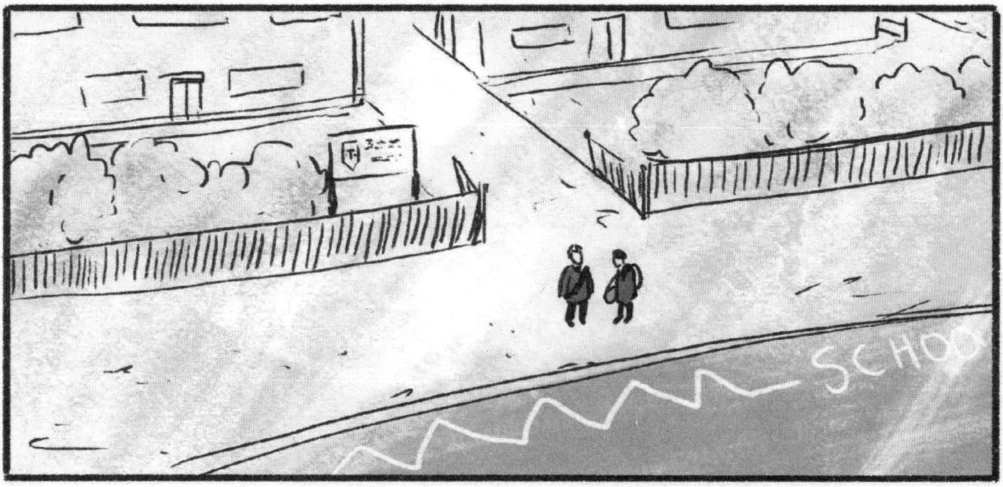

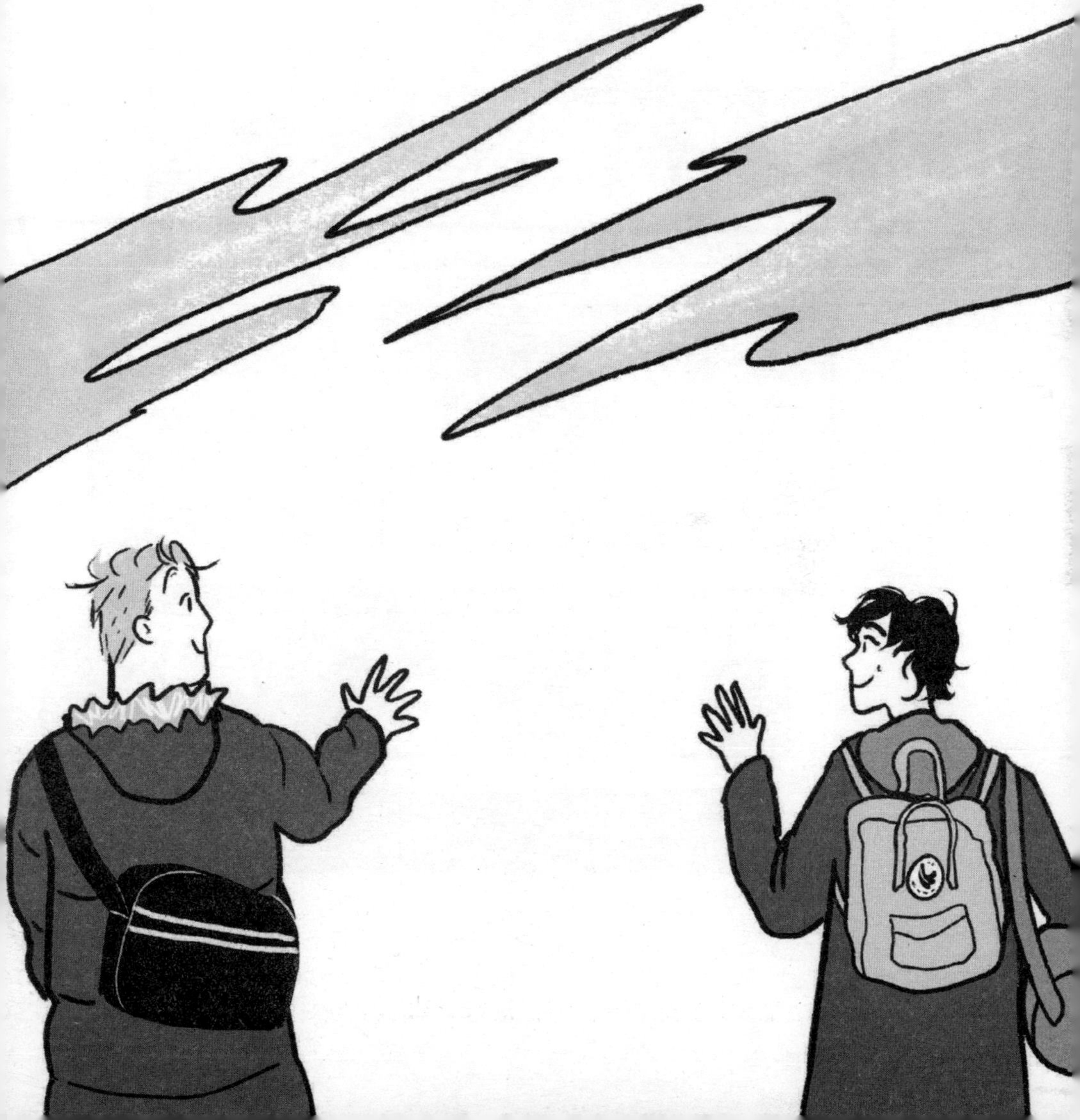

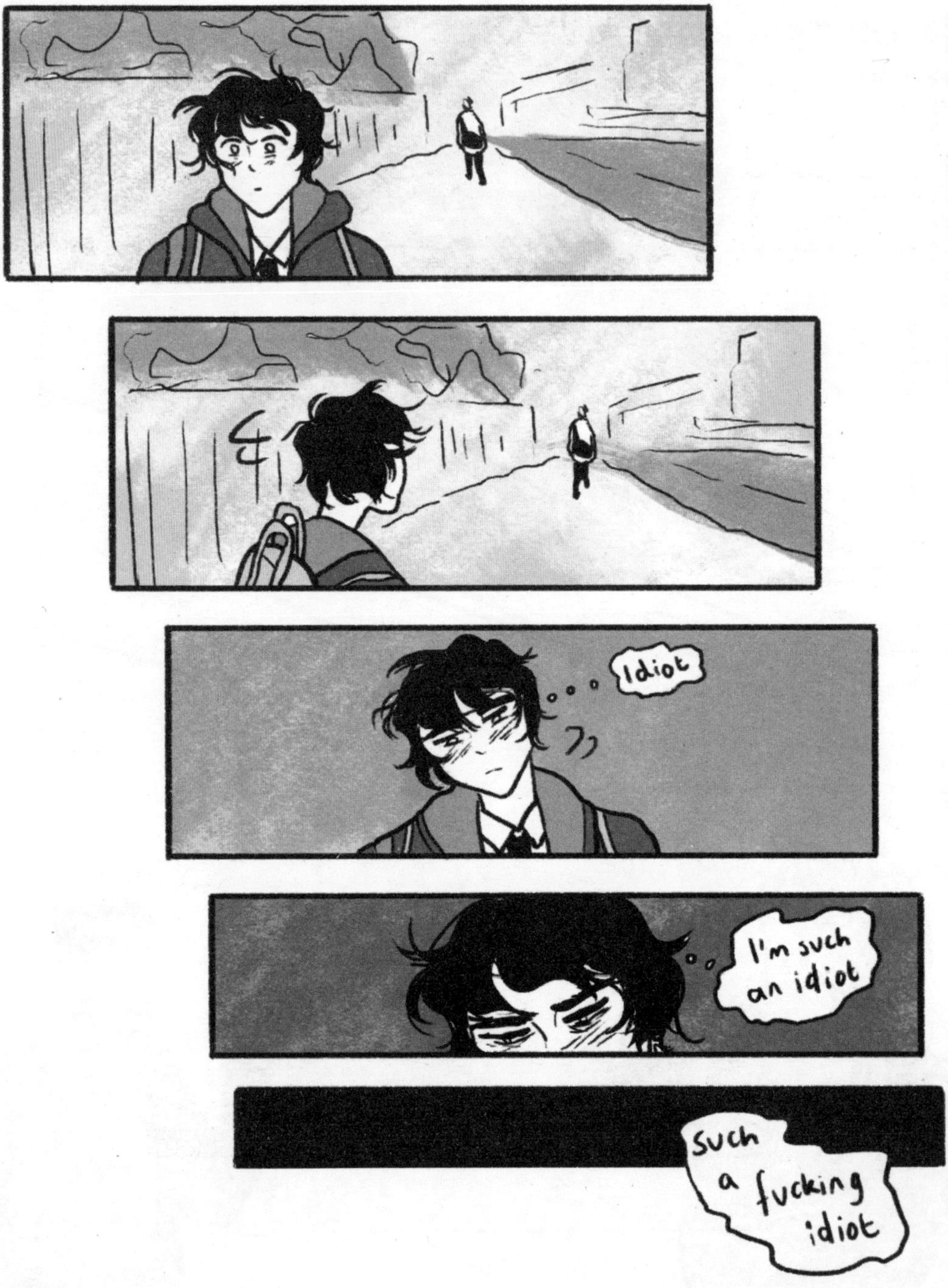
Idiot
I'm such an idiot
such a fucking idiot

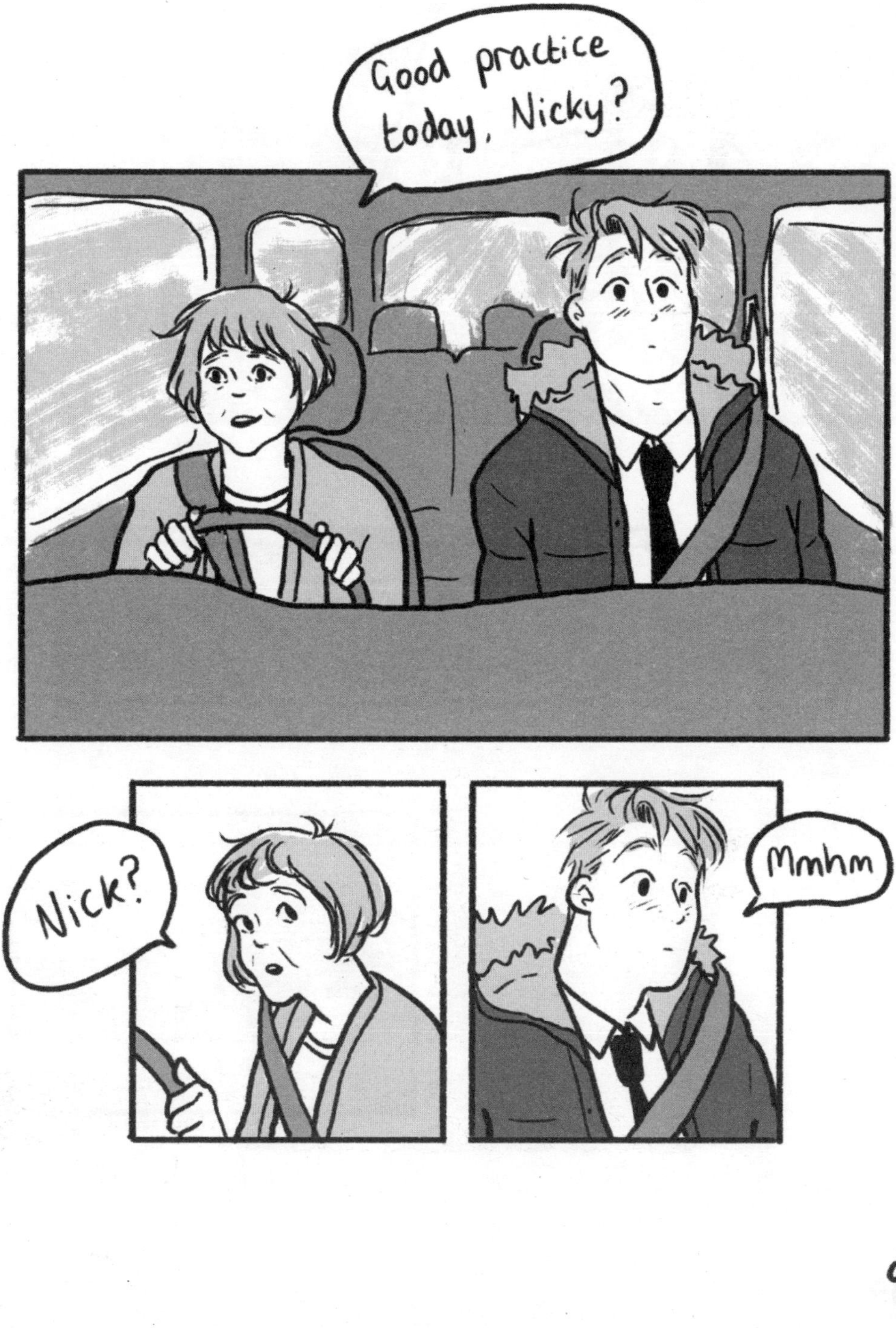
Good practice today, Nicky?
Nick?
Mmhm

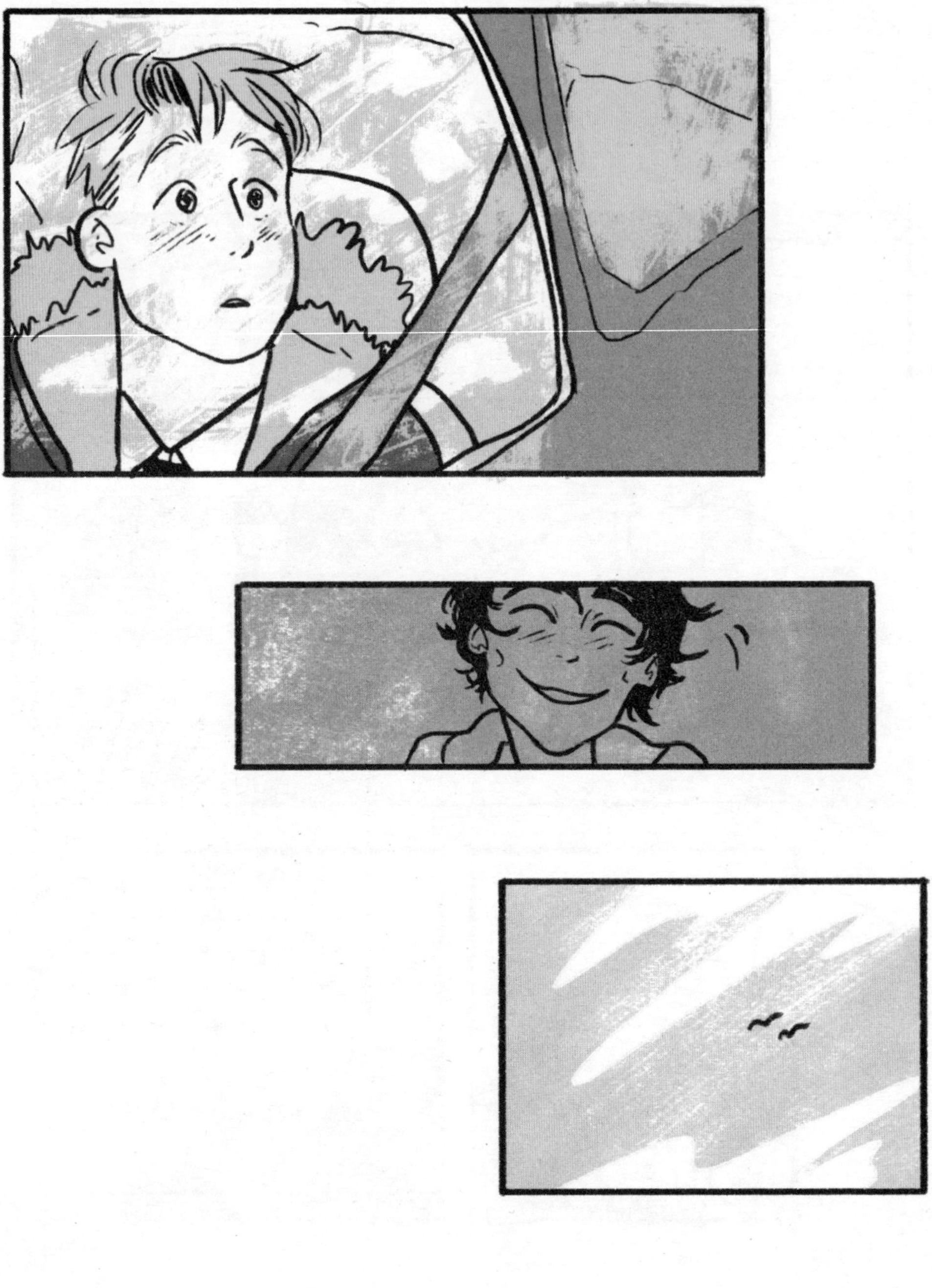

2.CRUSH

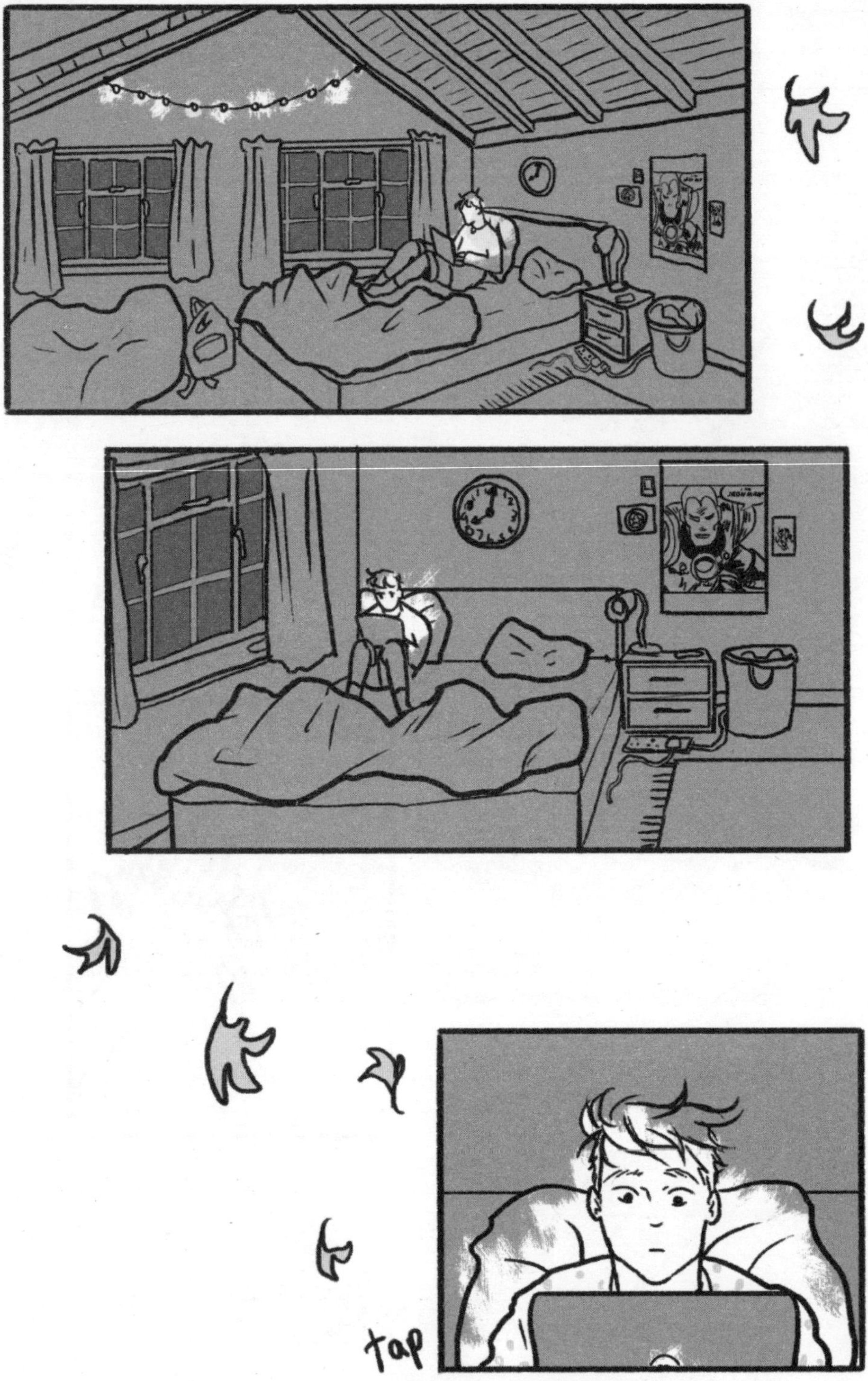
tap
tap tap

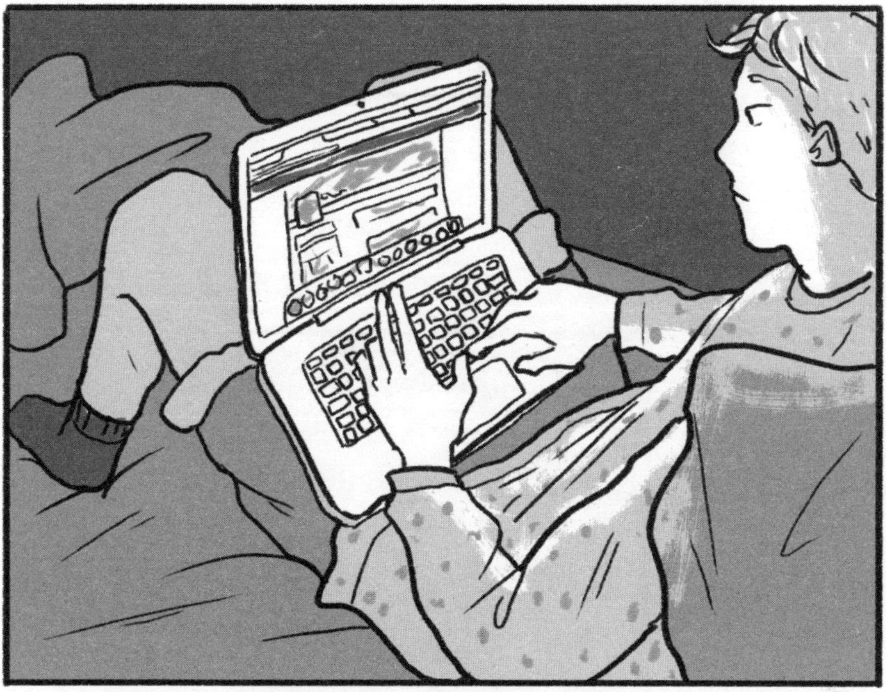

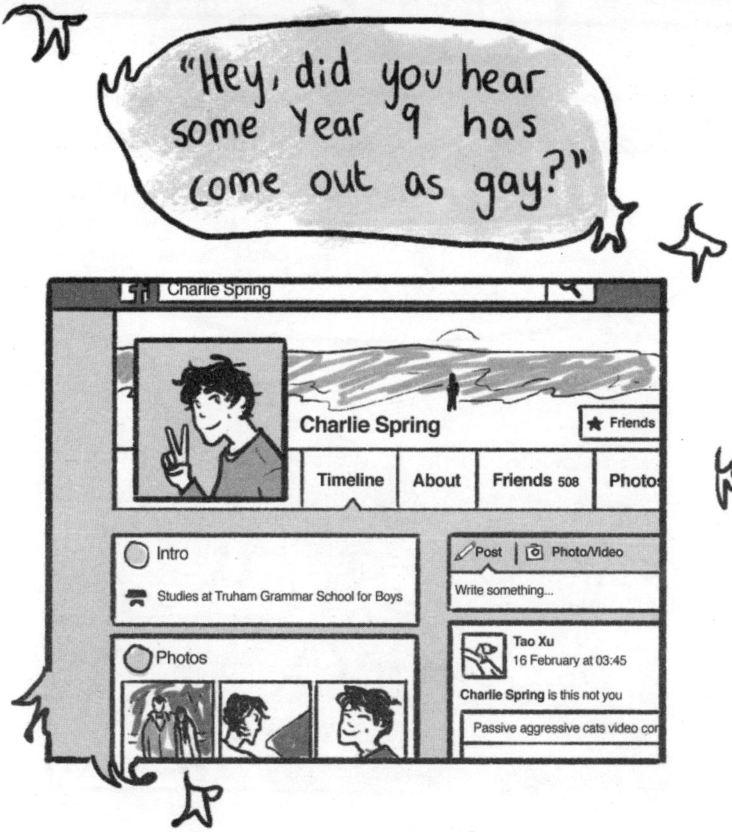
"Hey, did you hear some Year 9 has come out as gay?"
Charlie Spring
Charlie Spring
Friends
Timeline
About
Friends 508
Intro
Studies at Truham Grammar School for Boys
Post
Photo/Video
Write something...
Photos
Tao Xu
16 February at 03:45
Charlie Spring is this not you
Passive aggressive cats video co

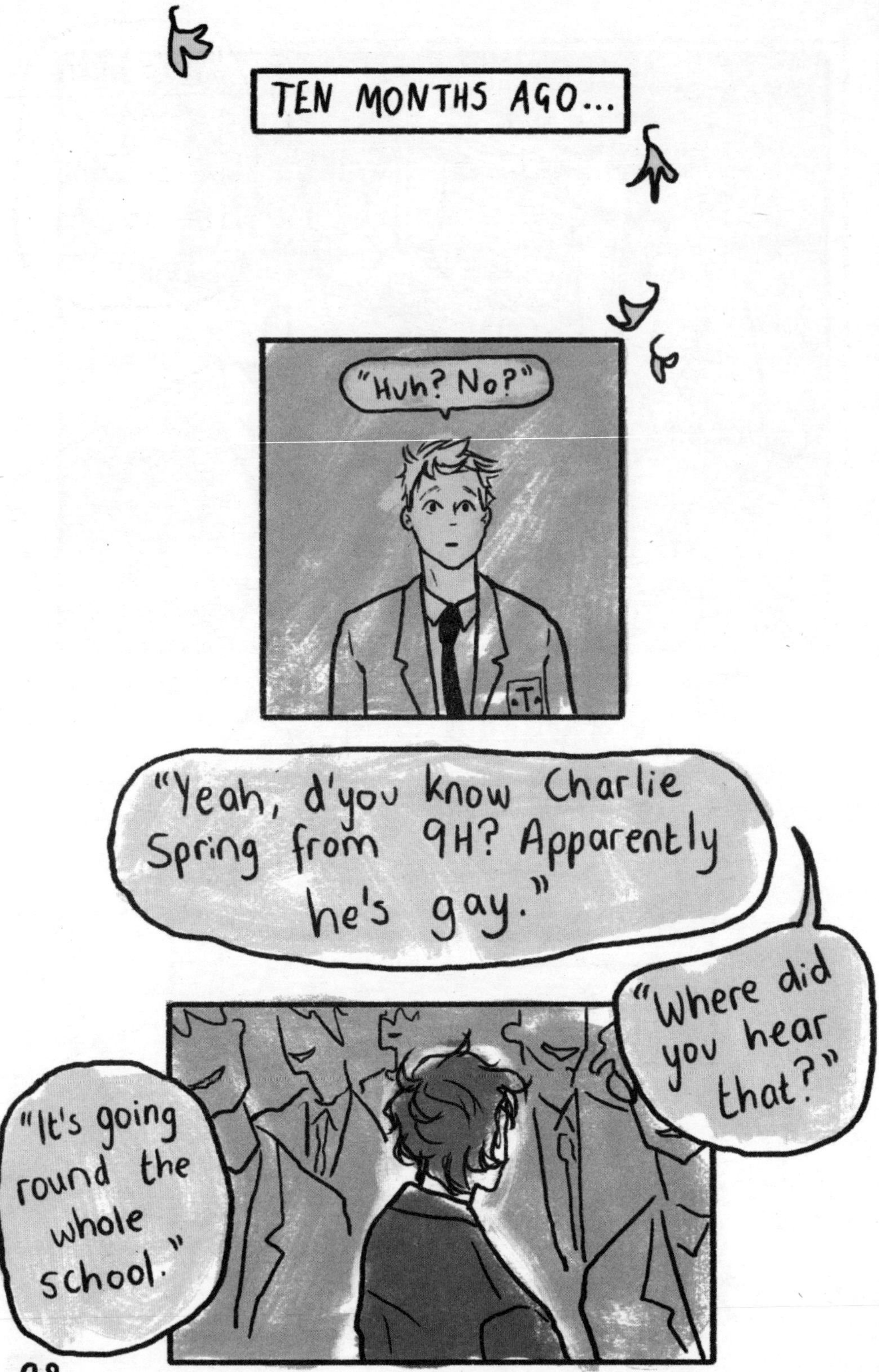
TEN MONTHS AGO...
"Huh? No?"
"Yeah, d'you know Charlie Spring from 9H? Apparently he's gay."
"Where did you hear that?"
"It's going round the whole school."

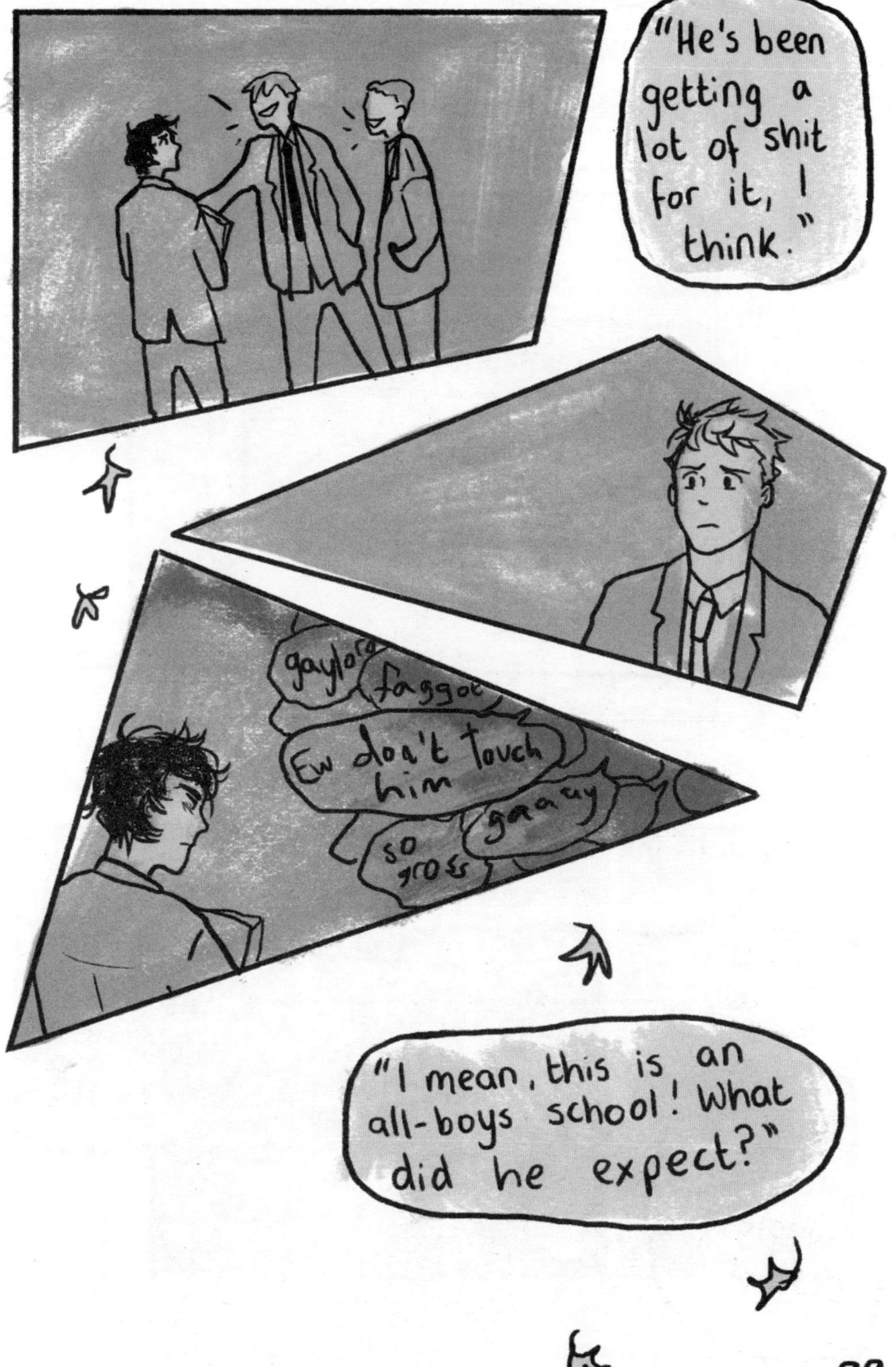
"He's been getting a lot of shit for it, I think."
faggot
Ew don't touch him
gaaay
so gross
"I mean, this is an all-boys school! What did he expect?"

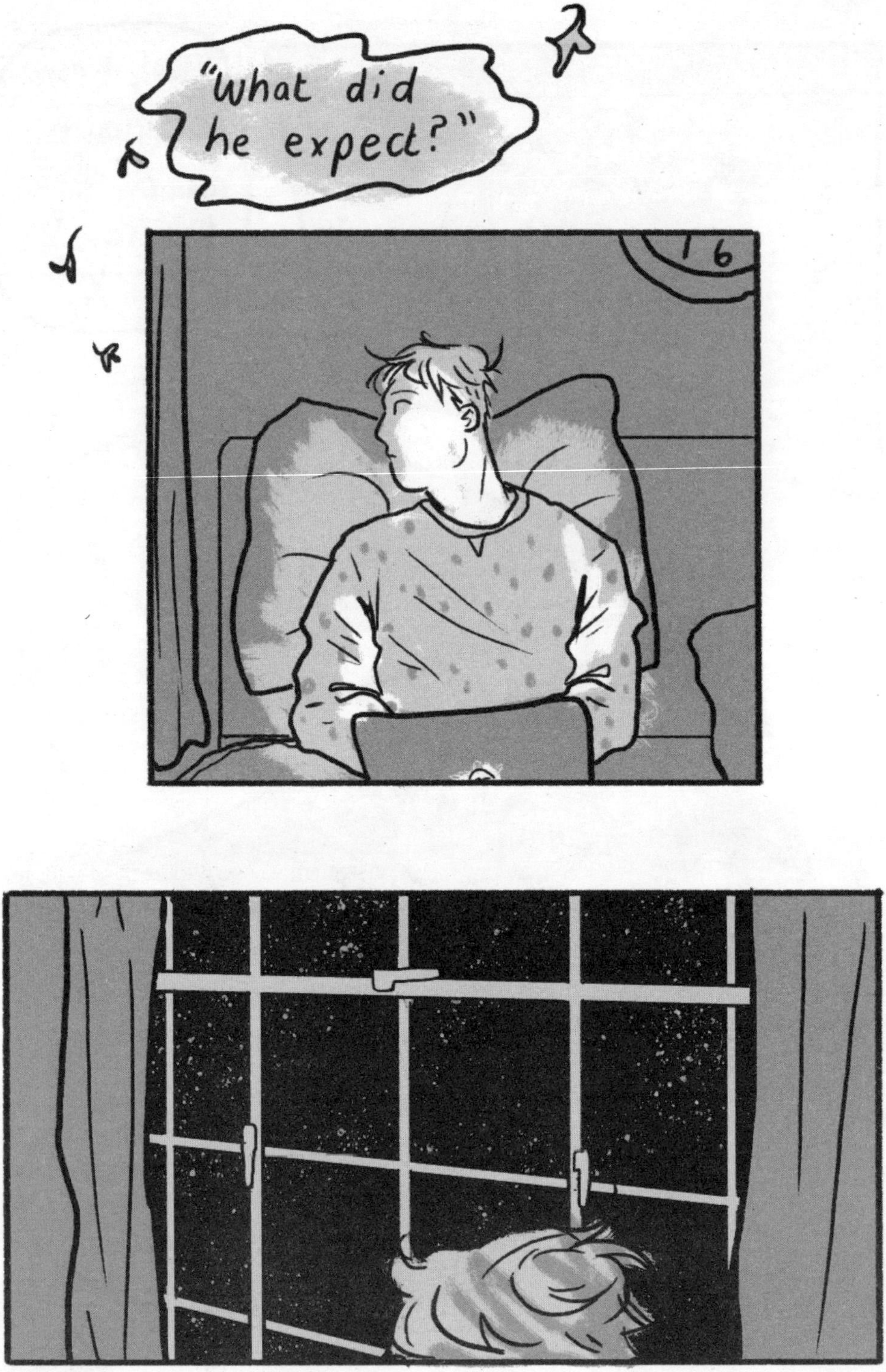
"What did he expect?"

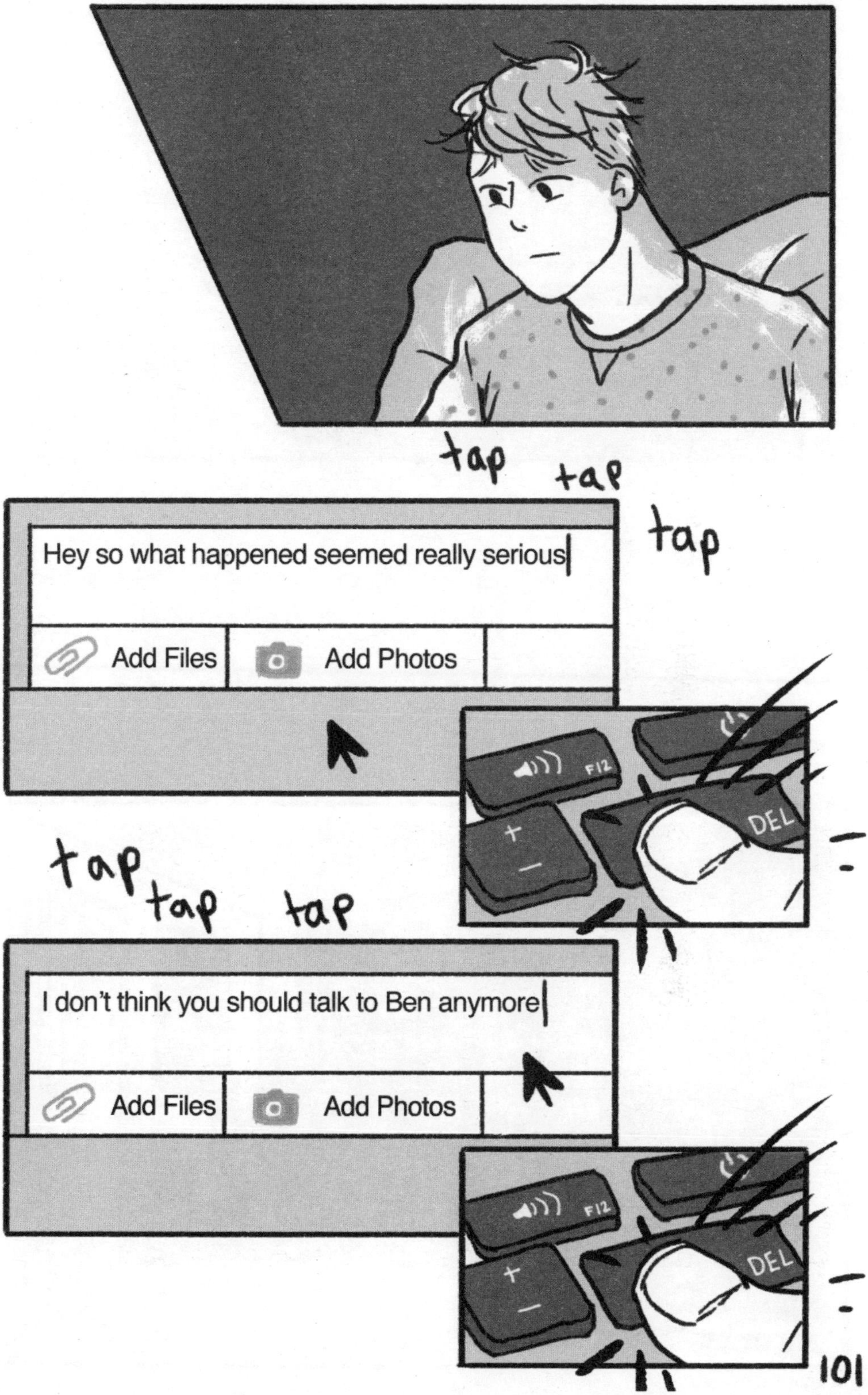
tap
tap
tap
Hey so what happened seemed really serious
Add Files
Add Photos
F12
DEL
tap
tap
tap
I don't think you should talk to Ben anymore
Add Files
Add Photos
F12
DEL

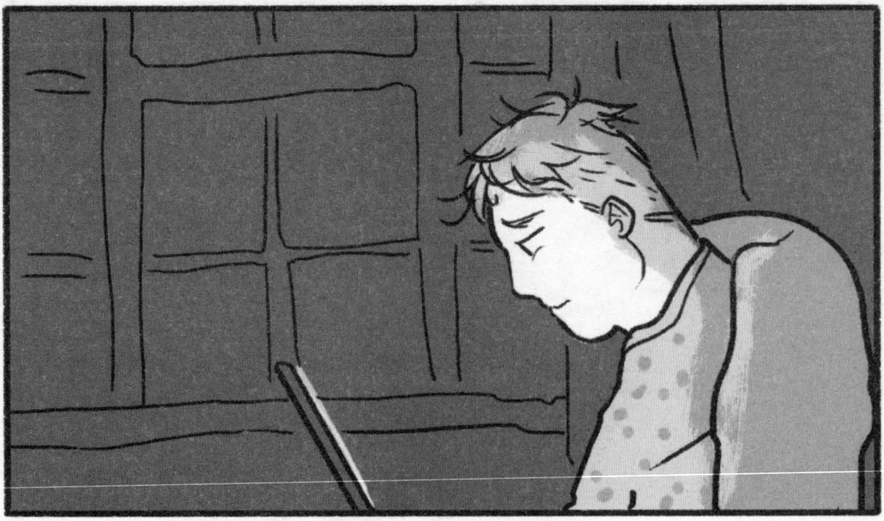

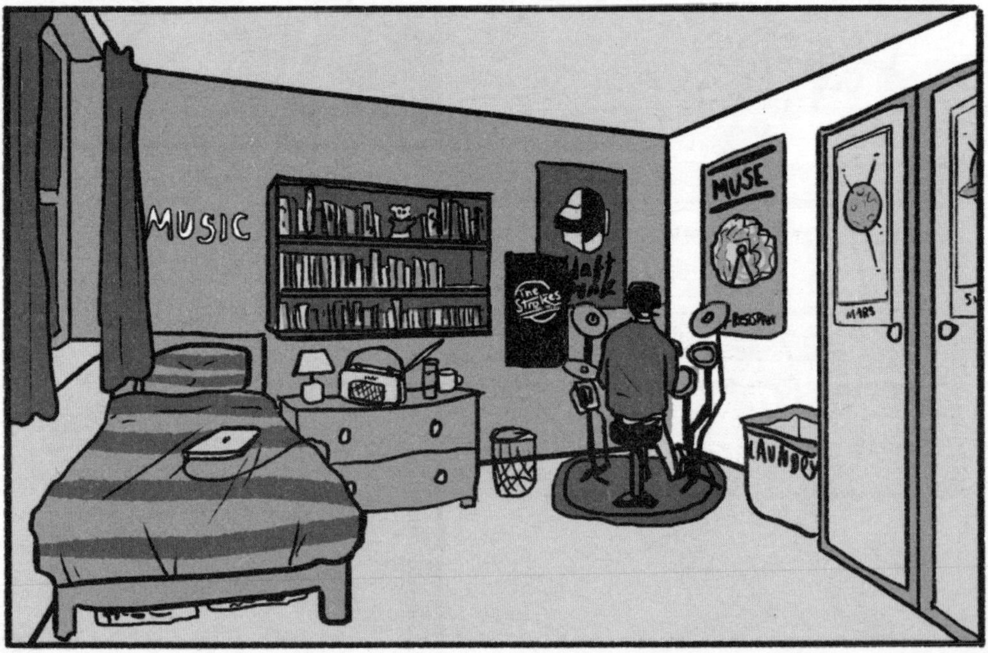
MUSIC
The Strokes
MUSE
MARS

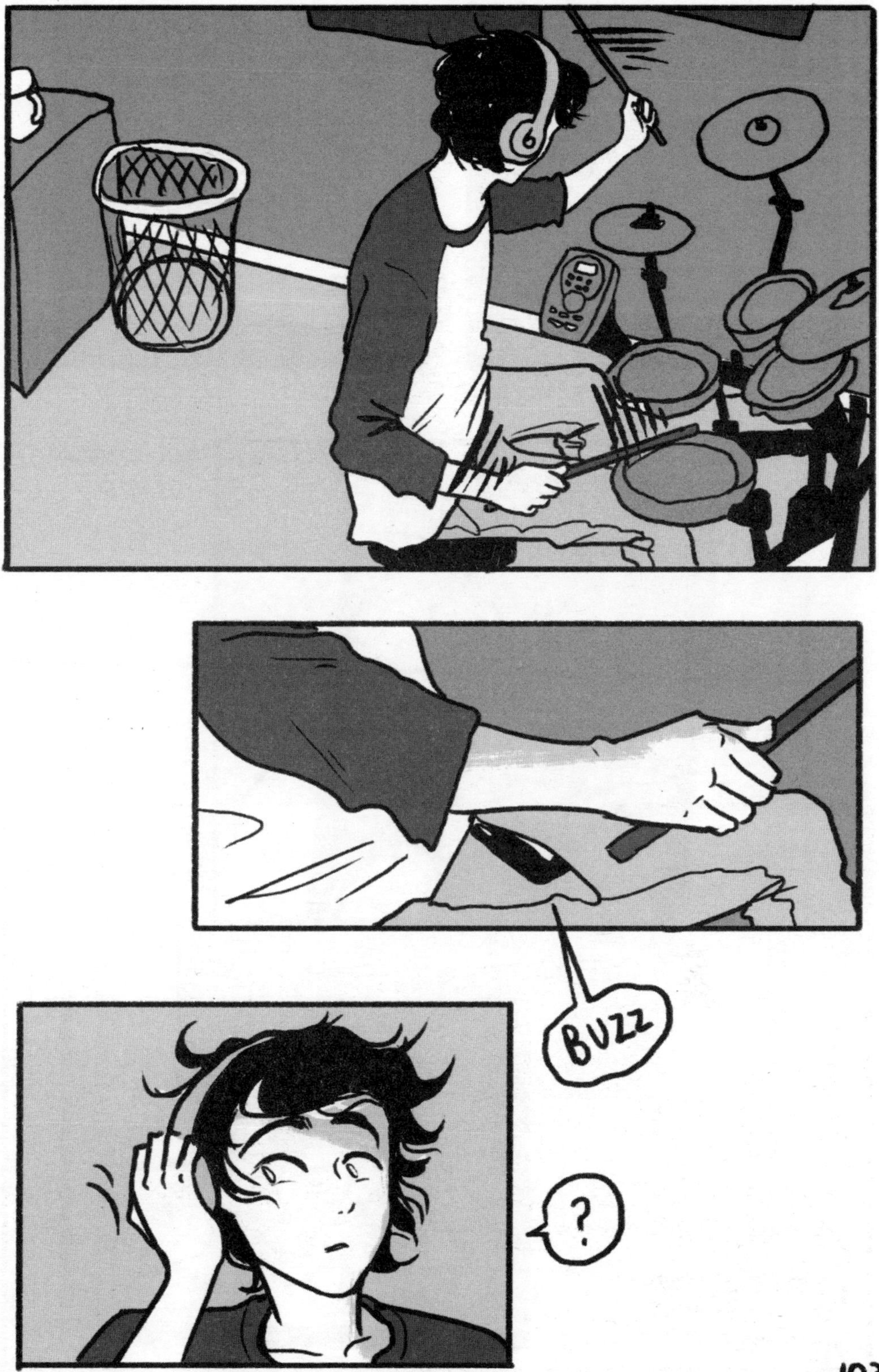
BUZZ
?

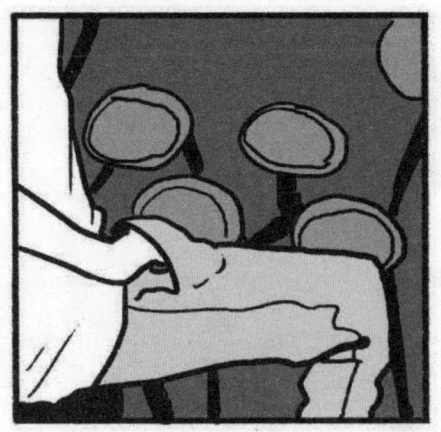

20:13
Friday 26 February

Nick Nelson
Hey, just wanted to check you're
okay. Ben's such a dick!!!

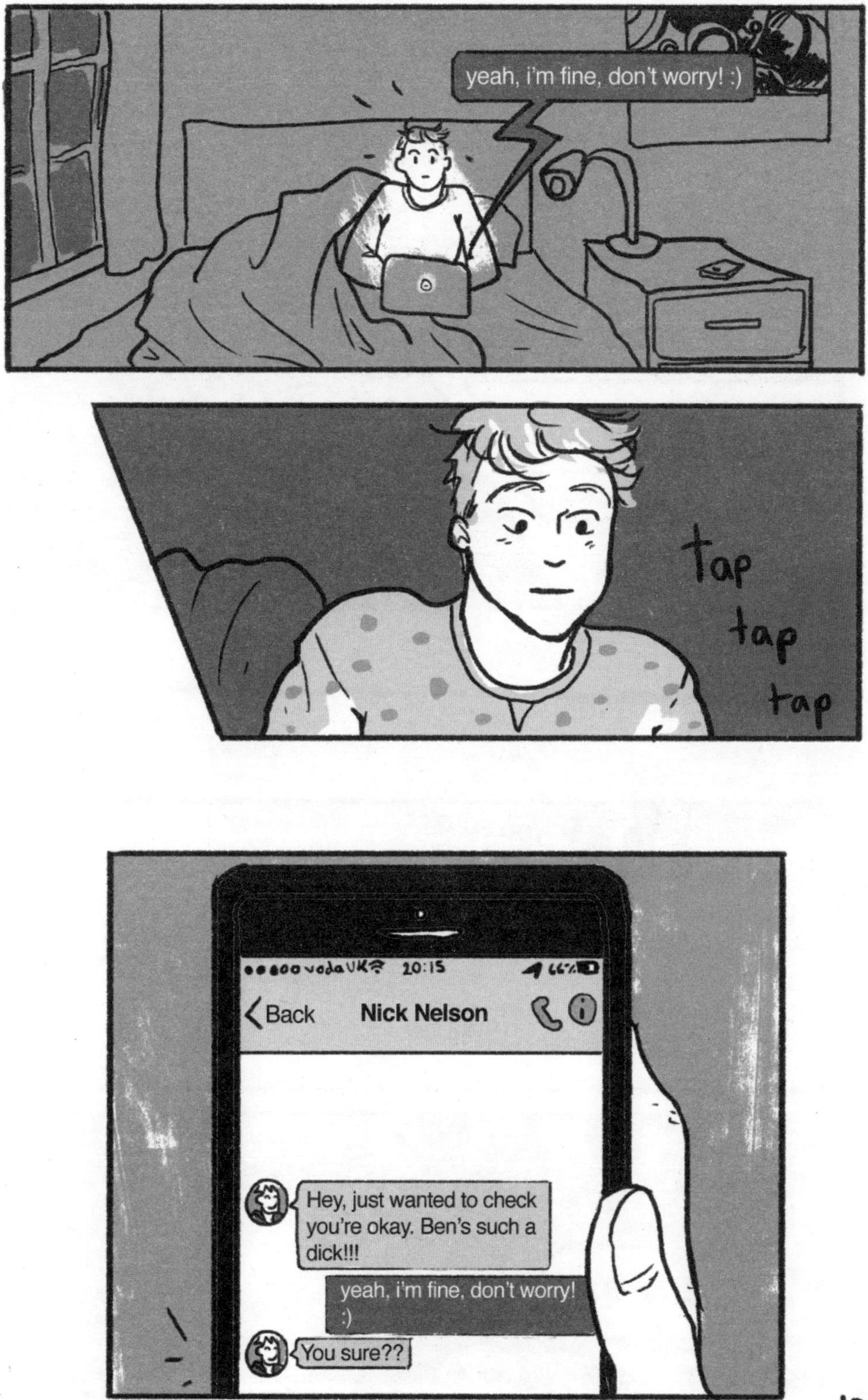
yeah, i'm fine, don't worry! :)
tap
tap
tap
20:15
Back
Nick Nelson
Hey, just wanted to check you're okay. Ben's such a dick!!!
yeah, i'm fine, don't worry! :)
You sure??

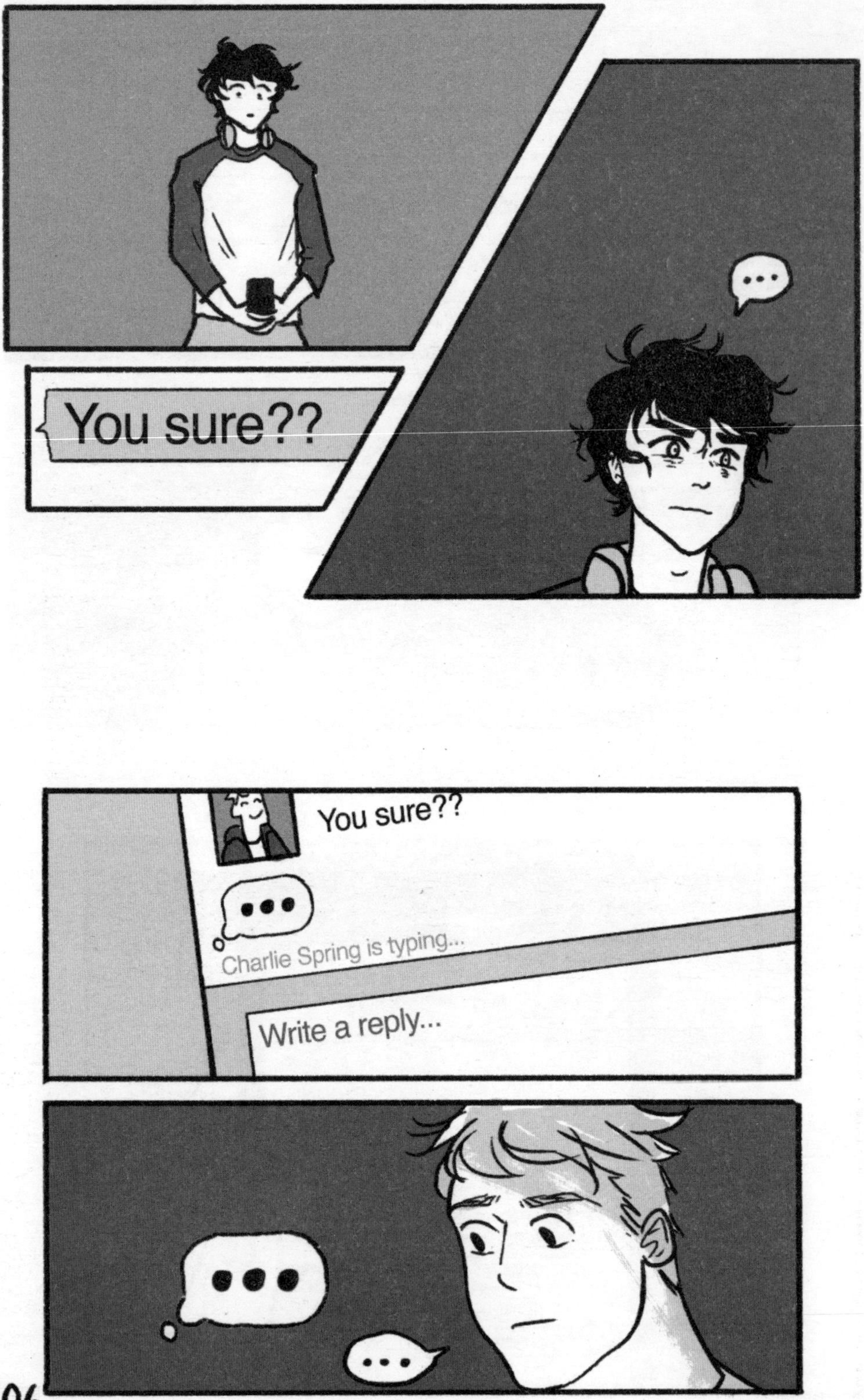
You sure??
You sure??
Charlie Spring is typing...
Write a reply...

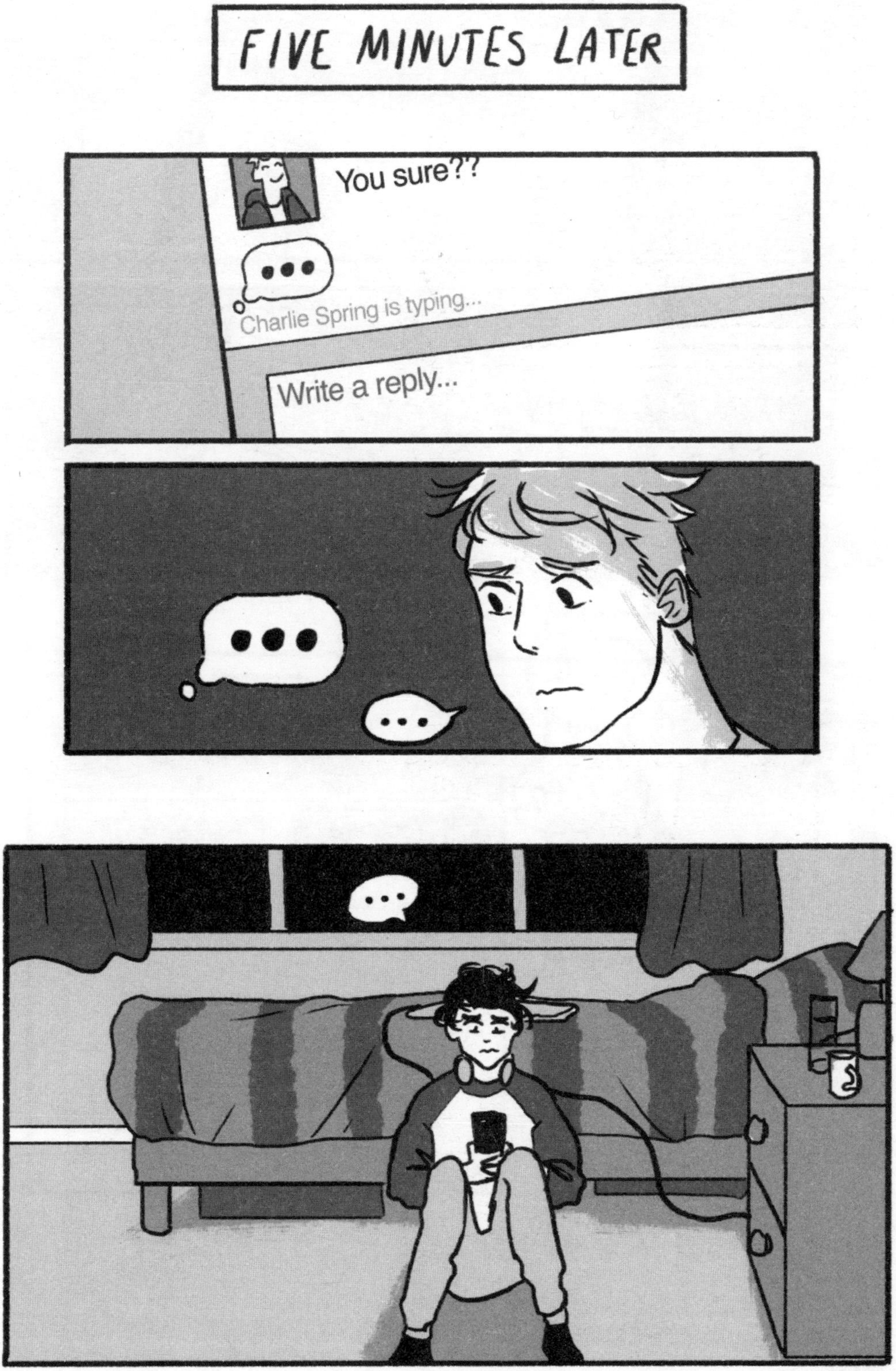
FIVE MINUTES LATER
You sure??
Charlie Spring is typing...
Write a reply...

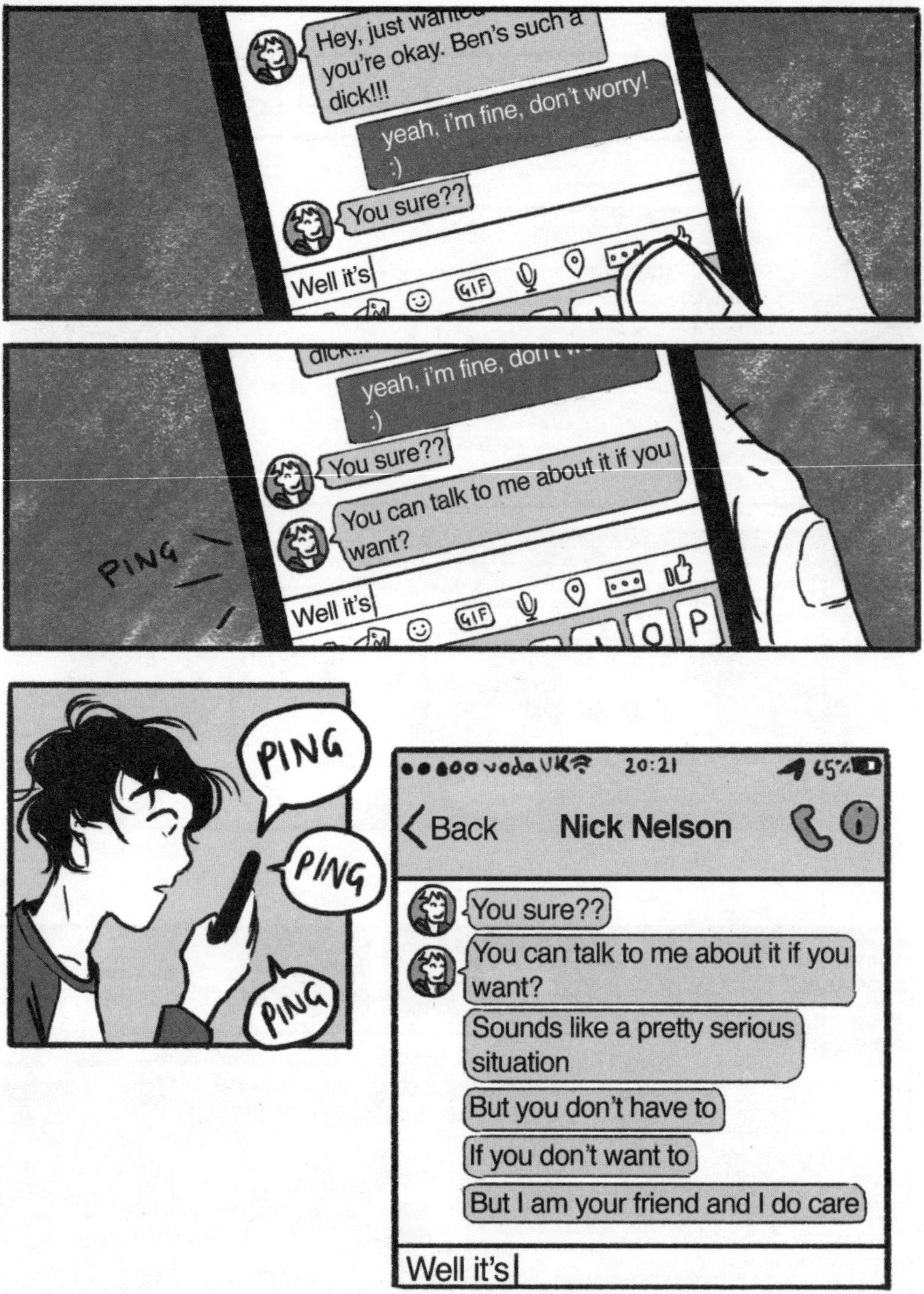

Hey, just
you're okay. Ben's such a
dick!!!
yeah, i'm fine, don't worry!
:)
You sure??
Well it's
GIF
yeah, i'm fine,
:)
You sure??
You can talk to me about it if you
want?
PING
Well it's
GIF
PING
PING
PING
vodaUK
20:21
65%
Back
Nick Nelson
You sure??
You can talk to me about it if you want?
Sounds like a pretty serious situation
But you don't have to
If you don't want to
But I am your friend and I do care
Well it's

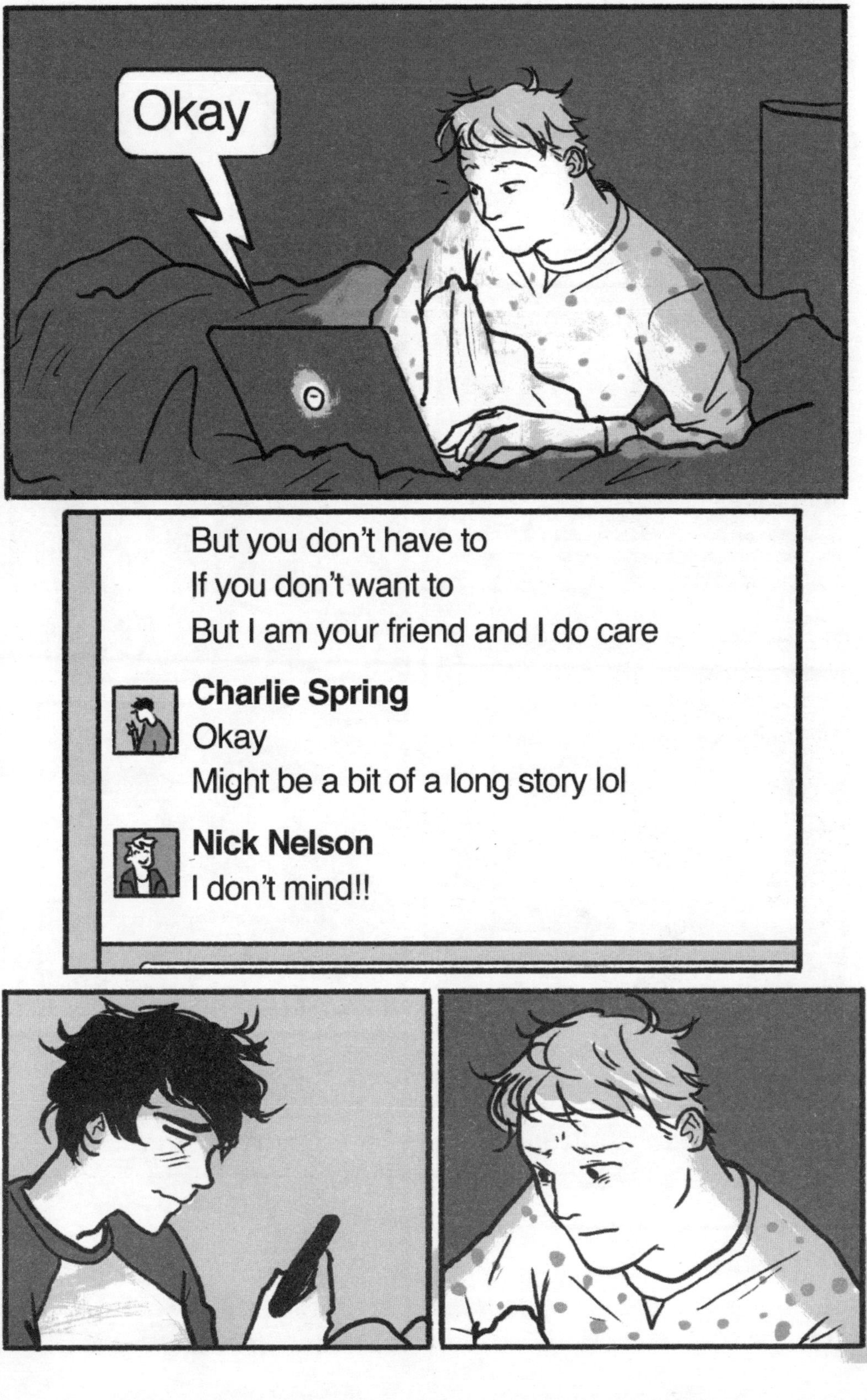
Okay
But you don't have to
If you don't want to
But I am your friend and I do care
Charlie Spring
Okay
Might be a bit of a long story lol
Nick Nelson
I don't mind!!

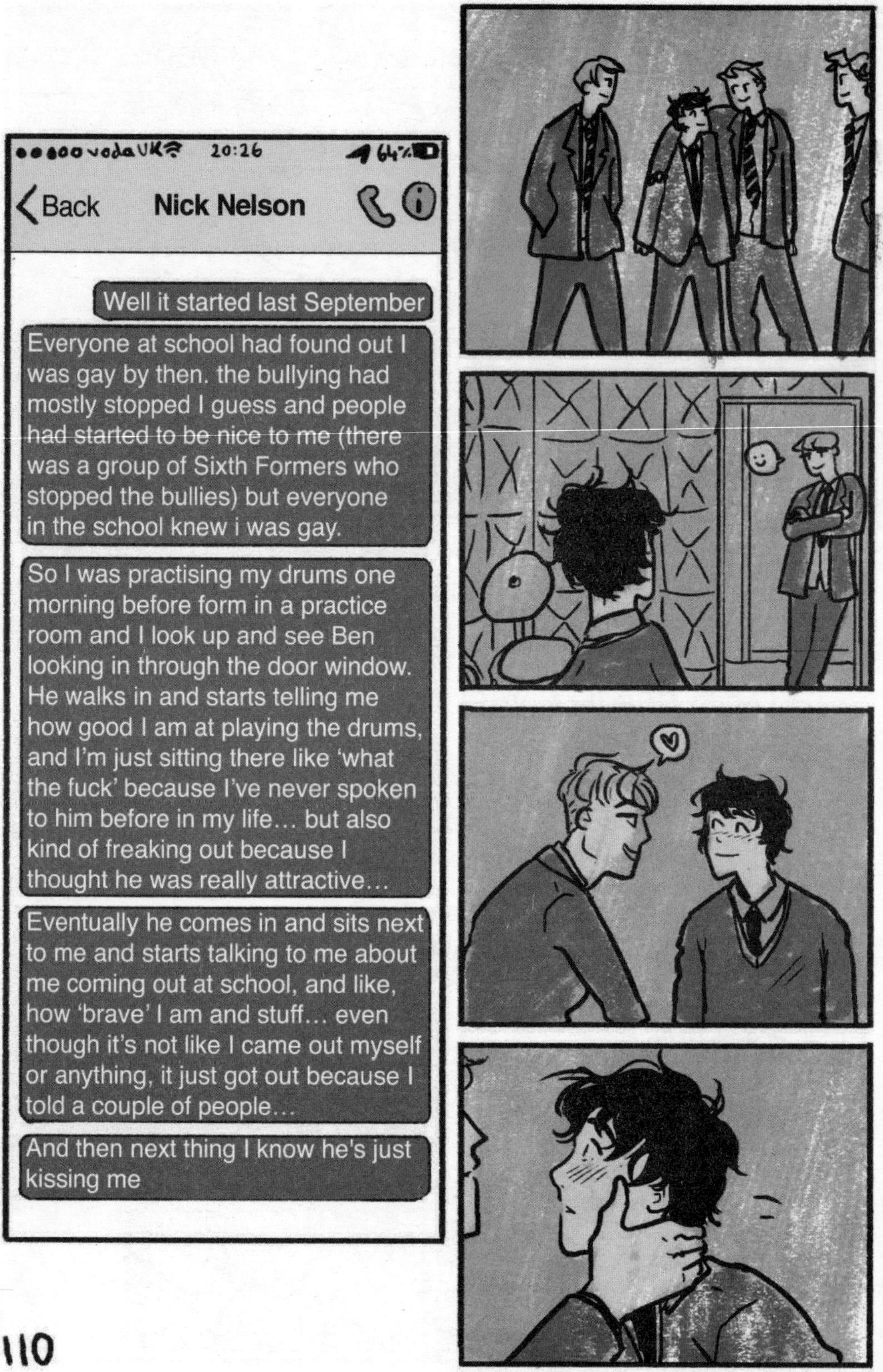
●●●○○ vodaUK 20:26 64%
Back
Nick Nelson
Well it started last September
Everyone at school had found out I was gay by then. the bullying had mostly stopped I guess and people had started to be nice to me (there was a group of Sixth Formers who stopped the bullies) but everyone in the school knew i was gay.
So I was practising my drums one morning before form in a practice room and I look up and see Ben looking in through the door window. He walks in and starts telling me how good I am at playing the drums, and I'm just sitting there like 'what the fuck' because I've never spoken to him before in my life… but also kind of freaking out because I thought he was really attractive…
Eventually he comes in and sits next to me and starts talking to me about me coming out at school, and like, how 'brave' I am and stuff… even though it's not like I came out myself or anything, it just got out because I told a couple of people…
And then next thing I know he's just kissing me

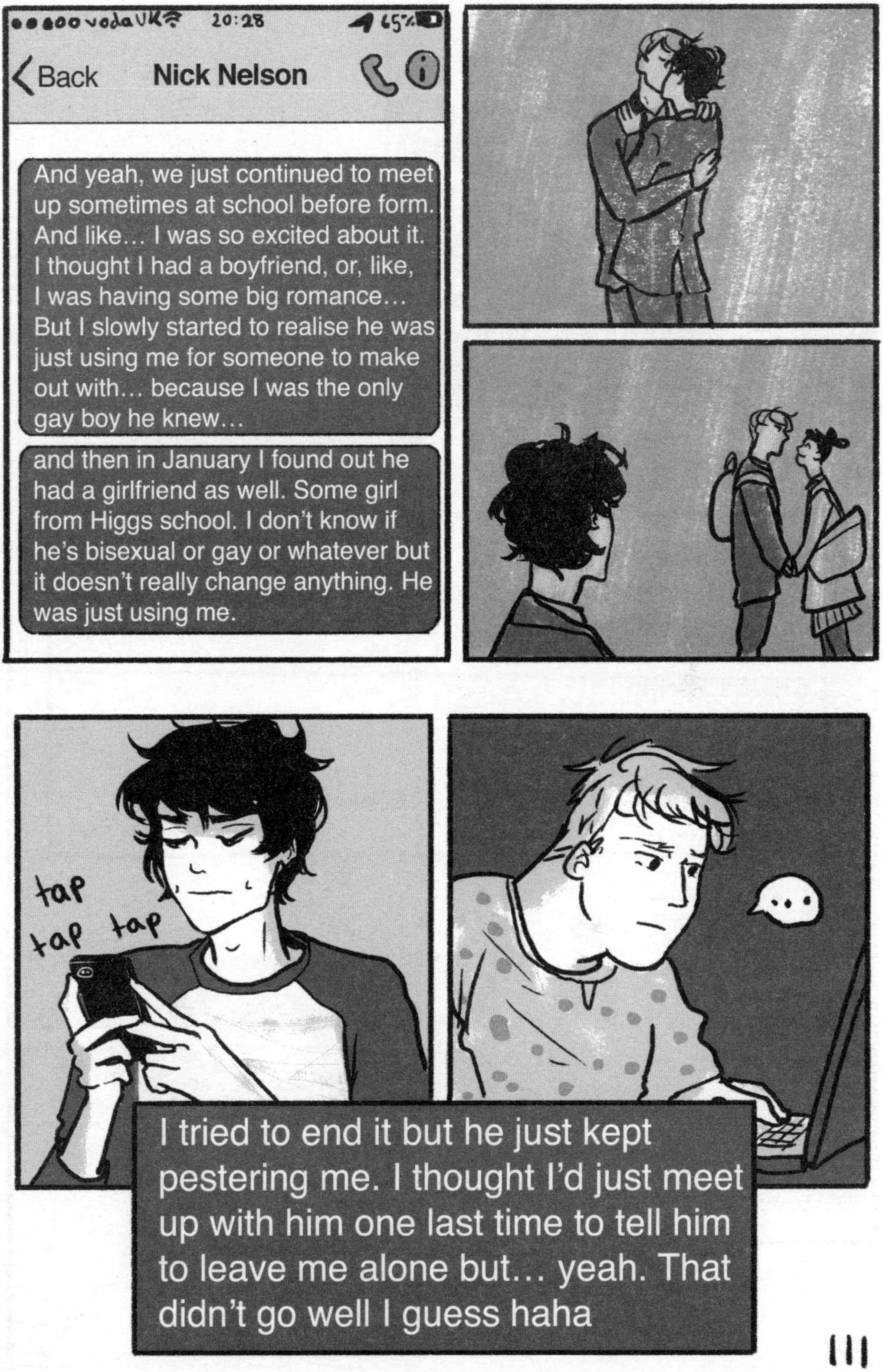
●●●○○ vodaUK 20:28 65%
Back
Nick Nelson
And yeah, we just continued to meet up sometimes at school before form. And like… I was so excited about it. I thought I had a boyfriend, or, like, I was having some big romance… But I slowly started to realise he was just using me for someone to make out with… because I was the only gay boy he knew…
and then in January I found out he had a girlfriend as well. Some girl from Higgs school. I don't know if he's bisexual or gay or whatever but it doesn't really change anything. He was just using me.
tap
tap tap
...
I tried to end it but he just kept pestering me. I thought I'd just meet up with him one last time to tell him to leave me alone but… yeah. That didn't go well I guess haha

tap tap tap

Nick Nelson
FUCK I hate Ben so much. I knew he was a dick, but... jesus.

Please don't ever talk to him again

Charlie Spring
I definitely won't!!!!

Nick Nelson
I will kick his ass if he tries to come near you

Thank you for being there

Generally or in the music block?

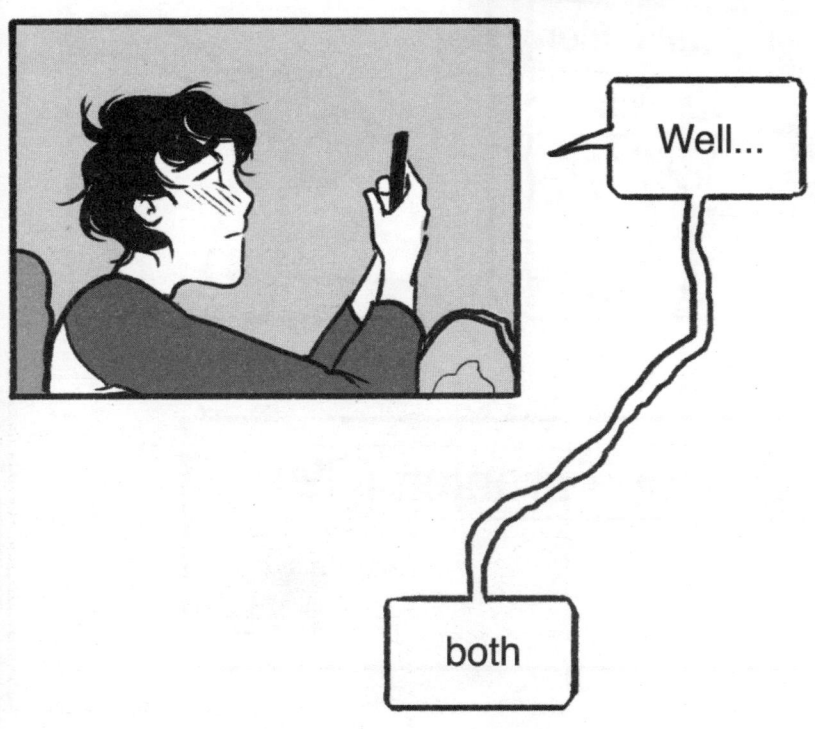

Well...

both

Not a problem
Not a problem
I love talking to you
Not a problem
I'm so glad we're frien
Not a problem

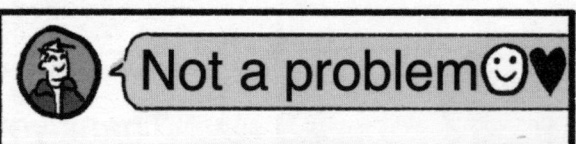

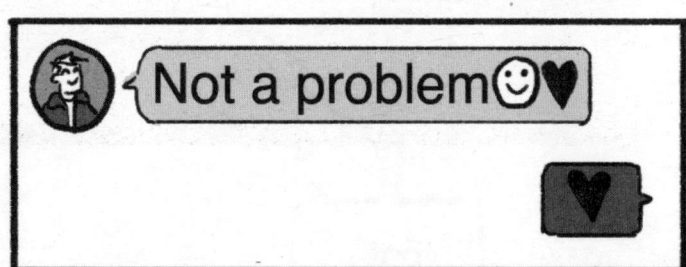

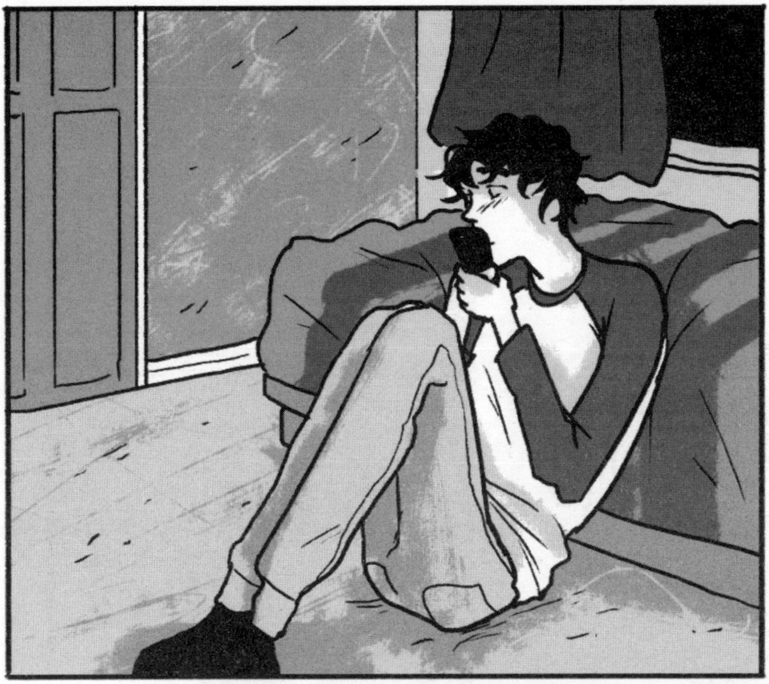

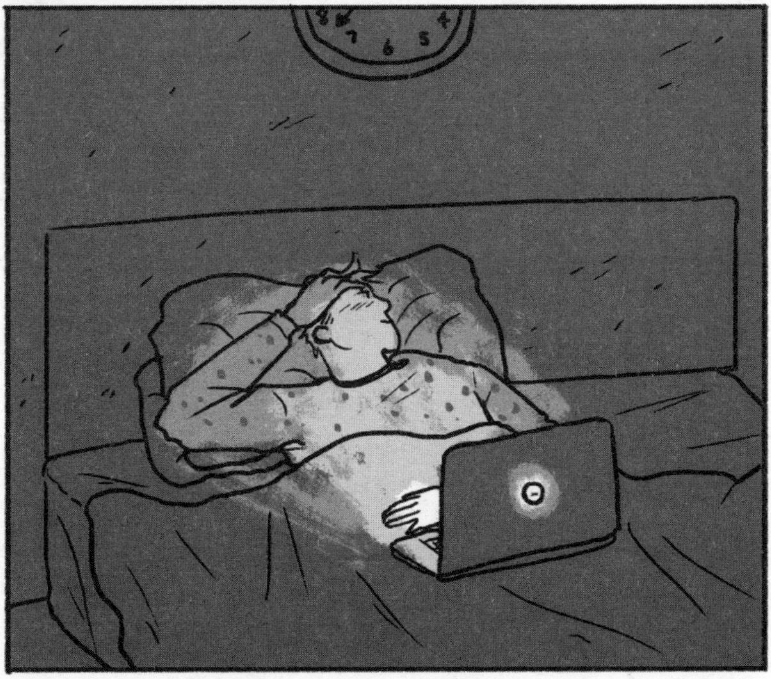

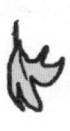

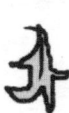

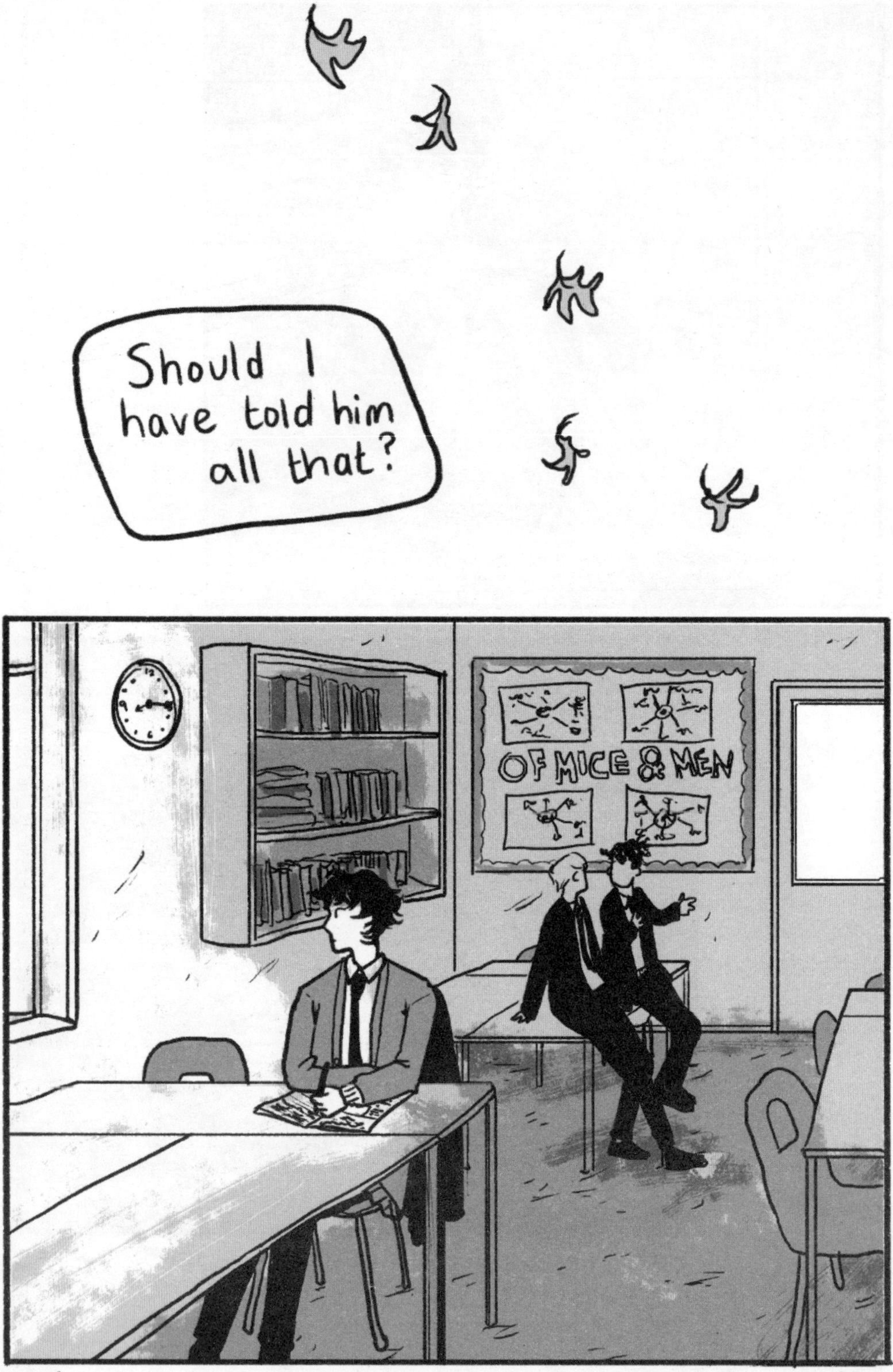
Should I have told him all that?
OF MICE & MEN

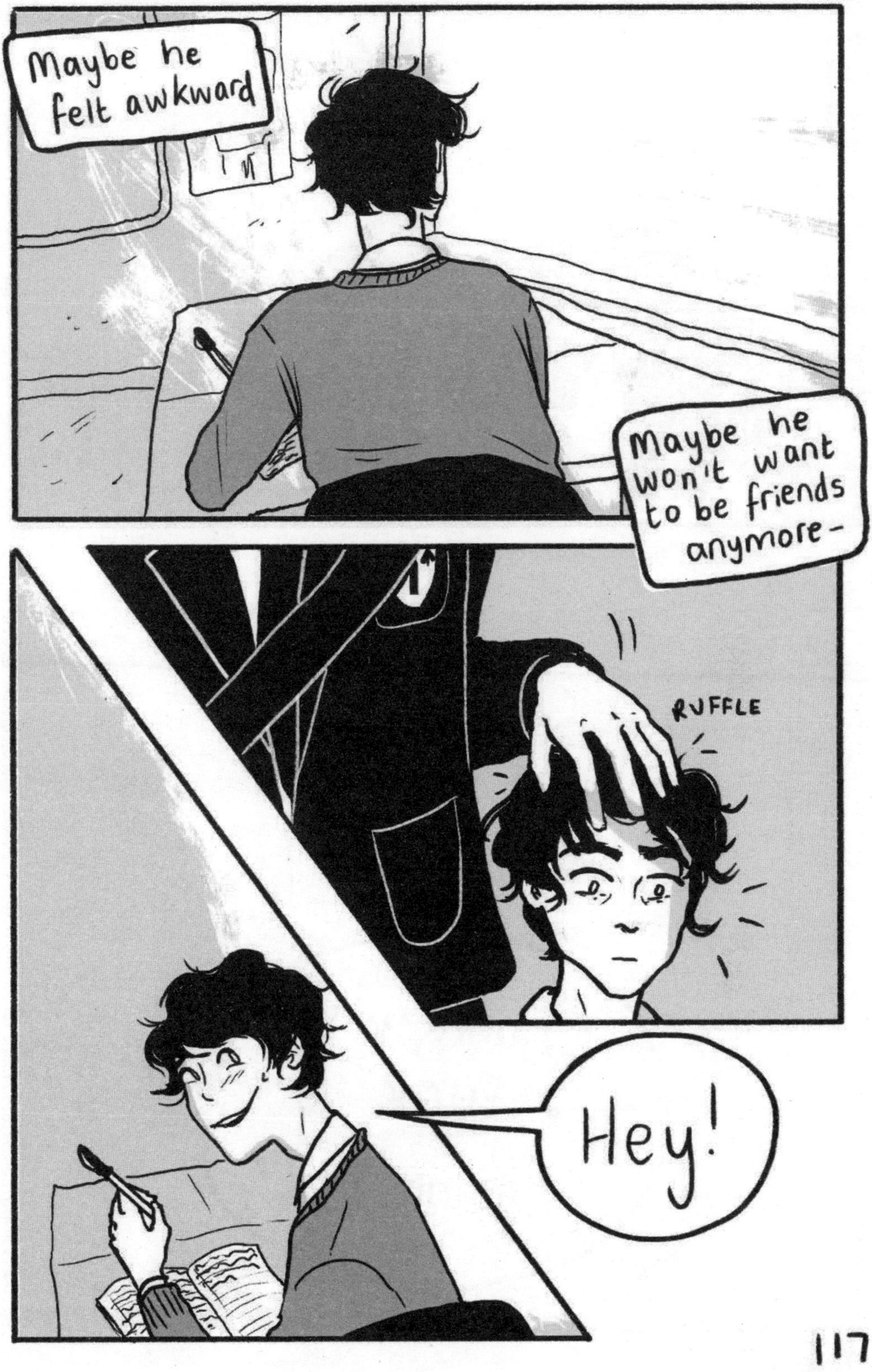
Maybe he felt awkward
Maybe he won't want to be friends anymore-
RUFFLE
Hey!

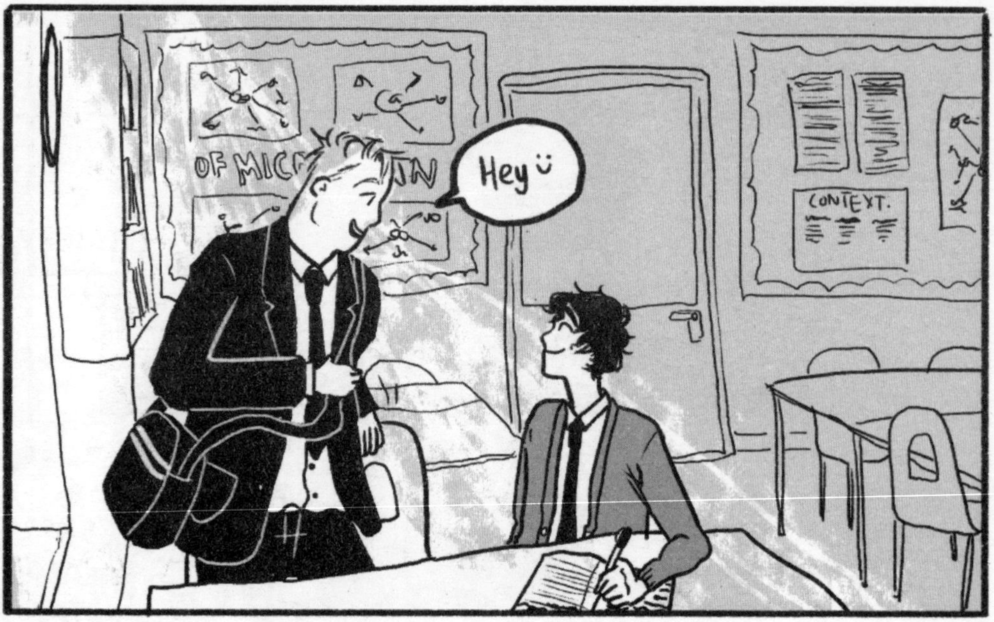
CONTEXT.
Hey

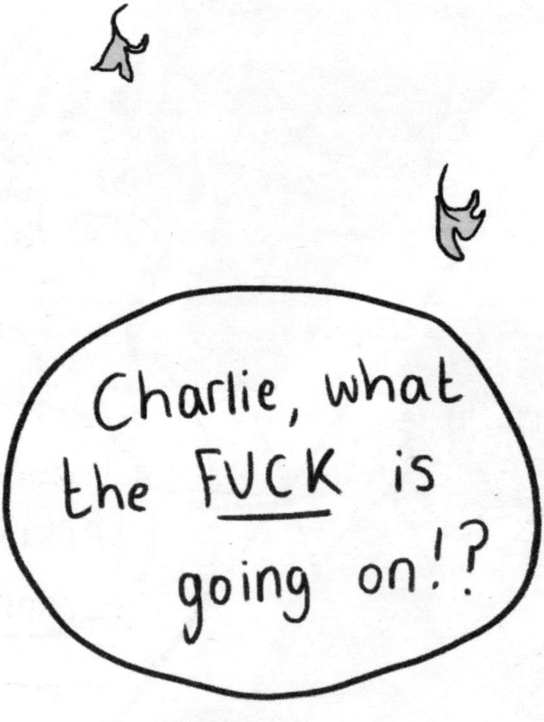
Charlie, what the FUCK is going on!?

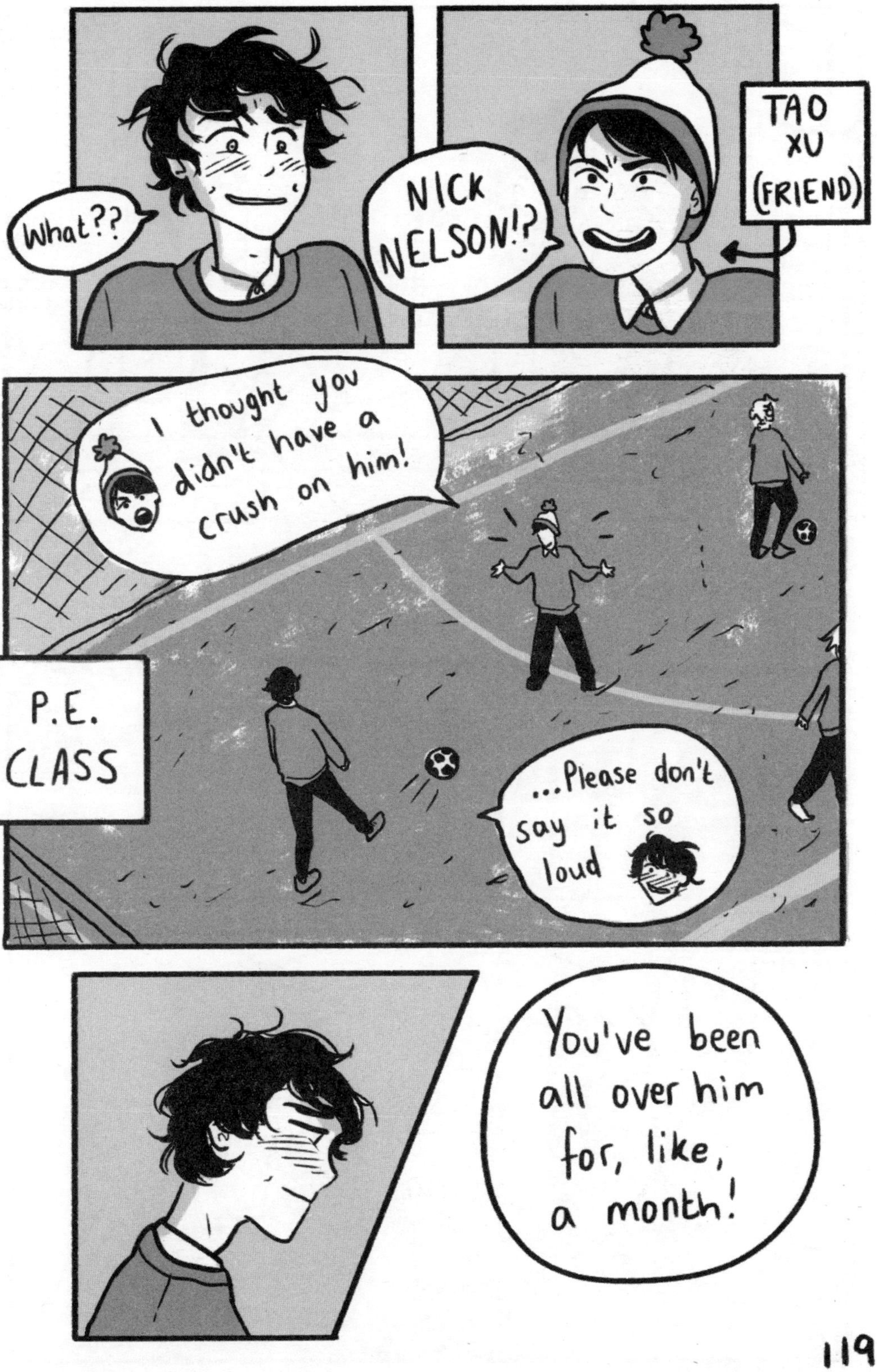
What??
NICK NELSON!?
TAO XU (FRIEND)
P.E. CLASS
I thought you didn't have a crush on him!
...Please don't say it so loud
You've been all over him for, like, a month!

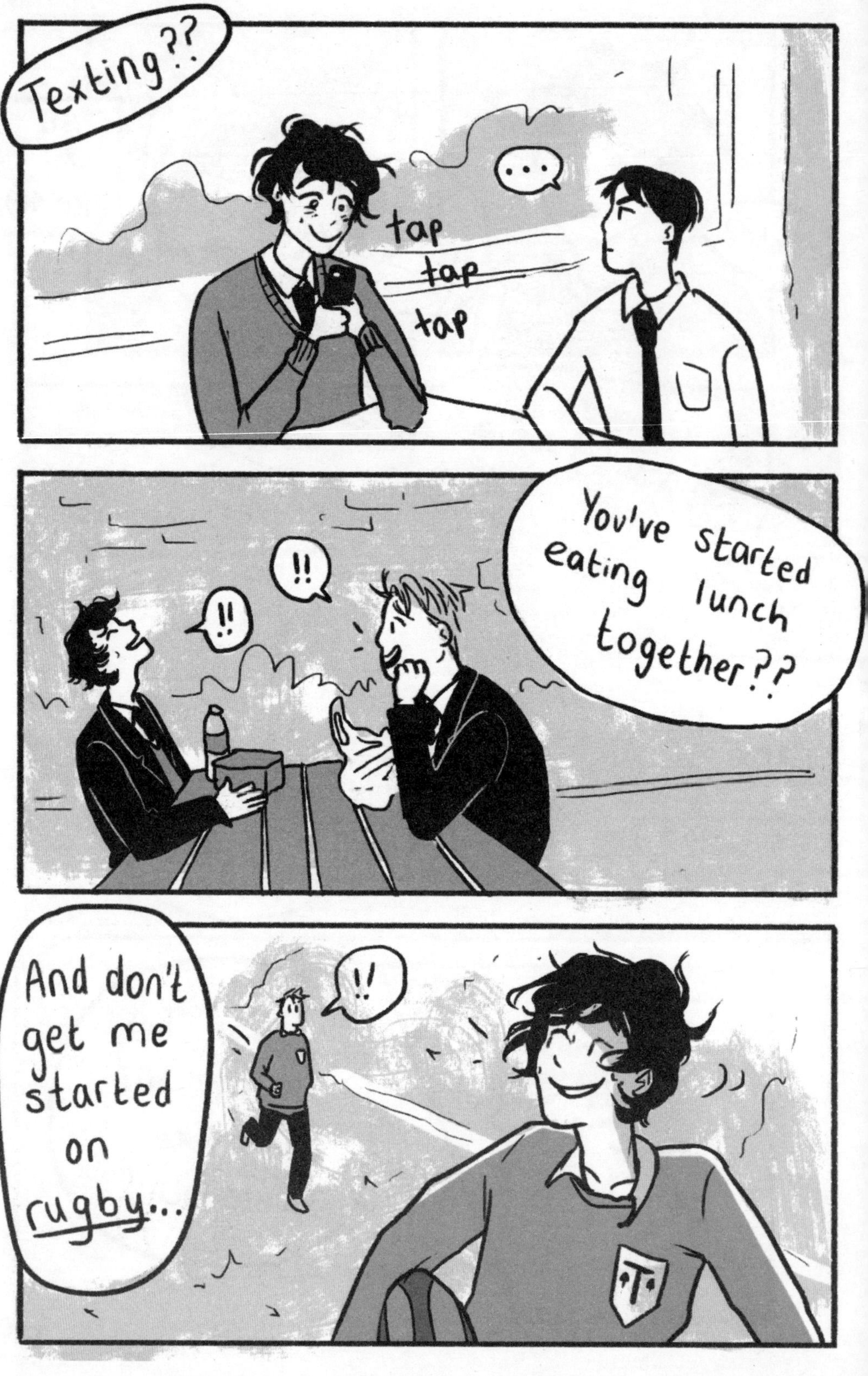
Texting??
...
tap
tap
tap
You've started eating lunch together??
!!
!!
And don't get me started on rugby...
!!

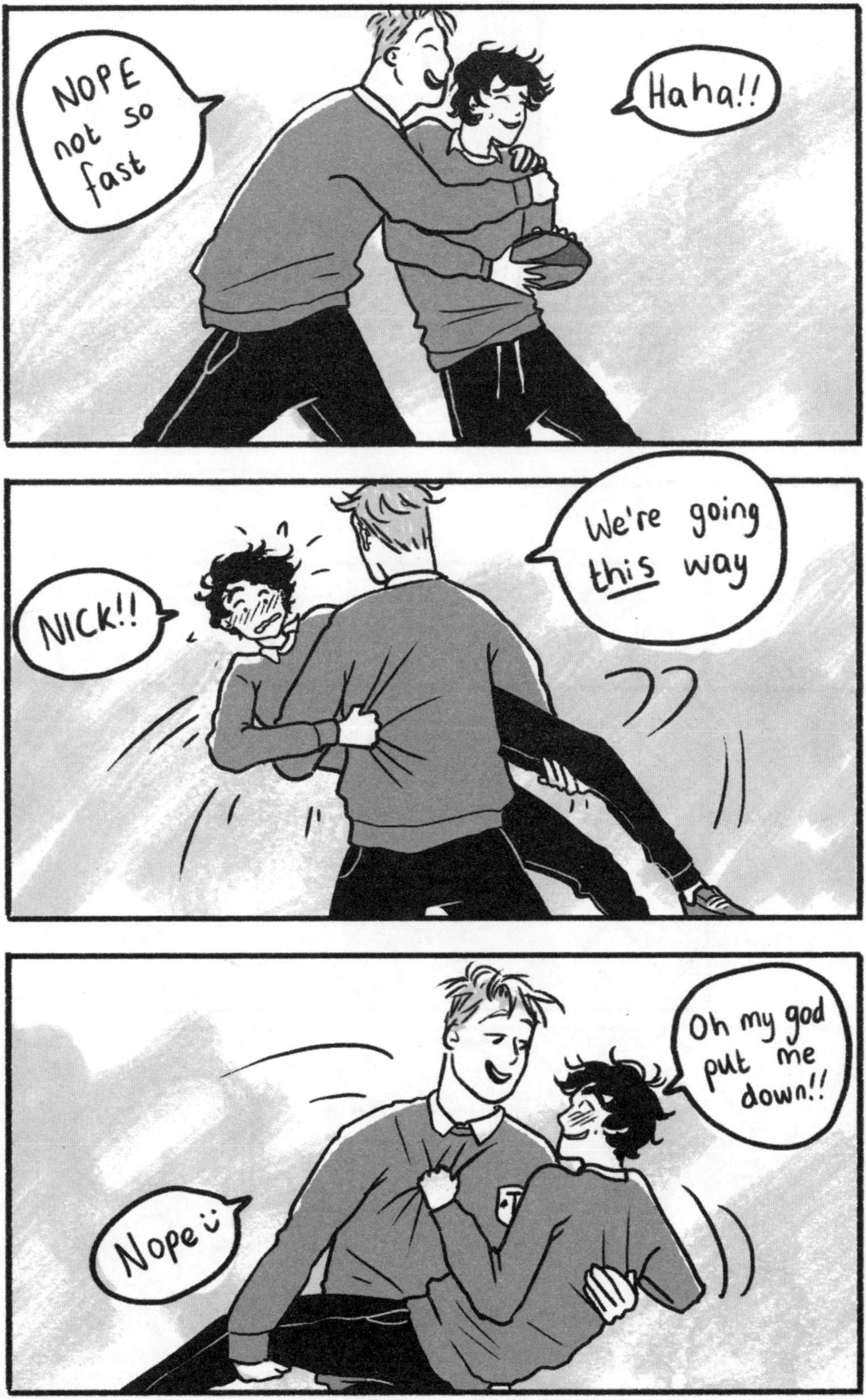
NOPE not so fast
Haha!!
NICK!!
We're going this way
Oh my god put me down!!
Nope

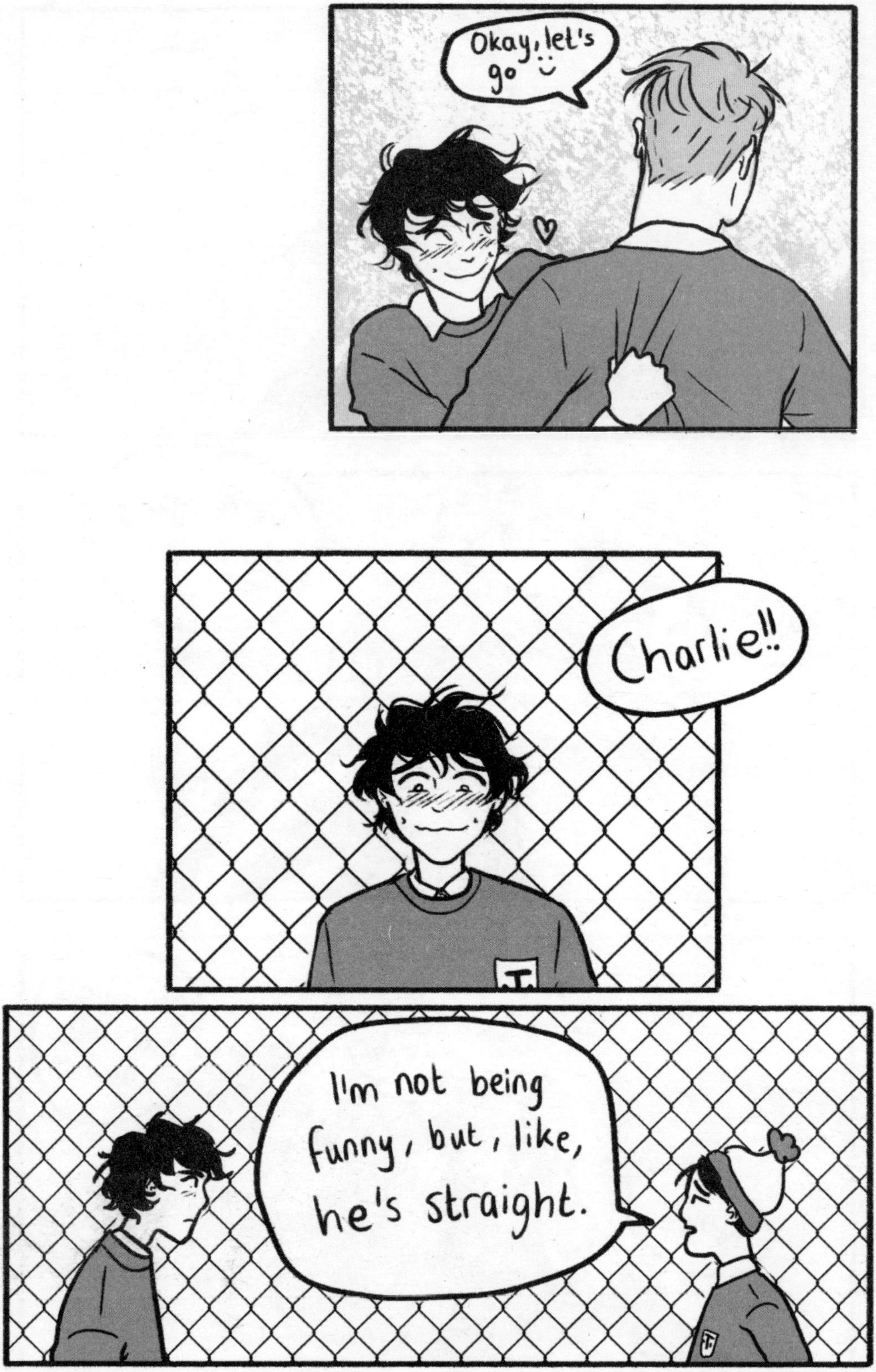
Okay, let's go
Charlie!!
I'm not being funny, but, like, he's straight.

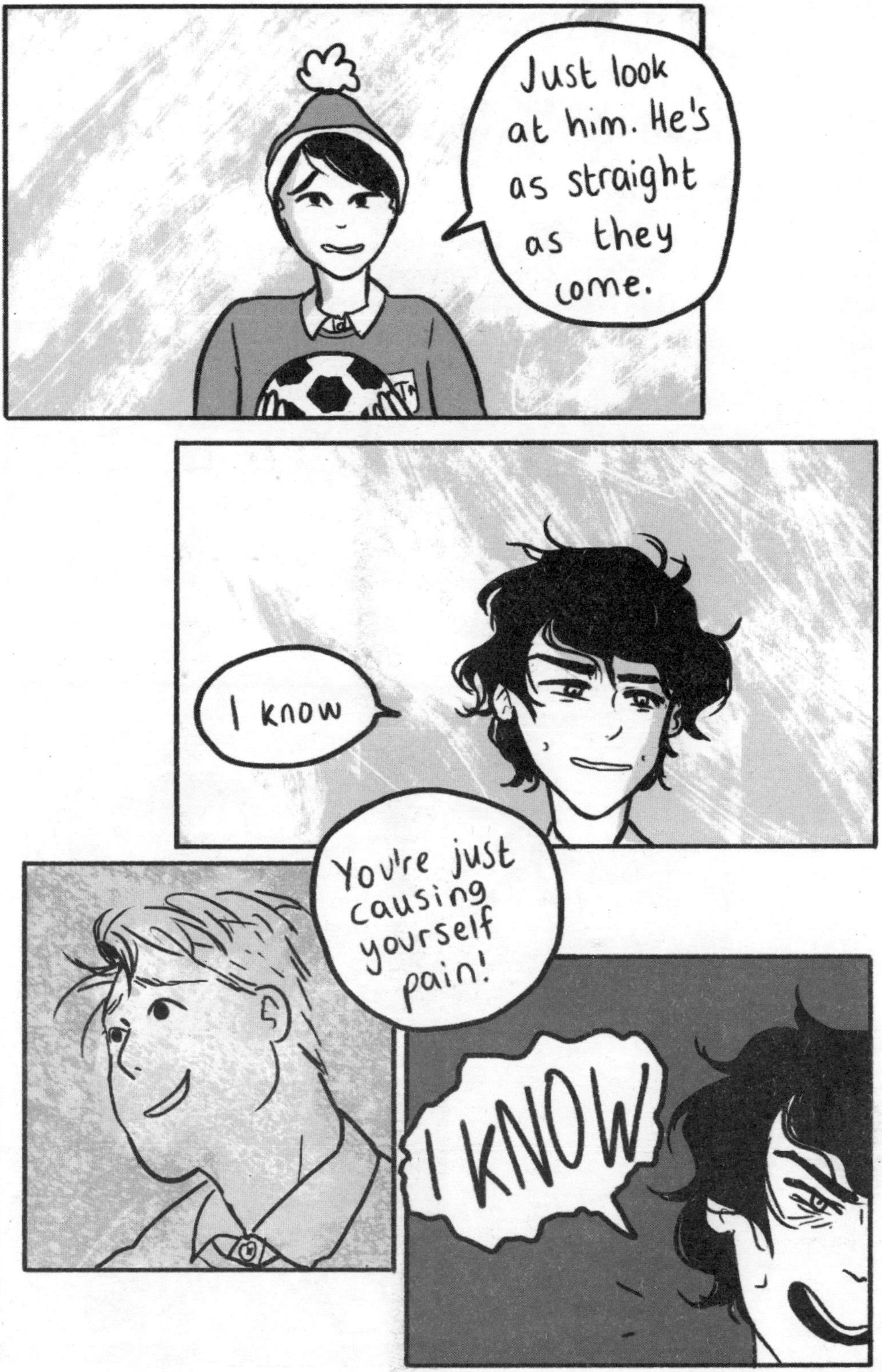
Just look at him. He's as straight as they come.
I know
You're just causing yourself pain!
I KNOW

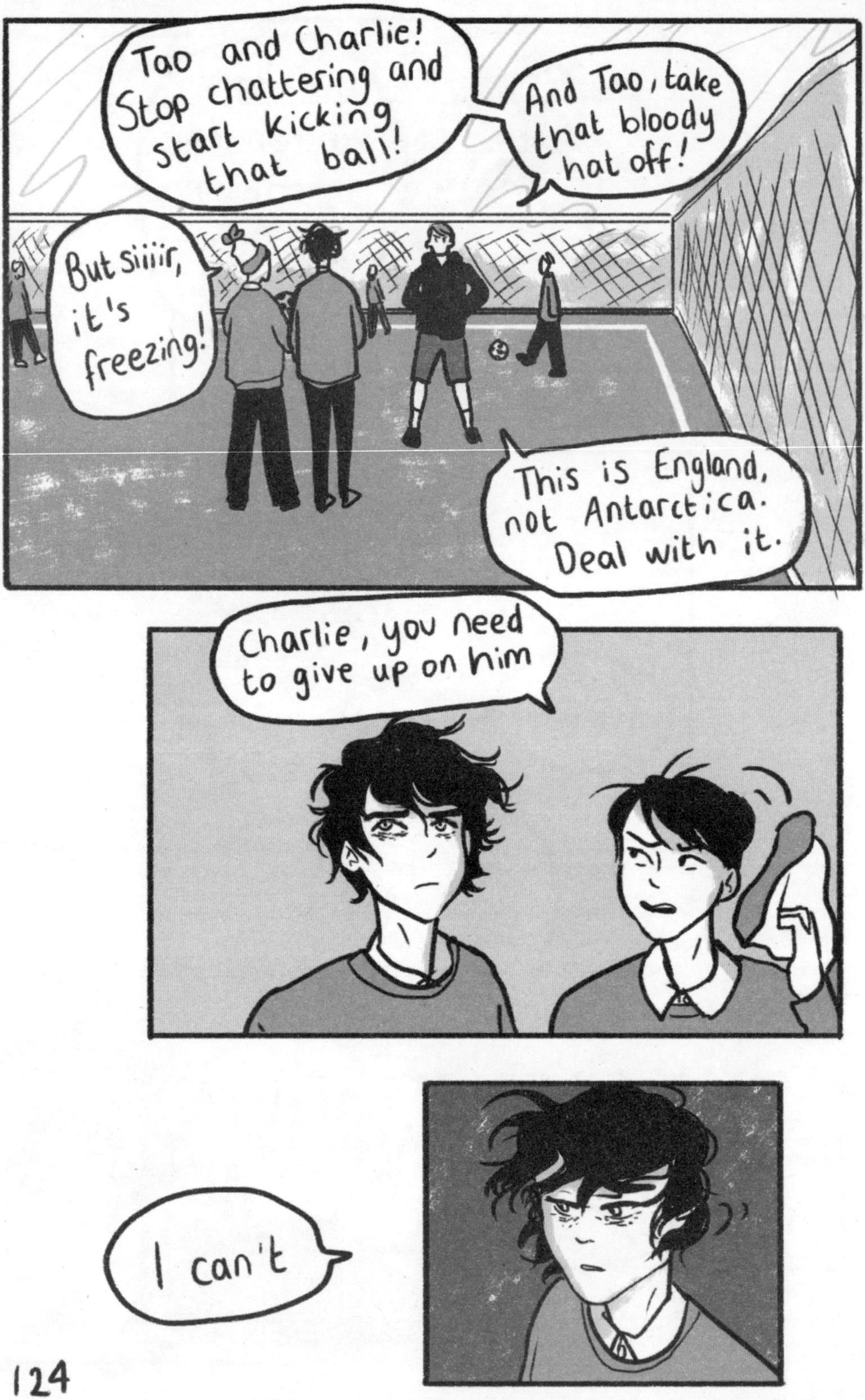
Tao and Charlie! Stop chattering and start kicking that ball!
And Tao, take that bloody hat off!
But siiiir, it's freezing!
This is England, not Antarctica. Deal with it.
Charlie, you need to give up on him
I can't

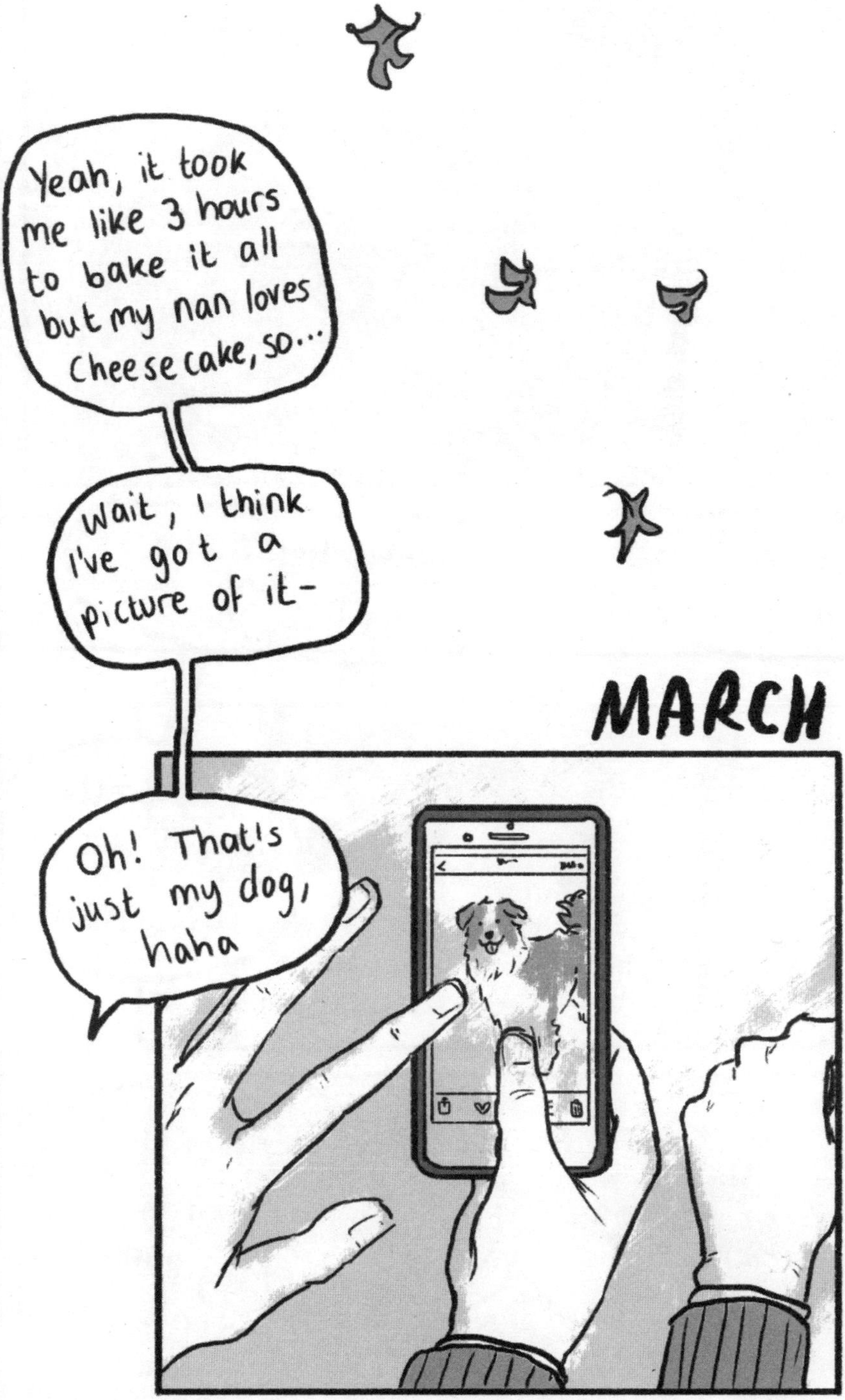
Yeah, it took me like 3 hours to bake it all but my nan loves cheesecake, so...
Wait, I think I've got a picture of it-
MARCH
Oh! That's just my dog, haha

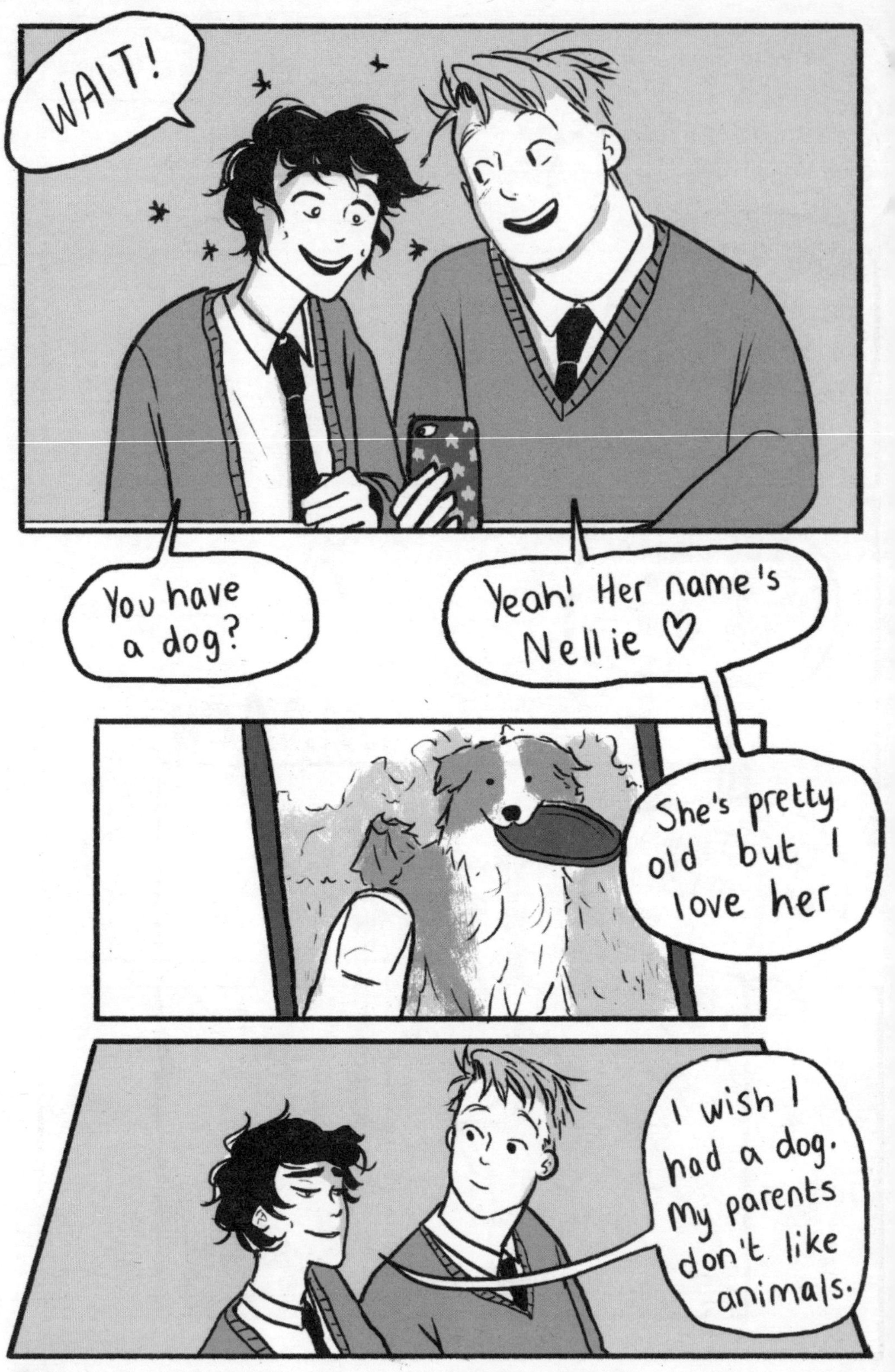
WAIT!
You have a dog?
Yeah! Her name's Nellie ♡
She's pretty old but I love her
I wish I had a dog. My parents don't like animals.

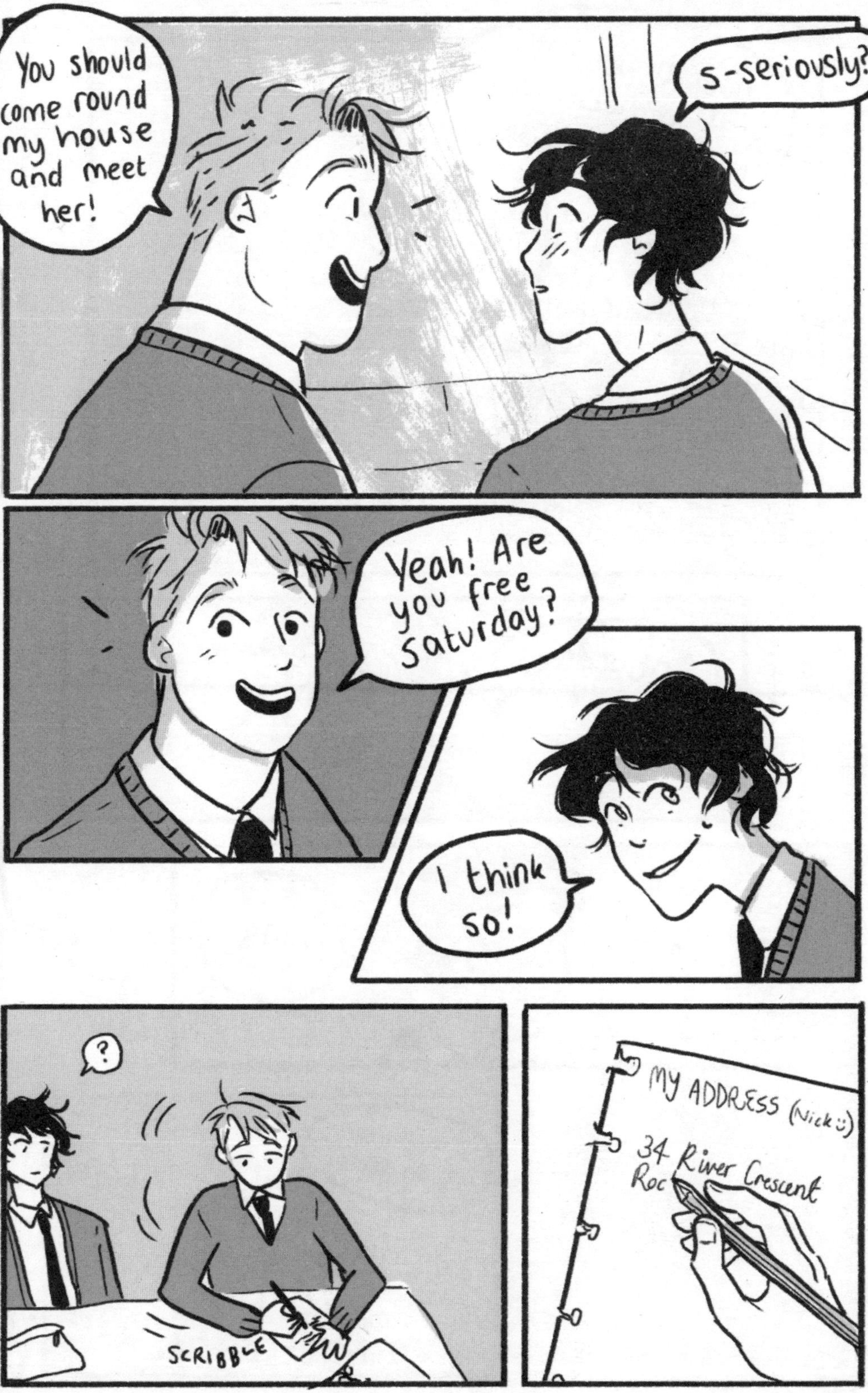
You should come round my house and meet her!
S-seriously?
Yeah! Are you free Saturday?
I think so!
?
SCRIBBLE
MY ADDRESS (Nick :))
34 River Crescent
Roc

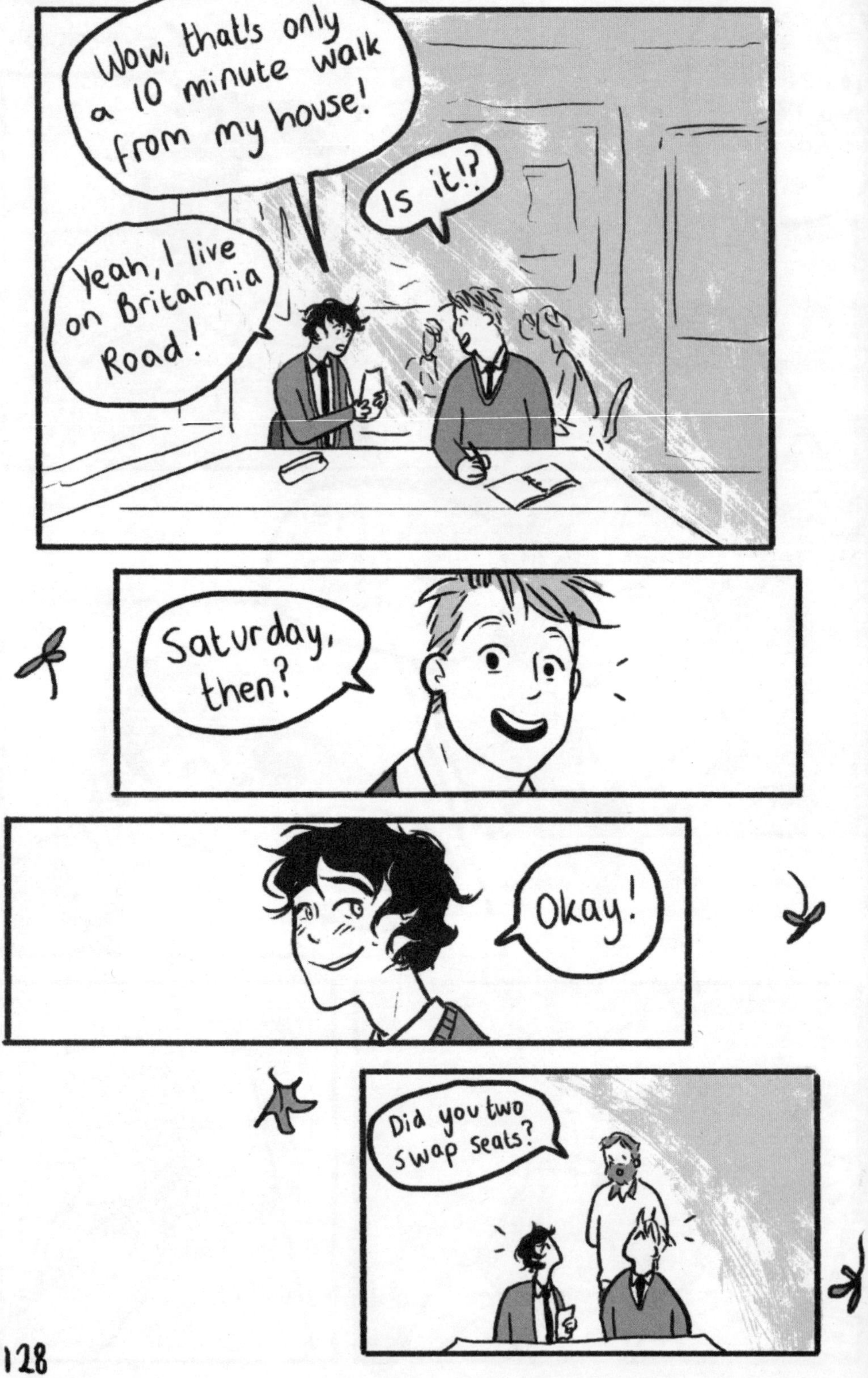
Wow, that's only a 10 minute walk from my house!
Yeah, I live on Britannia Road!
Is it!?
Saturday, then?
Okay!
Did you two swap seats?

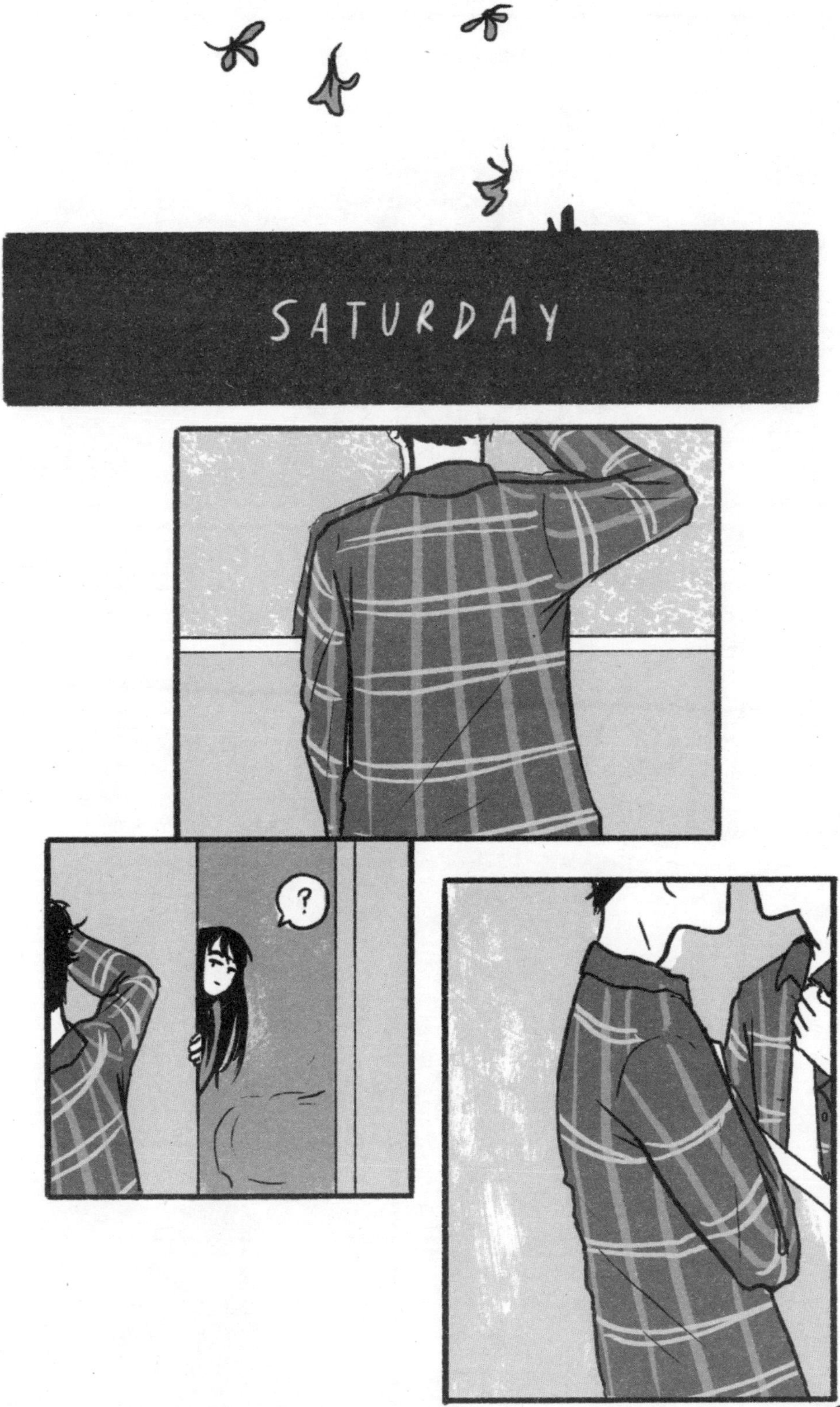
SATURDAY
?

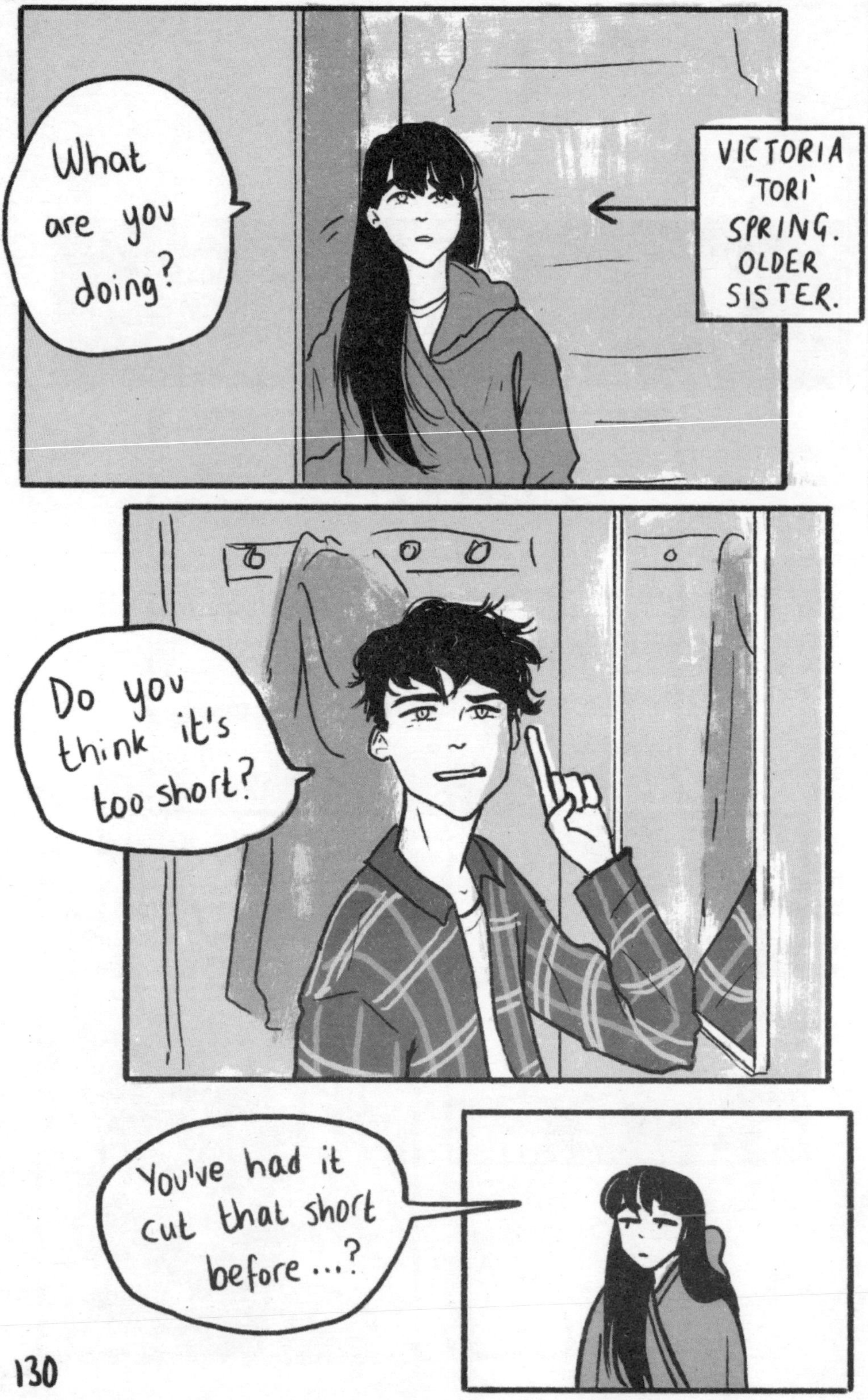
What are you doing?
VICTORIA 'TORI' SPRING. OLDER SISTER.
Do you think it's too short?
You've had it cut that short before ...?

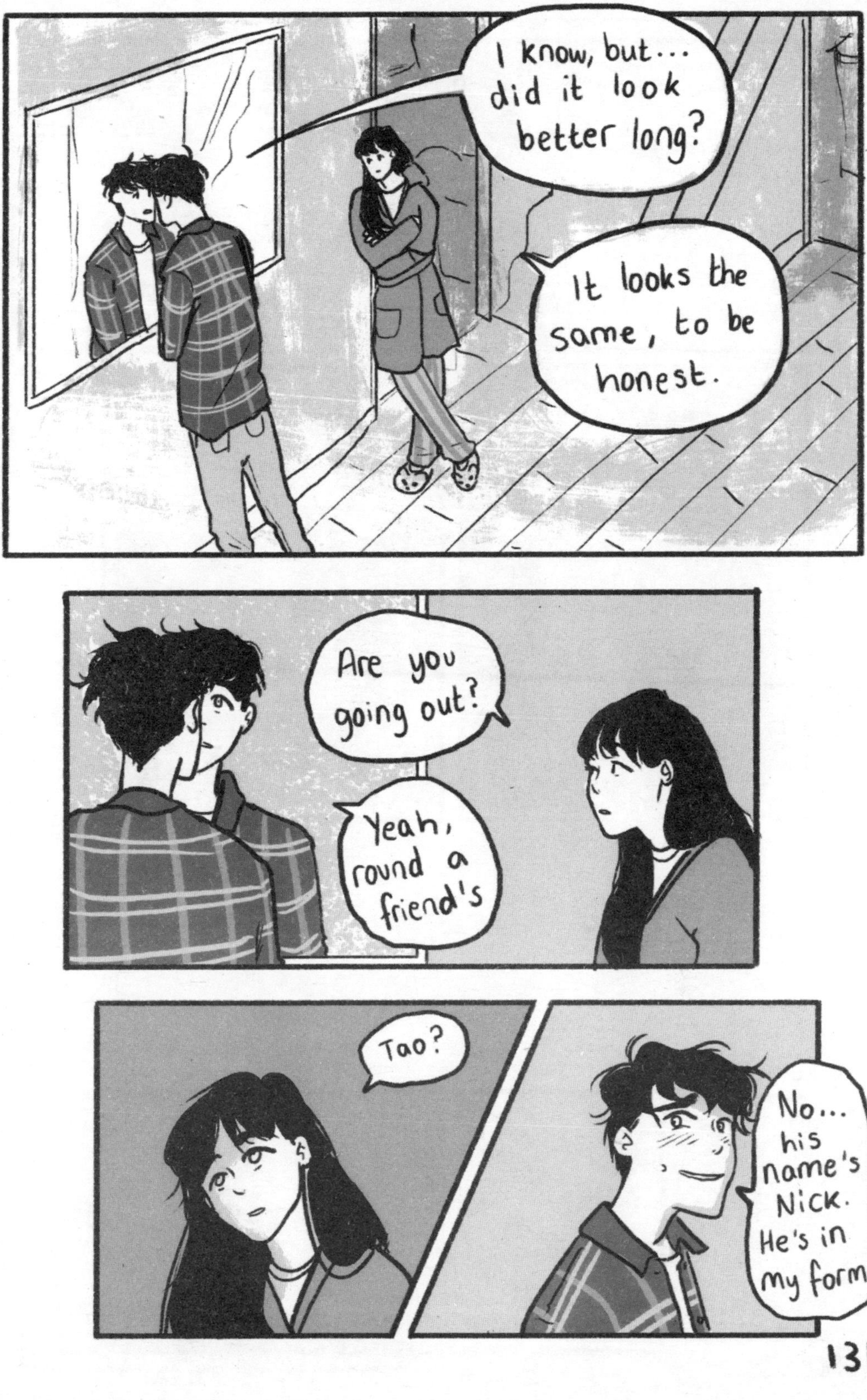
I know, but... did it look better long?
It looks the same, to be honest.
Are you going out?
Yeah, round a friend's
Tao?
No... his name's Nick. He's in my form.

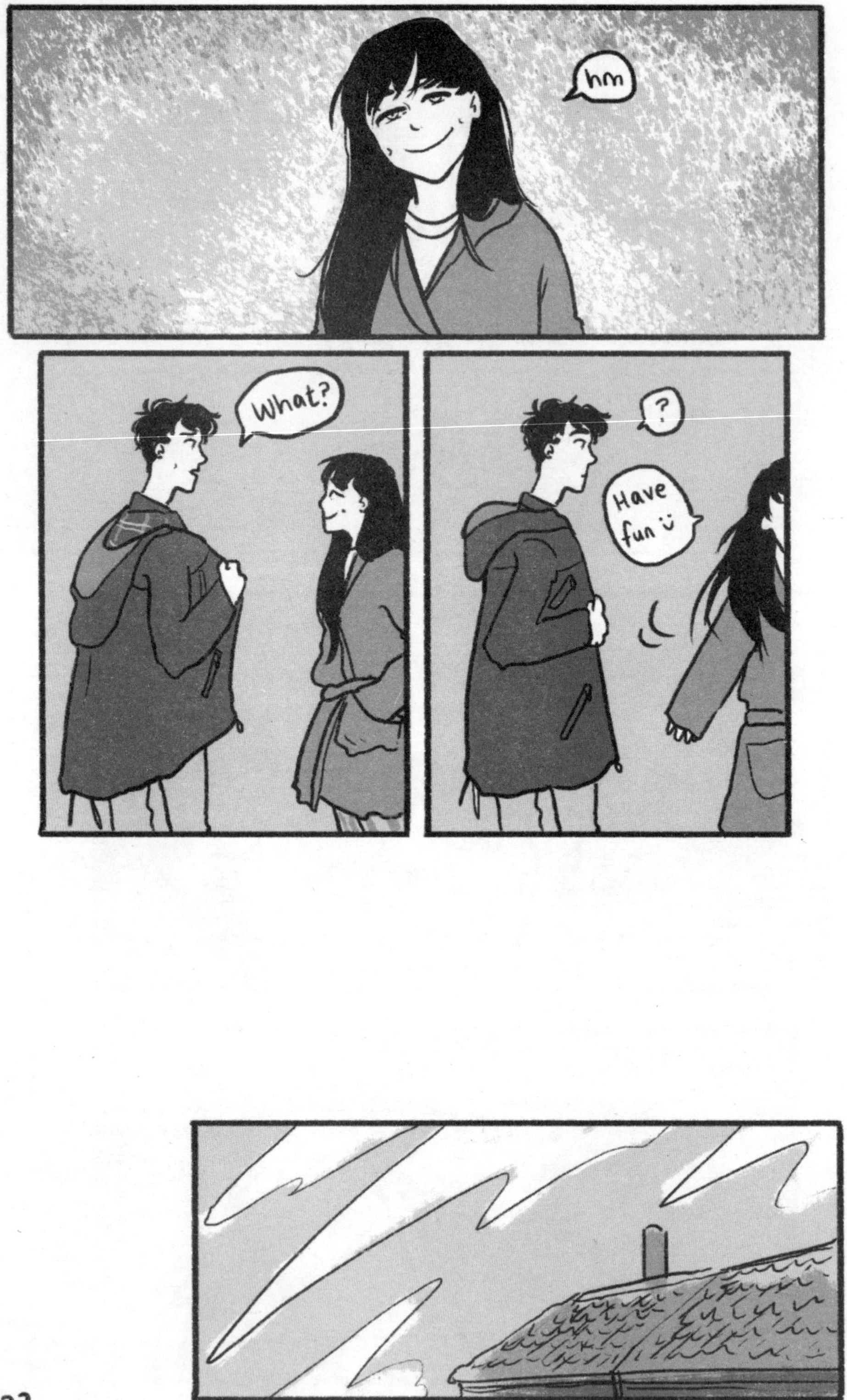
hm
What?
?
Have fun

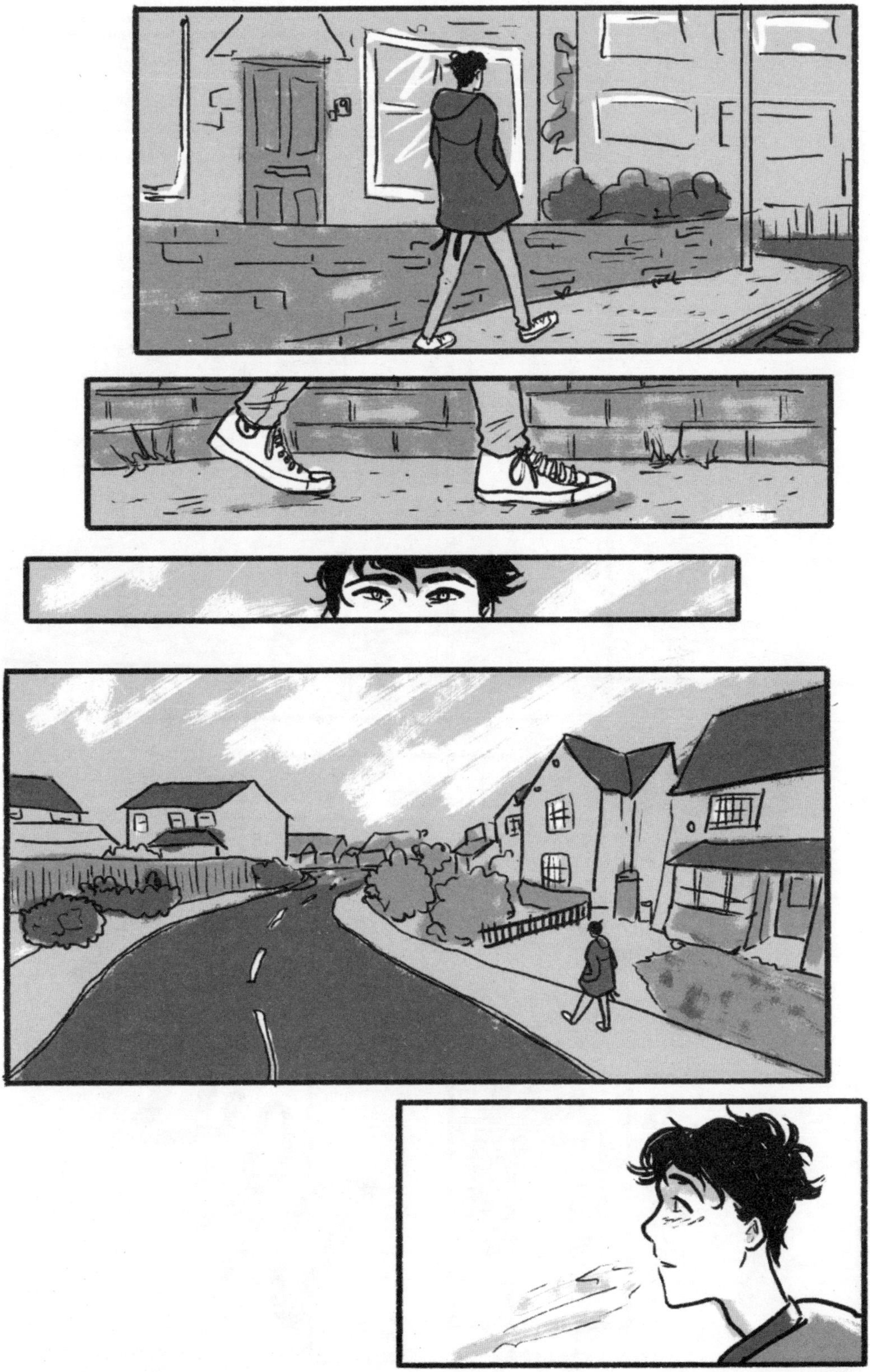

PRESS

DRRRING

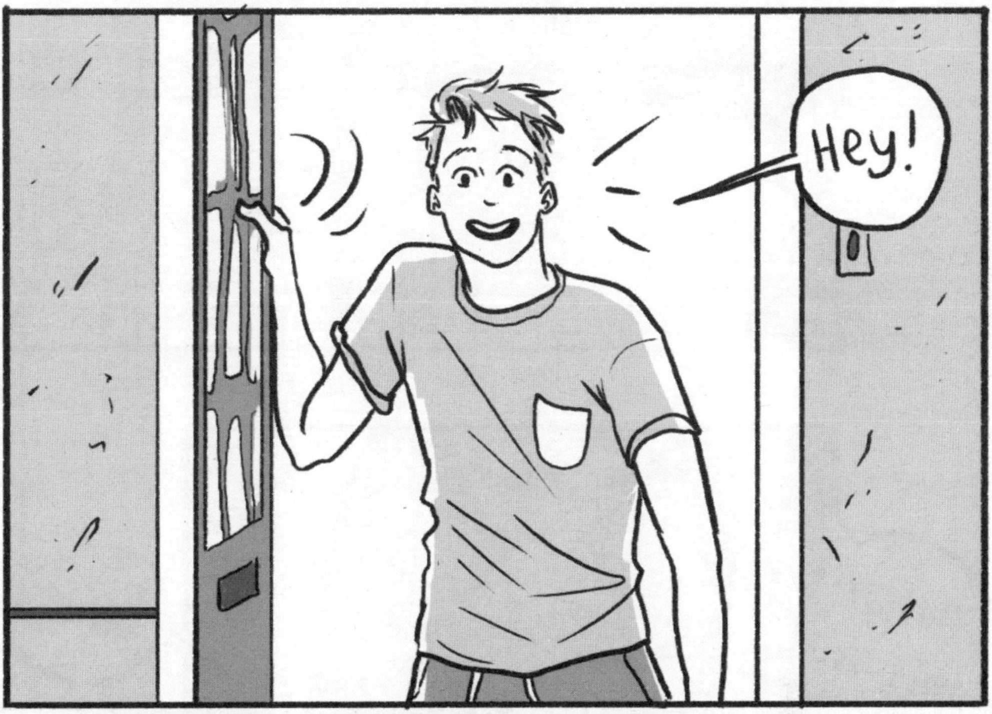
Hey!

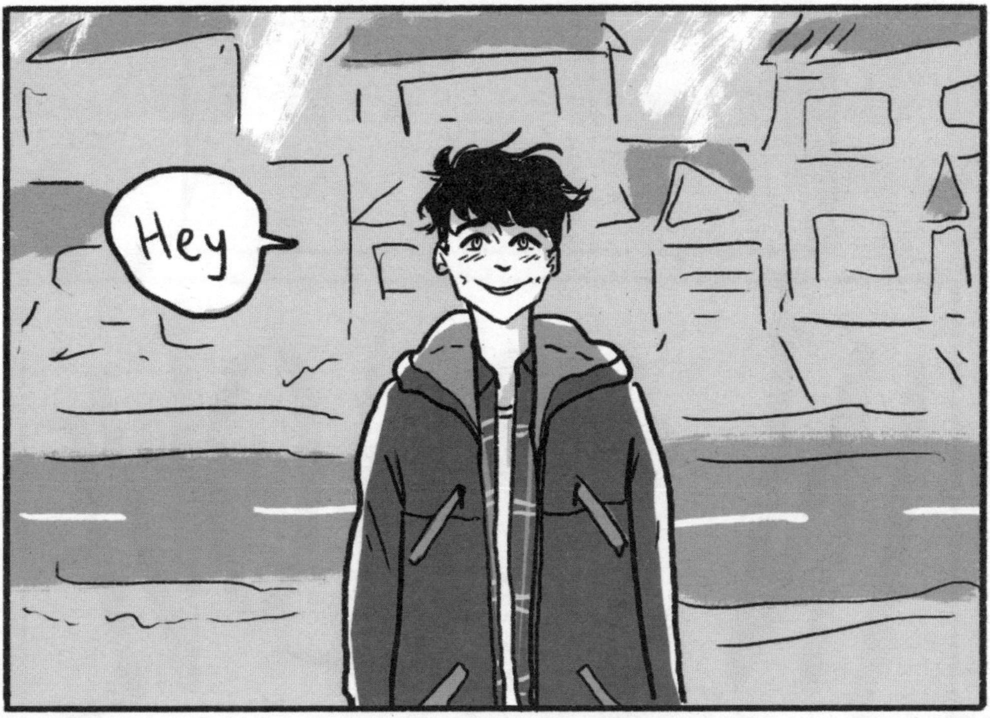
Hey

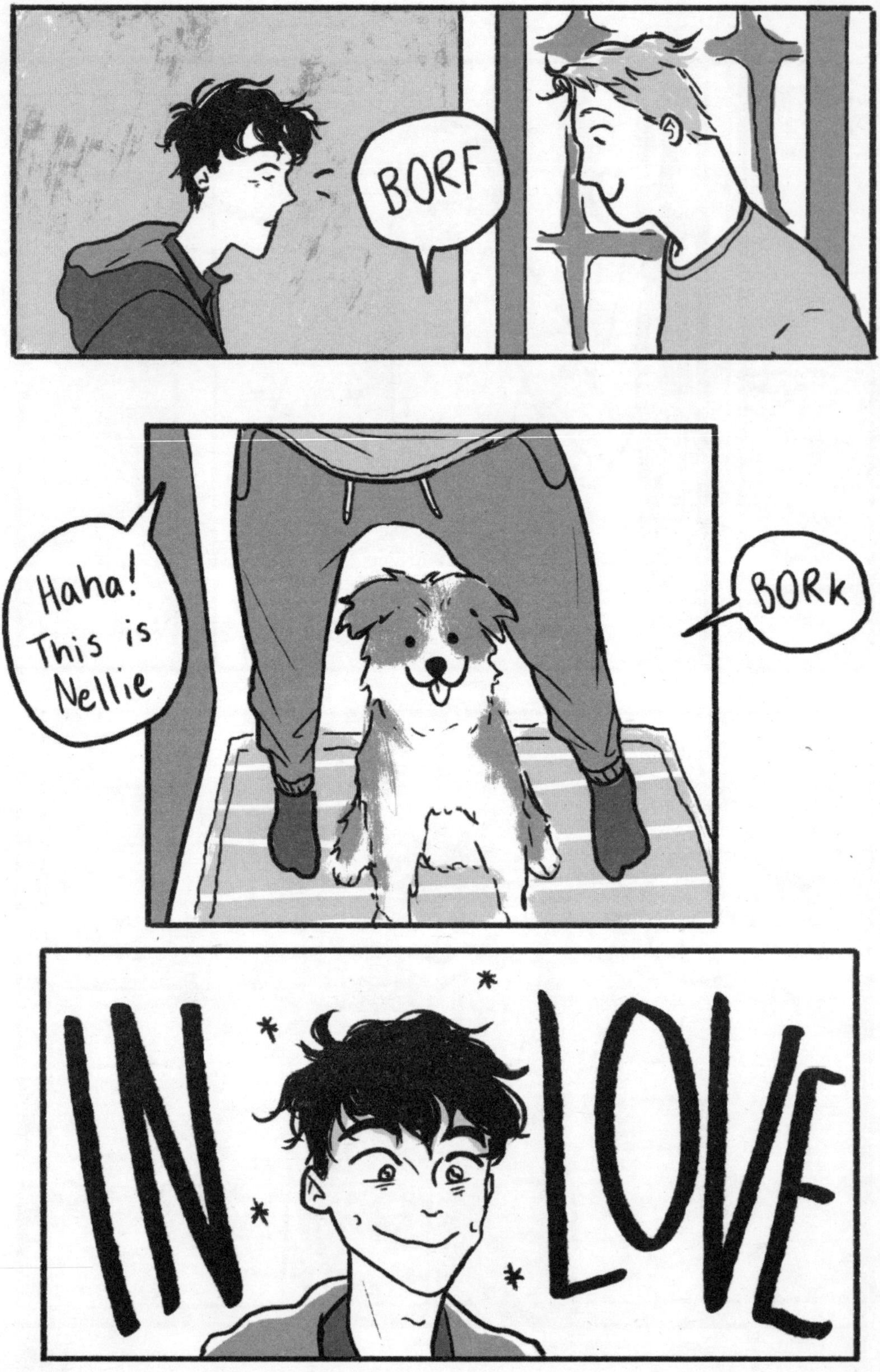
BORF
Haha! This is Nellie
BORK
IN LOVE

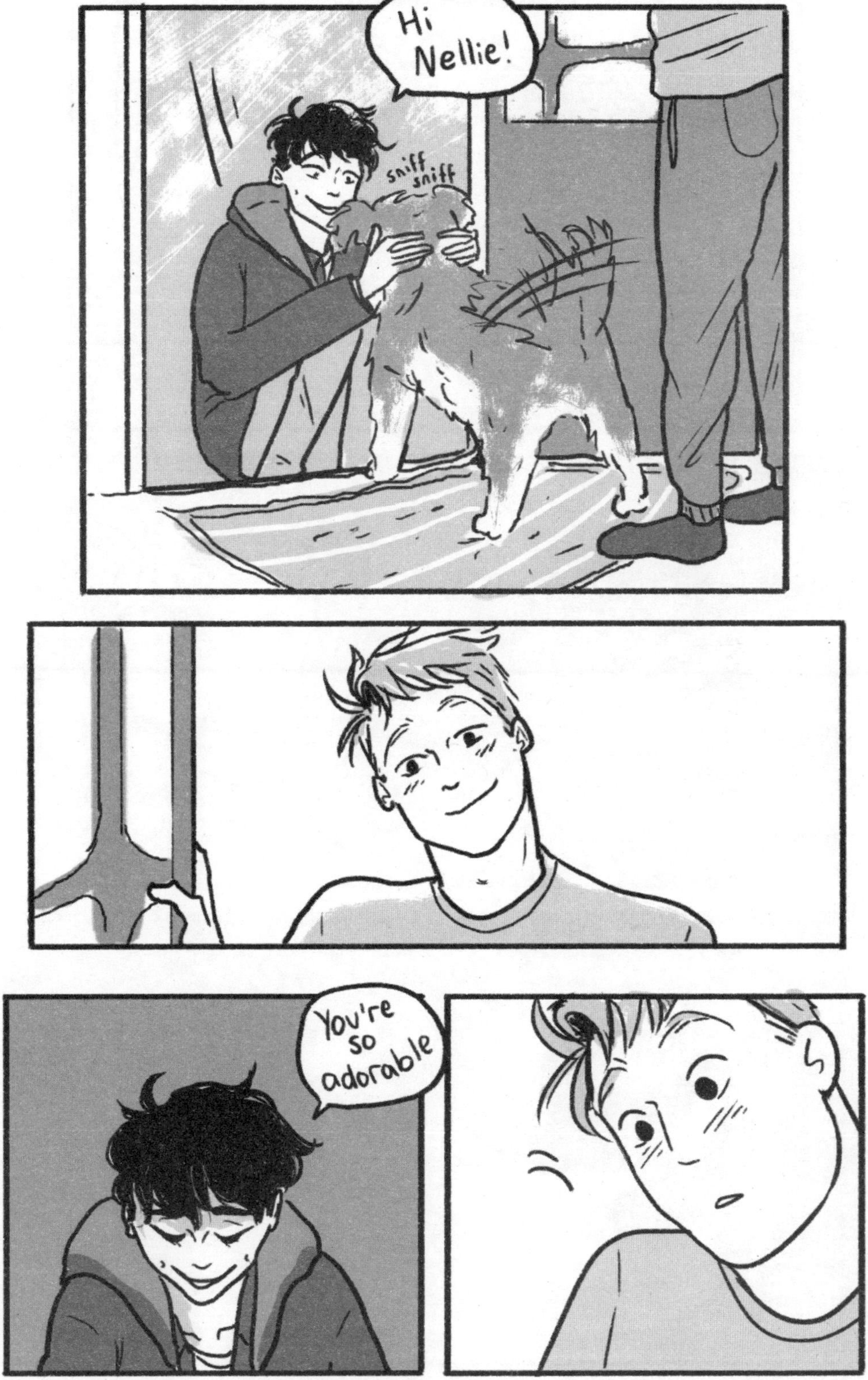
Hi Nellie!
sniff sniff
You're so adorable

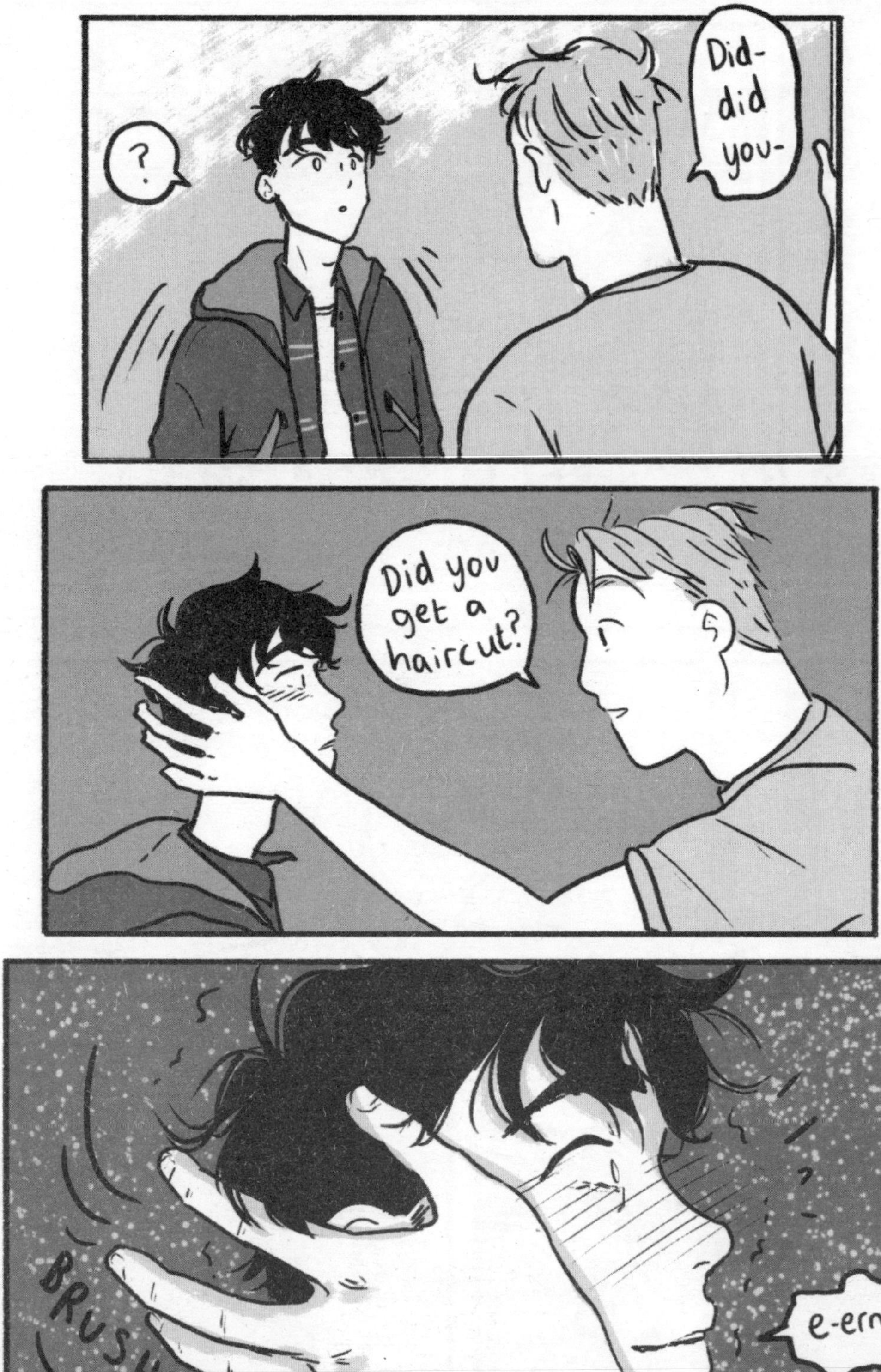
?
Did-
did
you-
Did you
get a
haircut?
BRUSH
e-erm

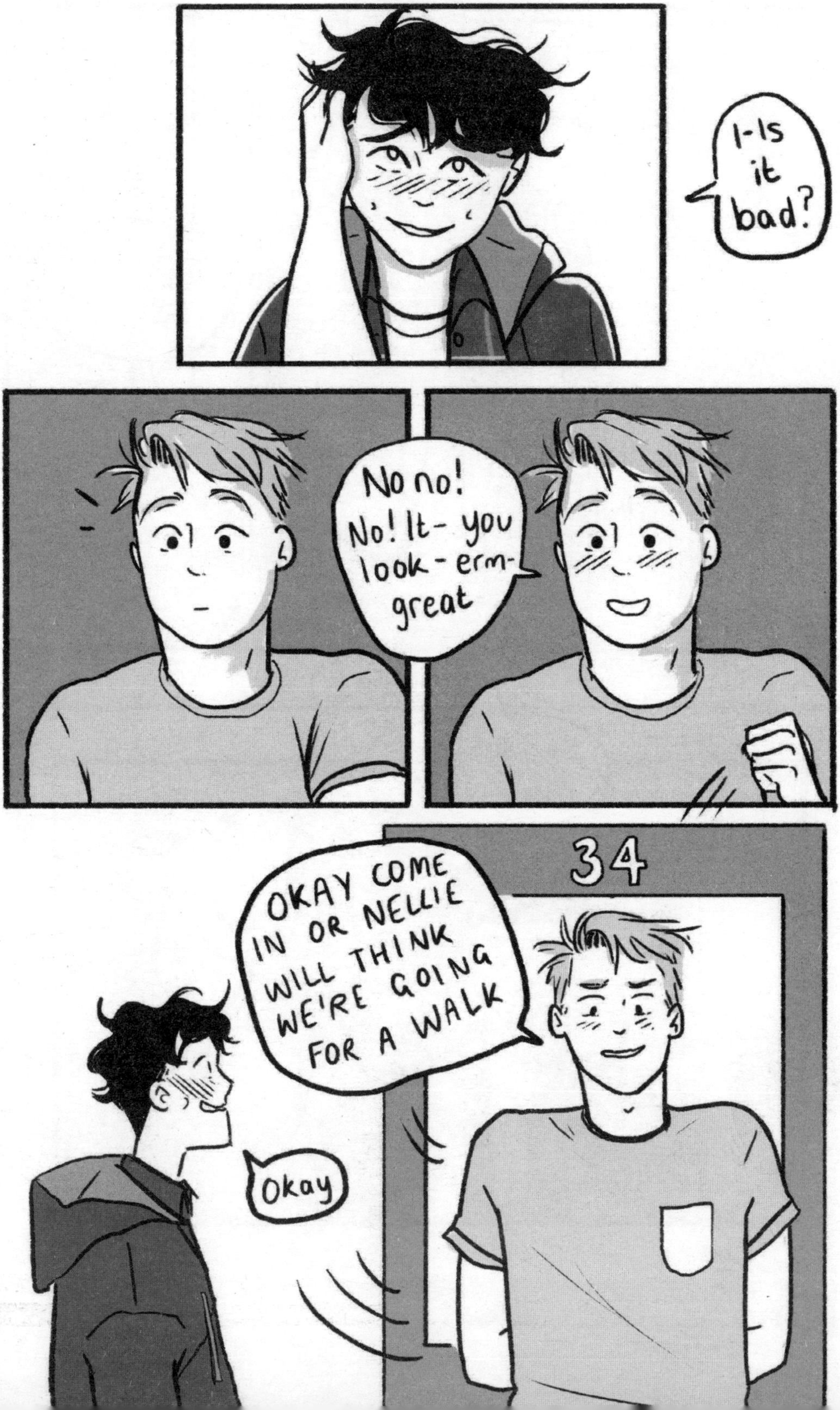
I-Is it bad?
No no! No! It- you look - erm- great
34
OKAY COME IN OR NELLIE WILL THINK WE'RE GOING FOR A WALK
Okay

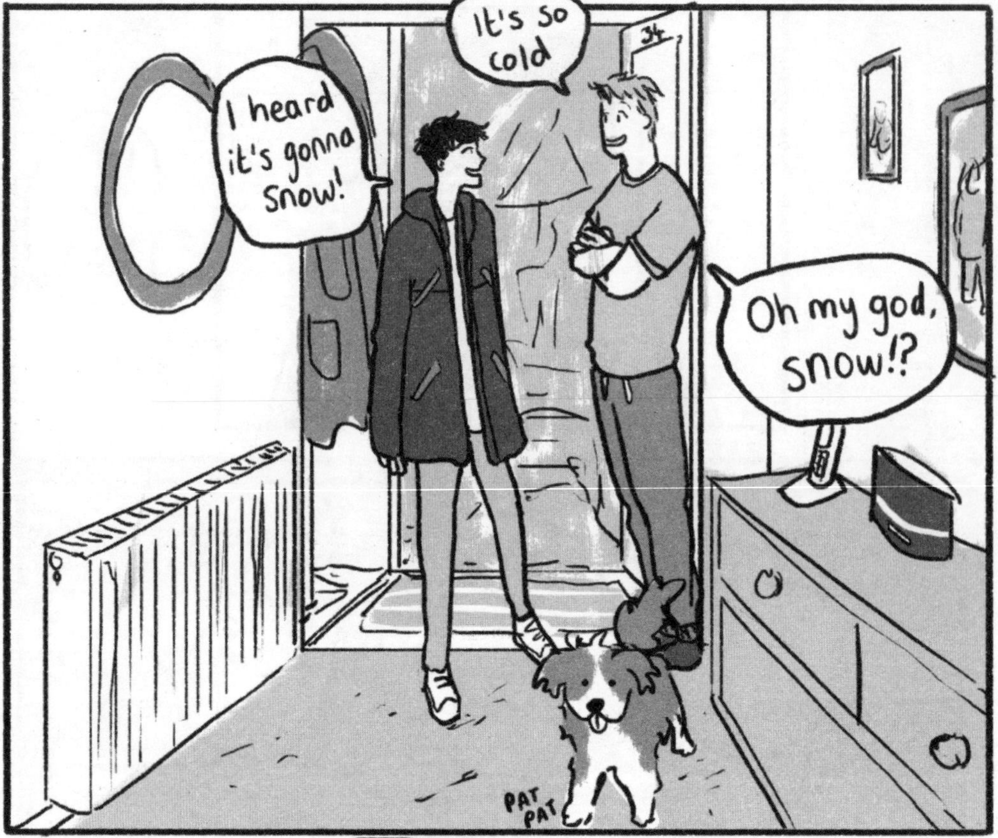
It's so cold
I heard it's gonna snow!
Oh my god, snow!?
PAT PAT

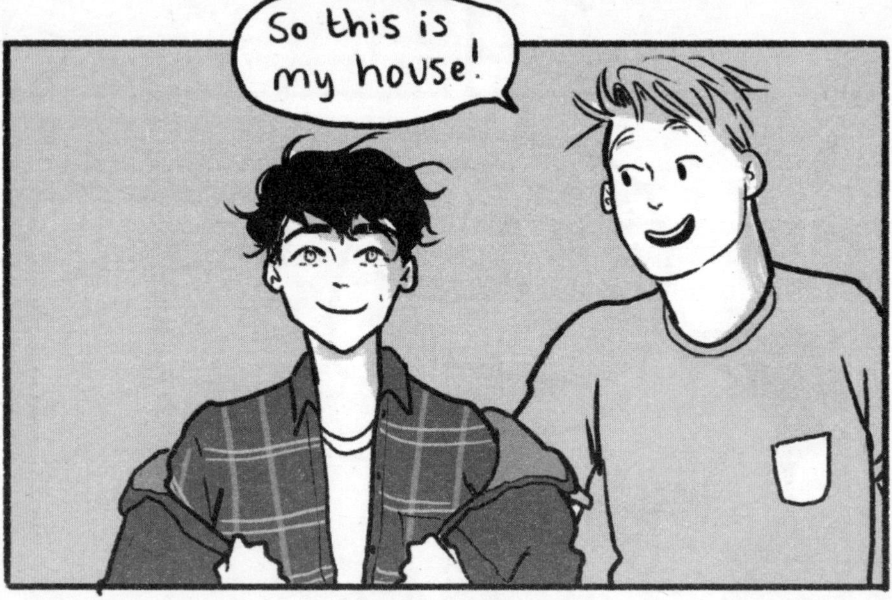
So this is my house!

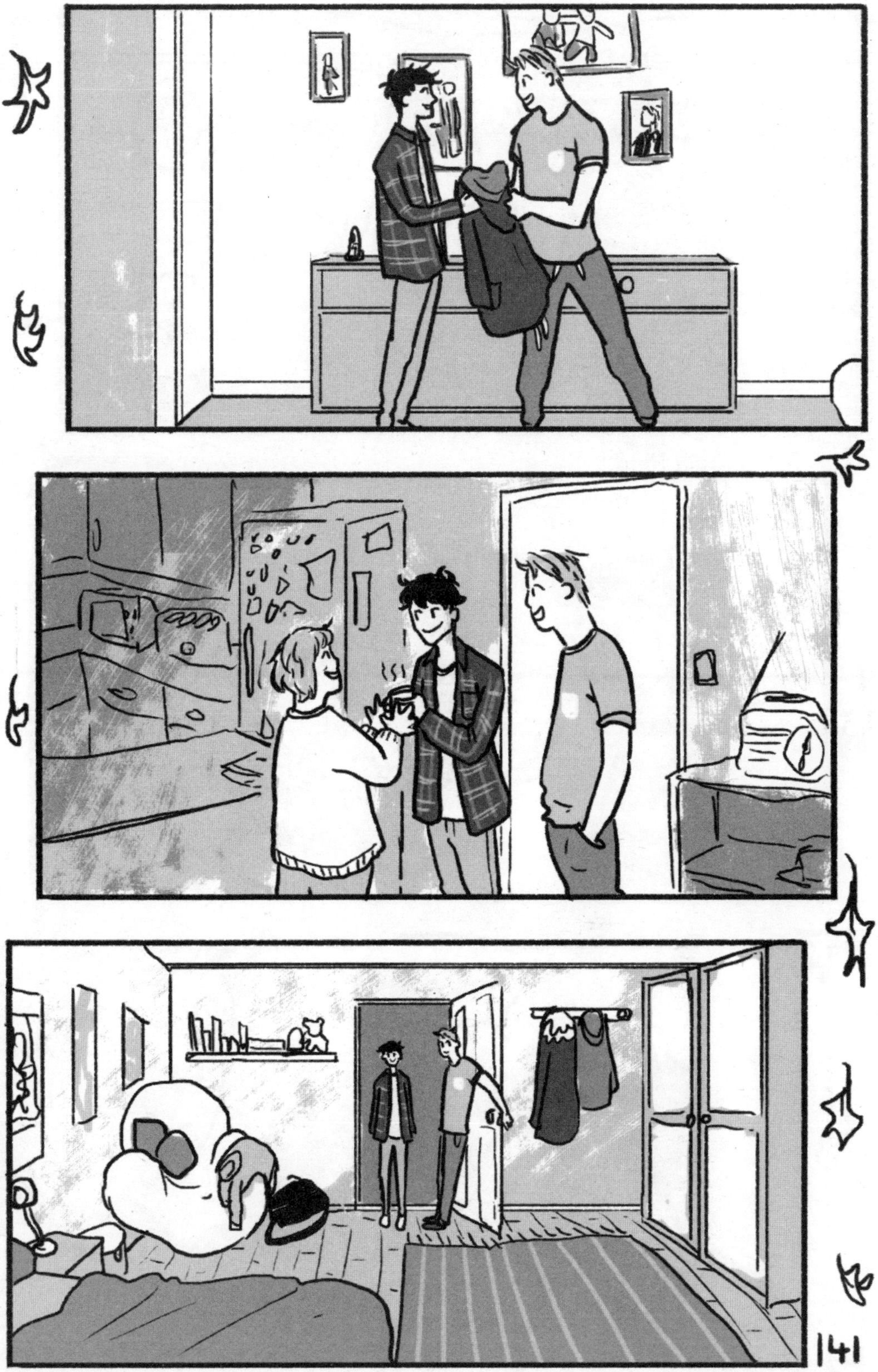

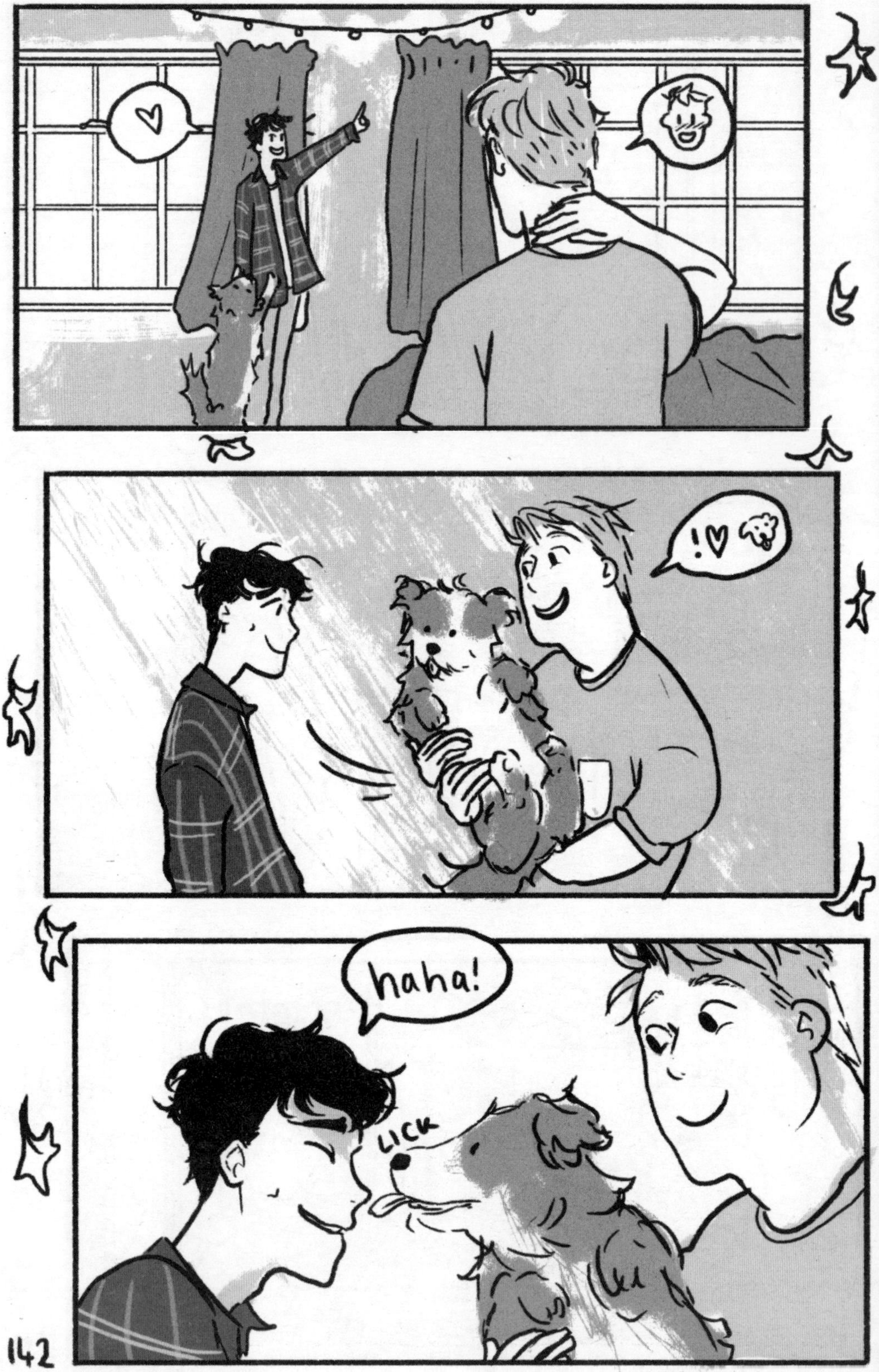
haha!
LICK

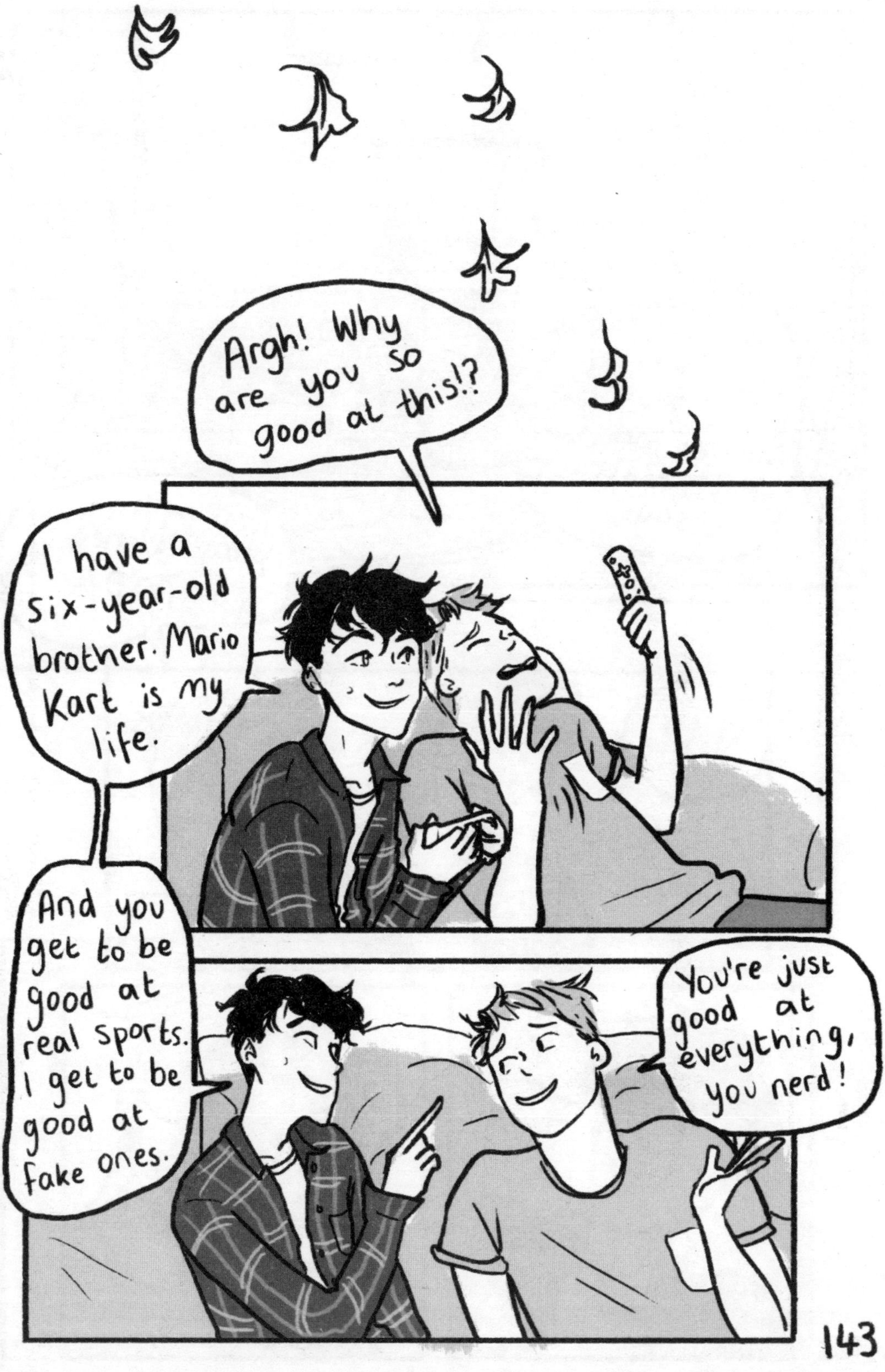
Argh! Why are you so good at this!?
I have a six-year-old brother. Mario Kart is my life.
And you get to be good at real sports. I get to be good at fake ones.
You're just good at everything, you nerd!

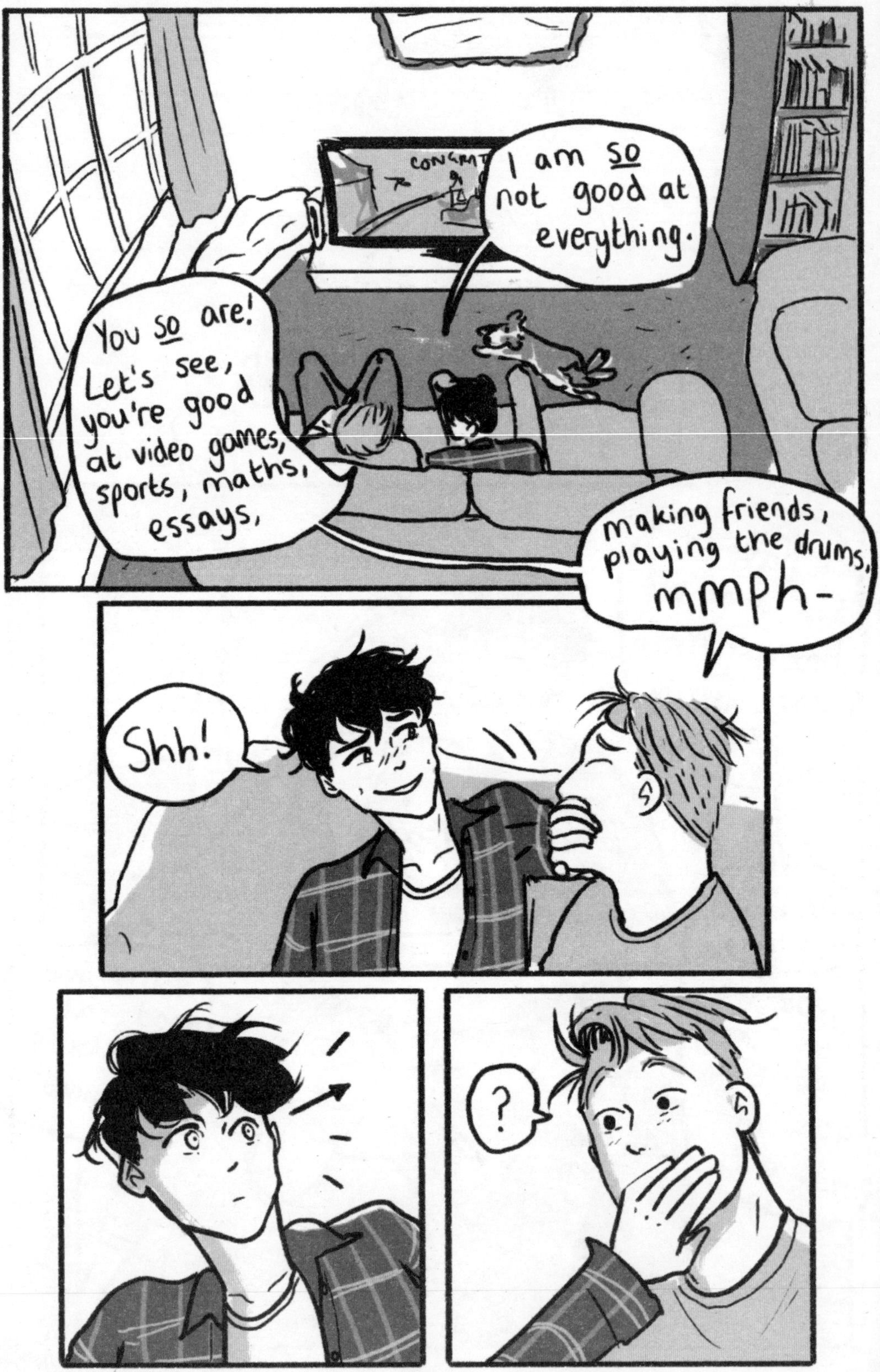

CONGRAT
I am SO not good at everything.
You SO are! Let's see, you're good at video games, sports, maths, essays,
making friends, playing the drums, mmph-
Shh!
?

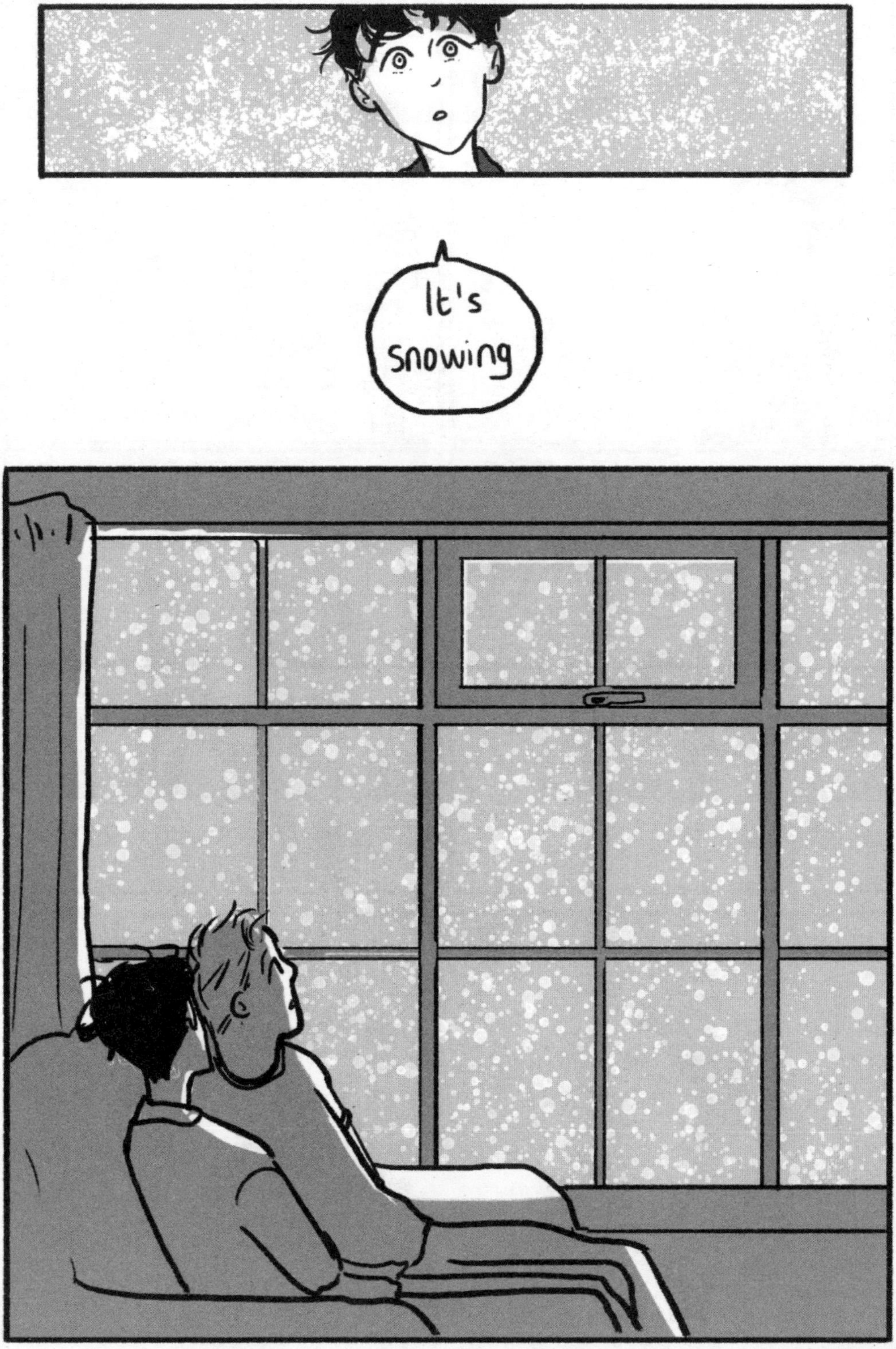
It's snowing

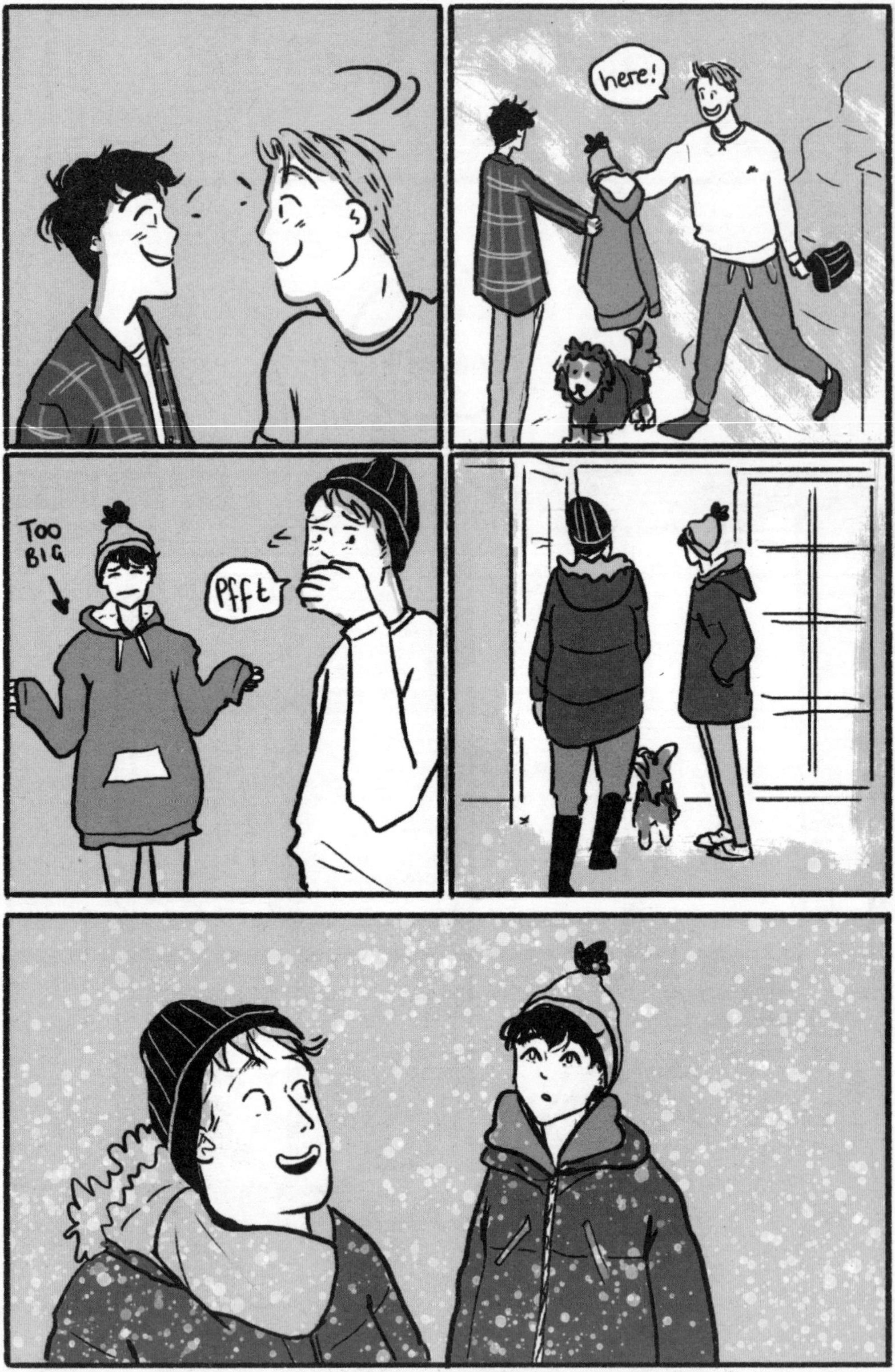
here!
TOO BIG
Pfft

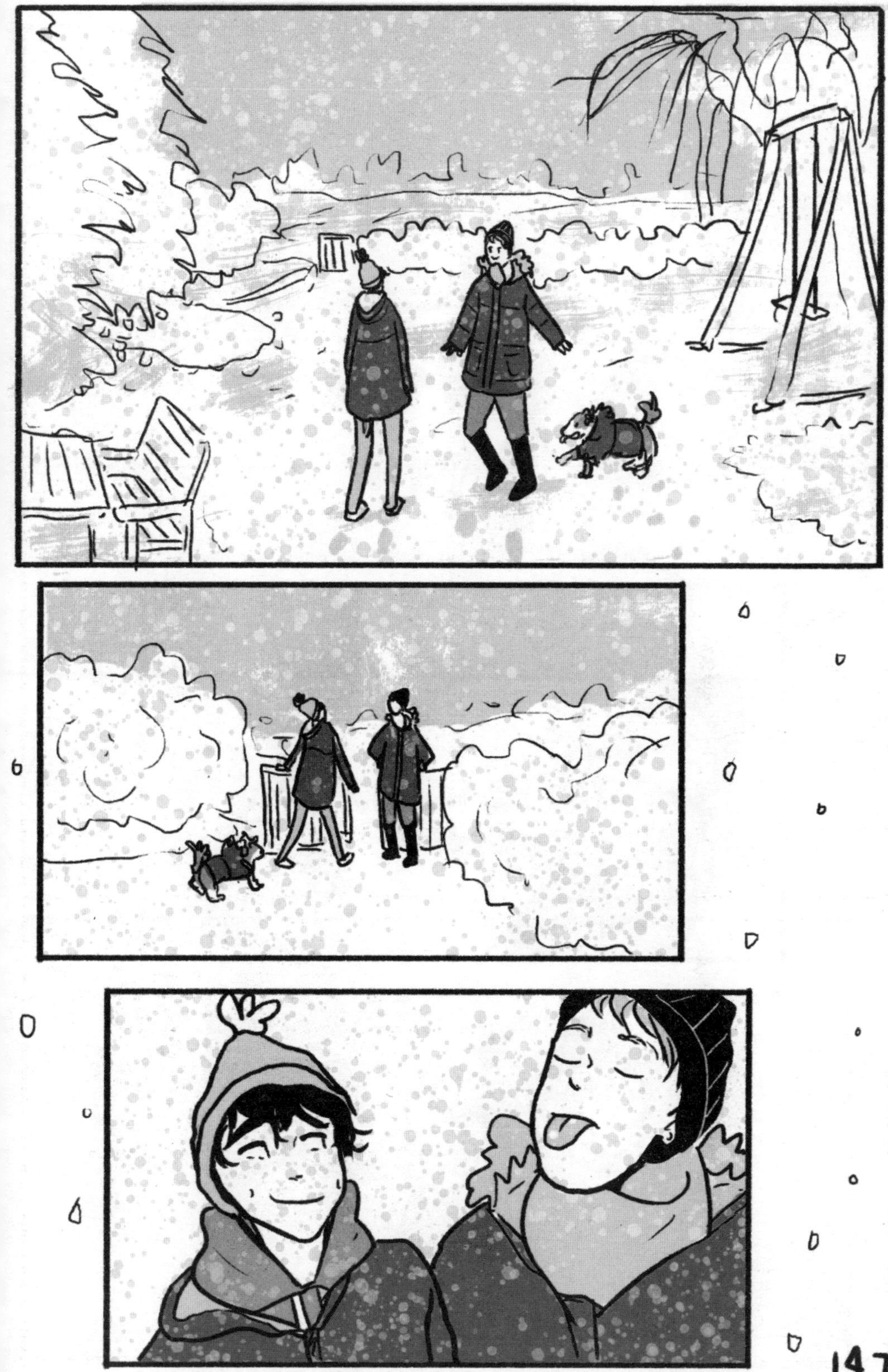

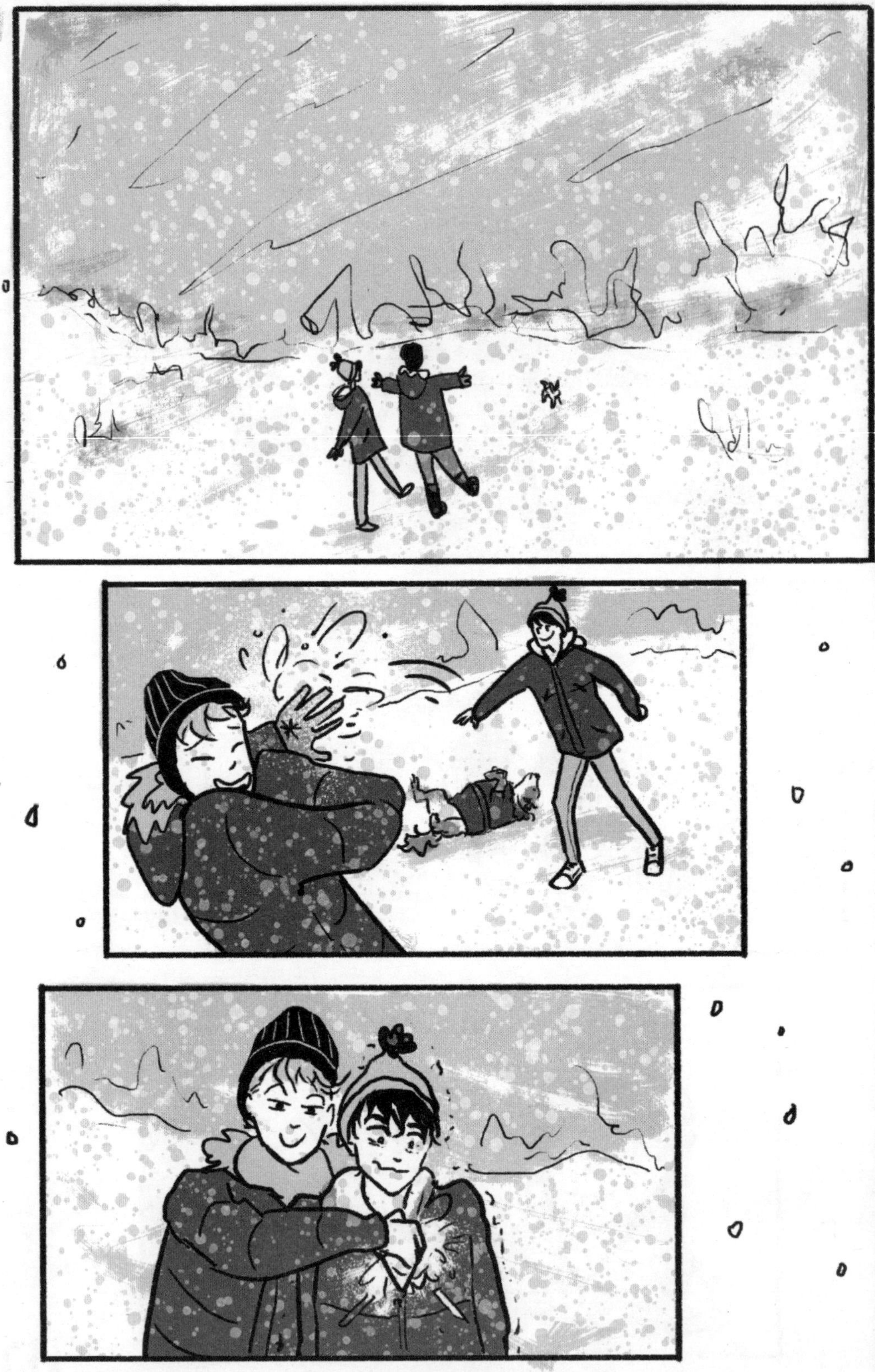

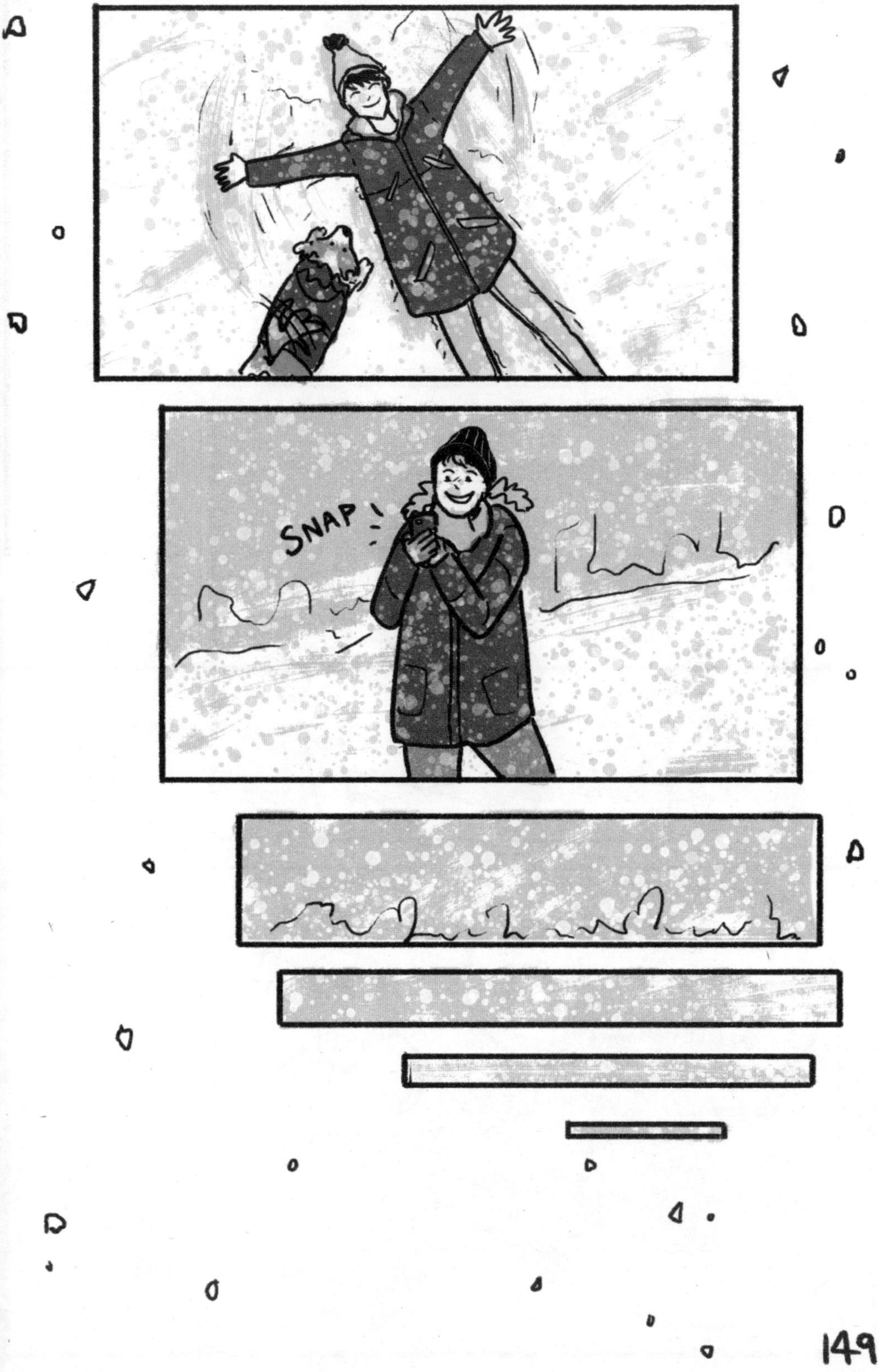
SNAP!

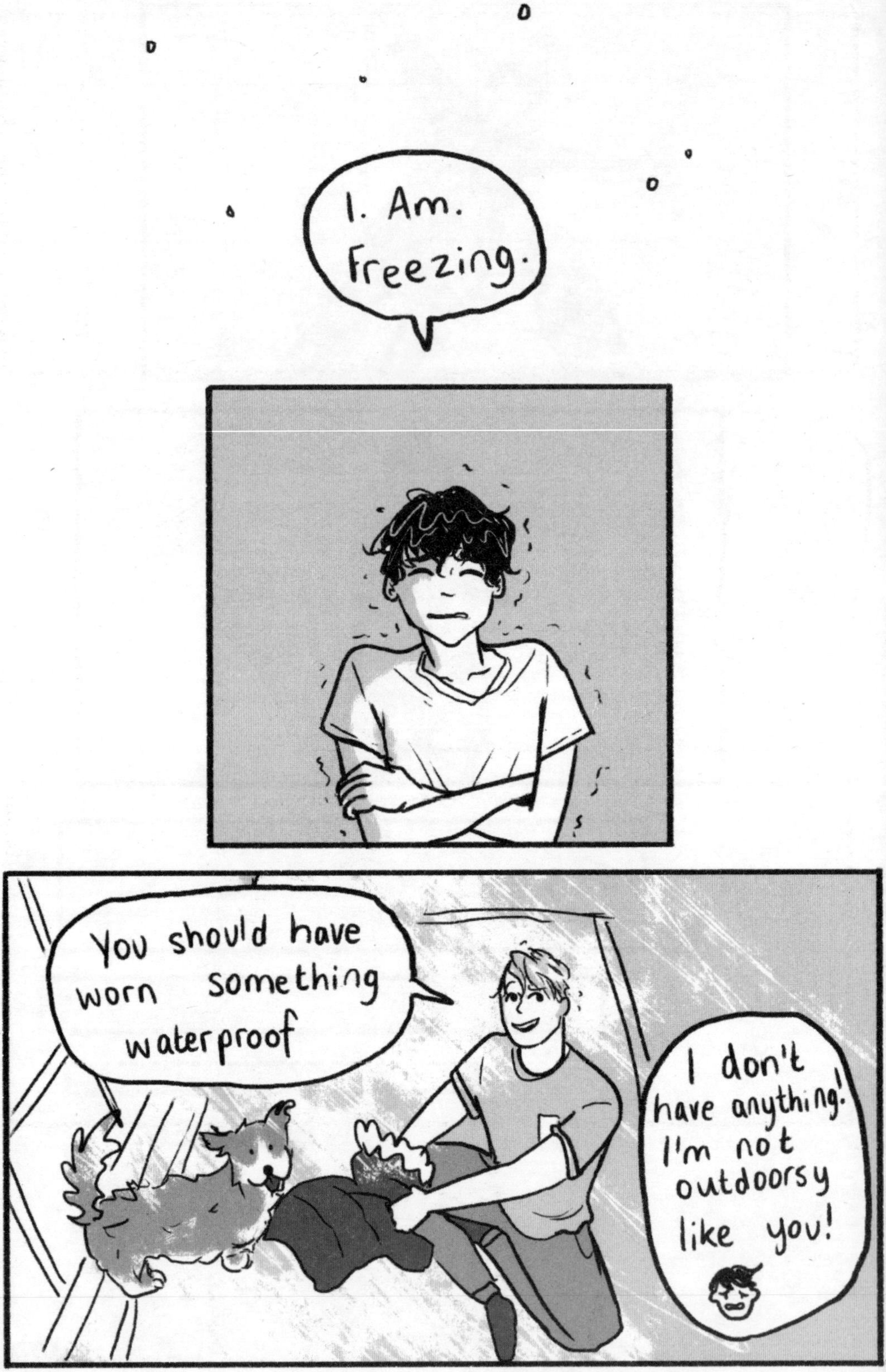
I. Am. Freezing.
You should have worn something waterproof
I don't have anything! I'm not outdoorsy like you!

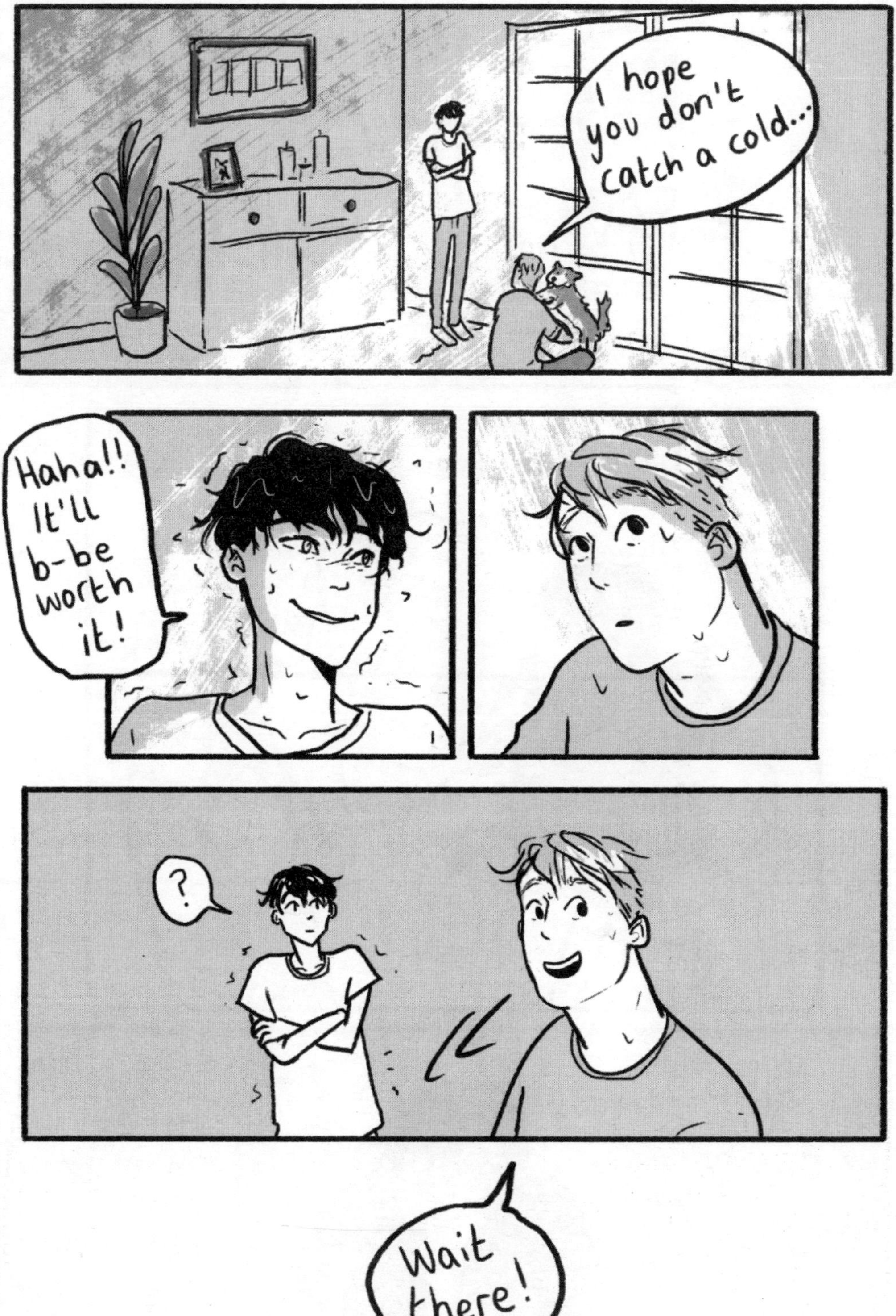
I hope you don't catch a cold...
Haha!! It'll b-be worth it!
?
Wait there!

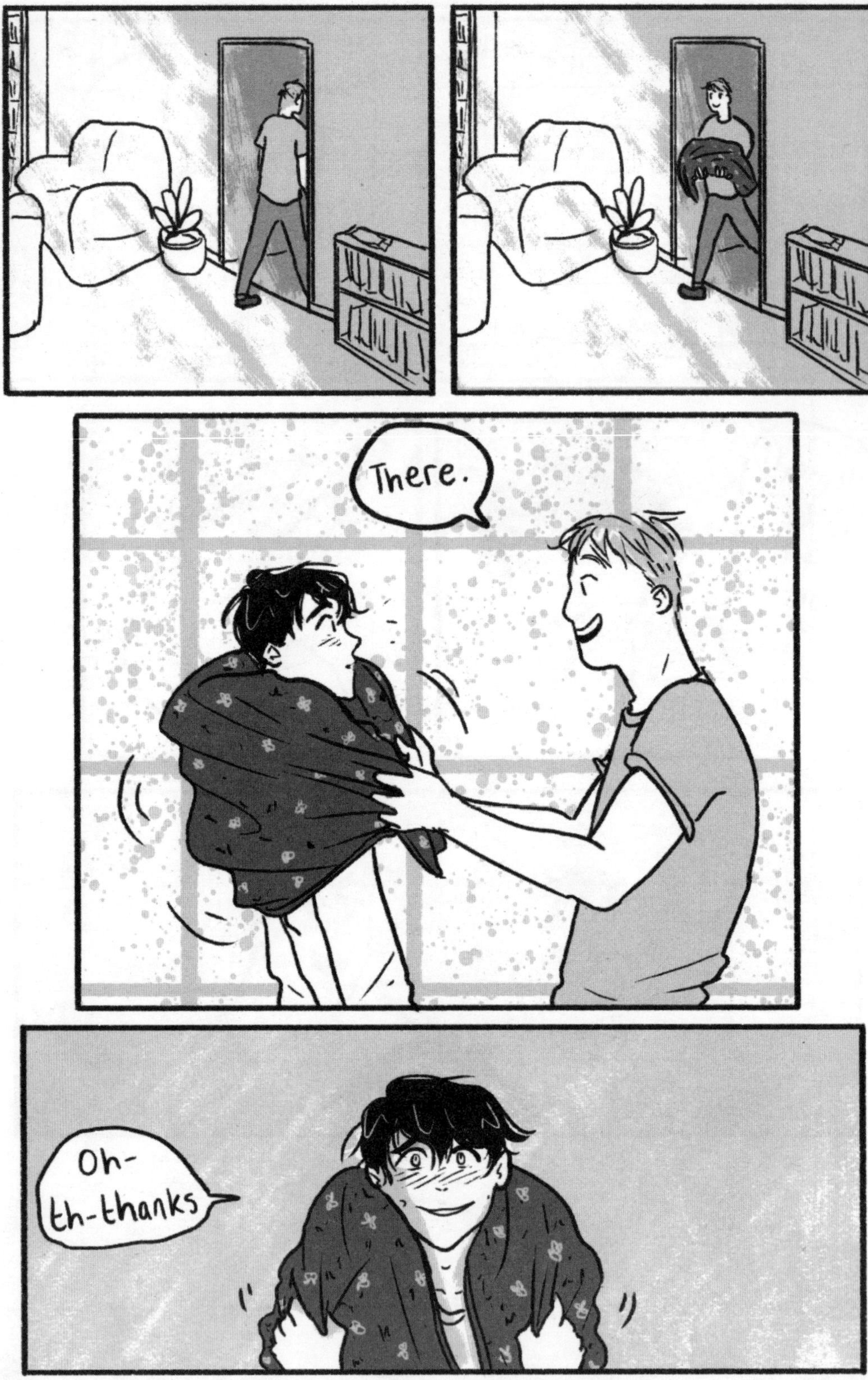
There.
Oh-
th-thanks

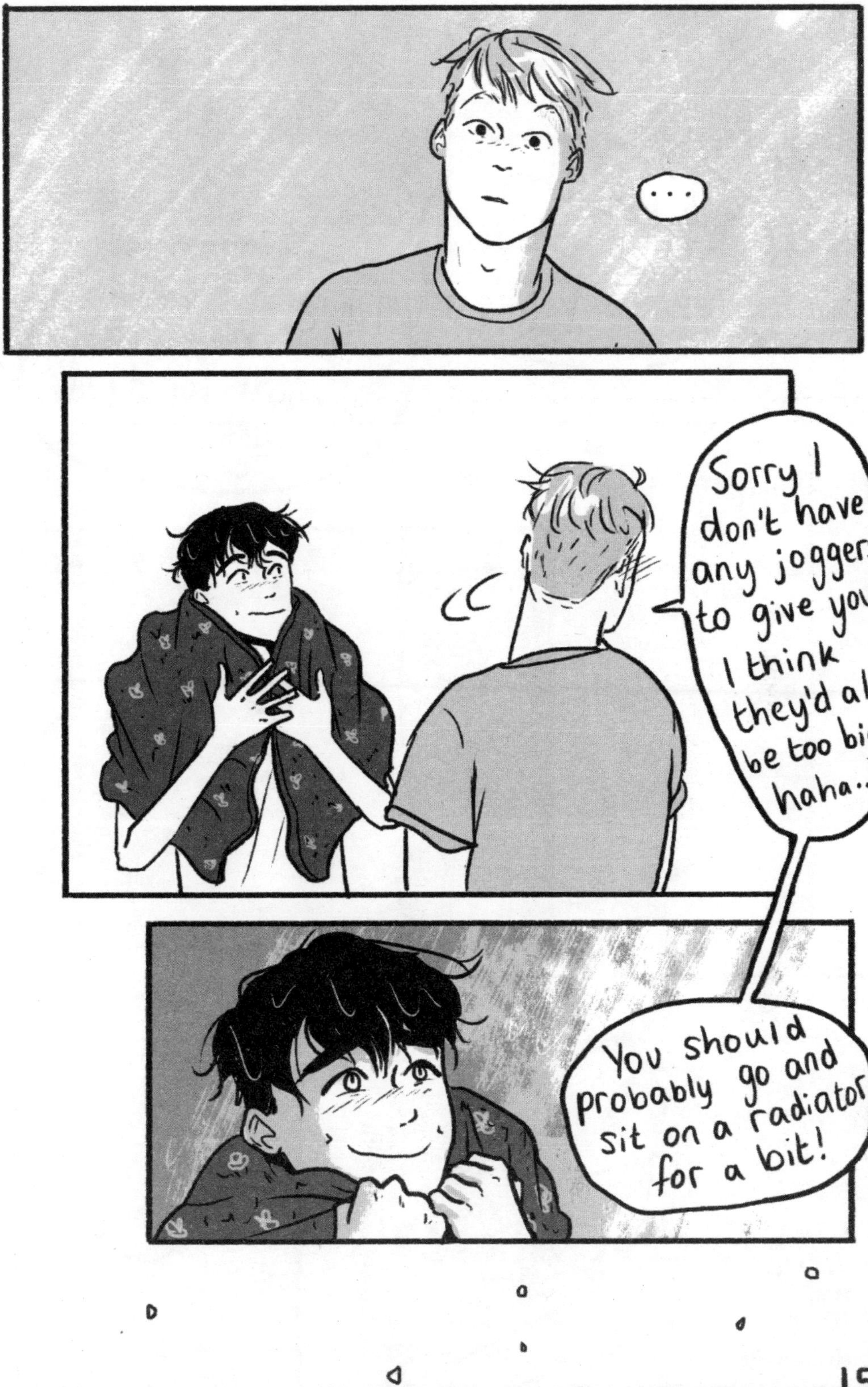
...
Sorry I don't have any joggers to give you, I think they'd all be too big haha...
You should probably go and sit on a radiator for a bit!

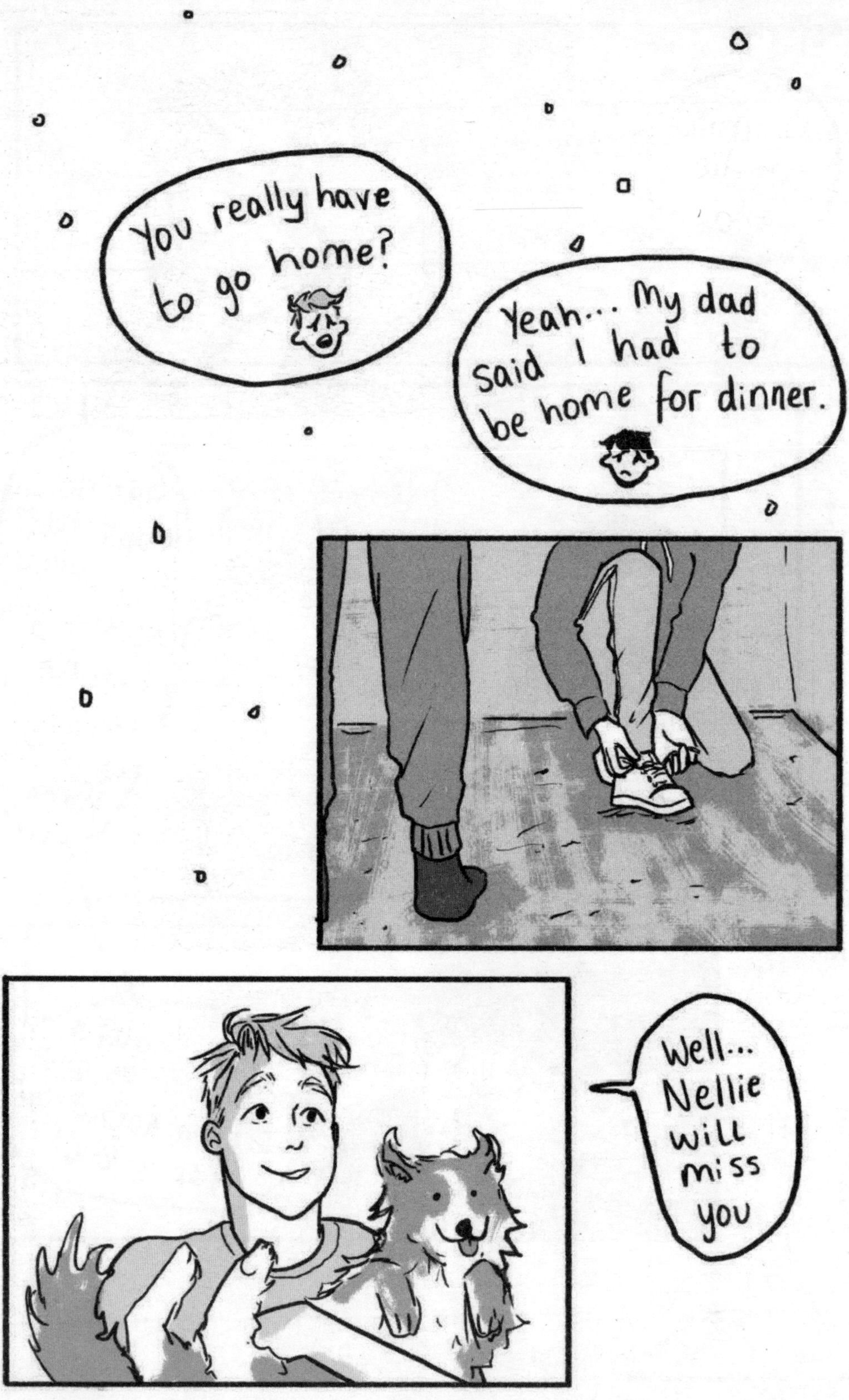
You really have to go home?
Yeah... My dad said I had to be home for dinner.
Well... Nellie will miss you

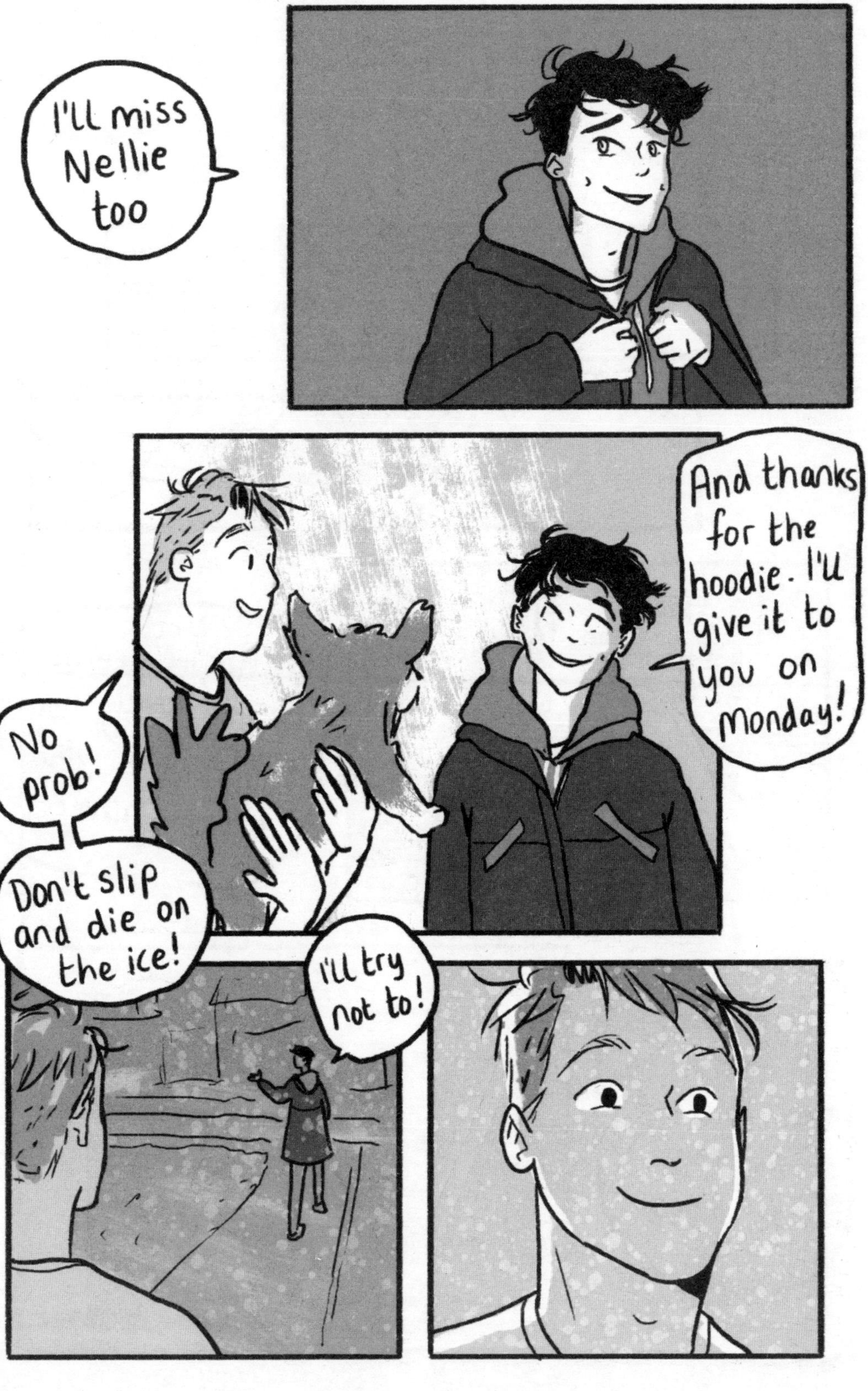
I'll miss Nellie too
And thanks for the hoodie. I'll give it to you on Monday!
No prob!
Don't slip and die on the ice!
I'll try not to!

CLICK

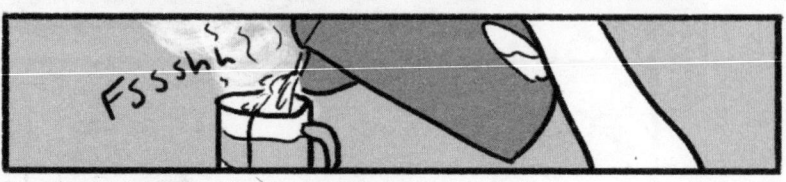

FSSShh

?

Charlie seems like a lovely boy. When did you meet him?

A couple of months ago. He's in my form group.

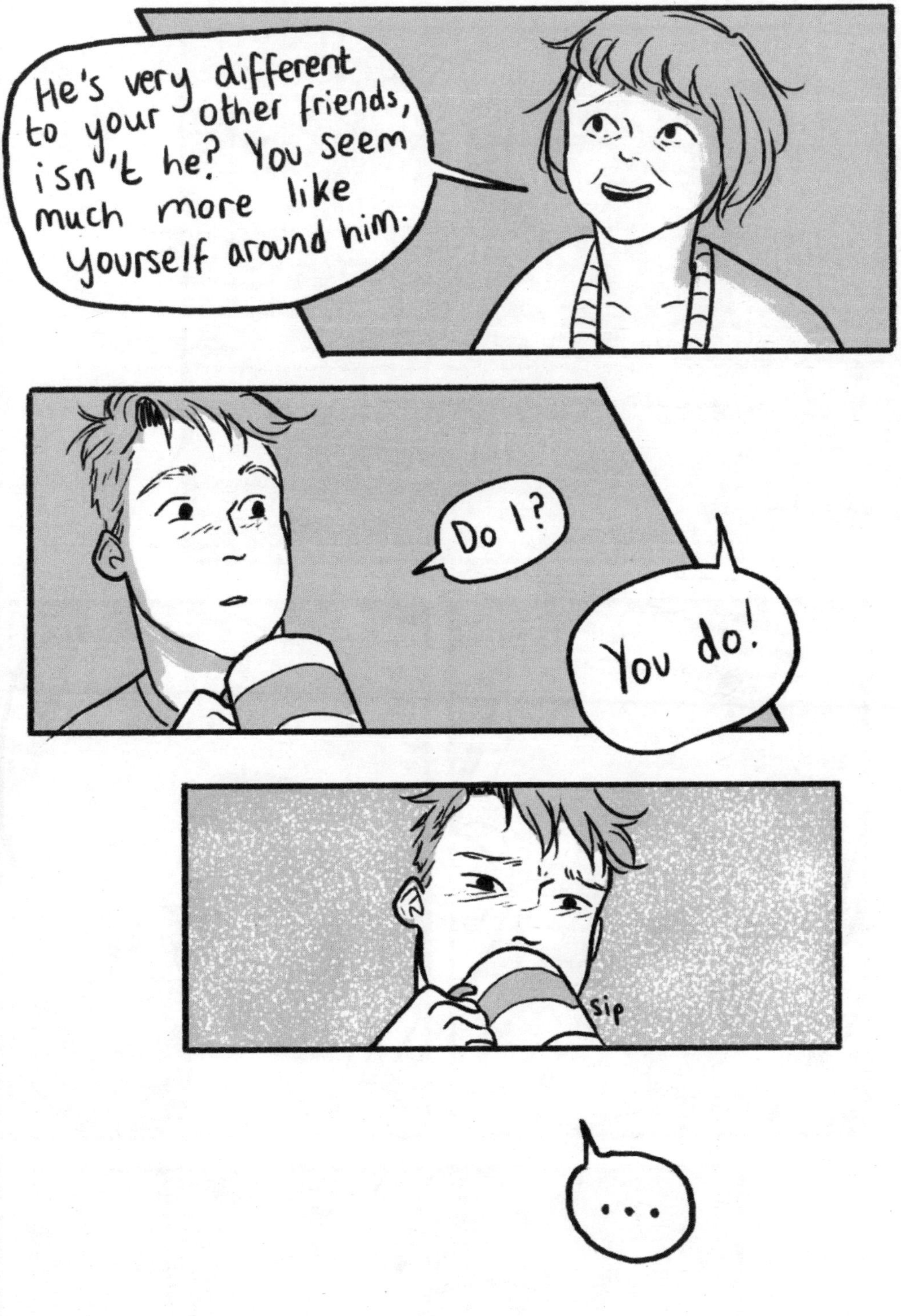
He's very different to your other friends, isn't he? You seem much more like yourself around him.
Do I?
You do!
sip
...

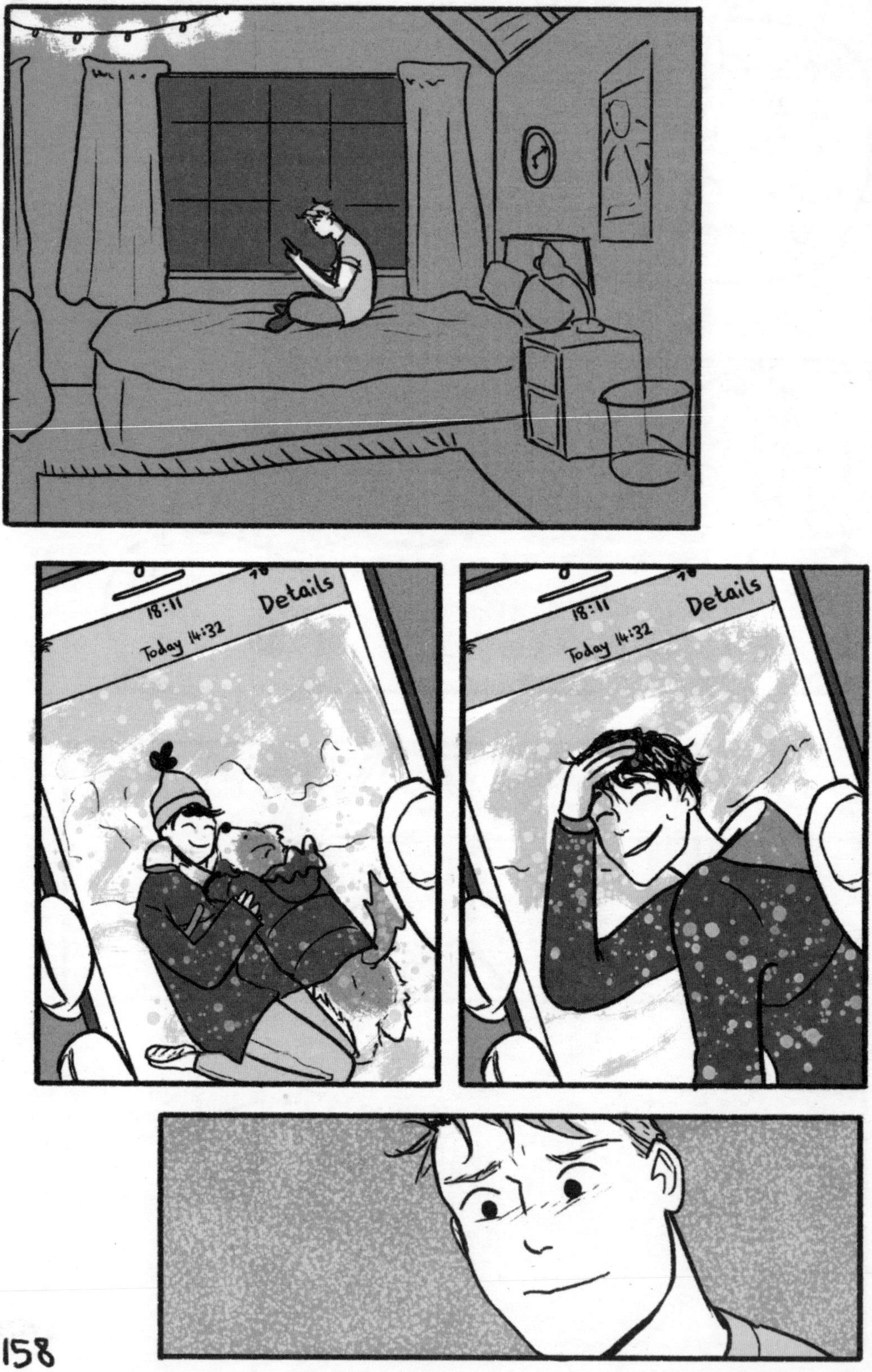
18:11
Details
Today 14:32
18:11
Details
Today 14:32

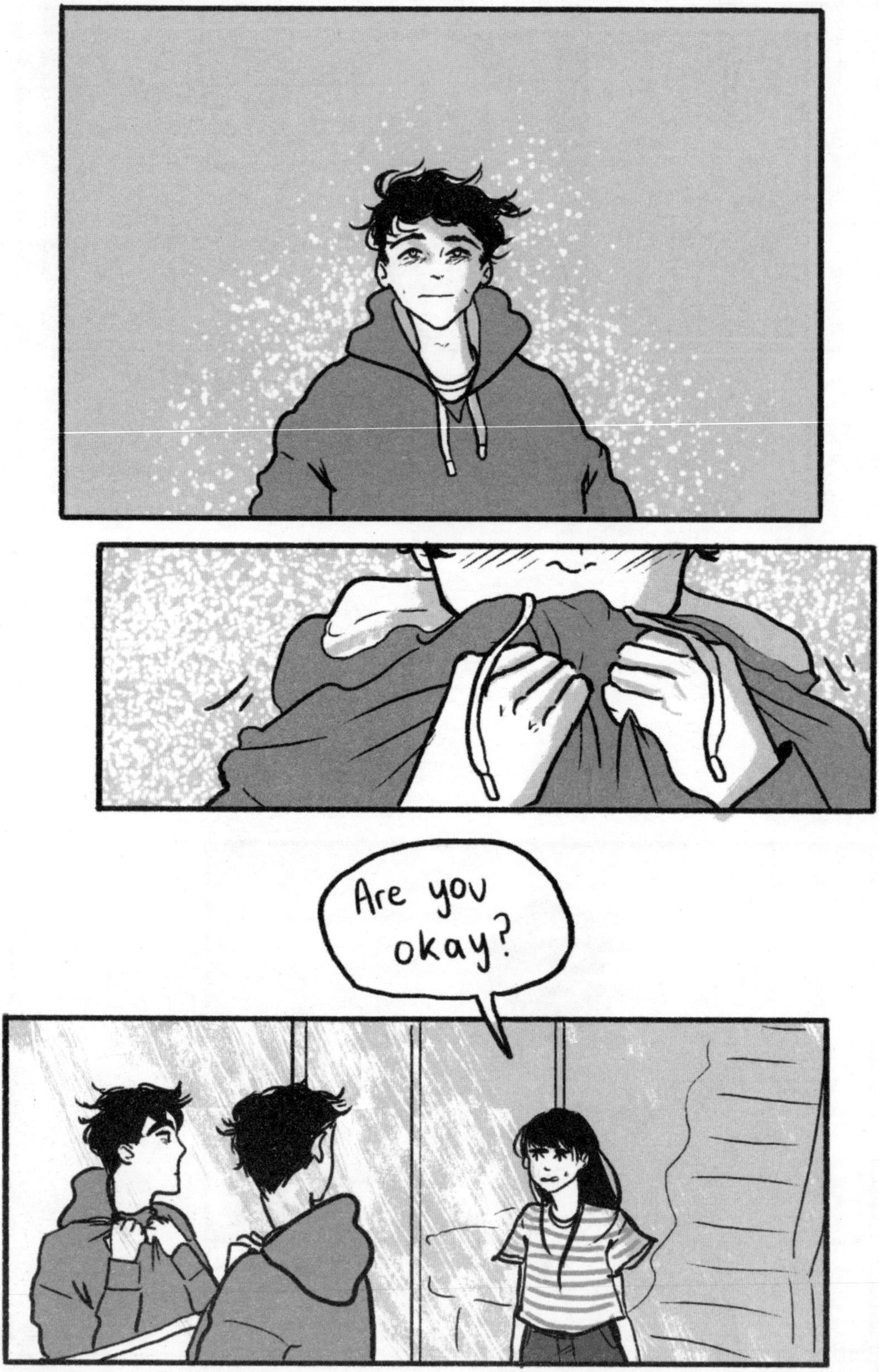
Are you okay?

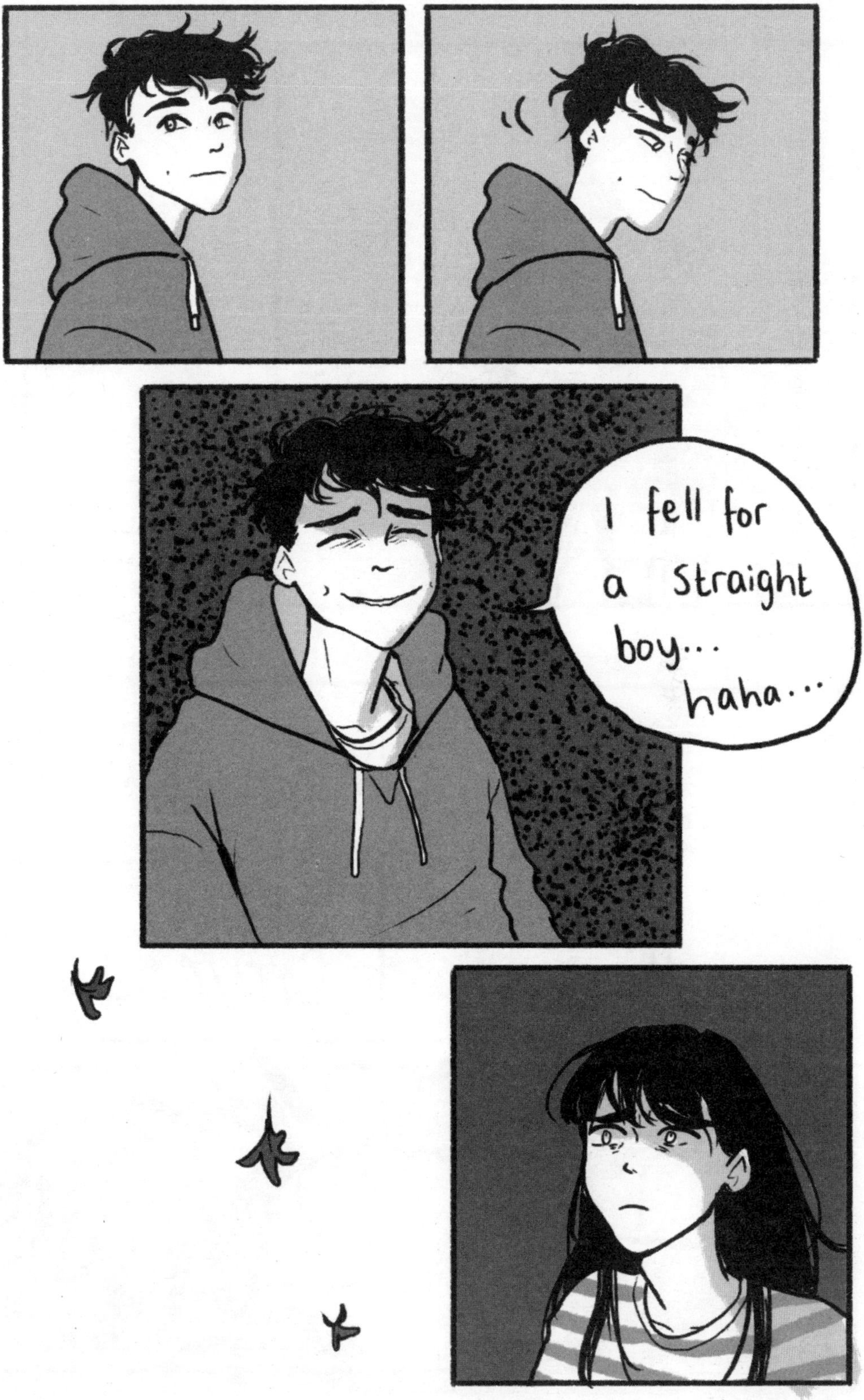
I fell for a straight boy... haha...

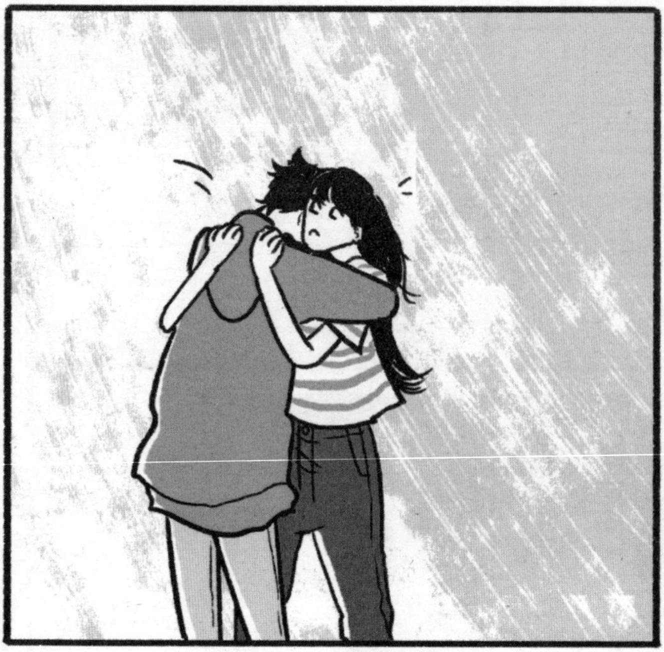

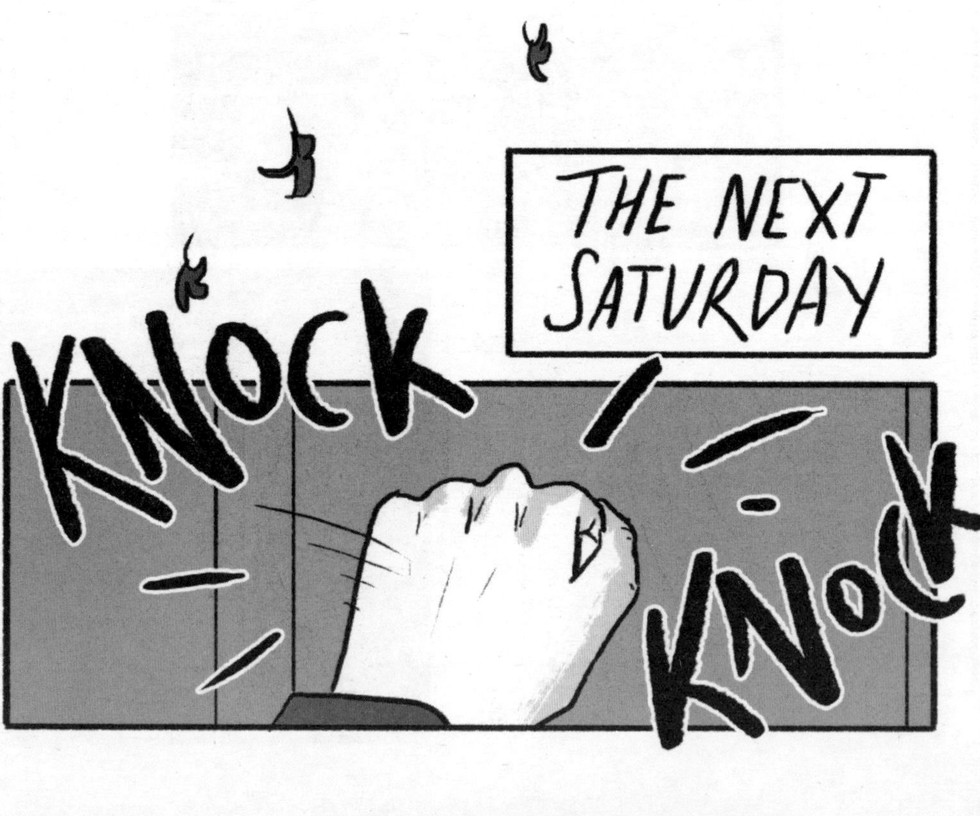
THE NEXT SATURDAY
KNOCK
KNOCK

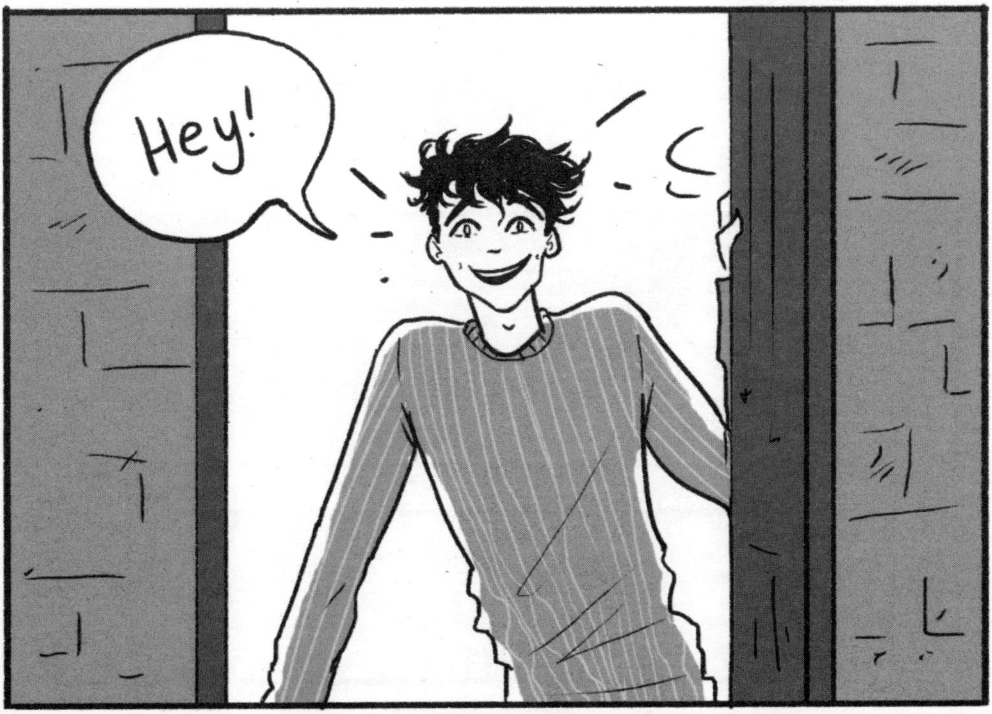
Hey!

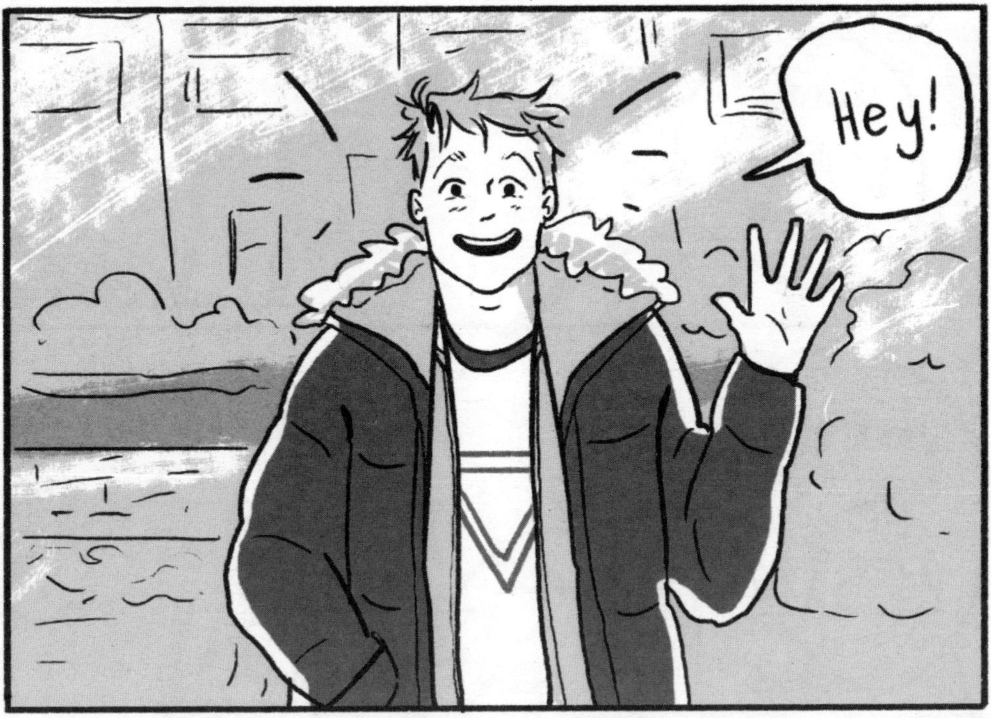
Hey!

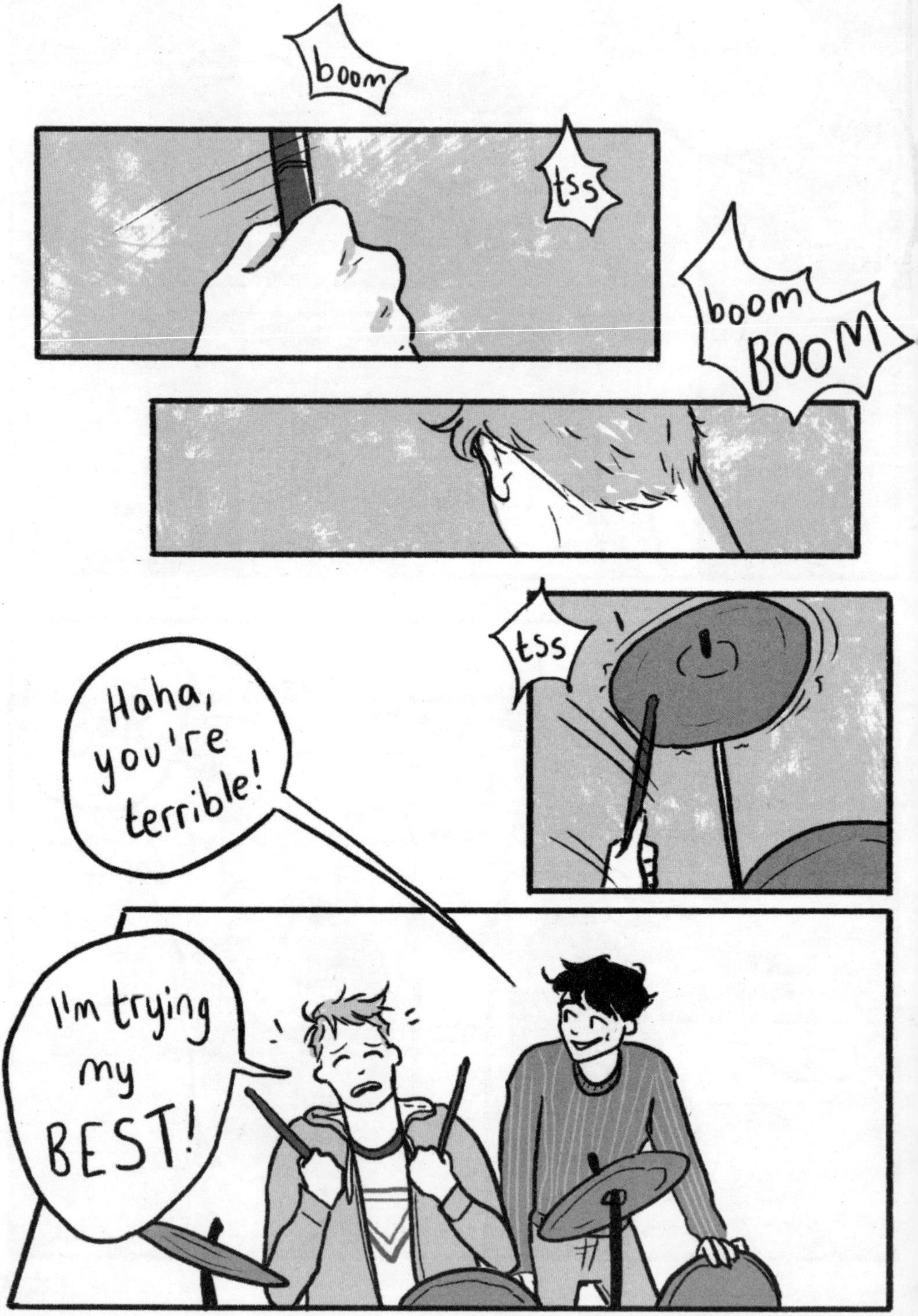
boom
tss
boom BOOM
tss
Haha, you're terrible!
I'm trying my BEST!

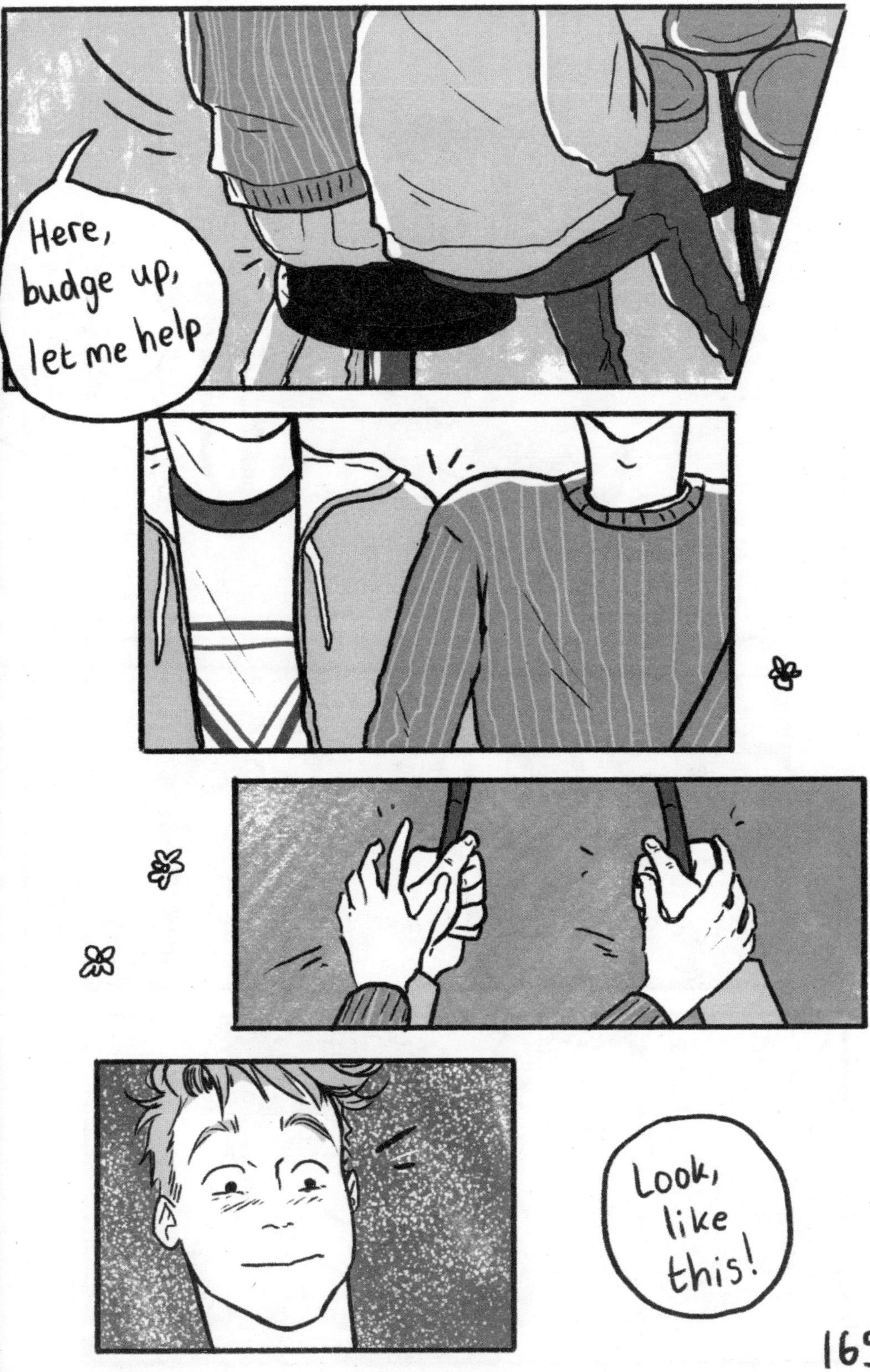
Here, budge up, let me help
Look, like this!

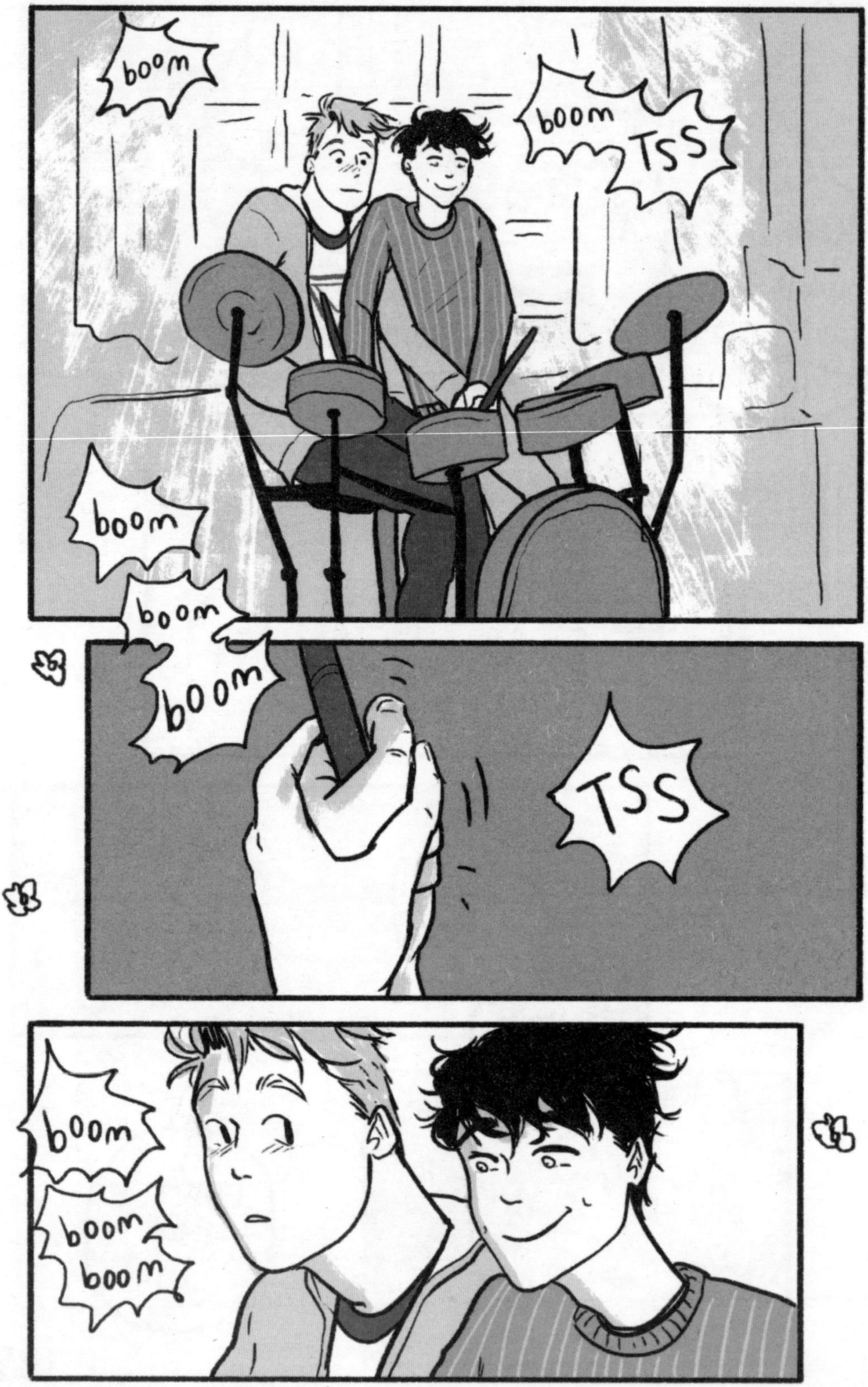
boom
boom
TSS
boom
boom
boom
TSS
boom
boom
boom

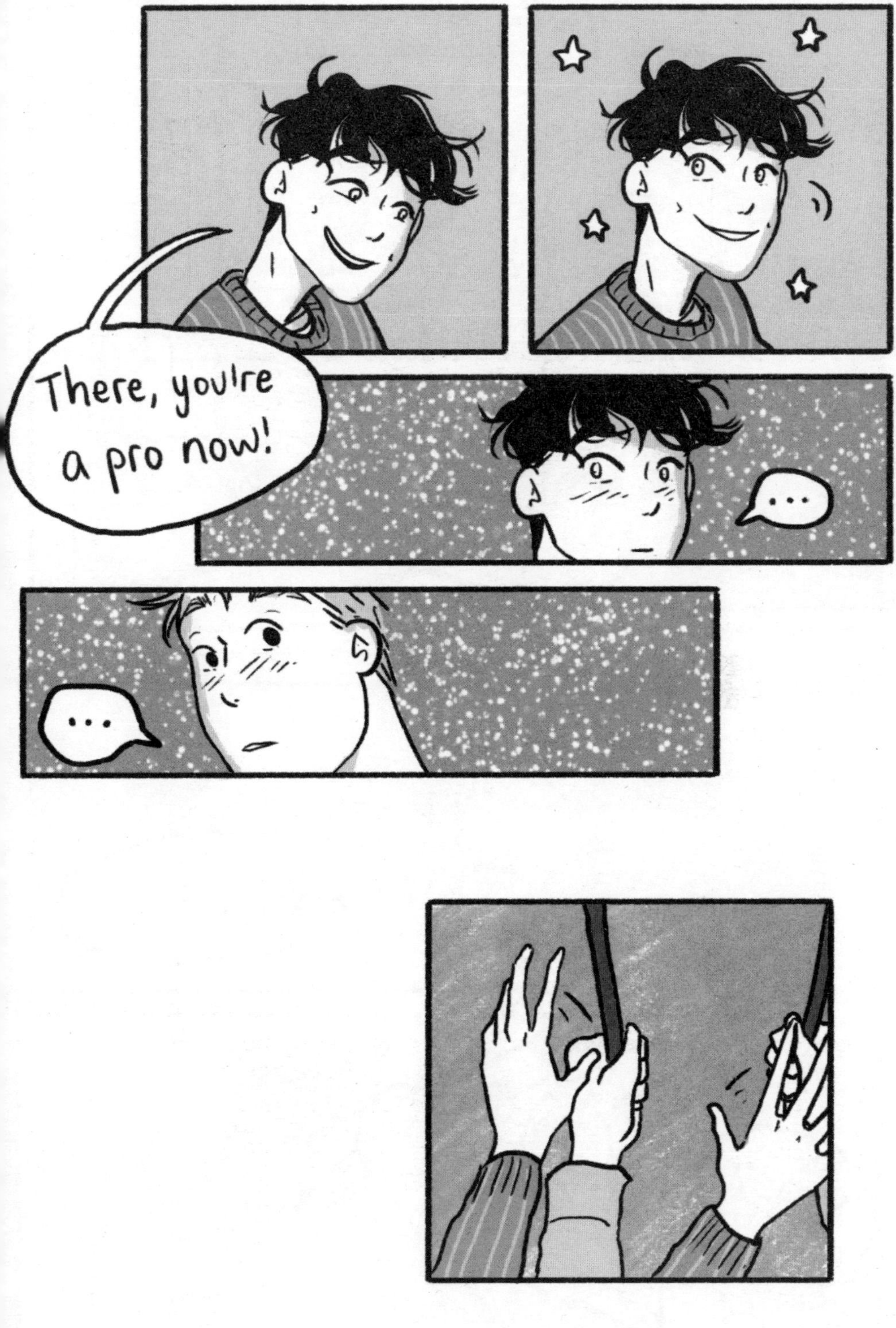
There, you're a pro now!
...
...

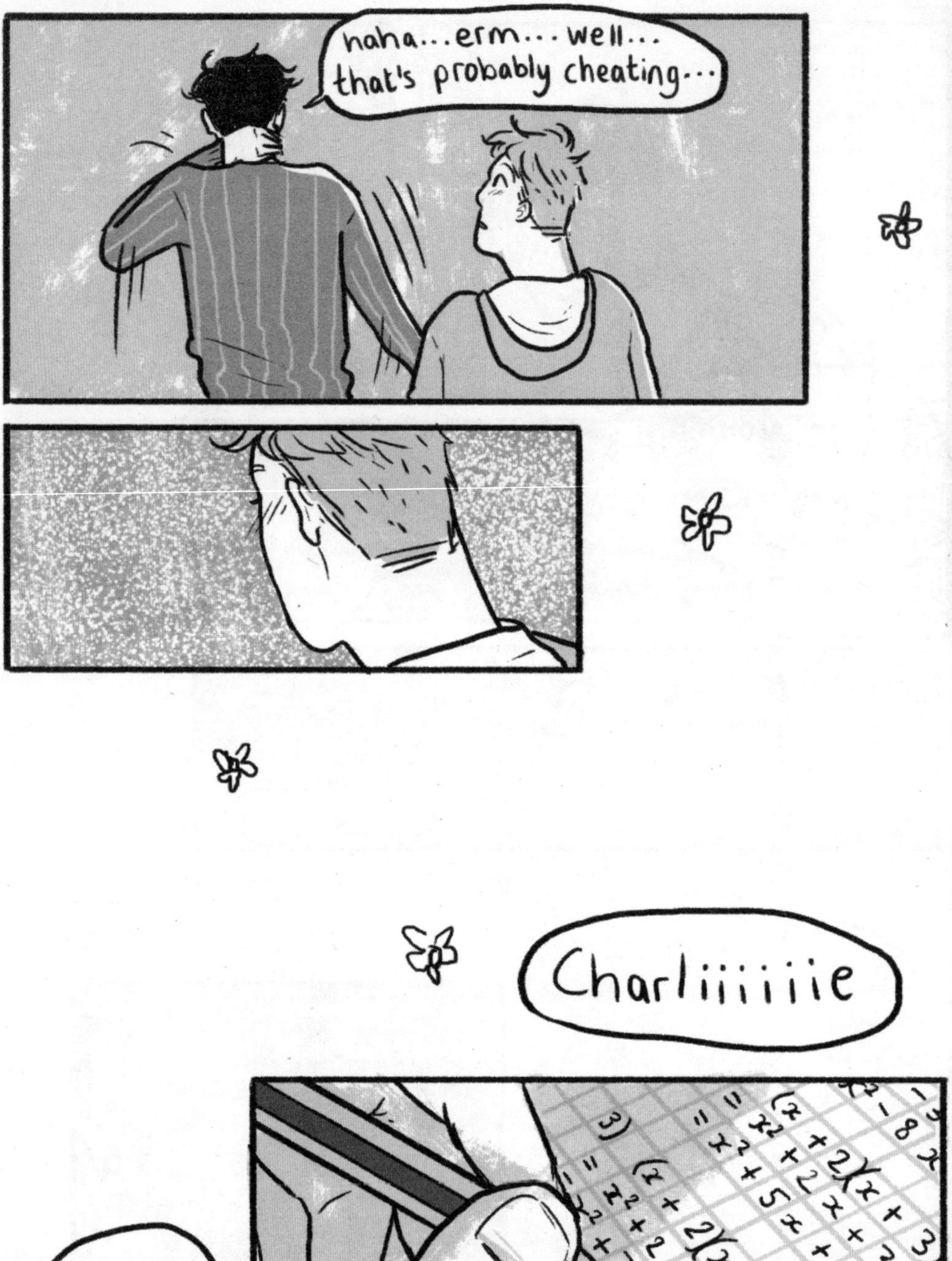
haha... erm... well... that's probably cheating...
Charliiiiiie
Yeah?

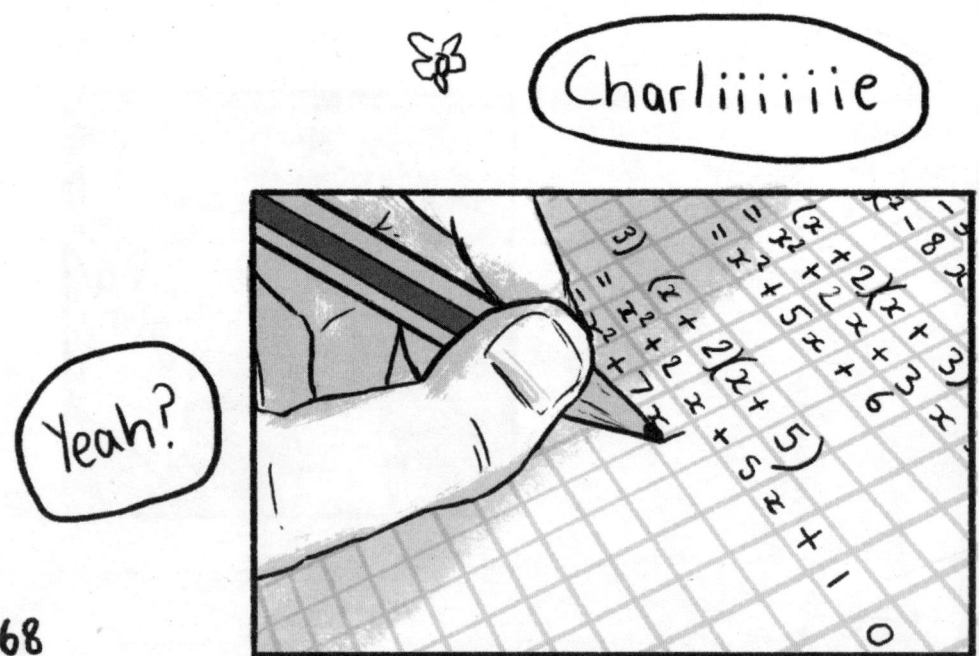

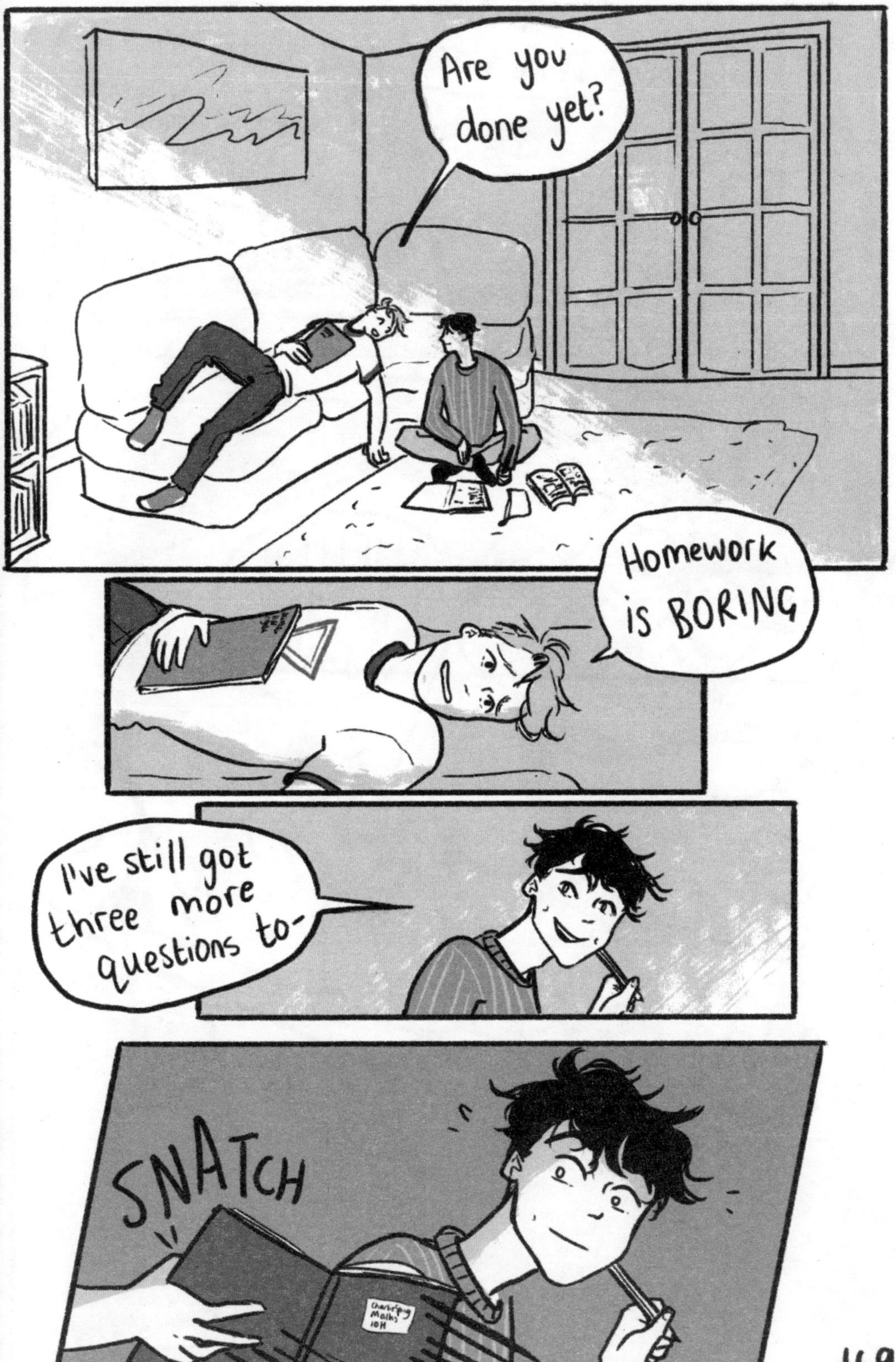
Are you done yet?
Homework is BORING
I've still got three more questions to-
SNATCH

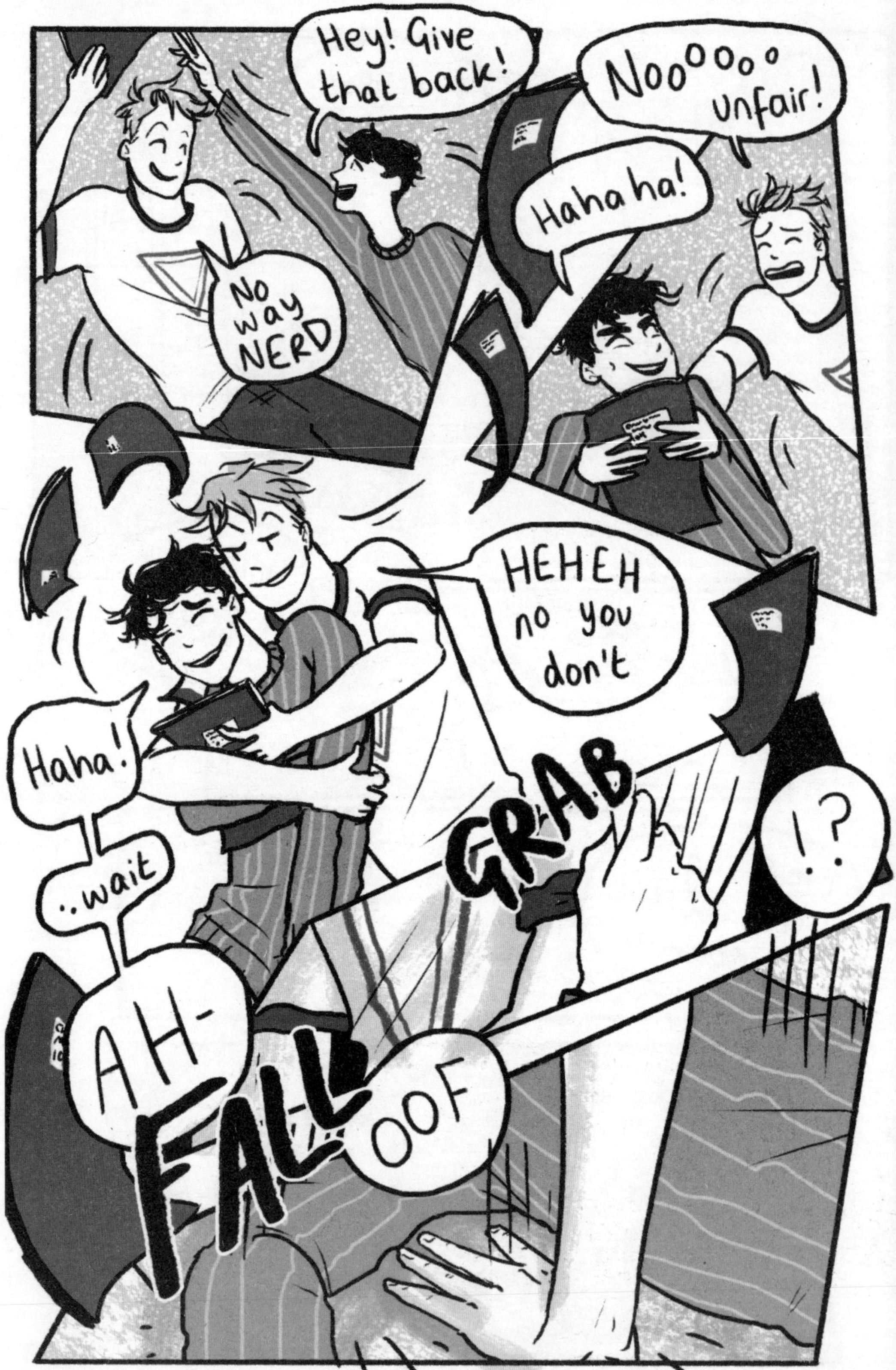
Hey! Give that back!
No way NERD
Nooooo unfair!
Hahaha!
HEHEH no you don't
Haha!
..wait
GRAB
!?
AH-
FALL
OOF

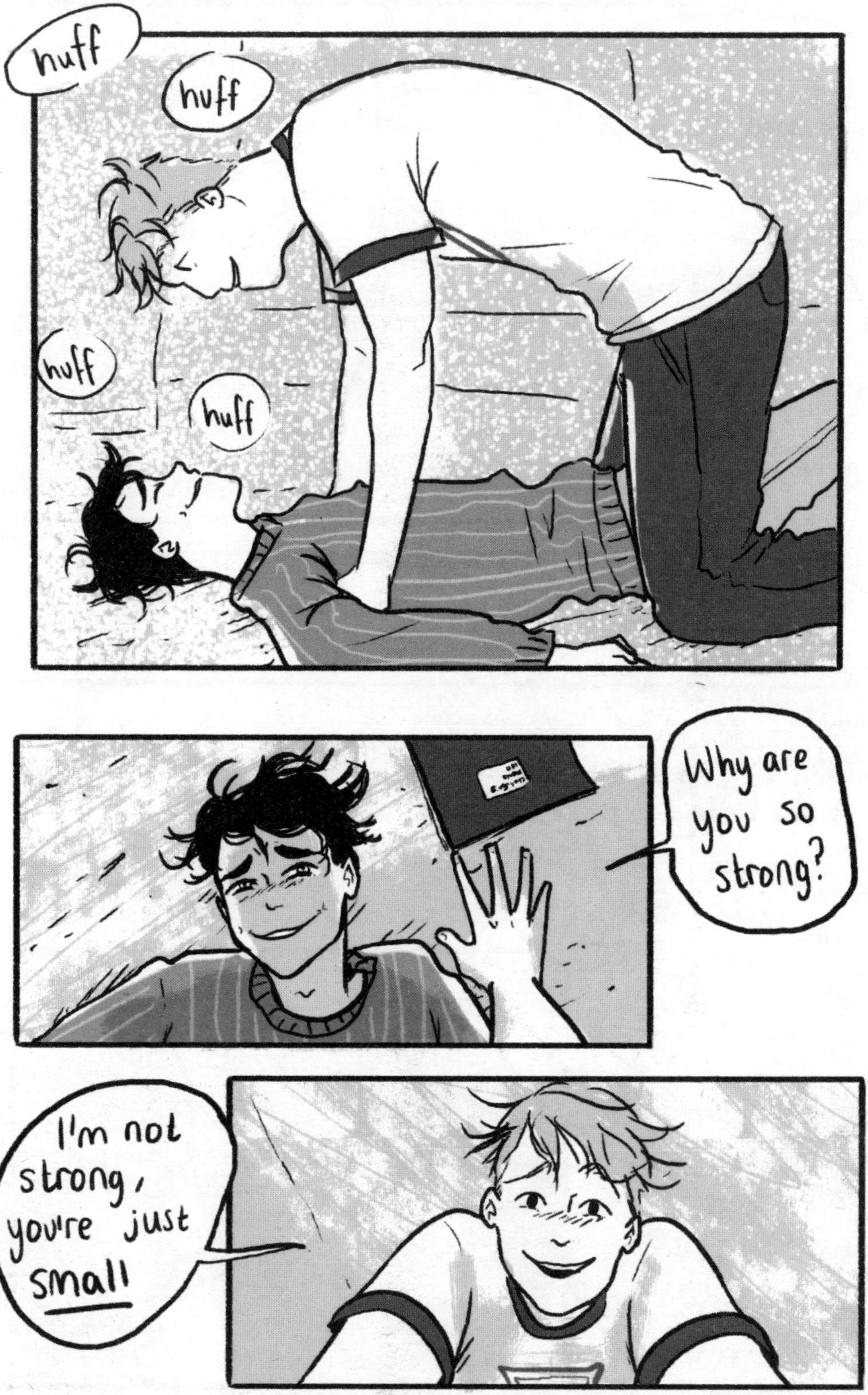
huff
huff
huff
huff
Why are you so strong?
I'm not strong, you're just small

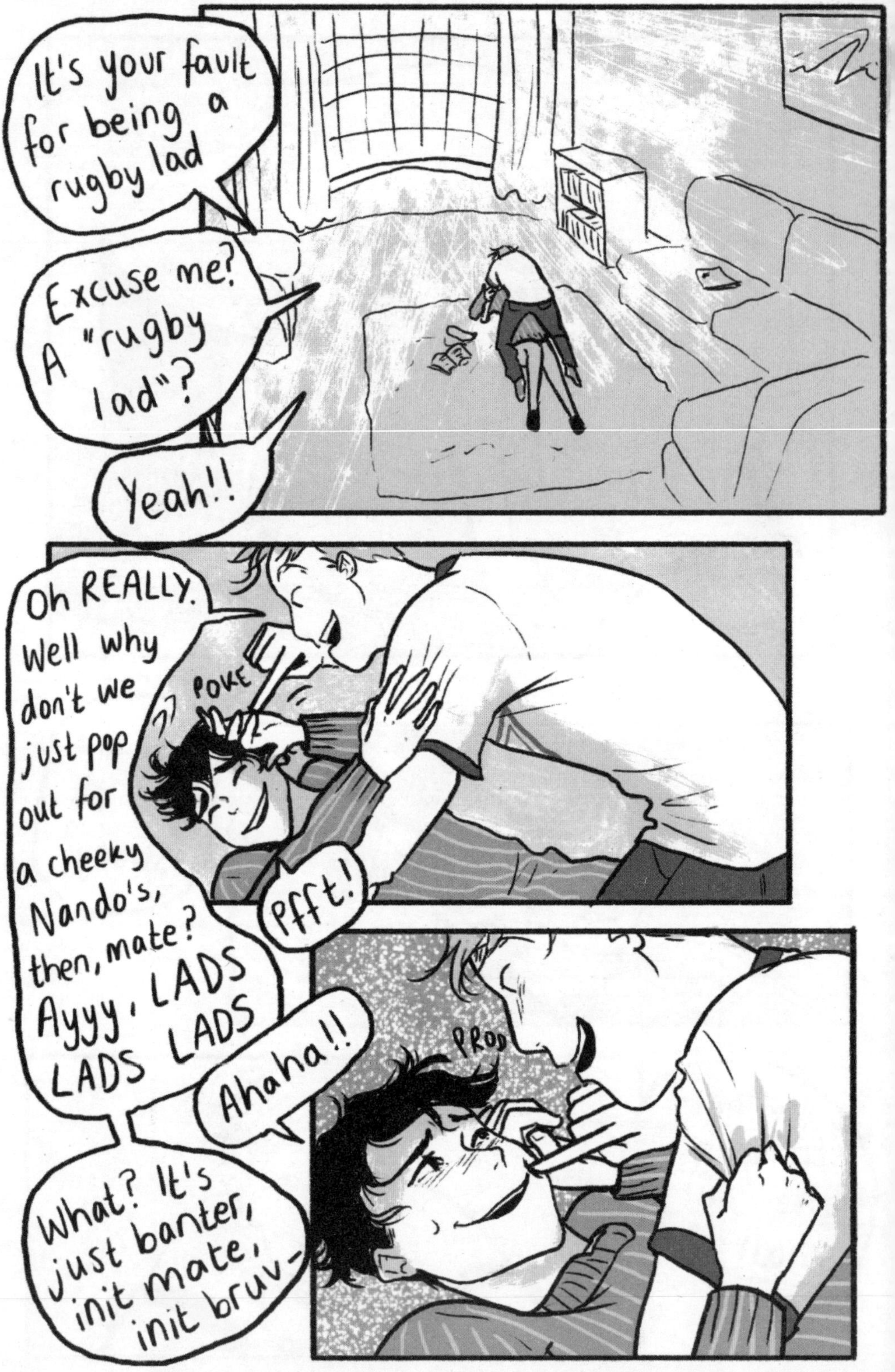
It's your fault for being a rugby lad
Excuse me? A "rugby lad"?
Yeah!!
Oh REALLY. Well why don't we just pop out for a cheeky Nando's, then, mate? Ayyy, LADS LADS LADS
POKE
Pfft!
PROD
Ahaha!!
What? It's just banter, init mate, init bruv–

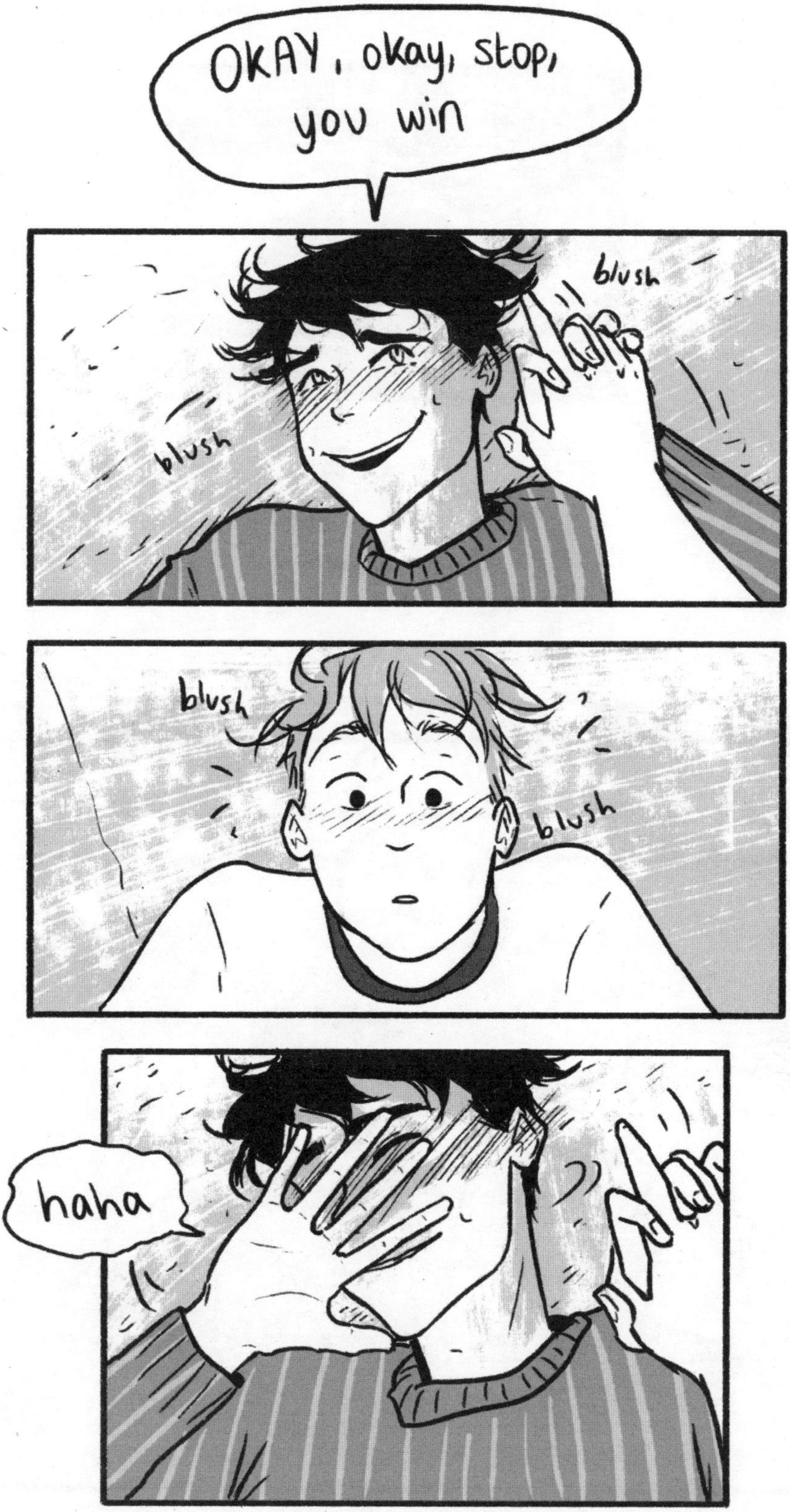
OKAY, okay, stop, you win
blush
blush
blush
blush
haha

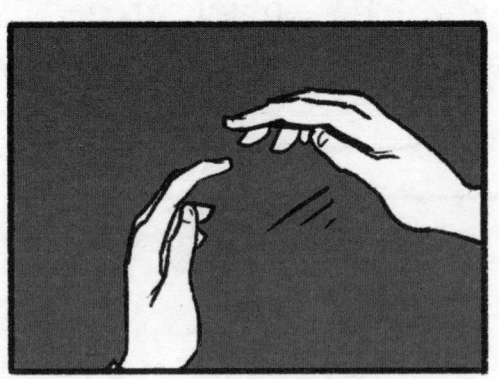

ROLL

?

Mario Kart?

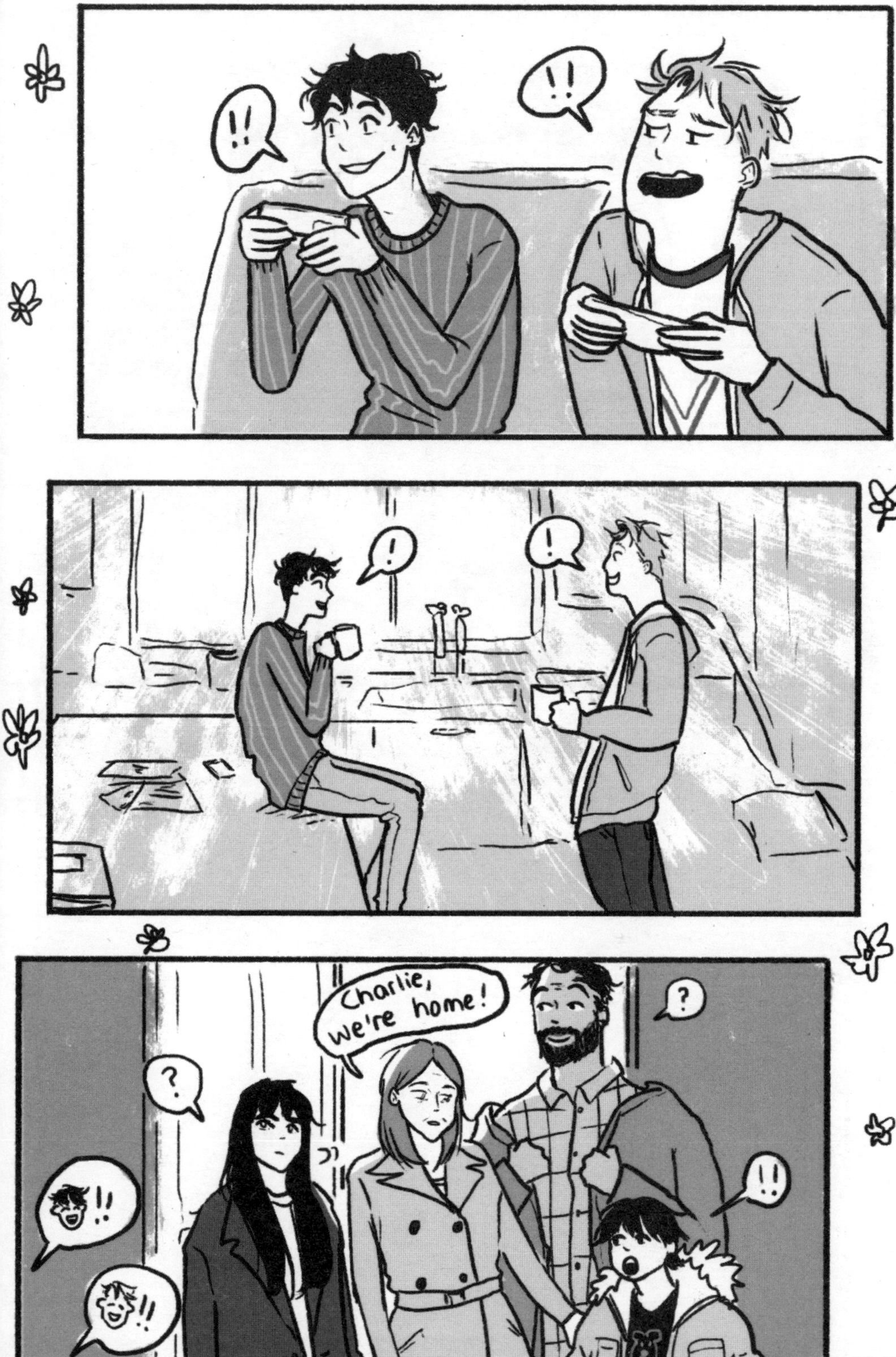
!!
!!
!
!
?
Charlie, we're home!
?
!!
!!
!!

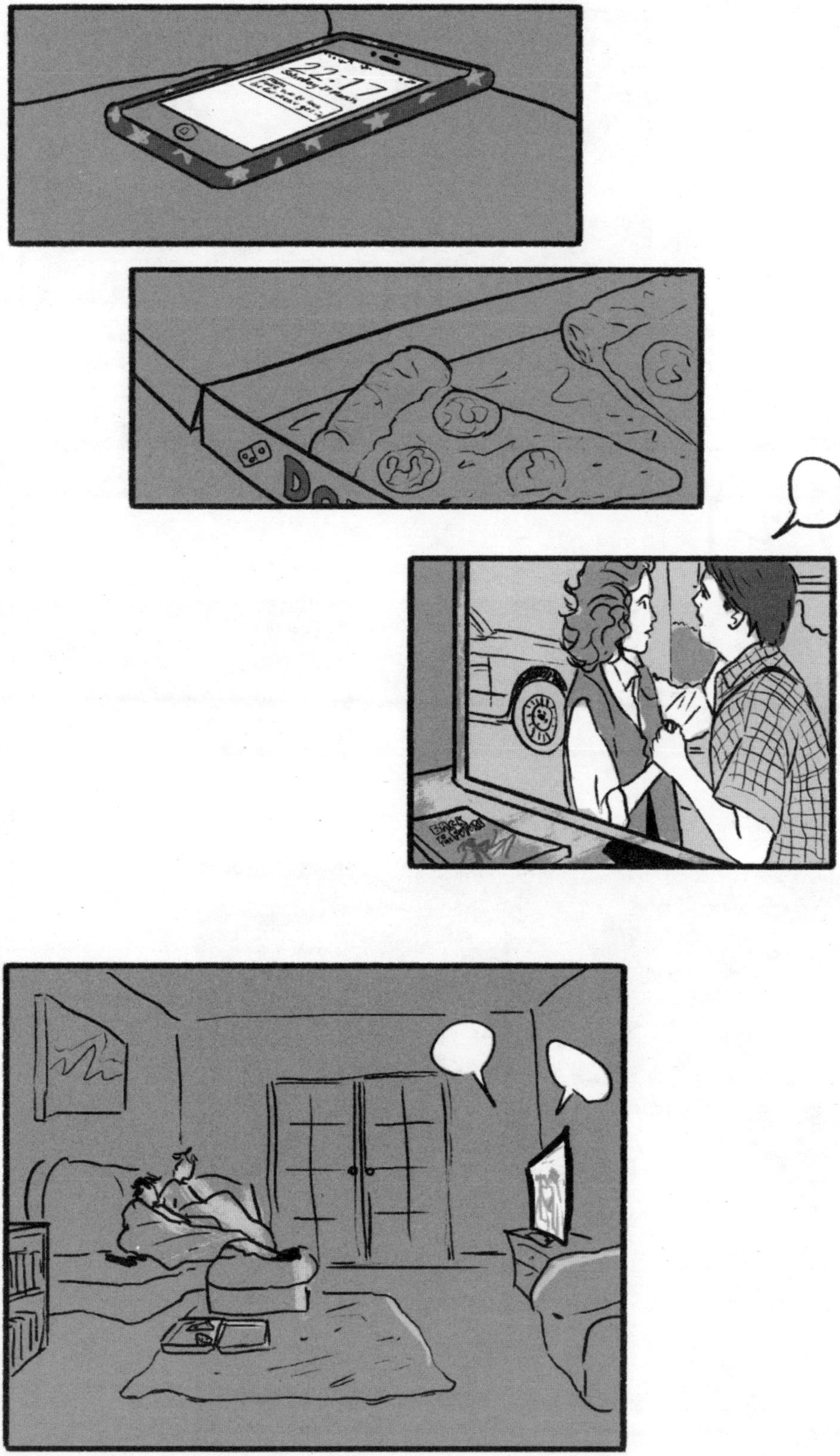
22:17

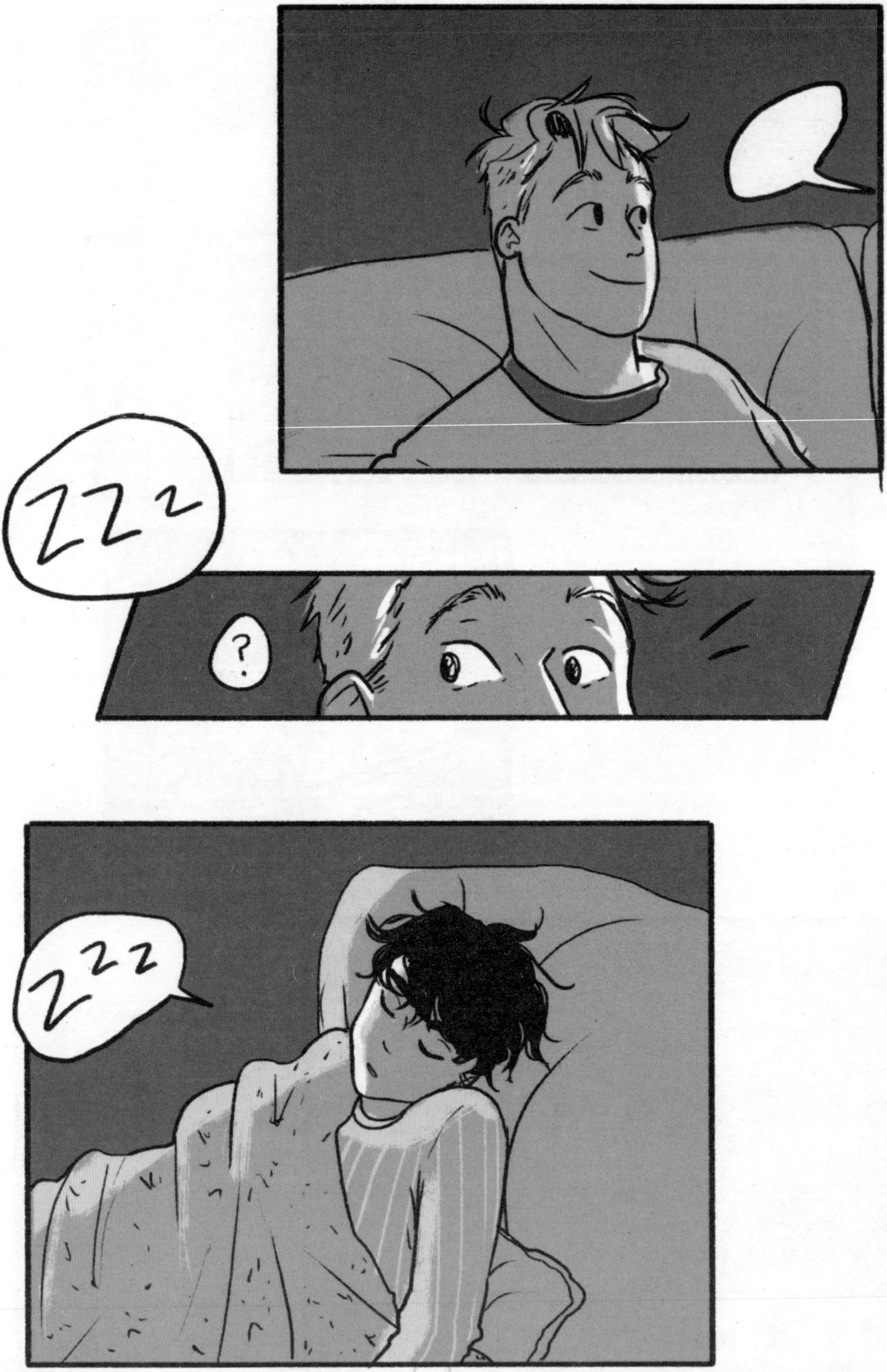
ZZz
?
Zzz

Zz

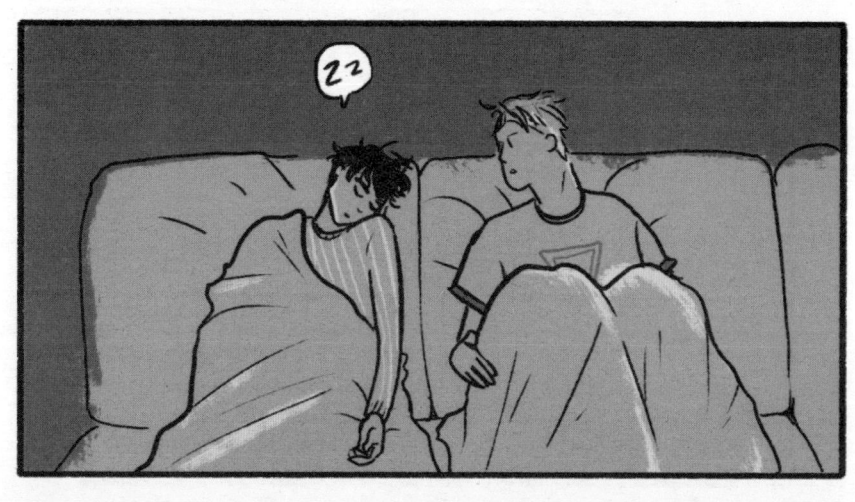

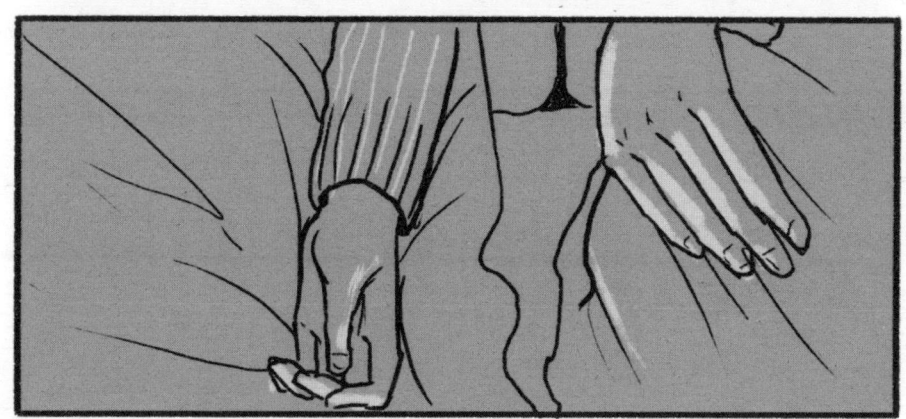

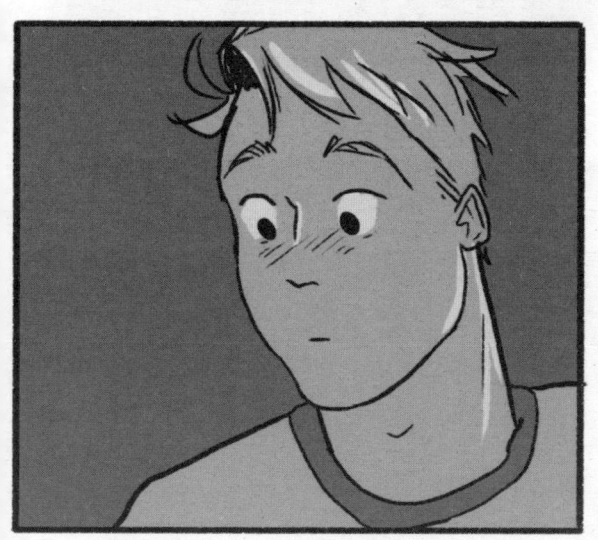

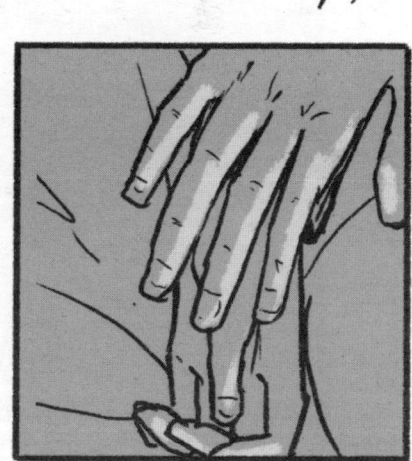

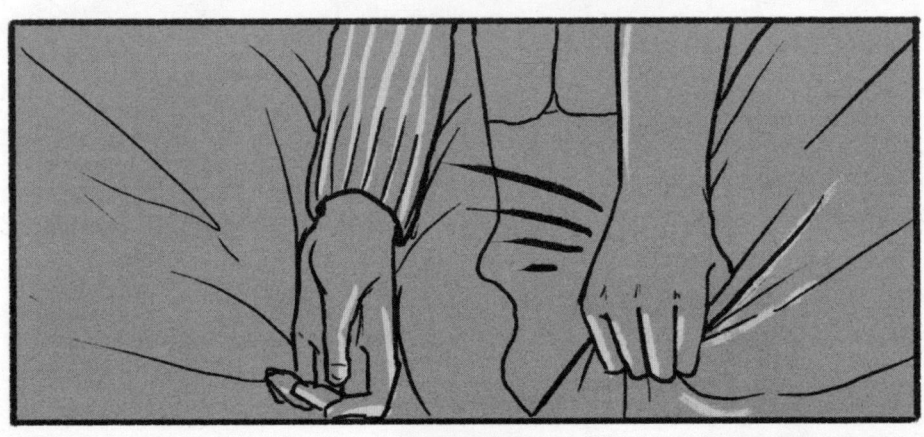

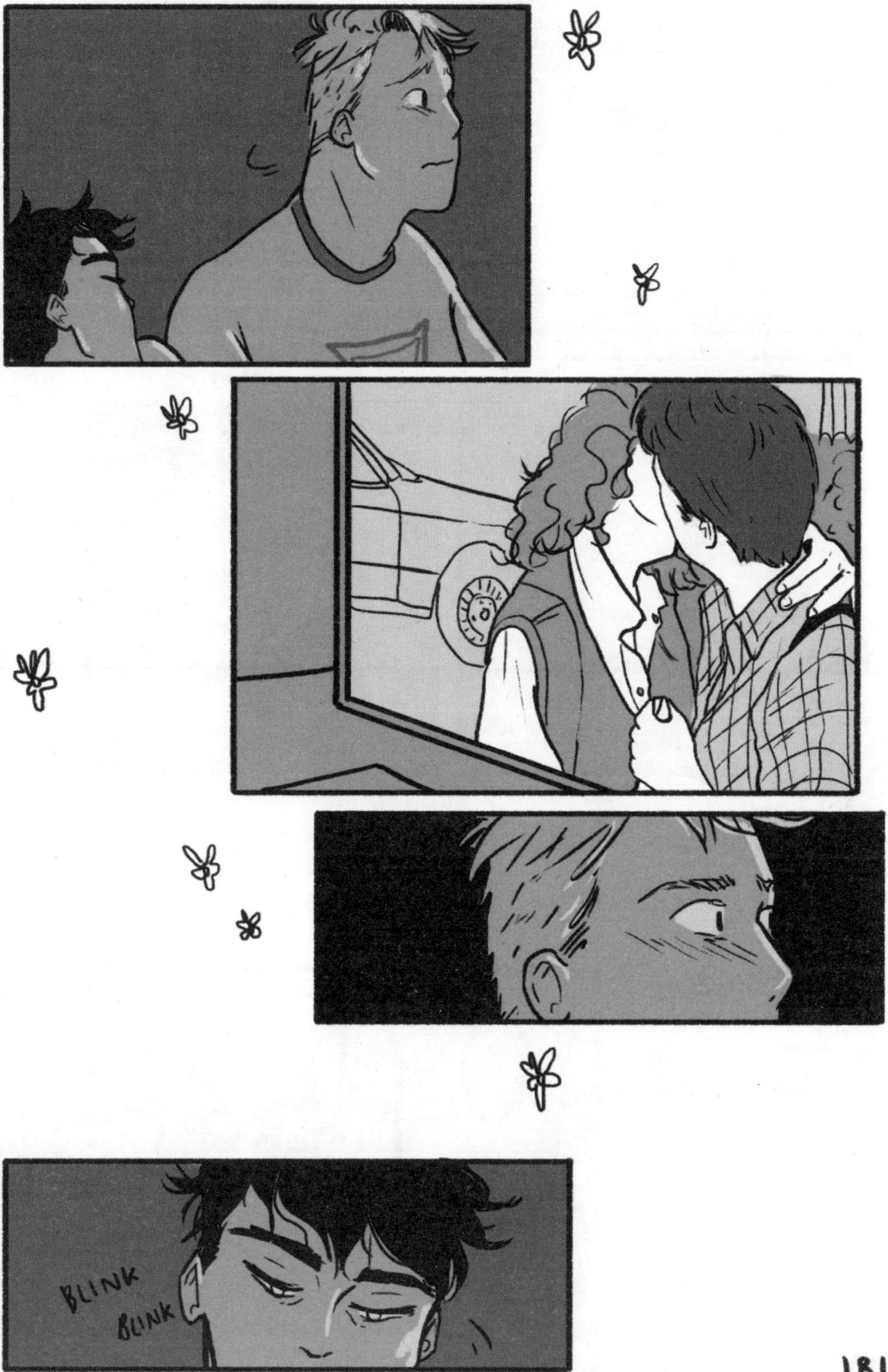
BLINK
BLINK

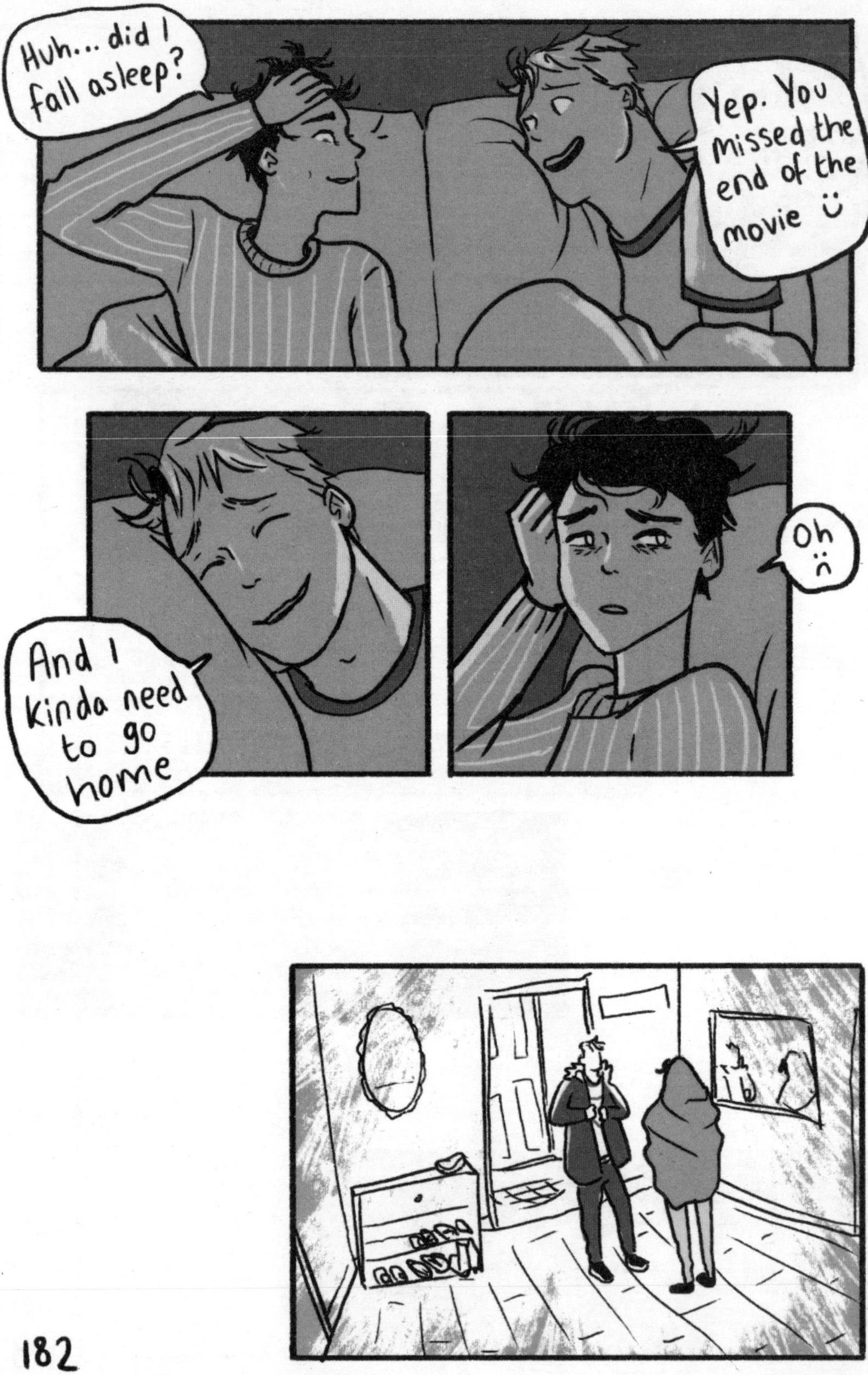
Huh... did I fall asleep?
Yep. You missed the end of the movie :)
And I kinda need to go home
Oh :(

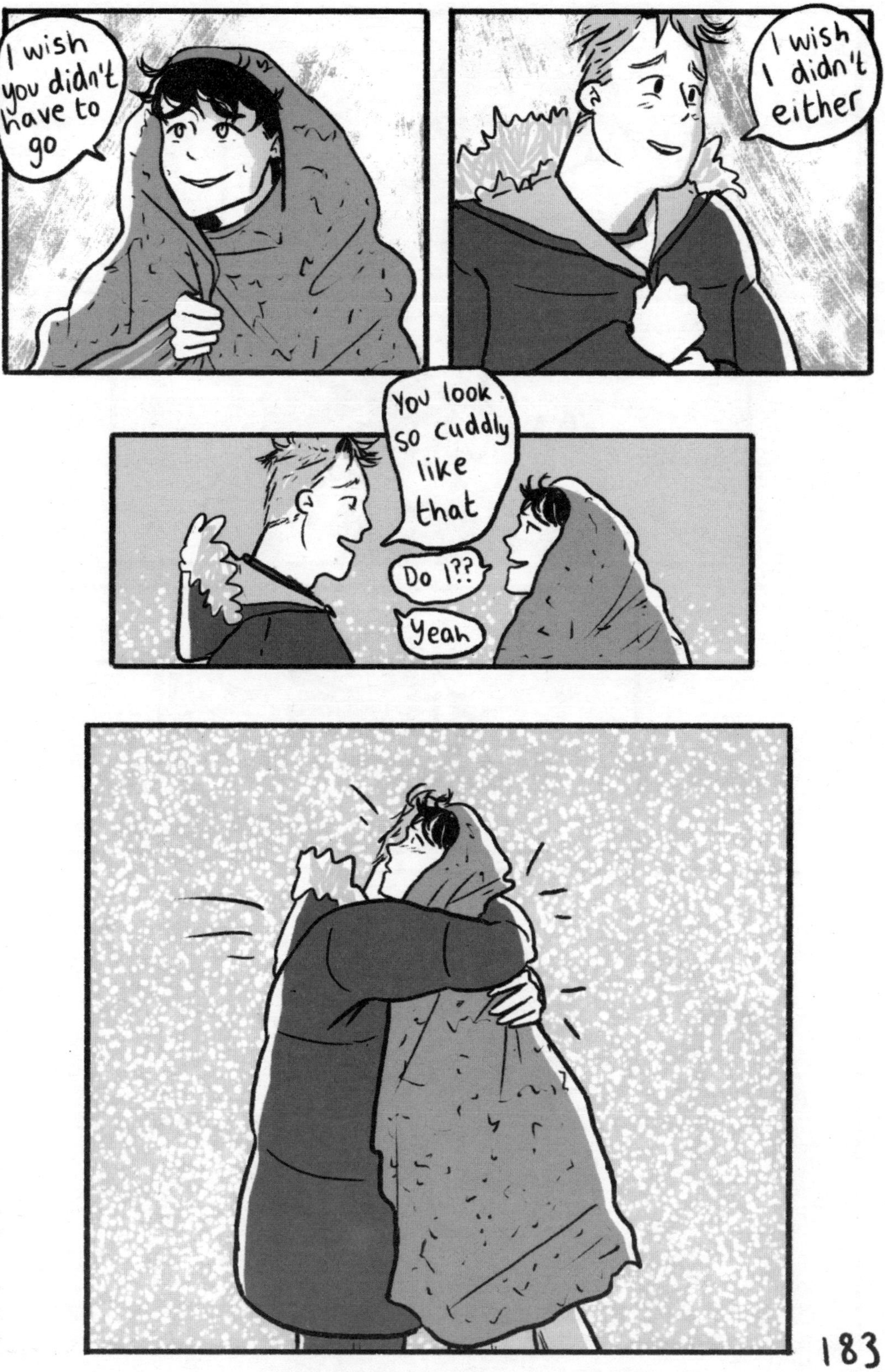
I wish you didn't have to go
I wish I didn't either
You look so cuddly like that
Do I??
Yeah

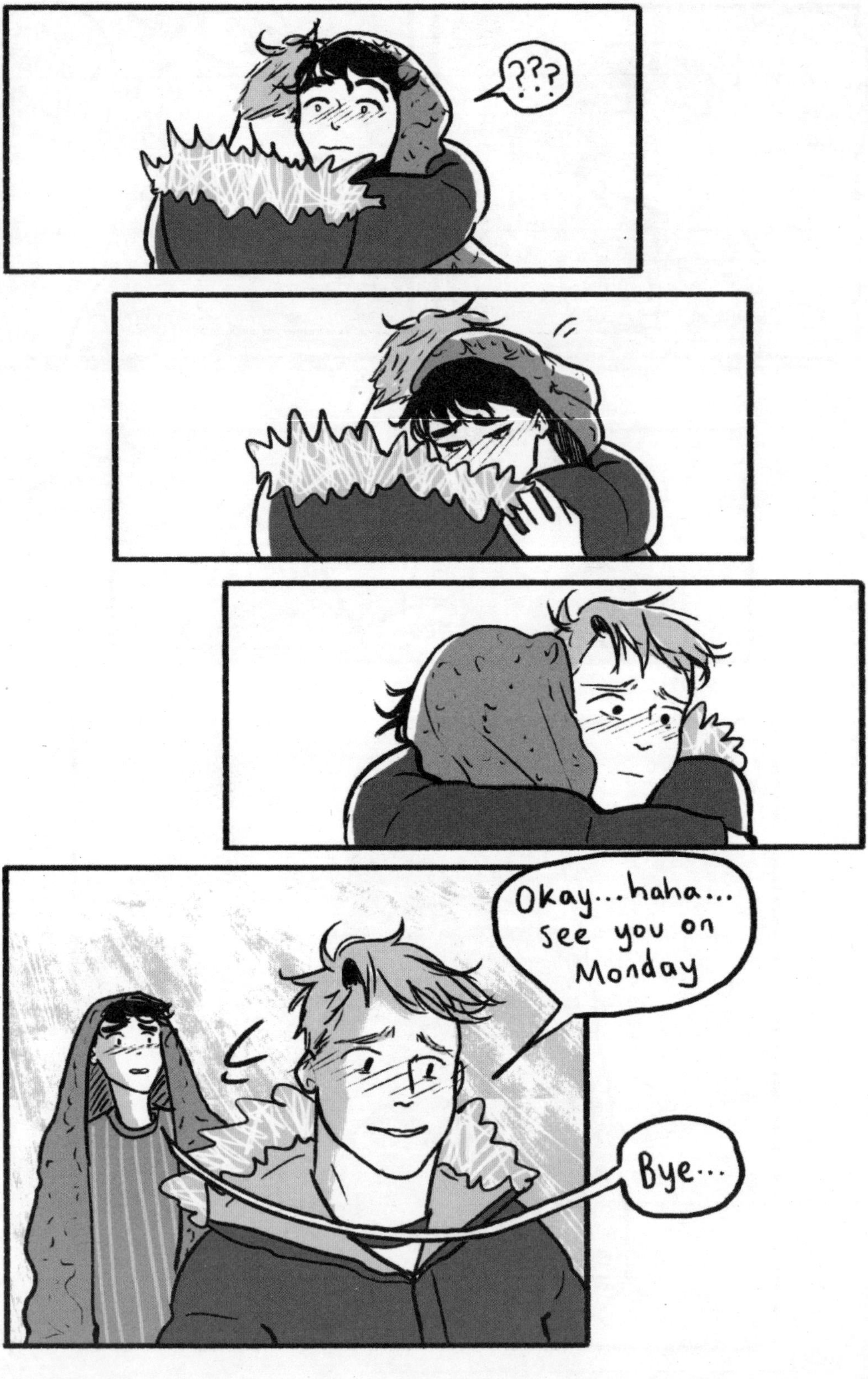
???
Okay... haha... see you on Monday
Bye...

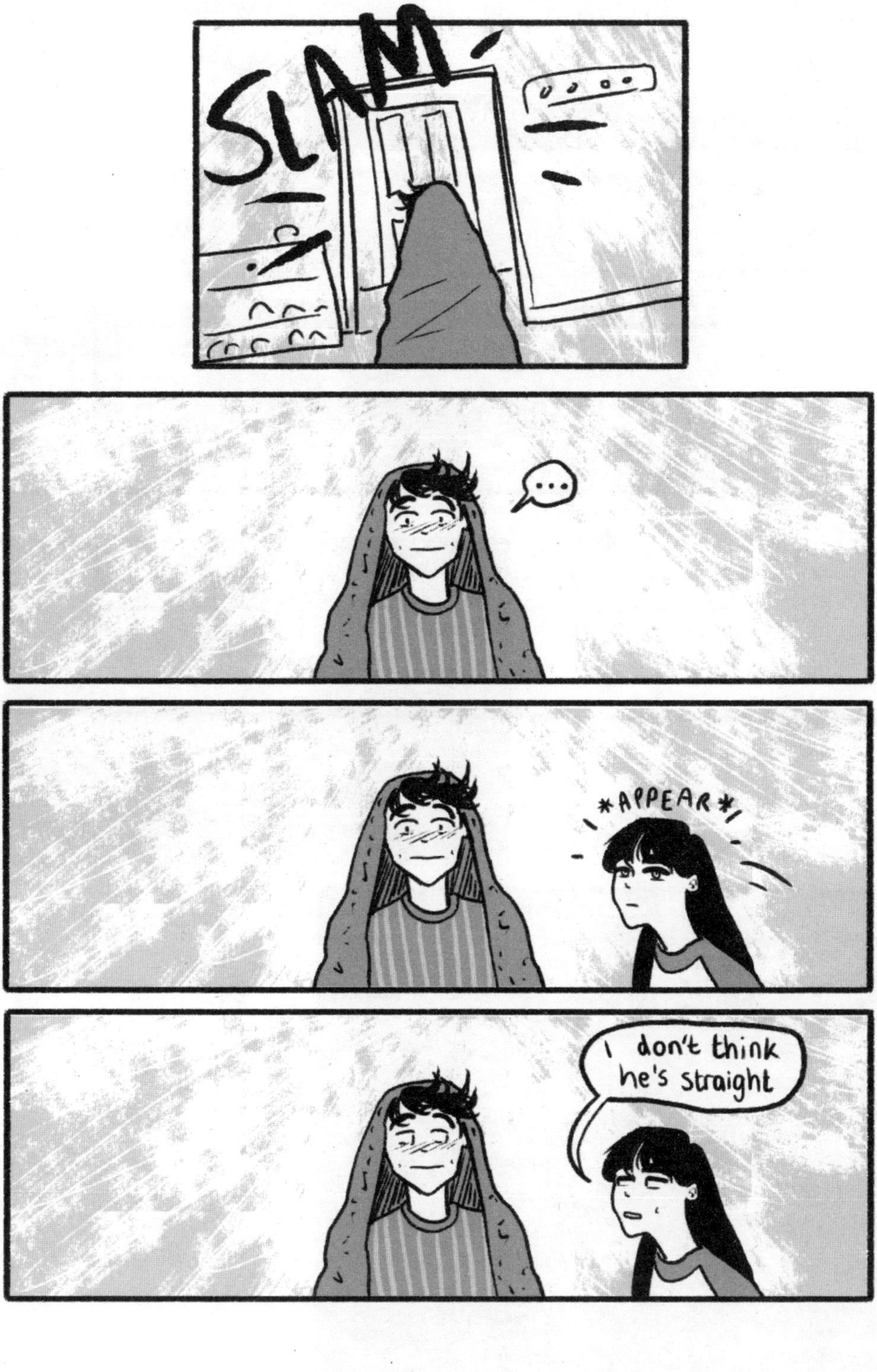
SLAM
...
APPEAR
I don't think he's straight

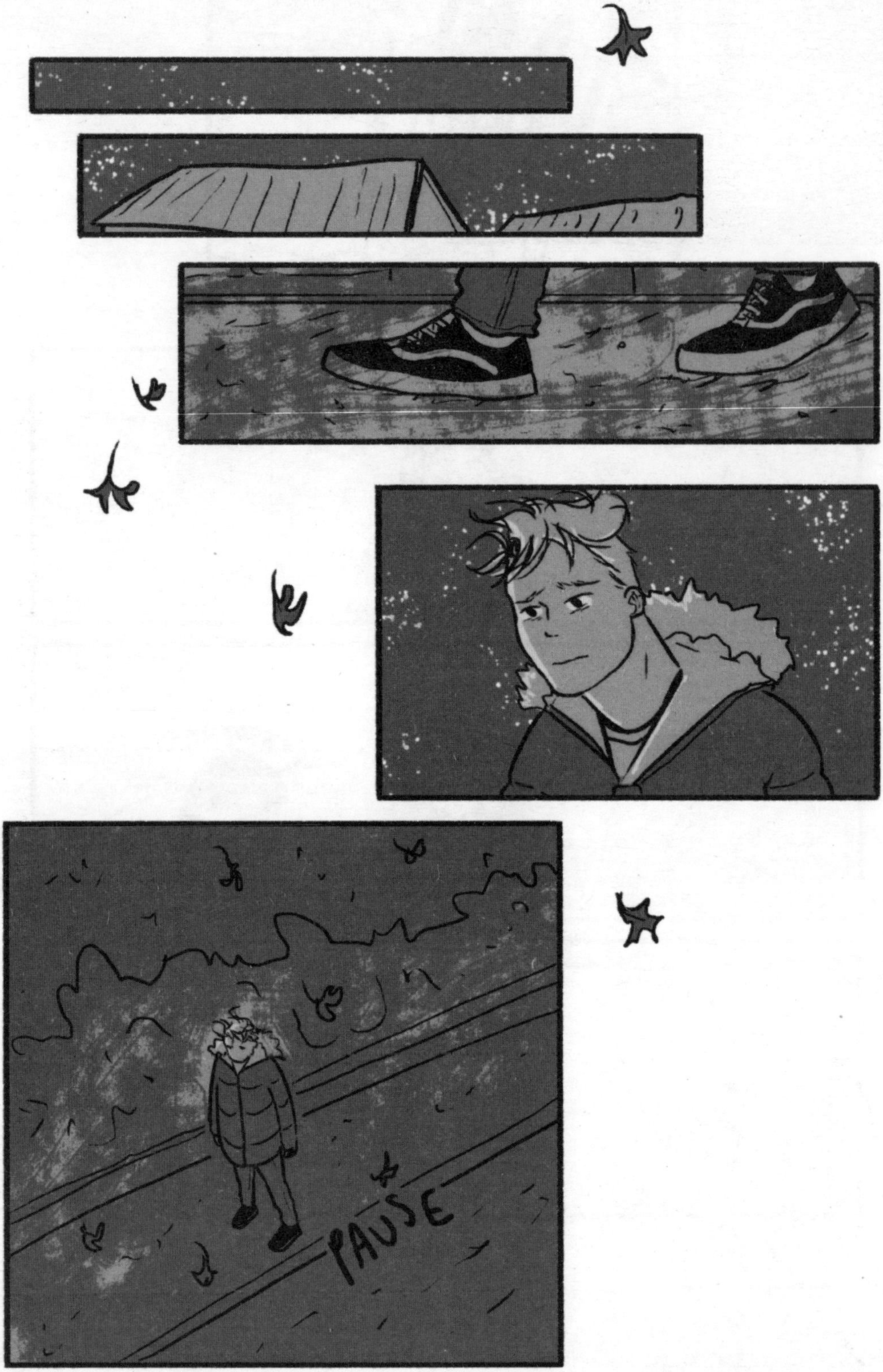
PAUSE

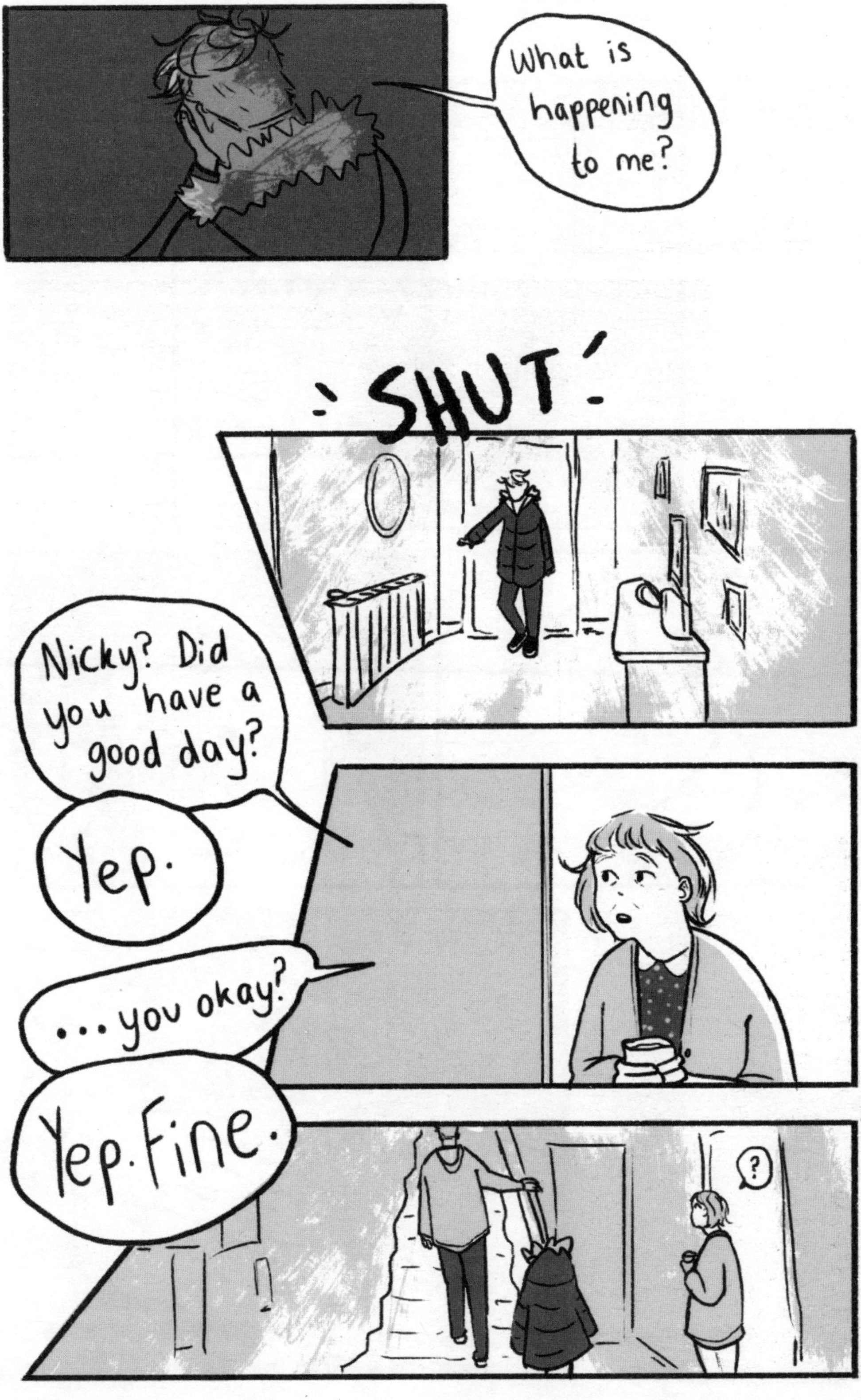
What is happening to me?
SHUT
Nicky? Did you have a good day?
Yep.
...you okay?
Yep. Fine.
?

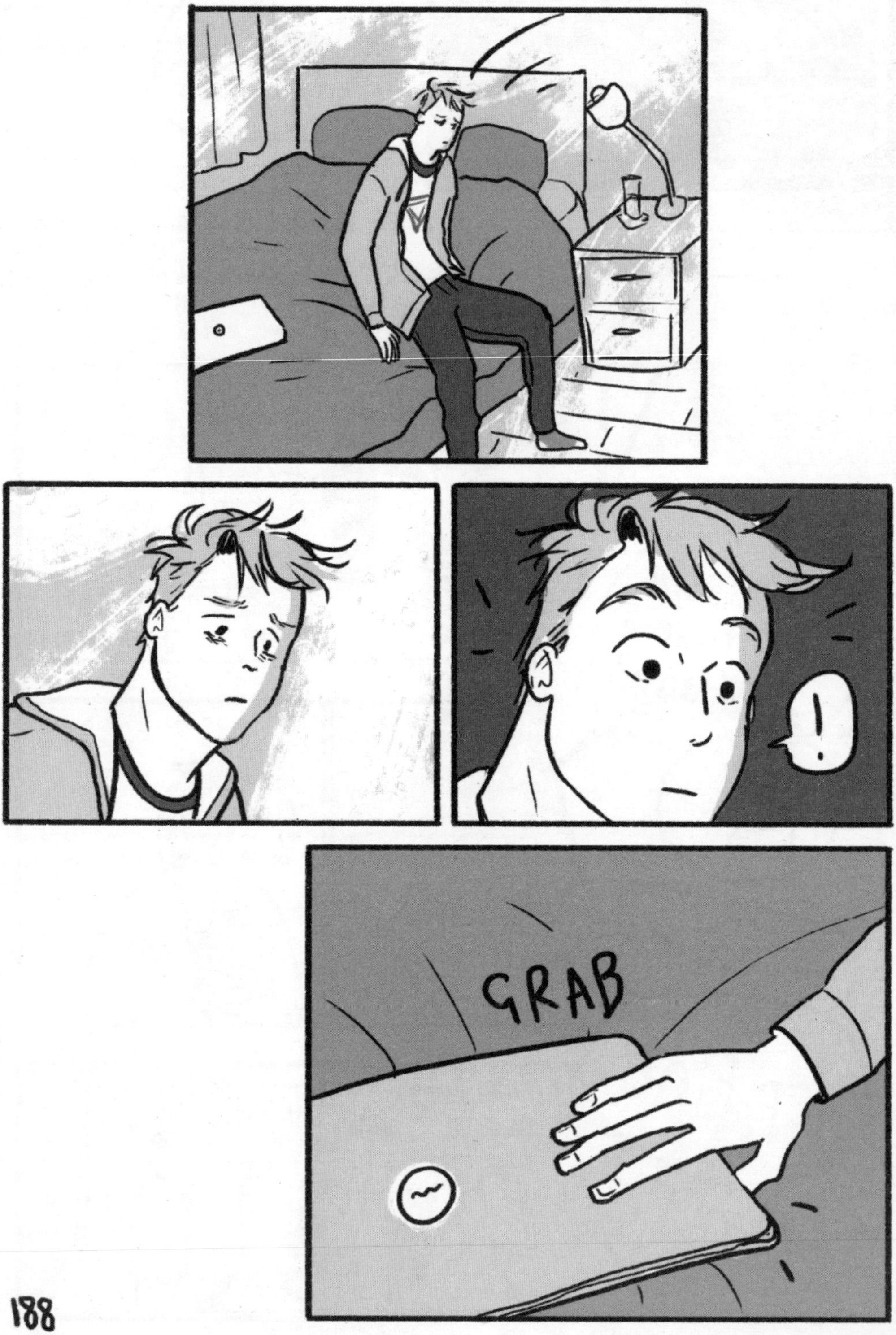
!
GRAB

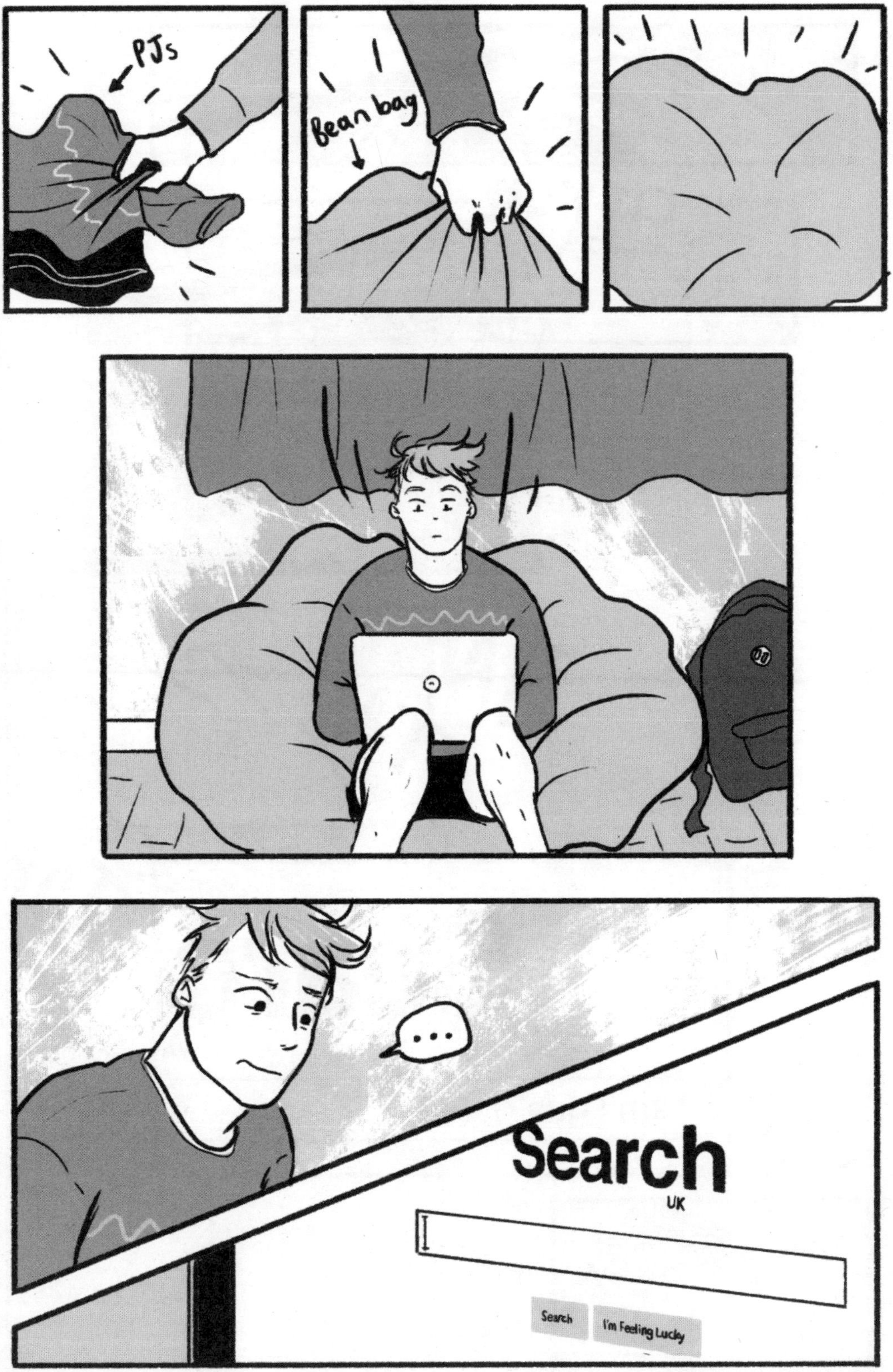
PJs
Bean bag
...
Search
UK
Search
I'm Feeling Lucky

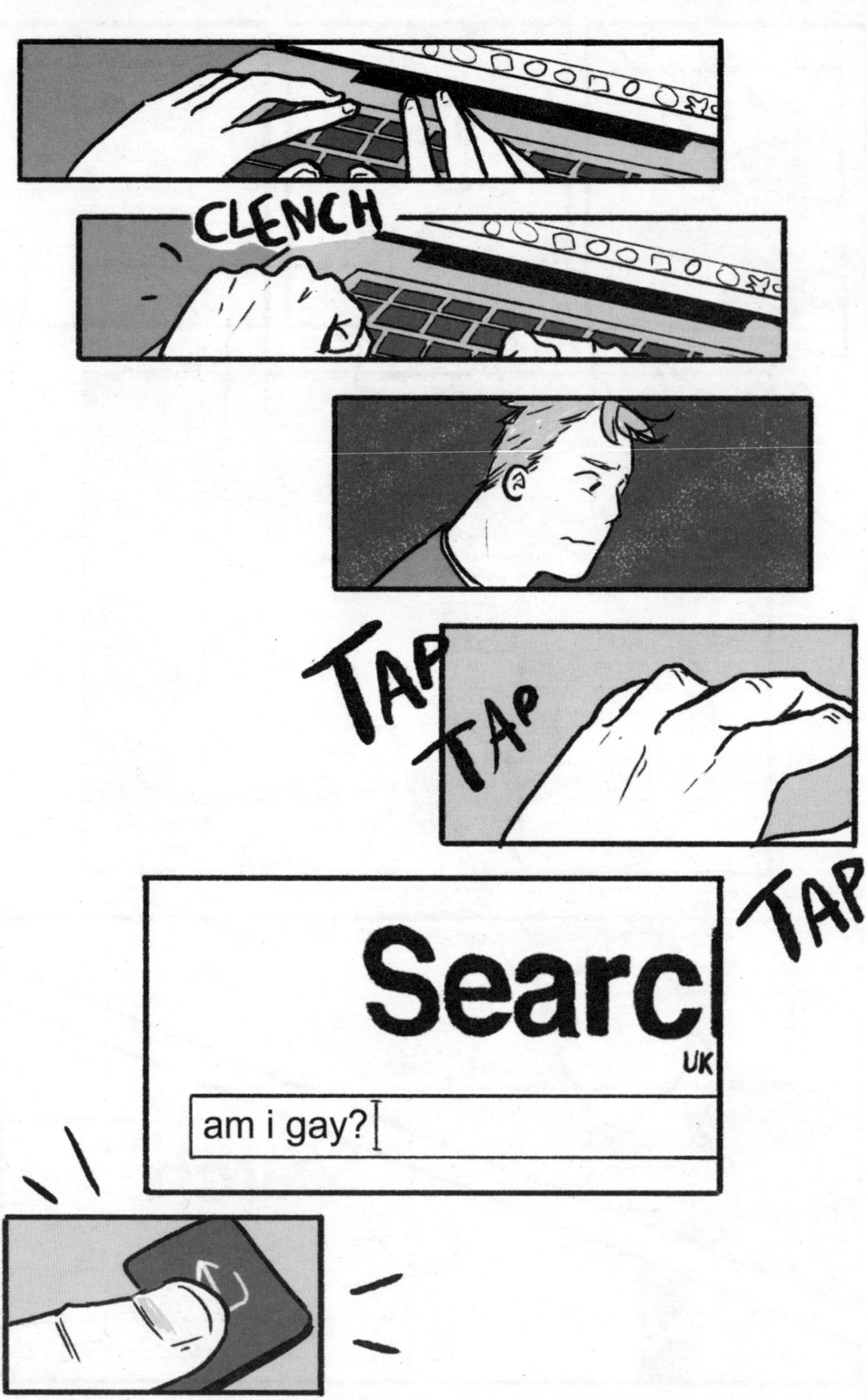
CLENCH
TAP
TAP
TAP
Searc
UK
am i gay?

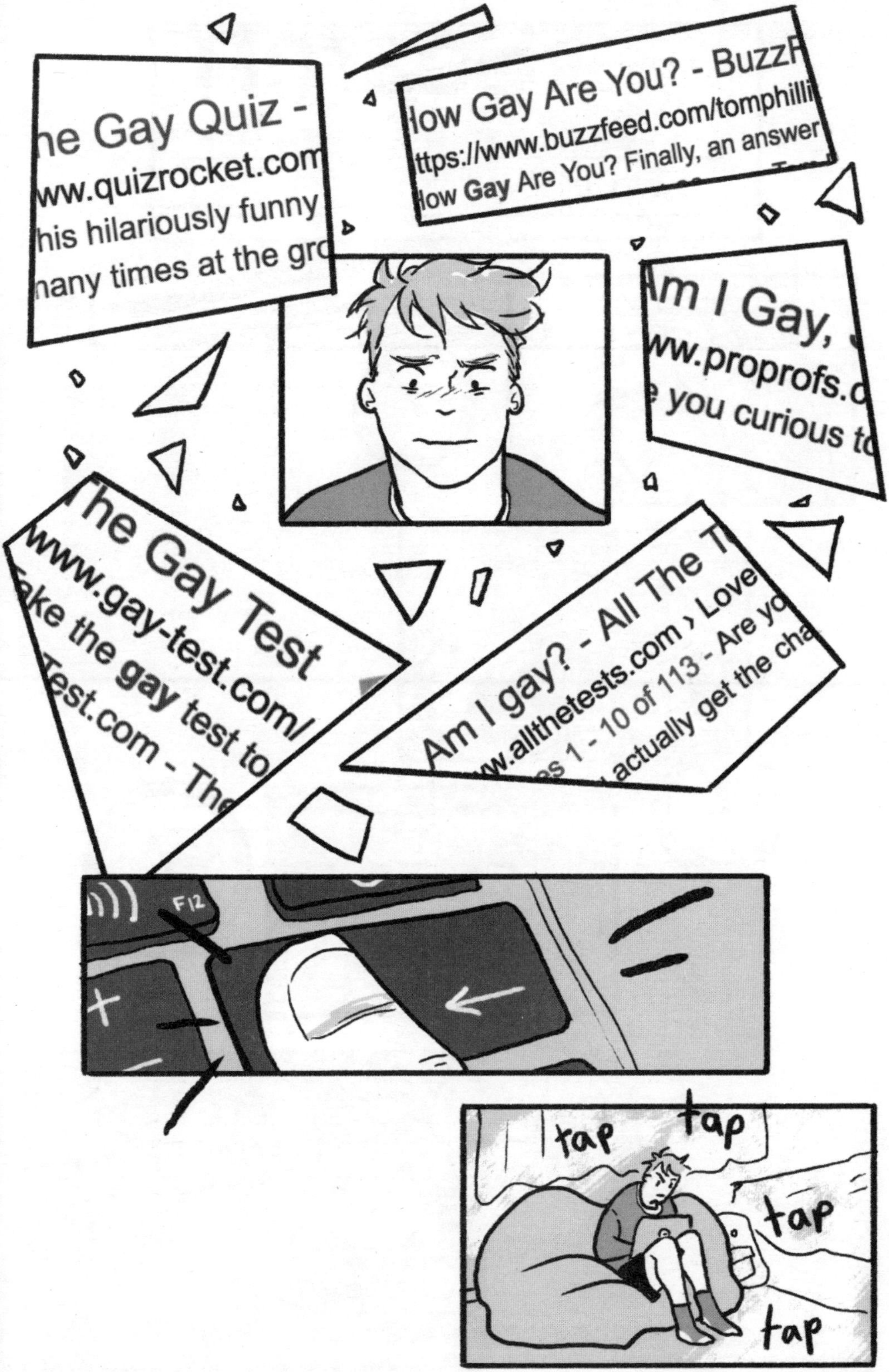

he Gay Quiz -
ww.quizrocket.com
his hilariously funny
nany times at the gro
How Gay Are You? - BuzzF
https://www.buzzfeed.com/tomphilli
How Gay Are You? Finally, an answer
Am I Gay,
ww.proprofs.c
e you curious to
The Gay Test
www.gay-test.com/
Take the gay test to
Test.com - The
Am I gay? - All The T
www.allthetests.com › Love
es 1 - 10 of 113 - Are yo
actually get the cha
F12
tap
tap
tap
tap

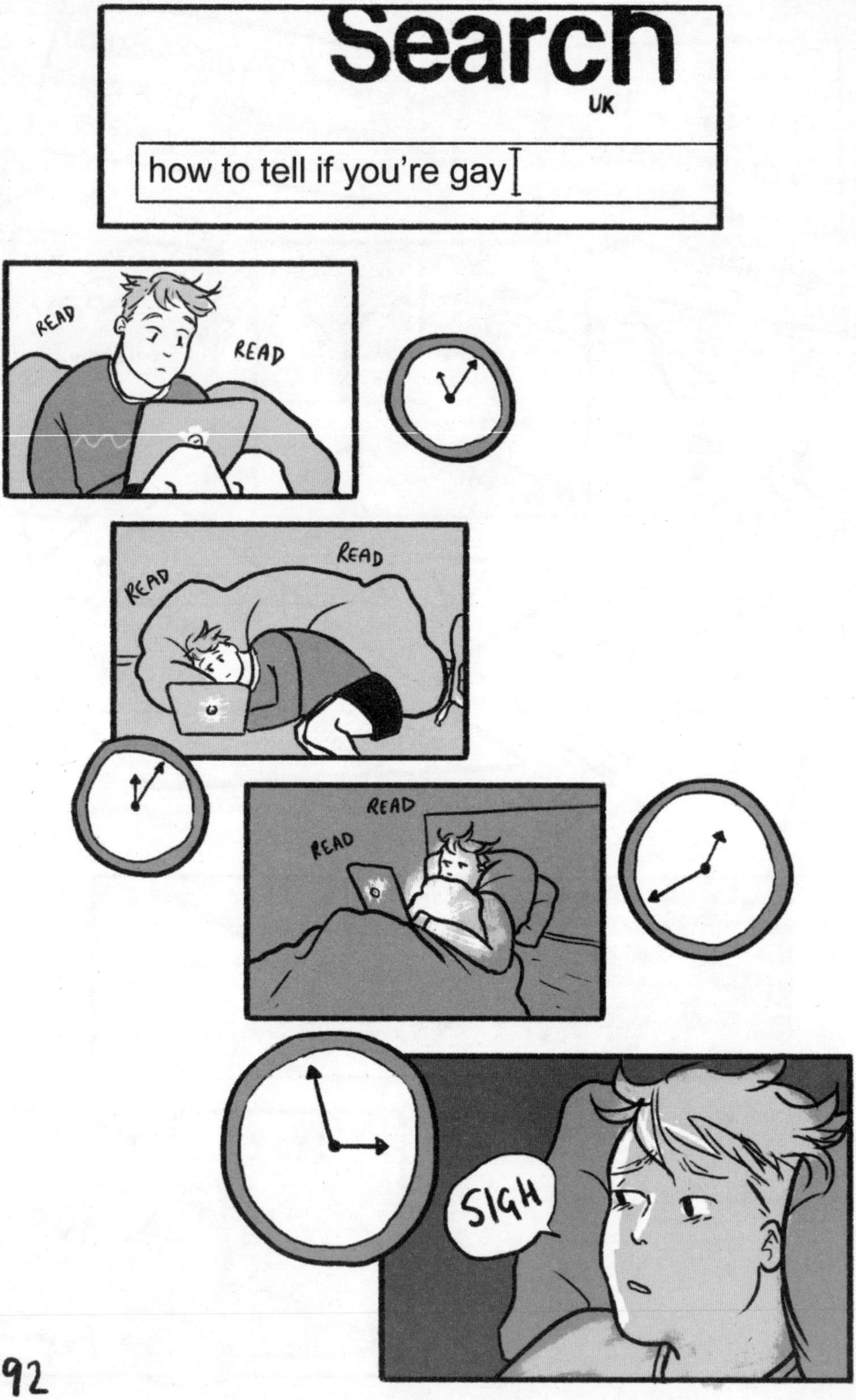
Search
UK
how to tell if you're gay
READ
READ
READ
READ
READ
READ
SIGH

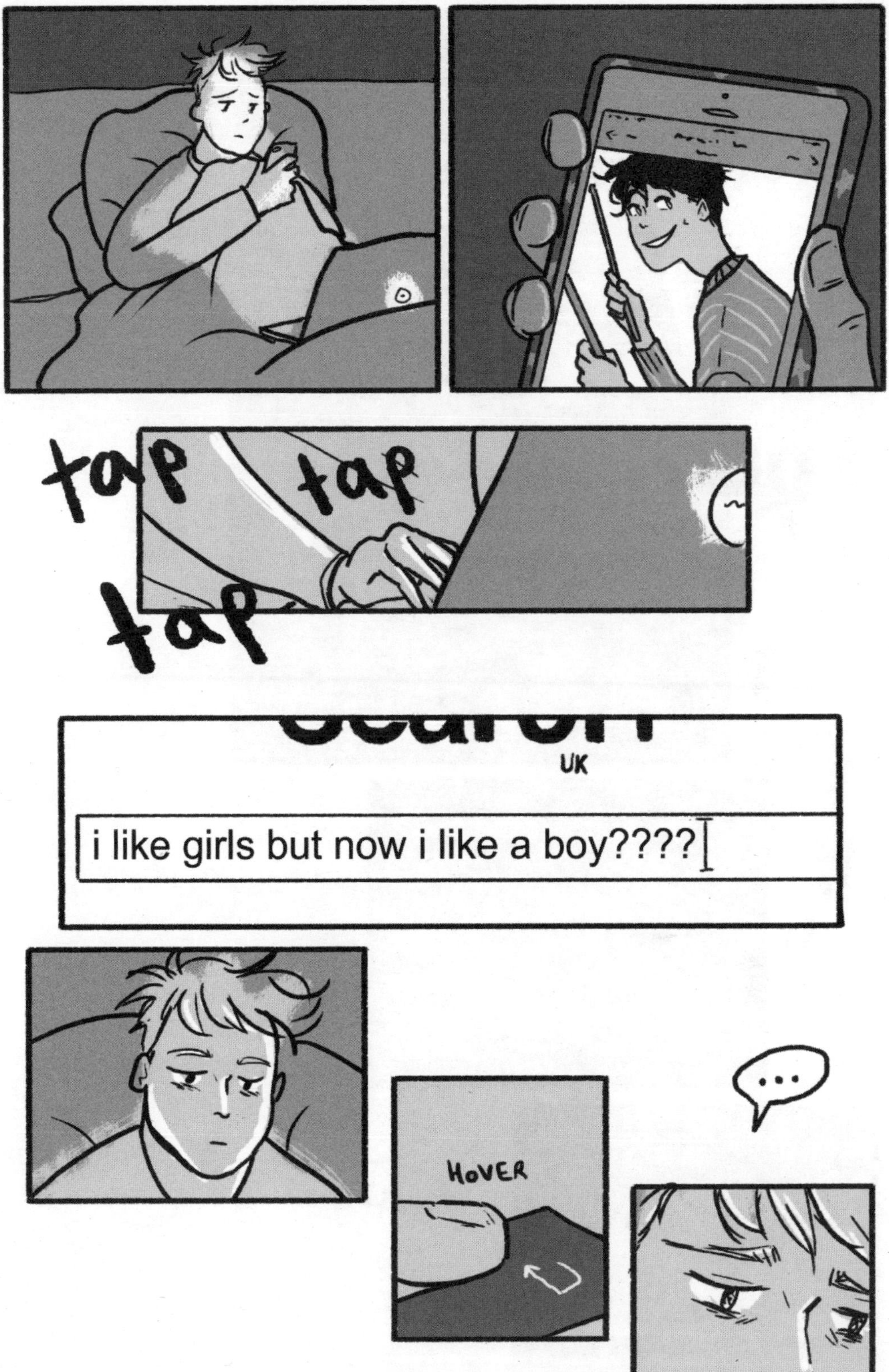

tap tap tap
UK
i like girls but now i like a boy????
HOVER
...

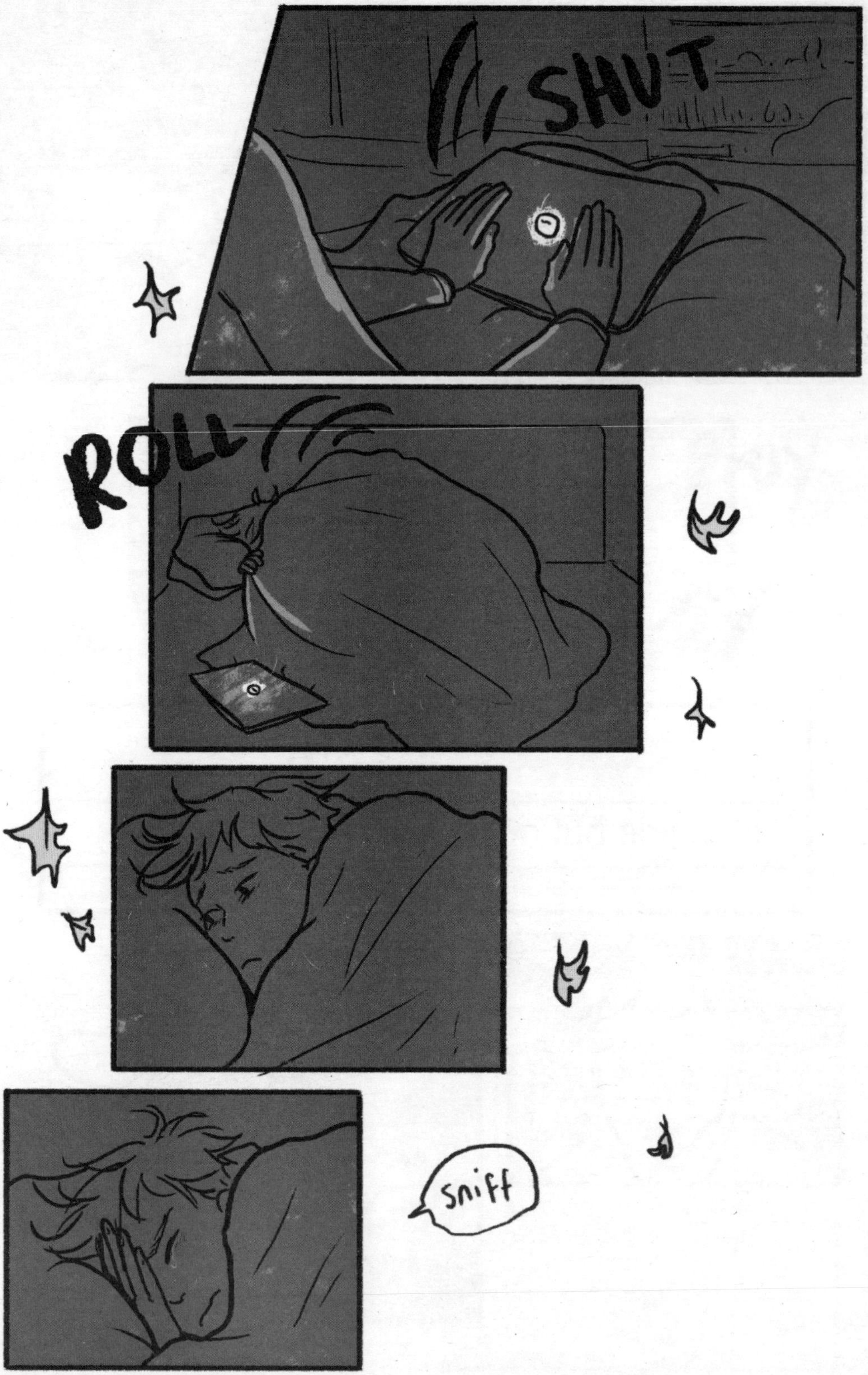
SHUT
ROLL
sniff

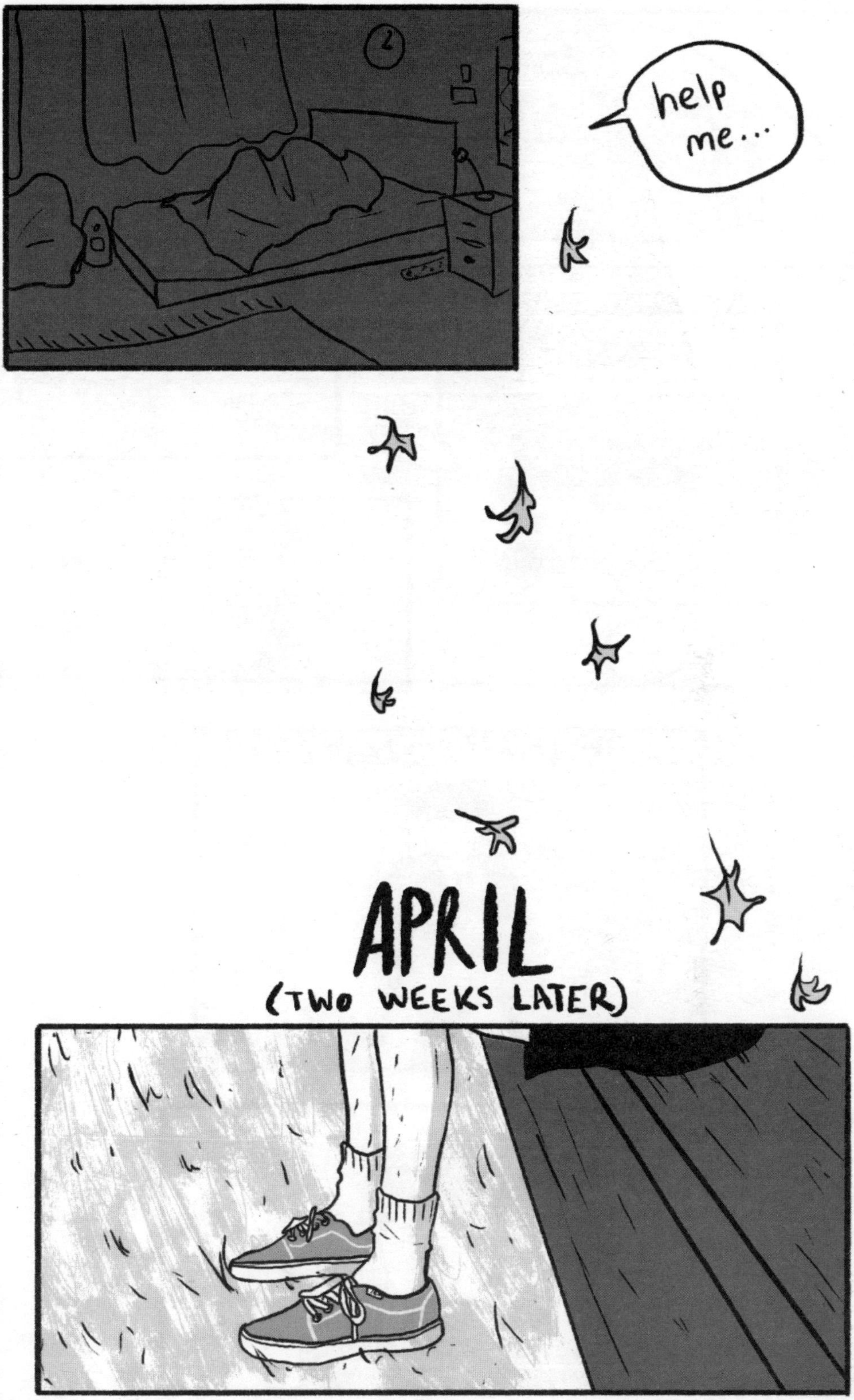
help me...
APRIL
(TWO WEEKS LATER)

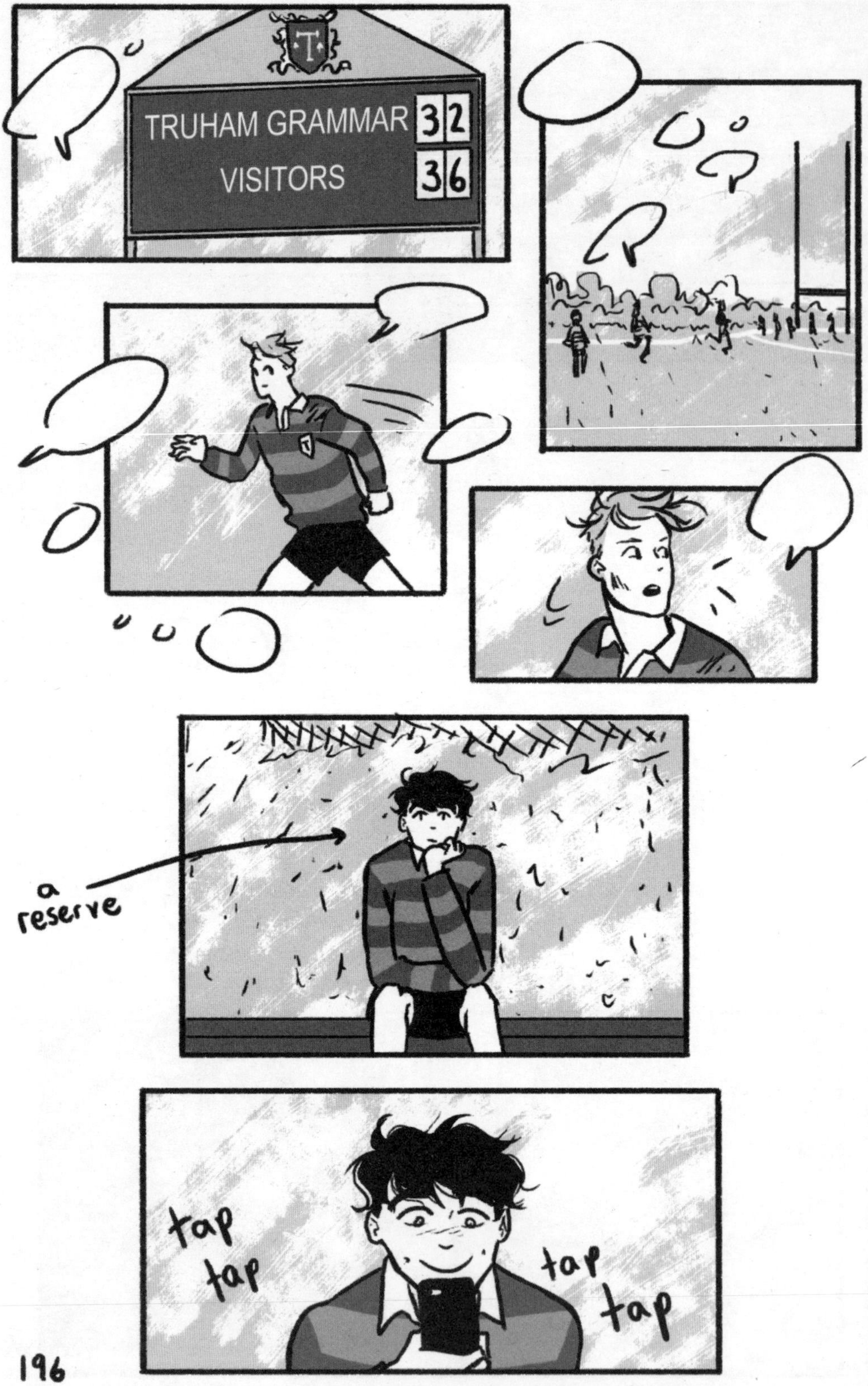
TRUHAM GRAMMAR 32
VISITORS 36
a reserve
tap tap
tap tap

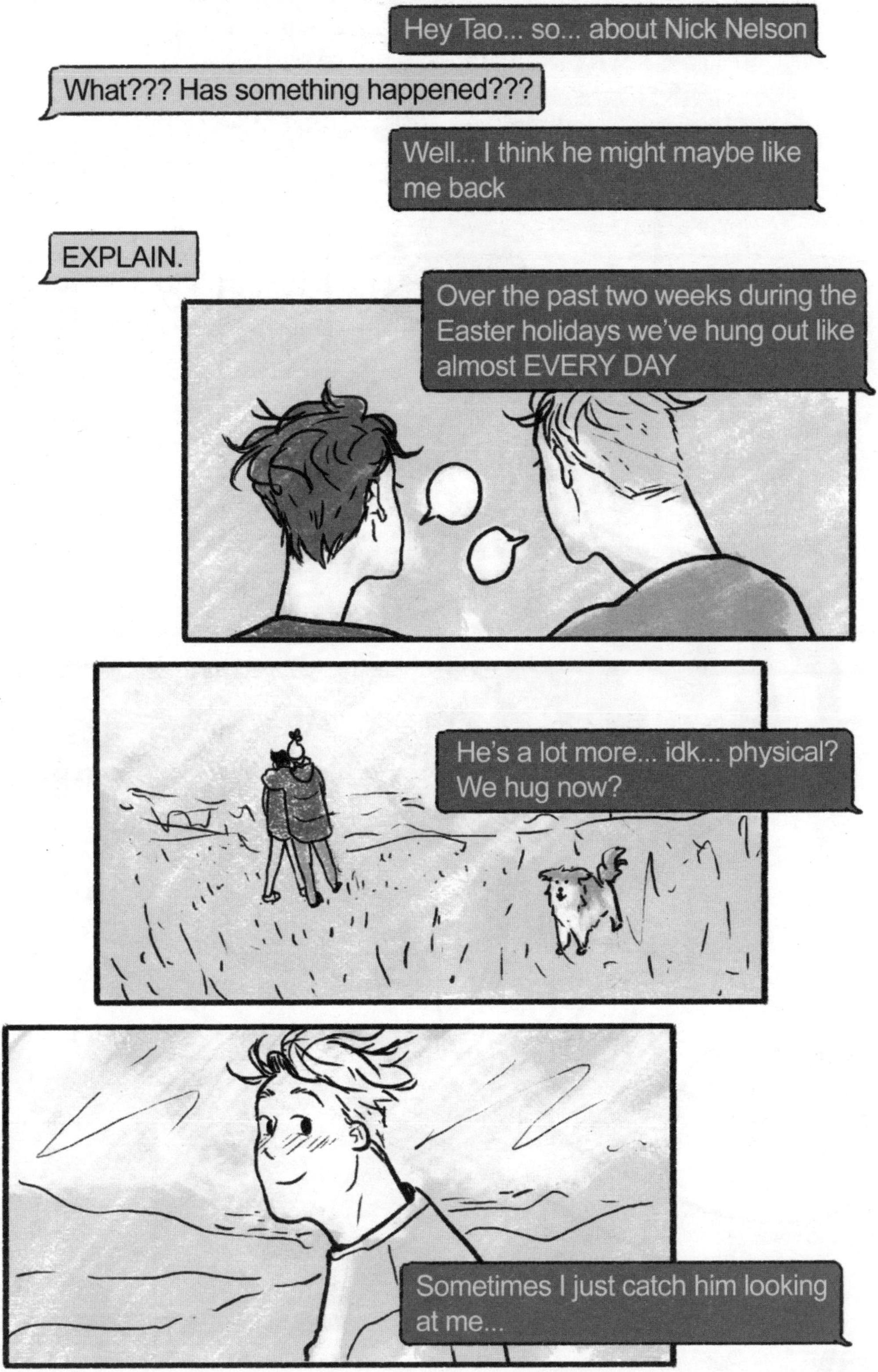
Hey Tao... so... about Nick Nelson
What??? Has something happened???
Well... I think he might maybe like me back
EXPLAIN.
Over the past two weeks during the Easter holidays we've hung out like almost EVERY DAY
He's a lot more... idk... physical? We hug now?
Sometimes I just catch him looking at me...

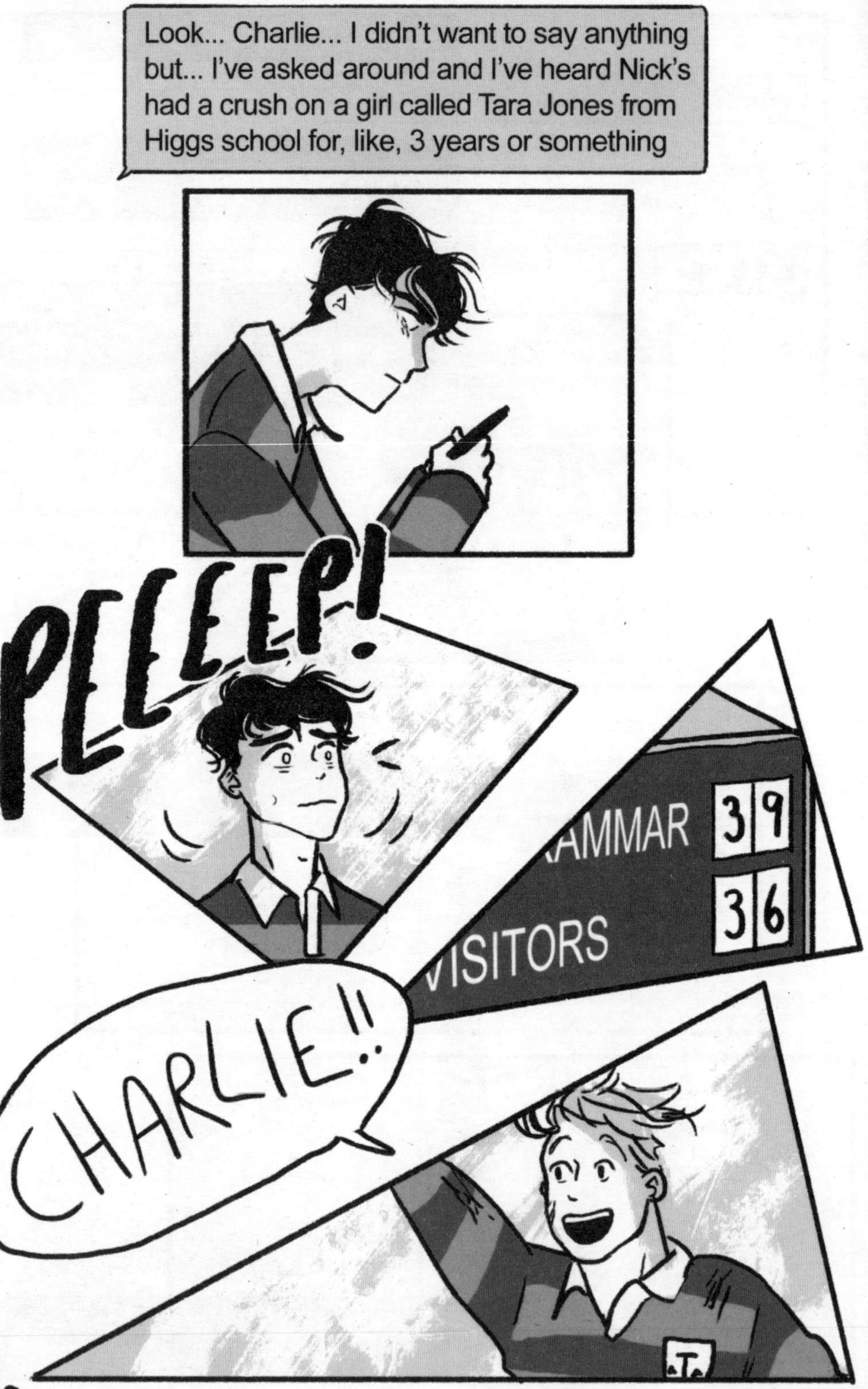
Look... Charlie... I didn't want to say anything but... I've asked around and I've heard Nick's had a crush on a girl called Tara Jones from Higgs school for, like, 3 years or something
PEEEEP!
AMMAR 39
VISITORS 36
CHARLIE!!

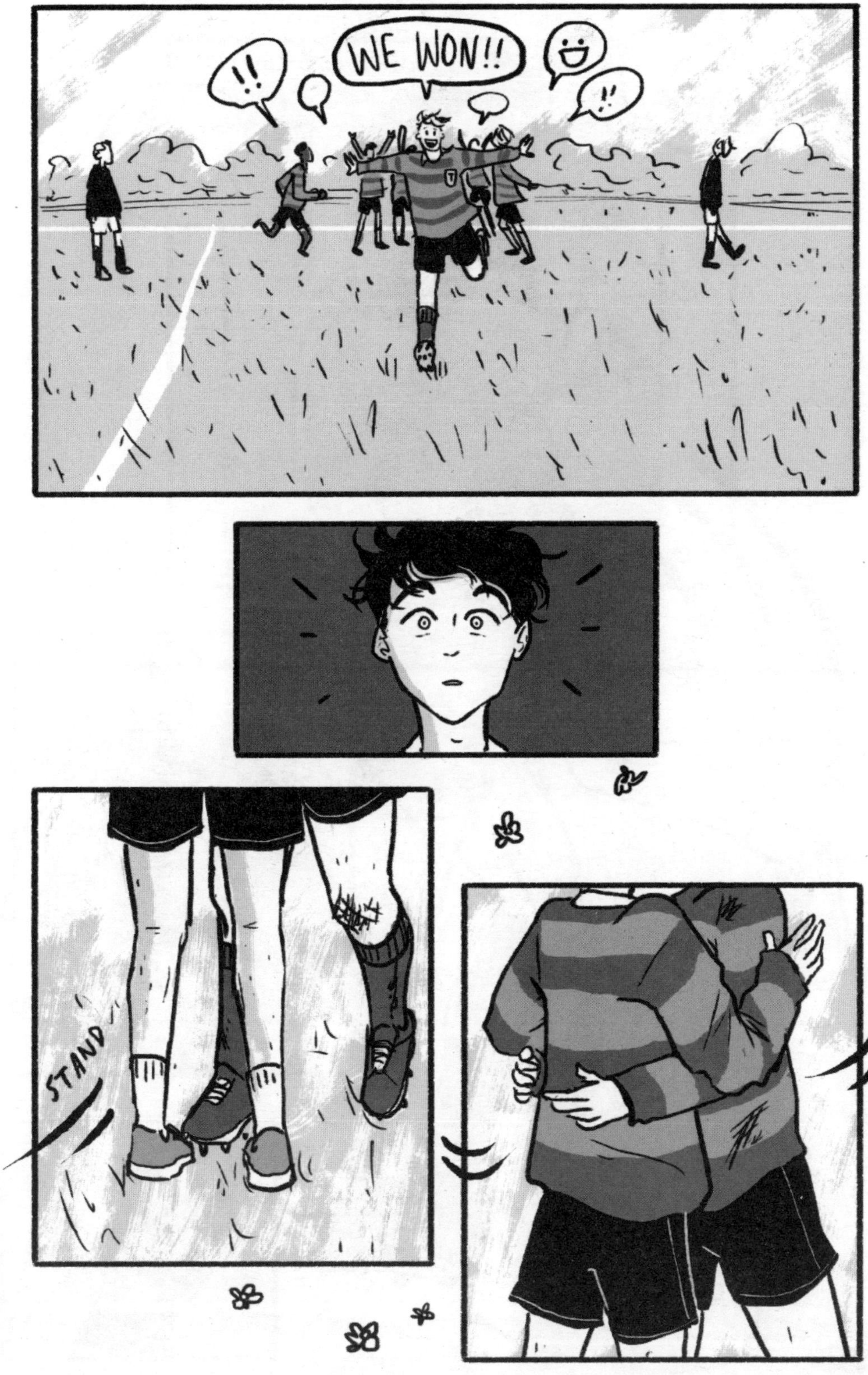
!!
WE WON!!
!!
STAND

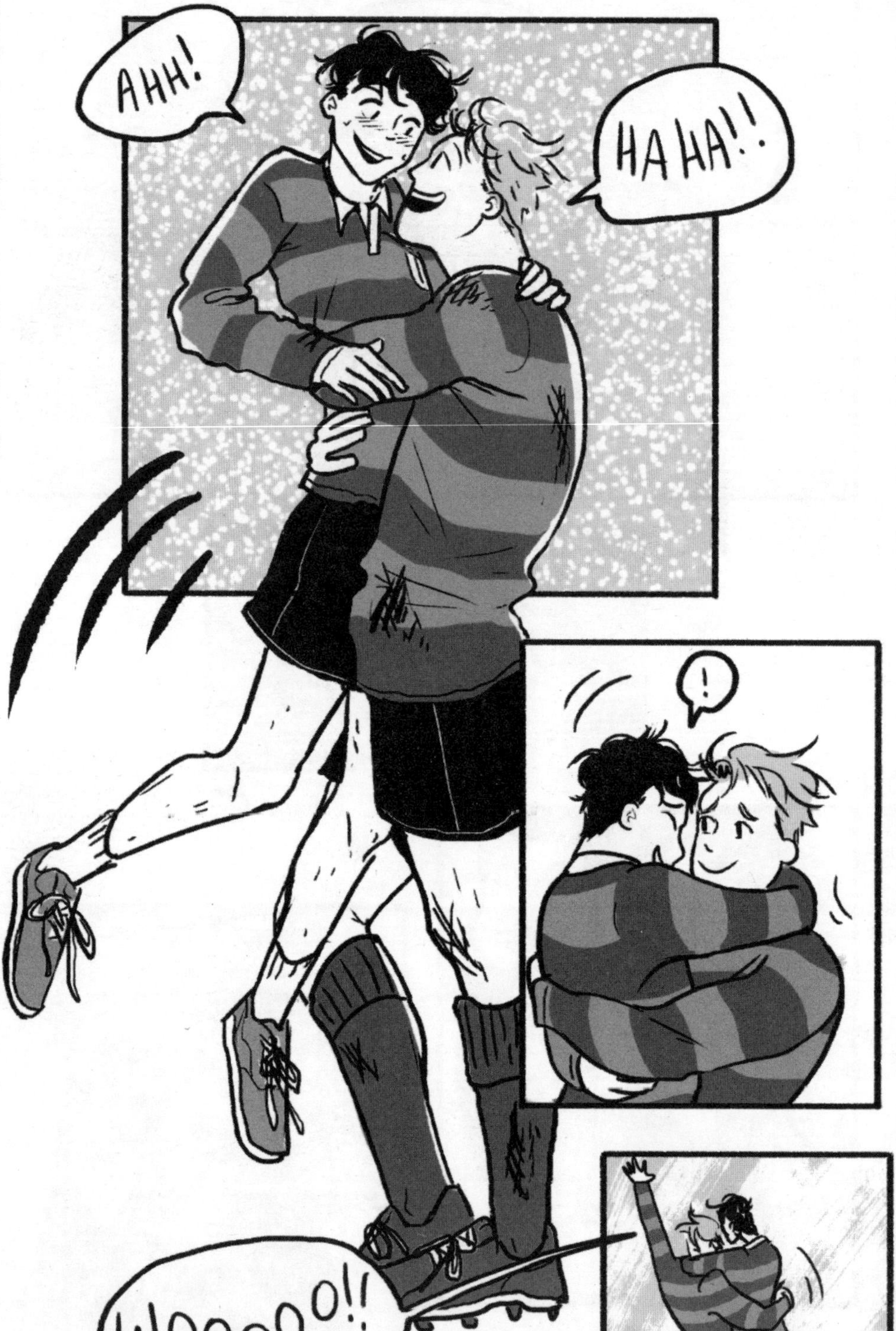
AHH!
HA HA!!
!
WOOOOO!!

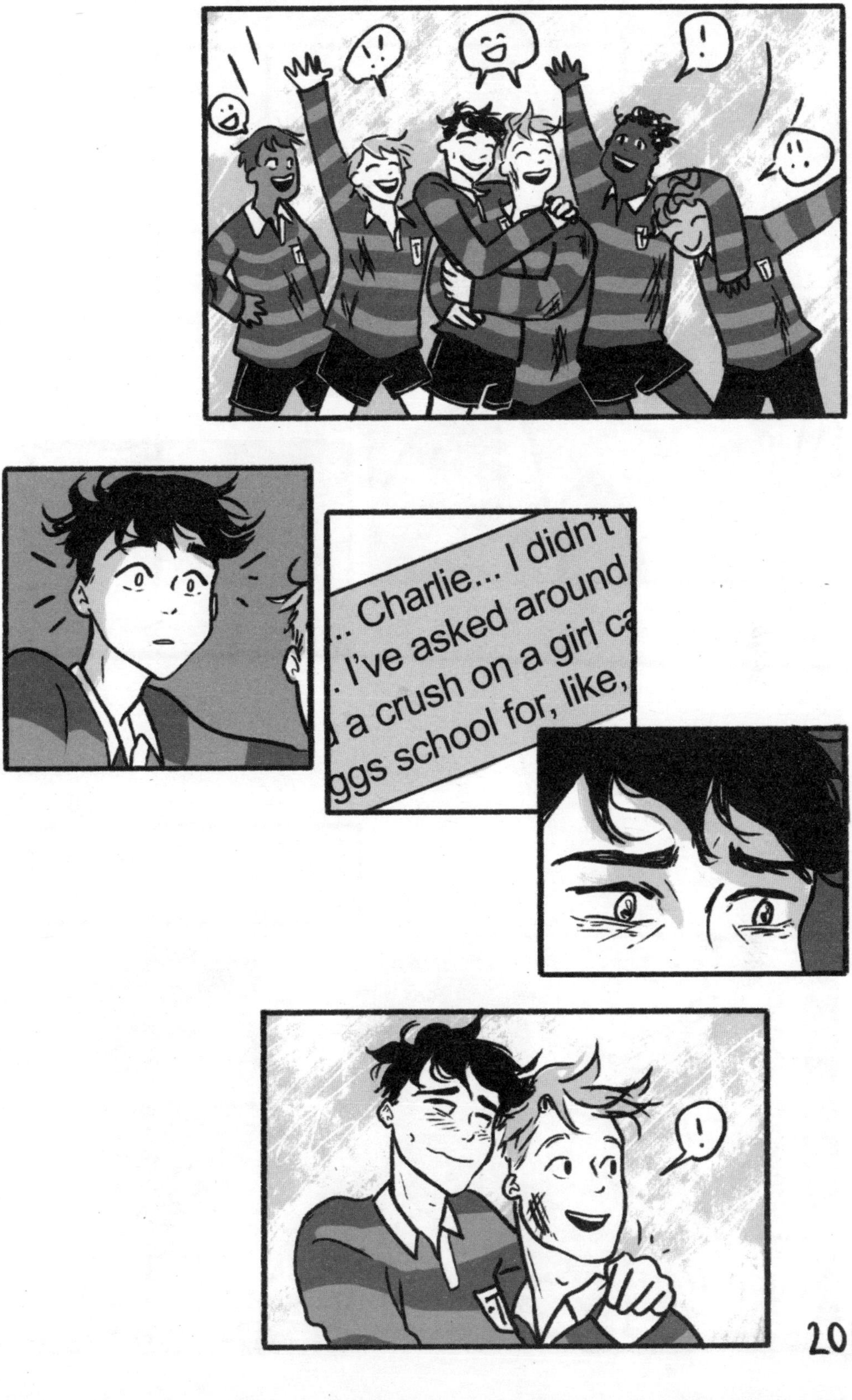
... Charlie... I didn't
. I've asked around
a crush on a girl ca
ggs school for, like,

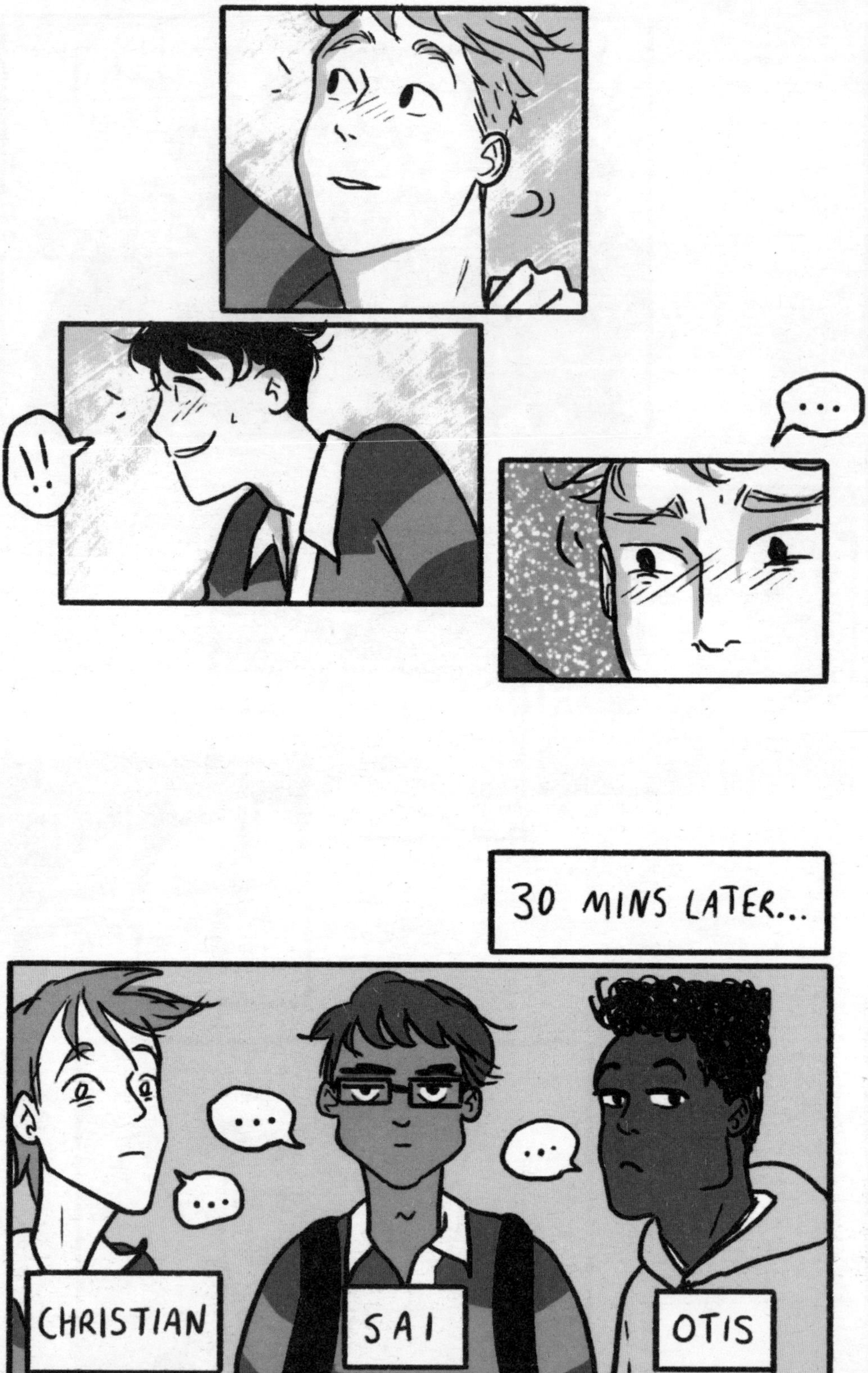
!!
...
30 MINS LATER...
...
...
...
CHRISTIAN
SAI
OTIS

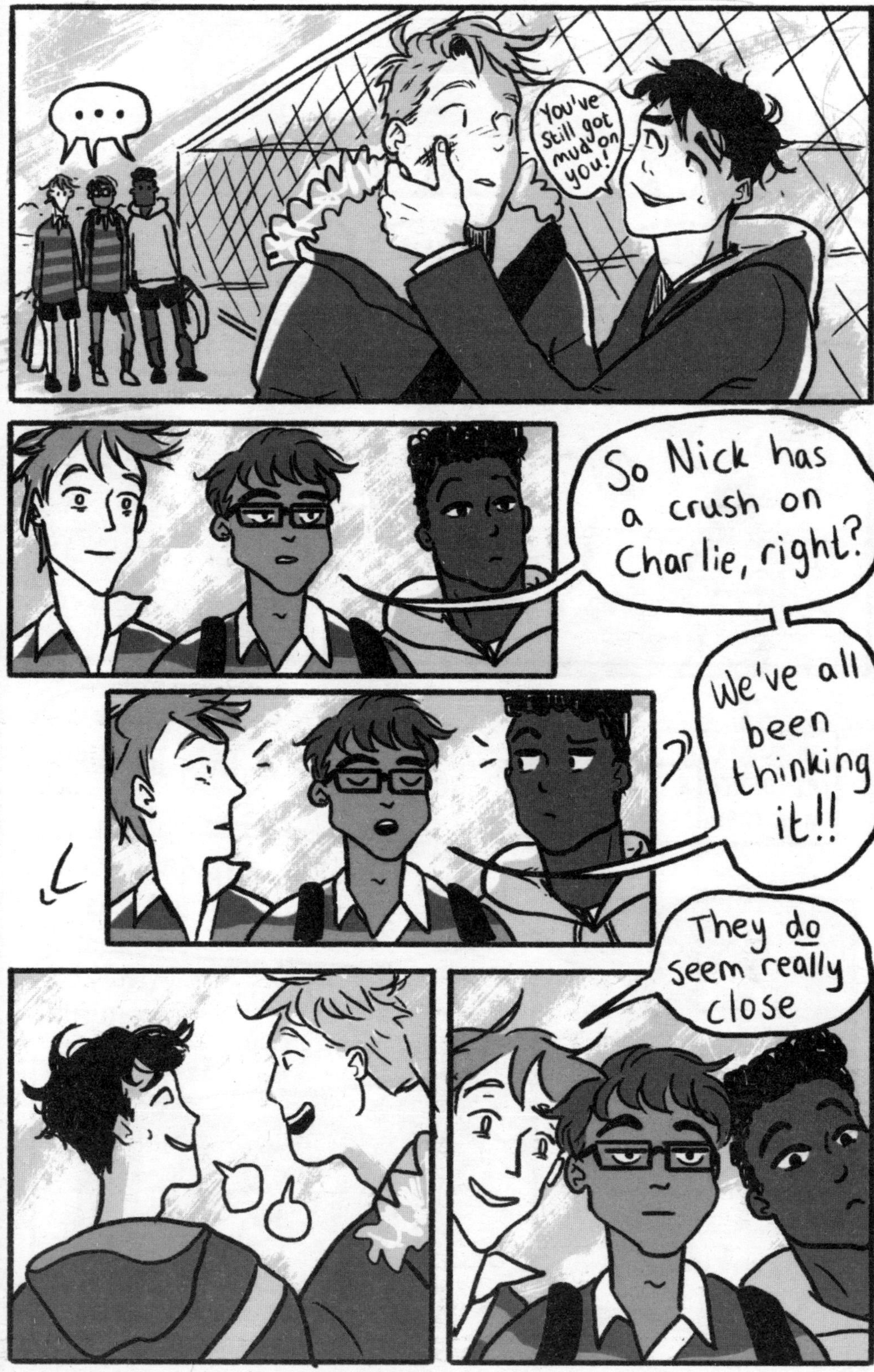
...
You've still got mud on you!
So Nick has a crush on Charlie, right?
We've all been thinking it!!
They do seem really close

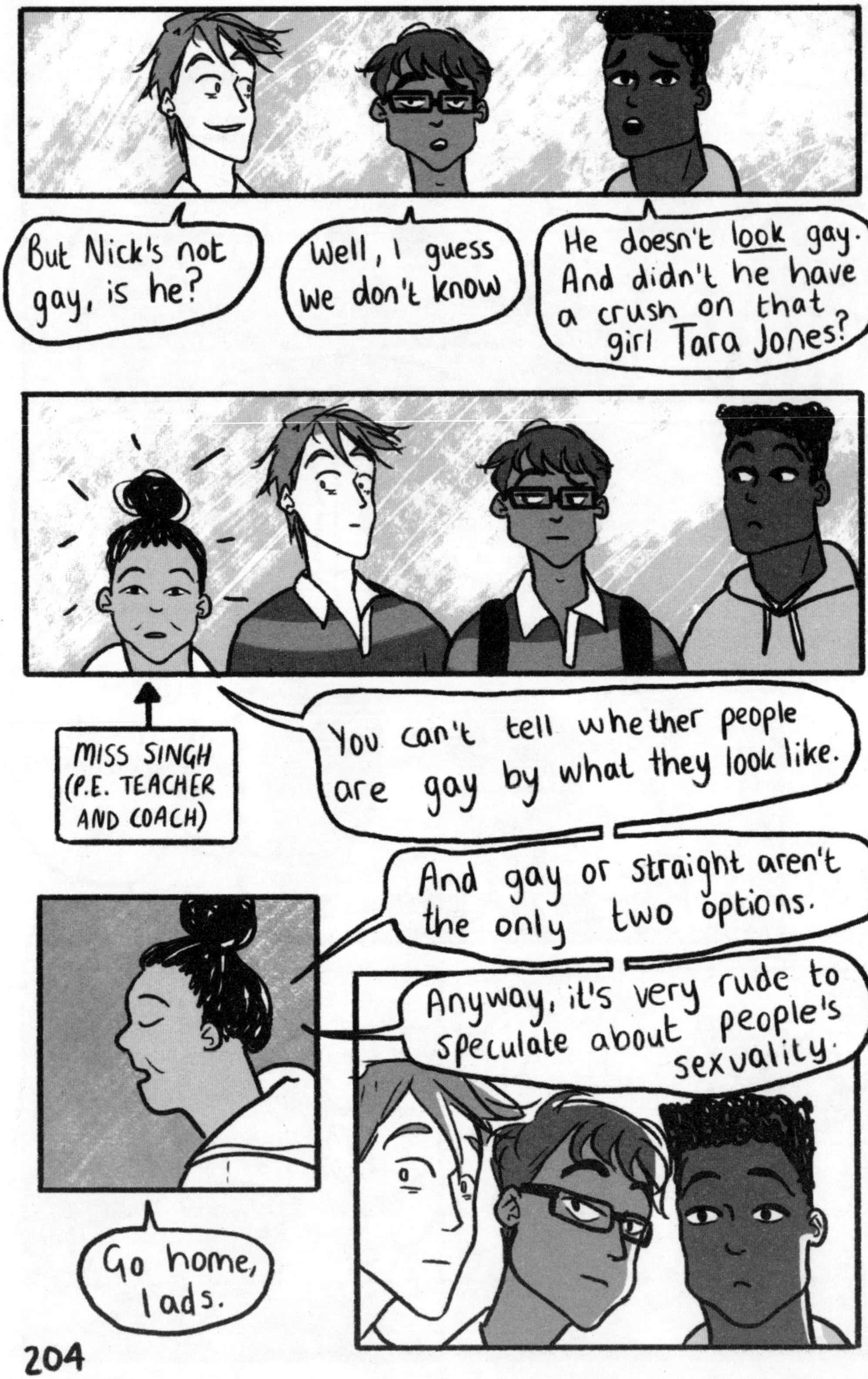

But Nick's not gay, is he?
Well, I guess we don't know
He doesn't look gay. And didn't he have a crush on that girl Tara Jones?
MISS SINGH (P.E. TEACHER AND COACH)
You can't tell whether people are gay by what they look like.
And gay or straight aren't the only two options.
Anyway, it's very rude to speculate about people's sexuality.
Go home, lads.

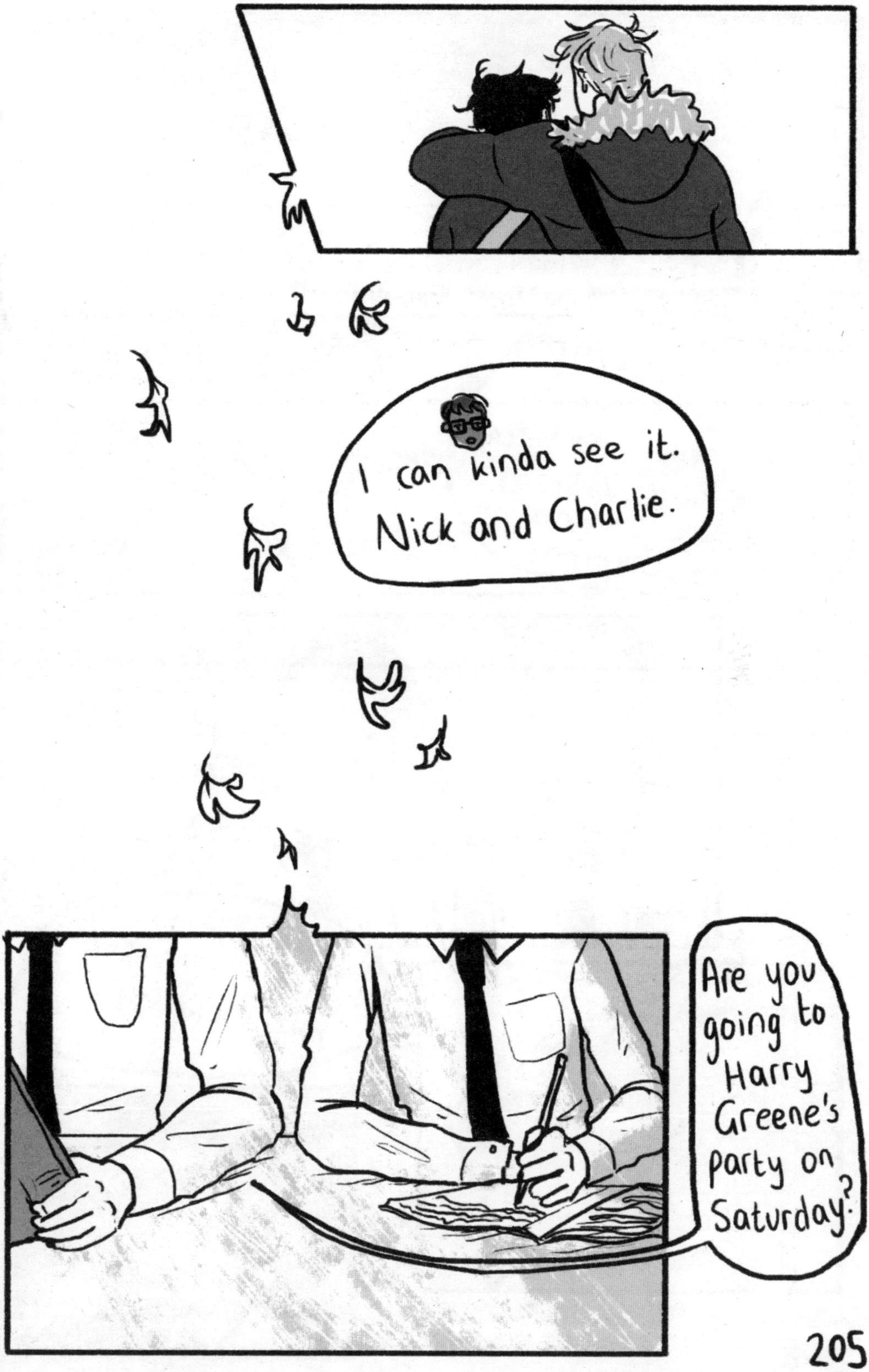
I can kinda see it. Nick and Charlie.
Are you going to Harry Greene's party on Saturday?

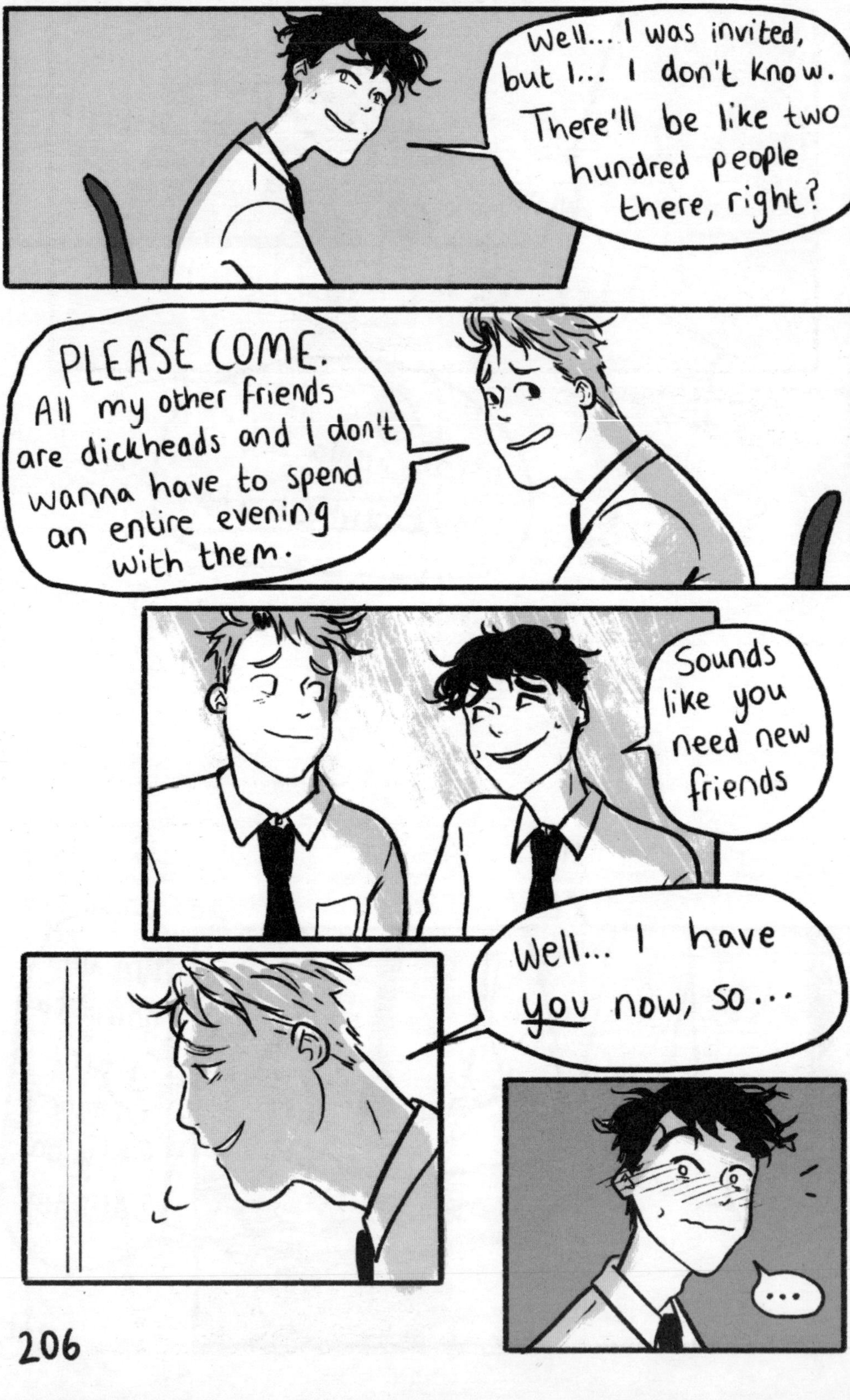
Well... I was invited, but I... I don't know. There'll be like two hundred people there, right?
PLEASE COME. All my other friends are dickheads and I don't wanna have to spend an entire evening with them.
Sounds like you need new friends
Well... I have you now, so...
...

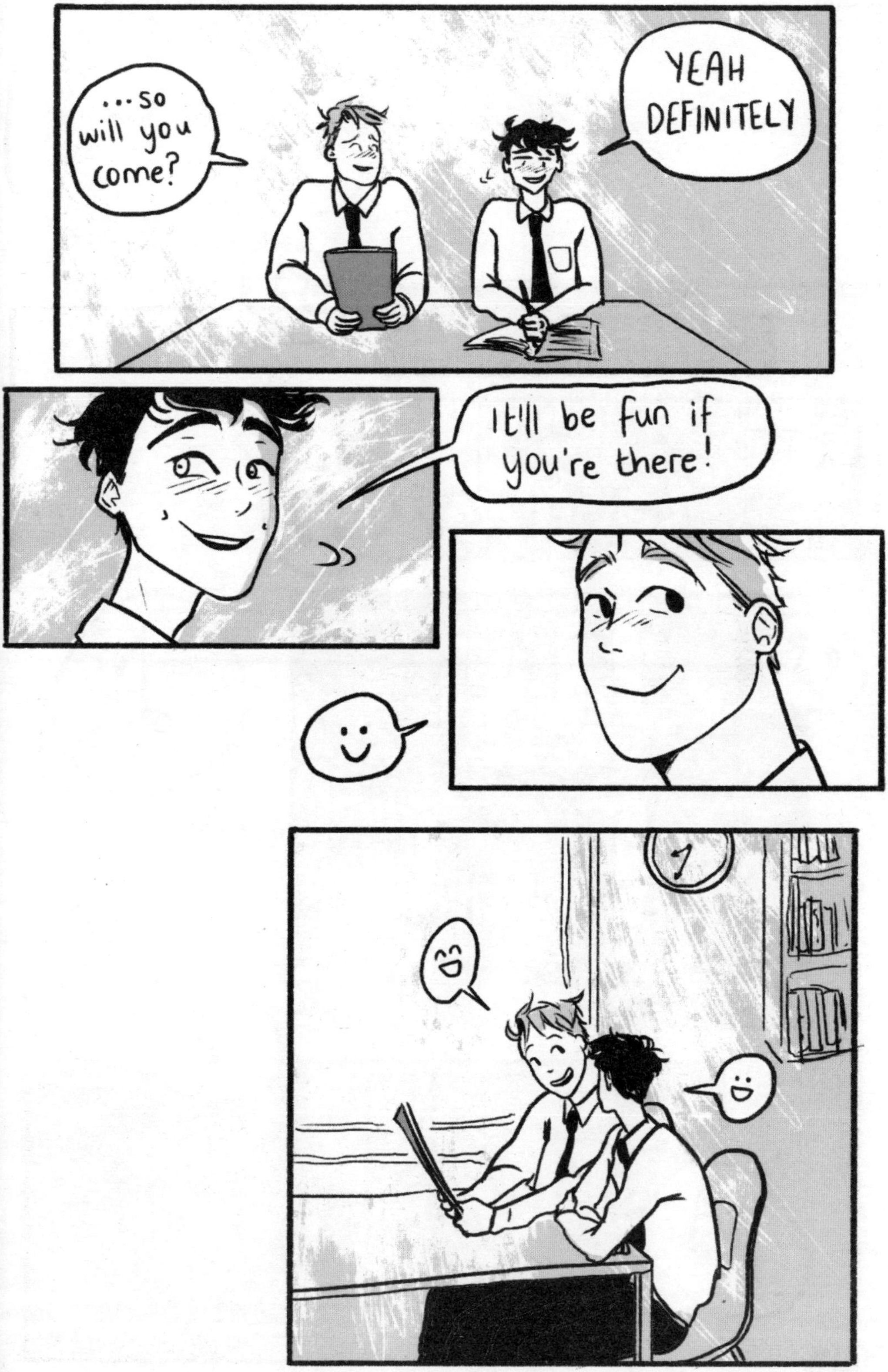
...so will you come?
YEAH DEFINITELY
It'll be fun if you're there!

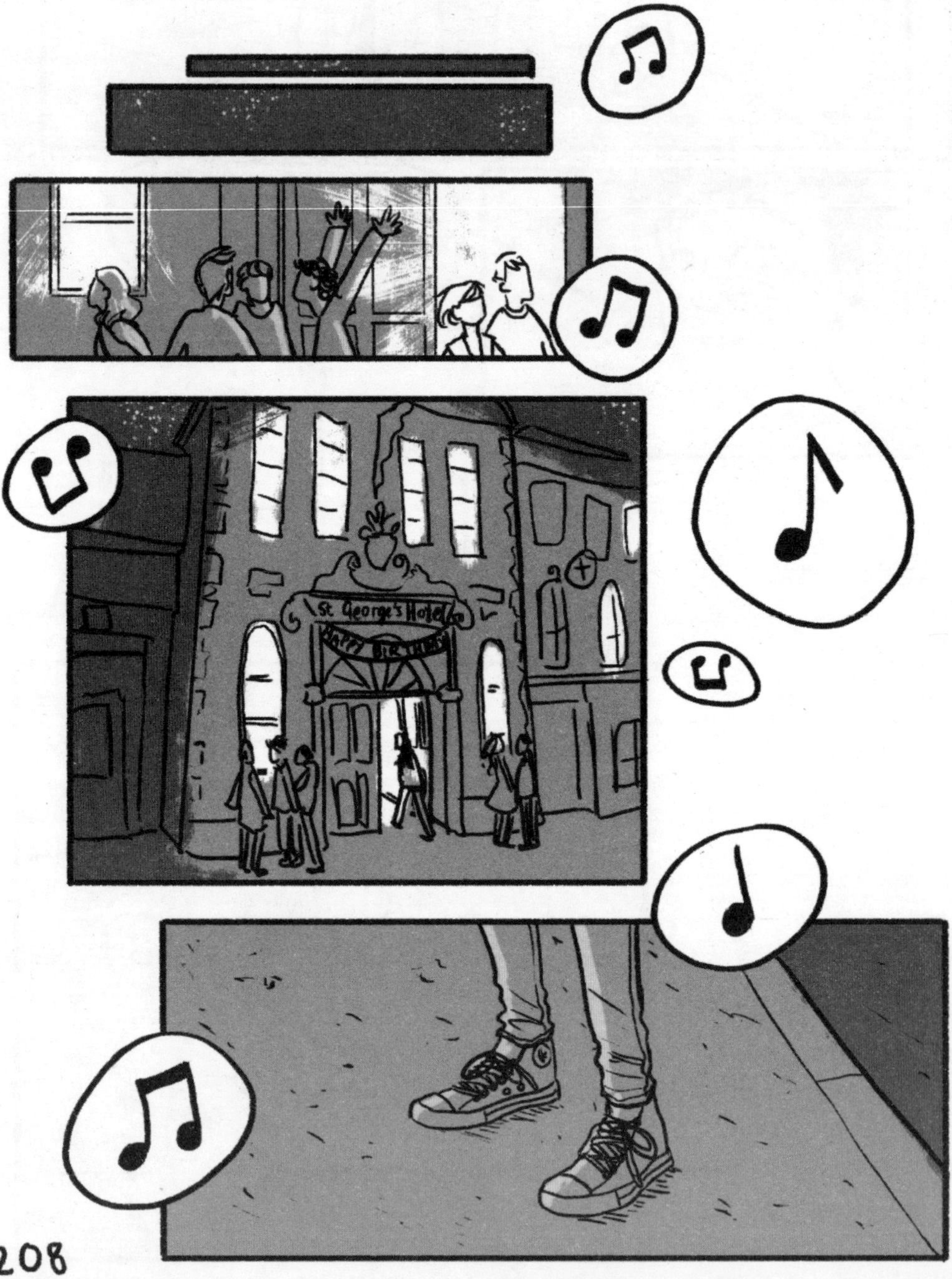
St George's Hotel

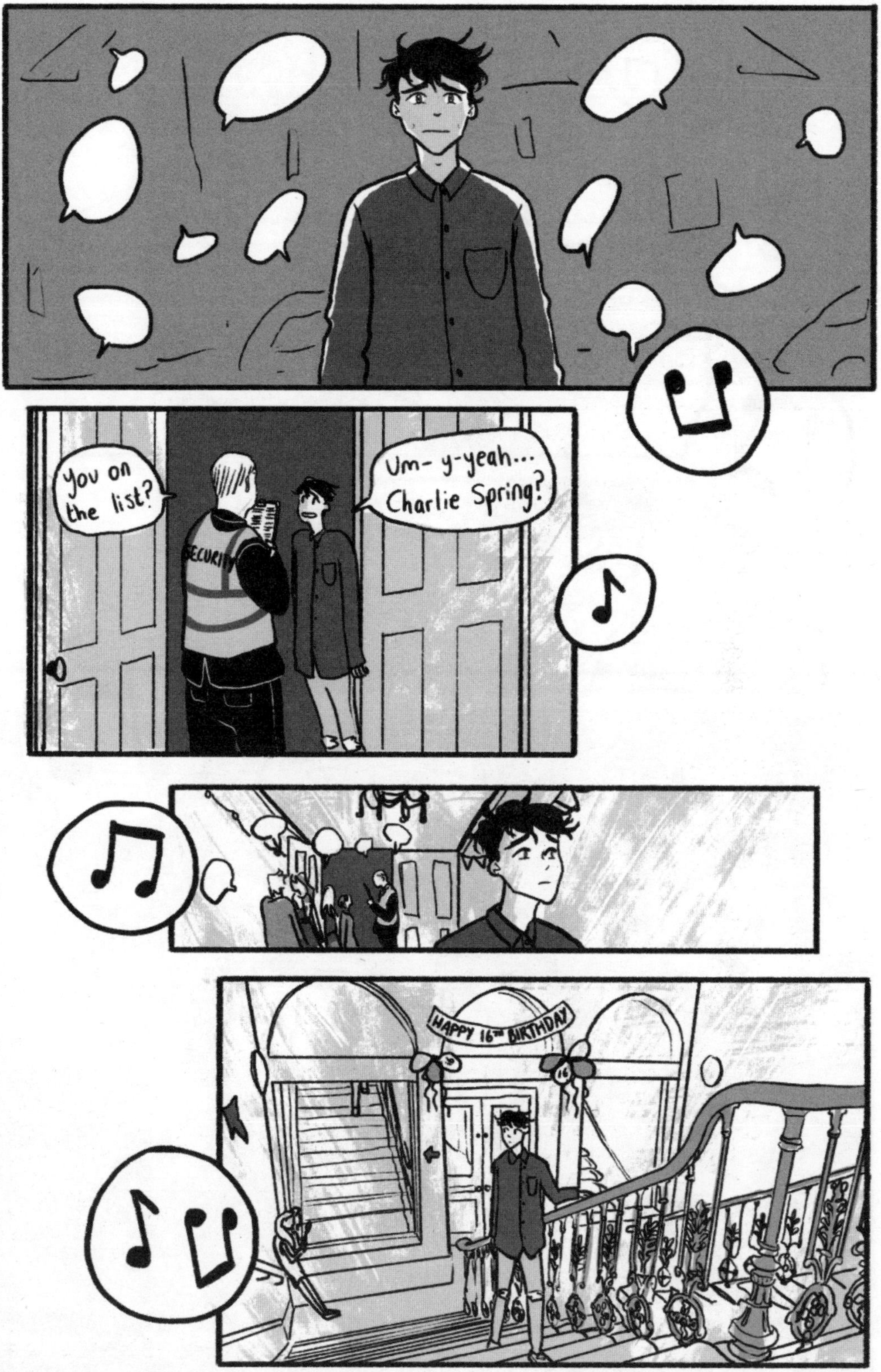
You on the list?
Um- y-yeah... Charlie Spring?
SECURITY
HAPPY 16TH BIRTHDAY

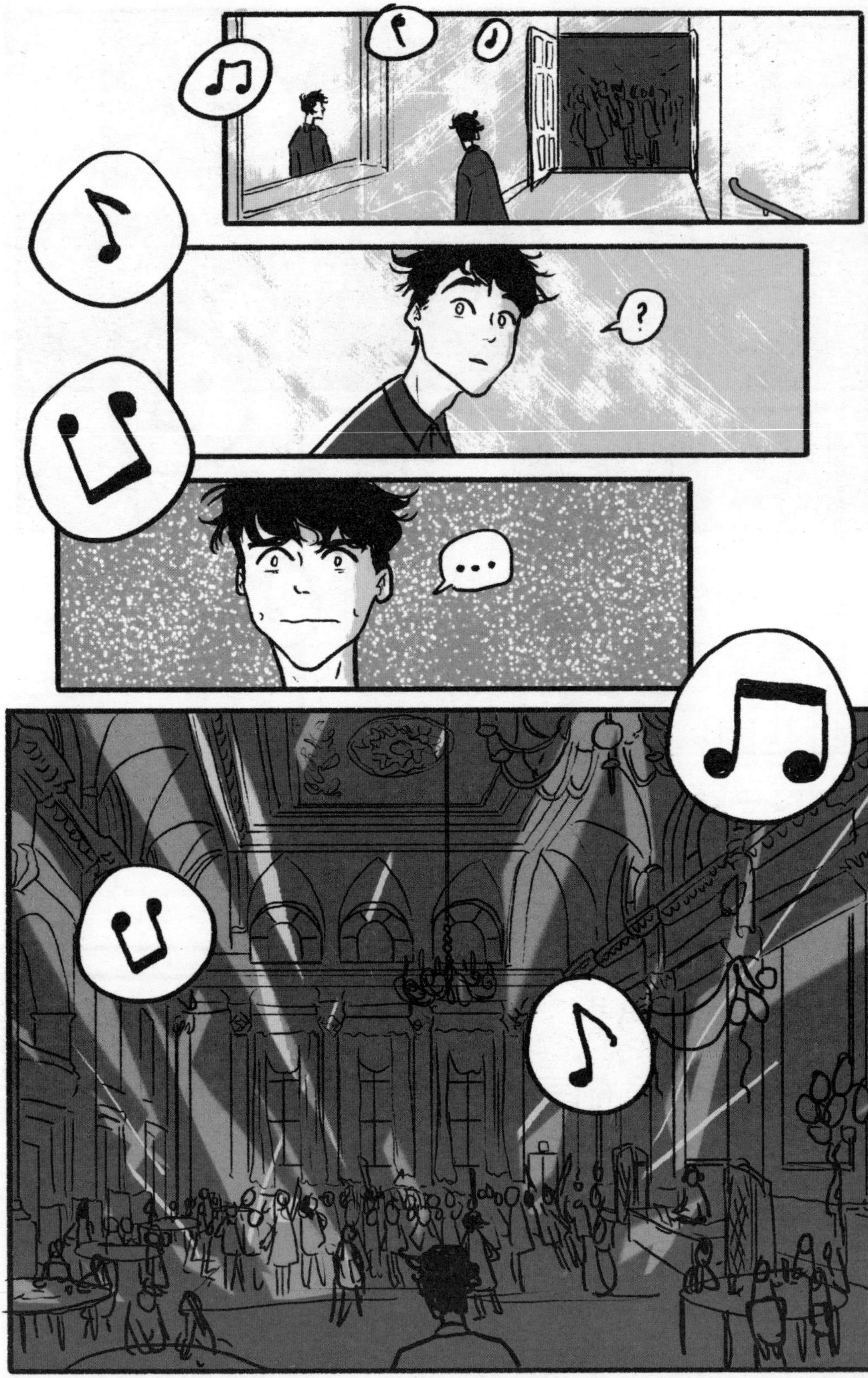
?
...

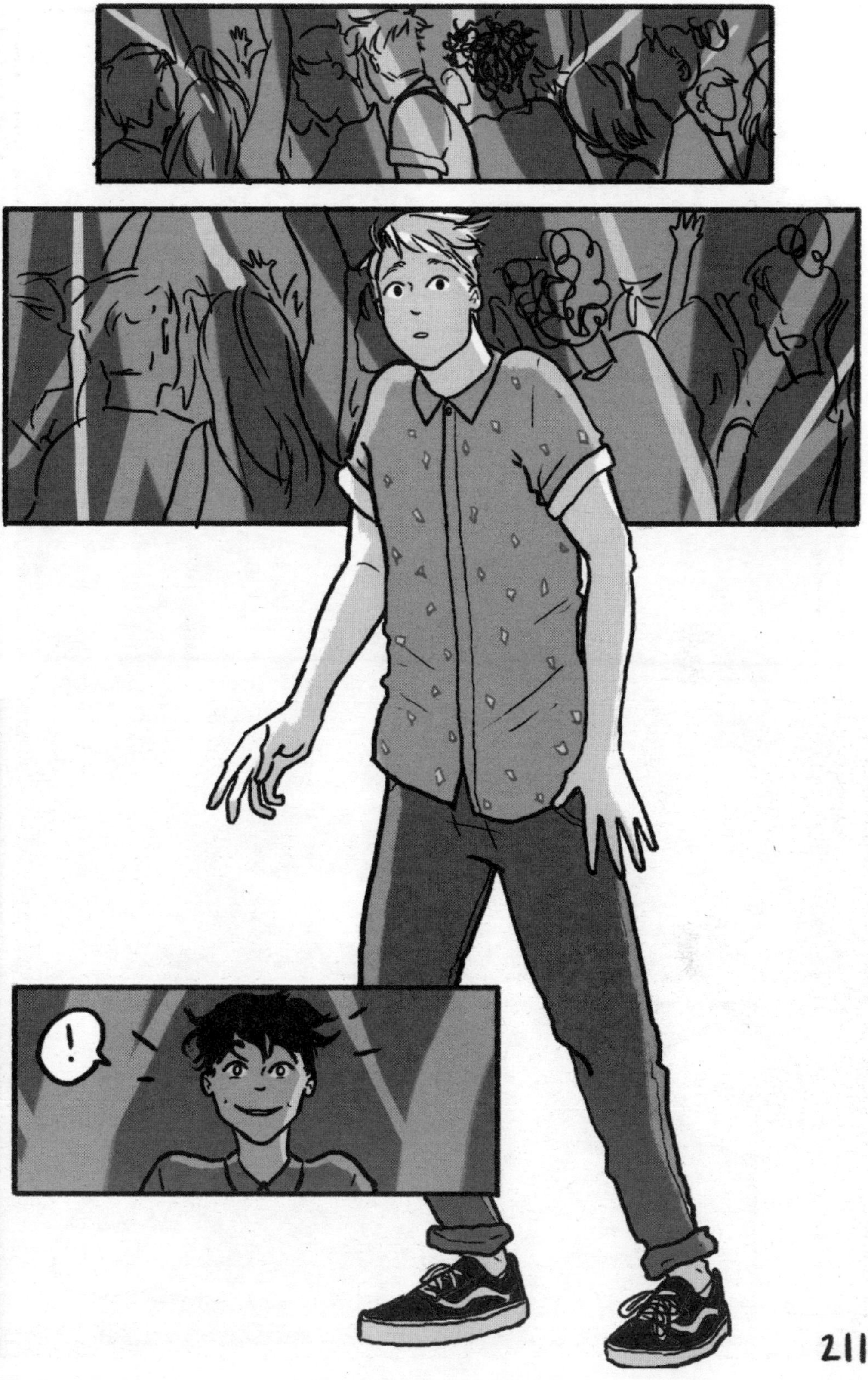
!

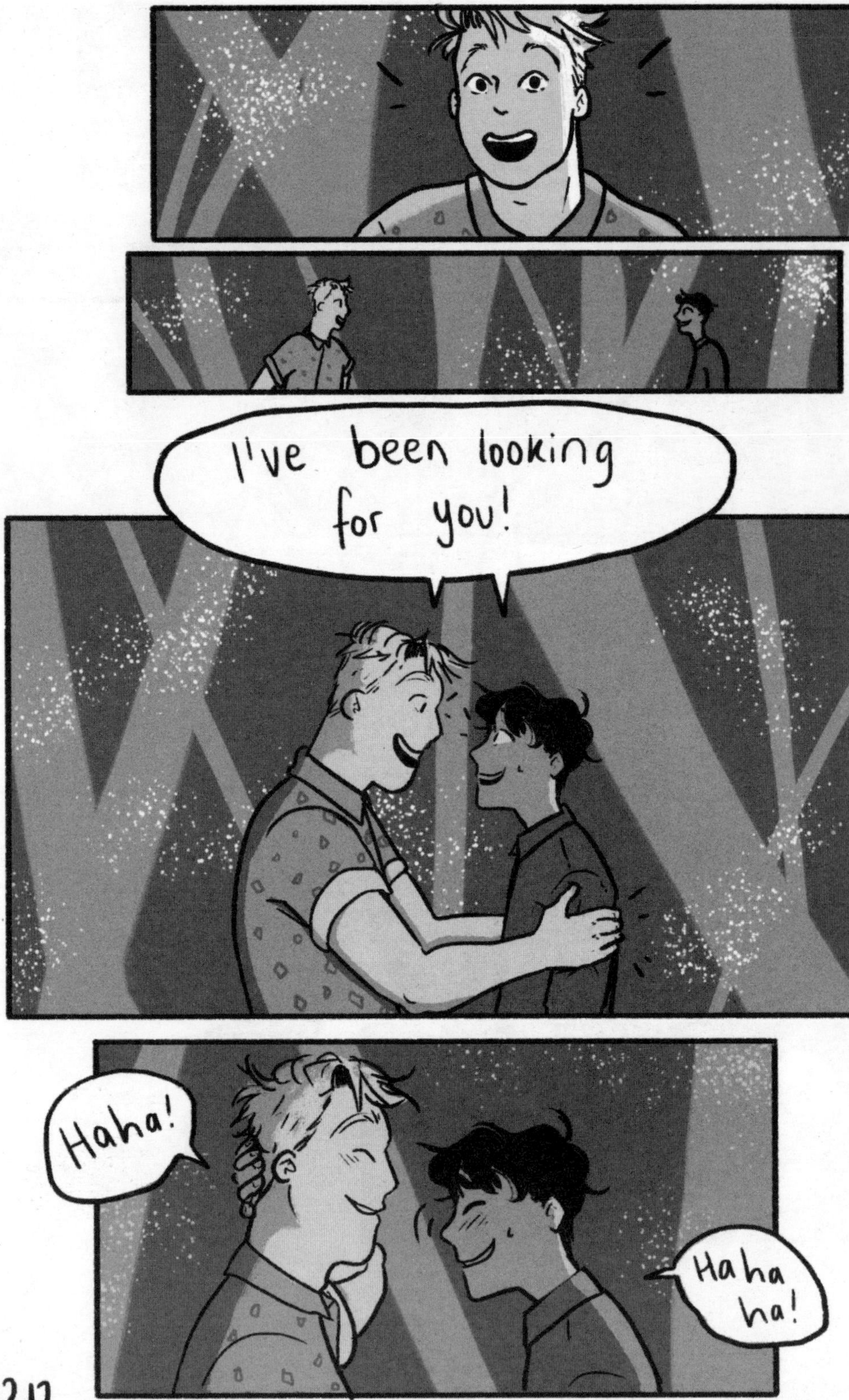
I've been looking for you!
Haha!
Haha ha!

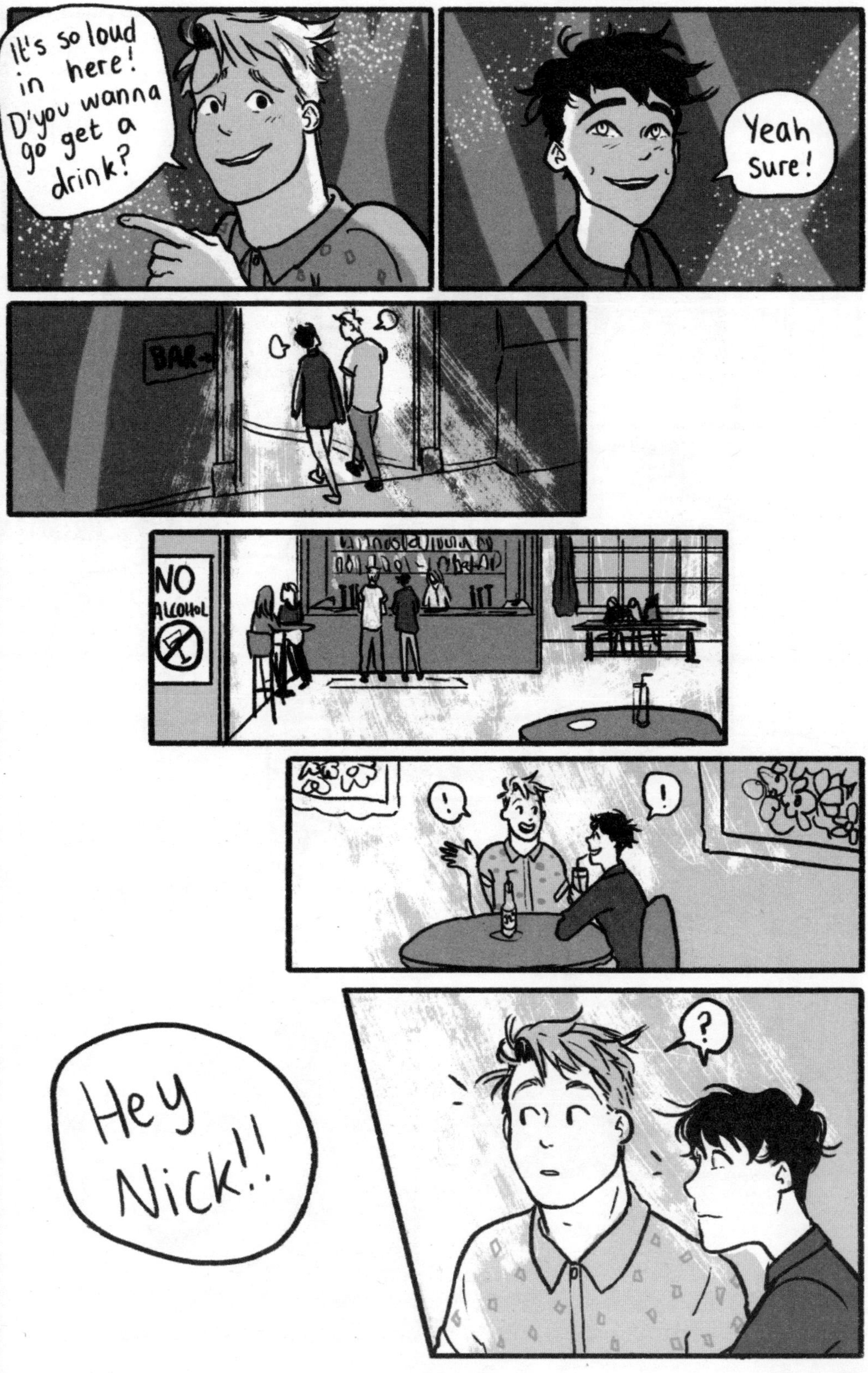
It's so loud in here! D'you wanna go get a drink?
Yeah sure!
BAR
NO ALCOHOL
!
!
?
Hey Nick!!

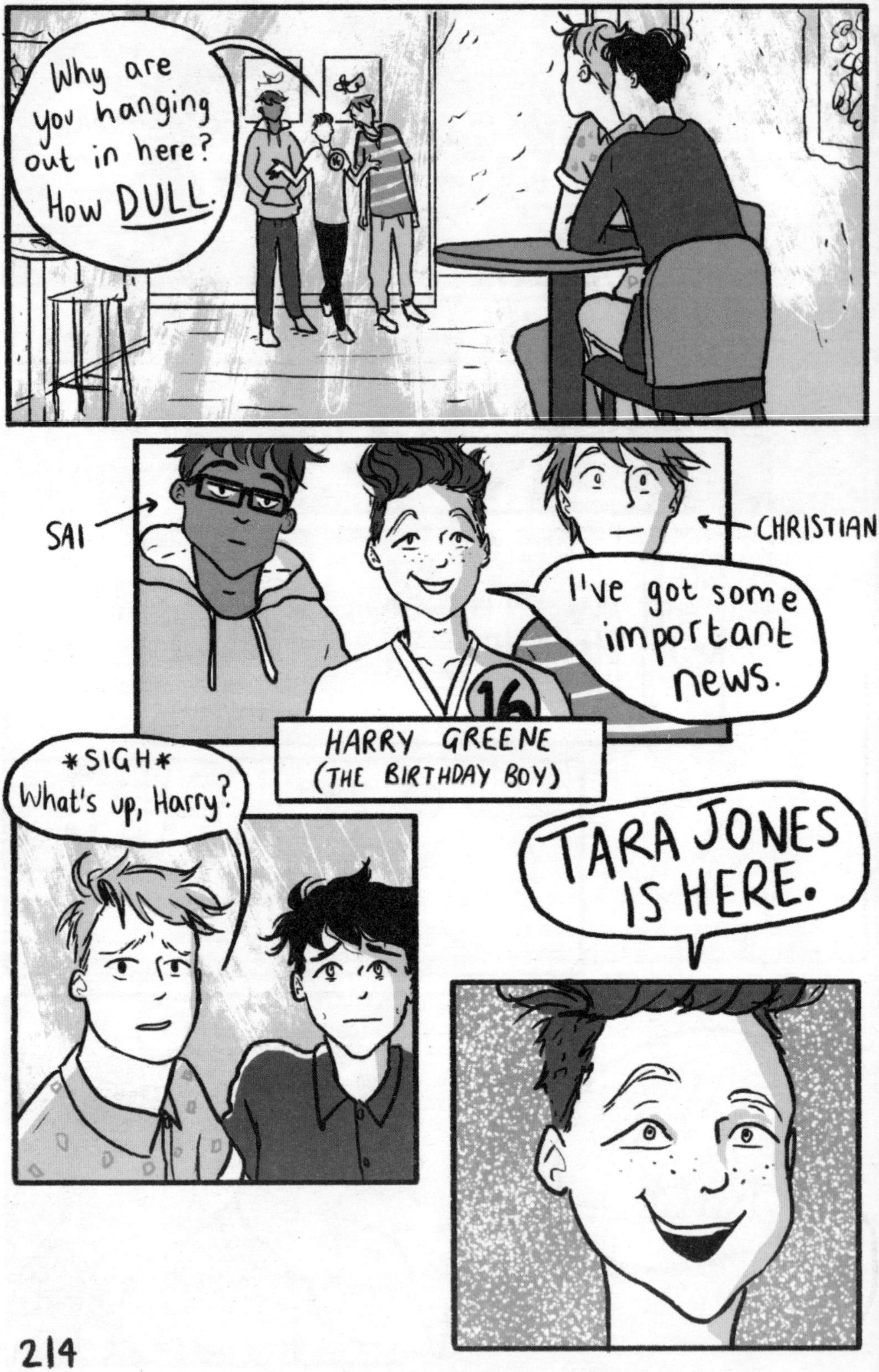
Why are you hanging out in here? How DULL.
SAI
CHRISTIAN
I've got some important news.
HARRY GREENE (THE BIRTHDAY BOY)
SIGH What's up, Harry?
TARA JONES IS HERE.

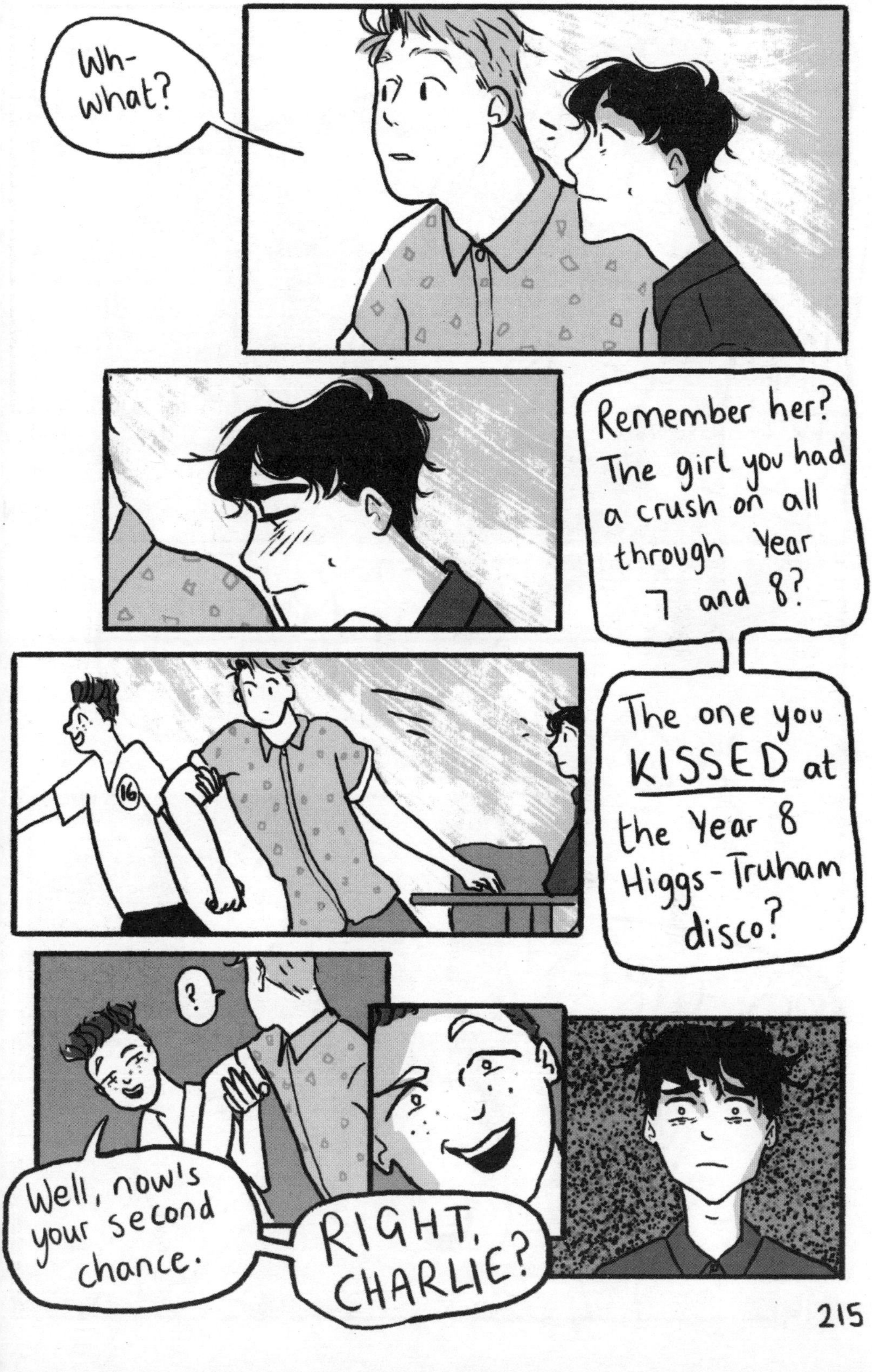
Wh-
what?
Remember her? The girl you had a crush on all through Year 7 and 8?
The one you KISSED at the Year 8 Higgs-Truham disco?
?
Well, now's your second chance.
RIGHT, CHARLIE?

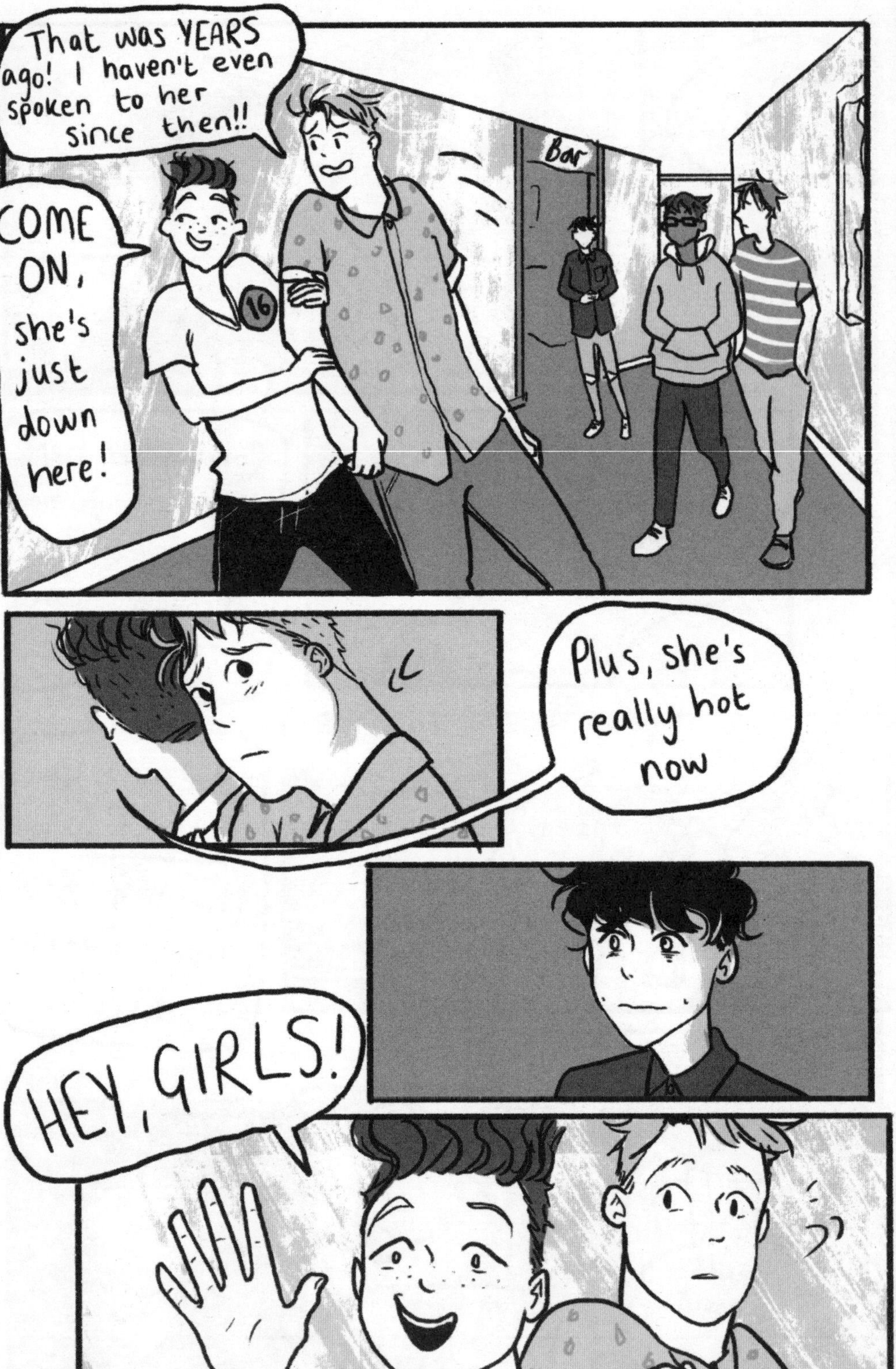
That was YEARS ago! I haven't even spoken to her since then!!
COME ON, she's just down here!
Bar
Plus, she's really hot now
HEY, GIRLS!

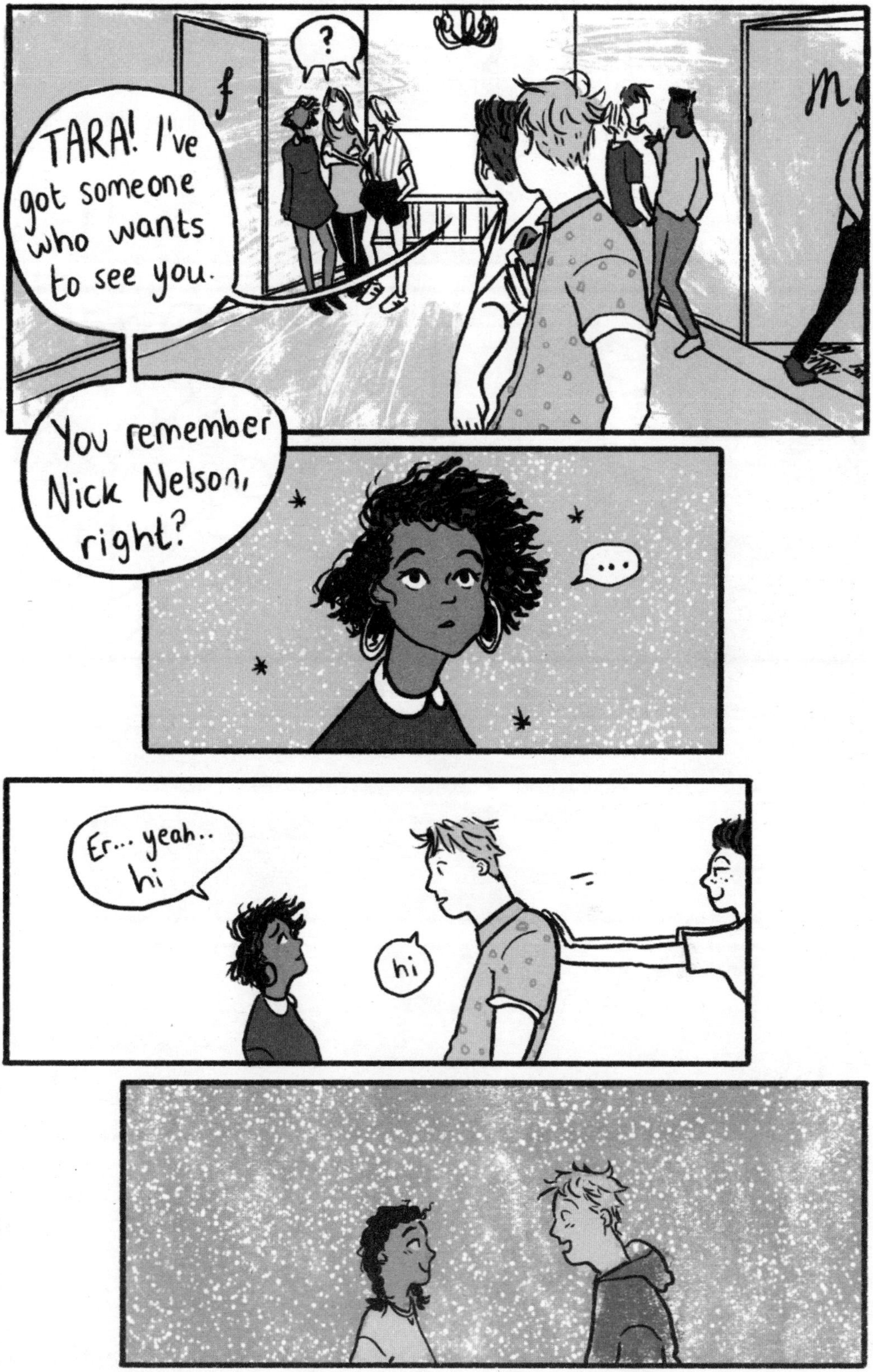
?
TARA! I've got someone who wants to see you.
You remember Nick Nelson, right?
...
Er... yeah.. hi
hi

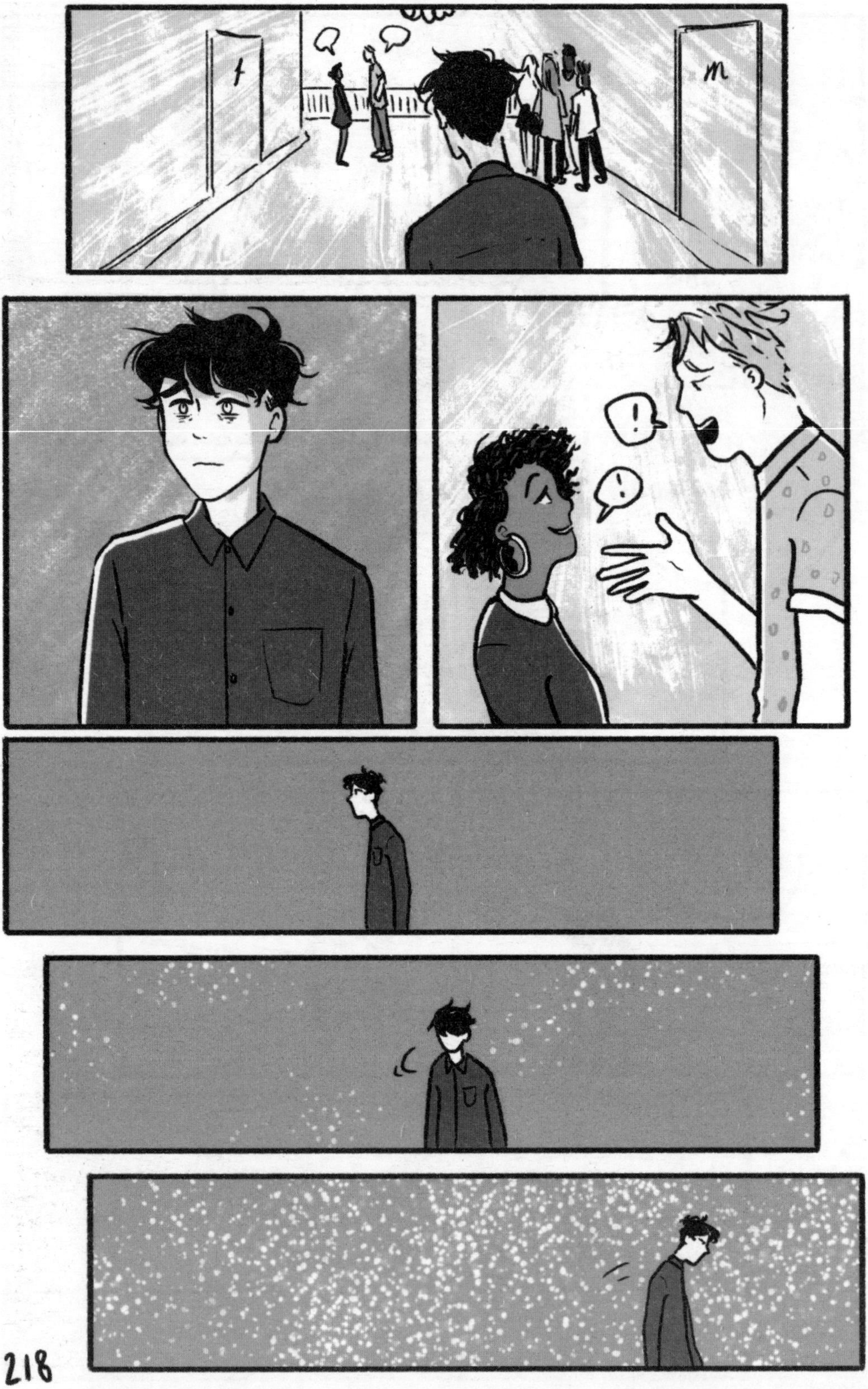
f
m
!
!

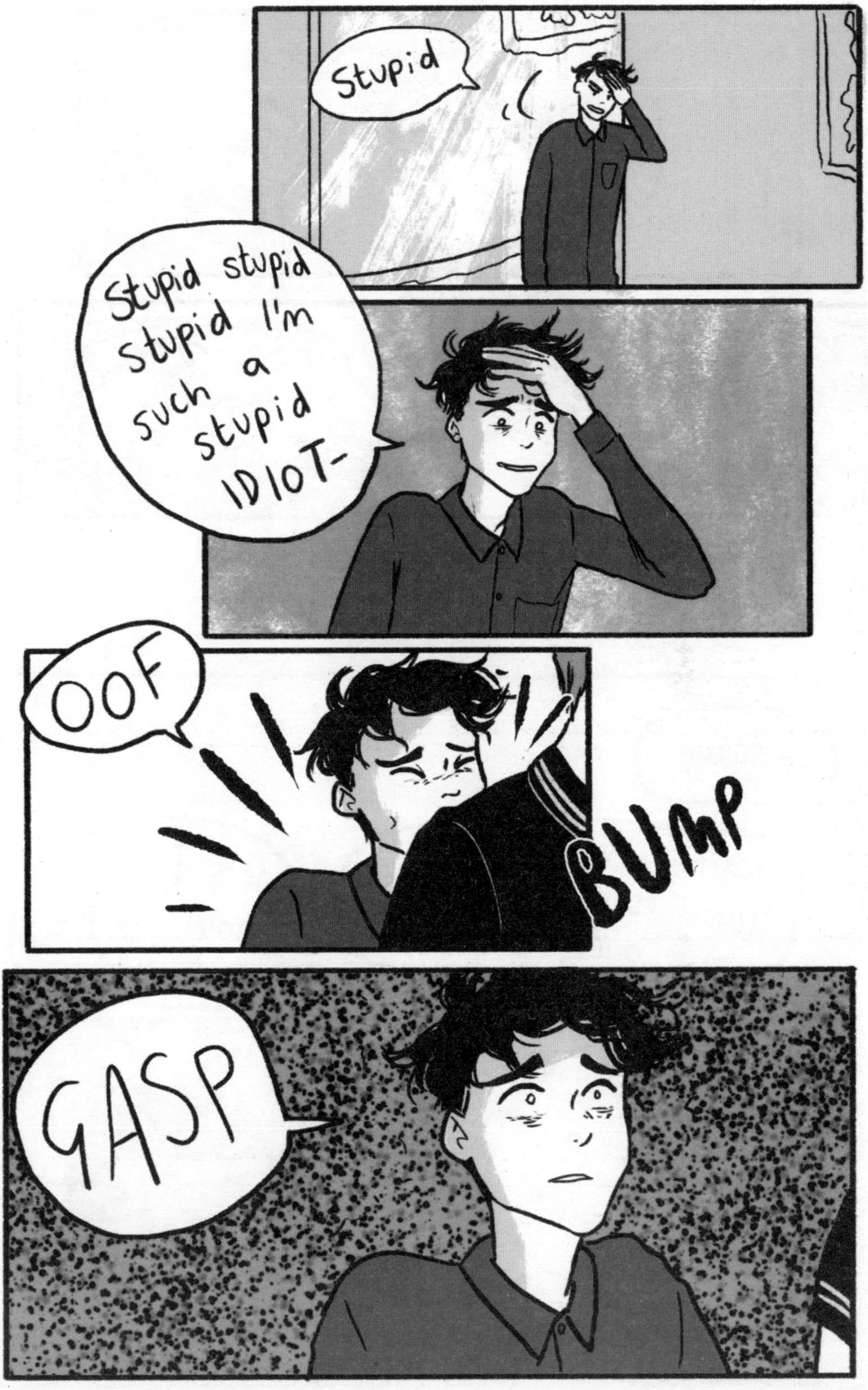
Stupid
Stupid stupid stupid I'm such a stupid stupid IDIOT-
OOF
BUMP
GASP

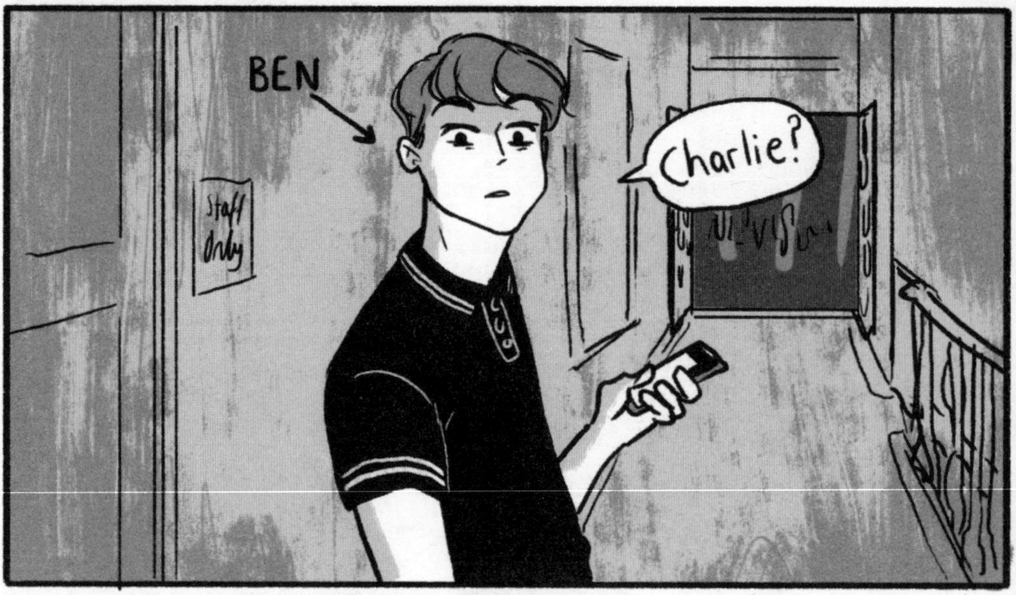
BEN
Staff Only
Charlie?

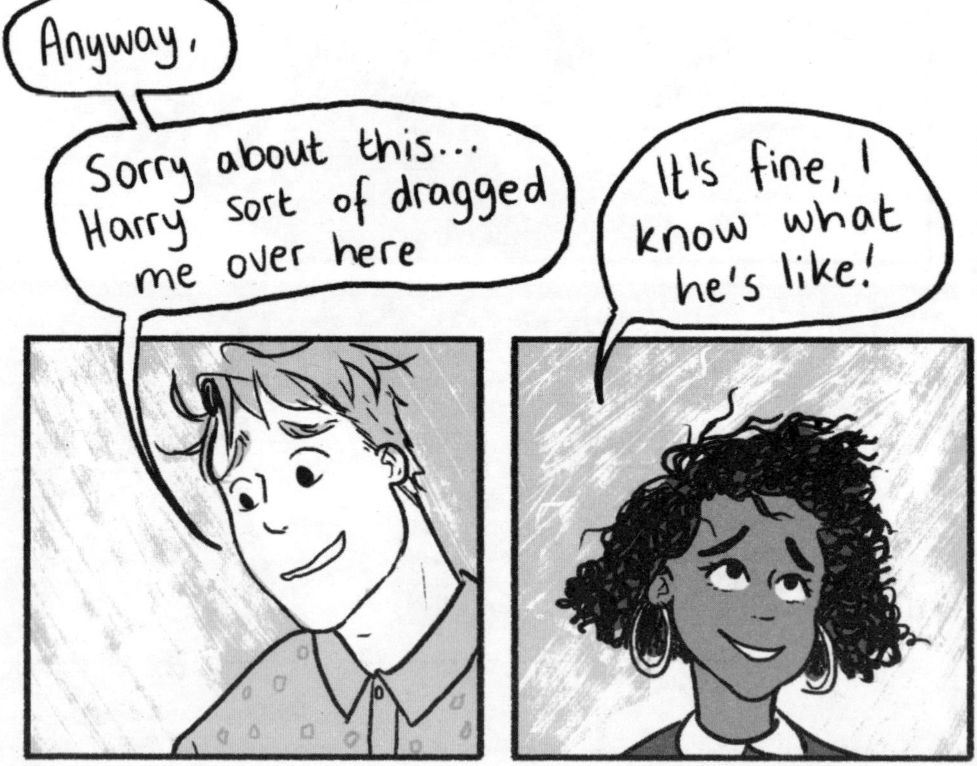
Anyway,
Sorry about this... Harry sort of dragged me over here
It's fine, I know what he's like!

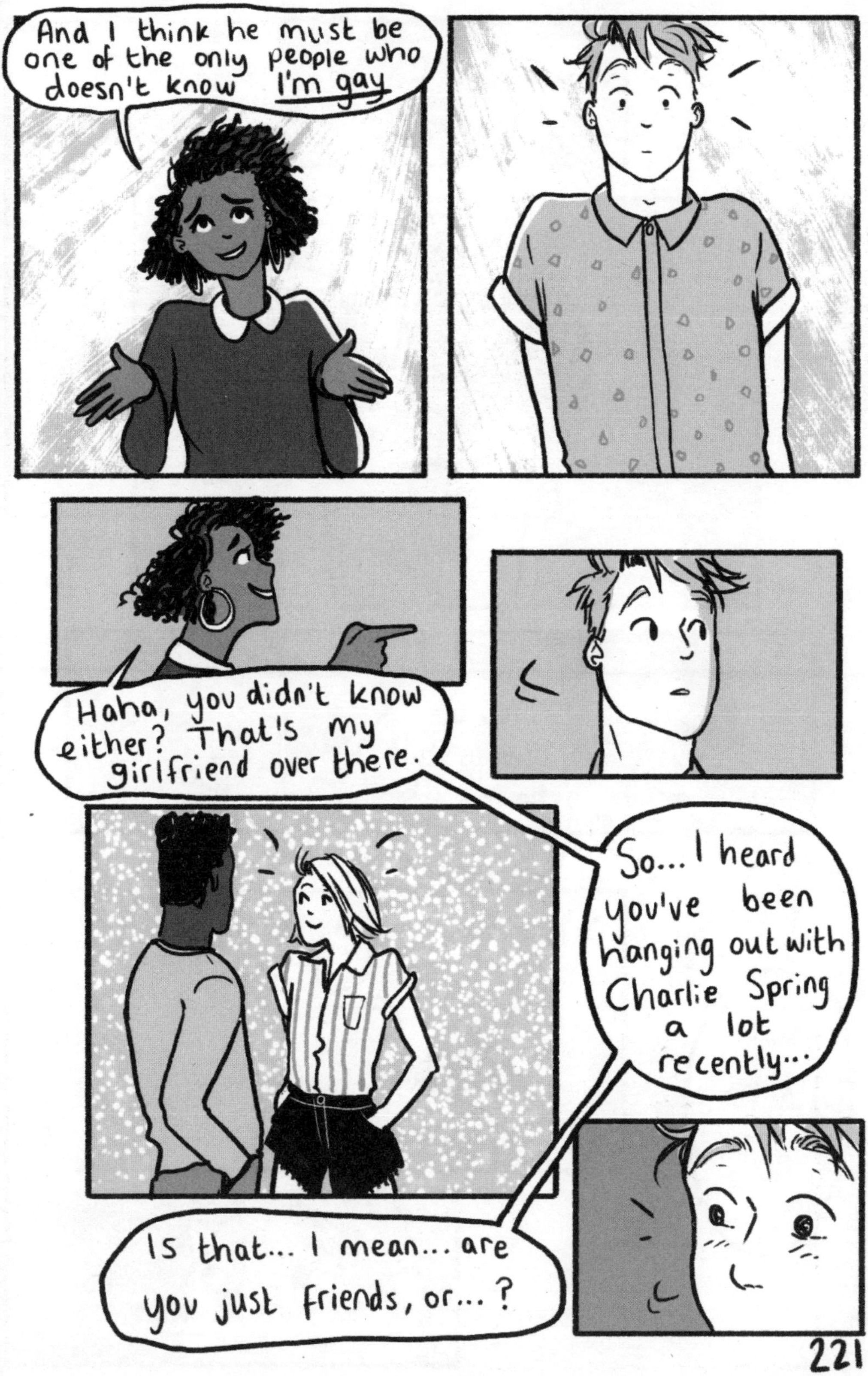
And I think he must be one of the only people who doesn't know I'm gay
Haha, you didn't know either? That's my girlfriend over there.
So... I heard you've been hanging out with Charlie Spring a lot recently...
Is that... I mean... are you just friends, or...?

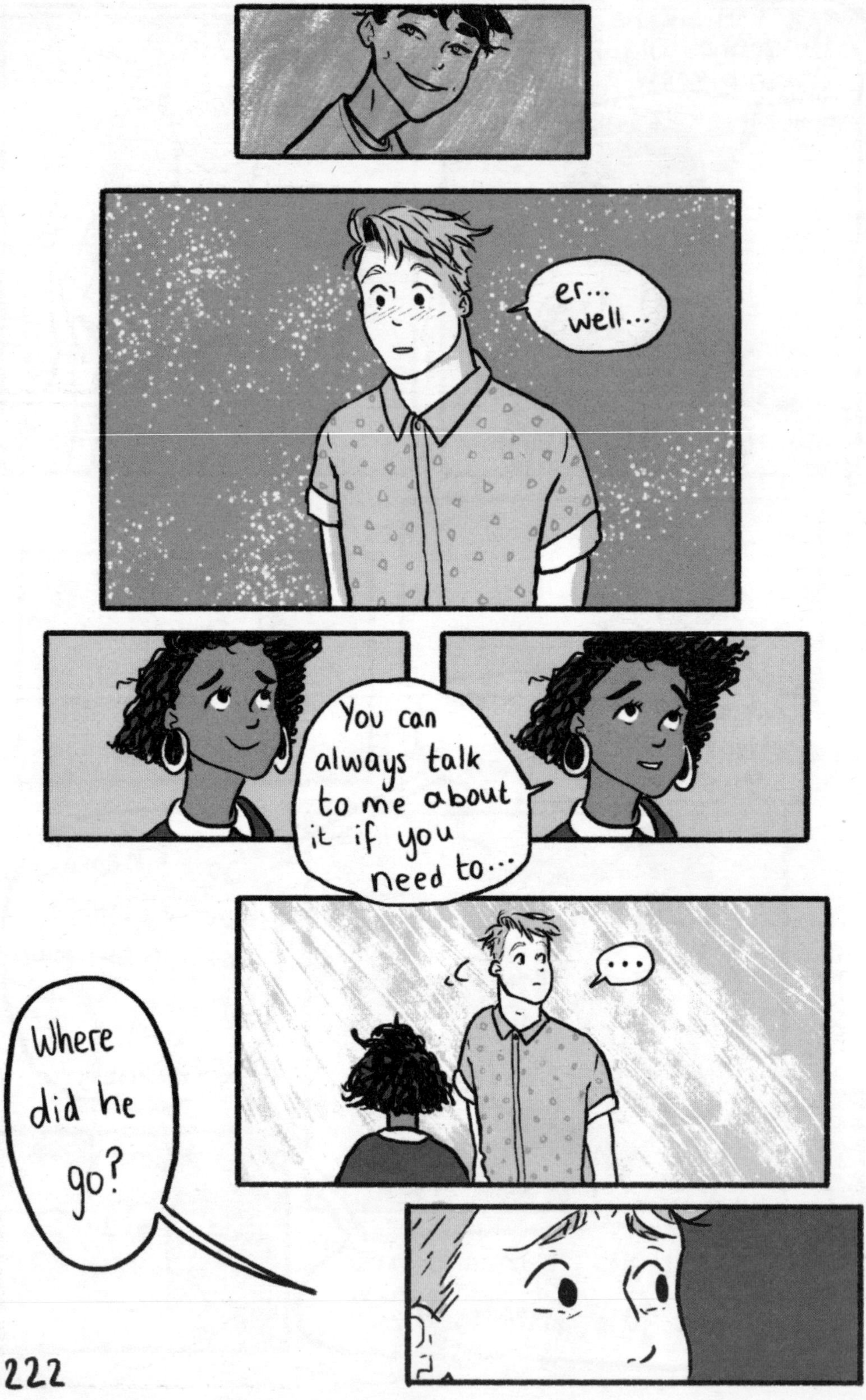
er... well...
You can always talk to me about it if you need to...
...
Where did he go?

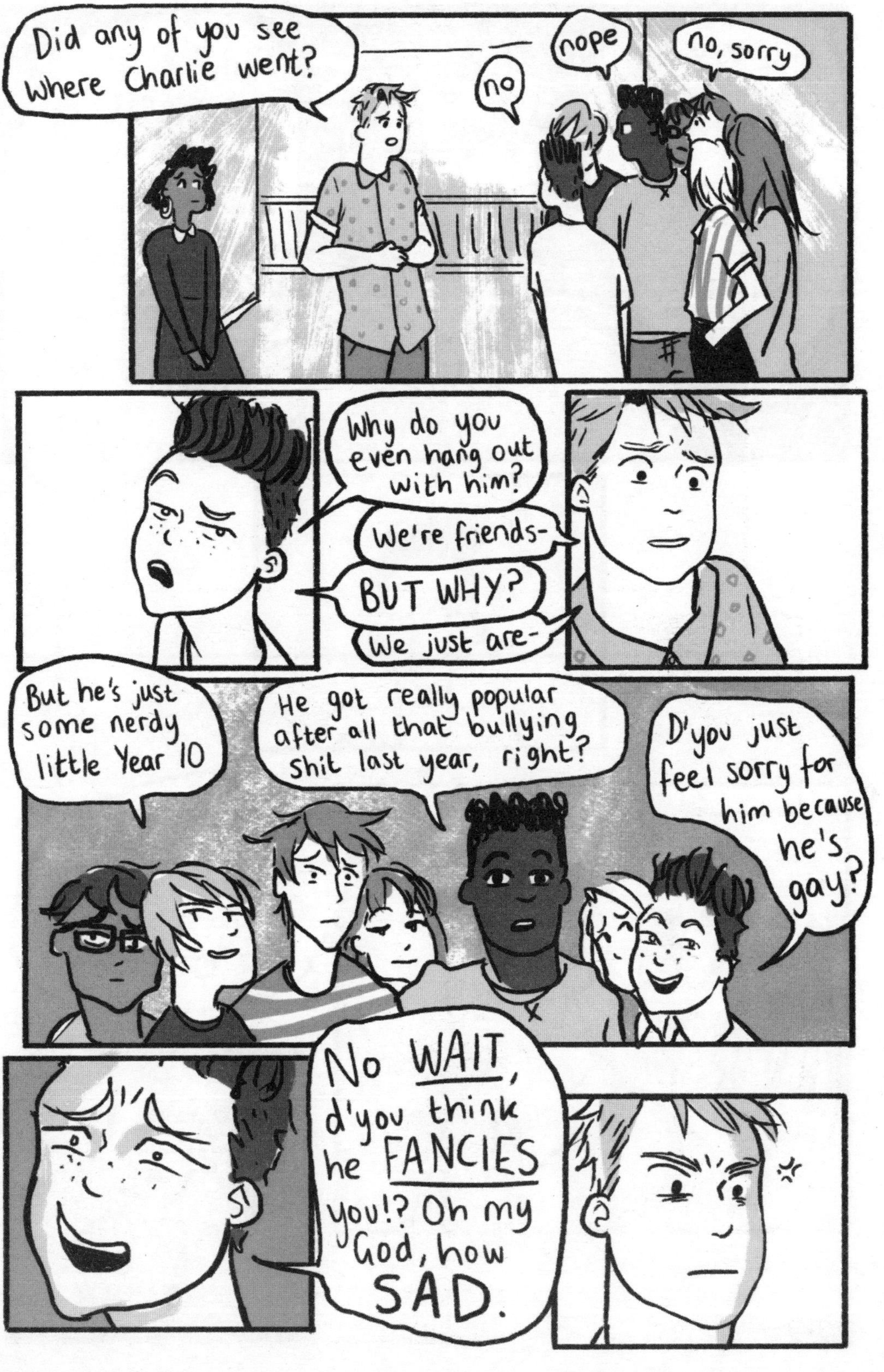
Did any of you see where Charlie went?
no
nope
no, sorry
Why do you even hang out with him?
We're friends-
BUT WHY?
We just are-
But he's just some nerdy little Year 10
He got really popular after all that bullying shit last year, right?
D'you just feel sorry for him because he's gay?
No WAIT, d'you think he FANCIES you!? Oh my God, how SAD.

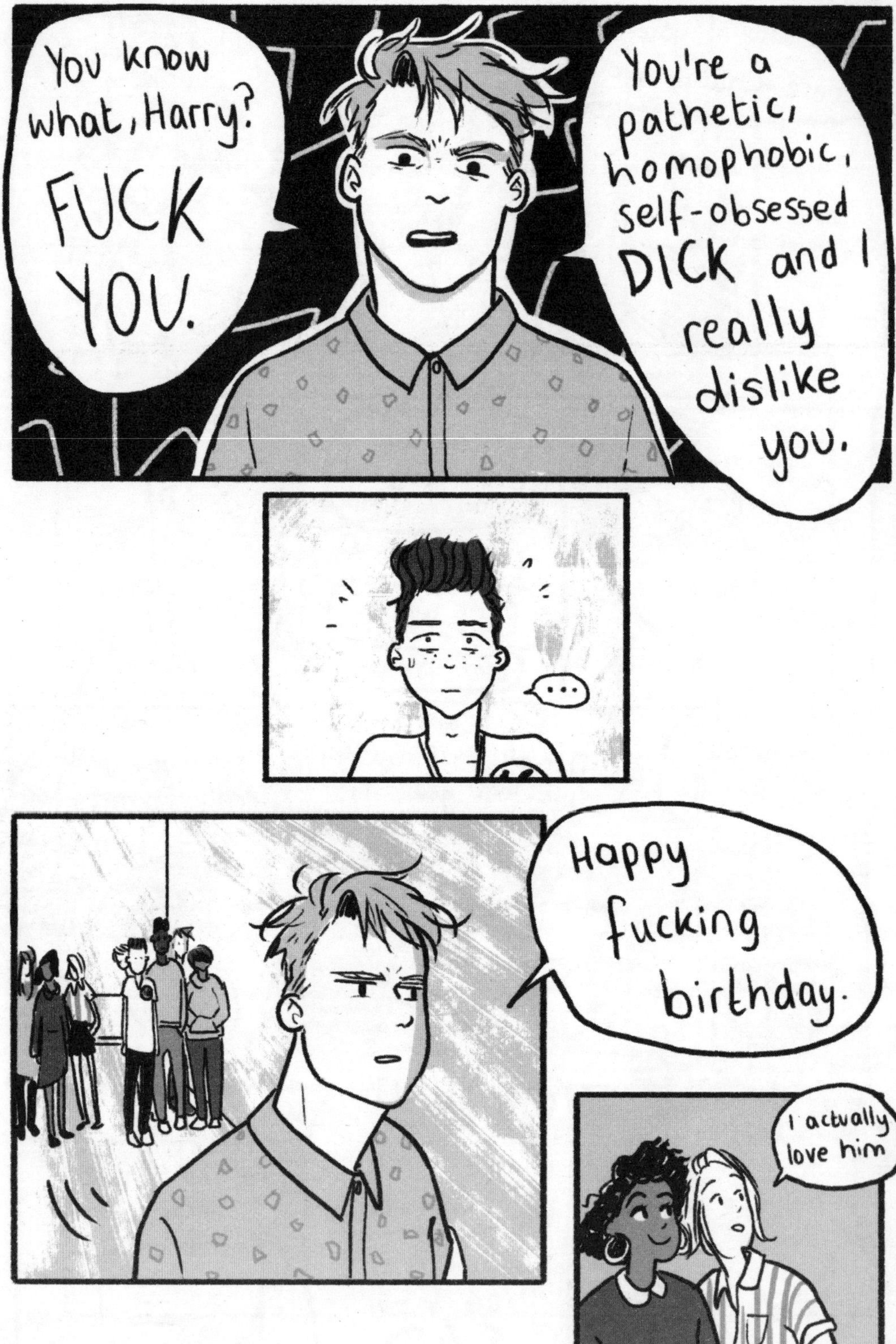
You know what, Harry? FUCK YOU.
You're a pathetic, homophobic, self-obsessed DICK and I really dislike you.
...
Happy fucking birthday.
I actually love him

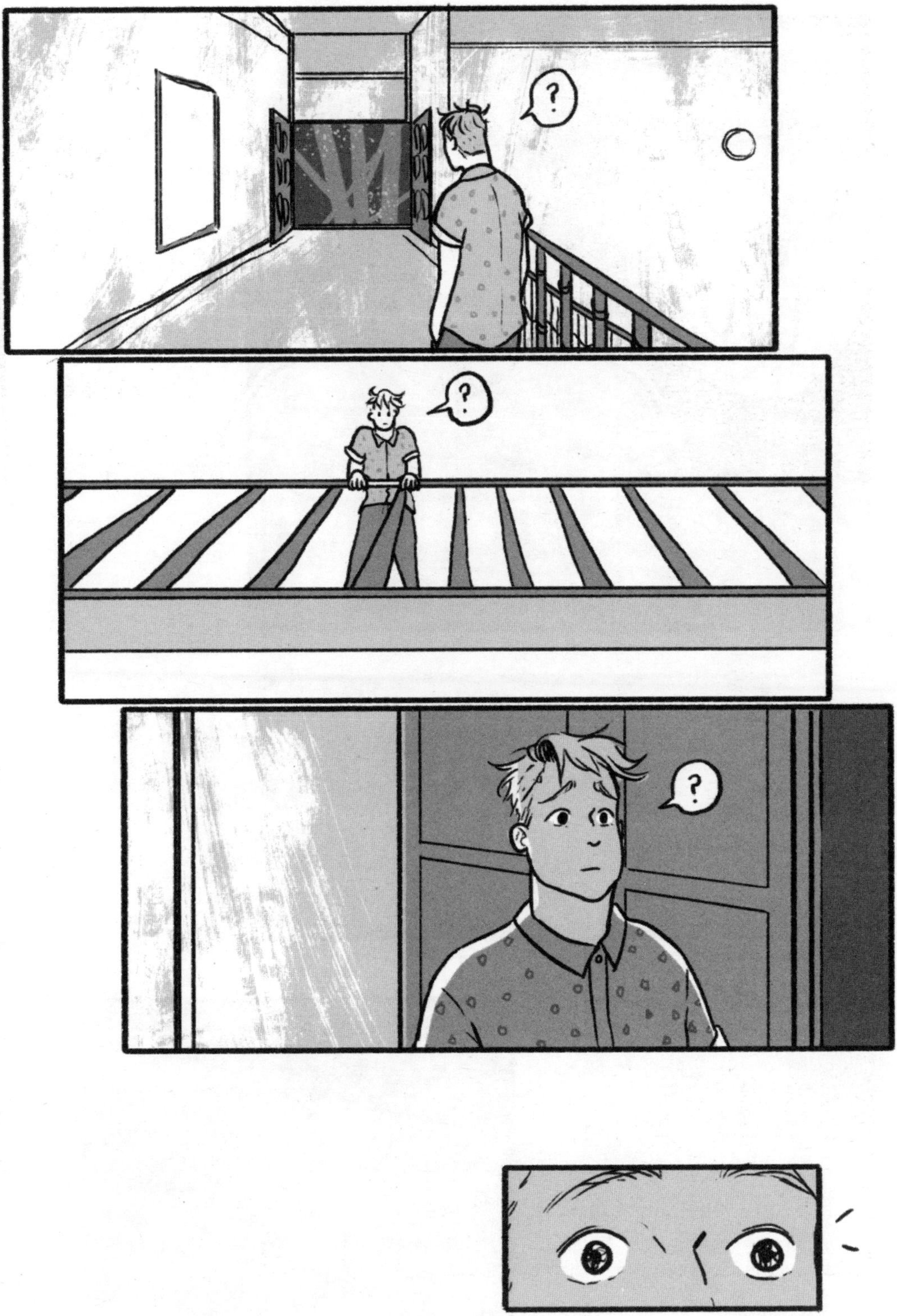
?
?
?

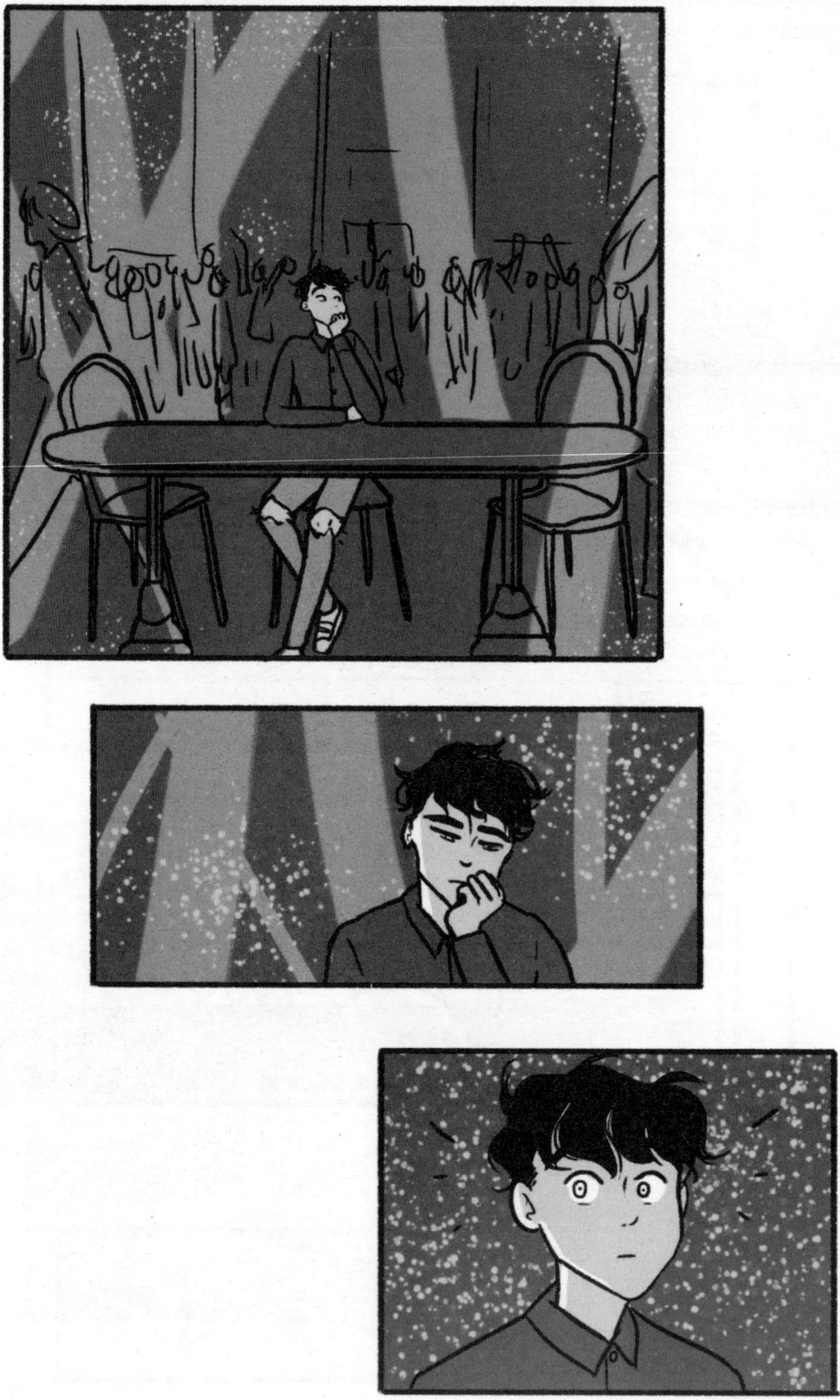

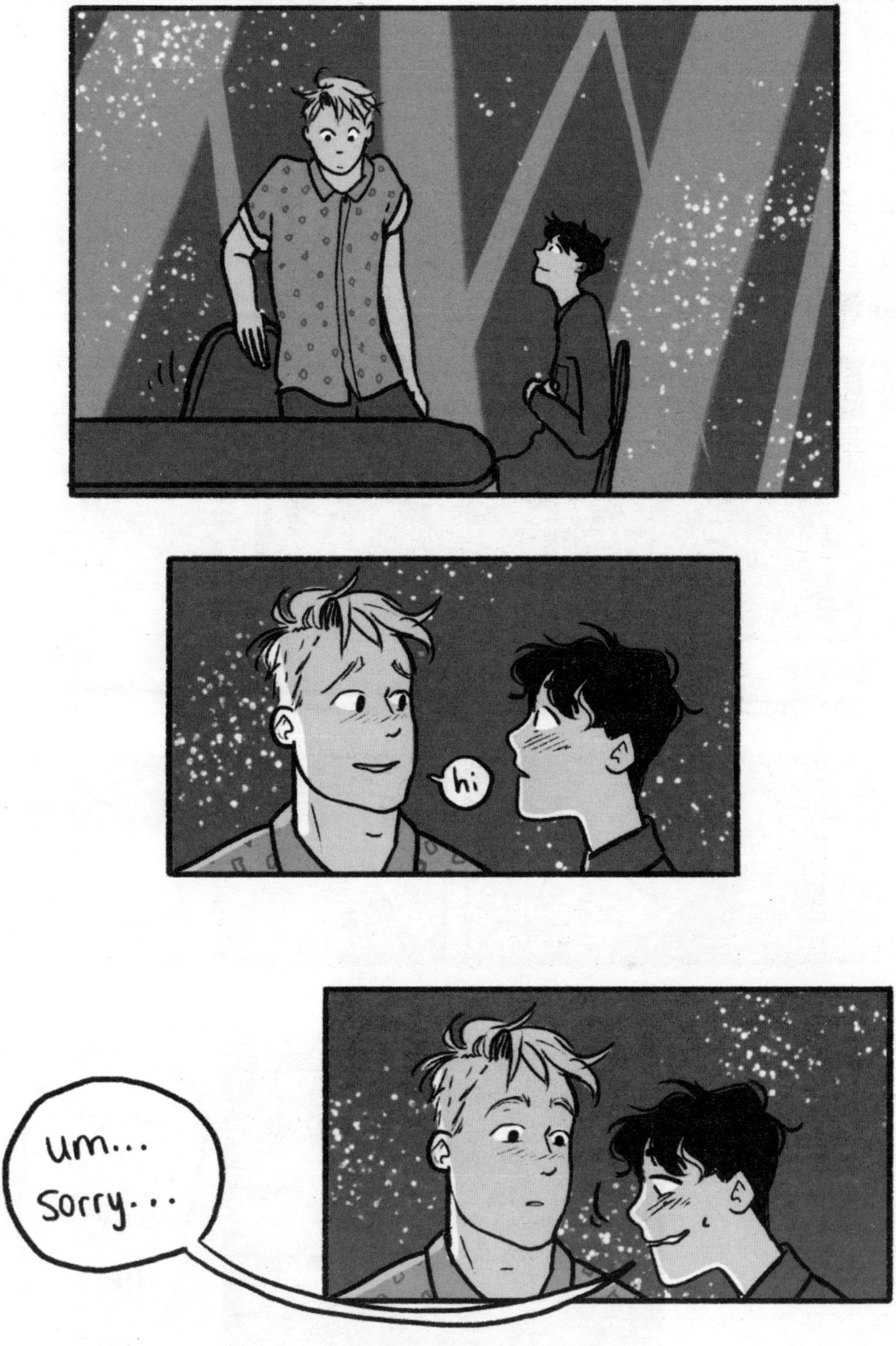
hi
um...
sorry...

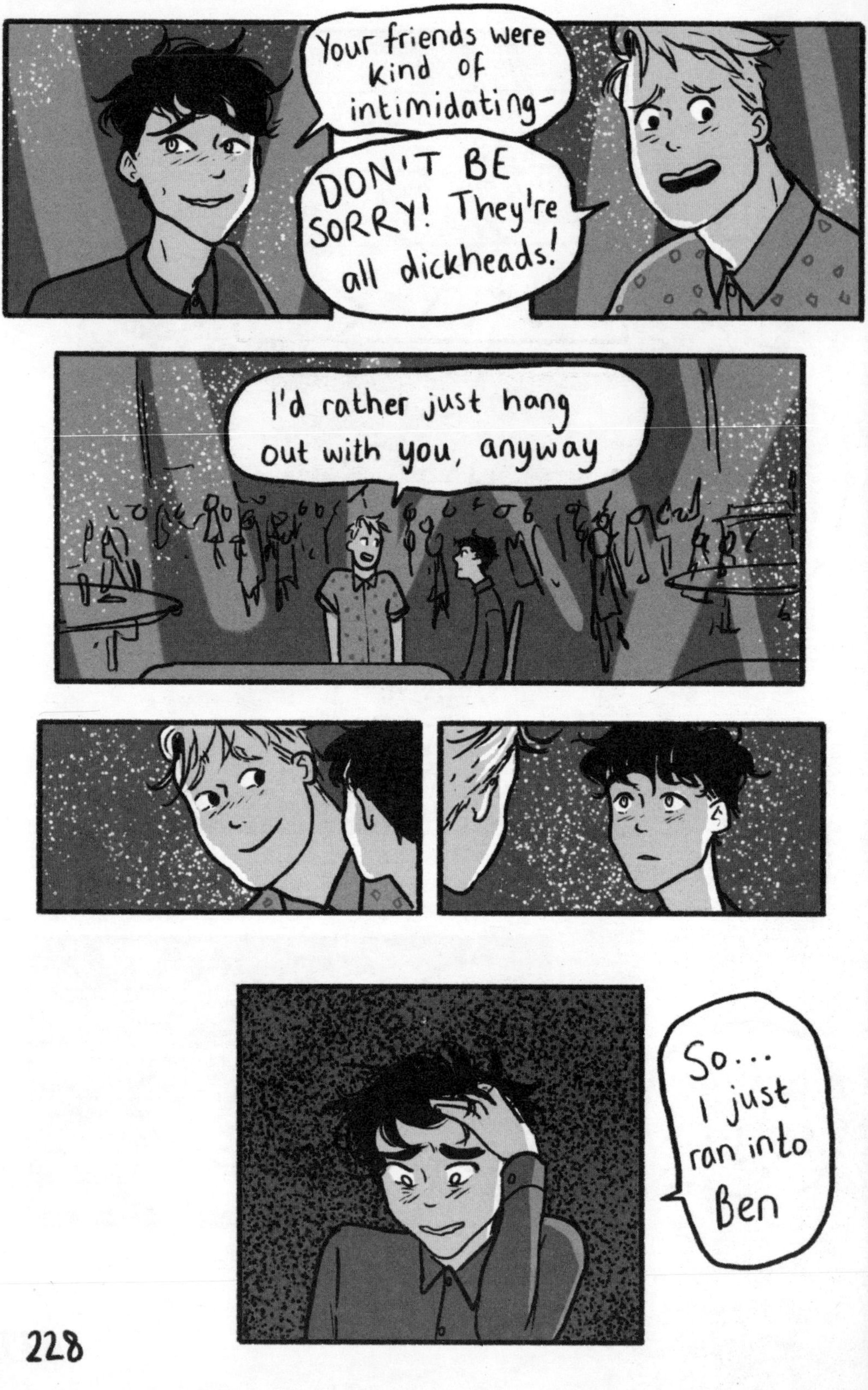
Your friends were kind of intimidating-
DON'T BE SORRY! They're all dickheads!
I'd rather just hang out with you, anyway
So... I just ran into Ben

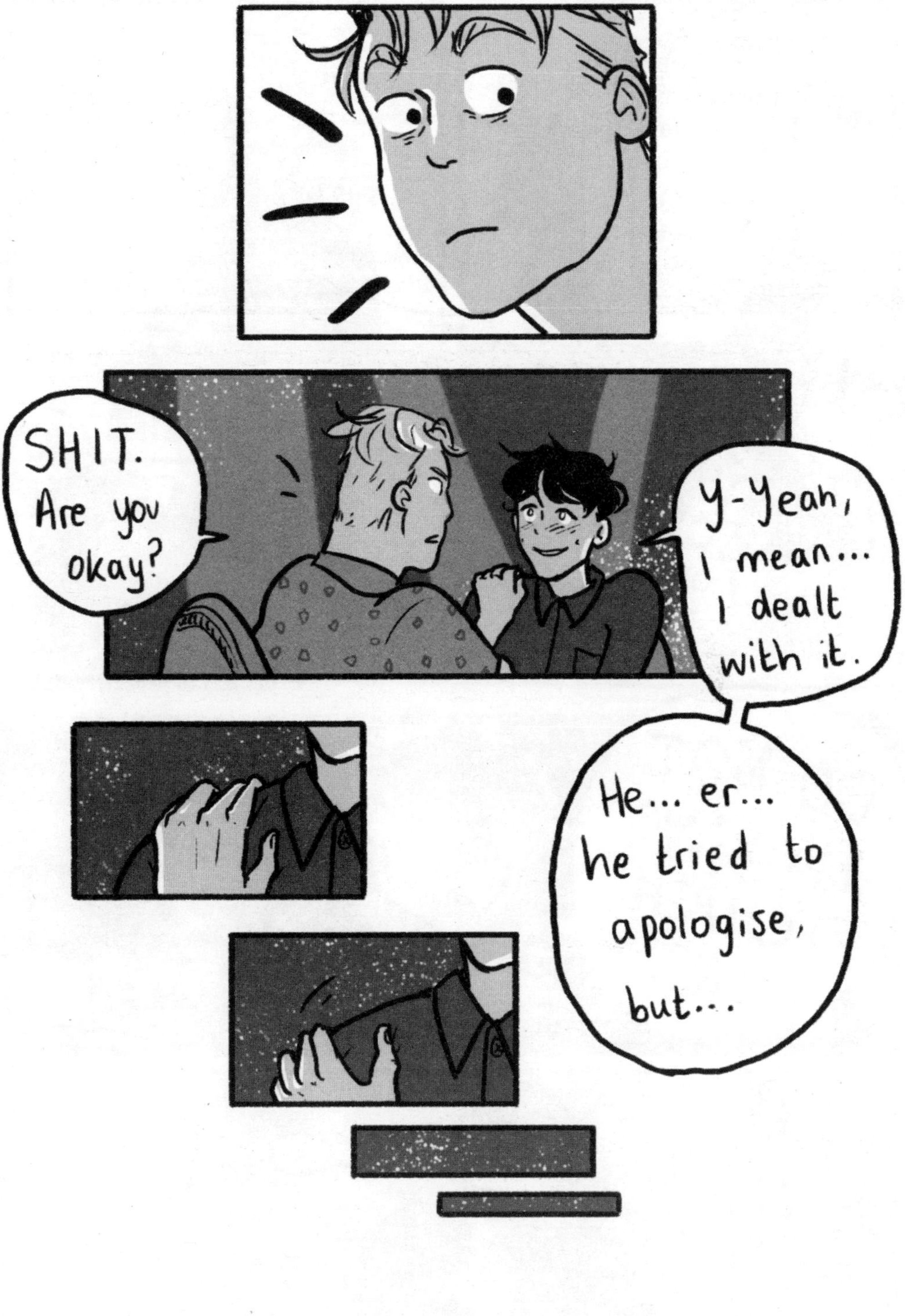
SHIT. Are you okay?
Y-Yeah, I mean... I dealt with it.
He... er... he tried to apologise, but...

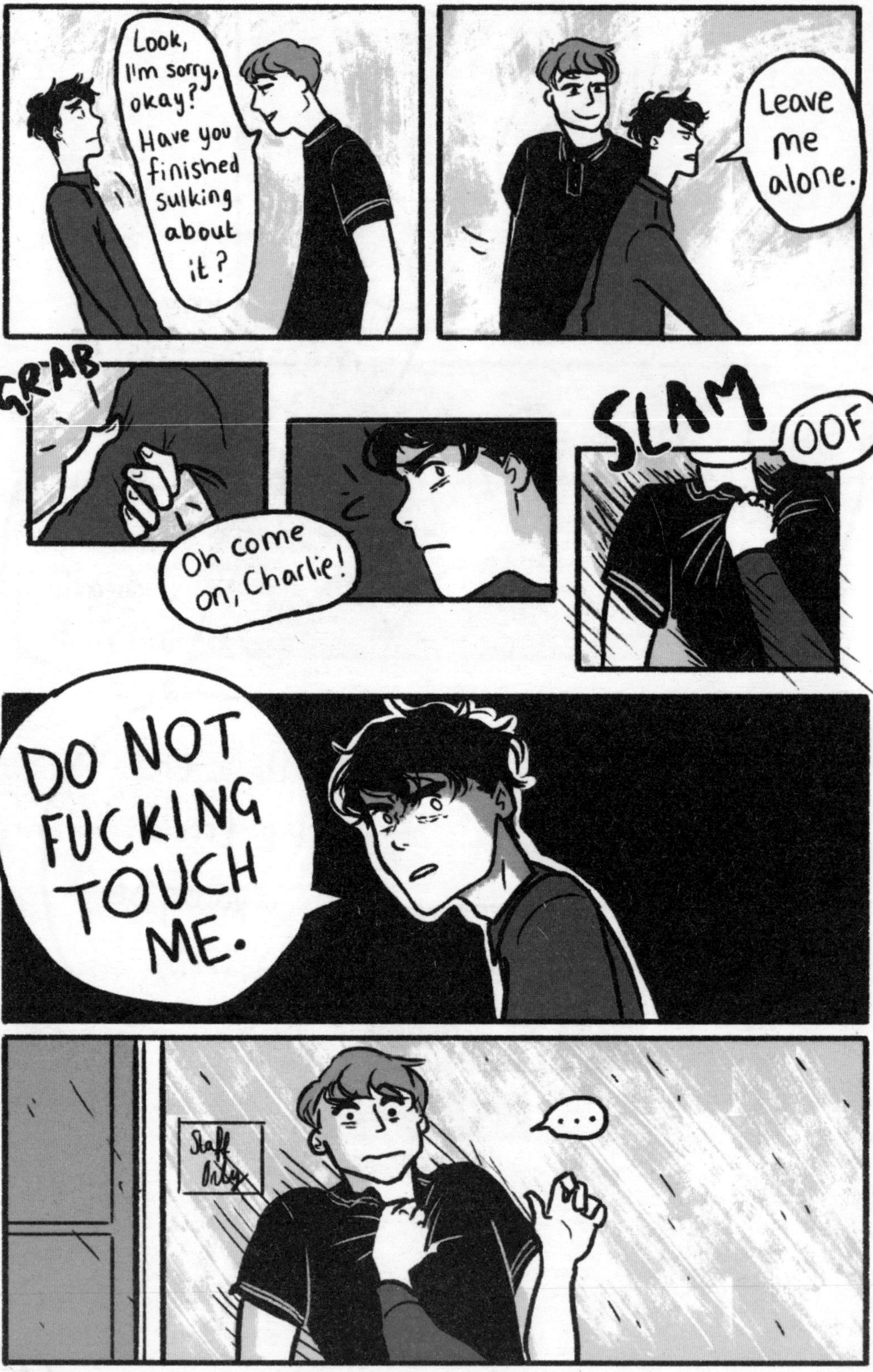
Look, I'm sorry, okay? Have you finished sulking about it?
Leave me alone.
GRAB
Oh come on, Charlie!
SLAM
OOF
DO NOT FUCKING TOUCH ME.
Staff Only
...

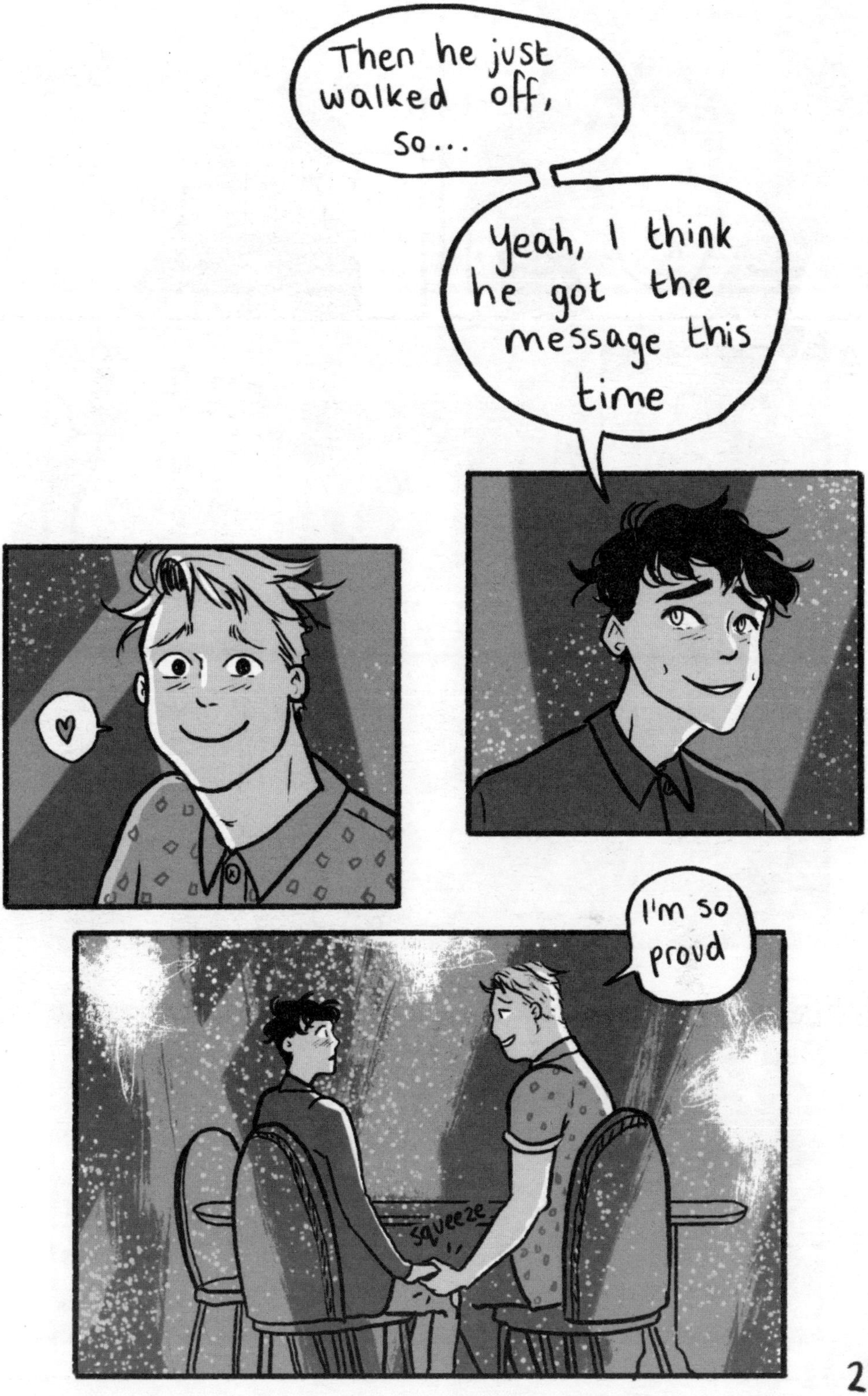
Then he just walked off, so...
Yeah, I think he got the message this time
♡
I'm so proud
squeeze

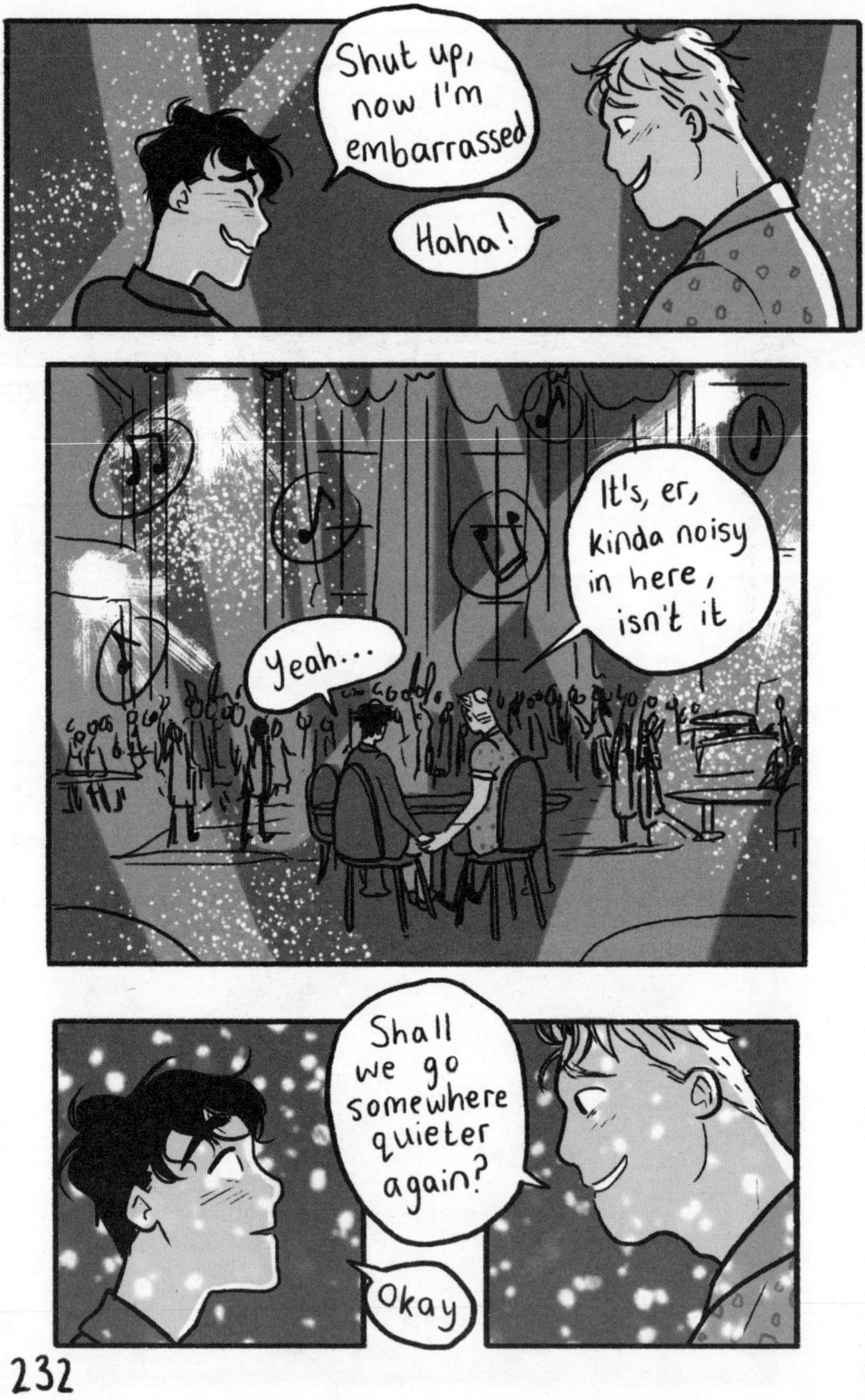
Shut up, now I'm embarrassed
Haha!
It's, er, kinda noisy in here, isn't it
Yeah...
Shall we go somewhere quieter again?
Okay

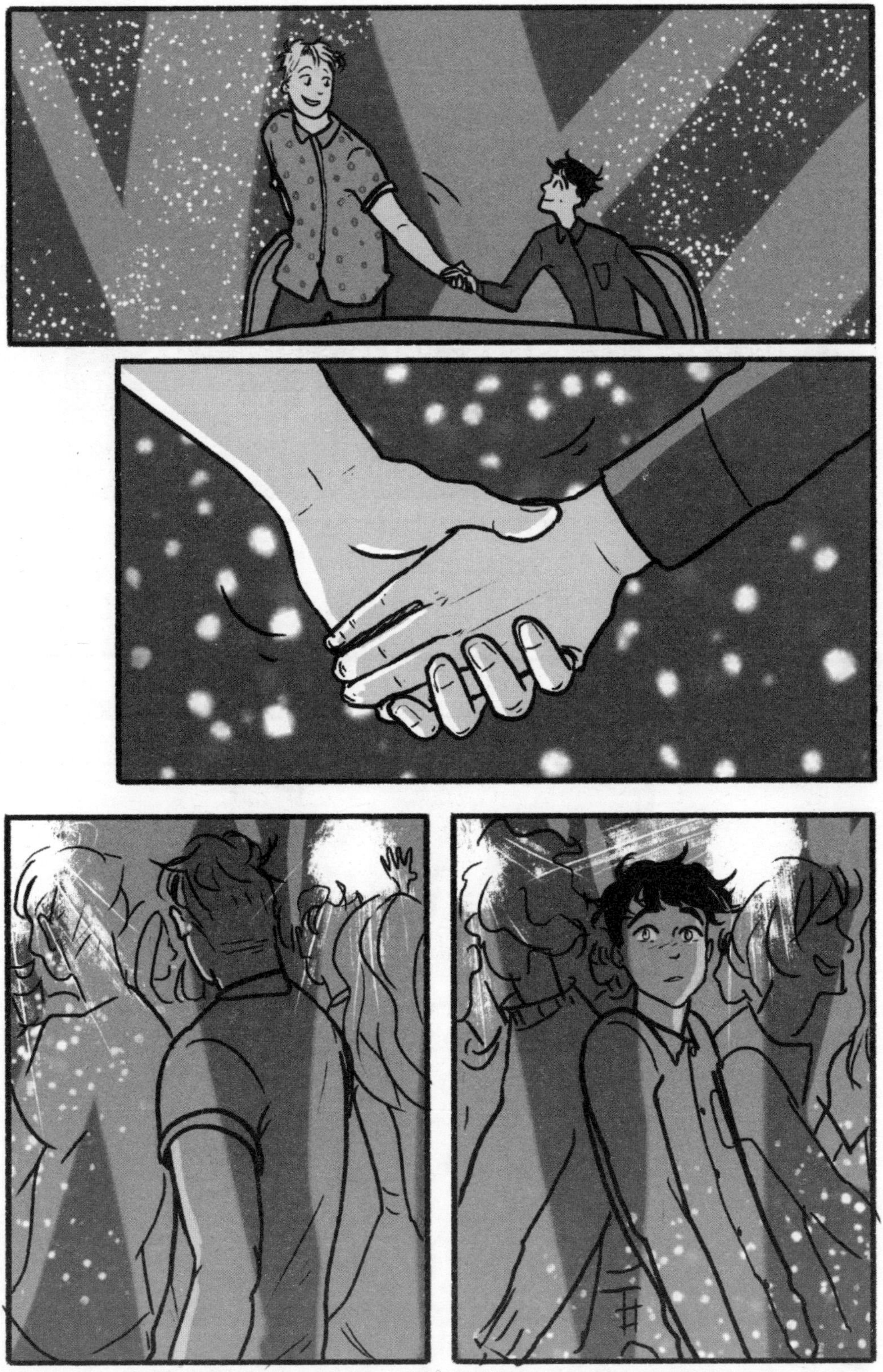

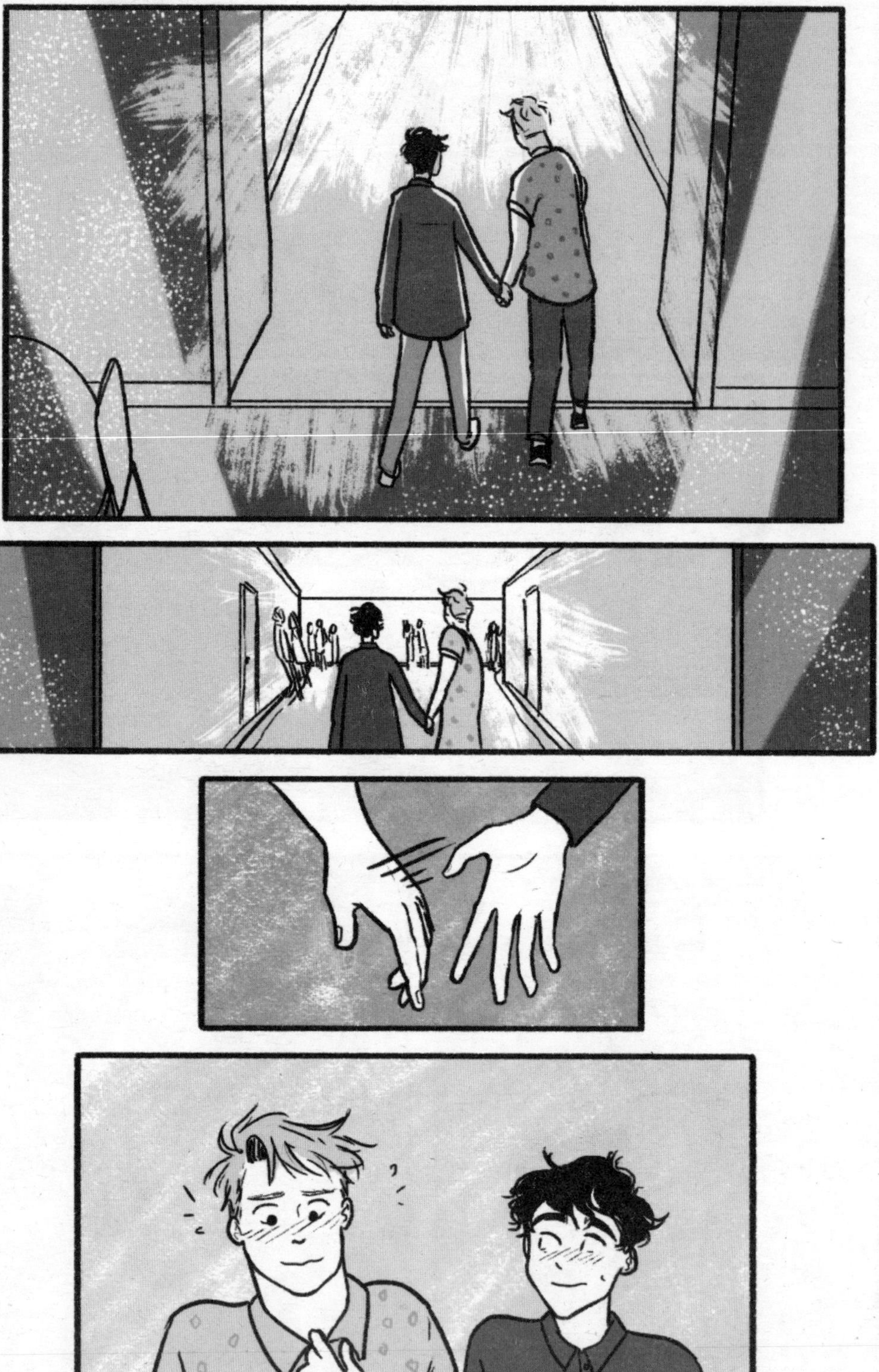

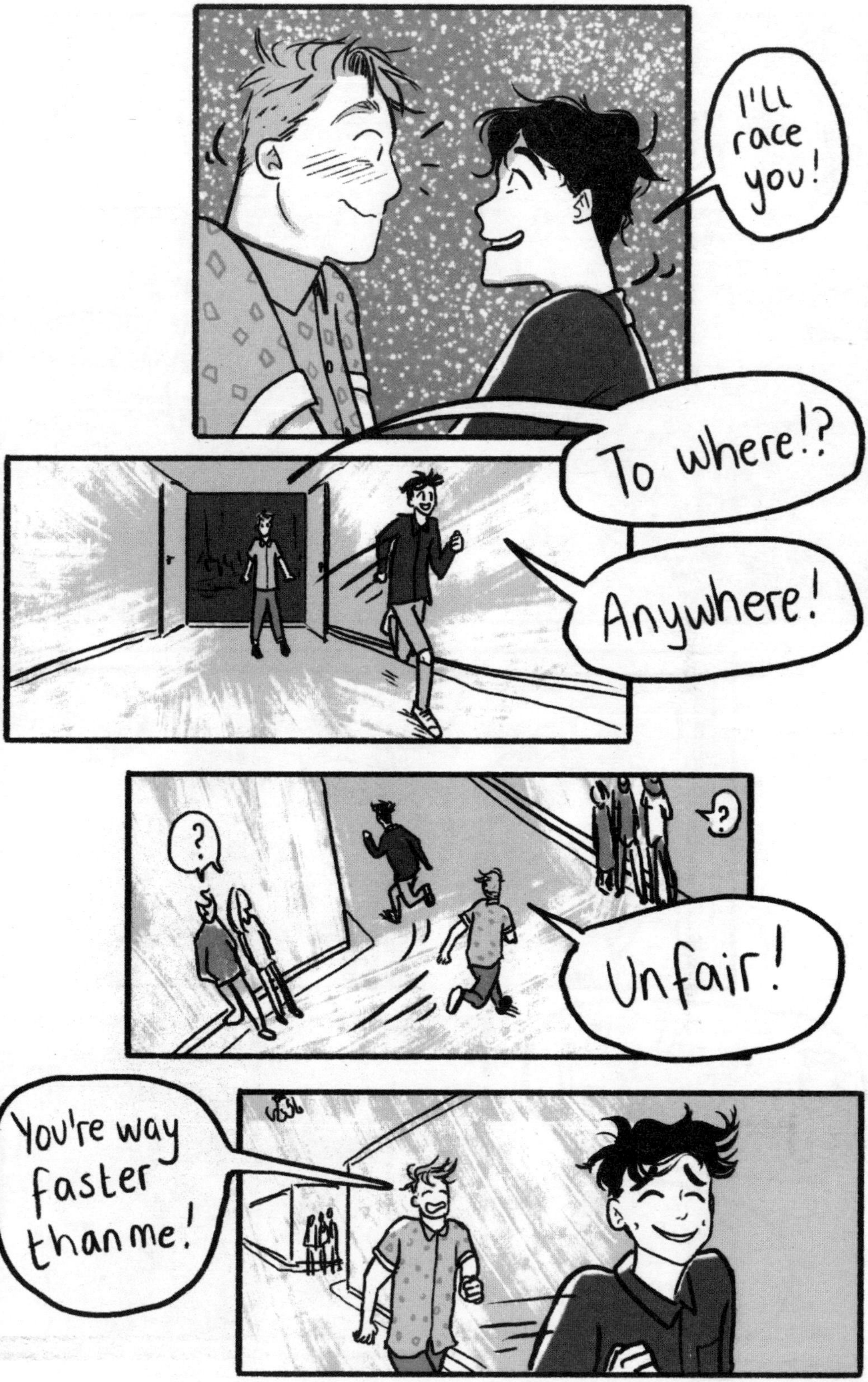
I'll race you!
To where!?
Anywhere!
?
?
Unfair!
You're way faster than me!

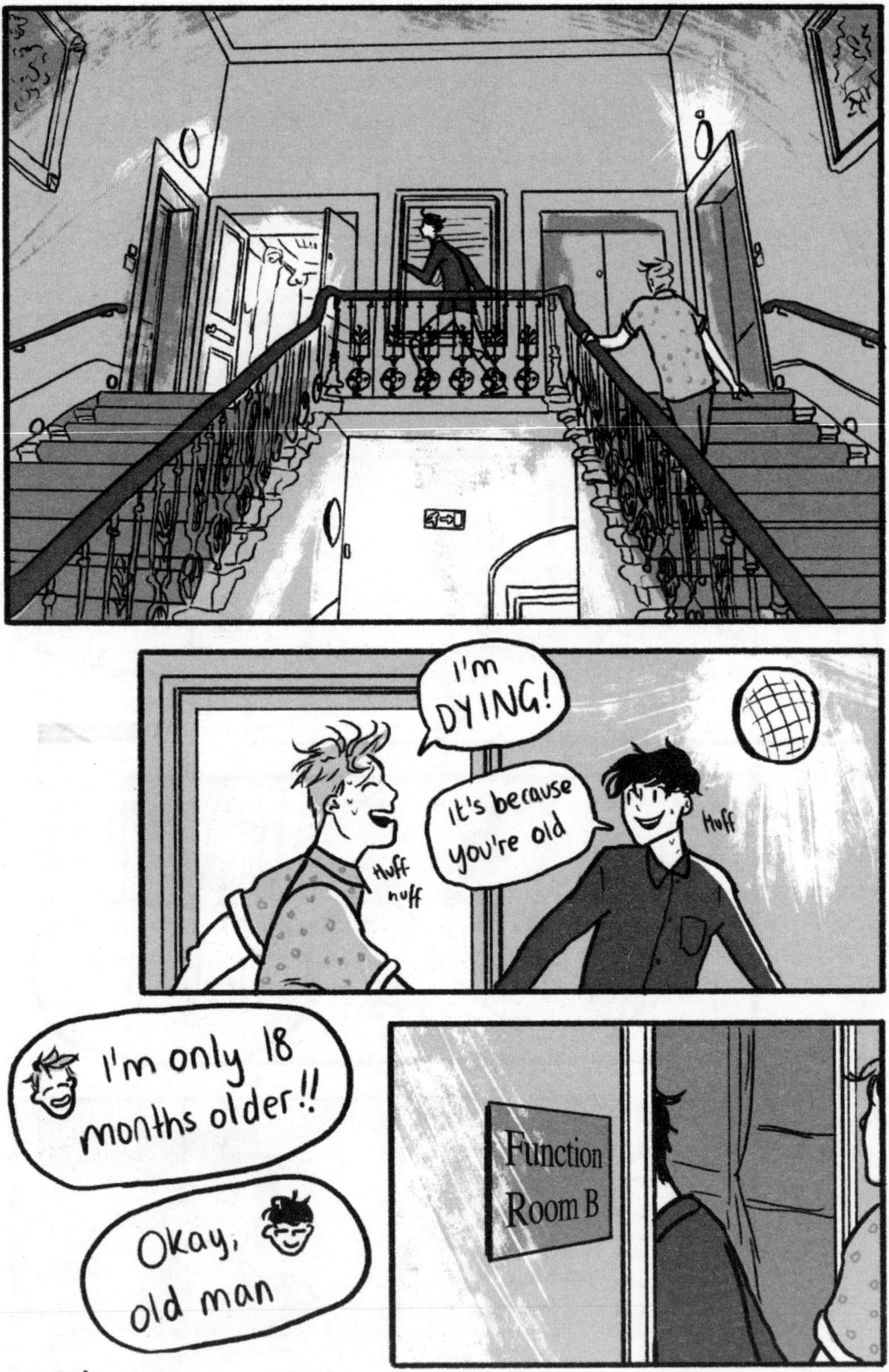
I'm DYING!
It's because you're old
Huff nuff
Huff
I'm only 18 months older!!
Okay, old man
Function Room B

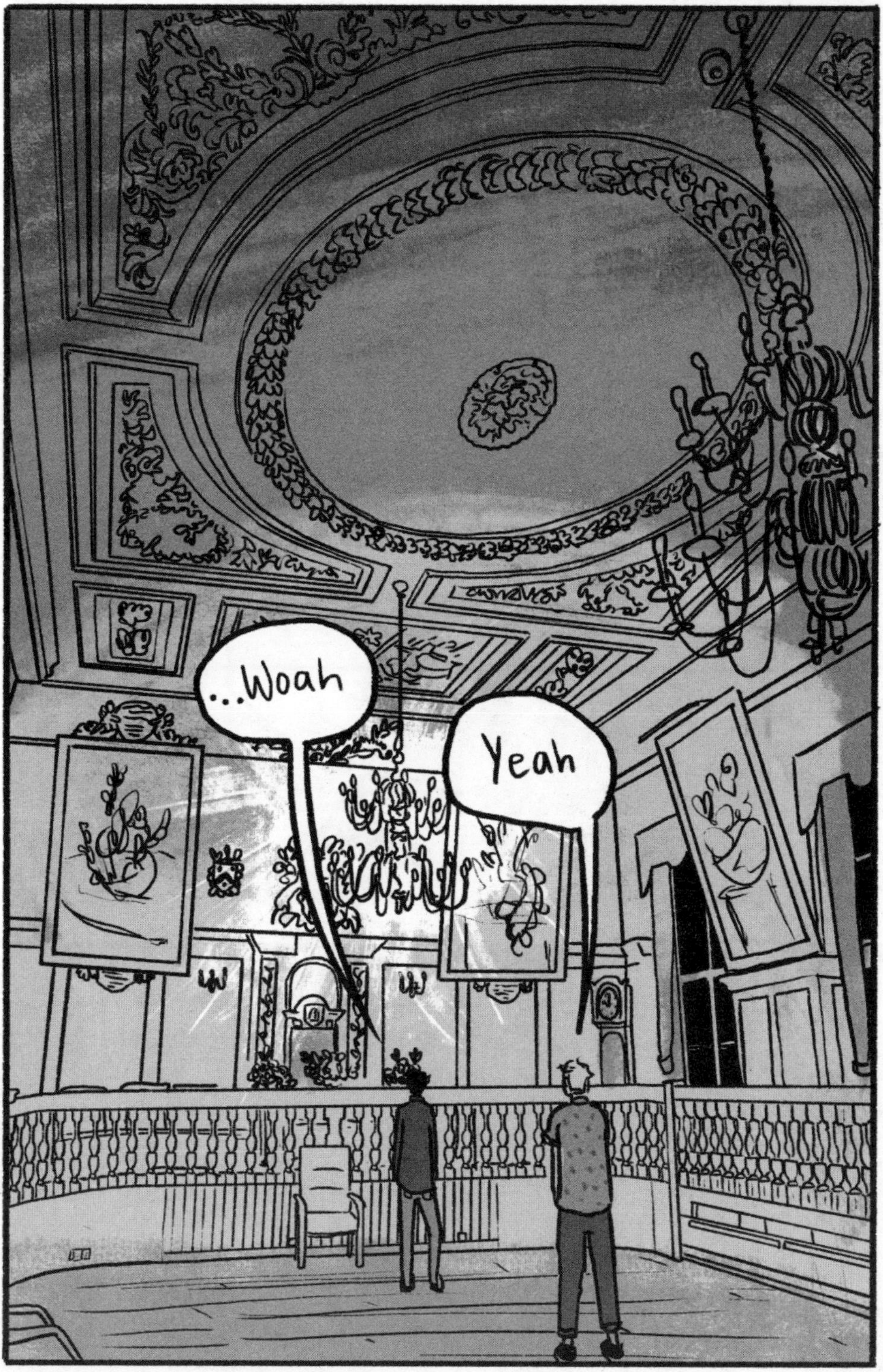
...Woah
Yeah

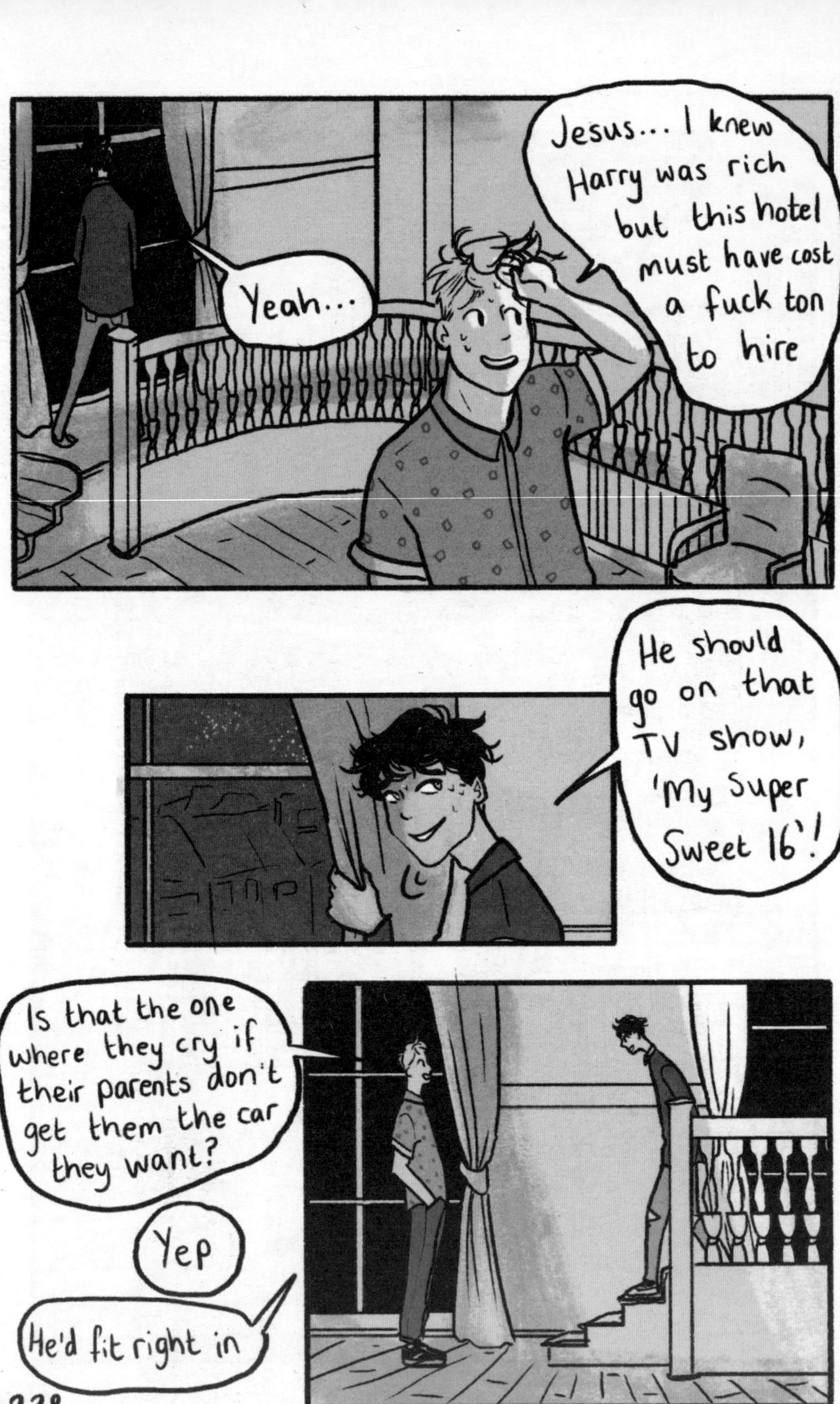
Jesus... I knew Harry was rich but this hotel must have cost a fuck ton to hire
Yeah...
He should go on that TV show, 'My Super Sweet 16'!
Is that the one where they cry if their parents don't get them the car they want?
Yep
He'd fit right in

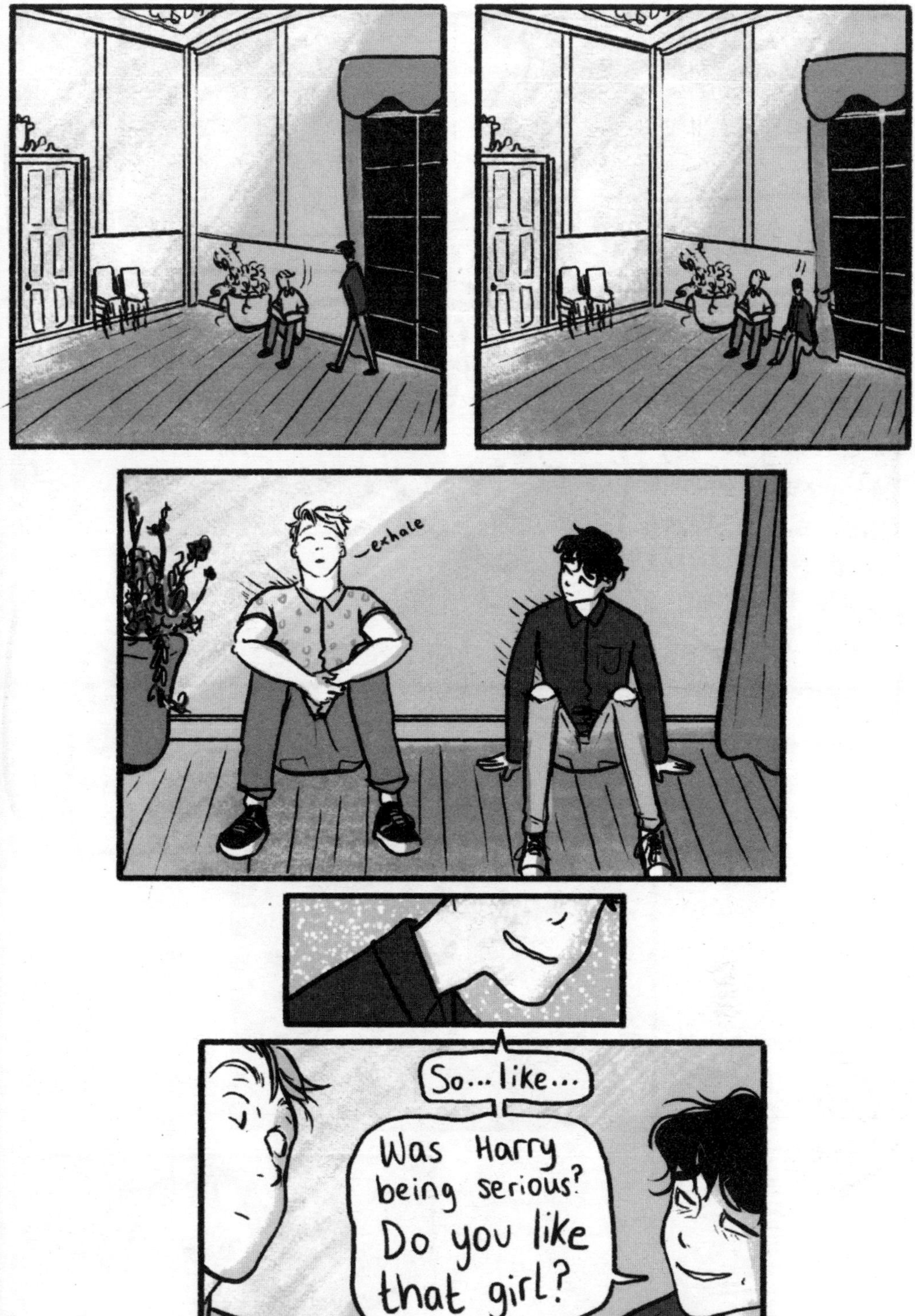
exhale
So... like...
Was Harry being serious? Do you like that girl?

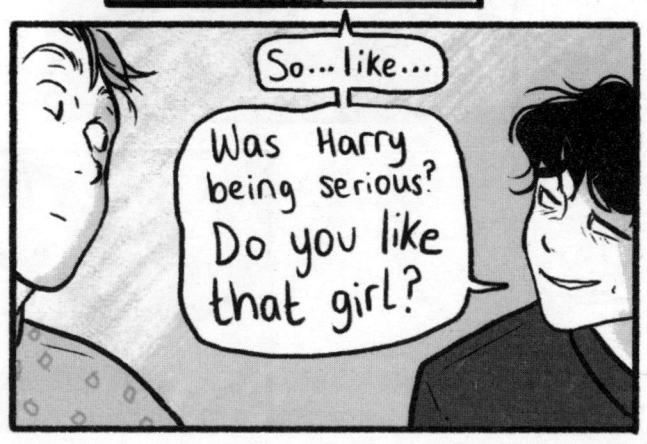

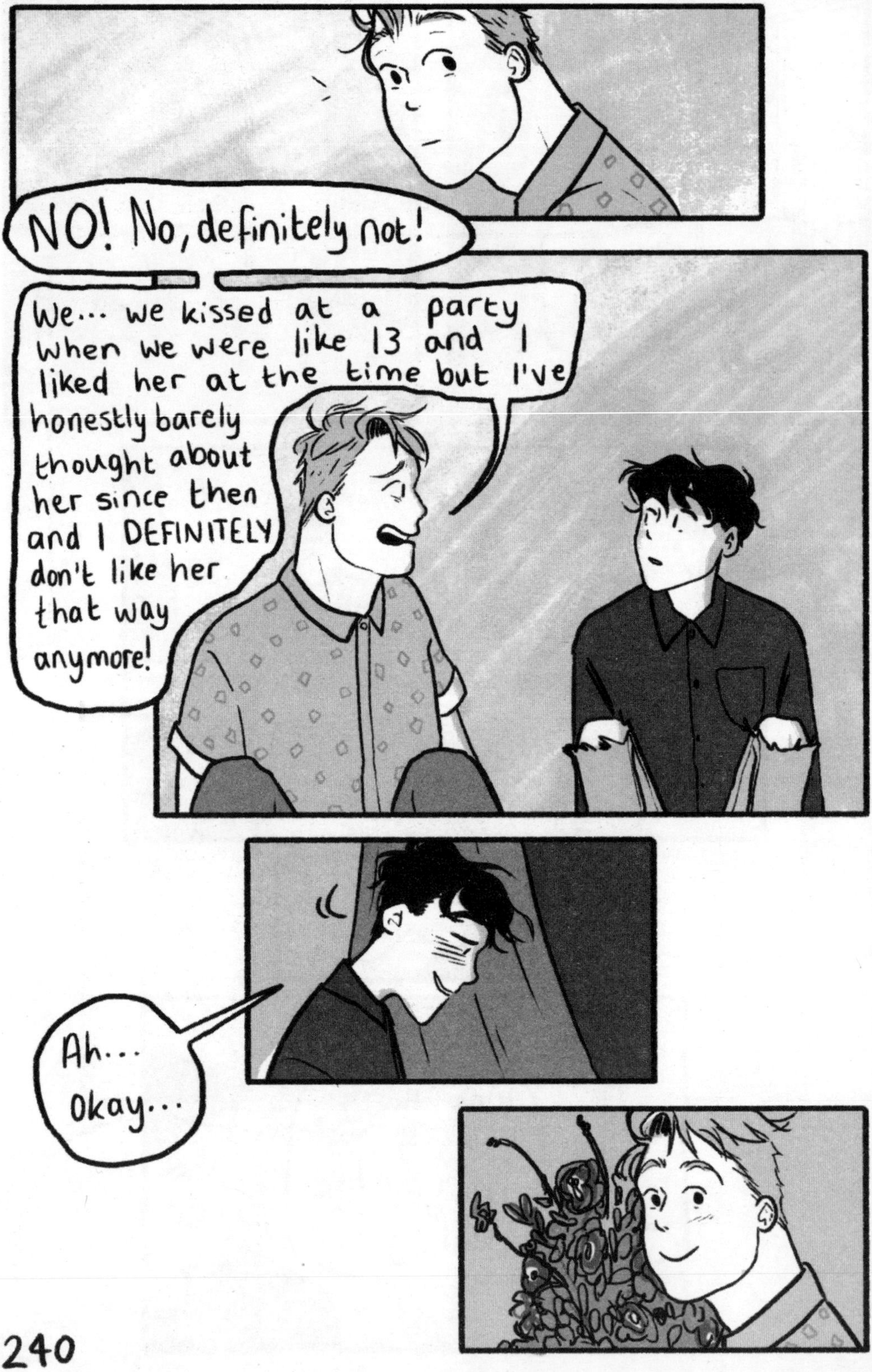
NO! No, definitely not!
We... we kissed at a party when we were like 13 and I liked her at the time but I've honestly barely thought about her since then and I DEFINITELY don't like her that way anymore!
Ah... okay...

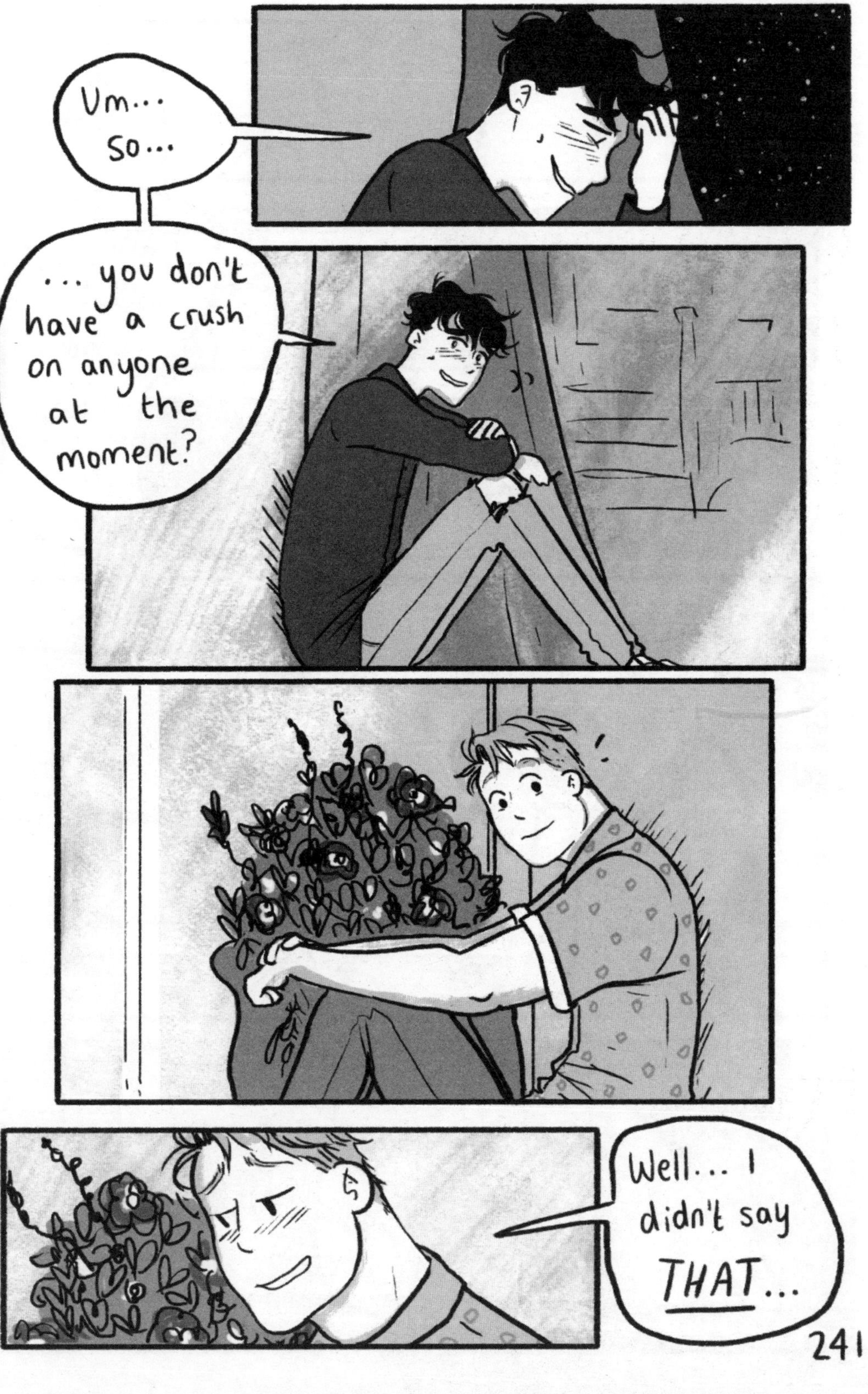
Um... so...
... you don't have a crush on anyone at the moment?
Well... I didn't say THAT...

...I've asked around... had a crush on a girl cal... Higgs school for like, 3 ye...

Haha... what's she like, then?

...

You're just gonna assume they're a she?

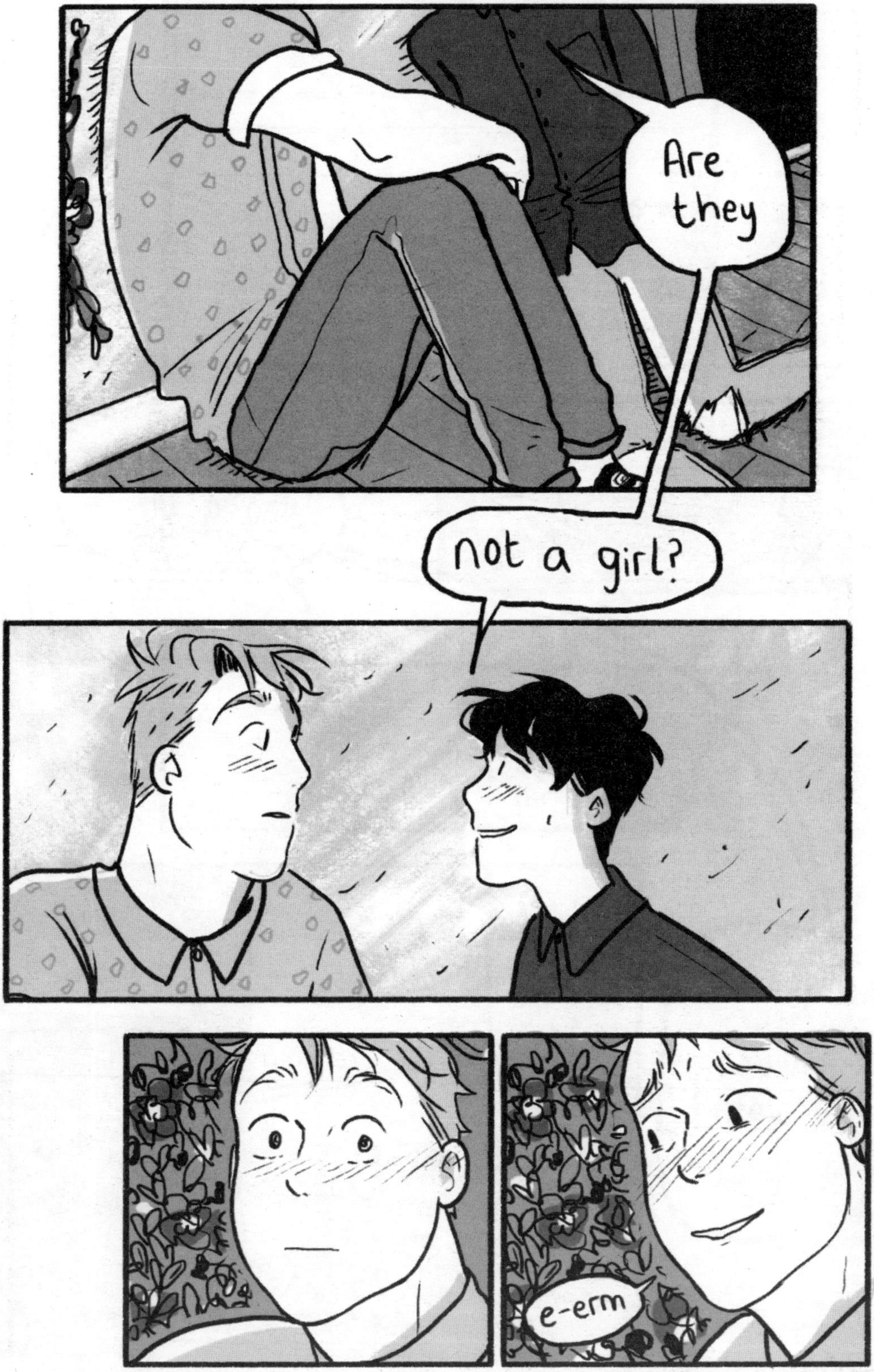
Are they
not a girl?
e-erm

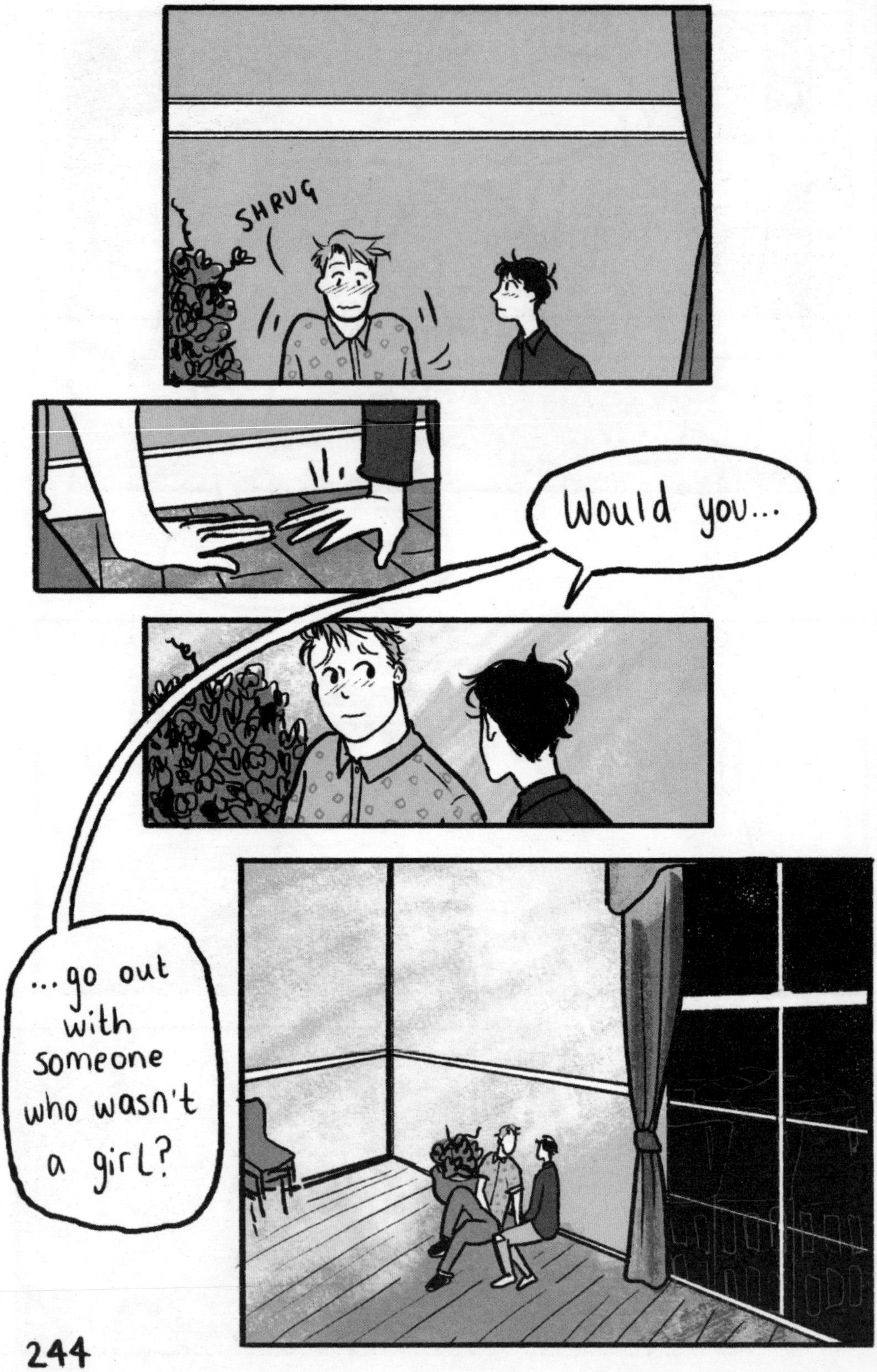
SHRUG
Would you...
...go out with someone who wasn't a girl?

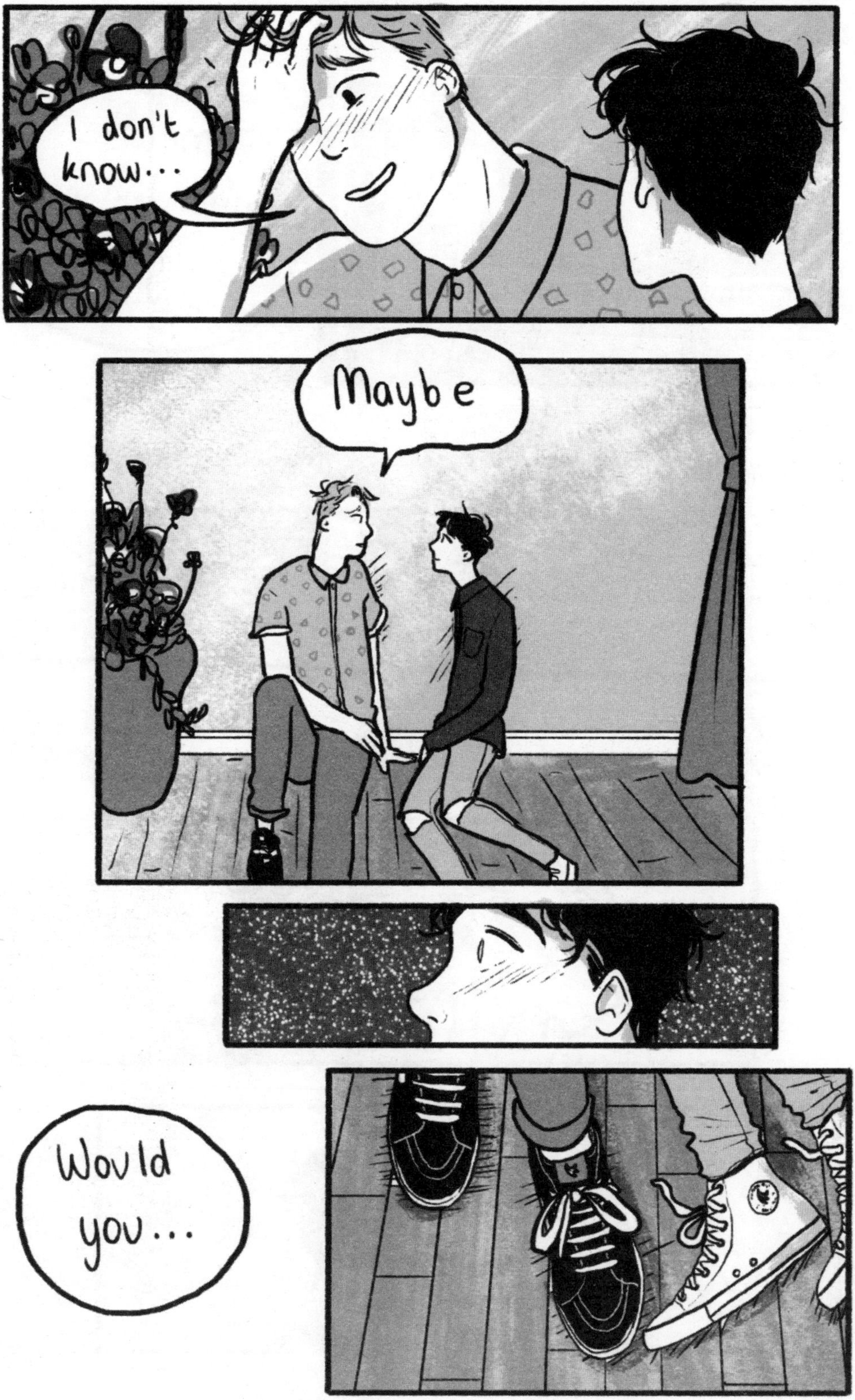
I don't know...
Maybe
Would you...

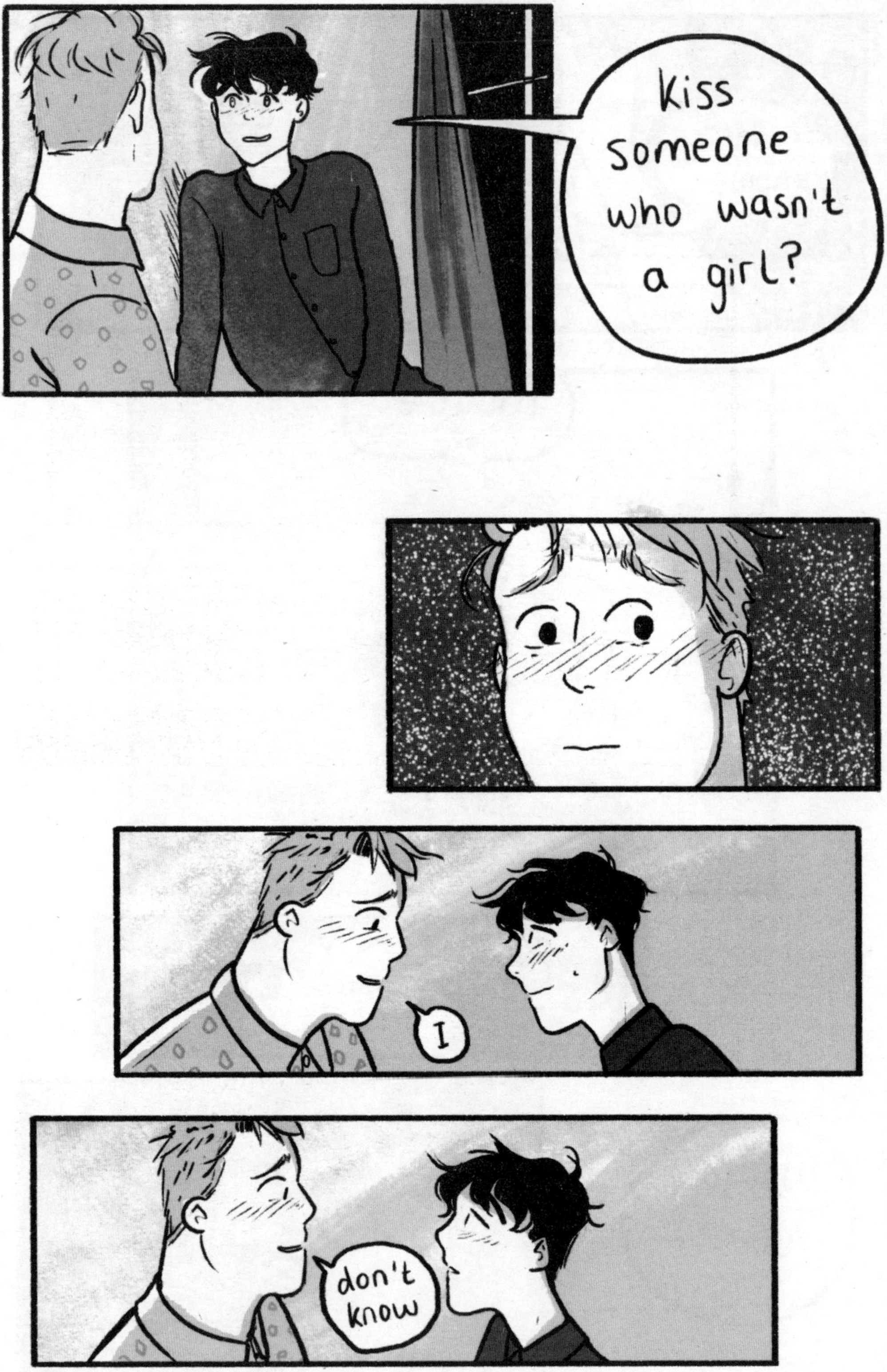
Kiss someone who wasn't a girl?
I
don't know

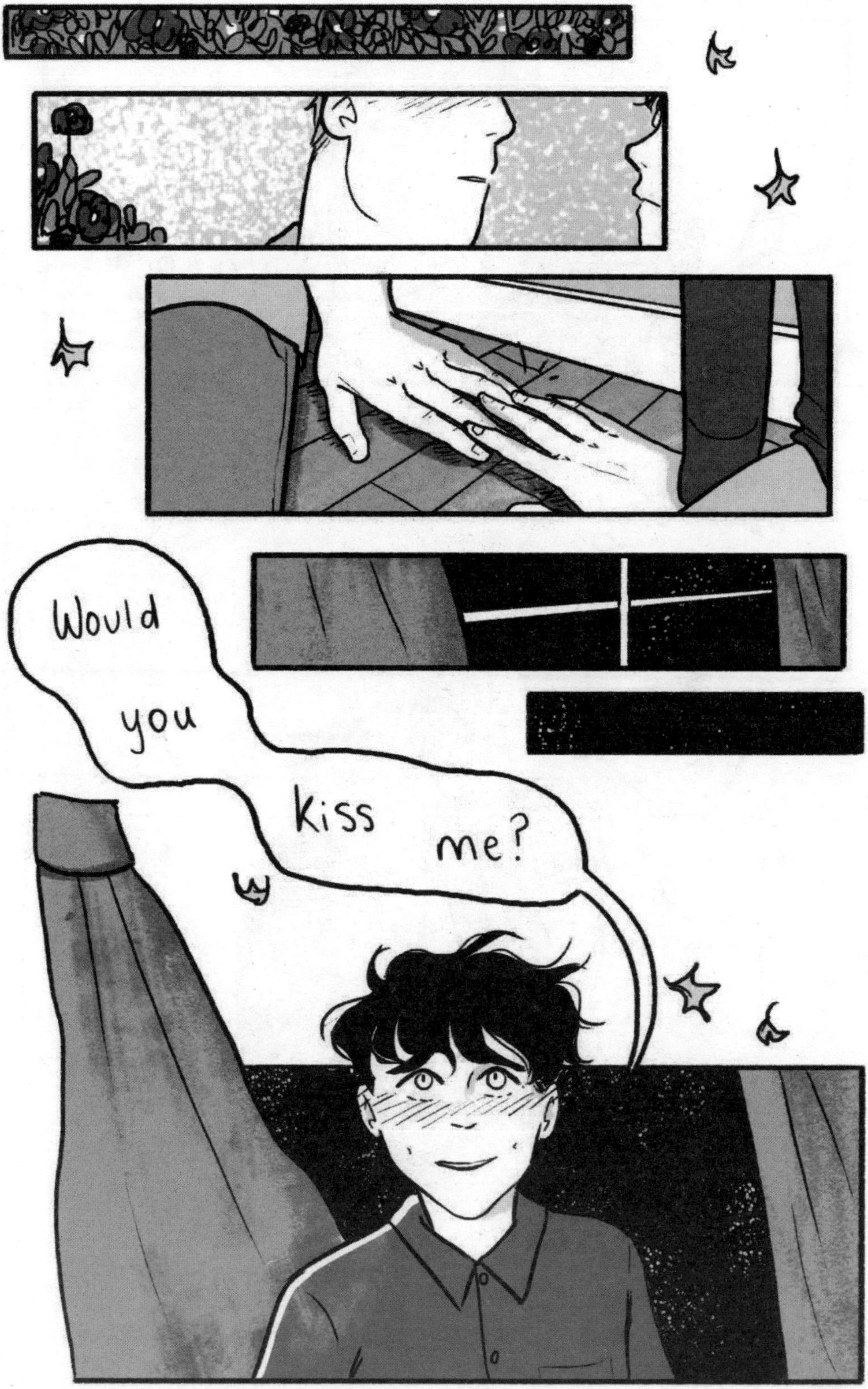
Would you kiss me?

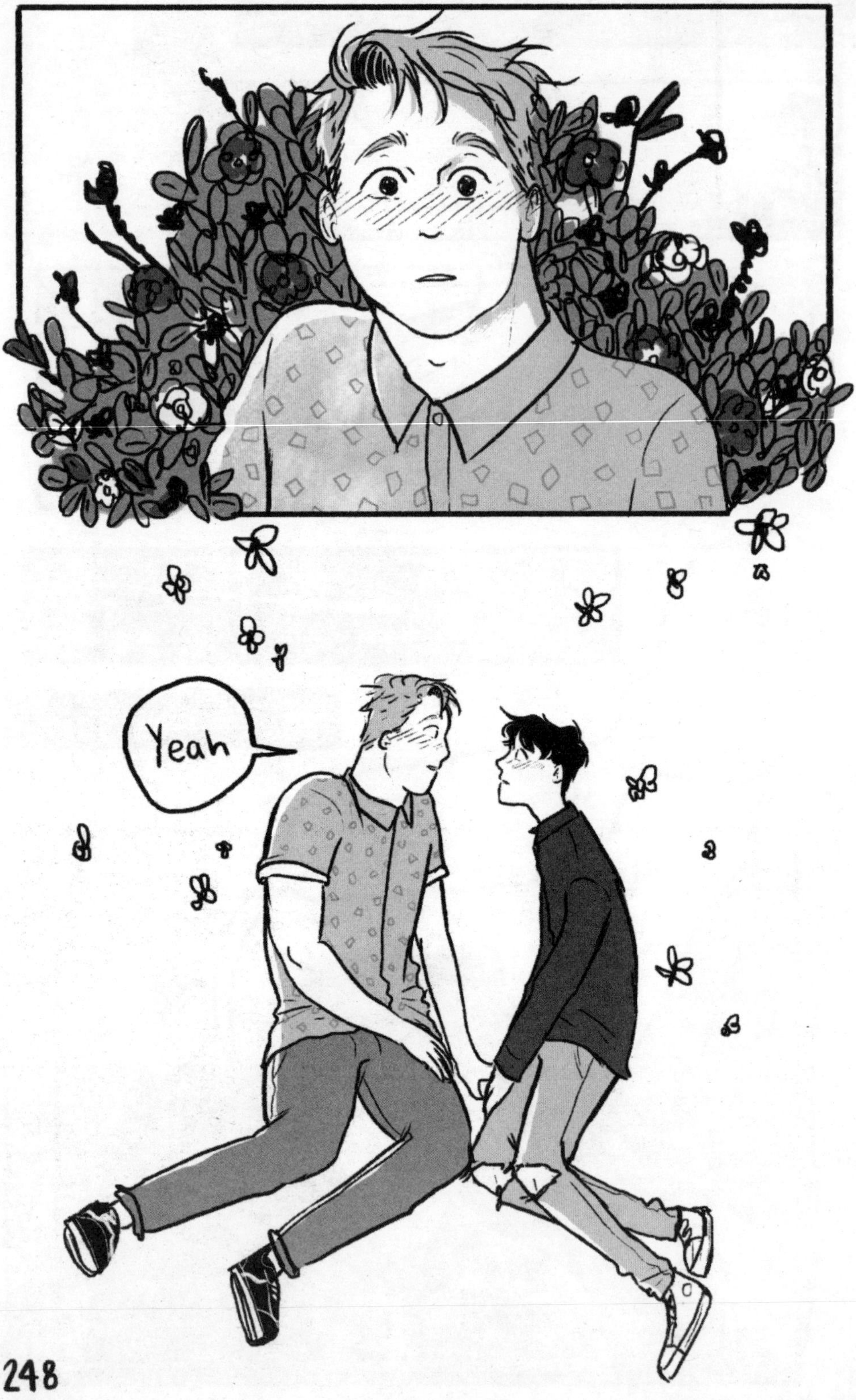
Yeah

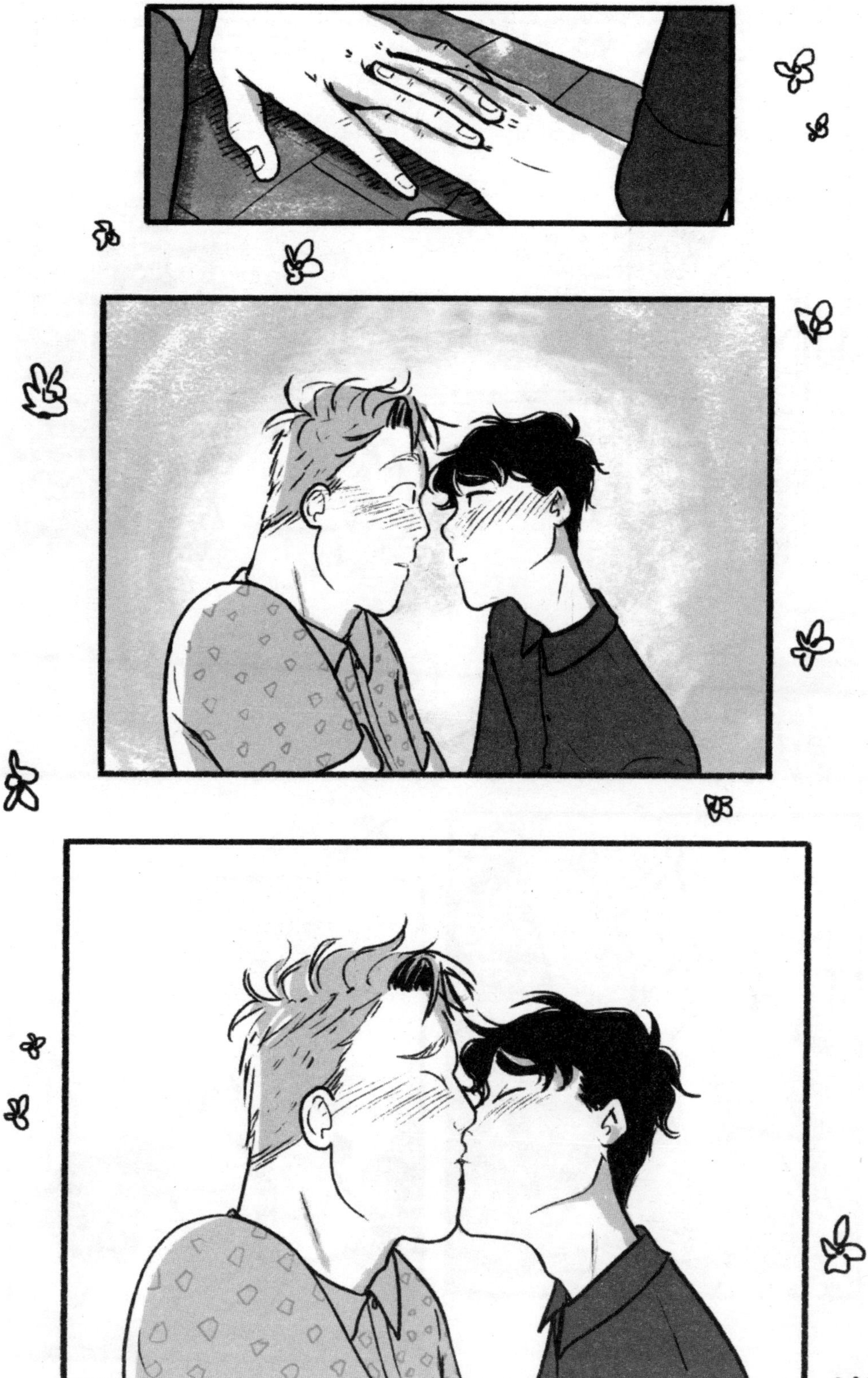

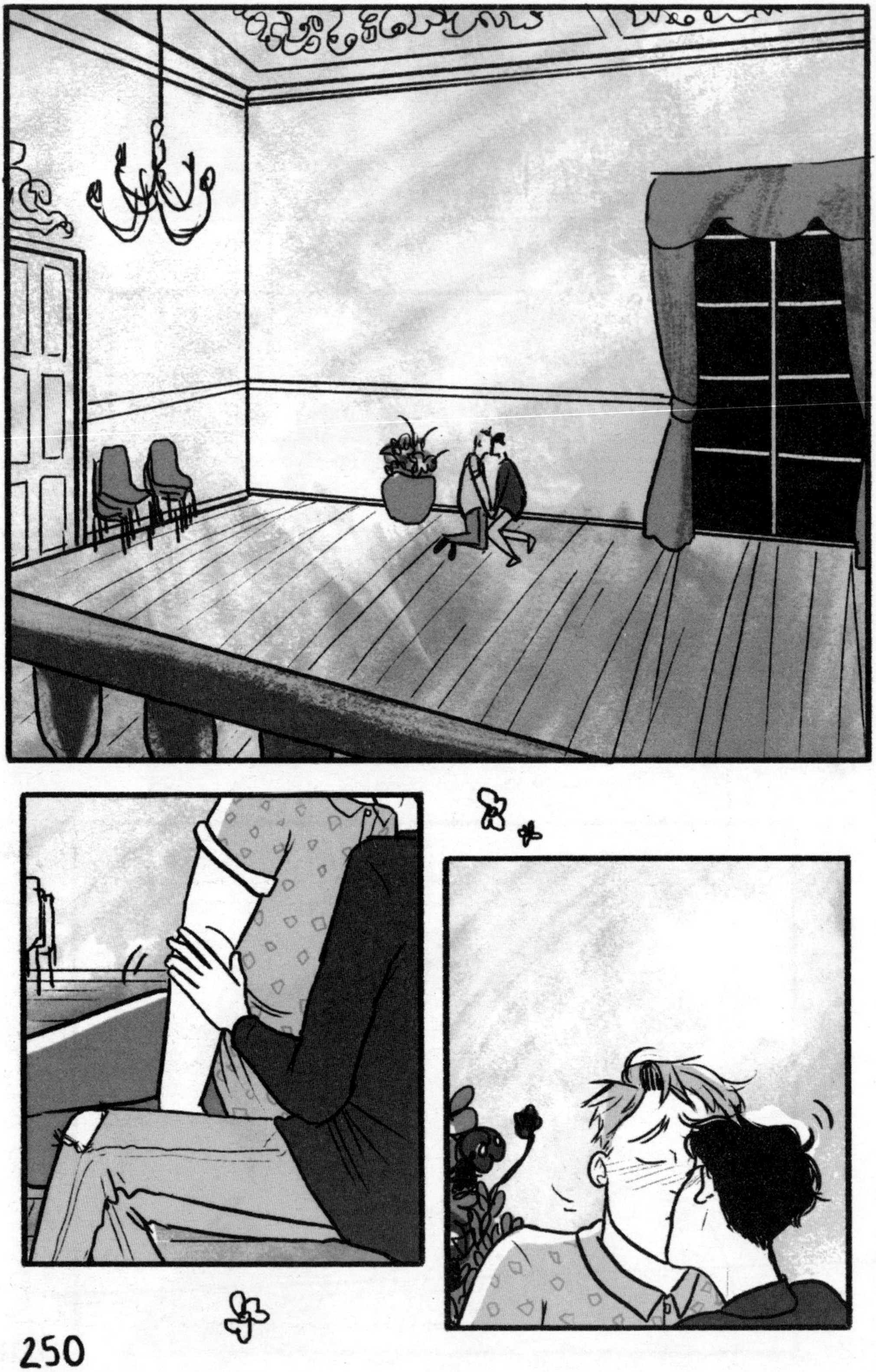

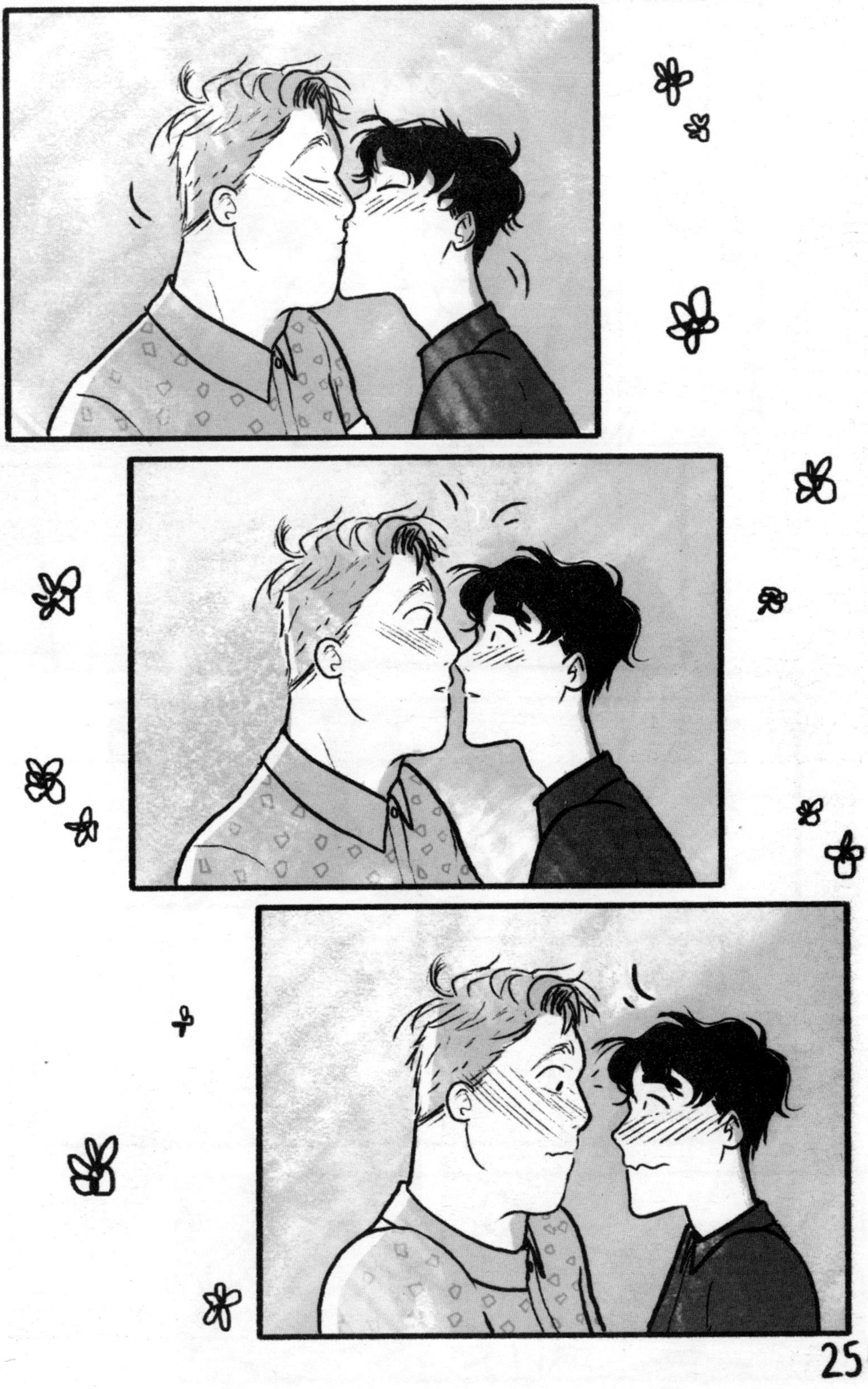

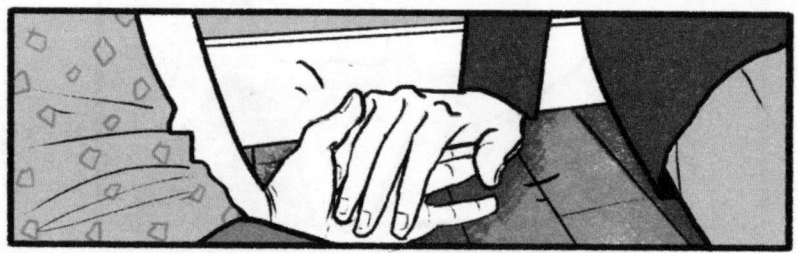

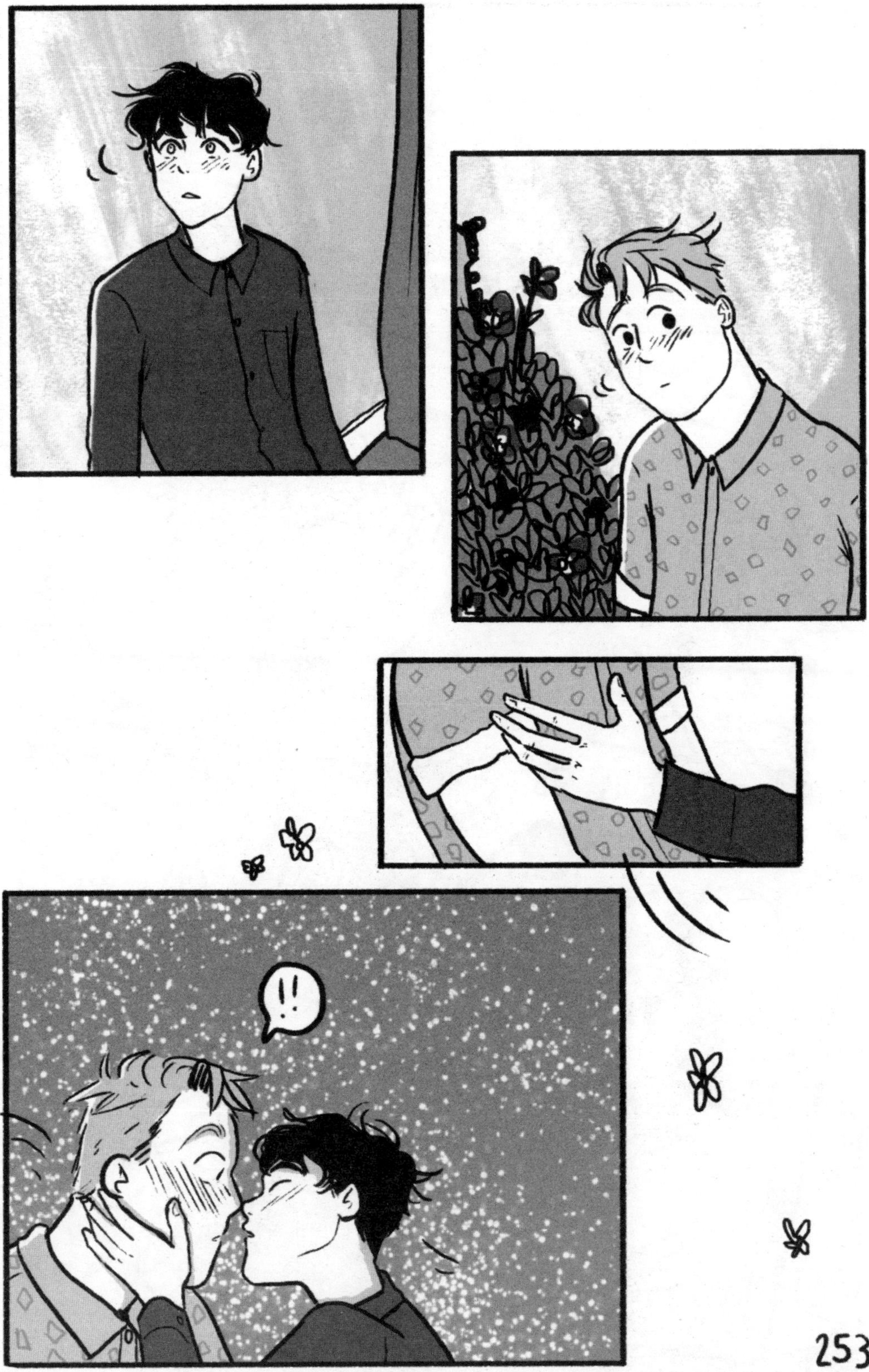
!!

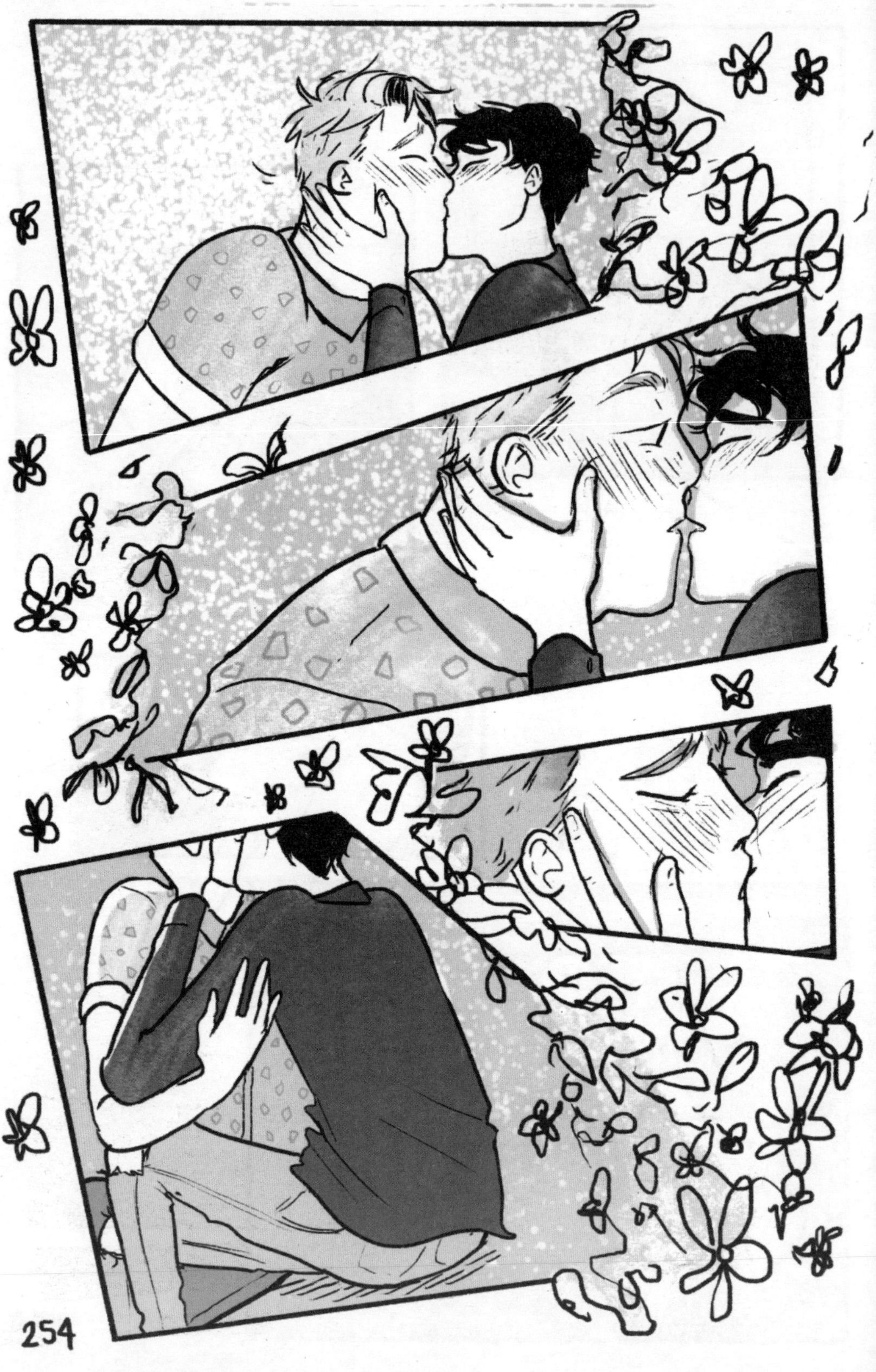

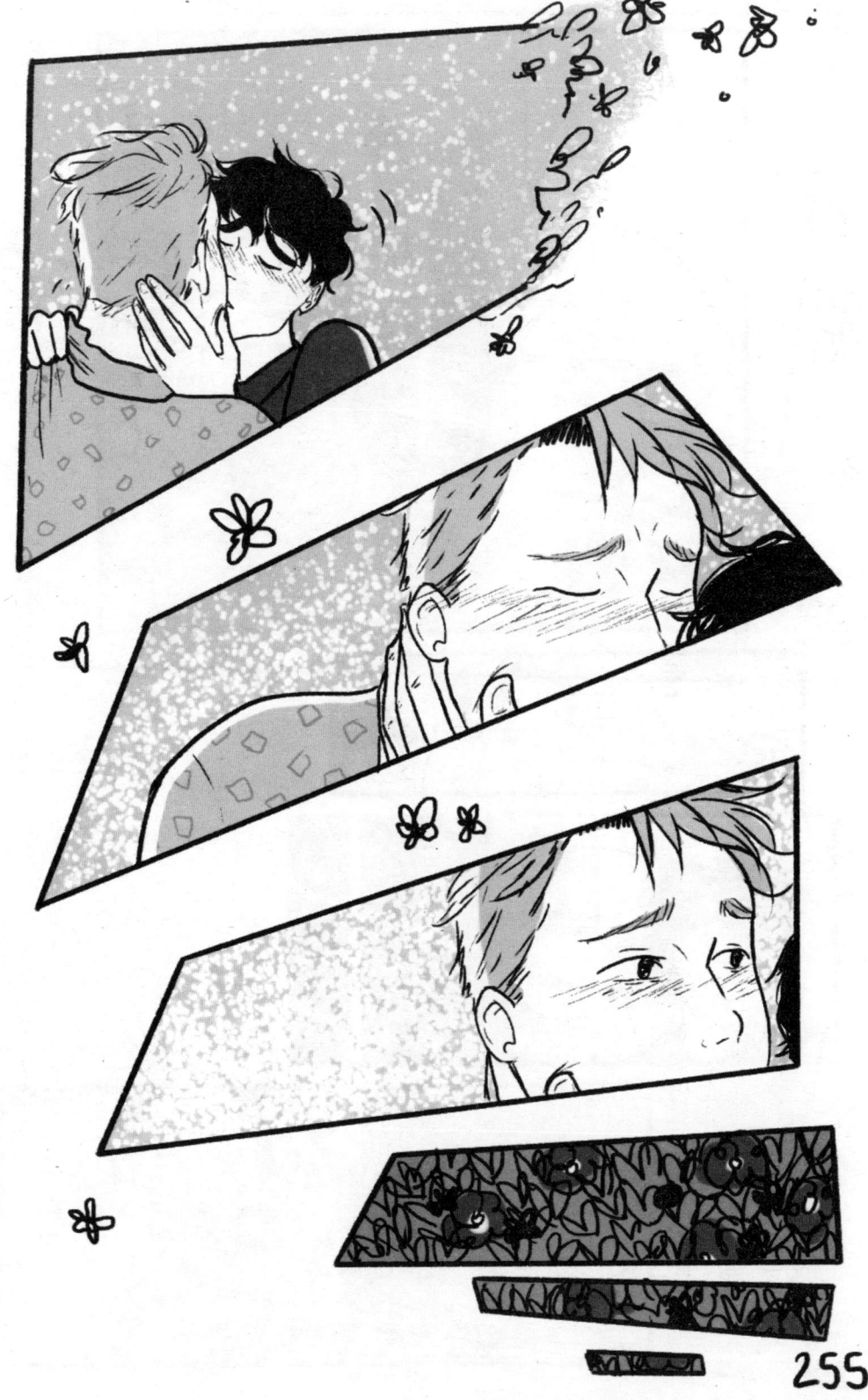

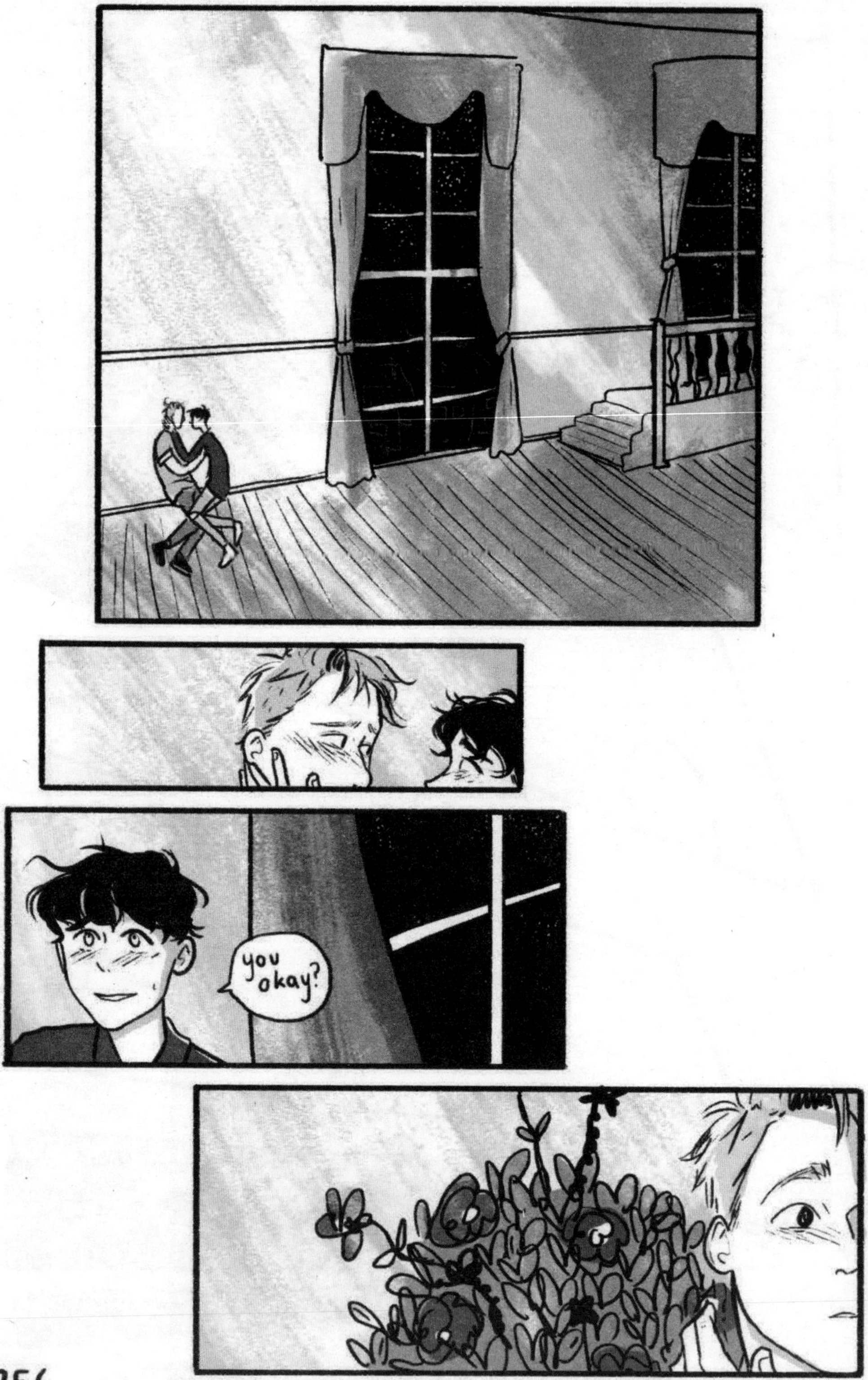
you okay?

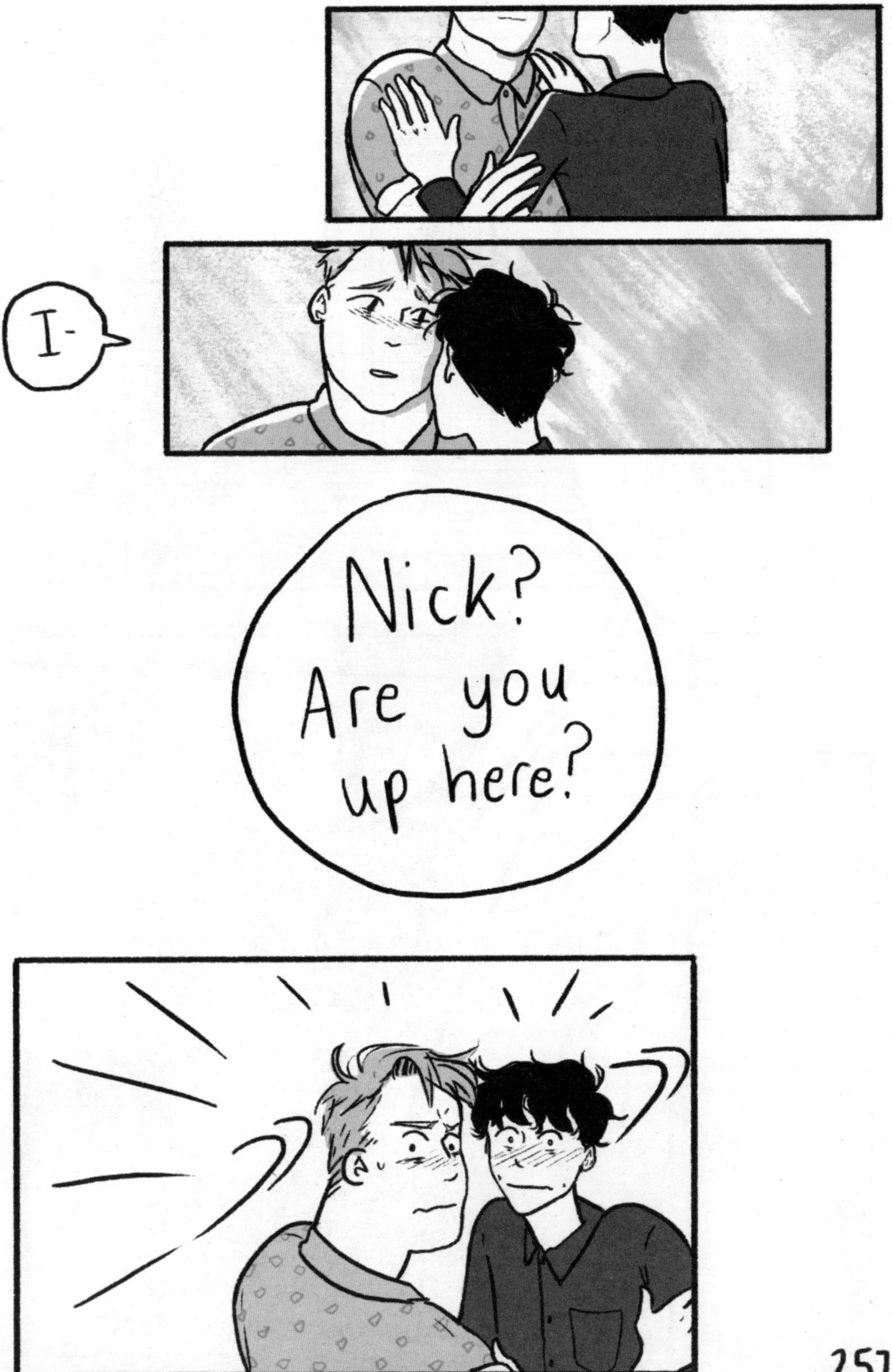
I-
Nick? Are you up here?

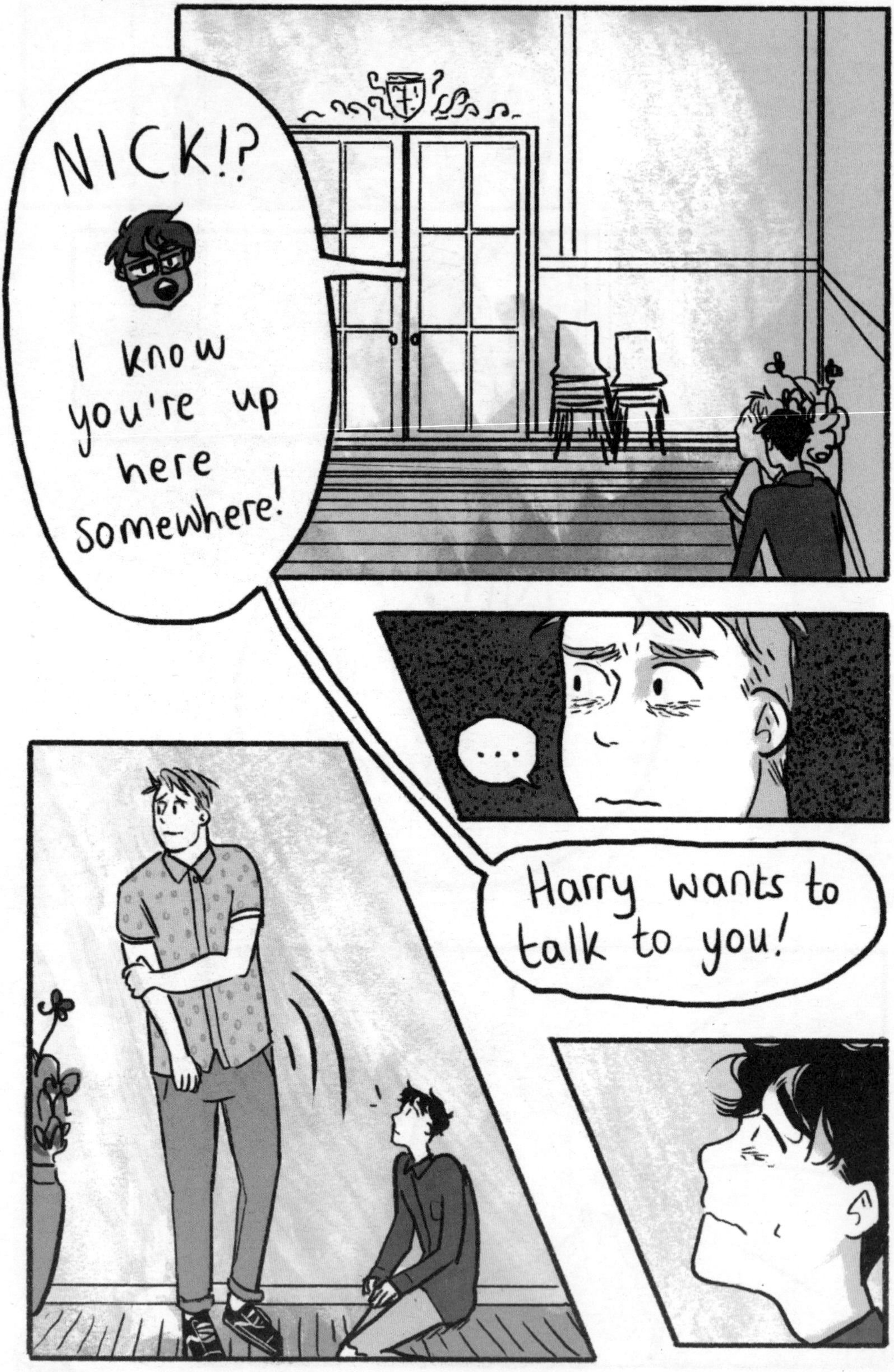
NICK!?
I know you're up here somewhere!
...
Harry wants to talk to you!
!

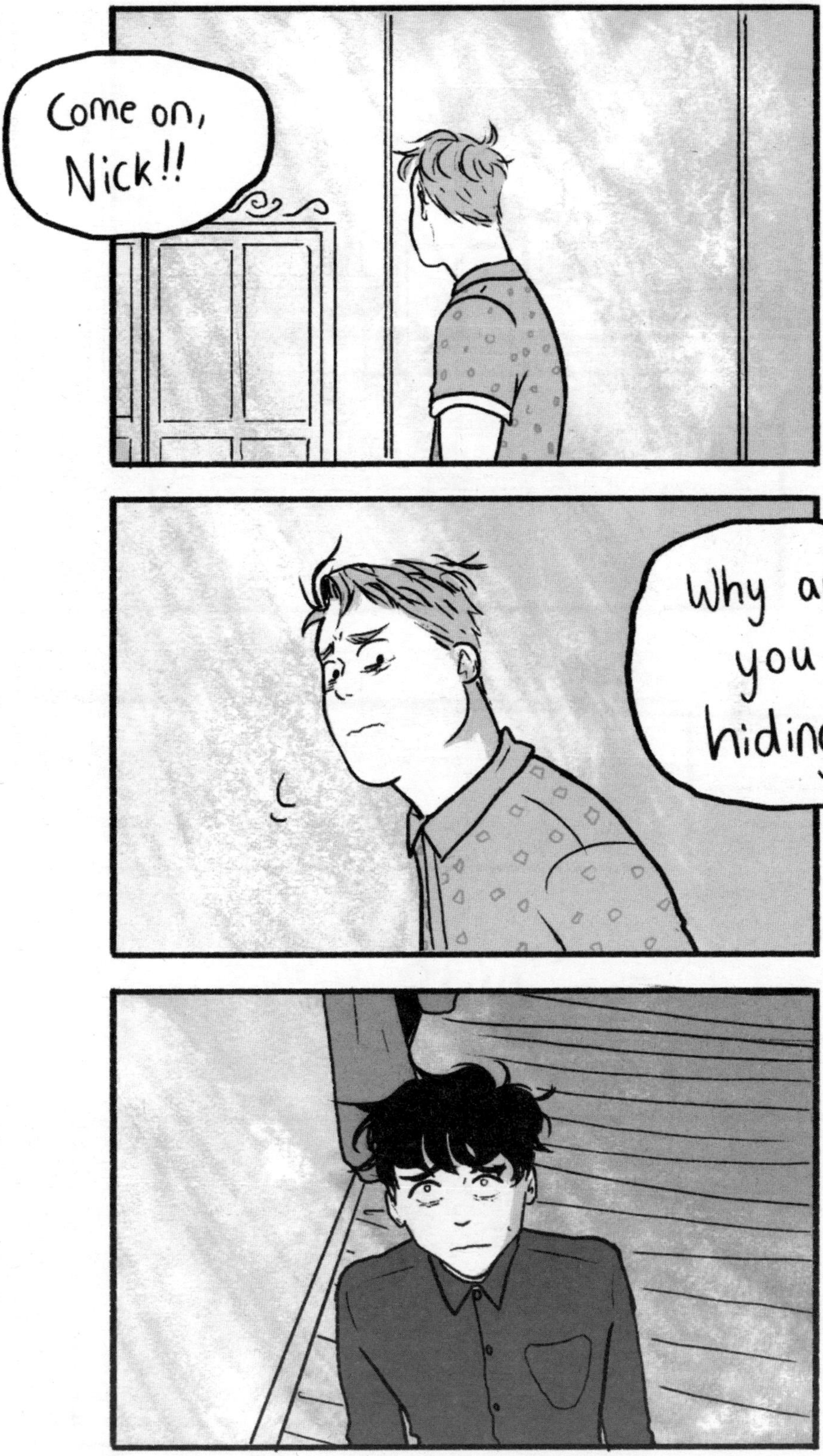
Come on, Nick!!
Why are you hiding?

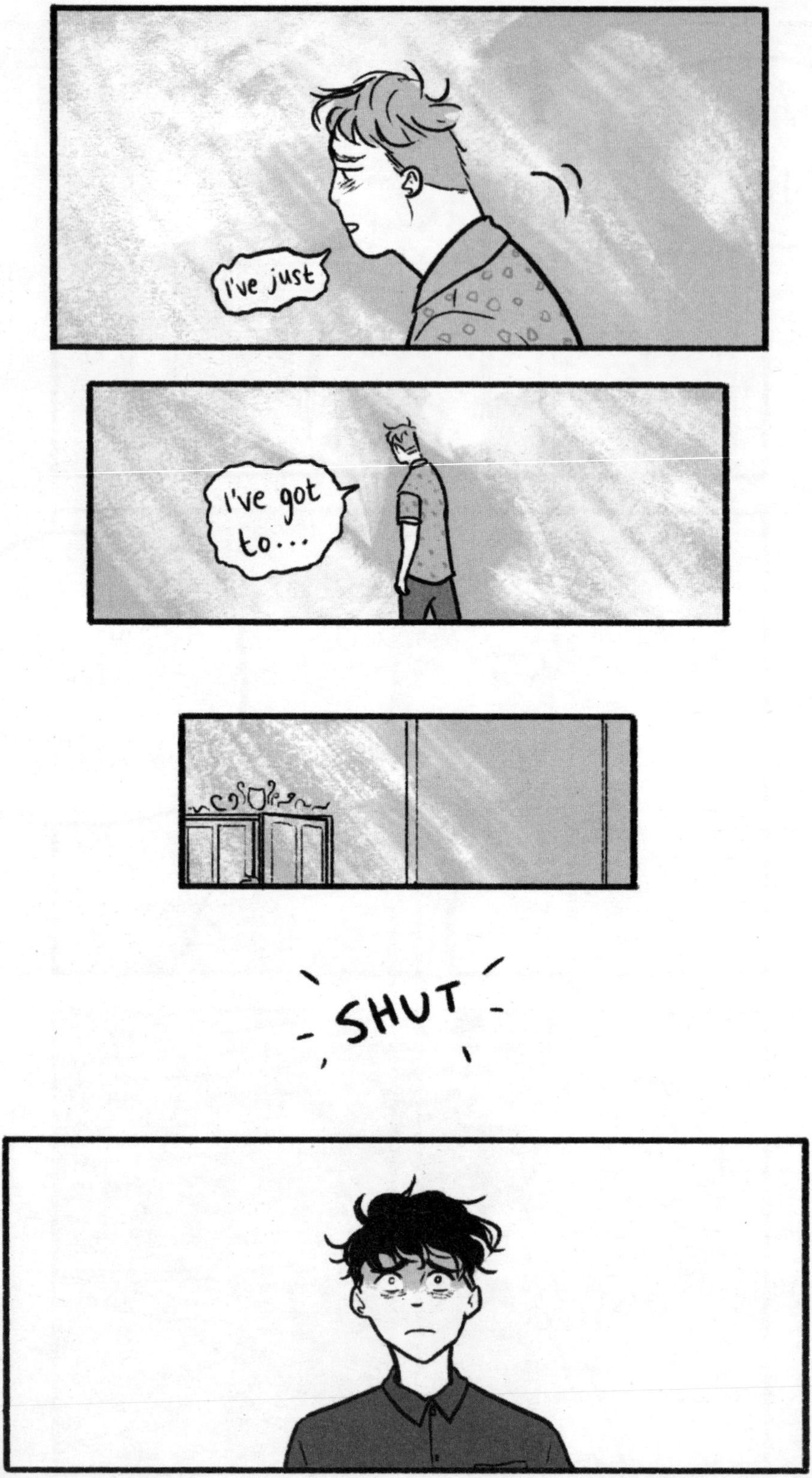

I've just
I've got to...
SHUT

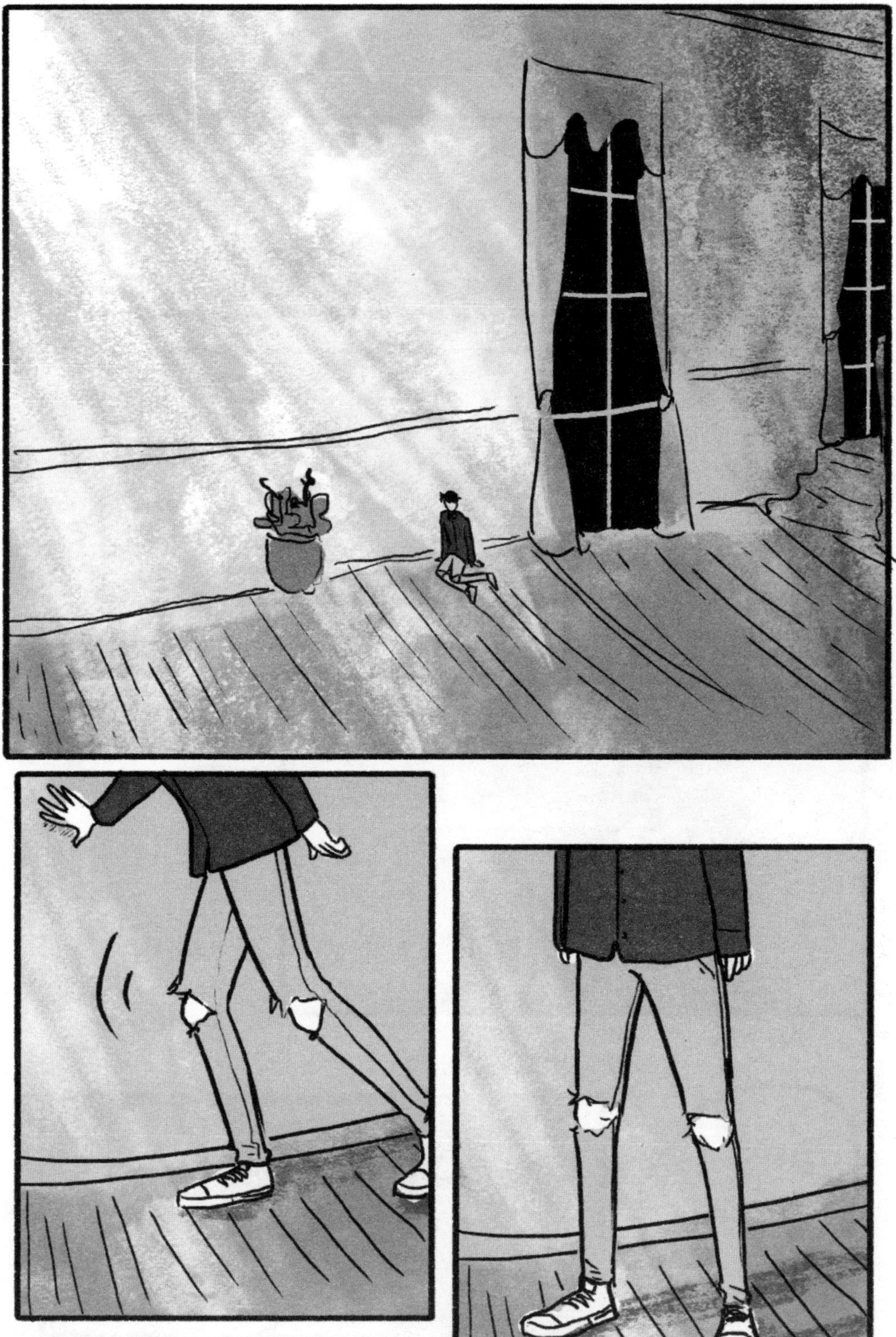

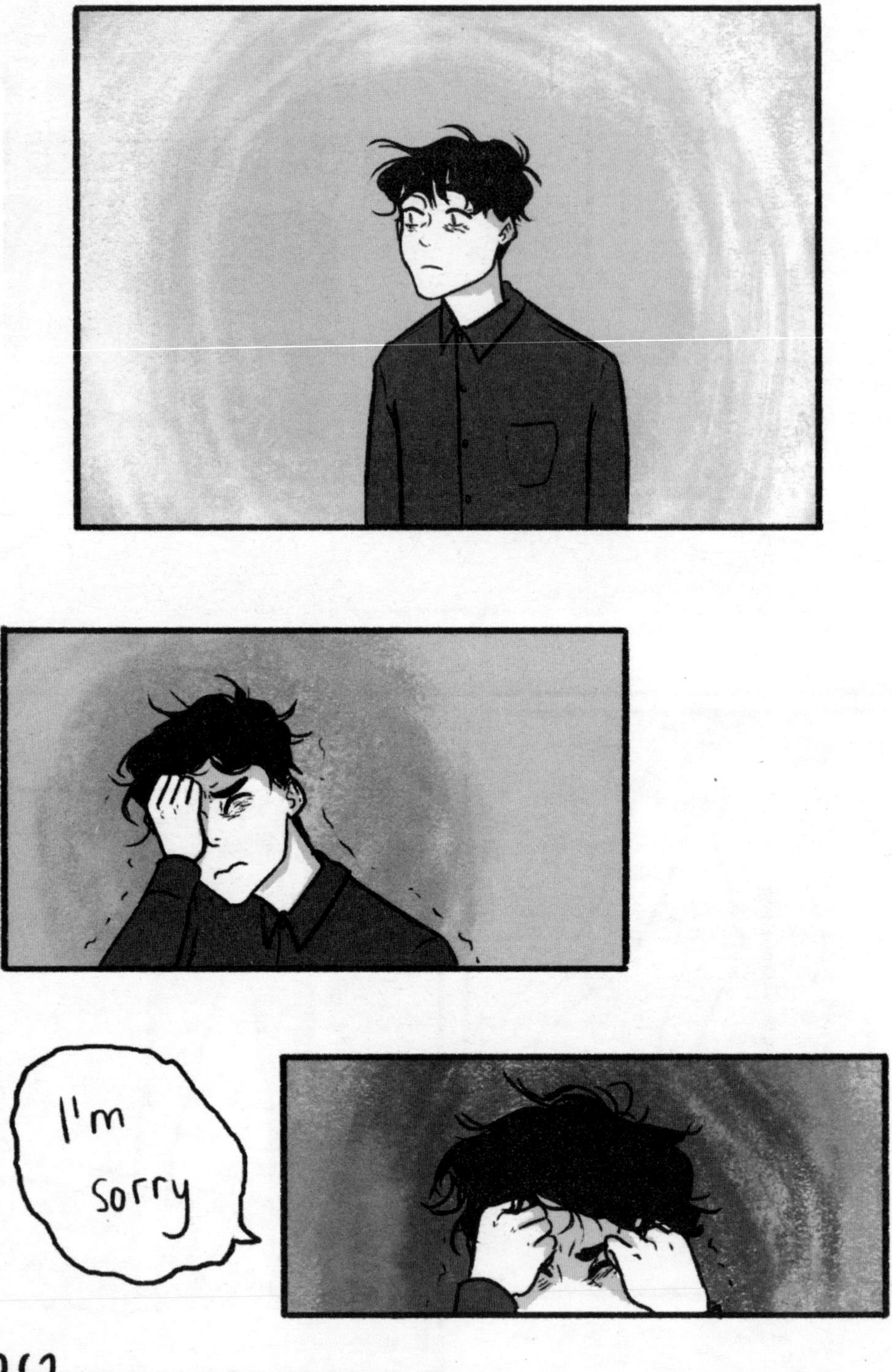
I'm sorry

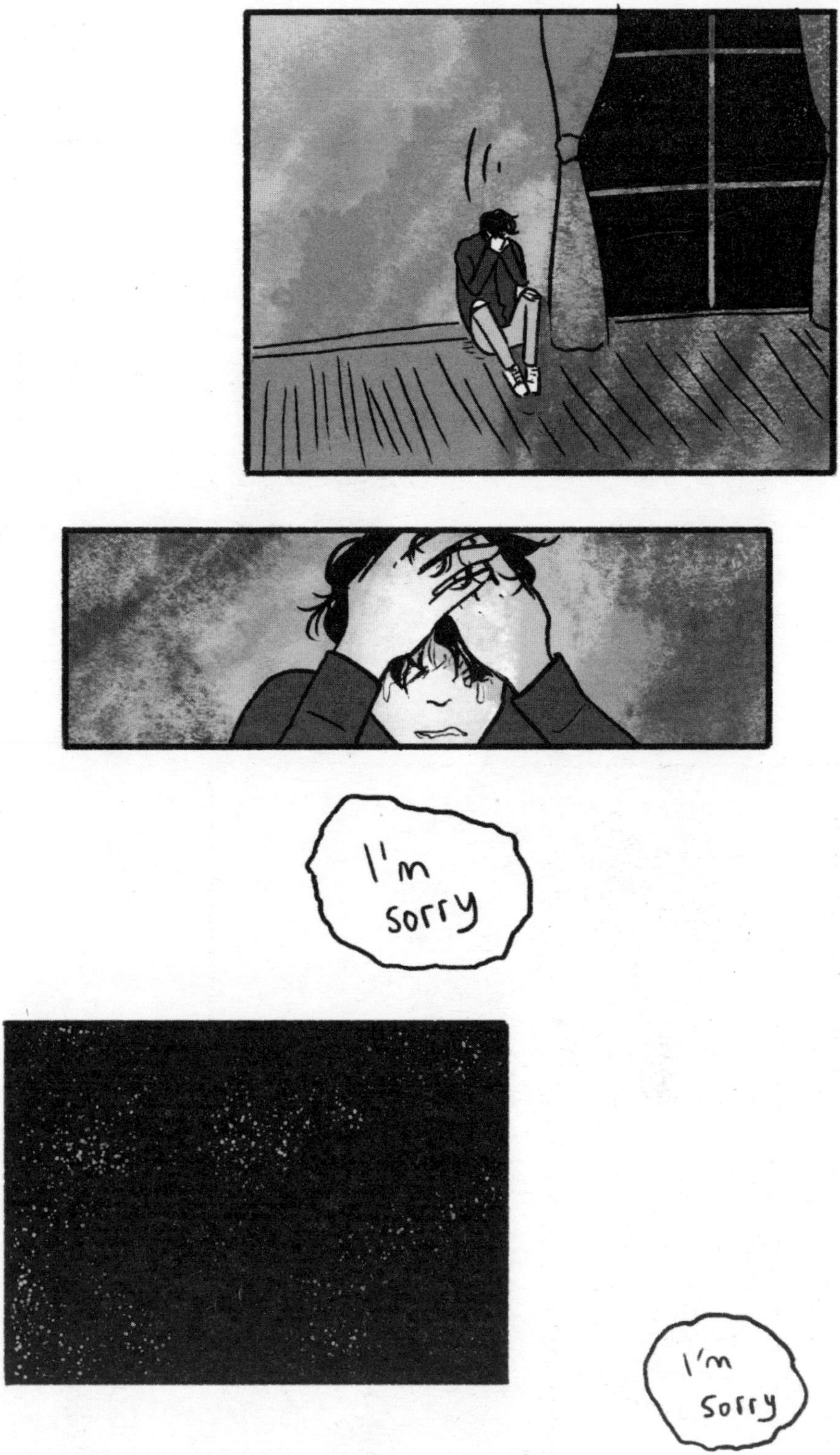
I'm sorry
I'm sorry

Heartstopper continues in Volume 2!

FSSSSSSHHHHH
...hi
TOKYO
N-Nick

Read more of the comic online:

heartstoppercomic.tumblr.com
tapas.io/series/heartstopper

Read on for an exclusive peek:

script extracts from the

Netflix live-action TV show!

EPISODE ONE, SCENE 3

INT. TRUHAM GRAMMAR, FORM ROOM – DAY

Charlie – dejected and glum after being stood up – enters his
new form room. The room is already full of boys chatting,
joking, and unpacking bags – a hubbub of morning chaos.
Charlie looks small and isolated against it all. He is *not* in
the mood.

MR. LANGE is sitting at a messy teacher's desk, ignoring the
classroom madness. On the whiteboard behind him in large,
untidy letters: 'Mr. Lange', and the form name, 'Hamlet 5'.

Feeling pretty miserable, Charlie approaches Mr. Lange.

> MR. LANGE
> Well, if it isn't Charlie Spring!
> Happy New Year!

> CHARLIE
> Hi, sir.

> MR. LANGE
> Come to join the ranks of Hamlet
> house?

> CHARLIE
> Apparently so.

Mr. Lange squints at his sheet of paper.

> MR. LANGE
> Let's see... where did I put you on
> the seating plan... Ah yes! You're
> over there. Next to *Nicholas
> Nelson*.

Mr. Lange points toward the corner of the room. While Mr.
Lange continues to speak, Charlie turns to look, but his view
of the seats – and Nick – is obscured by the other students
in the class.

> MR. LANGE (CONT'D)
> (rambling)
> He's in Year 11, so only one year
> older than you! One of the rugby
> boys, too, I think. I'm sure you'll
> get along swimmingly. Or you can
> just sit in silence for the rest of
> the year. Really doesn't affect me
> in any way whatsoever.

Charlie turns away and begins to walk over to his seat, but as he does, the students part like the red sea and reveal NICK NELSON (16, Year 11, a gentle rugby lad). Nick is sitting at a table, a window behind him with light streaming in, twiddling a pen in one hand. Totally in his own world.

Charlie stops walking. For the first time, his melancholy expression drops. Instead, he's... intrigued.

Nick, noticing he's being watched, glances towards Charlie. For a brief second, their eyes meet.

Then their view of each other is obscured again by other students in the class.

Charlie continues walking towards Nick and sits down in the seat next to him. As he does so, Nick looks up at him casually.

Once sat down, Charlie looks back at him. Their gaze lasts a moment too long, prompting a shy smile and a greeting from Charlie:

> CHARLIE
> (a little nervous)
> Hi.

> NICK
> (warm)
> Hi.

HEARTSTOPPER MOMENT: As they speak, animated leaves swirl around them, a flutter of warm feelings. A spark of something. Neither of them quite sure what.

EPISODE TWO, SCENES 21-24

EXT. OUTSIDE NICK'S HOUSE - DAY

Charlie is hyping himself up to ring the doorbell of Nick's house. He raises a hand, lowers it, raises it again, adjusts his hair, and finally-

He rings the doorbell.

Nick is there in seconds, yanking the door open with a sunshine smile on his face.

> NICK
> Hey!

                         CHARLIE
              Hey!

A small 'boof' sound causes Charlie to look down - because
there is Nellie, Nick's border collie. She's adorable.

                         NICK
              This is Nellie!

Charlie is in love. He bends down to pet Nellie. Nellie is
very happy to meet Charlie.

                         CHARLIE
              Hi Nellie! You're so adorable!

Nick looks at Charlie petting Nellie. Charlie looks...
different. As Charlie stands up, it clicks.

                         NICK
              You got a haircut!

Nick raises a hand and very lightly brushes back some strands
of Charlie's hair. Charlie has a minor meltdown internally.

                         CHARLIE
              Erm- is it- is it bad?

Nick suddenly realises what he's doing and wrenches down his
hand.

                         NICK
              No! No! You look- It looks great!

A pause.

                         NICK (CONT'D)
              Okay you'd better come in or Nellie
              will think we're going for a walk.

                         CHARLIE
              Okay!

INT. NICK'S BEDROOM - DAY

Nick and Charlie are sprawled on Nick's bed playing Mario
Kart. Charlie wins, not for the first time.

                         NICK
              How are you so good at this!?

                         CHARLIE
              You get to be good at real sports.
              I get to be good at fake ones.

                    NICK
You're just good at everything.

                    CHARLIE
No I'm not!

                    NICK
You are. You're a proper little
nerd.

                    CHARLIE
I'm *not*!

                    NICK
Let's see; you're good at video
games, literally all school
subjects but especially maths,
playing the drums, befriending
dogs, and you *are* good at sports,
like, you can run *so* fast-

Charlie slaps a hand over Nick's mouth.

                    CHARLIE
Shut up!!

There's a pause as they're both laughing, lost in the moment,
looking at each other... until Charlie looks over Nick's
shoulder, out the window.

                    CHARLIE (CONT'D)
Oh my God.

                    NICK
          (turning)
What?

Snow is falling.

                    CHARLIE
It's snowing.

They look at each other, grinning.

MONTAGE: NICK AND CHARLIE PLAYING IN THE SNOW - DAY

- In the Nelson house hallway, Nick appears from upstairs and
hands Charlie one of his hoodies. Charlie puts it on - it's
way too big. Adorable.

- They head into Nick's back garden (with Nellie, of course),
trudging through the snow and through a gate at the back.

Behind Nick's house is a large empty field, leading onto woodland and countryside.

- Nick sticking his tongue out, eating the snow.

- The boys running into the field - vast, white, magical as the snow settles.

- A snowball fight breaks out - snowballs are tossed back and forth, Nellie trying to get involved, Nick stuffing snow down Charlie's coat, Charlie getting him in the back of the head.

- Charlie falling into the snow to make a snow angel. Nick snaps a photo of him on his phone, then another when Charlie sits back up, covered in snow. Nick sitting down next to him. Taking a selfie of them together.

HEARTSTOPPER MOMENT: Nick and Charlie lay down in the snow together, and they start talking, sharing silly ideas.

We don't hear them speak, but we see Nick gesture up at the sky, wanting it to snow heavier. And 2D animated snowflakes, in the style of the Heartstopper comic, start mixing with the real snow.

As the two boys lay there, talking, the snow around them morphs into animation, looking sketched like in the comic. Slowly we zoom out from above, Nick and Charlie just looking at each other and talking for a while, everything a little more magical this way.

INT. NICK'S HOUSE, KITCHEN - EVENING

Nick is making a cup of tea. His mum, Sarah, is at the kitchen table with her iPad.

>   SARAH
>   Charlie seems like a lovely boy.
>   When did you meet him?

>   NICK
>   A couple of months ago. He's in my
>   form.

>   SARAH
>   He's very different to your other
>   friends, isn't he? You seem much
>   more like yourself around him.

>   NICK
>   Do I?

SARAH
You do!

Nick sips his tea. That's... something to think about.

EPISODE TWO, SCENES 38-43

EXT. CHARLIE'S HOUSE, FRONT DOOR - DUSK

In a reversal of their earlier greeting at Nick's house, Charlie opens the front door to his house to find Nick there.

NICK
Hey!

CHARLIE
Hey!

INT. CHARLIE'S BEDROOM - DUSK

Nick is sitting at Charlie's electric drum kit, trying his best to play a drum beat. He quite clearly does not have a good sense of rhythm nor much hand-leg coordination.

Charlie is standing just behind him, watching with a grin.

CHARLIE
You're terrible!

NICK
I'm trying my best!

CHARLIE
Here, budge up, let me help.

Charlie squeezes onto the drum stool next to Nick. They're closely pressed together. Charlie puts his hands over Nick's and helps him tap out a simple rock beat.

Nick is hyper-focused on Charlie's hands. His fingers. The feeling of their skin together. Then he turns a little to look at Charlie. Charlie is engrossed in the beat.

After finishing the drum beat, Charlie smiles at Nick.

CHARLIE (CONT'D)
There, you're a pro now!

They look at each other for a long moment.

Then Charlie's hands are gone as he awkwardly gets up from the stool. Away from Nick.

> CHARLIE (CONT'D)
> Haha... erm... well, that's
> probably cheating though.

Nick is... confused. What just happened?

INT. CHARLIE'S HOUSE, LIVING ROOM - NIGHT

It's dark in the living room. Only the glare from the TV and a lamp illuminate Nick and Charlie, who are watching a movie while tucked up in blankets.

We focus on Nick, a little sleepy. Nick looks over at Charlie. Charlie is asleep. He looks... adorable. Nick thinks he looks adorable.

Charlie's hand lays outstretched on his lap, palm up. Nick looks at it, and-

Total silence. Like Nick's heart stops.

HEARTSTOPPER MOMENT: An urge. Nick wants to take Charlie's hand. He raises his own hand very slowly. Carefully. An experiment.

He moves his hand to hover a couple of inches over Charlie's hands. Around their hands, in **ANIMATION:** a spark.

Nick moves his hand away, shaken. Surely he doesn't want to-

He moves his hand again. His fingers flex, imagining the feeling of slotting his fingers around Charlie's. The sparks fizz again, a twinkle, their hands at the centre of the world-

And then he whips his hand away again. It is very clear to Nick what he's feeling now.

INT. CHARLIE'S HOUSE, HALLWAY - NIGHT

Nick and Charlie stand opposite each other in the hallway. Nick's in his coat, ready to go home, while Charlie's still wrapped up in a blanket.

> CHARLIE
> I wish you didn't have to go.

                    NICK
          I wish I didn't either.
               (a beat)
          You look so cuddly like that.

                    CHARLIE
          Do I?

                    NICK
          Yeah.

Nick suddenly wraps his arms around Charlie and pulls him
close... a HUG.

Charlie is shocked. For a moment he can't even believe this
is real. Then he's raising his arms and hugging Nick back.
Praying the moment never ends.

But of course it does. Nick moves very quickly away, averting
his eyes and opening the front door.

                    NICK (CONT'D)
          Okay!! See you on Monday!!

The door slams. Nick is gone.

Charlie stands very still, shell-shocked.

Tori appears out of nowhere, sipping her usual glass of
lemonade through a straw.

                    TORI
          I don't think he's straight.

INT. CHARLIE'S BEDROOM - NIGHT

Charlie is sat on his bed, duvet over his head, messaging the
group chat.

Charlie: [what does it mean when hot straight boy hugs you
for like a full ten seconds]

Tao: [he was probably imagining you were tara]

Charlie: [SHHH LET ME DREAM]

Elle: [okay charlie don't ask how i know this, but... tara
definitely doesn't like nick back.
[there's ZERO chance of tara and nick becoming a thing.]

Charlie sits up, staring at the message. *A spark of hope.*

INT. NICK'S BEDROOM - NIGHT

Nick kicks his shoes into a corner and pulls his hoodie off.

He sits down heavily on the edge of his bed and takes out his phone, tapping intensely. He brings up Instagram. First up on screen - a selfie from Imogen. He pauses, abruptly reminded of his 'other self', the person who 'should' like Imogen - and then he scrolls past it.

And there's a post from Charlie - a photo of him in the snow. One Nick took. The caption: **snow day :)**

Nick closes Instagram and opens up his photos. There are more photos of Charlie. Many more. Nick picks one and gazes at it, at *Charlie*, smiling candidly at Nick behind the camera.

Nick grabs his laptop and flops onto his beanbag. He opens it up, opens the browser and clicks on the search bar. He stays like that, looking at the empty search bar, hands hovering over the keyboard.

This is it. This is the moment that will change everything.

We see Nick's face: nerves, shock at himself, a tiny bit of excitement. But mostly fear.

We see him type out a few words. And then we see the screen.

In the search bar: **am I gay?**

He presses enter.

EPISODE THREE, SCENES 22-24

INT. ST. GEORGE'S HOTEL, CORRIDOR - NIGHT

They run. They're racing, speeding through opulent corridors, past teenagers and giant mirrors and statues, up carpeted stairways and through doors, laughing, Nick trying to reach Charlie but he's too fast.

Charlie, still ahead, turns and enters a function room, and Nick tumbles in after him, and then-

INT. ST. GEORGE'S HOTEL, FUNCTION ROOM - NIGHT

The race is over and they stand very still, taking in the splendour around them:

The function room is intricately decorated in the Georgian style with an embellished ceiling, large old paintings, columns, flowers, and big curtains.

> CHARLIE
> Woah.

> NICK
> Yeah.

Charlie immediately starts exploring. Nick watches.

> CHARLIE
> How did Harry hire this entire
> place!?

> NICK
> He's, like, extremely rich.

> CHARLIE
> He should have gone on *My Super
> Sweet Sixteen*.

> NICK
> So he could cry when his parents
> got him the wrong colour
> Lamborghini?

> CHARLIE
> Exactly.

Nick goes to sit down on the floor against a wall. Charlie joins him.

It's silent for a moment. Nick and Charlie look very small in the big room with its huge ceiling. There are maybe thirty centimetres between them.

> CHARLIE (CONT'D)
> (cautious)
> So... like... was Harry being
> serious? D'you like Tara?

The question catches Nick off-guard.

                    NICK
          What- no! No, definitely not! I
          mean- I *used* to- like, we kissed
          once at a party when we were like
          thirteen and I liked her at the
          time but I've honestly barely
          thought about her since then and I
          definitely don't like her that way
          anymore.

                    CHARLIE
          Ah. Okay.

A pause. Nick wonders if he's overdone it. Charlie feels like
there's hope.

                    CHARLIE (CONT'D)
          So... you don't have a crush on
          anyone at the moment?

Another pause. Nick looks at Charlie, surprised, and...
suddenly extremely nervous.

                    NICK
          Well... I didn't say *that*.

This is not the answer Charlie was expecting.

                    CHARLIE
          Oh... What's she like, then?

                    NICK
          You're just gonna assume they're a
          'she'?

Charlie's *properly* shook now - what is *happening?*

                    CHARLIE
          Are they... not a girl?

                    NICK
          Erm...

Nick looks away. Flustered. Feeling like he's shared too
much.

He just shrugs mysteriously. It says enough.

Charlie is fully turned to face him now. He *has* to ask-

                    CHARLIE
          Would you... go out with someone
          who wasn't a girl?

Nick fiddles with his fingers. Shy. But feeling like he can
tell Charlie.

> NICK
> I don't know... Maybe.

A pang of hope. Charlie shuffles a fraction closer to Nick.

> CHARLIE
> Would you... kiss someone who
> wasn't a girl?

This question is scarier. Nick's voice is quieter as he says-

> NICK
> I don't know.

But then he turns to look at Charlie- and then they're both
fully looking at each other, transfixed, magic-

And Charlie moves a little closer so he can brush the tips of
his fingers against Nick's before asking in a soft voice-

> CHARLIE
> Would you kiss me?

HEARTSTOPPER MOMENT: A flower display behind Nick starts
blossoming, **ANIMATED** flowers appearing behind him and framing
the soft, surprised, excited expression on Nick's face.

Nick exhales. They link their fingers together. This is the
moment that changes everything.

> NICK
> Yeah.

And very slowly, nervously, cautiously, *excitedly*, Nick and
Charlie KISS FOR THE FIRST TIME.

It lasts only a few silent moments. More nerves than anything
else.

When they move apart, they just look at each other for a
brief moment- then they *realise what's just happened*. They
both turn away simultaneously. Still touching hands.

A pause. Neither Nick nor Charlie seem to know what to do or
say next. And then-

Nick is the first to turn back. Just a little. He moves his
hand so he can properly hold Charlie's.

It surprises Charlie. He turns back too. They're looking at
each other again.

And then there's <u>ANOTHER KISS</u> – this time, *fireworks*.

Not just an experiment. They *know this feels right*.

HEARTSTOPPER MOMENT: The **ANIMATED** flowers are everywhere, swirling around them, growing, flying.

When they draw back this time, it's slower, calmer, less awkward. They don't look away from each other.

>   CHARLIE
>   You okay?

Nick takes a moment. He's processing.

>   NICK
>   I–

But he's immediately interrupted by a voice calling for him in the corridor outside the room.

>   HARRY (O.S.)
>   NICK! You up here?

And that's when Nick starts to panic.

He scrambles to his feet, not really knowing what to do, staring at the closed door.

>   HARRY (O.S.) (CONT'D)
>   I just want to talk, mate. Why are
>   you hiding?

Nick looks back to Charlie. Charlie is looking up at him – like he knows what Nick is going to do.

Nick walks to the door... and leaves the room.

<u>INT. ST. GEORGE'S HOTEL, CORRIDOR – NIGHT</u>

Nick has rejoined Harry and his mates. Harry is talking to him, but Nick isn't listening – he's staring into the air over Harry's head, paralysed by what's just happened, in turmoil, not knowing what he should do–

>   HARRY
>   –and like, it's all just banter,
>   isn't it? The lads can see it's
>   banter, you can see it's banter,
>   there's no need to start anything
>   just because you're in a bad mood
>   at my birthday party–

Nick isn't listening to Harry. He's made his decision. He interrupts Harry mid-sentence.

> HARRY (CONT'D)
> -and like, I consider you a good
> mate, I mean, I invited you here,
> so I-

> NICK
> Yeah, I guess I was just in a mood.

> HARRY
> Yeah. Exactly. So we're good?

> NICK
> (reluctant)
> Yeah.
> (a beat)
> I'm just gonna go find the loo.

He turns around and walks off.

SCHOOL UNIFORM:

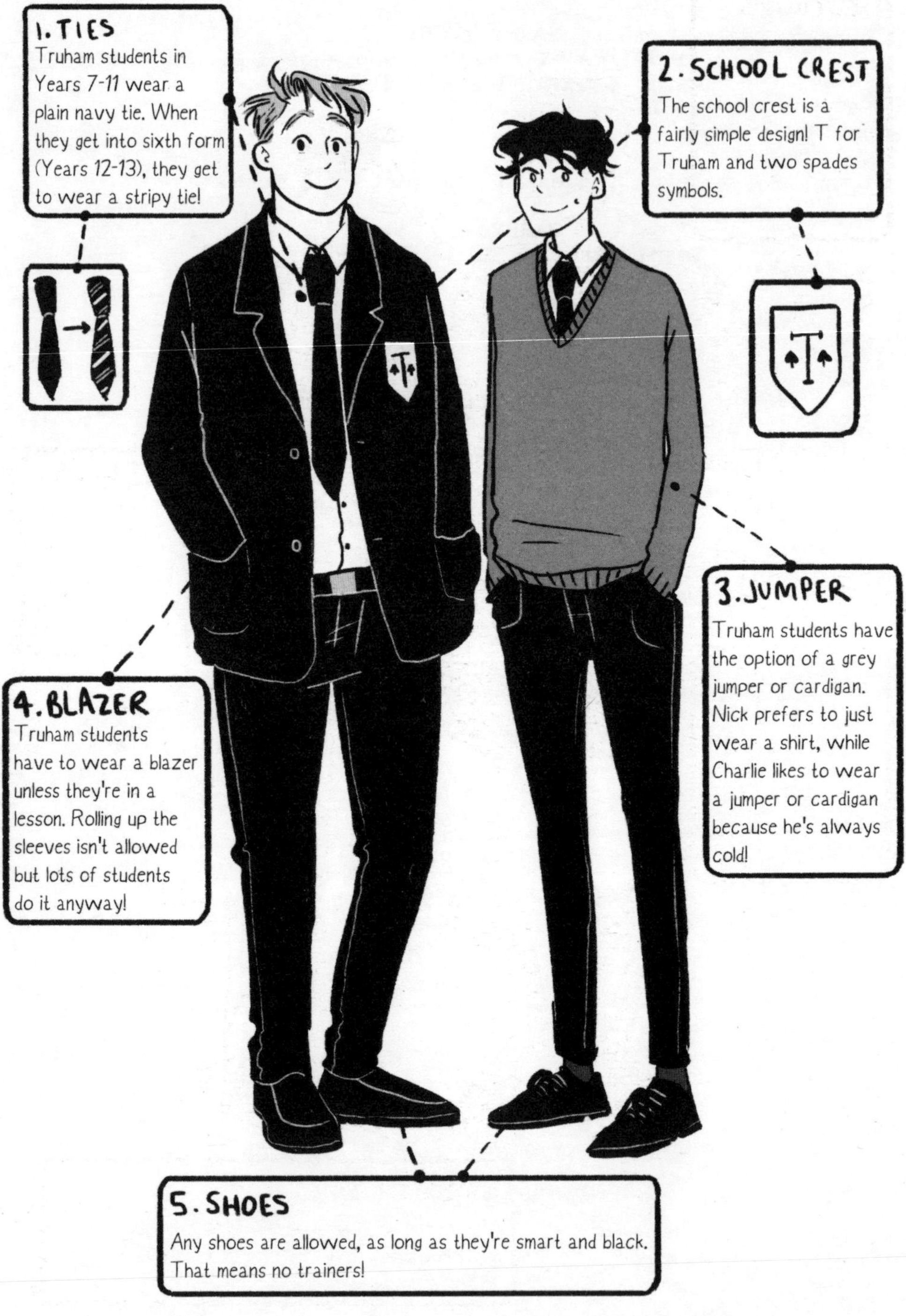

1. TIES
Truham students in Years 7-11 wear a plain navy tie. When they get into sixth form (Years 12-13), they get to wear a stripy tie!
2. SCHOOL CREST
The school crest is a fairly simple design! T for Truham and two spades symbols.
T
3. JUMPER
Truham students have the option of a grey jumper or cardigan. Nick prefers to just wear a shirt, while Charlie likes to wear a jumper or cardigan because he's always cold!
4. BLAZER
Truham students have to wear a blazer unless they're in a lesson. Rolling up the sleeves isn't allowed but lots of students do it anyway!
5. SHOES
Any shoes are allowed, as long as they're smart and black. That means no trainers!

RUGBY UNIFORM:

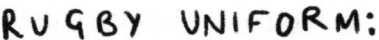

1. COLOURS
Their rugby uniform mainly consists of a striped navy/light blue rugby shirt. They only wear their uniform for official matches, though.

2. SHORTS
The team usually just wear their P.E. shorts for matches. Charlie doesn't enjoy this during the winter.

3. SOCKS
Players are supposed to wear long navy sports socks for matches. As you can see, Charlie is yet to get himself a pair.

4. SHOES
Nick loves rugby, so he has his own pair of studded rugby boots. Charlie isn't so passionate about the sport so he just sticks with a pair of Vans.

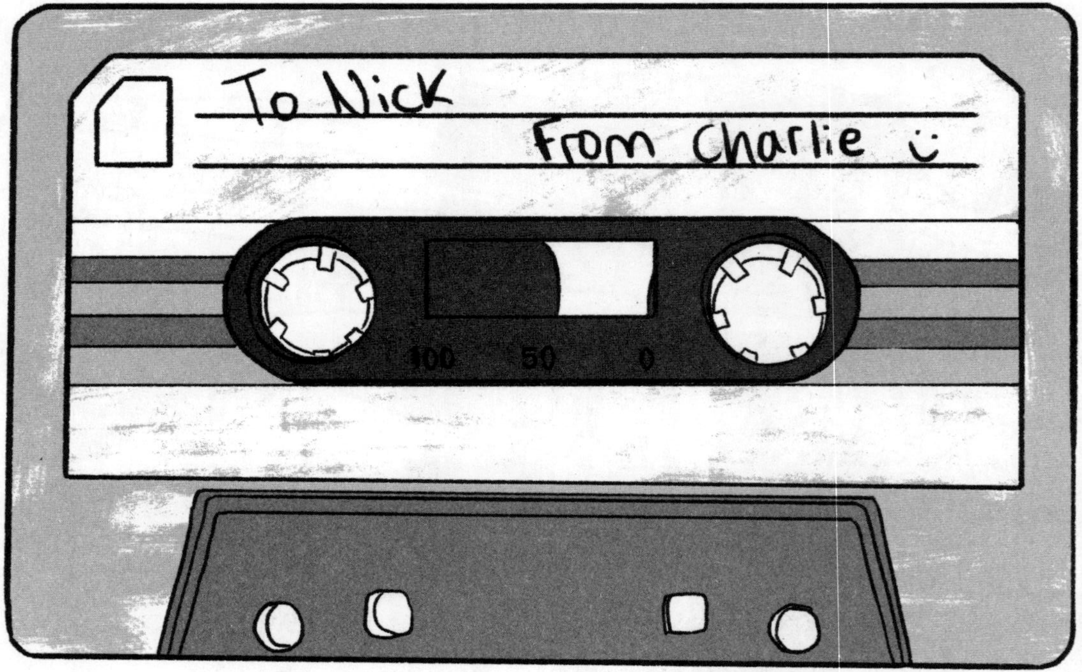
To Nick
From Charlie :)
100 50 0

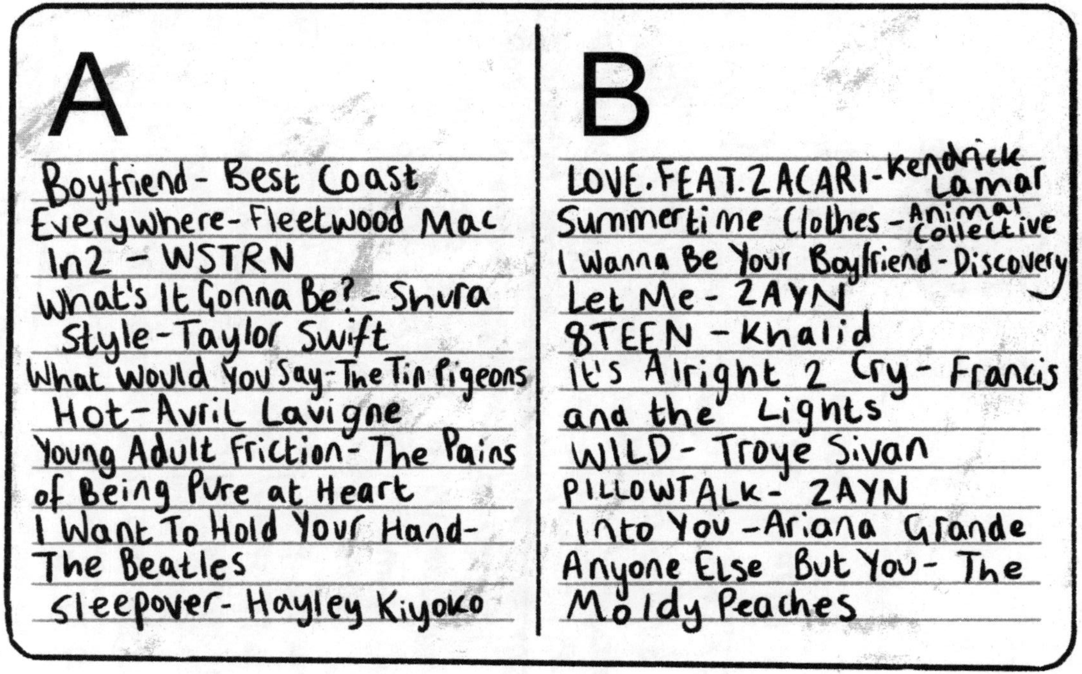
A
Boyfriend - Best Coast
Everywhere - Fleetwood Mac
In2 - WSTRN
What's It Gonna Be? - Shura
Style - Taylor Swift
What Would You Say - The Tin Pigeons
Hot - Avril Lavigne
Young Adult Friction - The Pains of Being Pure at Heart
I Want To Hold Your Hand - The Beatles
Sleepover - Hayley Kiyoko
B
LOVE. FEAT. ZACARI - Kendrick Lamar
Summertime Clothes - Animal Collective
I Wanna Be Your Boyfriend - Discovery
Let Me - ZAYN
8TEEN - Khalid
It's Alright 2 Cry - Francis and the Lights
WILD - Troye Sivan
PILLOWTALK - ZAYN
Into You - Ariana Grande
Anyone Else But You - The Moldy Peaches

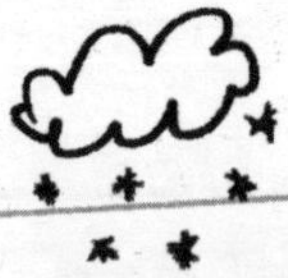

Saturday 20th March

Hung out with Charlie all day!! He came over and we went out in the snow with Nellie which was so much fun!! I really like hanging out with Charlie, like **WAY** more than my other friends. I feel like I can actually just relax and be myself around him, and we still have such a good time and joke around, I swear I can't stop smiling when we're hanging out. I know it's weird but I honestly don't think I've ever liked a friend this much before... I sort of dread seeing my other friends, like they're kind of annoying and being around them is stressful.

But when I'm with Charlie I don't want the day to end??

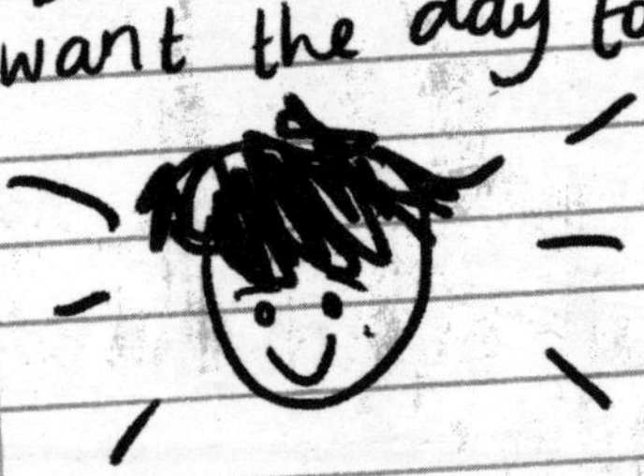

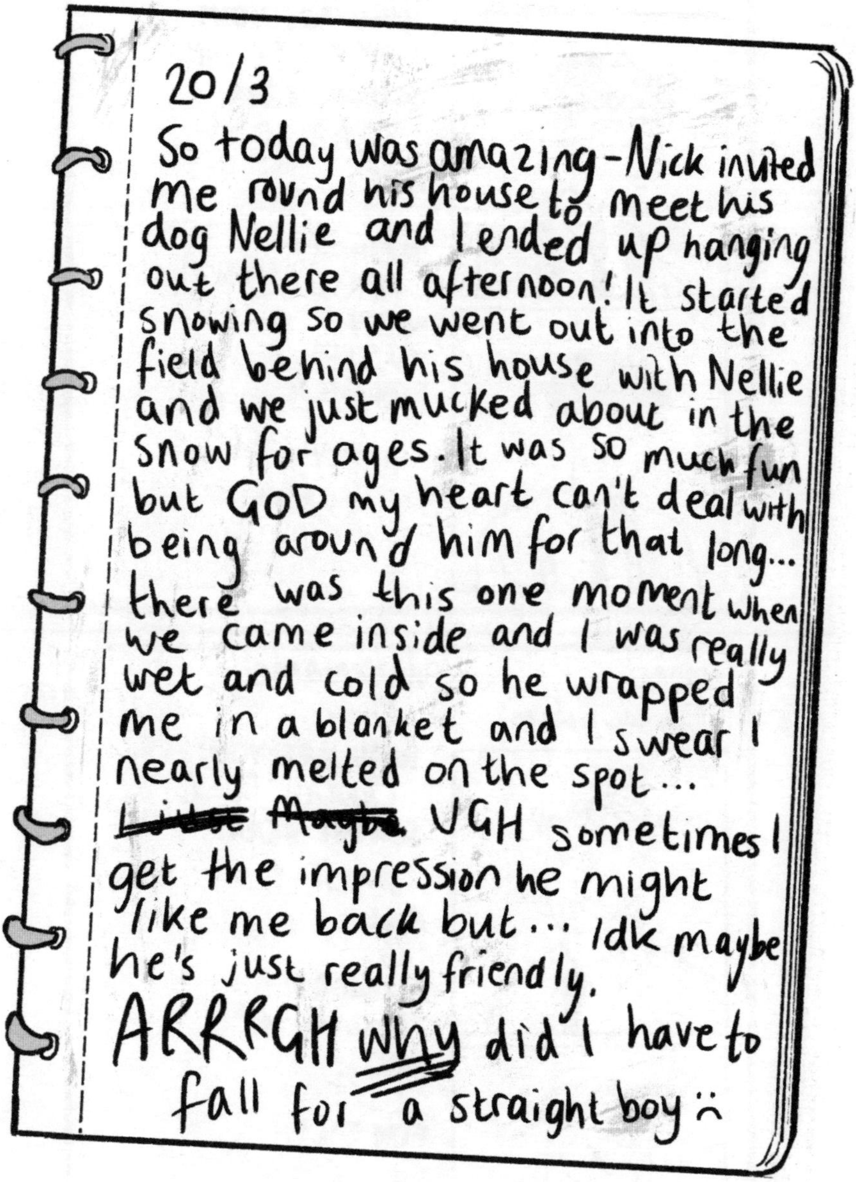
20/3
So today was amazing – Nick invited me round his house to meet his dog Nellie and I ended up hanging out there all afternoon! It started snowing so we went out into the field behind his house with Nellie and we just mucked about in the snow for ages. It was so much fun but GOD my heart can't deal with being around him for that long... there was this one moment when we came inside and I was really wet and cold so he wrapped me in a blanket and I swear I nearly melted on the spot...
~~Like~~ ~~Maybe~~ UGH sometimes I get the impression he might like me back but... Idk maybe he's just really friendly.
ARRRGH why did I have to fall for a straight boy :(

NAME:
CHARLES SPRING

NICKNAME:
CHARLIE

WHO ARE YOU:
NICK'S FRIEND

SCHOOL YEAR:
YEAR 10

AGE:
14

BIRTHDAY:
APRIL 27TH

MBTI:
ISTP

FUN FACT:

I LOVE TO
READ!

NAME:
Nicholas Nelson

NICKNAME:
Nick

WHO ARE YOU:
Charlie's friend

SCHOOL YEAR:
Year 11

AGE:
16

BIRTHDAY:
September 4th

MBTI:
ESFJ

FUN FACT:

I'm great at
baking cakes

NAME:
Tao Xu

NICKNAME:
Tao
WHO ARE YOU:
Charlie's friend
SCHOOL YEAR:
Year 10
AGE:
15
BIRTHDAY:
September 23rd
MBTI:
ENFP
FUN FACT:

I have a film
review blog

NAME:
Victoria Spring

NICKNAME:
Tori
WHO ARE YOU:
Charlie's sister
SCHOOL YEAR:
Year 11
AGE:
16
BIRTHDAY:
April 5th
MBTI:
INFJ
FUN FACT:

I HATE (ALMOST)

EVERYONE

NAME:
Benjamin Hope

NICKNAME:
Ben

WHO ARE YOU:
Charlie's ex

SCHOOL YEAR:
Year 11

AGE:
16

BIRTHDAY:
December 1st

MBTI:
ENTP

FUN FACT:
I can skateboard

NAME:
Tara Jones

NICKNAME:
Tara

WHO ARE YOU:
Nick's old crush

SCHOOL YEAR:
Year 11

AGE:
15

BIRTHDAY:
July 3rd

MBTI:
INFP

FUN FACT:
I love dance!
(especially ballet)

NAME:
HARRY GREENE

NICKNAME:
HARRY

WHO ARE YOU:
NICK'S CLASSMATE

SCHOOL YEAR:
YEAR 11

AGE:
16

BIRTHDAY:
APRIL 17TH

MBTI:
ESTJ

FUN FACT:
I HAVE OVER 20k INSTA FOLLOWERS

NAME:
Nellie Nelson

NICKNAME:
Nellie

WHO ARE YOU:
Nick's dog

SCHOOL YEAR:
N/A

AGE:
65 (dog years)

BIRTHDAY:
Unknown

MBTI:
ESFP

FUN FACT:

Boof!

Author's note

Nick and Charlie have been in my heart for a very long time.

As many of you know, they both first appeared in my debut YA novel, 'Solitaire'. Charlie is the younger brother of the narrator, Tori, and Nick is his doting, protective boyfriend. Neither of them are particularly major characters, but in the novel, aged 17 and 15 respectively, they are in a firm, loving, supportive relationship. That's where my desire to tell their story began. How did they get to this point? And where will they go from here?

In my spare time during my A-Levels, I filled an entire sketchbook with my first attempt at telling the backstory of Nick and Charlie. Then I started again, my art slightly better, and filled another sketchbook with a second attempt at the comic. I remember spending hours at a time just sitting and drawing in bed, not even listening to music in the background, completely lost and in love with the story of Nick and Charlie. It brought me peace in a way not even writing my novels could.

In 2016, aged twenty-one and my art greatly improved, I launched Heartstopper. It started small, but slowly its audience grew and grew. At the time of editing this author's note, Heartstopper has over 70,000 followers across Tumblr and Tapas. People come to the story for all sorts of reasons - for the realistic romance, for the LGBT+ rep, for the art, for the drama. But I think most of all people have been drawn to Heartstopper because it brings them comfort.

It brings me that too.

Alice x

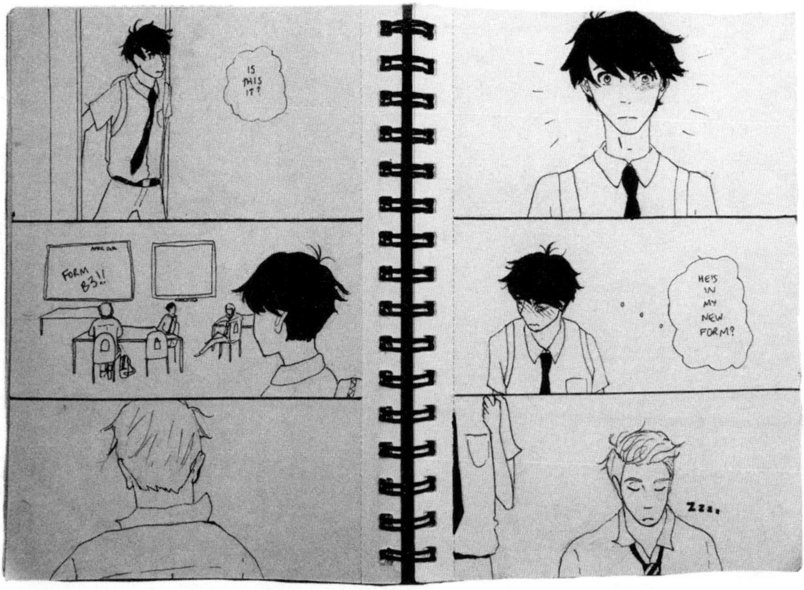
IS THIS IT?
FORM B3!!
HE'S IN MY NEW FORM?
ZZZ.

From a Nick and Charlie comic I drew in 2013

Love and thanks to my Patreon patrons, Kickstarter supporters,
and all readers of HEARTSTOPPER over the past couple of years.
This book wouldn't have been possible without you.

A huge thanks also to my agent, Claire Wilson, to my editor, Rachel Wade,
and to the whole team at Hachette Children's. Thank you for showing
HEARTSTOPPER so much love.

Finally, a special shout-out to those amazing people who gave a
little more to the Kickstarter:

JT Taylor, Lorna Burch, Kyle Sanders, Ade Mayr,
Ruben Molina Fernandez, Lucy Powrie, Shannon Baillie, Annie Furlong-Muir,
David Browne, Isobel, Lucy McGlasson, Jake Fraser, Charlotte Dreyfus,
Manon Pothin, Lowen Crombie, Chloe Zargarpour, Liang Hai, Katie Gibson,
Whitney Gravelle, Daphne Tonge (Illumicrate), Tory Schorsch, Jamie Destouet,
Janintserani Herrera, Peter Stromberg, Elise Buchanan,
Bella Beecham, Orlee Pnini, and John H. Bookwalter Jr.

ALSO BY ALICE OSEMAN:

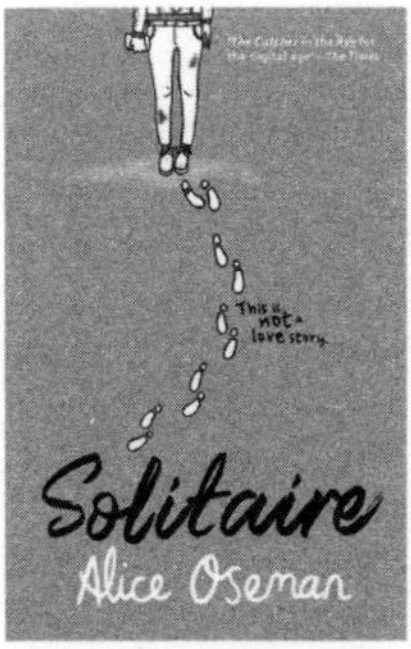
Solitaire
Alice Oseman

SOLITAIRE

Read the novel Nick and Charlie first appeared in!

A pessimistic sixteen-year-old girl, a teenage speed skater with a penchant for solving mysteries, and a series of anonymous pranks at school by an online group who call themselves 'Solitaire'.

Alice's debut novel tells the story of Tori Spring.

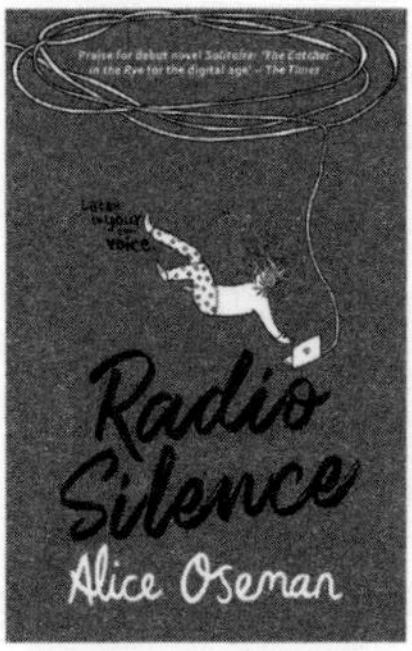
Radio Silence
Alice Oseman

RADIO SILENCE

Everyone thinks seventeen-year-old Frances is destined for a top university - including herself. But, in secret, Frances spends all her free time drawing fan art for a sci-fi podcast, 'Universe City'. And when she discovers that the creator of the podcast lives opposite her, Frances begins to question everything she knew about herself and what she wants from life.

What if everything you set yourself up to be was wrong?

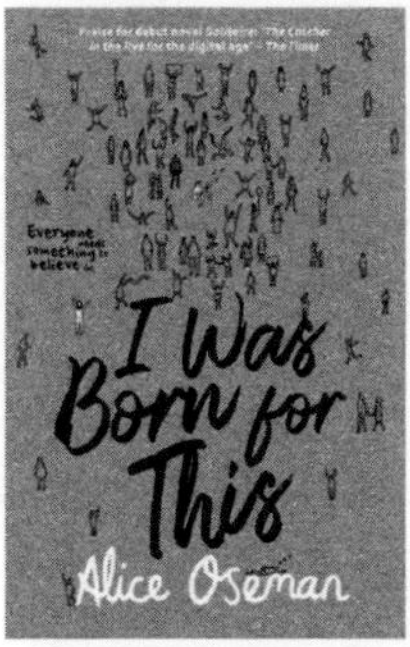
I Was Born for This
Alice Oseman

I WAS BORN FOR THIS

Angel, a massive fangirl of boyband 'The Ark', is headed to London to see The Ark live for the first time. Jimmy, frontman of The Ark, is struggling to deal with how famous he and his bandmates are becoming.

Over one week in August, Angel and Jimmy's lives begin to intertwine in mysterious ways, and when Angel and Jimmy are unexpectedly thrust together, they will discover just how strange and surprising facing up to reality can be.

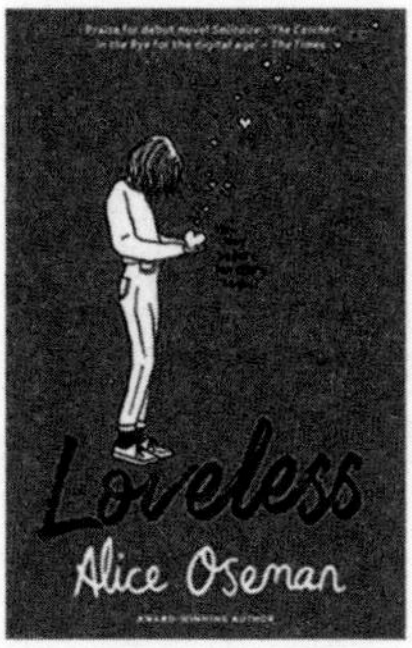
Loveless
Alice Oseman

LOVELESS

Georgia has never been in love, never kissed anyone, never even had a crush – but as a fanfic-obsessed romantic she's sure she'll find her person one day.

But when her romance plan wreaks havoc amongst her friends, Georgia ends up in her own comedy of errors, and she starts to question why love seems so easy for other people but not for her. . .

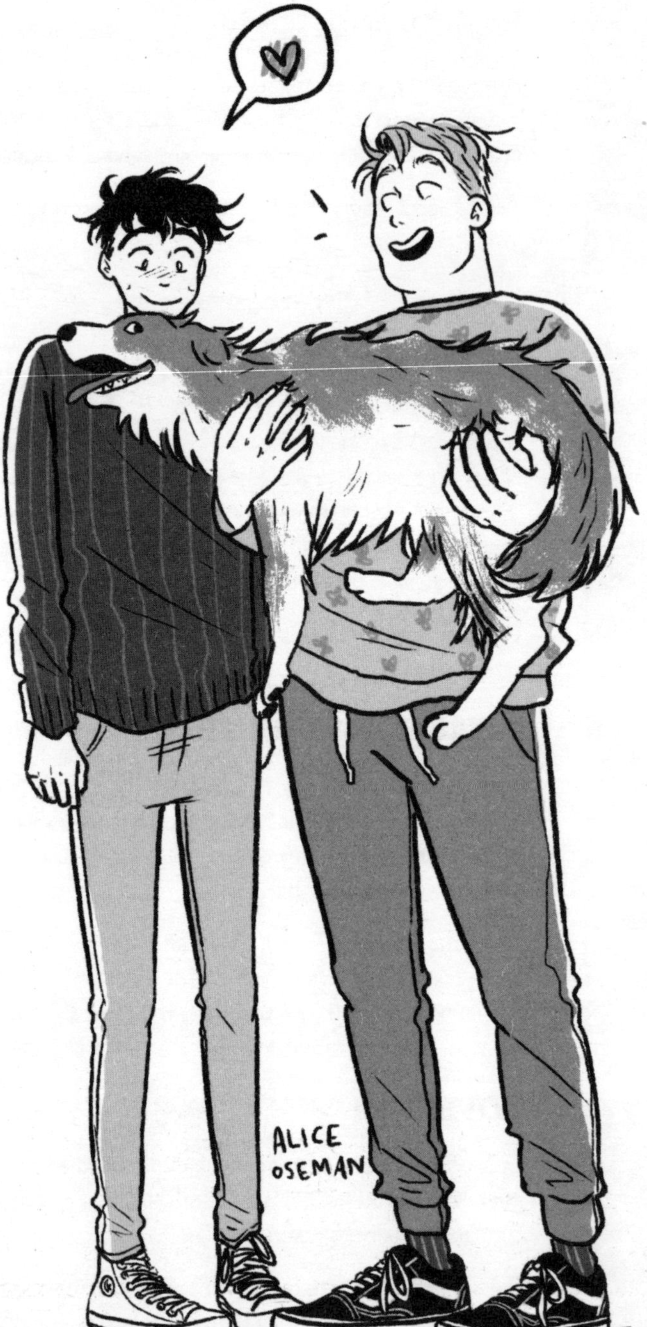

!
ALICE
OSEMAN